MOTHER of LEARNING

I

nobody103
AKA
DOMAGOJ KURMAIĆ

Wraithmarked
CREATIVE

MOTHER OF LEARNING: ARC 1
Book One of the *Mother of Learning* series
nobody103, Domagoj Kurmaić
Copyright © 2021, 2022 Domagoj Kurmaić. All rights reserved.

Editor: Taya Latham
Proofing: Laura Jorstad
Cover Illustration: Mansik Yang YAM
Front Endsheet: Daniel Kamarudin
Back Endsheet: Asur Misoa
Front Page Illustration: Schastny Sergey
Map: Soraya Corcoran
Cover Design and Interior Layout: STK·Kreations
Art Direction: Bryce O'Connor
Additional Cover Elements by Noob Model :D
(https://tinyurl.com/NoobModel3-BlueMagicCircle)

Trade paperback ISBN: 978-1-955252-19-5
Hardcover ISBN: 978-1-955252-18-8

Worldwide Rights
1st Edition

Published by Wraithmarked Creative, LLC
www.wraithmarked.com

CHAPTER 001

Good Morning Brother

Zorian's eyes abruptly shot open as a sharp pain erupted from his stomach. His whole body convulsed, buckling against the object that fell on him, and suddenly he was wide awake, not a trace of drowsiness in his mind.

"Good morning, brother!" an annoyingly cheerful voice sounded right on top of him. "Morning, morning, *MORNING*!!!"

Zorian glared at his little sister, but Kirielle just smiled back at him cheekily, still sprawled across his stomach. She was humming to herself in obvious satisfaction, kicking her feet playfully in the air as she studied the giant world map

Zorian had tacked to the wall next to his bed. Or rather, pretended to study—Zorian could see her watching him intently out of the corner of her eyes for a reaction.

This was what he got for not arcane-locking the door and setting up a basic alarm perimeter around his bed.

"Get off," he told her in the calmest voice he could muster.

"Mom said to wake you up," she said matter-of-factly, not budging from her spot.

"Not like this, she didn't," Zorian grumbled, swallowing his irritation and patiently waiting until she dropped her guard. Predictably, Kirielle grew visibly agitated after only a few moments of this pretend disinterest. Just before she could blow up, Zorian quickly grasped her legs and chest and flipped her over the edge of the bed. She fell to the floor with a thud and an indignant yelp, and Zorian quickly jumped to his feet to better respond to any violence with which she might decide to retaliate. He glanced down on her and sniffed disdainfully. "I'll be sure to remember this the next time I'm asked to wake *you* up."

"Fat chance of that," she retorted defiantly. "You always sleep longer than I do."

Zorian simply sighed in defeat. Damn the little imp, but she was right about that.

"So…," she began excitedly, jumping to her feet, "are you excited?"

Zorian watched her for a moment as she bounced around his room like a monkey on caffeine. Sometimes he wished he had some of that boundless energy of hers. But only some.

"About what?" Zorian asked innocently, feigning ignorance. He knew what she meant, of course, but constantly asking obvious questions was the fastest way of frustrating his little sister into dropping a conversation he'd rather not have.

"Going back to academy!" she whined, clearly aware of what he was doing. He needed to learn some new tricks. "Learning magic. Can you show me some magic?"

Zorian let out a long-suffering sigh. Kirielle had always treated him as something of a playmate of hers, despite him doing his best not to encourage her, but usually she remained within certain unspoken boundaries. She was downright impossible this year, though, and Mother was wholly unsympathetic to his pleas to rein her in. All he did was read all day long, she said, so it wasn't as if he was doing anything *important*. Thankfully the summer break was over and he could finally get away from them all.

"Kiri, I have to pack. Why don't you go pester Fortov for a change?"

She scowled at him unhappily and then perked up, as if remembering something, and ran out of the room. Zorian's eyes widened when he realized what she was up to a second too late.

"No!" he yelled as he ran after her, only to have the bathroom door slammed into his face. He pounded on the door in frustration. "Damn it, Kiri! You had all the time in the world to go to the bathroom *before* I woke up!"

"Sucks to be you," was her only answer.

After hurling a few choice curses at the door, Zorian stomped off back to his room to get dressed. She would be inside for ages, he was sure, if only to spite him.

Quickly changing out of his pajamas and putting on his glasses, Zorian took a moment to look around his room. He was pleased to note Kirielle hadn't rummaged through his stuff before waking him up. She had a very fuzzy notion of (other people's) privacy.

It didn't take Zorian long to pack—he had never really unpacked, to be honest, and would have gone back to Cyoria a week ago if he thought Mother would have allowed it. He was just packing his school supplies when he realized with irritation that some of his textbooks were missing. He could try a locator spell, but he was pretty sure he knew where they had ended up. Kirielle had a habit of taking them to her room, no matter how many times Zorian told her to keep her sticky little fingers away from them. Working on a hunch, he double-checked his writing supplies and, sure enough, found they had been greatly depleted.

It always happened—every time he came home, Kirielle would raid his school supplies. Putting aside the ethical problems inherent in breaking into your brother's room in order to steal his things, what on earth was she doing with all those pencils and erasers? This time he specifically bought extras with his sister in mind, but it still wasn't enough. He couldn't find a single eraser in his drawer, and he had bought a whole packet of them before coming home. Why Kirielle couldn't simply ask Mother to buy her some books and pens of her own was never really clear to Zorian. She was the youngest, and the only daughter, so Mother was always happy to spoil her—the dolls she talked Mother into buying her were five times more expensive than a couple of books and a stack of pencils.

In any case, while Zorian had no delusions about ever seeing his writing supplies again, he really needed those textbooks. With that in mind, he marched off to his sister's room, ignoring the 'Keep out!' warning on the door, and quickly found his missing books in their usual location—cunningly hidden under the bed, behind several conveniently placed stuffed animals.

His packing done, he went downstairs to eat something and see what Mother wanted from him.

Though his family thought he simply liked to sleep in, Zorian actually had a reason for being a late riser. It meant he could eat his food in peace, as everyone else had already had breakfast by then. Few things annoyed him more than someone trying to strike up a conversation while he was eating, and that was precisely the time when the rest of his family was most talkative. Unfortunately, that

4

peace seemed beyond reach this morning. He hadn't even finished his descent to the kitchen when Mother pounced on him, having already found something about him she didn't like.

"You don't really intend to go out looking like that, do you?" she asked.

"What's wrong with this?" asked Zorian. He was wearing simple brown trousers and a clean white shirt. A little plain and utilitarian, but little different from the outfits other boys of similar age wore when they went to the city. It seemed just fine to him.

"You can't go out looking like that," his mother said with a long-suffering sigh. "What do you think people will say when they see you wearing that?"

"Nothing?" Zorian tried.

"Zorian, don't be so difficult," she snapped at him. "Our family is one of the pillars of this town. We're under scrutiny every time we leave the house. I know you don't care about such things, but appearances are important to a lot of people. You need to realize you're not an island, and you can't decide things as if you were alone in the world. You are a member of this family, and your actions inevitably reflect on our reputation. I will not let you embarrass me by looking like a common factory worker. Go back to your room and put on some proper clothes."

Zorian restrained himself from rolling his eyes just long enough to turn his back on her. Maybe her guilt trip would have been more effective if this was the first time she tried it on him. Still, it wasn't worth the argument, so he changed into a pricier set of clothes—a more colorful shirt made from the fine dyed linen his mother preferred and a more elaborate jacket with ivory buttons and whatnot. It was excessive, considering he'd be spending the whole day in the train, but his mother nodded approvingly when she saw him coming down the stairs. She had him turn and pose like a show animal for a while before pronouncing him 'fairly decent'. He went to the kitchen and, to his annoyance, Mother followed after him. No eating in peace today, it seemed.

Father was thankfully on one of his 'business trips', so Zorian wouldn't have to deal with him today.

He entered the kitchen and frowned when he saw a bowl of porridge already waiting for him on the table. Usually he made his own breakfast, and he liked it that way, but he knew his mother never accepted that. This was her idea of a peace gesture, which meant she was going to ask something of him he wouldn't like.

"I figured I'd prepare something for you today, and I know you've always liked porridge," she said. Zorian refrained from mentioning he hadn't liked it since he was about eight. "You slept longer than I thought you would, though. It's gone cold while I've waited for you."

Zorian rolled his eyes and cast a slightly modified 'heat water' spell on the porridge, which was instantly returned to a pleasant temperature.

He ate his breakfast in silence while Mother talked to him at length about a crop-related dispute one of their suppliers was involved in, dancing around whatever topic she wanted to broach. He effortlessly tuned her out. It was practically a survival skill for every child in the Kazinski family, as both Mother and Father were prone to protracted lectures on every subject imaginable, but doubly so for Zorian, who was the black sheep of the family and thus subjected to such monologues more frequently than the rest. Thankfully, his mother thought nothing of his silence, because Zorian was always as silent as possible around his family—he had learned many years ago that this was the easiest way of getting along with them.

"Mother," he interrupted her, "I just woke up via Kiri jumping on me, I haven't had a chance to go to the bathroom, and now you're pestering me while I'm eating. Either get to the point or wait a couple of minutes while I finish breakfast."

"She did it again?" his mother asked, amusement obvious in her voice.

Zorian rubbed his eyes, not saying anything, before surreptitiously pocketing an apple from the bowl on the table while his mother wasn't looking. There were a lot of annoying things Kirielle did again and again, but complaining about it to Mother was a waste of time. No one in this family was on *his* side.

"Oh, don't be like that," his mother said, noticing his less-than-pleased reaction. "She's just bored and playing with you. You take things way too seriously, just like your father."

"I am nothing like my father!" Zorian insisted, raising his voice and glaring at her. This was why he hated eating with other people. He returned to his breakfast with renewed vigor, eager to finish this as soon as possible.

"Of course you're not," Mother said airily, before suddenly switching the subject. "Actually, this reminds me of something. Your father and I are going to Koth to visit Daimen."

Zorian bit the spoon in his mouth to prevent himself from making a snide comment. It was always Daimen this, Daimen that. There were days when Zorian wondered why his parents had three other children when they were clearly so enamored of their eldest son. Really, going to another continent just to visit him? What, were they going to die if they didn't see him for a year?

"What's that got to do with me?" Zorian asked.

"It will be an extended visit," she said. "We'll be there for about six months, most of it spent traveling from one place to another. You and Fortov will be at the academy, of course, but I'm worried about Kirielle. She's only nine and I don't feel comfortable bringing her along with us."

Zorian winced internally, finally catching on to what she wanted of him. Hell. No.

"Mother, I'm fifteen," he protested.

"So?" she asked. "Your father and I were already married when we were your age."

"Times change. Besides, I spend most of the day at the academy," Zorian responded. "Why don't you ask Fortov to take care of her? He's a year older and he has his own apartment."

"Fortov is in his fourth year," his mother said sternly. "He's going to graduate this year so he has to focus on his grades."

"You mean he said no," Zorian concluded out loud.

"And besides…," she continued, ignoring his remark, "I'm sure you're aware of how irresponsible Fortov can be at times. I don't think he's fit to raise a little girl."

"And whose fault is that?" Zorian grumbled quietly, loudly dropping his spoon and pushing the plate away from him. Maybe Fortov was irresponsible because he knew Mother and Father would simply dump his responsibilities onto Zorian if he just played dumb long enough. Didn't that ever occur to her? Why did it always fall to him to deal with the little imp? Well, he wasn't going to get saddled with this! If Fortov was too good to take care of Kirielle, then so was Zorian!

Plus, the little tattletale would undoubtedly report everything he did back to Mother without a second thought. The best thing about attending a school so far from home was that he could do whatever he wanted with his family being none the wiser, and there was no way he was going to give that up. Really, this was just a transparent ploy by his mother to spy on him, so she could lecture him some more about family pride and proper manners.

"I don't think I'm fit for that either," continued Zorian a little louder. "You said only a few minutes ago that I'm an embarrassment to the family. We wouldn't want to corrupt little Kiri with my uncaring attitude, now would we?"

"I didn't—"

"No!" Zorian shouted, cutting his mother off before she could argue otherwise.

"Oh, have it your way," she huffed in resignation. "But really, I wasn't suggesting—"

"What are you talking about?" Kirielle called out from behind him.

"We were discussing what a rotten brat you are," Zorian shot back.

"No you weren't!"

Zorian just rolled his eyes and rose from his seat, intending to go to the bathroom, only to find an irate little sister blocking his path. Really, what was up with her today?

Fortunately, that was the moment there came a knock, and all three of them turned in surprise to the house door, set in the far wall of the room.

"I'll get it," Zorian muttered after a brief pause, knowing that Mother would demand that one of them open the door and that Kirielle wouldn't budge from her spot any time soon. She could be very stubborn when she wanted.

That was how Zorian found himself staring at a bespectacled woman with neatly-cut brown hair, dressed in a khaki-colored suit of obviously-expensive make, and cradling a thick book in her arm.

The woman gave him an appraising glance, adjusting her glasses. "Zorian Kazinski?"

"Uh, yeah?" he said, unsure how to react to this development.

"I am Ilsa Zileti, from Cyoria's Royal Academy of Magical Arts. I'm here to discuss the results of your certification."

Zorian could feel the blood drain from his face. They sent an actual mage to talk to him!? What did he do to warrant this!? Mother was going to skin him alive!

"You aren't in trouble, Mister Kazinski," she said, smiling in amusement. "The academy has a habit of sending a representative to third year students to discuss various matters of interest. I confess I should have visited you sooner, but I have been a tad busy this year. You have my apologies."

Zorian stared at her for a few seconds.

"May I come in? I've always felt rather awkward lingering on a stoop…"

"Huh? Oh!" said Zorian. "Forgive my manners, Miss Zileti. Come in, come in."

"Thank you," she accepted politely, stepping into the house.

After a quick introduction of his mother and sister, Ilsa asked Zorian if he had somewhere they could discuss school matters privately. Mother—as astute as she could be insufferable—quickly decided she had to go to the town market, taking Kirielle with her. Zorian was left alone in the house with the mage, who promptly scattered various papers across the kitchen desk.

"So, Zorian," she began. "You already know you passed the certification."

"Yes, I got the written notice," Zorian said. "Cirin doesn't have a mage tower, so I was going to pick up the badge when I got back to Cyoria."

Ilsa simply handed him a sealed scroll. Zorian inspected the scroll for a few seconds and then tried to break the seal so he could read it. Unfortunately, the seal was quite tough to break. Unnaturally so, even.

He frowned. Ilsa wouldn't have given him the scroll like this if she didn't think he had the ability to open it. A test of some sort? He wasn't anyone terribly special, so this would have to be something pretty easy. What skill did every recently-minted mage possess that would…

Oh. He almost rolled his eyes when he realized what this was all about. He channeled some mana into the seal and it promptly snapped itself in half, allowing Zorian to finally unroll the scroll. It was written in very neat calligraphy and appeared to be some kind of proof of his identity as a first circle mage. He glanced back at Ilsa, who nodded approvingly, confirming to Zorian that he had just passed a test of some sort.

"You don't really have to pick up your badge until you finish school," she said. "The badge is pretty expensive and nobody is going to bother you about it unless you plan to open a shop or otherwise sell your magical expertise. If you get questioned about it, just refer them to the academy and we'll clear things up."

Zorian shrugged. While he did intend to break away from his family, he'd prefer to wait until graduation, and that was two years away. He motioned on for her to continue.

"That's the easy part finished, then. Now…," she began searching the pockets of her suit as though looking for something, "the records say you lived in the academy housing for the past two years. I assume you intend to continue?"

Zorian nodded just in time for Ilsa to pull out a rather strange key, which she promptly handed to him. He turned the thing over in one hand as he examined it. Zorian knew how locks in general worked, and could even pick simpler ones with enough time, but he couldn't figure out how this key was supposed to work—it had no 'teeth' to fit in with the tumblers inside the lock. On a hunch, he channeled some mana into it, and faint golden lines immediately lit across the surface of the metal. He looked at Ilsa with a silent question.

"Housing for third years works differently than you are used to," she told him. "As you're likely aware, now that you are a certified first circle mage, the academy is authorized to teach you spells of the first circle and above. Since you'll be handling sensitive material, greater security is required, so you'll be moving into a different building. The lock on your door is keyed to your mana, so you'll have to channel some of your personal mana into the key like you did just now before it will unlock."

"Ah," said Zorian. Idly he spun the key in his hand, wondering how exactly they got a hold of his mana signature. Something to research later, he supposed.

"Normally I would be explaining to you in detail what it means to be a third year student at Cyoria's magical academy, but I hear you have a train leaving soon, so why don't we jump straight to the main reason I'm here: your mentor and electives. You can ask me anything you wish to know afterwards."

Zorian perked up on this, especially the mention of 'mentor'. Each third year was given a mentor that they met with once a week, who was supposed to teach students in ways not possible in a standard class format, and otherwise help them reach their maximum potential. A choice of one's mentor could make or break one's magical career, and Zorian knew he had to choose carefully. Fortunately, he had asked around among older students to find out which ones were good and which ones were bad, so he figured he would at least be able to get an above-average one.

"So which mentors can I choose from?" Zorian asked.

"Well, actually, I'm afraid you can't," Ilsa said. "Like I said, I was supposed to get to you sooner. Unfortunately, all but one of the mentors have filled their quota of students at this point."

Zorian had a bad feeling about this… "And this mentor is?"

"Xvim Chao."

Zorian groaned, burying his face in his hands. Of all the teachers, Xvim was widely agreed upon as the *worst* mentor you could possibly get. It just had to be him, didn't it?

"It's not that bad," Ilsa assured him. "The rumors are mostly exaggerated, and mostly spread by students unwilling to do the kind of work Professor Xvim requires of his charges. I'm sure a talented, hard-working student such as yourself will have no problems with him."

Zorian snorted. "I don't suppose there is any chance to transfer to another mentor, is there?"

"Not really. We've had a really good pass rate last year, and all of the mentors are swamped with students as it is. Professor Xvim is the least burdened of the available mentors."

"My, I wonder why," Zorian mumbled. "All right, fine. What about electives?"

Ilsa handed him another scroll, this one unsealed, containing a list of all elective classes offered by the academy. It was long. *Very* long. You could sign up for practically anything, even things that weren't of strictly magical nature: things like advanced mathematics, classical literature, and architecture. It was to be expected, really, since Ikosian magical tradition had always been inextricably connected to other intellectual pursuits.

"You can choose up to five but no fewer than three electives this year. It would be a lot more convenient for us if you did it now, so that we can finalize the schedules over the weekend before the classes start. Don't be too intimidated by the sheer size of the list. Even if you choose something that doesn't appeal to you, you can switch to a different elective during the first month of school."

Zorian frowned. There were a lot of electives and he wasn't quite sure which ones he wanted to take. He'd already gotten shafted in the mentor department, so he really couldn't afford to screw up here. This would take a while.

"Please don't take this the wrong way, Miss Zileti, but would you mind if we take a short break before we go any further with this?"

"Of course not," she said. "Is something the matter?"

"Not at all," assured Zorian. "It's just that I *really* need to go to the bathroom."

Probably not the best way to make a first impression. Kirielle was so going to pay for putting him in this position.

Zorian trailed after his family in silence as they entered Cirin's train station, ignoring Fortov's exuberant greeting to some 'friends' of his. He scanned the crowd on the platform for any familiar faces but, predictably, came out empty. He didn't really know all that many people in his hometown, as his parents loved reminding him. He felt his mother's gaze on him as he unsuccessfully searched for an empty bench, but refused to look back at her—she would take that as permission to initiate conversation, and he already knew she would ask him why he wasn't joining Fortov and his friends.

Because they're immature jackasses, just like Fortov, that's why.

He sighed, looking at the empty train tracks with annoyance. The train was late. He didn't mind waiting as such, but waiting in crowds was pure torture. His family would never understand, but Zorian hated crowds. It wasn't any tangible thing, really—it was more like large gatherings of people projected some kind of presence that weighed down on him constantly. Most of the time it was annoying, though it did have its uses. His parents stopped taking him to church when they realized that dragging him into a small hall packed with people resulted in vertigo and fainting in a matter of minutes. Fortunately, the train station wasn't currently crowded enough to produce such intense effects, but Zorian knew prolonged exposure would take its toll. He hoped the train wouldn't take *too* long because he didn't relish spending the rest of the day with a headache.

Fortov's loud laughter broke him out of such gloomy musings. His older brother didn't have such problems, that's for sure. He was cheerful, sociable, and had a smile that could light up the world. The people he was surrounded with were clearly enthralled with him, and he stood out among them at first glance, despite having the same thin build that Zorian did. He just had that kind of presence around him. He was like Daimen in this way, only Daimen had actual skills to back up his charm.

He scoffed, shaking his head. Zorian didn't know for sure how Fortov had been accepted into a supposedly elite institution like Cyoria's magical academy, but he strongly suspected Father had greased a few palms to get Fortov in. It wasn't that Fortov was stupid, so much as lazy and completely unable to focus on a task, no matter how critical. Not that most people knew that, of course. The boy was charming as hell and very adept in sweeping his inadequacies under the metaphorical rug.

His father always joked that Fortov and Zorian each got a half of Daimen in them: Fortov got his charm, and Zorian his competence.

Zorian had never liked his father's sense of humor.

A whistle pierced the air, and the train entered the station with a high pitched squeal of metal wheels braking against the tracks. The original trains were steam-powered machines that billowed smoke wherever they went and consumed unholy amounts of coal to keep going, but this one was powered by the newer techno-magic engines that consumed crystallized mana instead. Cleaner, cheaper, and requiring less maintenance. Zorian could actually feel the mana radiating off the train as he approached, though his ability to sense magic was too underdeveloped to tell him any details. He had always wanted to look around the engine room of one of these things but could never figure out a good way to approach the train operators.

But that was a thought for another time. He gave a brief goodbye to Mother and Kirielle and entered the train to find himself a seat. He intentionally chose an empty compartment, something that was surprisingly easy to find. Apparently, despite the gathered crowd, few of them would be taking this particular train.

Five minutes later, the train gave another ear-splitting whistle and began its long journey towards Cyoria.

A sharp crackle sounded, followed by a ringing bell.

"Now stopping in Korsa," a disembodied voice echoed. The crackling sound again. "I repeat, now stopping in Korsa. Thank you."

The speakers protested one last time before turning silent.

Zorian released a long sigh of irritation and opened his eyes. He hated trains. The boredom, the heat, and the rhythmic thumping sounds all conspired to make him sleepy, but every time he finally drifted off to sleep, he was rudely woken by the station announcer. That this was the very purpose of that announcer—to wake up passengers who would sleep through their destination—was not lost on Zorian, but it was no less annoying because of it.

He looked through the window, only to see a train station like any other. In fact, it was completely identical to the previous five, down to the blue outline on the big white tablet saying 'Korsa'. Apparently the station builders were working off some kind of template these days. Looking at the station platform, he could see a large crowd of people waiting to get on the train. Korsa was a major trading hub, and a lot of newly minted merchant families lived here, sending their children to Cyoria's prestigious academy to become mages and mingle among children of other influential people. Zorian found himself wishing that none of his fellow students join him in his compartment, but he knew it was an idle dream. There were too many of them and his compartment was completely empty aside from him. He did all he could to make himself comfortable in his seat and closed his eyes again.

The first person to join him in his compartment was a chubby, glasses-wearing girl in a green turtleneck. She gave him a cursory glance and started reading a book in silence. Zorian would have been ecstatic with such an agreeable traveling companion, but soon enough a group of four other girls came in and took the remaining four seats for themselves. The newcomers were very loud and prone to giggling fits, and Zorian was sorely tempted to get up and find himself a new compartment to occupy. He spent the rest of the trip alternating between looking through the window at the endless fields they were passing and exchanging annoyed glances with the green turtleneck girl, who seemed similarly irritated by the other girls' antics.

He knew they were getting close to Cyoria when he could see trees on the horizon. There was only one city on this route that was this close to the Great Northern Forest, and the trains otherwise avoided getting close to so infamous a place. Zorian picked up his bag and went to stand by the exit. The idea was to be among the first to disembark, and thus avoid the usual crowding that always occurred once they got to Cyoria, but he was too late—there was already a crowd at the exit when he approached. He leaned on the nearby window and waited, listening to animated conversation between three first year students beside him, who were talking excitedly amongst themselves about how they were going to start learning magic and whatnot. Boy, were they going to be disappointed. The first year was all theory, meditation exercises, and learning how to access your mana consistently.

"Hey, you! You're one of the upperclassmen, aren't you?"

Zorian looked at the girl talking to him and suppressed a groan of irritation. He did not want to engage with anyone, much less an over-enthusiastic group of first years. He had been in the train since early morning, Mother had given him a nasty lecture because he hadn't offered Ilsa something to drink while she was in the house, and he was in no mood for anything.

Still, what was he supposed to do? Just stand there and not say anything?

"I suppose you could describe me as such," he said cautiously.

"Can you show us any magic?" she asked eagerly.

"No," said Zorian flatly. He wasn't even lying. "The train is warded to disrupt mana shaping. They had problems with people starting fires and vandalizing compartments."

"Oh," the girl said, clearly disappointed. She frowned. "Mana shaping?" she asked cautiously.

Zorian raised an eyebrow. "You don't know what mana is?" She was first year, yes, but that was elementary. Anyone who went through elementary school should know at least that much.

"Magic?" she tried lamely.

"Ugh," grunted Zorian. "The teachers would so fail you for that. No, it's not magic. It's what powers magic—the energy, the power that a mage shapes into a magical effect. You'll learn more about it in lectures, I guess. Bottom line is: no mana, no magic. And I can't use any mana at the moment."

This was misleading, but whatever. There was no way he was explaining the basics of spellcasting to some random first year, especially since she should already know this stuff.

"Um, okay. Sorry to bother you then."

With a lot of squealing and steam-letting, the train stopped at Cyoria's train station, and Zorian disembarked as fast as he could, pushing past the awed first-years staring at the sight before them.

Cyoria's train station was huge, a fact made obvious by the fact that it was enclosed, making it look more like a giant tunnel. Actually, the station as a whole was even larger, because there were four more 'tunnels' like this one, plus all the support facilities. There was nothing like it anywhere in the world, and virtually everyone was stupefied the first time they saw it. Zorian was too, when he first disembarked here. The feeling of disorientation was amplified by the sheer number of people that went through this terminal, whether they were passengers going in and out of Cyoria, workers inspecting the train and unloading luggage, newsboys shouting headlines, or homeless people begging for some change. As far as he knew, this massive flow of people never really ceased, even at night, and this was a particularly busy day.

He looked at the giant clock hanging from the ceiling and, discovering he had plenty of time, bought himself some bread from the nearby bakery and then set course for Cyoria's central plaza, intending to eat his newly acquired food while sitting on the edge of the fountain there. It was a nice place to relax.

Cyoria was a curious city. It was one of the most developed and largest cities in the world, which was, at first glance, strange, as Cyoria was dangerously close to monster-infested wilderness and wasn't in a favorable trade location. What really catapulted it to prominence was the massive circular hole on the west side of the city—probably the most obvious Dungeon entrance ever and the only Rank 9 mana well known to exist. The absolutely *massive* quantities of mana gushing out from the underworld had made the spot an irresistible magnet for mages. The presence of such a huge number of mages made Cyoria unlike any other city on the continent, both in the culture of the people living there and, more obviously, in the architecture of the city itself. A lot of things that would be too impractical to build elsewhere were routinely done here, and it made for an inspiring sight if you could find a good spot to watch the city from.

The large number of rats clustered at the bottom of the staircase he was approaching, on the other hand, was far less inspiring. They seemed to notice his approach, their many eyes tracking him, unnaturally focused and coordinated. He froze in his tracks, his horror at the sight rapidly rising. Their behavior was strange enough, but his heartbeat really sped up when he took notice of their heads. Was that… were their brains exposed!? He swallowed heavily and took a step back, slowly retreating from the stairwell before turning around and fleeing in a full sprint. He wasn't sure what they were, but those were definitely *not* normal rats.

He supposed he shouldn't be so shocked, though. A place like Cyoria attracted more than mages. Magical creatures of all breeds found such places just as irresistible. He was just glad the rats didn't pursue him, because he had nothing in the way of combat spells. The only spell he knew that could be used in a situation like this was the 'spook animals' spell, and he had no idea how effective that would have been against such clearly magical creatures.

Somewhat shaken but still determined to get to the fountain, he tried to circle the rat gathering by going through the nearby park, but luck just wasn't on his side today. The moment he approached one of the small bridges he had to cross to get through the park, his thoughts were interrupted by an unmistakable wail. Someone was crying on the bridge, loudly, and Zorian's rich experience with Kirielle told him it was probably a little girl.

Sure enough, as he stepped onto the bridge in front of him, he found a small black-haired girl crying her eyes out and blocking the path. Zorian stopped for a second to observe the situation and, finding no obvious reason for her distress, slowly walked over to see what the problem was.

He supposed he could have just pushed past her and left her there to cry, but not even he was that cold-hearted.

The girl didn't withdraw at his careful approach, so Zorian simply crouched down next to her and tried to get her attention by softly greeting her. That… didn't work too well. She just kept crying, ignoring his words. He spoke louder, asking her what was wrong. That did produce a response, but her attempts at speaking were so distorted by her crying and gasping for air that Zorian failed to understand a word she said.

In the end, it took him five full minutes just to get her to calm down enough to explain what had happened. There was probably a better way to calm down a crying child than calmly repeating that he couldn't help her until she told him what was wrong, but Zorian decided to play things safe. Poking her in the ribs a few times and telling her to stop being such a crybaby worked on Kirielle, but he felt it was a risky maneuver to pull on an unknown child he only just met.

"T-the b-bike!" she finally blurted out between hiccups. "It f-fell in!" she wailed.

Zorian blinked, trying to interpret this. Apparently realizing she wasn't making any sense, the girl pointed towards the creek running underneath the bridge. Zorian looked over the edge of the bridge and, sure enough, there was a children's bicycle half-submerged in the muddy waters.

"Huh," Zorian said. "Wonder how that happened?"

"It fell in!" the girl repeated, looking as if she was going to cry again.

"All right, all right, no need for waterworks. I'll get it out, okay?" Zorian said, eying the bicycle speculatively.

"You'll get dirty," she warned quietly. Zorian could tell from her tone of voice that she hoped he would get it out anyway.

"Don't worry, I have no intention of wading through that mud," Zorian said. "Watch."

He made a few gestures and cast a 'levitate object' spell, causing the bike to jerkily rise out of the water and into the air. The bike was a lot heavier than the objects with which he usually practiced, and he had to levitate the bike a lot higher than he was used to, but it was nothing outside his capabilities. He snatched the bike by its seat when it was close enough and placed it on the bridge.

"There," Zorian said. "It's all muddy and wet but I can't help you there. Don't know any cleaning spells."

"O-Okay," she nodded slowly, clutching her bicycle like it was going to fly out of her hand the moment she let go.

He bid her goodbye and left, deciding his relaxing time at the fountain just wasn't meant to be. The weather seemed to be worsening pretty quickly, too—dark clouds were brewing ominously across the horizon, heralding rain. He decided to simply join the diffuse line of students trudging towards the academy and be done with it.

It was a long way from the train station to the academy, since the station was on the outskirts of the city and the academy was right next to the Hole. Depending on how physically fit you were, and how much luggage you had to drag around, you could get there in an hour or two. Zorian wasn't particularly fit, what with his skinny physique and shut-in ways, but he had purposely packed light in anticipation of this journey. He joined the procession of students that was still streaming from the train station in the direction of the academy, ignoring the occasional first-year struggling with excessive baggage. He empathized with them because his asshole brothers hadn't warned him to keep the luggage at a minimum either, meaning he had been just like them the first time he arrived at the train station, but there was nothing he could do to help them.

The threat of rain and bad luck aside, he felt invigorated as he drew closer to academy grounds. He was drawing on the ambient mana suffusing the area around the Hole, replenishing the mana reserves he spent levitating that girl's bicycle. Mage academies are almost always built on top of mana wells for the express purpose of exploiting this effect. An area with such high ambient mana levels is a perfect place for inexperienced mages to practice their spellcasting. Anytime they run out of mana, they can supplement their natural mana regeneration by replenishing their mana reserves from their very surroundings.

Zorian took out the apple he still carried in his pocket and levitated it over his palm. It wasn't really a spell, so much as raw mana manipulation—a mana shaping exercise that was supposed to help mages improve their ability to control and direct magical energies. It looked like such a simple thing, but Zorian had needed two years to master it fully. Sometimes he wondered if his family was right and he really was *too* focused on his studies. He knew for a fact that most of his classmates had much more tenuous control over their magic, and it didn't appear to be inhibiting them too much.

He dismissed the mana construct holding the apple in the air and let it fall down on his palm. A drop of rain fell down on his palm along with the apple. Another raindrop soon followed it, splattering on his glasses.

He wished he had some kind of rain protection spell. That, or an umbrella. Either would work just fine, except an umbrella didn't require several years of training to use.

"Magic can be such a rip-off at times," said Zorian gloomily.

He took a deep breath and started running.

"Huh. So there *is* a rain protection spell," mumbled Zorian as he watched raindrops splattering upon an invisible barrier in front of him. He extended his hand over the edge of the barrier, and it passed unimpeded. He withdrew his now wet hand into the safety of the barrier and followed the boundary as far as his eyes could see. From what he could tell, the barrier encircled the entire academy compound (no small feat, as academy grounds were quite extensive) in a protective bubble that stopped the rain—and *only* rain—from penetrating it. Apparently the academy had upgraded its wards again, because they didn't have this feature the last time it was raining.

Shrugging, he turned around and continued towards the administration building. It was too bad the barrier didn't also dry you out when you passed it, because he was soaking wet. Thankfully, his bag was waterproof, so his clothes and textbooks weren't in any danger. Slowing down to a leisurely stroll, he studied the collection of buildings that made up the academy. The wards weren't the only thing that was upgraded; the whole place looked…prettified, for a lack of a better term. Every building was freshly painted, the old brick road was replaced by a much more colorful one, the flower patches were in full bloom, and the small fountain that hadn't worked for years was suddenly functional.

"Wonder what *that's* all about," he mumbled.

After a few minutes of contemplation, he decided he didn't care much. He would find out sooner or later, if it was of any importance.

The administration building was, predictably, mostly empty of students. Most of them were sheltering from the rain instead of pressing on like Zorian, and those who didn't live on academy grounds had no reason to come here today. That was perfect as far as Zorian was concerned, as it meant he could be done here quickly.

'Quickly' turned out to be a relative term. It took two hours of wrangling with the girl working at the administration desk before he had taken care of all the necessary paperwork. He asked about his class schedule, but was told it wasn't finalized yet and that he would have to wait until Monday morning. Come to think of it, Ilsa had mentioned the same thing. Before he left, the girl gave him a book of rules with which third-year students were expected to familiarize themselves before sending him on his way. Zorian idly flipped through the book while he searched for room 115, then tucked it into one of the more obscure compartments in his backpack, never to be looked at again.

Academy-provided housing was pretty terrible, and Zorian hadn't known a pleasant experience with it, but it was free and apartment space was severely overpriced in Cyoria. Even children of nobles often lived on academy grounds rather than in their own apartments, so who was he to complain? Besides, living so close to the lecture hall cut down on the travel time each morning and put him close to the biggest library in the city, so there were definitely good sides to it.

An hour later, he smiled to himself as he entered a fairly spacious room. He was even more pleased when he realized he had his own bathroom. With a shower stall, no less! It was a welcome change from having to share a cramped little room with an inconsiderate roommate and navigating a single communal bathroom with the whole floor. As far as furniture went, the room had a bed, a closet, a set of drawers, a work desk, and a chair. Everything Zorian needed, really.

Dropping his luggage on the floor, Zorian changed out of his wet clothes before collapsing on the bed with relief. He had two whole days before classes started, so he decided to postpone unpacking until tomorrow. Instead, he remained motionless on the bed, wondering for a moment why he couldn't hear the raindrops hitting the glass plane of the window next to his bed, before remembering the rain barrier.

"I've got to learn how to cast that," he mumbled.

His spell collection was extremely limited at the moment, consisting of about twenty simple spells, but he had plans to rectify that this year. As a certified first circle mage, he now had access to parts of the academy library he didn't before, and he planned on raiding them for spells contained within. Besides, this year's classes were supposed to be much more focused on practical spellcasting now that they'd proven themselves capable, so he should be learning plenty of interesting things in class, too.

Tired from the long journey, Zorian closed his eyes, intending to take a short nap.

He wouldn't wake up until the next morning.

CHAPTER 002

Life's
Little Problems

Although the academy loved saying they were an elite institution thanks to the excellent quality of the teaching staff, the truth was that the main reason for their supremacy was their library. Through contributions of its alumni, generous budget allocations by a number of former headmasters, quirks of local criminal law, and sheer historical accident, the academy had built a library without equal. You could find anything you wanted, regardless of whether the topic was magical or not—there was a whole section reserved for steamy romance novels, for instance. The library was so massive it had actually expanded into the tunnels beneath the city. Many of the lower levels were only accessible to guild mages, so it was only now that Zorian was allowed to browse their contents. Fortunately, the library was open during the weekend, so the very first thing Zorian did when he woke up was descend into these depths to see what he'd been missing these past two years and maybe fill out his spellbook a bit.

He was pleasantly surprised at the sheer number of spells and training manuals available to a first circle mage. There were more books and spells than he could master in a lifetime. Most of the spells were either highly situational or minor variations of each other, so he didn't feel the need to obsessively learn all of them, but he could already see this place would keep him busy all year round. A lot of them looked surprisingly easy and harmless, and he couldn't help but wonder why they were kept on the restricted level instead of being available to everyone. These could have been useful during second year.

He had skimmed the contents of several tomes in search of the rain barrier the academy incorporated into its ward scheme when he realized he had skipped breakfast and was getting awfully hungry, and that it was past noon. Reluctantly, he checked out a couple books to pore over in depth in the safety of his room and went to get something to eat.

There was no kitchen in his room, sadly, but the academy had a decent cafeteria available to students. The food they offered was cheap yet surprisingly edible. Still, it was something of a poor man's option, and most of the richer kids ventured out to eat in one of the many restaurants in the vicinity of the academy, rather than subject themselves to the dingy cafeteria. Expecting the familiar worn-down tables and chairs that didn't sit flat, Zorian's steps slowed in surprise as he entered the cafeteria. It was positively sparkling. New tables. New chairs. Freshly polished flooring. It was weird to see the place so... clean.

Shaking his head, he quickly loaded a couple plates on his tray, idly noting the cooks were a lot less stingy with the meat and other expensive parts of the dish than he remembered, and then started scanning the present students for familiar faces. Clearly something was happening here, and he hated being left outside the loop.

"Zorian! Over here!"

How fortunate. Zorian immediately set off towards the chubby boy gesturing for him to come over. Zorian had learned over the years that his exuberant classmate was firmly plugged into the academy gossip network, and knew pretty much everything and everyone. If anyone would know what was going on, it would be Benisek.

"Hello, Ben," Zorian said, placing his food tray on the table Benisek was using. He sat opposite of the other boy so they could face each other as they talked. "I'm surprised to see you in Cyoria so soon. Don't you usually come with the last train?"

"I should be asking you that!" Benisek half shouted. Zorian never understood why the boy had to be so loud all the time. "I came here so early but you're already here!"

"You came back two days before classes start, Ben," Zorian said, resisting the urge to roll his eyes at the other boy. Only Benisek would think that coming a couple days early was some great feat worth mentioning. "That's not all that early. And I just got back yesterday."

Being pretty hungry, Zorian took an opportunity to shove a forkful of green peas and fried potatoes into his mouth while he listened to Benisek's response. The peas were noticeably undercooked and the potatoes were very dry, and both could use a little more salt, but overall it was the level of quality that Zorian was used to receiving in the academy cafeteria.

"So did I," Benisek said. He wordlessly handed Zorian a salt shaker, as if reading his mind. "Damn. If you had contacted me, we could have arranged to travel together or something. You must have been bored out of your mind here, all alone for a whole day."

"Something like that." Zorian smiled politely, carefully separating the onions to one side of the plate so they wouldn't contaminate the rest of his meal, then liberally salting the rest.

"So, are you excited?" Benisek asked, suddenly changing the topic.

"About what?" Zorian asked. Funny, hadn't Kirielle asked him the exact same question?

"The start of a new year! We're third-years now. That's when the real fun starts."

Zorian blinked. To his knowledge, Benisek wasn't terribly concerned about his success in the arcane arts. He already had a guaranteed post in his family business, and was here simply to obtain the prestige of being a licensed mage. Zorian had half expected him to drop out immediately following certification, yet here he was, just as excited as Zorian to finally start delving into the real mysteries of magic. Zorian felt a twinge of guilt for writing Ben off so quickly. He really shouldn't be so presumptuous…

"Oh, that. Of course I'm excited. Though I must admit I never knew you actually cared about your education."

"What are you talking about?" asked Benisek, eying him strangely. "The girls, man, I'm talking about the girls. The younger ones *love* upperclassmen like us! The new batch of first-years will be all over us."

Zorian groaned. He should have known.

"Anyway," said Zorian, recovering quickly, "since I know you're always gossiping around—"

"Informing myself about the current state of things," Benisek cut in, his voice assuming a mock-lecturing quality.

"Right. What's with the academy being all sparkly and clean all of a sudden?"

Benisek blinked. "You didn't know? Oh man, people have been talking about this for months! Just which rock do you live under, Zorian?"

"Cirin is a glorified village in the middle of nowhere… as you very well know," Zorian said. "Now spill."

"It's the summer festival," Benisek said. "The whole city is getting ready for it, not just the academy."

"But there's a summer festival every year," Zorian said, confused.

"Yeah, but this year is special."

"Special?" Zorian asked. "How?"

"I don't know, some astrological bullshit," Benisek said, waving his hand dismissively. "Why does it matter? It's an excuse to have an even bigger party than usual. Don't look a gift horse in the mouth, I say."

"Astro—" began Zorian with a quirked eyebrow when something occurred to him. "Wait, you mean planetary alignment?"

"Yeah, that," Benisek agreed. "What's that anyway?"

"Do you have a couple of hours?"

"On second thought, I don't want to know," Benisek backpedaled, chuckling nervously. He stabbed his fork into a pile of fried potatoes and resumed eating. "Aren't you hungry?"

Zorian snorted. So easy to scare. The truth was that Zorian knew very little about planar alignments, and he probably couldn't speak about it for more than thirty seconds. It was a pretty obscure topic. Zorian strongly suspected that Benisek was right, and that it was being used simply as an excuse to have a bigger party.

He *was* hungry, though. They both focused on the food in front of them for a while.

"So, what did you do over the summer?" Benisek eventually asked.

Zorian groaned. "Ben, you sound like my elementary school literature teacher. 'Now, children, for your homework you will write a short essay about what you did during the summer holidays.'"

"I'm just being polite," Benisek said, eying his empty glass for a few seconds before eventually deciding to do nothing to refill it. Probably too lazy to walk to the nearest water tank. "No need to snap at me because you wasted your summer away."

"Oh, and you spent it productively?" Zorian challenged.

"Well, not voluntarily," Benisek admitted sheepishly. "Father decided it was time I start learning the family craft, so I spent all summer helping him and acting as his assistant."

"Oh."

"Yeah," Benisek went on, clacking his tongue. "He also made me choose estate management as one of my electives. I hear it's a really tough class, too."

"Hm. Can't say my summer was particularly stressful. I spent most of my time reading fiction and avoiding my family," Zorian said. "Mother tried to dump my little sister on me this year, but I managed to talk her out of it."

"I feel for you." Benisek shuddered, stabbing his fork into one of the sausages on his plate. "I've got *two* younger sisters and I think I'd die if they came to live with me here. They're both utter nightmares! Anyway, what did you take for your electives?"

"Engineering, Mineral Alchemy, and Advanced Mathematics."

"Eh!?" Benisek blanched, a sausage suspended in the air half way to his mouth. "Man, you're really taking this seriously, aren't you? I guess you're gunning for a spot in one of the spell forges, huh?"

"Yeah," Zorian said.

"Why?" Benisek asked. He looked genuinely baffled by Zorian's decision. "Designing magic items… that's a tough, demanding job. Surely your parents could find you a spot in their business?"

Zorian gave him a strained smile. Yes, no doubt his parents already had a spot all planned out for him.

"I'd rather starve out in the streets."

Benisek raised an eyebrow at him, but then simply shook his head with pity. "I think you're crazy, personally. Who did you choose as your mentor?"

"I didn't get to choose," Zorian scoffed. "There was only one left by the time it was my turn to do so. I'm mentored under Xvim."

Benisek actually dropped his spoon at this, staring at him in shock. "Xvim!? But that guy's a nightmare!"

"I know," Zorian said, releasing a long-suffering sigh.

"God, I'd probably transfer if I got assigned to that asshole," Benisek said. "You're a lot braver a man than I, that's for sure."

"So, who did you choose?" Zorian asked curiously.

"Carabiera Aope," Benisek said, immediately brightening.

"Please don't tell me you chose your mentor based on appearance."

"Well, not *just* based on appearance," Benisek said, brandishing his spoon. "They say she's pretty tolerant…"

"You don't want to do any extra work," Zorian surmised.

"This whole thing is like a vacation to me," Benisek acknowledged. "I get to postpone employment for two years and have some fun in the meantime. You're only young once, you know?"

Zorian shrugged. Personally, he found learning about magic and gathering knowledge to be fun all by itself, but he knew all too well that very few people shared this opinion with him.

"I suppose," Zorian said. "So, is there anything else that everyone knows that I missed while under my rock?"

He spent another hour or so conversing with Benisek, touching upon a variety of topics. It was particularly interesting to hear which of their classmates would be joining them this year and which wouldn't. Zorian had thought the certification exam was a bit on the easy side, but apparently he was mistaken, since roughly a quarter of their classmates would not be joining them. He did notice that most of the failed students were civilian-born, but this wasn't terribly unusual—mage-born students had parental support when learning magic and a reputation to live up to. He was pleasantly surprised that one particular asshole wouldn't be joining them this year: apparently Veyers Boranova lost his temper on his disciplinary hearing and got himself expelled from the academy. He wouldn't be missed. Honestly, that boy was a menace and it was a disgrace they hadn't expelled him sooner. Fortunately, it seemed there were some things that just couldn't be overlooked, even if you were an heir of Noble House Boranova.

He left when Benisek started discussing pros and cons of various girls in their class, not willing to get dragged into such a discussion, and went back to his room to get some reading done. He hadn't even opened the first book properly when he was interrupted by a knock on the door. Very few people cared to track him down to his room, so he actually had a pretty good idea of who it was before he even opened the door.

"Hi, Roach!"

Zorian stared at the grinning girl in front of him, contemplating whether to take offense at the insulting nickname before shooing her inside. In the past, while he was still crushing on her, the nickname had kind of hurt. Now it was just slightly annoying. Taiven promptly ran inside and jumped on his bed like a little kid. Really, what had he ever seen in her? Besides a beautiful older girl who was fairly nice to him and had a propensity to wear form-fitting clothes, that is.

"I thought you graduated," he said.

"I did," she answered, taking one of the spellbooks he borrowed from the library into her lap to leaf through it. Seeing how she had already taken over his bed, he sat down on the chair in front of his work desk. "But you know how it goes—there are always too many young mages and never enough masters willing to take them under their wing. I'm working as a class assistant for Nirthak. Hey, if you took nonmagical combat you will get to see me all the time!"

"Yeah, right," Zorian snorted. "Nirthak blacklisted me in advance, just in case I got any ideas."

"Really!?"

"Yeah. Not that I would ever sign up for a class like that anyway," Zorian said. Except maybe to watch Taiven get all sweaty and puffed up in that tight outfit she always wore whenever she trained.

"Pity," she said, seemingly engrossed in his book. "You really should put on some muscle one of these days. Girls like boys who exercise."

"I don't care what girls like," Zorian snapped. She was starting to sound like his mother. "Why are you here anyway?"

"Oh, calm down, it was just a thought," she said with a dramatic sigh. "Boys and their fragile little egos."

"Taiven, I like you, but you're really treading on thin ice here," Zorian warned.

She tossed the book aside and looked at him. "I came here to ask if you would join me and a couple of others on a job tomorrow."

"A job?" Zorian asked suspiciously.

"Yeah. Well, more like a mission. You know those job postings people tack onto the big board inside the administrative building?"

Zorian nodded. Whenever a mage in the city wanted something done for cheap, he posted a 'job offer' for interested students. The payout was generally miserable, but students had to collect 'points' by doing these, so everyone had to do a number of them. It was considered 'practical learning'. Most people didn't start doing these before their fourth year, unless they really needed the money, and Zorian fully intended to follow this tradition.

"A pretty nice one got posted this morning," Taiven said. "It's actually just a simple find and retrieve in the tunnels below the city that—"

"A sewer run!?" Zorian cut her off. "You want me to go on a sewer run?"

"It's good experience!" Taiven protested.

"No," said Zorian, crossing his arms. "No way."

"Oh, come on, Roach, I'm begging you!" Taiven whined. "We can't apply until we find a fourth member of the team! Would it kill you to make this tiny sacrifice for your old friend?"

"It very well might!" Zorian said.

"You'll have three other people to protect you!" she assured. "We've been there hundreds of times and nothing really dangerous ever happens down there. The rumors are just that: rumors."

Zorian snorted and looked away. Even if they really did keep him safe, it was still a trek through smelly, disease-ridden tunnels with three people he didn't really know who probably resented having to bring him along for the sake of a formality.

Besides, he still hadn't forgiven her for that fake date she invited him on. She may not have known he was crushing on her at the time, but it was still a pretty insensitive thing she did that evening.

He might feel a little more inclined to help if she stopped calling him 'Roach'. It was not nearly as cute as she thought it was.

"Okay, how about a bet?" she tried.

"No."

She let out an affronted cry. "You didn't even hear me out!"

"You want to fight," Zorian said. "You *always* want to fight."

"So?" she pouted. "You chickening out? You're admitting you'd lose to a girl?"

"Absolutely," Zorian deadpanned. Both of Taiven's parents were martial arts practitioners, and they had taught her how to fight since she could walk. Zorian wouldn't last five seconds against her in hand-to-hand combat.

Hell, he doubted anyone at the academy would do much better.

Taiven waved her hands in the air in a frustrated gesture and promptly collapsed on his bed. For a moment Zorian actually thought she was accepting defeat. Then she sat up and folded her legs under her until she was sitting in a lotus position. The smile on her face gave

Zorian a bad feeling.

"So," she began cheerfully. "How have you been?"

Zorian sighed. This was *not* how he had intended to spend his weekend.

Monday morning came early—pure torture after sleeping in had become habit, but Zorian managed to pull himself out of bed at the appropriate hour. He had many flaws, but a lack of self-discipline wasn't one of them.

He had managed to fend off Taiven after three hours of verbal wrangling, though he was in no mood for anything after that and put off reading for another day after her visit. In the end, he spent the entire weekend lazing around, actually somewhat impatient for classes to start.

The first class of the day was Essential Invocations, and Zorian wasn't quite sure what it was supposed to teach. Most of the other classes on his schedule had a clear subject of study made apparent by the class name, but 'invocation' was a general term. Invocations were what most people thought about when someone said 'magic'—a few arcane words and strange gestures and poof! Magic effect. It was actually more involved than that—a *lot* more involved—but the visible part drew all the attention. Whatever the class was, clearly the academy felt it was important enough to schedule it every day of the week.

As he approached the classroom, he noticed a familiar person standing in front of the door with a clipboard in her hands. This, at least, was a familiar sight. Akoja Stroze had been the class representative for his group since their first year, and she took her position *very* seriously. She gave him a harsh look when she noticed him, and Zorian wondered what he had done to annoy her now.

"You're late," she stated when he got close enough.

Zorian raised an eyebrow at this. "The class doesn't start for at least ten more minutes. How can I be late?"

"Students are supposed to be present and ready fifteen minutes before the class starts," she stated.

Zorian rolled his eyes. This was ridiculous, even for Akoja. "Am I the last person to arrive?"

"No," she conceded after a short silence.

Zorian walked past her and entered the classroom.

A gathering of mages was unmistakable. You could always tell when you encountered one. Their appearance and fashion sense gave them away unerringly, especially in Cyoria where mages from all over the world sent their children. Many of his classmates came from established magical families, if not outright Houses, and mage lineages often produced children with noticeable peculiarities, either due to bloodlines or because of secret enhancement rituals to which they subjected themselves to produce effects such as green hair, soul-bonded twins, or tattoo-like markings—all of which were examples exhibited by his classmates.

Shaking his head to clear his thoughts, Zorian went towards the front of the classroom, throwing polite greetings to those few classmates he knew a little better than the rest. No one really tried to talk to him—there was no bad blood, but neither was he particularly close to any of them.

He was just about to sit down when frantic hissing interrupted him. He glanced to his left, watching his classmate whisper soothingly to the orange-red lizard in his lap. The animal was staring at him intently with its bright yellow eyes, nervously tasting the air with its tongue, but didn't hiss again when Zorian carefully lowered himself into the chair.

"Sorry about that," the boy said. "He's still a little uneasy around strangers."

"Don't worry about it," Zorian said, waving the apology away. He didn't know Briam all that well, but he did know the boy's family bred fire drakes for a living, so it wasn't altogether unexpected to see him with one. "I see your family has given you a fire drake of your own. Familiar?"

Briam nodded happily, scratching the lizard's head absent-mindedly. The creature closed its eyes in contentment. "I bonded with him over the summer holidays," he said. "Familiar bond is a little strange at first, but I think I'm getting the hang of it. At least I've managed to talk him out of breathing fire at people without permission, else I would have to put a fire-suppressant collar on him, and he hates that thing."

"The school won't bother you about bringing it to class?" Zorian asked curiously.

"Him," Briam corrected. "And no, they won't. You can bring a familiar to class if you've reported them to the academy and can get them to behave. And, of course, as long as they're reasonably sized."

"I hear fire drakes can get pretty big."

"They do," Briam agreed. "That's why I wasn't allowed to have one until now. In a few years, he'll be too big to follow me into the classroom, but by then I'll be finished with my education and back at the ranch."

Satisfied the creature wouldn't try to take a bite out of him during class, Zorian let his attention wander elsewhere. He mostly spent his time studying the girls as covertly as possible. He blamed Benisek for this, since he usually wasn't in the habit of ogling his classmates. No matter how cute some of them were…

"Hot, isn't she?"

Zorian jumped in surprise at the voice behind him and cursed himself for being caught so unawares.

"I don't know what you're talking about," he said quickly, turning as calmly as possible in his seat to face Zach. The cheery, smiling face of his classmate told him he wasn't fooling anyone.

"Don't be so flustered," Zach told him happily. "I don't think there's a single boy in class who doesn't occasionally daydream about our resident red-headed goddess."

Zorian snorted. Actually, he wasn't looking at Raynie at all, but at the girl she was talking to. Not that he was going to correct Zach about that. Or anything, really. Zorian had mixed feelings about Zach. On the one hand, the raven-haired boy was charming, confident, handsome, and popular—and thus reminded Zorian uncomfortably of his brothers. But on the other hand, Zach was never mean or inconsiderate to Zorian and would often chat with him when everyone else was content to ignore him. As a result, Zorian was never quite sure how to act around him.

Regardless, Zorian never discussed his tastes in women with other boys. The academy rumor mill churned about who liked who, and Zorian knew all too well how even relatively innocuous rumors could make your life miserable for years to come.

"From your wistful tone, I'm guessing she's still immune to your charm," Zorian said, trying to shift the focus of the conversation away from him.

"She's tricky," Zach agreed. "But I've got all the time in the world."

Zorian raised an eyebrow at that, not sure what the other boy was implying. All the time in the world?

Thankfully, he was saved from further conversation when the door creaked open and the teacher entered the classroom. Zorian was honestly surprised to see Ilsa walk into class with the huge green book that all teachers carried, though he really shouldn't have been. He already knew Ilsa was a teacher at the academy, so there was nothing unusual about her teaching this class. She gave him a smile before setting the book down on her desk and clapping her hands together to silence those students who were too engrossed in their own conversations to notice the teacher in the room.

"Settle down everyone, the class has started," Ilsa said, accepting the list of present students from Akoja, who remained standing beside Ilsa at attention, like a soldier in front of a superior officer.

"Welcome, students, to your first class of the new school year. I am Ilsa Zileti and I will be your teacher for this class. You are third-year students now, meaning you have passed your certification and joined us in our… illustrious magi community. You have proven yourself to be intelligent, driven, and capable of bending mana—the lifeblood of magic—to your will. But your journey is just beginning. As all of you have noticed, and many of you have complained about, you have only been taught a handful of spells so far, and all of them are mere cantrips. You'll be pleased to know this injustice ends now."

A cheer erupted from the students, and Ilsa allowed them to go wild for a second before gesturing for silence. She certainly had a flair for theatrics.

Much like the students, really—that cheer certainly wasn't because they were honestly unable to contain their excitement.

"But what exactly are spells?" she asked. "Can anyone tell me?"

"Oh great," Zorian mumbled. "A review session."

Hesitant mumbling erupted in the classroom until Ilsa pointed to one particular girl, who repeated her answer of 'structured magic'.

"Indeed, spells are structured magic. To cast a spell is to invoke a particular mana construct. A construct that is, by its very nature, limited in what it can do. This is why structured spells are also called bounded spells. The shaping exercises you have been doing for the past two years, the ones that you all think are a useless chore, are unstructured magic. In theory, unstructured magic can do anything. Invocations are simply a tool to make your life easier. A crutch, some would say. To cast a bounded spell is to sacrifice flexibility and force mana into a rigid construct that can only be modified in minor ways. So why does everyone prefer invocations?"

She waited for a few moments before continuing. "In an ideal world, you would learn how to perform all your magic in an unstructured manner, bending it to your will as you please. But this is not an ideal world. Unstructured magic is slow and hard to learn, and time is precious. And besides, invocations are good enough for most purposes. They can do amazing things. Many of the things you can accomplish with invocations have never been reproduced using unstructured magic. Others…"

She paused and took out a pen from her pocket and placed it on the table before casting what Zorian recognized as a simple 'torch' spell. The pen erupted in soft light that illuminated the room. Well, at least now he knew why the curtains were closed in the classroom. It was hard to effectively demonstrate light spells in broad daylight. The spell was nothing new to Zorian, though, since they had been taught how to cast it last year.

"The 'torch' invocation is one of the simplest spells, and one that you should already know by now. It is comparable to the light-emitting shaping exercise that you should *also* know by now."

Ilsa then launched into an explanation about the relative advantages and disadvantages of the 'torch' spell compared to the shaping exercise and how it related to structured vs. unstructured magic in general. For the most part, it was nothing that Zorian hadn't known from books and lectures already, and Zorian amused himself by drawing various magical creatures in the margins of his notebook while she talked. From the corner of his eye, he could see Akoja and a number of other people furiously writing everything down, even though this was just a review session and they almost certainly had all of this already written in their last year's notebooks. He didn't know whether to be impressed with their dedication or disgusted by their single-mindedness. He did notice, however, that some of the students had animated their pens to copy down the entire lecture while they listened. Zorian personally preferred to write notes, but he could see how such a spell would be useful, so he quickly jotted down a reminder to find the spell they used to do that.

Ilsa then began discussing dispelling, another topic they had covered exhaustively during the previous year and also one of the key areas they had to be proficient in to pass the certification process. To be fair, it was a complex and vital topic. There is no one-size-fits-all solution to effectively dispelling a structured spell, and without knowing how to dispel your own spells, experimenting with structured magic could be disastrous. Still, one would think the academy would assume they knew it by now and move on.

Somewhere along the line, Ilsa decided to spice up her explanation with examples and performed some kind of summoning spell that resulted in several stacks of ceramic bowls popping into existence on her table. She told Akoja to distribute the bowls to everyone, and then had them use the 'levitate object' spell to make the bowls hover over their tables. Compared to levitating that little girl's bicycle out of the river, this was insultingly easy.

"I see you've all managed to levitate your bowls," Ilsa said. "Very good. Now I want you to cast the de-illuminator spell on it."

Zorian raised his eyebrows at this. What would that achieve?

"Go on," Ilsa urged. "Don't tell me you have already forgotten how to cast it?"

Zorian quickly made a couple of gestures and whispered a short chant while concentrating on the bowl. The item in question wobbled for a second before finally dropping out of the air like any normal heavier-than-air item. A plethora of clattering sounds informed him that this wasn't an isolated occurrence. He glanced towards Ilsa for an explanation.

"As you can see, the 'levitate object' spell can be dispelled by the 'de-illuminator' spell. An interesting development, don't you agree? What does a spell designed to snuff out sources of magical light have to do with hovering objects? The truth, my young students, is that 'de-illuminator' is simply a specialized form of a general-purpose disruptor spell, which breaks down the structure of a spell in order to make it go away. While not designed with 'levitate object' in mind, it is still capable of affecting it if you supply it with enough power."

"Why didn't you tell us to just dispel it normally, then?" one of the girls asked.

"A topic for another time," Ilsa said without missing a beat. "For now, I want you to take notice of what happened when you dispelled the spell on the bowl. It dropped like a rock, and if it had not been magically strengthened, it would have probably shattered upon impacting the table. This is the main problem inherent in all disruptor spells. Disruptor spells are the simplest form of dispelling, and virtually every spell can be disrupted if you put enough power into the disruptor. However, sometimes disrupting the spell can have worse consequences than letting it run its course. This is especially true for higher-order spells, which almost always react explosively to disruption because of the vast amount of mana that goes into their casting. Not to mention that 'enough power' can be far more than any mage can provide. Now, please place your bowl on the table and put a few torn pages from your notebook into it."

Zorian was somewhat surprised by Ilsa's sudden request, but did as she said. He had always found tearing paper to be cathartic, so he filled the bowl with a bit more than necessary, and then waited for further instructions.

"I want you all to cast the 'ignite' spell on the paper, followed immediately by the de-illuminator on the resulting fire to dispel it," Ilsa said.

Zorian sighed. This time he had caught on to what she was doing, and knew the flames would not be dispelled by the de-illuminator, but he did as she said anyway. The flames didn't even flicker, and the fire died out on its own when it ran out of fuel.

"I see all of you can cast the ignite spell perfectly," Ilsa said. "I suppose I shouldn't be surprised. Heating things is very easy to do with magic. That and explosions. None of you managed to dispel the flames, though. Why do you suppose that is?"

Zorian snorted as he listened to several other students trying to guess the answer. 'Guess' being the operative word, because they seemed to be throwing random answers around in hopes of making something stick. Normally he never volunteered for anything in class—he disliked the attention—but he was getting tired of the guessing game and Ilsa didn't seem willing to supply the answer herself until someone figured it out.

"Because there's nothing to dispel," he called out. "It's just a regular fire, started by magic but not fueled by it."

"Correct," Ilsa said. "This is another weakness of disruptor spells. They break down mana constructs, but any fundamentally non-magical effects caused by the spell are unaffected. With that in mind, let us return to our immediate problem…"

Two hours later, Zorian filed out of the classroom with his fellow classmates, actually a bit disappointed. He learned precious little during the lecture, and Ilsa said she would spend an entire month rounding out their basics before moving on to more advanced material. Then she assigned them an essay on the topic of dispelling. It was shaping up to be a relatively boring class, since Zorian had a pretty good grasp of the basics, and they had essential invocations five times a week—that is to say, every day. Joy.

The rest of the day was uneventful. The remaining four classes were purely introductory, outlining what material would be covered for each class and other such details. Essential Alchemy and Operation of Magical Items looked promising, but the other two classes were just more of the same thing they'd had for the past two years. Zorian wasn't sure why the academy felt that they needed to continue learning about the history of magic and magical law into the third year of their education, unless they were deliberately trying to annoy everyone. This was especially true because their history teacher, an old man by the name of Zenomir Olgai, was very enthusiastic about his subject and gave them an assignment to read a two-hundred-page history book by the end of the week.

It was a poor way to start the week, in Zorian's opinion.

The next day opened with Combat Magic, which was taught in a training hall instead of a classical classroom. Their teacher was an ex-battlemage named Kyron. It only took one look at him for Zorian to realize this was not going to be the average class.

The man standing in front of them was of average height, but he looked as if he was chiseled out of stone—bald, grim-faced, and very, very muscular. He had a rather prominent nose and he was completely shirtless, proudly displaying his chest muscles. He carried a combat staff in one hand and the ever-present green teacher's book in the other. Had someone described the man to Zorian, he would have thought it funny, but there was nothing funny about facing this person in the flesh.

"Combat magic isn't really a category of spells as such," Kyron said in a loud, commanding voice, more like a general commanding recruits than a teacher talking to students. It was probably the quietest class Zorian had ever been in. Even chatterboxes like Neolu and Jade were silent. "More like a way of casting magic. To use spells in combat, you need to cast them fast, and you need to overcome your opponent's defenses. This means they inevitably require a lot of power and that you shape the spell in an instant... which means that classical invocations you learn in other classes are *useless!*" He slammed his staff into the floor for emphasis, and his words reverberated throughout the training hall. Zorian could swear the man was empowering his voice with magic somehow. "Chanting a spell takes several seconds, if not longer, and most of your opponents will kill you before you finish. Especially today, in the aftermath of the Splinter Wars, when every fool is armed with a gun and educated in ways to effectively combat mages."

Kyron waved his hand and the air behind him shimmered, revealing a transparent phantasm of a minotaur over him. The creature looked fierce and angry, but it was clearly an illusion.

"A lot of combat spells used by mages of old relied on people being awed by magic, or unfamiliar with its limitations. Today, every child that went through elementary school knows better than to be scared away by an obvious illusion like this one, much less a professional soldier or a criminal. Most of the spells and tactics you will find in the library are hopelessly obsolete."

Kyron stopped and rubbed his chin in thought. "Also, it is somewhat hard to focus on spellcasting when someone is actively trying to kill you," he remarked offhandedly. "As a consequence of all this, nobody casts combat spells as classical invocations anymore. Instead, people use spell formulas, like the one imprinted on my staff, to cast specific spells with greater speed and ease. I won't even be teaching you how to cast combat spells without these items, since teaching you how to use classical invocations effectively in battle would take years. If you're really curious, you can always browse the library for the right chants and gestures and practice on your own."

Then he handed them each a rod of magic missile and had them practice firing the spell at the clay dolls on the other end of the training hall, until their mana ran out. While he was waiting for the girl in front of him to run out of mana, Zorian studied the spell rod in his hand. It was a perfectly straight piece of wood that fit well into Zorian's hand and could be grasped at each of the two ends without any change in effect—that being a bolt of force emerging from the tip of the rod pointing away from the caster.

When it was finally his turn, he realized that casting with the aid of a spell formula was almost insultingly easy. He didn't even have to think about it much, just point the rod in the desired direction and channel mana through it. The spell formula in the rod did almost everything by itself. The real problem was that 'magic missile' took a lot more mana than any other spell that Zorian had encountered, and he burned through his mana reserves in only eight shots.

Drained of mana and a little disappointed in how quickly he ran out, Zorian observed Zach as he fired magic missile after magic missile with lazy confidence. Zorian couldn't help but feel a bit envious of the boy—the amount of mana Zach had to have used by then was easily three or four times greater than Zorian's maximum. And Zach didn't appear to be slowing down at all, either.

"Well, I'm going to let you all go, even though the class isn't officially over yet," Kyron said. "You're all out of mana, with the exception of Mister Noveda here, and combat magic is all about practice. As parting words, I must caution you to use your newly acquired combat magic with restraint and responsibility. Otherwise, I will personally hunt you down."

If it were any other professor saying this, Zorian would have laughed, but Kyron might just be crazy enough to do it.

Then it was time for spell formula class, which was the branch of magic that was used to build the focusing aids they had used in their combat magic class. Their teacher, a young woman with gravity-defying orange hair that stood up like the flame of a candle, reminded Zorian of Zenomir Olgai with her enthusiasm for her subject. Zorian actually liked spell formula, but not quite as much as Nora Boole thought was appropriate. Her 'recommended reading' included twelve different books and she immediately announced that she would be organizing bonus lectures each week for those interested in learning more. Then she gave them 'a short test' (it had sixty questions) to assess how much they remembered from their last two years. She then wrapped up the class by telling them to read the first three chapters from one of the books on her recommended reading list for the next day.

After that, the rest of the day was like a relaxation period in comparison.

Zorian knocked on the door in front of him, nervously fidgeting in place. The first week of school was rather uneventful, aside from finding out that Advanced Mathematics was also taught by Nora Boole, and she was similarly enthusiastic about that subject as well, giving them another preliminary test and more 'recommended reading'. Still, it was now Friday, and it was time to meet his mentor.

"Come in," a voice sounded from the room, and Zorian swore he could feel the impatience in the voice already, like the man felt Zorian was wasting his time before he even saw him. He opened the door and came face to face with Xvim Chao, the notorious mentor from hell.

The man in front of him didn't look imposing at first glance. He was of average height and build, clean shaven, with short black hair and a flat, stoic expression on his face. His hands were folded together on the table in front of him, his back straight, and he remained motionless like a statue as Zorian entered the office.

Despite the man's inscrutable bearing and flat facial expression, Zorian could tell straight away that Xvim didn't think much of him.

"Zorian Kazinski? Sit down, please," Xvim ordered, not even bothering to wait for an answer. Zorian barely caught the pen the man threw at him the moment he sat down.

"Show me your basic three," his mentor ordered, referring to the shaping exercises they were taught in their second year. His voice was polite, but firm.

He had heard about this part. No one had ever mastered the basic three enough to impress Xvim. Sure enough, Zorian had barely begun levitating the pen when he was interrupted.

"Slow," Xvim pronounced. "It took you a full second of concentration to snap into a proper mindset. You must be faster. Start over."

Start over. Start over. Start over. He kept saying that, again and again, until Zorian realized it had been a whole hour since they had begun. He had completely lost track of time in his attempt to focus on the exercise instead of his growing desire to ram the pen into Xvim's eye socket.

"Start over."

The pen immediately rose into the air, before Xvim was even done talking. Really, how could he possibly get any faster than this with the exercise?

He lost focus when a marble collided with his forehead, disrupting his concentration.

"You lost focus," Xvim admonished.

"You threw a marble at me!" protested Zorian, unable to quite accept that Xvim had really done something so childish. "What did you expect would happen!?"

"I expected you to maintain focus on the exercise *anyway*," Xvim said. "Had you truly mastered the exercise, such a minor disturbance would not have impeded you. It seems I have once again been regretfully proven right: the inadequacy of current academy curricula has stunted the growth of another promising student. It seems we have to start with the very basics of mana shaping. We will go through each of the basic three until you can do them flawlessly."

"Professor, I had those exercises mastered a year ago," Zorian protested. He was *not* wasting his time with the basic three. He had already spent too much time refining those in his opinion.

"You have not," Xvim said, sounding as if he was affronted Zorian would even suggest such a thing. "Being able to perform the exercise reliably is not the same as mastering it. Besides, doing this will teach you patience and how to control your temper, which is *clearly* something you are having trouble with. Those are important skills for a mage to have."

Zorian's lips pressed themselves into a thin line. The man was intentionally pissing him off, Zorian was sure of it. Apparently the rumors were right and these sessions were going to be one giant exercise in frustration.

"Let us start with the levitation exercise," Xvim said, oblivious to Zorian's musings. "Start over."

He was starting to hate those two words.

CHAPTER 003

The
Bitter Truth

I f someone had asked Zorian at the end of the
first week what classes he thought he would
have the most trouble with, he would have
answered Spell Formulas and Advanced Mathematics. Combat Magic maybe. Two weeks later,
he could safely say the answer was Warding.

Warding, the art of protecting things with
magic, was a surprisingly complex field. It was
necessary to take into account the material, dimen-
sions, and geometry of the object to be protected,
as well as what existing magic was present and
how it might react with the ward—or you could
just slap a general-purpose warding invocation on

your target and hope for the best. But the professor would fail you for that answer, so that wasn't an option in the classroom.

But these complexities aside, the class should have been a breeze, or at least not this confusing. Zorian was a patient, methodical person when it came to magecraft, and he had slogged through worse offenders than warding with decent results. The problem was that their teacher, a stern woman with hair cut so short she might as well have gone all the way and shaved her head completely, didn't know how to teach. At all. Oh, she clearly knew the subject matter very well, but she simply didn't know how to translate that knowledge into a proper lecture. She was leaving a lot of things out of her lectures, apparently not realizing that just because they were obvious to *her*, they were not obvious to her students. The textbook she assigned for the class wasn't much better, and read more like a manual for a professional warder than a student's textbook.

Question 6: You are tasked with building a research outpost on a first degree mana well in the Sarokian Highlands. The building is meant to support a staff of four at any particular time, and the prospectors have expressed concerns over a heavy presence of winter wolf packs and an infestation of borer wasps in the surrounding area. You have a budget of 25,000 pieces and are assumed to be a certified second circle warder.

Assuming only mana extracted from the mana well is available for powering the wards, which combination of wards do you feel would be the best choice for the outpost? Explain your reasoning.

Draw basic floor-plans of the planned outpost and explain how the room placement and shape of the building itself affect ward effectiveness.

Do you think the issue of the borer wasp infestation is best resolved by using a vermin repellant ward or by careful choice of building materials? Explain your reasoning.

Assume that you are commissioned to build not one but five outposts. The budget remains the same. How does this change your answer? Do you believe it is better to make the wards identical for all five outposts or do you feel some amount of difference between them is in order? Explain the advantages and disadvantages of each approach.

Zorian rubbed his eyes in frustration. How was he supposed to answer a question like this? He didn't take the architecture elective and wasn't aware that you had to take it to do well in your warding class. Not to mention that the question assumed they knew what the market rates were for buying the necessary materials, or that they knew where the Sarokian Highlands were. Zorian was quite good at geography, and he had no idea, though considering the presence of monsters like winter wolves, he suspected they were somewhere in the northern forest.

At the very least he knew how to answer the third part of the question. The correct answer was definitely wards. Even if the outpost was made inedible to borer wasp larvae, it would still make a prime place to build a nest. Considering how territorial those insects were, you didn't want them living anywhere near you. Theoretically, the 'careful choice of materials' options would free up mana that would otherwise be spent on maintaining vermin repellant wards, but those wards required very little mana flow to stay active. Especially if they were keyed specifically to borer wasps.

His thoughts were interrupted by a girlish giggle coming from the back of the classroom. Zorian didn't even have to turn around to know what was happening. Zach was entertaining the students around him again. He wished the teacher would penalize the guy for the disruption he was causing, especially in the middle of an exam, but Zach was a bit of a darling to the stern woman because he was the only student acing her exams. No doubt the guy had already finished his test with 100% accuracy. Which, by the way, made no sense whatsoever. During their first two years, Zach had been a below-average student more distinguished because of his charm than magical talent. Kind of like a nicer version of Fortov, actually. This year, though, he was acing everything. *Everything*. He had a wealth of knowledge and a work ethic he hadn't had at the end of their second year, far in excess of what could be gained through the normal passage of time.

How does one improve so drastically in the span of a single summer?

Fifteen minutes later, Zorian threw his pencil down on the table, calling it quits. He had only filled in eight out of ten questions, and he wasn't sure how correct these eight were, but it would have to do. He would have to set aside a couple days for warding self-study because the lectures were making less and less sense with every passing day. The only other student that stayed in the classroom as long as he did was Akoja, and she handed in her paper only a few seconds after he did and followed him outside. Of course, they stayed in the classroom so long for very different reasons. He stayed so he could scrape in a few stray points. She stayed because she was a perfectionist who wanted to triple check everything.

"Zorian, wait!"

Zorian slowed down and allowed Akoja to catch up to him. The girl could be insufferable sometimes, but she was a good person overall and he didn't want to snap at her just because the test didn't go the way he wanted.

"How do you think you did back there?" she asked.

"Badly," he answered, not seeing the point in lying.

"Yeah, me too."

Zorian rolled his eyes. Their definitions of 'badly' differed greatly.

"Neolu finished in only half an hour," said Akoja after a brief silence. "I bet she'll get a perfect score again."

"Ako..." Zorian sighed.

"I know everyone thinks I'm jealous but that's not normal!" said Akoja in a hushed but agitated voice. "I'm pretty smart and I study all the time and I'm still having problems with the material. And we've both been in the same class as Neolu for the past two years and she was never this good. And... and now she's beating me in every single class!"

"Kind of like Zach," said Zorian.

"Exactly like Zach!" she agreed. "They even hang out together, two of them and one other girl I don't know, behaving like... like they're in their own private little world."

"Or like they're a couple," said Zorian, before frowning. "Triple? What's the word for a romantic relationship between three people?"

Akoja scoffed. "Whatever. The point is the three of them do nothing but waste time together and antagonize the teachers and get perfect scores anyway. They even refused the chance to get transferred to first tier groups, can you believe that!?"

"You're too worked up over this," Zorian warned.

"Aren't you a little bit curious how they do it?" asked Akoja.

"Of course I am," said Zorian. "It's hard not to be. But what can I do about it? Besides, Zach has never done anything to me. I don't want to cause problems for him just because he has suddenly discovered his inner prodigy."

Zorian squeezed to the left of the hallway as Benisek suddenly swooped in so he could walk beside them, simply popping up from behind a corner like an eavesdropping ghost. Sometimes Zorian wondered if the chubby boy could *smell* gossip.

"I know what you mean," Benisek said. "I always thought Zach was no good at anything. You know, like me."

"Hah. Well, there's no way he got this good at everything over one summer break," Zorian said. "I guess he was pulling the wool over our eyes all this time."

"Man, that's so stupid," said Benisek. "If I were that good I'd make sure everyone knew it."

"I don't think he was faking lack of skill for two years straight," Akoja huffed. "He would have slipped at least occasionally."

"Well, what's left then?" Zorian asked. He refrained from listing some of the more obscure ways such a rapid growth could be accomplished with magic, because most of them were criminal and he was sure the academy checked Zach to make sure he wasn't a shapeshifting imposter or possessed by the ghost of a long-dead mage.

"Maybe he knows the answers in advance," she suggested.

"Only if he's an oracle," Benisek said. "Boole gave him an oral exam last Tuesday when you went home early, and he was rattling off answers like he swallowed the textbook."

The conversation died down as all three filed into the alchemy classroom, which was really more of a big workshop than a typical classroom. There were about twenty tables, each one full of various containers and other equipment. All ingredients for the day's lesson were already set out in front of them, though some would require additional preparation before they could be used in whatever process they were learning about that day. Zorian was pretty sure they weren't going to be putting live cave crickets into the boiling solution, for instance.

Alchemy, like warding, was a complicated art, but their teacher knew her stuff *and* knew how to teach, so Zorian wasn't having any issues with the class. Technically they had to work in groups of two or three students because there were not enough tables and equipment, but Zorian always paired up with Benisek, which translated to working alone in practice. The only problem was getting Benisek to shut up and stop distracting him during class.

"Hey Zorian," Benisek whispered to him not so quietly. "I never noticed it until now, but our teacher is kind of hot!"

Zorian gritted his teeth. The blasted idiot couldn't keep his voice down if his life was on the line. There was no way she didn't hear that.

"Benisek," he hissed back to his partner, "I need good grades in alchemy to get my dream job when I graduate. If you screw this up for me I will never speak to you again."

Benisek grumbled mutinously before returning to his ogling. Zorian refocused on grinding the borer wasp husks into a fine powder needed for the particular type of glue they were supposed to be making.

Admittedly, Azlyn Marivoski did look surprisingly good for a fifty-year-old woman. Some kind of cosmetic treatment probably—she *was* their alchemy teacher, after all. Maybe even a true youth potion, though those were really rare and usually imperfect in some way.

"I don't see why you like this class so much," grumbled Benisek. "I'm not even sure I'd call it magical. You don't need mana for it. It's all searching for herbs this, cutting the roots the right way that... it's like cooking. Hell, we're making glue, of all things. You should leave that to girls."

"Benisek..."

"It's true!" he protested. "Even our teacher is a girl. A hot girl, but still. I read somewhere that alchemy traces its roots back to witches' covens, with their potions and what not. Even now the best alchemical families are descended from witches. I bet you didn't know that, huh?"

As a matter of fact, Zorian did know that. He was, after all, tutored in alchemy by an honest-to-gods traditional witch before he went to the academy. She was so traditional, in fact, that she shunned the name 'alchemy' and referred to her skill strictly as 'potion making'.

But that wasn't the sort of stuff you wanted people to know, for a wide variety of reasons.

"If you don't shut up right now, I won't let you partner with me anymore," Zorian told him seriously.

"Hey!" protested Benisek. "Who's going to help me with that stuff, then? I'm not good at this!"

"I don't know," said Zorian innocently. "Maybe you should find some girl to help you."

Fortunately, the teacher was currently too busy fawning over Zach's newest masterpiece to pay attention to Zorian's table. Somehow the boy had managed to make some kind of enhancement potion out of the provided ingredients, and that was apparently very impressive. Azlyn didn't appear to mind that Zach completely ignored the assignment to make magical glue and did his own thing.

Zorian shook his head and tried to concentrate on his own work. He wondered whether he would have gotten the same reaction if he did something like that, or if he would be accused of showing off. The few times Zorian tried to wow the teachers he was simply told to work on his basics and not get cocky, because arrogance kills. Was it because Zach was the heir of Noble House Noveda? Or something else?

It was in moments like these that he understood exactly how Akoja felt about all this.

"And that concludes today's lesson," said Ilsa. "Before you leave, however, I have an announcement to make. As some of you know, the academy traditionally organizes a dance on the eve of the summer festival. This year is no exception. The dance will take place in the entrance hall next Saturday. For those of you who are unaware, attendance is *mandatory* this year."

Zorian groaned, slamming his forehead into the table in front of him, causing the rest of the class to snicker. Ilsa pointedly ignored his reaction.

"For those of you who don't know how to dance, dance lessons will be held every day at eight in the evening in room six. Those of you who do know how to dance still have to come to at least one of these lessons to prove so. I will not have you embarrass me on the night of the dance. Dismissed. Miss Stroze, Mister Kazinski, stay after class, please."

"Oh great," Zorian mumbled. He probably should have restrained himself from reacting so strongly to the pronouncement. Truthfully, he intended to skip the dance, regardless of how mandatory it was. Did Ilsa realize that? No, he could detect no disapproval in her posture, and he was pretty sure she'd be rather annoyed if she sensed his plans.

"Now then…," Ilsa began when he and Akoja were the only students left, "I assume you both know how to dance?"

"Sure," said Zorian.

Akoja fidgeted. "Umm… I'm not very good at it."

"No matter," Ilsa said. "We'll iron out any gaps you may have easily enough. The reason I told you to stay behind is that I want you to help me with the dance lessons."

Zorian considered refusing outright. It wasn't something he wanted to spend his time on, but he figured this could be a favor that would make Ilsa forgive him a transgression or two. Like, say, not showing up to the mandatory dance? Before he could express his tentative agreement, however, Akoja decided in his place.

"How can we help?" she said, clearly pleased they were chosen for this 'honor'. Zorian raised an eyebrow at the way she presumed to speak for him, but let it slide for the moment.

"We only have five days to teach everyone how to dance," Ilsa said. "That's why we're going to use magic to help."

"Animation spells," Zorian guessed.

"Yes," Ilsa said, then quickly moved to explain for Akoja's benefit. "There is a spell that will guide a person's limbs and body through whatever dance it is designed for. It's not really suitable as a substitute for dancing skill, but if you practice dancing while you're under its effects, you will learn a lot faster than you would otherwise."

"How does that work?" Akoja asked.

"The spell moves you around like a puppet on a string until you learn how to move along with it, if only to make the feeling of something jerking you around go away," said Zorian. "Eventually you no longer need the spell to dance correctly."

"I see you have personal experience with this method," Ilsa said with a smile.

Zorian resisted the urge to scowl. Getting put under that spell by Daimen was one of his childhood traumas. It wasn't amusing at all.

"I sincerely hope you intend to give students a choice to refuse," Zorian said.

"Of course," Ilsa agreed. "Though, those who refuse this method will have to attend at least three sessions instead of one, so I expect most will choose this option instead of the traditional one. In any case, I want you two to help me cast the spell on people during the lessons. I expect I'll have to dispel and recast the spell often, and I could use some help."

"And why did you choose us, specifically?" Zorian asked.

"You both have decent control over your magic and you seem responsible enough to be taught such a spell. Animation spells targeting people are restricted material, after all, and not something normally available to students."

Huh. So how did Daimen get a hold of it then? In his second year, no less?

Well, whatever. At least knowing how to cast the spell would make it easier to counter it in the future.

"Anything else?" Ilsa asked. "Very well, then. Come to my office after the last class and I'll set up some dummies for you to practice on before moving on to people. Poorly controlled, the spell is intensely uncomfortable. We don't want to give anyone traumas."

Zorian narrowed his eyes. He didn't. Not even Daimen would… oh, who was he kidding? Of course he would have. Practicing such a spell on your own little brother was right up Daimen's alley.

"Miss Stroze, you can leave. I have something else to discuss with Mister Kazinski."

Ilsa began to speak the moment Akoja was gone, catching Zorian somewhat by surprise. He shook his head to clear his thoughts, trying to ignore his annoyance with Daimen in favor of paying attention to what Ilsa was saying.

"So Zorian," she said with a faint smile. "How are you getting along with your mentor?"

"He's having me work on my basic three," Zorian told her flatly. "We're still on the levitation exercise."

Yes, even after four weeks, Xvim was still making him levitate a pencil over and over again. Start over. Start over. Start over. The only thing Zorian learned in those sessions was how to dodge marbles that Xvim kept throwing at him. The jerk seemed to have an endless supply of those things.

"Yes, Professor Xvim likes his students to have a firm grasp of the basics before moving on to advanced topics," Ilsa agreed.

That or he hates his students. Zorian personally thought his theory was a lot more plausible.

"Well, I just wanted to tell you that you might be able to change mentors soon," Ilsa said. "One of my students will be dropping out after the summer festival, and I'll have a vacancy to fill. Unless something comes up, you're almost certain to be the one I pick. That is, if you're actually interested in a transfer."

"Of course I'm interested!" Zorian burst out, much to Ilsa's amusement. He frowned for a moment. "Unless you also plan to throw marbles at me? Is that some kind of standard training method?"

"No," Ilsa chuckled. "Xvim is special that way. Well, I just wanted to see how you feel about this before doing anything. Have a nice day."

It was only after he was out of the classroom that he realized this development greatly complicated his plan to skip out on the dance. He couldn't afford to annoy his (potential) new mentor too much, else he'd be stuck with Xvim for the rest of his education.

Well played, professor. Well played.

"Why can't we just cast that spell ourselves once the dancing starts?"

Zorian let out a long-suffering sigh. "You can't make an animation spell do something you don't know how to do yourself. You don't know how to dance, hence you cannot animate anyone to dance either. Also, how are you going to break the spell once the dance ends if you can't move your arms where you want them to be? This really isn't the sort of spell you should be casting on yourself."

Really, there were so many problems with that idea that Zorian struggled to put them all into words. Were these people thinking before speaking?

"So how many dances do we have to learn?"

"Ten," said Zorian, bracing himself for the cries of outrage.

Sure enough, a rumble of complaints erupted after that statement. Thankfully, Ilsa took over the lesson at this point, instructing everyone to pair up and scatter throughout the spacious room to give everyone enough space. Zorian could already feel a headache coming and cursed himself for letting Ilsa talk him into this. Even though room six was fairly spacious, there were a lot of people and the invisible pressure they gave off was particularly strong today.

"You all right?" Benisek asked, putting his hand on Zorian's shoulder.

"I'm fine," Zorian said, shrugging the hand off. He didn't like to be touched much. "I just have a slight headache. Did you need help with something?"

"Nah, you just looked like you could use some company, standing all alone in your little corner," Benisek said. Zorian decided not to tell him that he was intentionally standing on the sidelines unless he was needed. Benisek wasn't the sort of person who understood the need for some breathing room. "Say, who is your date for the dance anyway?"

Zorian suppressed a groan. Of course Benisek would want to talk about *that*.

Relationships weren't something Zorian thought about often. The chances that one of his classmates would agree to date him were minuscule. For one, such a relationship would quickly be noticed by the rest of their classmates, and the resulting merciless teasing was something few relationships could survive for any appreciable length. Secondly, and perhaps more importantly, all teenage girls liked older guys. Dating a guy that was two or three years her senior seemed to be a status symbol for a girl, and a majority of them loudly disparaged the male population their own age as crass and immature. When they were in their first year, all the girls wanted to date third-years. Now that they were in their third year, all the girls wanted to date apprenticed graduates. Since there were plenty of guys willing to play along, the chances that some girl in his class would give him the time of day were negligible.

And the girls that weren't his classmates? To most of them he wasn't Zorian Kazinski, but 'brother of Daimen and Fortov Kazinski'. They had this image of what he ought to be like, and once it became obvious that the real him didn't match their expectations, they inevitably became bored or upset.

Besides, all this romantic stuff... well.

"Well?" Benisek prodded.

"I'm not going," Zorian said.

"What do you mean 'I'm not going'?" Benisek said cautiously.

"Just what I said," Zorian said. "I'm skipping out on the whole dance thing. Turns out I had an alchemy-related accident and have to stay in my room for the evening."

It was perhaps a bit cliché, but whatever. Zorian had already found a particularly tricky potion that was supposed to make a person more outgoing and sociable—something that was entirely plausible for him to try to make. It would make a person very ill when prepared incorrectly but wouldn't actually kill. If he played it right it would seem like an honest mistake instead of a way to weasel out of the dance.

"Oh come on!" protested Benisek, and Zorian had to pinch him to make him lower his voice. The last he needed was to have Ilsa overhear him. "It's the summer festival! A special summer festival, with the whole... parallel... thingy..."

"Planar alignment," Zorian offered.

"Whatever. The point is that you have to be there. Everyone who is anyone is coming!"

"I'm a nobody."

Benisek sighed. "No, Zorian, you're not. Look, Zorian, we're both merchant kids, right?"

"I don't like where this is going," Zorian warned.

Benisek ignored him. "I know you don't like to hear this but—"

"Don't. Just don't."

"You have a duty to your family to put on a good face. Your behavior reflects on them, you know."

"There is nothing wrong with my behavior," snapped Zorian, aware that he was attracting stares of nearby people but not caring at the moment. "You're free to go to whatever you want, but leave me out of it. I'm a nobody. A third son of a minor merchant family from the middle of nowhere. People here don't give a fuck about me. They don't even know who I am. And I like it that way."

"Okay, okay!" protested Benisek, gesturing wildly. "Dude, you're making a scene…"

"Whatever," scoffed Zorian. "Leave me alone and go away."

The nerve! If anyone should take a look at the impression he was leaving it was Benisek! The irresponsible leech would have been dumped into a tier three group if it wasn't for Zorian's constant help, and this was how Benisek repaid him? Why was he even hanging out with that guy?

Zorian clenched his hand, trying to calm down. Stupid summer festival and stupid dance. The funny thing was that unlike most people who hate those kinds of events, Zorian wasn't strictly *bad* at them. He knew how to dance, he knew how to eat without embarrassing himself, and he knew how to talk to people. He had to know these things, because his parents used to drag him along with them when attending these kinds of events, and they made sure he knew how to behave himself properly once there.

But he hated it. He had no words to describe how much events such as these sickened him. Why should he be forced to attend something he loathed when the academy had absolutely no right to demand it of him?

No, they had no right at all.

Hesitantly, Zorian knocked on the door to Ilsa's office, wondering why she had called him there. There was no way…

"Come in."

Zorian peeked inside and was promptly told to have a seat while Ilsa calmly sat behind her desk, drinking something out of a cup. Probably tea. She looked calm and serene, but Zorian could detect an undercurrent of disapproval in her posture.

"So, Zorian," Ilsa began. "You've been doing quite well in my class."

"Err, thank you, professor," said Zorian. "I try."

"Indeed, one could say you're one of the best students in your group. A student I intend to take under my wing after this whole festival rush dies down. An example to everyone, and just as much a representative of your class as Miss Stroze."

Oh, this was *bad*.

"I don't—"

"Are you excited about the dance this Saturday?" asked Ilsa, seemingly changing the topic.

"Yes, I am," Zorian lied smoothly, a radiant smile blooming on his face. "It sounds like a lot of fun."

"That's good," Ilsa said, smiling back at him. "Because I heard that you plan to boycott the event. It was rather upsetting, I must say. I was rather clear that attendance is mandatory, I believe."

Zorian fought to keep himself from grimacing. He should find something horrible to do to Benisek. A spell that causes the target's tongue to feel like it's on fire or something… or maybe piercing pain in the genital region…

"Just a bunch of nasty rumors, professor," Zorian said smoothly. "I would never dream of intentionally boycotting the dance. If I am unable to attend—"

"Zorian."

"Professor, why is it so important that I show up there, anyway?" asked Zorian, a bit of crankiness seeping into his voice. He knew it was a bad idea to blow up on a teacher, but damn this whole thing was *pissing him off*! "I have a medical condition, you know? Crowds give me headaches."

She snorted. "They give me headaches, too, if it makes you feel any better. I can give you a potion for that. The fact is I'm one of the organizers of the dance, and if too many students are absent, I'll end up with a black mark on my record. Especially if someone as prominent as you were to not show up."

"Me? Prominent!? I'm just an average student!" Zorian protested.

"Not nearly as average as you think," Ilsa said. "Just getting this far requires extraordinary intelligence and dedication, especially for a civilian-born student who wasn't exposed to magic your entire life. People keep an eye out for people like you. Also, you're Daimen's younger brother, and we both know how famous he is."

Zorian's lips stretched into a thin line. He was sure the last reason was what it all came down to in the end, and all the other arguments were just excuses and attempts to butter him up. Even with his brother a whole continent away, Zorian still couldn't escape from his shadow.

"You don't like to be compared to him," she guessed.

"No," Zorian admitted in a clipped tone.

"Why is that?" she asked curiously.

Zorian considered side-stepping the question—his family was a sore subject for him—but uncharacteristically decided to go for honesty. He knew it wouldn't do much, but he felt like venting at the moment.

"Everything I do is always compared to Daimen and, to a slightly lesser extent, Fortov. It has been that way since I was a child, before Daimen ever became famous. My parents have never been shy about playing favorites, and since they were always interested chiefly in social achievements, I was always found wanting. My family has no use for a withdrawn bookworm, and made that abundantly clear over the years. Until recently, they ignored me completely, treating me more like I was my sister's babysitter than their son."

"But something happened recently that caused them to take notice of you?"

"Fortov happened," Zorian growled out. "He bombed several exams, had to be bailed out by Father's connections. He has shown himself to be generally unreliable, which is a problem, because he was supposed to be the spare heir for the family business, just in case Daimen dies on one of his escapades. So now I am suddenly taken out of the metaphorical closet so they can groom me for the role."

Ilsa nodded. "But you don't want to be the spare?"

"I don't want to be involved in Kazinski family politics, period. I am not a part of that family. Never was. At best, I was only ever a loosely aligned associate. I appreciate them feeding me and funding my education, and I'm willing to reimburse them for that when I get a job, but they have no right to ask something like that of me. I won't hear it. I have my own life and my own plans, none of which involve playing second fiddle to my older brother and wasting time on insipid social events where people suck up to each other non-stop."

He decided to stop there because he was just making himself angrier and angrier. Plus, he suspected Ilsa didn't empathize with him much. Most people thought he was simply being overdramatic about his family. They weren't the ones who had to live with them.

When she realized he wasn't going to say anything more, Ilsa leaned back and took a deep breath. "I empathize with you, Zorian, but I'm afraid such comparisons are unavoidable. For what it's worth, I think you're shaping up to be a fine mage yourself. Not everyone can be a prodigy like Daimen."

"Right," said Zorian, refusing to look at her.

She sighed, running her hand through her hair. "You make me feel like the villain here. Family issues aside, why are you so bothered by this? It's a party. I thought all teenagers liked parties. Are you concerned about finding a date? Just ask some first-years and they'll jump at the chance. They can't attend unless invited by an upperclassman."

Zorian released a sigh of his own. He wasn't looking for a way to find a date. He had no doubt that simply dropping his last name would net him some impressionable giggly first-year for the evening. He was looking for a way out. Something that Ilsa wasn't willing to provide him with, it seemed.

"I'm not getting a date," Zorian told her, rising from his seat. "I may have to come to the dance, but I'm pretty sure that bringing a date is not mandatory. Have a nice day."

He was surprised that Ilsa didn't try to contradict him as he left. Maybe this whole dance thing wouldn't be such a chore.

Zorian trudged through the corridors of his residence building wearily, not in any real hurry to get to his room. The teachers had refrained from giving them any substantial homework over the weekend, knowing that everyone would be too preoccupied with the summer festival to get any work done. Normally all that free time would be a godsend to Zorian, but just thinking about what he would have to endure tomorrow was enough to make him lose the will to do anything fun or productive, so he fully intended to go to sleep the moment he arrived at his room.

As he turned a corner, he noted that someone was already in a celebratory mood. The walls of the corridor he was passing through were full of colorful splotches in vivid yellow, green, and red.

"Zorian! Just the man I was looking for!"

Zorian jerked in shock at the loud voice behind him and whirled around to face the man who invaded his personal space. He scowled at the grinning idiot in front of him.

"Why are you here, Fortov?" he asked.

"What, I can't visit my little brother?" he protested. "You too good to hang out with big bro?"

"Cut the crap, Fortov. You never come to *me* when you just want to hang out with someone. What do you need help with, now?"

"That's totally not true," Fortov huffed. "You're my favorite brother, you know?"

Zorian stared at him impassively for a few seconds. "Daimen isn't here so you'll settle for me, huh?"

"Daimen is an asshole," Fortov snapped. "Ever since he got famous, he's always too busy to help out his younger brother. I swear, that guy only thinks about himself."

"The hypocrisy is thick with this one," Zorian mumbled.

"Sorry, I didn't catch that."

"Nothing, nothing. So, what kind of trouble are you in now?"

"Um, I might have promised a friend I'd make her an anti-rash potion," Fortov said sheepishly.

"There is no such thing as an anti-rash potion," huffed Zorian. "There is, however, an anti-rash *salve*, which is applied directly to the affected skin instead of being imbibed like a potion is. This just shows what a total dunderhead you are when it comes to alchemy. What the hell were you thinking, promising your friend something like that?"

"I kind of pushed her into a purple creeper patch during our wilderness survival class," Fortov admitted. "Please, you have to help me! I'll find you a girlfriend if you do!"

"I don't want a girlfriend!" Zorian shouted irritably. Least of all the kind of girlfriend Fortov would set him up with. "Look, why are you bothering me about this? Just go to the apothecary and buy some."

"It's Friday evening. All stores are closed in preparation for the celebration tomorrow."

"Well, that's too bad, because I can't help you," said Zorian. "First two years are all theory and lab safety, and I'm just starting my third year. We haven't done any serious alchemy in class so far."

So true and yet such a bald-faced lie. He hadn't done all that much alchemy in class, but he had done quite a bit of private study in his free time. He could make an antidote for the purple creeper rash easily, but why should he spend his expensive alchemical ingredients?

"Oh man, come on. You can speak three different languages and you know all the silly shaping exercises they make us learn, but you can't even do something so basic? What the hell are you doing in your room all day long if not learning how to do stuff like that?"

"You're one to talk!" Zorian snapped. "You're a year older than me, you should be perfectly capable of doing this yourself."

"Eh, you know I never cared for alchemy. Too fiddly and boring for me," Fortov said with a dismissive wave. "Besides, I can't even make vegetable soup without ruining Mom's kitchenware. Do you really want me around alchemical equipment?"

Well, when he put it that way…

"I'm tired," Zorian said. "I'll make it tomorrow."

"Are you crazy!? Tomorrow is too late!"

"It's not like she'll die of a goddamn rash!" said Zorian irritably.

"Please, Zorian, I know you don't care about these kinds of things, but she's crushing on this boy and—"

Zorian immediately tuned him out. That was pretty much all he needed to know about this 'emergency'.

"—and if my friend's rash isn't fixed by then she won't be able to go and she'll *never forgive me*! Please, please, please—"

"Stop it."

"—please, please, please, please—"

"I said stop it! I'll do it, okay? I'll make the damn salve, but you owe me big time for this, you hear?"

"Yup!" he said cheerfully. "How much time do you need?"

"Meet me at the fountain in about three hours," Zorian sighed.

Zorian watched Fortov as he ran away, probably eager to disappear before Zorian could change his mind or make concrete demands. He shook his head and went back to his room to retrieve the necessary alchemical reagents. The academy had an alchemical workshop students could use for their own projects, but you had to bring your own ingredients. Fortunately, he had everything he needed for this particular task.

The workshop was totally empty aside from him, but that wasn't very unusual. Most people were preparing for the dance and were unlikely to do some last-minute alchemy practice. Unfazed by the eerie silence of the workshop, Zorian scattered the reagents across the table and set to work.

Ironically, the main ingredient of the anti-rash salve was the very plant that was the cause of this mess—the purple creeper, or more accurately its leaves. Zorian had already left them to dry in the sun, and now they only had to be ground to powder. This was generally the most annoying part of the procedure, as purple creeper leaves released a cloud of irritating dust into the air if they were simply crushed with a standard mortar and pestle set. The textbooks he read had all sorts of fancy ways to deal with this, usually involving expensive equipment, but Zorian had a much simpler solution: he wrapped the leaves in a damp piece of cloth, then wrapped the whole thing in a piece of leather, and then hammered the resulting lump until he felt no resistance. The irritating dust would bond with the cloth and the leaf pieces wouldn't.

After mixing the leaf dust with ten drops of honey and a spoonful of oblia berry juice, he put the whole thing over a low fire, stirring the contents until they achieved uniform color and consistency. Then he removed the bowl from the fire and sat while he waited for the stuff to cool.

"That was very impressive work," a feminine voice sounded behind him. "Nice improvisation with the creeper leaves. I'll have to remember that trick."

Zorian recognized the owner of the voice though, and Kael wasn't really female, despite some nasty rumors. He turned around to face the morlock boy, studying his bone white hair and intense blue eyes for a moment before returning his attention to cleaning the alchemical equipment he had used. No reason to get barred from using the workshop because he failed to clean up after himself.

He struggled to formulate a response while Kael was inspecting the salve with a practiced eye. The boy was rather mysterious, having only joined their group this year by transferring from gods know where, and not being very talkative. Plus, he was a morlock.

How long had the boy been watching him? Zorian had a tendency to lose track of his surroundings when he worked on something, so he couldn't be sure.

"It's nothing special," Zorian finally said. "Now your work… that's impressive. I get the notion that you're on a whole different level from the rest of us when it comes to alchemy. Even Zach can't beat you most of the time, and he seems to be acing everything these days."

The white-haired boy smiled mildly. "Zach doesn't have the passion for the subject. Alchemy requires a craftsman's touch and a lot of patience, and no matter how extensive his knowledge is, Zach just doesn't have the mindset for it. You do. If you had as much practice with alchemy as Zach apparently does, you'd surpass him for sure."

"Ah, so you think he has prior experience, too?" Zorian inquired.

"I do not know him as well as you do. I only recently joined your class. Still, one does not get as proficient in this field as Zach apparently has in a matter of months. He works with the practiced ease of someone who has been doing alchemy for years."

"Like you."

"Like me," Kael confirmed. "I hate to be rude, but are you finished here? I'd like to make something myself today."

Zorian apologized to the boy for the hold-up, which the morlock waved off as something of little importance, and bid him goodbye.

As he walked away, it occurred to Zorian that he should have made some kind of sleeping potion for himself while he was at it. He had to get plenty of rest, because he certainly wouldn't get any the next night.

CHAPTER 004

Stars Fell

"**I**'m coming, I'm coming," Zorian grumbled, stomping towards the door. Really, why all the frantic knocking? Who exactly was so desperate to get into his room? He wrenched the door open and found himself staring at Akoja's disapproving face. "Ako? What are you doing here?"

"I should be asking you that," she said. "Why are you still at home? The dance is—"

"Two hours away," Zorian interrupted. "I can get to the dance hall in ten minutes."

"Honestly Zorian, why do you always have to wait for the last possible moment to do something? Don't you realize what a bad example you're setting?"

"Time is precious," Zorian said. "And I will repeat my question: what are you doing here? I don't think it's your usual habit to seek people out when they're not early enough for your tastes."

"Miss Zileti told me to get you."

Zorian blinked. It seemed Ilsa wanted to make sure he didn't 'forget'. Hah. While the idea *had* occurred to him, he knew that would never fly.

"She also said you couldn't find a date, so that will be me for the evening," Akoja continued in a more subdued tone, suddenly finding the doorframe interesting enough to merit examination.

Zorian scowled. How does 'refuse to bring a date' become 'couldn't find a date'? It seemed that Ilsa, like his mother, had a tendency to 'translate' his words into whatever was most convenient to her purposes. The two of them would get along quite well, Zorian suspected.

"Anyway, get dressed so we can go already," Akoja said, suddenly regaining her confidence. "You might be fine with cutting things close, but I'm not."

Zorian stared at her for a full second, trying to decide what to do. He was tempted to slam the door in her face and refuse to participate in this farce, but he supposed it wasn't Akoja's fault that she got roped into it. In all likelihood she had more pleasant plans for the evening than accompanying a surly boy who loathed the experience. He shooed her into the room and went into the bathroom to get dressed.

He really had to marvel at Ilsa's manipulation skills, though. If it was just him going to this thing, he would have arrived dressed in casual clothes, spent the absolute minimum of time there before leaving, and avoided people like a plague throughout the entire evening. Now? He didn't want to ruin Akoja's evening, which meant he would have to make at least a token effort. Yes, Ilsa and his mother would get along like two peas in a pod...

The walk to the dance hall was a quiet one. Zorian refused to strike up a conversation, despite sensing that Akoja found the silence awkward. The silence suited him just fine, and he knew he would be comfortable with very few things this evening. He would enjoy the peace while it lasted.

Which wasn't long. The ten-minute walk to the hall the academy had set aside for the event passed too quickly, as far as Zorian was concerned, and the moment they approached the entrance, they were greeted by the sight of a large gathering of excited students engaged in animated discussions.

Zorian paled a little at the sight of the dense throng. He was getting a headache just by looking at them.

Sadly, no matter how much he pleaded with Akoja, she refused to let them wait on the outskirts of the gathering until the start of the dance. As revenge, Zorian 'accidentally' managed to get separated from Akoja when they were ushered inside and got himself lost in the crowd. He chuckled to himself, wondering how long it would take her to find him again. He'd be shocked if it was less than half an hour, since he was quite adept at avoiding the notice of a particular person at a party without drawing attention from the other party goers.

For a supposedly simple school dance, the entire event was surprisingly lavish. The tables were overflowing with food, much of it so exotic that Zorian couldn't identify it, and the hall was decorated with high-quality paintings and animated carvings that moved in a pre-programmed manner. Hell, even the tablecloths were decorated with complicated lace and so delicate they had to have been made of something monstrously expensive. Many of his fellow students were openly gaping at their surroundings and even Zorian, who had been at these kinds of events many times before, was a little shocked. Then he shrugged and did his best to blend into the crowd so Akoja couldn't find him.

He meandered through the tables overflowing with food, occasion-ally sampling one of the dishes when he saw something interesting, observing the other people and painstakingly avoiding notice from anyone who might be inclined to strike up a conversation with him. He could see why Ilsa was so determined to make everything about the dance run smoothly. The sheer expense of the thing aside, it wasn't just the students that were present. There were also representatives from various guilds, Houses, societies, and organizations. And not just from the Alliance, but also from abroad, even other continents. He could see at least one man in the distinctive light blue Abnazia military uniform, a small delegation from Hsan, and a dark-skinned woman in a gown so colorful Zorian doubted anyone failed to notice her by now. He idly wondered what this dance was *really* about, since these people wouldn't be here for a mundane school dance, before deciding he didn't really care. People like this lived in their own world and their standards of 'important' differed from mere mortals like him.

An hour later the first dance was about to start and Zorian made his way to Akoja. She was fuming and didn't appear to believe him when he claimed he had honestly gotten lost and couldn't find her, but she managed to restrain herself from blowing up at him. He led her to the dance floor and didn't retaliate when she 'accidentally' stepped on his toes a couple of times.

"People were asking for you," she said finally, having tired of abusing his toes for the moment.

"Well, I was around," Zorian said with a small smirk. "All they had to do was look for me."

"No reason why you can't seek them out now, though," Akoja remarked.

"But Ako, we're dancing. There is no way I'd leave a beautiful girl like you for anything. I've left you unattended for too long as it is," Zorian said, not a trace of mocking in his voice. It was a practiced skill.

She glared at him, but Zorian could see she liked the compliment.

Sadly, it didn't stop her from dragging him off to meet one group of people after another soon afterwards. Zorian hated being put on display like that, but he suspected Akoja was under orders from Ilsa, so he didn't snap at her. He was surprised his stalling had worked for as long as it had, really. Zorian found himself memorizing various faces, names, and titles, despite not caring much. It was instinctive to him by now, and he did it even when he didn't mean to—the legacy of his family's failed attempt to turn him into a socialite.

"Kazinski? Oh, are you by chance related to—"

"Daimen and Fortov Kazinski, yes," Zorian said, doing his best to keep the annoyance out of his voice. The woman who had asked beamed in response.

"Oh my, how fortunate," she said. "I must say your brother isn't half bad with the violin." She gestured towards the stage, where the academy music club was playing a slow, relatively quiet song. Fortov was officially an ordinary orchestra member, but was obviously the most prominently placed musician on the stage. His presence, as usual, attracted attention and comments. "What instrument do you play?"

"None," Zorian said, his voice flat. His family had tried to teach him how to play an instrument, since it was a fashionable thing to learn among the rich (and those pretending to be so), but were thwarted by the fact that Zorian was almost entirely tone-deaf. He had no ability to play music at all. Truth be told, he wasn't particularly interested in it either, though he could certainly feign interest when doing so was polite. It was one of his mother's bigger disappointments that he had no talent in this area, since Daimen and Fortov were both relatively decent at music, Daimen at piano and Fortov on the violin. They weren't prodigies by any means, but they were skilled enough to impress the kind of people that frequented events like this. "I don't have much of an ear for music, unlike my brothers. Personally, I'm more interested in how the orchestra fills the entire hall evenly with sound, with everyone hearing them at the right volume, regardless of how near or how far they're sitting in relation to the stage."

Sadly, neither the woman nor anyone else gathered around them could answer that question. Apparently nobody else even noticed it until he mentioned it. In fact, Zorian got a distinct notion that people felt it was an irrelevant detail and that he was strange for even mentioning it. Bah—no appreciation for magic from these people. Why, then, were they attending a dance at a mage academy?

Thankfully, Akoja decided to have mercy on him at this point and led them to a nearby table to get something substantial to eat. A couple of other students from their class joined them and a casual conversation settled in around them. Zorian didn't contribute much, since he found the conversation to be mostly aimless drivel that was of no interest to him. He still nodded and chuckled at appropriate times, of course, brushing off an occasional comment about him being 'too quiet' and needing to 'lighten up'.

He was just about to dig into the piece of cake in front of him when Akoja nudged him with her knee. He glanced at her with an unvoiced question.

"Wrong fork," she mumbled.

Zorian looked down at the fork in his hand and realized he was supposed to use the tiny fork reserved for desserts. He shrugged and stabbed the cake with the giant fork in his hand anyway.

"I know," he mumbled back.

That seemed to be the straw that broke the camel's back.

"Zorian," she burst out, her voice carrying a pleading note in it. "Why are you being so difficult? It's just one night. I know I'm not what you wanted for your date…"

"It's not that," Zorian interrupted her. "It's not like I wanted a date, anyway. I was going to come alone to this thing."

She stared at him in shock. She seemed emotionally crushed, and Zorian didn't understand why.

"Y-You'd rather go alone than with m-me?" she asked.

Aw *crap*.

All this time he thought Akoja was roped into this to keep an eye on him, but what if she had *wanted* to go with him? That...

She fled before he could figure out something to say.

He swore under his breath and buried his face in his hands. And to think he had nearly convinced himself the night might not be so terrible.

An hour later he was pretty sure Akoja was no longer in the dance hall and that she wasn't going to come back. He didn't really want to chase her through the streets in the middle of the night, so he refrained from following her outside. Besides, what was he supposed to say to her? He wouldn't know where to even start. He thought about going home himself, but in the end he simply climbed up onto the roof of the dance hall and observed the stars. He wasn't going to get much sleep tonight, anyway.

To keep his mind occupied, he silently named all the stars and constellations he could see. Due to his interest in the topic as a child and the Astronomy class they had in their first year at the academy, he knew quite a bit. It was a full hour before he ran out of things to name and describe.

Monday was going to be awkward. Zorian had no doubt their little drama was overheard and would be *the* topic of conversation for several weeks to come. Considering that Akoja was a bit of a teacher's pet in most of the subjects, the teachers could very well decide to make his life more difficult as well.

Damn it all.

It was the sound of fireworks that broke him out of his thoughts. It was midnight, apparently, and the festival had officially started. Zorian relaxed a little as he watched various fireworks blossom against the night sky, each exploding in its own unique way. It was beautiful. Most of them dissolved into quickly fading motes of light after the initial explosion, but a couple of them remained whole and consistently bright, more like flares than fireworks. They arced through the sky before dipping down and falling back to earth like falling stars. He frowned. Strange. Shouldn't they be exploding by now?

The flare falling closest to him slammed into the nearby academy residence building and detonated. The explosion was so loud and so bright that Zorian was momentarily blinded and deafened, stumbling back and collapsing to his knees as the entire building shook beneath his feet.

Blinking spots out of his vision, his ears still ringing from the sound of the explosion, Zorian scrambled back to his feet. He stared at the spot where the stricken residence building once stood. Nearly the entire building had been leveled to the ground, everything flammable in the vicinity of the impact site was burning, and strange flaming shapes were emerging from the epicenter of the destruction.

Wait a minute... that was *his* residence building!

He collapsed to his knees again as the implications of this hit him. If he had opted to stay in his room like he had originally planned, he'd be dead right now. It was a sobering thought. But what the hell was happening here!? That was no firework, that's for sure! It looked and sounded more like a high level artillery spell.

Though the ringing in his ears made it difficult to discern at first, Zorian noticed the faint sounds of celebration had stopped. Looking over the city he saw that what had happened to the residence building wasn't an isolated occurrence: wherever one of the flares hit, it had left devastation in its wake. He only had a few seconds to ponder this before he noticed another batch of flares start ascending into the sky from the distance. This particular barrage was not masked by fireworks, so it was pretty obvious that they *were* artillery spells. The academy was under attack.

As the flares started dropping back to earth, Zorian began to panic. What the hell was he supposed to do!? Running away would be pointless since he didn't know what the flares were targeting. He could very well be running straight into the area of effect if he ran blindly. Wait a minute, why did *he* have to do anything? The building was full of capable mages. He should just notify them and have them handle it. Zorian got to his feet, his head rushing with blood and adrenaline, and raced to the stairs that would take him down into the dance hall.

He had barely stepped onto the top stair when he ran into Ilsa and Kyron.

"Zorian! What are you doing here?" Ilsa demanded.

"Err, I just went out for some fresh air," Zorian fumbled. "But that's not important right now!"

"I agree," Kyron said. "Kid, what was that blast? Don't tell me this is something you did?"

"Hardly," Zorian said. "Some kind of flares are falling all over the city, destroying everything they hit. Looks like some kind of powerful artillery spell."

Ilsa and Kyron shared a look before turning back to him.

"Go join Akoja and the others in the dance hall," Ilsa told him. "We'll see what is happening and teleport everyone into the shelters if necessary."

They both pushed past him and rushed to the roof, leaving Zorian to stumble into the dance hall in a daze. Akoja… Akoja wasn't in the dance hall. She left. Because of him. She was out there, maybe even already dead…

He shook his head and banished such thoughts out of his mind. He took out his divination compass and quickly cast a divination spell to locate her. He wasn't sure if it would work, since the spell he used could only find people you were familiar with—in other words, friends and family. Thankfully, it seemed that being classmates with her was enough of a connection for the spell to function. The needle of the compass spun wildly, then slowed to a stop, quivering toward the north.

He took a deep breath to steel his nerves. He was liable to get himself killed, but… well, it was kind of his fault. He didn't think he could live with himself if Akoja ended up dead because of him.

Like a ghost, he weaved between agitated students and foreign dignitaries, ignored and unhindered, until he was near the exit. He slipped out of the building and then broke into a run in the direction indicated by the compass.

Trolls were, as a whole, pretty nasty creatures. While variations existed among the subspecies, all of them were three-meter-tall humanoids with tough leather skin and supernatural regenerative abilities so strong they were able to reattach severed limbs simply by holding them to the matching stump for a few moments. The most numerous and famous subspecies was the forest troll, which had vivid green skin and roamed throughout the great forested expanse in the north.

As Zorian watched a troop of trolls strut through the streets, smashing windows and howling unintelligibly, he reflected that it was fortunate the acrid smoke wafting from the nearby burning buildings masked his scent. His textbooks all said a forest troll's sense of smell was frighteningly good.

Under less ominous circumstances, he would have wondered what such a large gathering of forest trolls was doing in the middle of a human city, relatively far away from their native lands, but the blades and maces they were holding told him all he needed to know. Those were weapons too advanced to have been produced by the trolls themselves, who were highly primitive and lacked such metal working skills. They were war trolls. Somebody had armed these creatures and set them loose on the city.

When they had stomped around a corner and out of sight, Zorian relaxed a little and tried to figure out what to do. He was such an idiot. Why, oh why did he have to run off without getting some help from the teachers first? Then again, he had assumed the flares were the only danger, in which case getting to Akoja wouldn't be an issue, assuming a stray flare didn't get him. Instead, he found the city overrun with monsters. This wasn't merely a terrorist attack like he had thought. It was a full-blown invasion! Sadly, the option to return to the dance hall was closed to him, since a lot of the invading forces were converging towards the academy, cutting off his path of retreat. With that in mind, Zorian set out towards Akoja, following the compass needle. He kept to the shadows, knowing the invaders would quickly notice anyone caught in the open, such as that boy standing... over... there...

Was that Zach?

"Over here!" Zach shouted, standing confidently in the middle of the ruined street, his hands cupped around his mouth to make his voice carry further. He was clearly trying to be as provocative and attention-grabbing as possible. "I'm over here you stupid animals! Come and get me!"

Zorian gaped at the reckless stupidity of what he was witnessing. What the hell was that idiot doing!? No matter how talented a student he was, there was no way Zach could stand up to the sort of monstrosities that were stalking the city at the moment. But it was too late to do anything. Attracted by Zach's shouting, the trolls came running back, unleashing a single collective battle cry before charging at the boy foolish enough to demand their attention. Zorian could tell from Zach's posture that he intended to fight the trolls, which he thought was pretty crazy. What could he, a mere student, do against a creature that could regenerate from nearly any wound done to it? Only fire and acid could do permanent harm, and they didn't—

Zach grasped his staff firmly in his right hand, his other hand outstretched in the direction of the charging trolls. A roaring fireball erupted from his palm, surged through the darkness at terrifying speed, and exploded in the middle of the troll formation. When the flames cleared, only charred corpses remained.

Zorian was shocked. A proper fireball like that was a third circle spell and required a sizable amount of mana to cast, much more than any academy student had. Even Daimen could not have cast that spell when he was Zach's age. Yet not only had Zach successfully done it, he didn't even appear drained from the action. Indeed, when a flock of iron beaks descended from the sky and attacked Zach, raining their deadly feathers at the boy, he erected a pale, faintly glowing shield—a freaking aegis!—around himself and peppered the birds with tiny fireballs that homed in on their targets, like magic missiles made out of fire.

A steady stream of monsters converged on Zach's location from the surrounding streets. More war trolls, more iron beaks, and a large pack of winter wolves, too. Zach showed no hint of fear or surprise at this, taking the entire horde on directly with one advanced combat spell after another.

Zorian was transfixed by the sight of his classmate effortlessly fighting off hordes of monsters single-handedly... so much so that he almost failed to notice that one of the winter wolves attacking Zach had stealthily broken off from the main pack and was sneaking up on him. Almost. Thankfully, some primal instinct alerted him to the danger and he threw himself to the side, narrowly avoiding the creature's deadly pounce.

Zorian cursed himself as he watched the winter wolf reorient itself with startling ease for something so large, ready for another attack. He really should have expected to be targeted, considering the amount of attention Zach was drawing to the area. He should have used Zach as a distraction and fled while he had the chance. Now it was too late. Zorian knew he was not fast enough to outrun a winter wolf, and he had no combat spells with which to defend himself. Or rather, no spell rods and other tools. If he survived the evening, he would definitely make it a priority to learn a few combat invocations, obsolete as they might be. That was a big if, though.

A shining bolt of force slammed into the winter wolf's head, causing it to explode in a gory mess of blood and bone fragments. Zorian didn't know whether to be disgusted that he was showered by some of the bloody mess or relieved he would live for a little while longer. He also noted that the effects of the bolt were stronger than a regular magic missile. He supposed this was just another example of Zach's baffling proficiency with combat magic.

"Zorian? What the hell are you doing here?"

Zorian straightened from his crouch and looked at Zach, noticing the trail of monstrous corpses left in the other boy's wake. Zorian eyed the staff in Zach's right hand and the belt full of spell rods. For all his apparent recklessness, Zach certainly came prepared. Zorian was tempted to ask the boy the very same question, but decided that would be needlessly antagonistic. Zach had just saved his life, after all. He decided to go for honesty. Maybe the other boy would be willing to help him get to Akoja, considering his awe-inspiring fighting skills.

"I'm searching for Akoja. She left the dance a while before the attack and it's kind of my fault."

Zach groaned. "Man, and I even went to the trouble of making sure you would be at the dance. It's like you want to get killed or something!"

"You?" asked Zorian incredulously. "You're the one that told Ilsa I wasn't planning to go? All this time I've blamed Benisek! How did you even know about it?"

"You always stay in your room and get killed in the initial barrage if I don't do something to stop it. And let me tell you, convincing you not to stay in your room without resorting to violence or getting Ilsa involved is a damn chore. You can really be a stubborn ass when you want to be," Zach said with a sigh.

Zorian stared at him, confused. The way Zach was talking, you'd think this kind of thing happened every day or something.

"But enough of that," said Zach cheerfully. "Let's go find Akoja before something eats her. You know the way?"

And so they did. They traveled through the burning streets of the city, leaving a trail of dead invaders behind them. Zach didn't even try to avoid the monsters, simply plowing through them like an angry god out for vengeance. At one point they were even attacked by a horde of skeletons and an enemy mage, but Zach simply made the earth beneath their feet open up and swallow them. Zorian dutifully kept his mouth shut and never questioned Zach about his seemingly inexhaustible mana reserves or his knowledge of advanced magic that should be beyond his access level and proficiency, content to enjoy the benefits of Zach's skill and talent. He would never have come this far without Zach's help, and he was honestly grateful for the boy's assistance. Zach could keep his secrets, whatever they were.

They eventually found Akoja barricaded in the upper floor of one of the houses. Apparently she was chased there by a pack of winter wolves and then refused to leave for fear that the creatures were waiting for her to come out. Smart, really. Smarter than what Zorian had done, that's for sure. Fortunately, there was no trace of winter wolves around the house at that point—not that Zach was likely to have had any trouble with them if they *were* present—so they moved to the slightly frustrating task of convincing Akoja that it was safe to unbarricade the door. It was clear her experience with the winter wolves had shaken her up pretty badly.

Zorian was certain she would blame him for causing her to leave the safety of the dance hall, so he was quite surprised when Akoja immediately latched onto him when she finally opened the door, hugging him and sobbing into his shoulder.

"I thought I was going to die!" she wailed. "There were these huge birds flinging iron feathers everywhere and the winter wolves and…"

Zorian opened his mouth in confusion, unsure how to deal with such an emotional outburst. He shot Zach a pleading look, but the boy merely grinned at him cheekily, apparently amused by the reaction.

"Ah, young love." Zach nodded to himself knowingly. "But I'm afraid you'll have to continue your heart-felt reunion back in the shelters."

"Yes!" Akoja shouted, lifting her face out of Zorian's shoulder. She ignored Zach's jab about them being in love, though Zorian suspected it was because she hadn't even heard that part. She was still clutching his torso with an iron grip, as if afraid he'd disappear if she let go. It was kind of painful but he refrained from telling her so. "The shelters! We'll be safe there!"

Zach flinched, his jaw tensing as he took half a step back before catching himself. It was so fleeting Akoja didn't appear to have noticed, but Zorian did. The shelters weren't safe? But it seemed they were safer than being out on the streets, because Zach appeared determined to go through with it.

"Great!" said Zach cheerily, clapping his hands in satisfaction. He took one of the spell rods out of his belt and handed it to Akoja. "You hold on too, Zorian."

"What is that?" Zorian asked, his hand hovering over, but not touching, the rod. The rod had none of the markings that might identify what it was for, which made Zorian leery of it. Using unknown magical objects without identifying their purpose was a big no-no if you wanted to remain healthy and live to old age.

"It's a teleport rod," Zach said. "It's programmed to transport whoever is holding it to the shelters. I've set it to a thirty second delay, so hold it before you're left behind."

"But what about you?" Akoja asked. "You need to come with us!"

"Ah, no," Zach said, waving her off. "I still have unfinished business here."

"Unfinished business!?" Akoja protested. "Zach, this isn't a game! These things are going to kill you!"

"I'm perfectly capable—"

Zorian wasn't sure what tipped him off, exactly. He just got a vague feeling of dread and knew he had to react immediately, much like when the winter wolf tried to get a jump on him earlier. Wrenching himself free from Akoja's grip with a sudden jerk, he pushed Zach out of the way of the incoming spell. An angry red ray surged through the air in front of them, passing right where Zach's head was only a few moments ago, and hit the wall behind them. The jagged beam of red light bit deep into the wall, gouging a deep trench in it and shrouding the area in a cloud of fine dust.

"Crap," Zach said. "He found me. Quick, hold the rod before—"

Akoja winked out of existence as the rod teleported her away to safety.

"—it activates," finished Zach in a long-suffering tone. "Damn it, Zorian, why didn't you hold on?!"

"You'd be dead if I had!" Zorian protested. He wasn't going to let a person who helped him so much tonight die from a stray spell if he could help it. Besides, whoever had cast it would surely fall to Zach's magical might, just like the rest of the creatures and enemy mages they had encountered so far. Just how talented could this enemy caster be, really?

A sudden gust of air blew the dust away and a gaunt humanoid figure stepped into view. Zorian gasped as he took in the appearance of the thing in front of them—a skeleton wreathed in sickly green light. Its bones were black with a strange metallic sheen, as if they were not bones at all, but rather a facsimile of a skeleton made out of some kind of black metal. Encased in gold-decorated armor, with a scepter held tightly in one of its skeletal hands and a crown full of purple gemstones, the creature looked like some long-dead king risen from the dead.

It was a lich. It was a thrice-damned *lich*! Oh, they were so going to die...

The lich swept its empty eye sockets over them. As Zorian's eyes met the black pits that once held the lich's eyes, an uncomfortable feeling washed over him, like the lich was peering into his very soul. The gaze lingered only a moment before the lich lazily shifted its attention to Zach, apparently dismissing Zorian as something of no consequence.

"So...," the lich spoke, its voice resonant with power, "you're the one who has been killing my minions."

"Zorian, run away while I deal with this guy," Zach said, clutching the staff in his hand.

Without waiting for a response, Zach launched a barrage of magic missiles towards the lich, who retaliated with a trio of purple beams as it erected an aegis around itself with a single wave of its bony hand. Two of the beams were aimed at Zach, but the third streaked toward Zorian's retreating form. He dodged at the last moment, causing the beam to impact the ground next to him. A sizeable explosion sent Zorian flying through the air to land in a heap as slivers of stone shrapnel pierced his legs. Zorian collapsed, pain burning through him, unable to take another step.

With every movement an agony, Zorian dragged himself behind a toppled cart, his eyes watering with dust and pain. He hoped it would shield him from at least some of the destructive power that was being thrown around in the battle. From this measure of safety, Zorian caught a glimpse of Zach, who was keeping the lich occupied enough that it didn't send any more spells after Zorian. He watched with growing unease as Zach and the lich exchanged various destructive spells that Zorian couldn't even identify, realizing with rising dread that his prediction of their grisly death was well founded. No matter how good Zach was, the lich was in another league entirely. The thing was toying with the other boy, and was bound to tire of the game sooner or—

Zorian winced as a spear-like red bolt punched straight through Zach's aegis and impaled the boy through his flank. He suspected the hit was in a non-vital spot only because the lich wished to gloat a little more, and his suspicious were all but confirmed when the creature didn't finish Zach off with anything destructive, opting instead to hurl Zach into the air with a single casual gesture. Zach collided with the wall near where Zorian was taking cover and groaned in pain.

The lich approached. Unhurried. Unconcerned that Zach was rising shakily to his feet, a spell rod clenched tightly in his left hand. Zorian could see that his right hand was pressed tightly against the bleeding wound on his flank. His staff was missing.

"You put up quite a fight, child," the lich said. "Impressive for someone who is supposed to be a mere academy student."

"Not… impressive enough," Zach gasped out, the spell rod dropping from his hand as he clutched the wound on his flank with both hands, apparently in great pain. "I guess… I'll have to… try harder… next time."

The lich chuckled. It was strange sound, hardly fitting the creature. It sounded way too normal, almost jovial and friendly in tone, rather than some sinister laugh. "Next time? Silly child, there will be no next time. There is no way I'm letting you live, surely you know that?"

"Bah," Zach spat, straightening himself with a grimace. "Enough talking, just get it over with."

"You seem surprisingly unconcerned at the prospect of your death," the lich remarked, equally unconcerned.

"Ah, whatever," said Zack, rolling his eyes. "It's not like I'll be dead for good."

Zorian looked at Zach incredulously, the pain in his legs a distant throbbing, not really understanding what Zach was getting at. The lich seemed to understand, though.

"Aaah, I see," the lich said. "You must be new to soul magic if you think this makes you invulnerable. I could just trap your soul in a soul jar, but I have a much better idea."

The lich casually gestured towards Zorian, and he suddenly felt his entire body freeze up as if it was encased in some alien force. Another wave and Zorian was hurled with great speed towards the shocked Zach. He slammed into the other boy and they both ended up on the ground in a tangle of limbs. Zorian flexed his fingers and was relieved that at least the unknown force paralyzing him was gone.

"It doesn't matter if your soul can be reincarnated elsewhere if someone mutilates it beyond recognition before it gets there," the lich said. "After all, the soul may be immortal, but no one said it cannot be altered or added to."

Dimly, Zorian could hear the lich chanting in some strange language that definitely wasn't standard Ikosian used in traditional invocations, but any curiosity about this was washed away by a new wave of pain and unidentifiable *wrongness* that suddenly slammed into him. He opened his mouth to scream, but then his world suddenly erupted into bright light before everything vanished into black.

CHAPTER 005

Start Over

Zorian's eyes abruptly shot open as sharp pain erupted from his stomach. His whole body convulsed, buckling against the object that fell on him, and suddenly he was wide awake, not a trace of drowsiness in his mind.

"Good morning, brother!" an annoyingly cheerful voice sounded right on top of him. "Morning, morning, *MORNING*!!!"

Zorian stared at Kirielle in shock, trying to understand what had happened. The last thing he remembered was the lich casting that spell at him and Zach, and then blackness. His gaze darted left and right, taking in his surroundings and confirming his suspicions—he was in his room, back in Cirin. That didn't make any sense, though. He was pleased that he survived the whole experience, but at the very least he expected to wake up in the hospital or something. And Kirielle shouldn't be this casual with him after he went through so harrowing an experience. Not even she was this inconsiderate. Besides, this entire scene was… eerily familiar.

"Kiri?"

"Um, yes?"

"What day is it?" Zorian asked, already dreading the answer.

"Thursday."

He scowled. "I mean the date, Kiri."

"First of Chariot. You're going to the academy today. Don't tell me you forgot," Kirielle prodded. Literally. She accompanied her words with a well-placed jab at his flank, sticking her bony little index finger in between his ribs. Zorian slapped her hand away, hissing in pain.

"I did not forget!" Zorian snapped. "I just…"

He stopped there. What was he supposed to tell her? Frankly, he didn't even know what he should tell himself.

"You know what?" he said after a moment of silence. "Never mind that, I think it's high time you got off of me."

Before Kirielle could answer, Zorian unceremoniously flipped her over the edge of the bed before jumping up himself.

He snatched his glasses from the set of drawers next to his bed and his eyes swept through his room with more attention to detail this time, seeking anything out of place, anything that might unmask this as a giant (if rather tasteless) prank. While his memory wasn't flawless, he had a habit of arranging his belongings in very specific ways to detect the rummaging of nosy family members. He found nothing massively out of place, so unless his mysterious re-enactor knew his system inside and out (unlikely) or Kiri had finally decided to respect the sanctity of his room while he was away (hell would sooner freeze over), this really was his room like he left it when he went to Cyoria.

Was it all a dream, then? It seemed altogether too real for a dream. His dreams had always been vague, nonsensical, and prone to evaporating from his memory soon after he woke up. *These* felt exactly like his normal memories—no talking birds, floating pyramids, three-eyed wolves, or other surreal scenes his dreams usually contained. And so much had happened, too. Surely a whole month worth of experiences was too much for a mere dream?

"Mom wants to talk to you," Kirielle told him from the floor, apparently not in any great hurry to get up. "But hey, can you show me some magic before you get down? Please? *Pretty please?*"

Zorian frowned. Magic, huh? Come to think of it, he had learned quite a bit of magic. Surely if this was all a particularly elaborate dream, all the magic he had learned in his classes would be completely bogus, right?

He made a couple of sweeping gestures and words before cupping his hands in front of him. A floating orb of light promptly materialized above his palms.

Huh. Not just an elaborate dream, then.

"That's amazing!" Kirielle gushed. She poked at the orb, only to have her finger pass straight through it. Not surprising, really, since it was just light. She withdrew her finger and stared at it, as if expecting to find it changed. Zorian mentally directed the orb to fly around the room and circle Kirielle a few times. Yep, he definitely knew the spell. He retained not just the memory of the casting procedure, but also the fine control he had developed with repeated practice. This was not the result of a mere vision, even a prophetic one.

"More! More!" demanded Kirielle.

"Oh, come on, Kiri." Zorian sighed. He really wasn't in the mood for her antics at the moment. "I indulged you, didn't I? Go find something else to amuse yourself now."

She pouted at him, but he was thoroughly immune to such things by now. Then she frowned for a moment and suddenly straightened as if remembering something.

Wait…

"No!" Zorian shouted, but he was already too late. Kiri ducked out of his reach, raced to the bathroom, and slammed the door behind her. "Damn it, Kiri, why now? Why not before I woke up?"

"Sucks to be you," she answered.

Zorian leaned forward until his forehead collided with the door. "I had forewarning and I still fell for it."

He frowned. Forewarning, indeed. Whatever his future memories were, they seemed to be fairly reliable. Was Cyoria really going to get invaded during the summer festival, then? What should he do about that? What *could* he do about that? He shook his head and marched back to his room. He would not even contemplate that sort of question until he found out more about what had happened to him. He locked the door so he would have some privacy and sat on his bed. He needed to think.

Okay. He had lived through a whole month of school before… something happened… and then he woke up in his room back in Cirin, as if the entire month never happened. Even with magic factored in, that was preposterous. Time travel was impossible. He didn't have any books in his room that discussed the topic at any appreciable length, but all of the passages that dealt with time travel agreed that it couldn't be done. Even dimensional magic could only warp time, speeding it up or slowing it. It was one of the few things mages agreed was beyond the ability of magic to accomplish.

How, then, was he living through it?

He was in the process of consulting the books in his room for any type of magic that could 'fake' time travel in some way when a knock on his door interrupted his thoughts, and he suddenly realized he was still in his pajamas and that Mother had wanted to talk to him quite a while ago. He quickly changed and opened the door to find himself under the scrutiny of two women, only one of whom was his mother.

He almost greeted Ilsa by name, but caught himself in time.

"A teacher from the academy has come to talk to you," his mother said, her disapproving stare telling him she was going to give him an earful once Ilsa left.

"Greetings," Ilsa said. "I am Ilsa Zileti, from Cyoria's Royal Academy of Magical Arts. I was hoping to speak to you about some matters before you leave. It won't take long."

"Of course," said Zorian. "Um, where do you…"

"Your room shall suffice," Ilsa said.

"I'll bring you something to drink," his mother said, excusing herself.

Zorian watched Ilsa as she unpacked various papers and placed them on his desk (what was she doing with those, anyway?), trying to decide how to proceed with this. If his future memories were valid, she should be handing him the scroll right about…

Yeah, there it was. Knowing the future was weird.

For the sake of appearances, Zorian gave the scroll a cursory examination before channeling mana into it. It was exactly how he remembered it—the calligraphy, the flowery language, the elaborate crest at the bottom of the document—and Zorian felt a wave of dread wash over him. What the hell had he gotten himself involved in? He had no idea what was happening to him, but it was big. *Very* big.

He had the urge to tell Ilsa about his predicament and seek her advice, but he restrained himself. It sounded like the most sensible thing to do—surely a fully trained mage like her was far more qualified for tackling this than he was. But what could he possibly say? That he was remembering things that hadn't happened yet? Yeah, that would go over well. Besides, considering the nature of his future memories, he could easily imagine ending up in a prison cell if a conspiracy to invade Cyoria was really discovered thanks to his warning. It wouldn't be difficult for the authorities to make the assumption that his shocking knowledge came from being a defector from the conspiracy. Certainly it was more plausible than time travel. An image of a government agent torturing him for information briefly flittered through his mind and he shuddered.

No, best to keep this to himself for now.

This decided, Zorian basically reenacted his memories of his initial interaction with Ilsa for the next ten minutes, not seeing the point in choosing differently this time. All of his choices had been made for reasons that were currently every bit as valid as they had been in his future memories. He didn't argue with Ilsa about Xvim this time around, though, since he already knew arguing over that topic was pointless, and he didn't request a bathroom break, since he already knew what electives he wished to take. Ilsa seemed completely indifferent to his strange decisiveness, apparently just as eager as he was to get this whole thing out of the way. Then again, why would she be surprised? She had no future memories to compare this entire encounter to, unlike him. Hell, she didn't even know him.

Zorian sighed and shook his head. They really did feel just like normal memories, and it was hard to ignore them. This is going to be one long month.

"Are you all right, Mr. Kazinski?"

Zorian glanced at Ilsa curiously, trying to divine why she asked him that. She glanced towards his hands—only for a moment, but Zorian caught it. His hands were shaking. He balled them into fists and took a deep breath.

"I'm fine," he said. An uncomfortable silence ensued, Ilsa apparently unwilling to press on with her closing speech while she continued to study him. "Can I ask you a question?"

"Of course," Ilsa said. "That's why I'm here."

"What do you think about time travel?"

She was clearly taken aback by the question. It was probably the last thing she expected him to ask, or at least close to the bottom of the list. She composed herself very quickly though.

"Time travel is impossible," Ilsa said firmly. "Time can only be dilated or compressed. Never skipped or reversed."

"Why?" asked Zorian, honestly curious. He had never actually seen an explanation for the impossibility of time travel, though that might be because he hadn't been terribly interested in the topic until now.

Ilsa sighed. "I admit I'm not particularly knowledgeable about the details, but our best theories indicate that going against temporal currents is utterly impossible. As in 'draw a square circle' impossible, not 'leap over the ocean' impossible. The river of time flows only in one direction. Beyond that, innumerable attempts have been made in recorded past, all ending in failure." She gave him a sharp look. "I sincerely hope you won't waste your talents on such a fool's quest."

"I was just curious," Zorian said defensively. "I was just reading a chapter discussing limitations of magic and wondered why the author was so certain time travel is impossible."

"Well, now you know," Ilsa said, getting up. "Now if that's all, I really should be going. I'll be happy to answer any further questions on Monday after class. Have a nice day."

Zorian watched her leave and shut the door behind her before collapsing back on his bed. Definitely a long month.

For once the train ride to the academy didn't put Zorian to sleep. He had subtly prodded Mother with some sensitive topics when she tried to scold him for shutting himself in his room that morning, and he was pretty sure by the time he boarded the train that he wasn't experiencing some kind of elaborate illusion, unless the illusionist was aware of some very closely kept family secrets. And he felt far too lucid for this to be an induced hallucination. As far as he could tell at the moment, he really had traveled back in time. He spent most of the train ride writing down everything of importance he could think of in one of his notebooks. He didn't really think the memories were going to fade any time soon, but it helped him organize his thoughts and notice details he might have otherwise missed. He noted that he'd forgotten to retrieve his books from under Kiri's bed in all the confusion, but decided it didn't matter. If the classes were anything like they were the last time around, he wouldn't need them for the duration of the first month.

It was that last spell the lich performed on him and Zach, Zorian was sure of it. The trouble was, Zorian had no idea what the spell was. Even the words were unfamiliar. Standard incantations used Ikosian words as their base, and Zorian knew enough Ikosian to get a general sense of a spell just by listening to what the caster was chanting. But the lich had spoken a different language for his incantation. Fortunately, Zorian had a really good memory and remembered most of the chant, so he wrote it down in his trusty notebook in phonetic form. He was pretty sure he wouldn't find the spell itself anywhere within his clearance level, as it was probably highly restricted knowledge and kept out of reach of first circle mages like him, but he would see about identifying the language and finding a proper dictionary in the academy library.

The other clue was Zach himself. The boy was capable of fighting a lich—a freaking *lich*!—for several minutes before succumbing to it. Even though the lich had been toying with him, this was still impressive. Zorian would put Zach on par with a third circle mage, perhaps even higher. What the hell was he doing with academy students then? Something was definitely strange about Zach, though Zorian had no intention of confronting the other boy directly until he knew more about what was going on. For all he knew, it could be one of those 'you know about us, so now we have to kill you' sort of things. He would have to tread carefully around the Noveda heir.

Zorian slammed the notebook shut and ran his hand through his hair as the train chugged onward. No matter how he looked at it, this whole situation was utterly crazy. Did he really have memories from the future or was he simply going insane? Both possibilities were terrifying. He was in no way qualified to tackle something like this on his own, but he didn't know how to get other people to help him without being carted off to either a madhouse or an interrogation chamber.

He resolved to think about it later. He needed to sleep on it before he decided on a course of action.

"Excuse me, is this seat free?"

Zorian glanced at the speaker and recognized her after a second of recollection. The nameless green turtleneck girl who had joined him in his train compartment at the Korsa stop. Of course, the last time she hadn't bothered to ask for permission before taking a seat. What changed? Ah, it didn't matter—what *did* matter was that last time she had soon been followed by four other girls. Very loud, very obnoxious girls. No way he was going to spend the rest of the train ride listening to their banter... *again*.

"Yeah," he nodded. "In fact, I was just leaving. This was Korsa, right? Good day, miss."

And then he quickly grabbed his luggage and went to search for another compartment, abandoning the girl to her fate.

Maybe these future memories were good for something after all.

Bam!

"Roach!"

Bam! Bam! Bam!

"Roach, open the thrice-damned door! I *know* you're in here!"

Zorian rolled over in his bed and groaned. What the hell was Taiven doing here so early? No wait… He snatched the clock from his dresser and brought it in front of his face… She wasn't early. He had slept past noon. Huh. He distinctly remembered going straight to the academy from the train station and falling asleep minutes after reaching his room, yet still he had overslept. Apparently dying and then waking in the past was tiresome business.

Bam! Bam! Bam! Bam! Bam!

"I'm coming, I'm coming!" shouted Zorian. "Stop banging on my door, already!"

Naturally, she just kept banging on it with more enthusiasm. Zorian smoothed down his messy hair and pulled on some clothes, then stomped towards the door. Wrenching it open, he gave Taiven a withering look…

…which she promptly ignored.

"Finally!" she said. "What the hell took you so long!?"

"I was sleeping," Zorian ground out.

"Really?"

"Yes," he ground out.

"But—"

"I was tired," Zorian snapped. "Very tired. And what the hell are you waiting for? Get inside."

She rushed inside and Zorian took a moment to collect himself before he confronted her. In his future memories, she hadn't visited him once after he had refused to go along with her mission to the sewers, which spoke volumes about her true feelings about this 'friendship' of theirs. Then again, he had hardly thought about her himself until now, so he probably shouldn't judge. In any case, he was even less inclined to join her on this mission the second time than he was in his future memories. He actually had more pressing matters to attend to this time, in addition to his general apprehensiveness that was still as valid now as it was then. Accordingly, he felt a lot less reluctance in simply blowing her off, and it only took him an hour to convince her to leave him alone.

That done, he immediately set out for the library, making a short detour to a nearby bakery for a quick bite to tide him over. Once in the library he started searching for books on the topic of time travel and trying to identify the language the lich used in his spell.

To call his search a disappointment would be a mild assessment. For one thing, there were no books on time travel. The topic was not considered a serious field of study, what with it being impossible and all. What little was written about it was scattered across innumerable volumes, hidden in unmarked sections and paragraphs of otherwise unrelated books. Piecing together these scattered mentions was an absolute chore and not all that rewarding either. None of it was useful in solving the mystery of his future memories. As for the language the lich had spoken, all of Zorian's efforts to identify it only brought him more frustration.

Despite a growing feeling of hopelessness, he spent the entire weekend sifting through library texts, finally abandoning that avenue of research when it became obvious it wasn't producing any results. On top of that, the library workers were starting to give him weird looks at his choice of literature and he didn't want to create any unfortunate rumors. Hopefully he would be able to trick Zach into revealing what the hell was going on when school started.

"You're late."

Zorian looked at Akoja's stern face in quiet contemplation. He was glad he wouldn't have to deal with any drama because of his disastrous evening with her—almost as glad as he was about the fact that he wasn't dead. But he couldn't help but wonder what her outburst the night of the dance had been about. She didn't really seem to have a crush on him, so why had his comment hit her so heavily?

"What?" she asked, and Zorian realized he had been staring at her a little too long. Oops.

"Ako, why are you telling me this when more than half the class isn't even here yet?"

"Because there is at least a chance you will listen, unlike them," Akoja admitted. "Also, someone like you should be an example to other students, instead of descending to their level."

"Someone like me?"

"Just get inside," she snapped irritably.

He sighed and went inside. It was probably for the best to leave things be. He had other problems to deal with, and she was far too rule-bound for his tastes anyway.

He didn't know what he had been expecting when he walked into the class. Everyone to stop what they were doing and stare at him, maybe? At least then he would have a reason for feeling so unnerved at attending his first class of the year for the second time. But of course they did no such thing. It wasn't a second time for them, and there was nothing visibly irregular about him for them to take notice. He quashed his unease and sat down in the back of the class, discreetly scanning new arrivals for signs of Zach. He was sure the other boy was connected to this somehow, and the mysterious boy appeared to be Zorian's best chance at understanding what was happening to him.

There was a brief commotion when Briam's fire drake familiar hissed up a storm and started chasing Briam's terrified neighbor across the classroom before Briam calmed it down. Apparently the magical reptile liked the unfortunate boy even less than it had Zorian. In any case, Ilsa came in soon after and started the class.

Zach never showed up.

Zorian spent the entire class in a daze, shocked at this turn of events. Where the hell was Zach? Everything had happened almost exactly as it had in his future memories so far, with Zach's absence being the first major deviation. This firmly cemented Zach as somehow connected to this madness, but it also put the boy out of Zorian's reach for the moment.

The lecture was even more annoying now than it was the first time he listened to it, since from his perspective he had gone through these review sessions less than a month before. Apparently Ilsa worked off some kind of a script, because the lecture was virtually identical to the one from his memory, the only difference being that Zach wasn't there to answer questions in competition with Akoja.

Funny how things seem clearer in retrospect. Zach was acting strange right from the start, in that very first lecture, but Zorian had thought nothing of it. Sure, Zach volunteering to answer the teacher's questions was out of character for the boy, but not completely implausible. It was just a review session anyway, and they had to know these things to pass the certification. It had taken two weeks before people really began to notice the extent of Zach's sudden improvement.

So many questions, so few answers. He could only hope that Zach would show up soon.

Zach didn't come to class that day, or the next, or the day after that. By Friday, Zorian was pretty sure the other boy wouldn't be showing up at all. According to Benisek, Zach simply disappeared from his family mansion on the very same day that Zorian took the train to Cyoria, and no hint of him had been seen since. Zorian didn't think he could cook up anything the investigators hired by the boy's guardian hadn't thought of doing, and he didn't want to attract attention to himself by asking around, so he reluctantly put the mystery of Zach aside for the moment.

His schoolwork was going well, at least. Thanks to his foreknowledge, he aced Nora Boole's surprise tests and didn't really have to study for any subject—a small refresher was sufficient to coast him through pretty much anything. Once the work required for warding class grew more difficult, that would probably change, but for the time being he had all the freedom he wanted to deliberate on what he should do about the rapidly approaching summer festival and the accompanying assault.

Sadly, with Zach absent, Zorian had hit dead ends in all the clues he had, and was now at a loss how to proceed.

"Come in."

Zorian opened the door to Xvim's office and defiantly met the man's gaze. He was pretty confident in the accuracy of his future memories by now, Zach's mysterious absence aside, so he knew this was going to be another exercise in frustration. He was tempted to boycott the meetings, but he suspected it was his stoic perseverance in the face of the man's antagonism that eventually convinced Ilsa to take him under her wing. Besides, he felt that he would be doing Xvim a favor if he quit—Zorian had a distinct feeling that the man was trying to get him to quit the last time around—and he was far too spiteful to give in to that. He sat down without prompting, a little disappointed that the man didn't remark upon his intentionally rude gesture.

"Zorian Kazinski?" Xvim asked. Zorian nodded and expertly snatched the pen the man had thrown at him out of the air, having anticipated it this time.

"Show me your basic three," the mentor ordered, not the least bit surprised at the feat of coordination.

Instantly, without even an extra deep breath, Zorian opened his palm and the pen practically jumped out of his hand and into the air.

"Make it spin," Xvim said.

Zorian's eyes widened. What happened to 'start over'? His current attempt wasn't any worse than what he had displayed during their last session before that fateful dance, and Xvim's only response that night had been 'start over', just like any other time. What changed *now*?

"Are you having problems with hearing?" Xvim asked. "Make it spin!"

Zorian blinked, finally realizing he should be focusing on the current session instead of his memories. "What? What do you mean 'make it spin'? That's not part of the basic three…"

Xvim sighed dramatically and slowly took another pen and levitated it over his own palm. Instead of just hanging in the air like Zorian's, however, Xvim's pen was spinning like the blade of a fan.

"I… have no idea how to do that," Zorian admitted. "We weren't taught how to do that."

"Yes, it is criminal how badly the classes are failing our students," Xvim said. "Such a simple variation of a levitation exercise should not be beyond the grasp of a certified mage. No matter, we shall correct this deficiency before we move on to other matters."

Zorian sighed. Great. No wonder no one ever mastered the basic three to Xvim's liking if the man kept redefining what 'mastered' meant. There were probably hundreds of 'small variations' of each of the basic three, enough to spend decades learning them all, so little wonder no one could exhaust them all in two measly years. Especially considering Xvim's standards.

"Go on," Xvim urged. "Start."

Zorian focused intensely on the pen hanging above his palm, trying to figure out how to do as Xvim asked. It ought to be relatively simple. He just had to affix a stabilization point in the middle of the pen and put pressure on the ends, right? At least, that's the first thing that popped into his head. He had just managed to get the pen to move a bit when he felt a familiar object impact his forehead.

Zorian glared at Xvim, cursing himself for forgetting about the man's damnable marbles. Xvim glanced at the pen that was still hovering over Zorian's palm.

"You didn't lose focus," Xvim remarked. "Good."

"You threw a marble at me," Zorian accused.

"I was hurrying you up," Xvim said, unrepentant. "You're too slow. You must be faster. Faster, faster, faster! Start over."

Zorian sighed and returned to his task. Yup, definitely an exercise in frustration.

Between his unfamiliarity with the exercise and Xvim's constant interruptions, Zorian only managed to get the pen to wobble by the end of the session, which was… a little humiliating, actually. His above average shaping skills were one of the few things that set him aside from his fellow mages, and he felt he should have done much better, despite Xvim's repeated attempts at sabotage. Fortunately, a book describing the exercise in detail was easy to find in the academy library, so he would hopefully master it by the following week. Well, not *master* it—not in the sense that Xvim wanted him to—but he at least wanted to know what he was doing before he tackled his next session with his mentor.

Of course, normally he wouldn't be willing to pour that much effort into a lousy shaping exercise, but he needed a distraction. At first, the entire time travel situation was so patently ridiculous that he found it easy to remain calm and collected. Some part of him kept expecting that the whole thing was a double dream or something, and that he would wake up one day and not remember a thing. That part was becoming panicked and agitated now that it had become obvious that the situation he faced was real. What the hell was he supposed to do? Zach's mysterious absence weighed heavily upon him, inflaming his paranoia and making him reluctant to tell anyone about the looming invasion. Zorian was not a fundamentally selfless person and didn't want to save people only to screw himself over in the end. Whatever had caused his future memories, they were in essence his second chance at life—he was pretty sure he died at the end of his future memories—and he had no intention of squandering this chance. He did consider it his ethical duty to warn people of the danger threatening the city, but there had to be a way to do it without destroying his life or reputation.

The simplest idea would be to warn as many people as possible (thus ensuring that at least some of them took him seriously) and do so face-to-face, since written communications could be ignored in a way that personal interactions could not. Unfortunately, that would almost certainly paint him as a madman until vindicated by the assault. *If* there was an assault, that is—what if the conspirators decided to lay low upon having their plans unmasked and the invasion didn't happen? What if nobody believed him until it was too late and then decided to turn him into a scapegoat in order to shift responsibility away from themselves? What if one of the people he tried to warn was part of the conspiracy and had him killed before he could tell anyone else? What if, what if… way too many what ifs. And he had a sneaking suspicion that one of those what ifs was responsible for Zach's disappearance.

As a result of these musings, the idea of staying anonymous appealed to him more and more with each passing day. The problem was that sending a message to a bunch of people without having it traced back to you was not at all simple when magic got involved. Divinations weren't all-powerful, but Zorian had only academic understanding of their limitations, and any precautions he might think to take probably wouldn't hold against a motivated search by a skilled diviner.

Zorian sighed and started outlining a tentative plan in his notebook, completely ignoring the history teacher's enthusiastic lecture. He had to figure out who to contact, what to put into the letters, and how to ensure they couldn't be traced back to him. He somehow doubted the government would allow authors to publish instructions on how to evade detection from law enforcement, but he would still check the library to see what they had on the topic. He was so caught up in his self-appointed task, furiously scribbling away while everyone else packed and filed out of the classroom, he barely noticed when the class ended. He definitely didn't notice Benisek peering over his shoulder.

"What are you doing?"

Zorian slammed his notebook shut in a reflexive maneuver and gave the other boy a nasty glare.

"It's impolite to look over other people's shoulders."

"Jumpy, aren't we?" Benisek smiled and dragged a chair, the legs scraping loudly on the floor, from the nearby table so he could sit opposite Zorian. "Relax, I didn't see anything."

"Not for the lack of trying," remarked Zorian. Benisek only grinned wider. "What do you want, anyway?"

"Just wanted to talk for a bit." Benisek shrugged. "You're been really withdrawn this year. You've got this frustrated look on your face all the time, and you're always busy even though it's only the start of the school year. Wanted to know what was bothering you, you know?"

Zorian sighed. "This isn't something you can help me with, Ben…"

Benisek made a strangled noise, apparently outraged by his remark. "What do you mean I can't help you!? I'll have you know I'm an expert on girl trouble."

Now it was Zorian's turn to make a strangled noise. "Girl trouble!?"

"Oh, come on." Benisek laughed. "Constantly distracted? Spacing out in the middle of the class? Making plans for sending anonymous letters? It's obvious, man! Who's the lucky girl?"

"There is no 'lucky girl'," Zorian growled. "And I thought you didn't see anything."

"Listen, I don't think sending anonymous letters is a good idea," Benisek said, completely ignoring his remarks. "That's so… first year, you know? You should just walk up to her and tell her how you feel."

"I don't have time for this." Zorian sighed and got up from his seat.

"Hey, come on…," protested Benisek, trailing after him. "Man, you're one touchy guy, did anybody tell you that? I was just…"

Zorian ignored him. He really didn't need this right now.

In retrospect, Zorian should have known that simply ignoring Benisek wasn't such a good idea. It only took two days for most of the class to 'know' that Zorian had a crush on someone, and their loud speculation was annoying as hell. Not to mention distracting. Still, his displeasure at the rumors evaporated when Neolu approached him one day and gave him a short list of books she claimed he might find useful. He had half a mind to set the list on fire, especially since the paper was decorated with dozens of little hearts, but in the end his natural curiosity won over and he went to the library to check them out. He figured that at the very least he'd get a good laugh out of them.

He got more than a good laugh—instead of silly love advice like he expected, the books Neolu recommended were all about making sure your letters and gifts couldn't be traced back to you with divinations and other magic. Apparently titling a book *Forbidden Love: Mysteries of Scarlet Letters Revealed* and framing it as relationship advice could get you straight past the usual censorship such topics would normally be subjected to.

Of course, he had no idea how reliable the advice in those books really was, and the librarian looked at him funny when he checked them out, but he was still pleased to have found them. If this whole thing worked out in the end he'd have to do something nice for Neolu.

As the summer festival approached, as the school grew preoccupied with dancing and dresses and dignitaries, Zorian prepared and plotted. He bought a stack of generic paper, pens, and envelopes in a store that looked too poor and disorganized to track their customers' purchases. He worded the letters carefully to avoid revealing any personal details. He made sure not to touch the paper with his bare hands at any point and that none of his sweat, hair, or blood ended up in the envelope. He deliberately wrote in a blocky, formal script that looked nothing like his normal handwriting. He even destroyed the pens, excess paper, and envelopes he didn't use.

And then, a week before the festival, he put the letters in different public postal boxes all over Cyoria and waited.

It was… nerve-wracking, to say the least. Nothing happened, though—no one came to confront him about the letters, which was good, but the lack of apparent response was disconcerting. Did no one believe him? Did the letters not reach their intended recipients? Were they being so subtle in their reaction that no disturbance was being made? The wait was killing him.

Finally, he had enough. On the evening before the dance, he decided he'd done everything he could and took the next train out of the city. His letters either would work or wouldn't, but the outcome was out of his hands and leaving the city guaranteed his safety. If anyone asked (though he doubted they would), he was prepared to use his trusty alchemical accident excuse. He messed up a potion and breathed in some hallucinogenic fumes, only coming to his senses when he was already outside of Cyoria. Yes, that's exactly what happened.

As the train sped away from Cyoria in the dead of night, Zorian suppressed his unease and feelings of guilt for doing so little to warn anyone of the approaching attack. What else could he have done? Nothing, that's what. Nothing at all.

After a while he fell into uneasy sleep, the rhythmic thumping of the train his lullaby, visions of falling stars and skeletons wreathed in green light haunting his dreams.

Zorian's eyes abruptly shot open as sharp pain erupted from his stomach. His whole body convulsed, buckling against the object that fell on him, and suddenly he was wide awake, not a trace of drowsiness in his mind.

"Good morning, brother!" an annoyingly cheerful voice sounded right on top of him. "Morning, morning, *MORNING*!!!"

Zorian gaped at his little sister incredulously, his mouth opening and closing periodically. What, again?

"Oh, you've got to be kidding me!" Zorian growled, and Kirielle quickly got off of him and scooted away fearfully. Apparently she thought his ire was directed at *her*. "Not you, Kiri, I… I just had a nightmare, that's all."

He couldn't believe this. It was happening *again*!? What the hell? He was glad the first time, since it meant he wasn't… *dead*. But now? Now it was just *freaky*. Why was this happening to him?

Oh, and while he was internally lamenting his fate, Kirielle barricaded herself in the bathroom once more. Gods damn it all!

CHAPTER 006

Concentrate and Try Again

Zorian stared at the endless fields blurring past him, the silence of the otherwise empty compartment only broken by the rhythmic thumping of the train's machinery. He looked calm and relaxed, but it was only a practiced façade and nothing more.

His mask of stoicism might have seemed silly, as there was no one around to judge him, but over the years, Zorian had found that acting calm on the outside helped him achieve calm more easily on the inside as well. He needed any help he could get in achieving inner peace now, because he was about to start panicking like a headless chicken.

Why was this happening again? The first time it had happened, he was dead sure the lich was responsible. The spell had hit him, and then he woke up in the past. Cause and effect. He hadn't been hit by some mysterious spell this time, though—not unless someone had snuck into the train compartment while he was sleeping, the academy fading into the night behind him. But he found this very unlikely. No, he had just dozed off and woken up in the past again, as if it was the most normal thing in the world.

Then again, it did highlight some things that had been bothering him until now. After all, why would the lich cast a time travel spell on him? It seemed rather counterproductive to the whole 'secret invasion' plot, especially when death was simpler. Time travel seemed too purposeful and complex to be an accidental side effect, and he seriously doubted the lich had used a spell whose effects it did not understand. Even a neophyte like him knew what a horrible idea it was to use a spell you don't understand in an uncontrolled environment, and the undead spellcaster wouldn't have reached the level it did if it was willing to do something so foolish for the sake of a couple of brats it had already defeated anyway. No, there was a simpler—if more troubling, somehow—explanation: the lich wasn't responsible for his time traveling problems. It really *had* been trying to kill them. Them, plural, because Zach had also been the target. The same Zach who had become shockingly good in all of his classes. The same Zach who had confronted trolls while armed to the teeth with combat magic that should be beyond any academy student. The same Zach who had been making very curious offhand comments for a month…

Perhaps it was Zach, not the lich, who had cast the time travel spell?

Zach being a time traveler would explain his vast abilities and inexplicable academic improvement quite nicely. Since this particular method of time travel seemed to just send a person's mind into their younger body, he could be of an arbitrarily large age, and what Zorian remembered of Zach's various comments led him to believe the boy had lived through this particular time period many times over. A mage with decades of experience and detailed foreknowledge would no doubt find third year curriculum laughably easy.

But even if Zach had been the one to cast the spell, there was still the question of why Zorian was thrown back in time, too. It could have easily been an accident—he knew that grabbing a mage in the process of casting a teleport spell could pull you along for the ride, and they had been tangled up with one another—but that didn't explain why Zorian was repeating this month for the *second* time. Zach had been absent all month long, and thus hadn't had the opportunity to cast *anything* at Zorian.

He didn't know what to think. Hopefully Zach would be present for questioning this time around.

"Now stopping in Korsa," a disembodied voice echoed, the faulty speakers crackling with signal noise every once in a while. "I repeat, now stopping in Korsa. Thank you."

What, already? A glance through the window revealed the familiar white tablet confirming their arrival at the trading hub. He was tempted to get off the train and spend the entire month fooling around and trying to forget this whole time travel business, but quickly dismissed it. Blowing off the beginning of the school year like that would be really irresponsible and self-destructive, even if going through another identical month of classes was anything but appealing. There was a possibility that he would be flung back into the past for the *third* time, of course, but that wasn't something he should rely on. There was no way the spell could keep sending him back indefinitely—it was bound to run out of mana sooner or later. Probably sooner, since time travel had to be pretty high level.

...right?

"Um..."

Zorian snapped out of his thoughts and finally noticed the boy peering into his compartment. He frowned. He had specifically chosen this compartment because it had been completely empty during his… second attempt at life. After he had left the green turtleneck girl to her giggling fate, his journey had been uninterrupted, so this time he had decided to be proactive and claimed the new compartment right from the start. Apparently it wasn't that simple. He supposed that his very presence attracted the boy—some people just plain liked company and would avoid empty compartments.

"Yes?" Zorian said politely, hoping the boy just wanted to ask him something instead of trying to find a seat.

He was mistaken.

"Do you mind if I sit here?"

"No, go right ahead," said Zorian, giving the boy a forced smile. Damn.

The boy smiled brightly at him and quickly dragged his luggage in. A lot of luggage.

"First-year, right?" Zorian asked, unable to help himself. So much for his plan on remaining silent and creeping the boy out into leaving the compartment. Oh well.

"Yeah. How did you know?"

"Your luggage. You do realize the academy grounds are pretty far from the main station, right? Your arms are going to fall off by the time you get there."

The boy blinked. Apparently he *didn't* know. "Um, it's really not that bad, is it?"

Zorian shrugged. "You better hope it doesn't rain."

The boy laughed nervously. "I'm sure I'm not that unlucky."

Zorian smirked. Ah, the benefits of foresight. Or was it hindsight? Language really wasn't designed with the possibility of time travel in mind.

"Ah! I didn't introduce myself!" the boy suddenly blurted out. "I'm Byrn Ivarin."

"Zorian Kazinski."

The boy's eyes lit up. "Like—"

"Like Daimen Kazinski, yes," Zorian said, suddenly finding the window incredibly interesting.

He could sense the boy staring at him expectantly, but if he wanted further elaboration from Zorian on the subject, he was about to be sorely disappointed. The last thing Zorian wanted to do was talk about his eldest brother.

"So, um, are you related to Daimen Kazinski or is your last name just a coincidence?" asked the boy after a lengthy pause.

Zorian pretended he couldn't hear him and instead retrieved his notebook from the neighboring seat and studied it intently. It was almost completely empty, since all his previous notes about the invasion and the mystery of his 'future memories' were now gone, lost in a future he left behind him. It wasn't much of a loss, since the vast majority of those notes had been worthless—hollow speculations and dead-end leads that hadn't got him any closer to solving this mystery. Still, he had written down a few things he remembered from his previous notes, like the spell chant the lich had uttered before killing him. Yes, Zach was likely responsible for all of this, but he couldn't be *sure...*

After judging the silence to have lasted for a fittingly awkward amount of time, Zorian looked up from his notebook to fixate a look of confusion on the waiting boy.

"Huh? Did you say something?" Zorian frowned slightly as if he honestly hadn't heard a word of the question he had been asked.

"Err, never mind," Byrn backpedaled. "It's not important."

Zorian gave the boy a genuine smile. At least he could take a hint.

He talked to the boy for a while, mostly just answering the boy's questions about first-year curriculum, before growing bored with it and starting to feign interest in his notebook again, hoping the younger boy would take the hint once more.

"What's so interesting about that notebook, anyway?" Byrn asked, either oblivious to Zorian's disinterest in continued conversation or deliberately ignoring it. "Don't tell me you're studying already?"

"No, these are just notes on some personal research," said Zorian. "It's not going too well so I'm a little frustrated with it. My mind keeps drifting to it." Especially when the alternative was talking to an overly inquisitive first-year.

"The academy library—"

"First thing I tried." Zorian sighed. "I'm not stupid."

The boy rolled his eyes at him. "Did you search for the books yourself or did you ask the librarian to help you? My mother works as a librarian, and they have these special divination spells that let them find things in minutes that would take you decades if you searched by title and skimming alone."

Zorian opened his mouth and then closed it again. Ask the librarian for help, huh? Okay, maybe he *was* stupid.

"Well… it's not really a topic I want to bother the librarian with," Zorian said. Which was true, but he knew he'd end up trying it anyway. "Maybe I could find the spells themselves in the spell repository? But no, if they are anything like other divination spells, it's using them correctly and interpreting the results that's the problem, not casting them…"

"You could always get a job in the library," the boy offered. "If the academy library is anything like the one my mother works in, they're always desperate for help. They teach their employees how to use those spells as a matter of course."

"Really?" Zorian asked, rather intrigued by the idea.

"It's worth a try," Byrn said, shrugging.

For the rest of the ride, Zorian stopped trying to evade conversation. Byrn had definitely earned some respect from him.

"Of course! We're always looking for help!"

Well... that was easy.

"We can't pay you much, understand—that miserable gnome of a headmaster cut our budget again!—but we're very flexible about hours and we've got a pretty friendly atmosphere here..."

Zorian waited patiently for the librarian to run out of steam. She was an unassuming middle-aged woman at first glance, but the moment she had begun speaking, he realized her looks were rather deceiving. She was cheerful and had an indescribable energy about her. Just standing around her made Zorian feel the same sort of pressure he felt when stuck in a crowd of people, and he had to rein in his instinct to step back as if from a raging fire.

"I'm guessing you don't get many work requests, then?" Zorian said. "Why is that? Shouldn't people be fighting tooth and nail to work in a place like this? It's a pretty famous library."

She snorted, and Zorian would have sworn he could *feel* the derision and a touch of bitterness in the seemingly innocuous sound. "Academy regulations require us to only hire employees that are first circle mages or higher. Most graduates have better paying and more glamorous options than this," she waved her hand towards rows or bookshelves around them, "reducing us to hiring students. Who are..."

She suddenly stopped and blinked, as if remembering something. "But anyway, enough of that!" she said, clapping her hands and beaming at him. "From this day on, you're a library assistant. Congratulations! If you have any questions, I'll be glad to answer them."

It was only through superhuman willpower that Zorian stopped himself from rolling his eyes at her. He hadn't agreed to anything, merely inquired about the *possibility* of employment… and she undoubt-edly knew that. But oh well, he *did* want the job, and not just because he was hoping to learn some nifty new spells and translate the lich's chant. He suspected that library employees got to access parts of the library that would normally be restricted to him as a first circle mage, and that was just too much of a temptation to pass up.

"Question one," said Zorian. "How often do I come to work?"

She blinked, surprised for a moment. No doubt she expected him to protest her presumptuousness. "Well… when *can* you come? Between the classes, and the need for study time and other commitments, most of our student employees work once or twice a week. How much time can you set aside for this?"

"The classes are pretty easy at this point," Zorian said. "We're mostly doing the review of our second year, which I know like the back of my hand. Setting aside one day for unexpected developments, I could be here four times a week. My weekends are mostly free, too, if you need any help then."

Zorian mentally berated himself for his slip up—classes hadn't even started yet, so how would he know what they would cover? Luckily, the librarian didn't seem to notice. Instead, her eyes lit up and she started shouting.

"Ibery!" she called out. "I've got a new partner for you!"

A bespectacled girl carrying an armload of books popped out of the small room adjacent to the information desk to see what was go-ing on. Oh. It was the green turtleneck girl (she was wearing it even now) that he had shared a compartment with…

…except he had chosen a seat on the other side of the train this time, so they had never met. Oh well, probably wouldn't have mat-tered anyway.

"I believe some introductions are in order," the librarian said. "I am Kirithishli Korisova, one of the few actual librarians in this place.

This pretty lady," she gestured towards the turtleneck girl, who blushed at the praise and shifted uncomfortably, clutching the stack of books tighter in her arms, "is our resident busy little bee, Ibery Ambercomb. Ibery has been working here since last year, and I don't know what I'd do without her. Ibery, this is Zorian Kazinski."

The girl suddenly perked up. "Kazinski? As in…"

"As in younger brother of Daimen Kazinski," Zorian said, unable to suppress a small sigh.

"Um…"

"Actually, I'm pretty sure she meant your *other* brother," Kirithishli said with a sly smile. "She's in class with Fortov and has a bit of a crush…"

She and a dozen other girls. Fortov never had a shortage of women throwing themselves at him.

"Miss Korisova!" Ibery protested.

"Oh, lighten up," Kirithishli said. "Anyway, Zorian here will be working with us pretty heavily for the foreseeable future. Go show him what to do."

And just like that, he was employed at the library. Only time would tell if he was wasting his time.

Much like the last time around, Zach hadn't shown up in class. Zorian was half-expecting it, but it was no less annoying. It cemented Zorian's suspicion that Zach was heavily involved in this mess, but the boy's absence made it impossible for Zorian to confront him about it. What was he supposed to do now?

For that matter, was he supposed to do *anything at all?* Last time he had been operating on the belief that if he didn't do something about the invasion, no one would. No one else had the strange future memories he did, after all. If his speculations were correct, though,

Zach had probably traveled through time *specifically* to stop the invasion—what other reason did he have to frequent this particular time period? Besides, he had been wandering the city during the attack, picking off attackers. With such an experienced time-traveling mage on the job already, Zorian would only get in the way.

The problem with that idea was that he was ultimately just guessing and had no idea if it was true or not. He could be dooming himself and the city through inaction, relying on a boy who, quite frankly, didn't inspire too much confidence in him. Zach reminded him of his brothers a little too much. And besides, hadn't Zach *lost* to the lich? Yeah.

Not knowing how to unravel the mystery presented to him, or even where to start, Zorian had thrown himself into schoolwork and his job at the library. Of course, thanks to going through this for the third time, the only issue he had with schoolwork was Xvim's grating insistence that his grasp on the pen-spinning exercise was abominable and that he had to do it over and over *and over again*. His time at the library, on the other hand, was… interesting, though not really in the way he had hoped it would be.

He hadn't learned any spells yet, though he suspected this was because there were so many other, more pressing things he had to learn before Kirithishli and Ibery decided to invest that kind of effort in him. Simply put, he wasn't very good at his job. The seemingly simple job of shuffling some books around was made immensely more complicated by the various library protocols and the all-important book classification scheme. Zorian had hoped to demonstrate basic proficiency with his duties before asking for favors, but it had been two weeks and he was beginning to understand that it would take him at least a couple of months to reach that level, and he didn't have that kind of time. The summer festival was getting closer.

Which was why, two weeks into his employment, he proceeded to corner Kirithishli after she had dismissed him for the day to ask her about the coveted book divinations. Ibery lingered, pretending to be busy sorting a stack of books, no doubt so she could eavesdrop. She sure was nosy for such a shy girl.

"Say, I've been meaning to ask a small favor of you," Zorian began.

"Go ahead," Kirithishli said. "You've helped us a lot, so I'll be happy to help if I can. It's not often we get such a competent worker."

"Eh!?" balked Zorian. "Competent? I barely know what I'm doing—if it weren't for your and Ibery's help I would wander around like a headless chicken."

"That's why I paired you with Ibery—to learn. And you are learning fast! Faster than I did when I first started at this job, that's for sure. To be honest I usually give only the simplest and most tedious jobs to student employees, but since you've proven to be more dedicated, I've given you the advanced course."

"Ah," Zorian said after a short silence. "I'm flattered." And he really was. "Anyway, I was wondering about book-finding divinations. I've been searching for a pretty obscure topic and I'm not getting anywhere with it."

"Ah!" Kirithishli said, slapping her forehead. "How could I forget about that!? Of course I'll teach you. We teach all our long-term employees those. They're a bit tricky to use, though, so it will take a while to learn how to use them properly. Ibery will show you how. Though you can always tell me what exactly you're looking for and I'll do my best to help you out. I know this library like the back of my hand."

For a moment, Zorian debated the wisdom of showing her the lich's chant. He suspected it was something that could get him into a lot of trouble just for asking about it, but he saw no other way. No doubt learning how to use those divinations took months—months he didn't have. He took out his notebook, ripped out the corresponding page, and handed it to the librarian.

Kirithishli arched her eyebrow at the text. Ibery gave up on all pretense of not paying attention and peered over the woman's shoulder to see what was on the slip of paper.

"It's phonetic spelling," Zorian clarified, "and I want to identify the language. I don't really know where to start."

"Hm, tricky," Kirithishli remarked. "Finding a written reference based on a phonetic pronunciation of a word you don't know is a tall order, even with divinations. You should just find an expert in languages to help you."

"You should try Zenomir," piped up Ibery.

"Our history teacher?"

"He also teaches linguistics," Ibery said. "He's a polyglot. Speaks thirty-seven languages."

"Woah."

"Yeah," Ibery agreed. "He should at least know what language that is, even if he can't read it. He's pretty helpful if you approach him nicely. I doubt he'll turn you away."

How interesting.

"Ah, Mister Kazinski, what can I do for you?"

Zenomir Olgai was old. *Really* old. He wore blue robes—actual robes, like the magi of ancient times—and had a carefully sculpted white beard. Despite his advanced age, he moved with a spring in his step and his eyes had a sharpness that most people half his age lacked. Zorian hadn't taken the linguistics elective, but he knew from his history class that Zenomir cared about his subject almost as much as Nora Boole did about runes and mathematics—though Zenomir at least understood that most students didn't share his passion for the subject.

"I was told you can help me with some translation," Zorian said after the professor had admitted him into a cozy, book-strewn office.

"I have a pretty fragmentary recording of an unknown language in phonetic form. I was hoping you could help me identify it. It's nothing like anything I've encountered so far."

Zenomir perked up at the notion of an unknown language and gingerly took the paper slip with the lich's chant from Zorian's hand. His eyes widened barely a second afterward.

"Where did you get this?" he asked quietly.

Zorian debated internally what to do and then settled for a measure of truth.

"I was attacked by someone a while ago. They used a spell with that chant as the incantation. I just wanted to know what it does."

Zenomir took a deep breath and leaned back, studying Zorian with those sharp eyes. "You're lucky it didn't hit," he said after a moment. "It's some kind of soul magic spell."

"Soul magic?"

"Necromancy," clarified Zenomir.

Zorian blinked. Necromancy? Well, it made sense for the lich to use that sort of spell, but what did necromancy have to do with time travel? Nothing. This was the most definite confirmation of Zach as a primary cause of his predicament that Zorian had found yet.

"So, wait, what is that language?" asked Zorian.

"Hm? Oh! Yes, the language. It's old Majara, spoken by many of the cultures that shared the continent of Miasina with the Ikosians before their rise to prominence. Many of the ruins in Koth are written in it and, sadly, it is the language in which many of the blackest rituals and necromantic spells are formulated. You won't find any books about it in public circulation, I'm afraid. But let's return to the matter of this assailant." Zenomir's thoughtful expression deepened into a frown. "This is the darkest of magic, and your attacker was up to no good if they used a spell like that on a student."

Deciding he couldn't completely backpedal now, Zorian nonetheless chose to refrain from mentioning time travel and settled for making something up. He told Zenomir he overheard a plan to invade the city during the summer festival, claiming he had at first dismissed it as some kind of prank because of its ludicrous nature. But when the two cloaked figures noticed him eavesdropping, they had attacked. As Zorian finished his fabrication, the professor folded his hands together in thought, then, apparently willing to take a third-year seriously, told Zorian to go home and leave everything up to him.

Huh. That went surprisingly well. At least Zenomir hadn't dragged him off to the police station or the headmaster, though he suspected something like that might be in his near future. After returning to his dormitory, he paced nervously in his room, unable to sleep and steadily losing the fight to keep his growing apprehension in check. Smart or not, the deed was done, and now the only thing he could do was wait and see what the consequences of his decision would be. For him and for everyone.

A knock on the door interrupted his aimless pacing. Strong, confident knocking that nonetheless only lasted for a second or two—and unlike the knocking of anyone who visited him regularly.

"Coming!" Zorian called out, suspecting it was someone coming to talk to him about the story he told Zenomir. "What can I—urk!"

Zorian stared dumbly at the blade sticking out of his chest, his mouth opening in an unvoiced scream. Through his shocked haze, he had just enough time to look at his assailant—a short figure dressed in loose black clothes and a featureless white mask—before the blade was painfully wrenched out of his body and then immediately inserted again into his chest cavity. Again and again and again…

By the time darkness consumed his vision, Zorian was actually glad he was dying. Being repeatedly stabbed in the chest *hurt*.

Zorian's eyes abruptly shot open as sharp pain erupted from his stomach. His whole body convulsed, buckling against the object that fell on him, and suddenly he was wide awake, not a trace of drowsiness in his mind.

"Good m-!"

Kirielle was cut off as Zorian shot upright, eyes wide in fright, gasping for breath. He had been killed! They killed him! He told someone about the attack and he was killed that very evening! How the hell had he been discovered that fast!? Was Zenomir in on the attack or were they just that well informed?

"Nightmare?" Kirielle asked.

Zorian breathed deeply, ignoring the phantom pain in his chest as he did so. "Yeah. Definitely a nightmare."

Zorian knew he should focus on what Ilsa was saying, but for the life of him his mind wouldn't stop dwelling on what had happened. In retrospect, he shouldn't have been so surprised by his death—an invasion of that scale could not, he reasoned, be kept secret without some significant inside help, so of course they'd find out about anyone raising an alarm about them! And besides, if stopping the invasion had as simple a solution as notifying law enforcement, surely Zach would have already done it and Zorian wouldn't be repeating this month for the third time.

That being said, he was starting to develop a healthy dose of respect for these… restarts. This was the second time he died and he only went through this month thrice. He seemed prone to dying. Hadn't Zach said something about Zorian always getting blown up in that initial barrage unless he did something about it?

Zorian snapped back into the real world when he realized Ilsa had stopped talking and was looking at him intently. He gave her a questioning look.

"Are you quite all right?" she asked while glancing at his hands. Why would she—

Oh.

His hands were shaking. He was probably quite pale, too, if the skin on his hands was of any indication. He rubbed his palms together a few times and then balled them up into fists to reassert control over them.

"Not quite," Zorian admitted. "But I will be. You don't have to worry about it."

She stared at him for a second longer and then nodded.

"Very well," she said. "Do you want me to teleport you to the academy? I can't imagine riding the train in the state you're in is going to be very pleasant for you."

Zorian blinked, at a loss for what to say. He disdained train travel at the best of times, so an offer like this was a godsend at the moment, but... why?

"I don't want to inconvenience you...," he tried.

"Don't worry, I was going there anyway," she said. "It's the least I could do for getting to you so late and taking the choice of your mentor away from you."

Well, that much was true. Xvim really was a horrible, useless mentor.

Zorian excused himself to tell Mother he was leaving—which took way too long in his opinion, since she wouldn't stop bombarding him with questions about teleportation, suddenly concerned for his safety. But at last he was able to collect his luggage and follow Ilsa outside. He was actually a little excited, having never teleported before. He'd have been even more excited, but the memory of being stabbed to death was still uncomfortably fresh, dampening his enthusiasm for the coming experience.

"Ready?" she asked.

He nodded.

"Don't worry, the rumors about the dangers of teleporting are mostly exaggerated," Ilsa said. "You can't get stuck inside solid objects—the spell doesn't work that way—and if something goes wrong, I'll know immediately and collapse the spell before dimensional ripples tear us apart."

Zorian scowled. He already knew that, but bit back his desire to tell her so—she obviously had heard his little exchange with Mother.

Ilsa started chanting and Zorian stood straighter, not wanting to miss—

The world rippled, then changed. Suddenly they were both standing in a well lit round room, a large magical circle carved into the marble floor beneath their feet. There was no disorientation, no flash of colors, no nothing—almost disappointing. He studied the room they were in a little more closely, trying to understand where they were.

"This is the teleport redirection point," Ilsa said. "The academy wards shunt every incoming teleport into this place for security reasons. Of course, that's assuming you're properly keyed in and have sufficient authorization to teleport in at all." She fixed him with a penetrating gaze. "Teleporting into a warded space is just one of the many dangers of the spell. Don't experiment with it on your own."

"Err… I'm pretty sure teleport is *far* above my access level," pointed out Zorian.

She shrugged. "Some students are capable of reconstructing a spell after seeing it performed only once. Once you know the chant and gestures, 80% of the work has already been done for you."

Zorian blinked. Why didn't he think of that?

"Would you mind casting that spell one more time?" he asked innocently. "Strictly for academic purposes, you see…"

She chuckled. "No. If it makes you feel any better, I doubt you have enough mana reserves to cast the spell even once."

As a point of fact, it *didn't* make him feel any better. He didn't care how dangerous it was, he'd learn the teleport spell as soon as he was able. He had just shaved off an entire day of train travel in an instant—the ability to do that kind of thing at will would be worth quite a lot of trouble to acquire. He let out a sigh as he and Ilsa exited the redirection chamber and parted ways. Emerging into one of the academic buildings, he took the shortest route to his dormitory, doing his best to avoid eye contact with anyone who crossed paths with him.

"I could get used to this kind of travel," Zorian mumbled to himself as he unlocked the door to his room and dropped his luggage to the floor in relief. "Too bad I could never fake distress convincingly enough, or else I'd be able to get Ilsa to take me along at the beginning of every restart."

He froze mid-step. He shouldn't be thinking like that. That was a dangerous assumption. He had no proof that the restarts would keep happening indefinitely. In fact, everything he knew about magic told him it *couldn't* be true—whatever spell had been put on him was going to run out of mana at some point and then there'd be no restart, no second chances... no return from the dead. He had to treat every restart as if it were his last, because it might very well be.

Though he had to admit that, despite it ending with him getting stabbed to death, the previous restart wasn't a complete disaster. At least he had all but confirmed it was Zach, and not the lich, that was responsible for this. Instead of researching unknown languages and time travel, it would probably be wiser to spend his efforts trying to find out where Zach kept disappearing to every time.

But not just yet. He deserved a little rest after being brought back from the dead.

He really should have known it wouldn't be that easy. The moment he tried to track down Zach, he was reminded of why he didn't do that in his very first restart. Zach was not only an heir of Noble House Noveda. He was the *only* living member of that House, the rest of his family having been killed in the Splinter Wars. Zach stood to inherit a sizeable financial empire and a legacy of several generations of mages once he came of age, so everything about him was scrutinized closely by a great number of interested parties. Consequently, his disappearance was a Big Deal, and a lot of people wanted to know where he went. Zorian was just one of these people, and if everyone else (and the people they hired) hadn't managed to track him down, he had very little chance to do so.

Needless to say, he didn't make any progress. As he suspected, the two girls Zach had hung out with during Zorian's original month were nothing special without the Noveda heir there to help them out and hang out with them (and asking people about the girls led to some pretty annoying rumors being spread around; honestly, can't a guy ask about a girl without everyone assuming he's got a romantic interest in her?), his house was sealed with some pretty heavy ward-work and his legal guardian could not be reached. To make it more difficult, if Zach had any close friends at the academy, they weren't among his classmates. Zorian wasn't a detective, and had no idea what else to look for. And considering that many professional detectives had already failed (and continued to fail) to track the boy down, he suspected it wouldn't help even if he *did* know a thing or two about tracking people down.

A month went by with little to show for it. Summer festival came, and Zorian once again boarded a train out of Cyoria, awake and alert as the night deepened and the minutes ticked away. He brought a pocket watch with him this time, and kept glancing at it every once in a while, silently praying that he wouldn't have to start over once again but wanting to know exactly when he got thrown back in case he did. Sure enough, his prayers went unanswered. Somewhere around two past midnight, he blacked out and woke up, once again, with Kiri on top of him, wishing him a good morning.

He probably should have admitted it to himself right then and there. He was a fairly smart person, after all, and not prone to deluding himself. But he was also stubborn and it took four more restarts before he finally accepted the truth of his predicament: he was stuck in some kind of time loop, and it wasn't going to end any time soon.

He didn't know how it was possible. Maybe the spell was powered by Zach's seemingly inexhaustible mana reserves instead of being limited to a fixed amount at the moment of casting. Maybe it was one of those rare self-sustaining spells. Hell, maybe it reached into the Heart of the World and drew power from the World Dragon itself! It didn't really matter how it worked, only that it did.

But this only came to him with the wisdom of hindsight. As he lived each of the restarts, he refused to accept it, and instead tried to live like he normally would. It was rather boring, yes, but what if this particular restart was the one where it ended? The restart where the consequences of his choices would not magically disappear at two past midnight on the night of the festival. And each time his watch ticked to that fateful moment and the next thing he knew was the pain and Kiri's voice.

He was through with that, though. He couldn't go on like this. Excluding the invasion bit, the month had been a bore even the first time around, and he had lived through it eight times already. He knew the first month curriculum well enough by now to get near-perfect scores in all subjects, even warding. It had little effect on how people treated him, as he found out. He was known to be capable, and his grades had always been very good, so people weren't really surprised when he aced all the exams or effortlessly performed a perfect magic missile on their very first combat magic class. It was within the realm of people's expectations, unlike Zach's sudden improvement. The only people whose behavior changed in response to his improvement were Akoja and Xvim. Akoja had become twice as annoying now that she apparently found a kindred soul. She began to insist that they check each other's work and asked him for help whenever she didn't understand something. Zorian had thought she'd be green with jealousy that he was beating her scores, but it seemed she was a lot less bothered to be outdone by *him* as opposed to by the likes of Zach and Neolu.

As for Xvim, Zorian's mentor took his superb scores as an indication that he should be held to an even higher standard. As such, not only did Xvim not declare his pen-spinning good enough to move on from, he had *demoted Zorian back to the regular levitation exercise.* In all honesty, Zorian wasn't terribly bothered by that—even if he did master the pen-spinning exercise to Xvim's satisfaction, no doubt he'd get nothing more than *another* minor variation of the basic three to practice.

But going through *another* boring month like that was out of the question. He took different electives this time—Astronomy, Architecture, and Geography of the Global Mana Flow—and he fully intended to lower his academic scores back to less exaggerated levels so Xvim and Akoja would remain their normal, more tolerable selves. He also intended to skip quite a few time-consuming homework projects to focus on his own personal studies, and he was going to spend a sizeable portion of his savings on alchemical supplies. Should this restart be the final one, he was going to be seriously inconvenienced by those choices, but it wouldn't be the end of the world, and he suspected the disruptions following in the wake of the invasion would render many of the normal concerns moot.

Then he walked into the Essential Invocations classroom on the first day of school and realized his plans would have to be adjusted.

Zach was finally back in class.

CHAPTER 007

Of Gaps
And Pretending

A t first, Zorian didn't even notice Zach's reappearance. That was noteworthy by itself, as Zach wasn't an easy person to overlook. The boy loved attention and seemed to have trouble staying still and quiet, something that had remained consistent even after Zach suddenly turned into some kind of a weirdo time traveler. That day, however, the normally loud and exuberant boy was eerily silent. He also eschewed his typical tactic of sitting in the back of the classroom, instead choosing a seat near the front. If his out of character behavior hadn't caused people to glance at him a bit too often, Zorian would have probably overlooked him.

He was so shocked to see the boy finally present in class that he momentarily halted in his tracks on his way to his seat, standing like an idiot in the middle of the classroom. Then, after a moment's thought, he set off towards the cause of his predicament.

His first instinct was to immediately march up to the boy and drag him away into some private corner to clear everything up, but Zach's subdued appearance gave Zorian pause. Zach's skin was pale and bloodless, and his breathing was quick and shallow, not at all as it should be. He looked sick. Thinking about it a little more carefully, Zorian realized that approaching the boy so directly would be a reckless and possibly dangerous course of action. His loss to the lich aside, Zach was vastly more powerful than Zorian, and Zorian had no idea how the other boy would react if he knew there was another person tagging along in his time traveling adventure. He'd need to confront him sooner or later, though, so he fully intended to make at least tentative contact. He scanned the front of the classroom, looking for a free seat near Zach that would allow him to study the other boy during the lecture.

He didn't have to look hard—Zach was sitting close to Briam, and every seat around Briam was empty. The cause was easy to divine: people were reluctant to get close to the angry-looking fire drake he was holding. As someone with future knowledge, Zorian knew their fears were well founded. While the young fire drake hadn't torched anyone (and sometimes Zorian wondered how much of that was thanks to the drake's youth and lack of ability, as opposed to having self-restraint) it hadn't hesitated to bite and scratch, and it was difficult to tell what would set it off. Fortunately, it seemed to tolerate Zorian better than most people, so he simply plopped down into the seat next to Briam and silenced the lizard's hissing with a glare. He stared at the fire drake's slitted yellow eyes until the reptile turned its head and left him alone.

"Wow, you shut him down in an instant," Briam said. "I wish *I* could control him that easily."

The fire drake snapped its jaws at the air in front of Briam's face, causing the boy to flinch back. Briam huffed in annoyance and apparently let the matter drop. Not for the first time, Zorian wondered just how smart that creature really was.

Then, doing his best to appear natural, Zorian turned to Zach sitting a bit further away from him.

"You look like hell," Zorian remarked.

Zach groaned and buried his face in his hands. "I *feel* like hell," he moaned. "What did that pile of bones do to me?"

Zorian's heart quickened. Zach no doubt expected his comment to be disregarded as a weird metaphor, but to Zorian it was definite confirmation that Zach was also a time traveler. No points for guessing who or what the mysterious 'pile of bones' was.

Now… how could he get Zach to talk more without revealing that he knew more than he should?

"Pile of bones?" Zorian asked, trying to keep his voice light.

Zach opened his mouth to respond but Ilsa chose that exact moment to walk into the classroom and Zach dropped the issue.

Zorian had to restrain himself from glaring at Ilsa as she smiled at him. Couldn't she have waited a few more minutes?

Ignorant of Zorian's internal grumbling, Ilsa accepted the list of present students from Akoja and began introducing herself and her class. It wasn't anything that Zorian hadn't heard eight times already, so he mostly ignored her in favor of keeping an eye on Zach and plotting how to extract time travel related information out of him.

Suddenly he realized that Ilsa had stopped talking and was looking in his direction. After a moment, he realized she was looking at Zach.

"Mr. Noveda, you look quite ill. Please tell me you didn't come to my class with a hangover."

The class erupted into laughter and Zach winced, either because loud noises bothered him in the state he was in or because he noticed the undercurrent of agitation in Ilsa's question. Either way he recovered quickly.

"It's not a hangover," protested Zach. "I just woke up like this, I swear."

"And you thought that coming to class like this was a good idea… why?" Ilsa prodded.

"Err… I honestly didn't think it would last this long. I figured it would pass in an hour or two," said Zach sheepishly.

Zorian frowned. If the sickness was a consequence of the spell the lich had targeted them with that evening, that would mean Zach had been suffering its effects for the past eight months or so, as Zach had been absent for that long. Why would Zach expect a condition that serious to pass 'in an hour or two'?

Why couldn't there be any simple answers in all this?

"Well, it didn't," Ilsa concluded. "While I appreciate your dedication to your studies," Zorian distinctly heard Ako snorting derisively in the background, "I must insist you go home or, better yet, visit a healer. You look like you're going to collapse any moment."

Before Zach could say anything, Zorian rose from his seat.

"I'll get him home," he said. Zach gave him a surprised look, but Ilsa just nodded and shooed them away.

Zorian picked up his bag and left with Zach in tow, very pleased with himself. He had created a legitimate excuse to talk to Zach in private *and* been given permission to skip a class he had already attended eight times by now. Could a victory be more complete?

"You didn't have to do that, you know," Zach remarked, trailing behind him. "I can get back home on my own. I don't feel *that* sick."

"But if I *hadn't* done that, I would've had to sit through two hours of boring review," countered Zorian.

Zach laughed, but his mirth quickly collapsed into a painful sounding cough.

"Damn," he wheezed. "He really did a number on me."

"Who is this someone you keep mentioning?" prodded Zorian.

"It's not important," Zach mumbled. He took a deep breath and fixed Zorian with a speculative look. "Hey. Want to go to the cafeteria and grab something to eat?"

"You think your stomach can handle it?" Zorian asked.

"You bet," Zach said, nodding. "I'm starving!"

Zorian shrugged and gestured for Zach to lead the way.

As they each collected some food, Zorian tried to determine if he should broach the subject of time travel immediately or wait for Zach to get used to his presence over the course of a few days. By the time they claimed a table near the windows, he still hadn't made up his mind.

"You know, I find this whole situation very amusing," Zach said between mouthfuls, shoveling noodles into his mouth and attempting to talk at the same time. Now *that* was very amusing. Zorian's mother always insisted he should aspire to behave 'like a noble'. She would have a heart attack if he ever adopted Zach's eating manners. "A good little student like you, skipping class to have lunch with a class delinquent. What is the world coming to? What would your mother say if she saw you now?"

"First of all, I'm not skipping class—I'm escorting you home," Zorian pointed out, ignoring a snort from Zach. "We just stopped for a meal so you wouldn't collapse from starvation before we get there." Another snort. "And my mother would go all sparkly-eyed at who I'm having lunch with and promptly forget I'm supposed to be in class."

"Ah. A social climber," Zach said, a sour expression on his face. "Say no more. At least you're male so she wouldn't try to pair us."

"Well, I do have a nine-year-old sister…"

"Don't go there," Zach warned.

"Fine," agreed Zorian. He didn't particularly want to continue in that avenue, anyway. "So, are you going to tell me who roughed you up or what?"

"You're a lot nosier than I remember," Zach said. "What makes you think someone roughed me up?"

"Your offhand comments aren't as oblique as you imagine them to be," Zorian said.

"Whatever," Zach scoffed. "I just breathed in some weird fumes while I was messing with my alchemy set yesterday, that's all."

Ah, the trusty 'alchemical accident' excuse. So cliché, yet so effective. Zorian had used it quite a few times himself. In any case, he wasn't willing to let go so easily. He decided to risk it and try to provoke a reaction from the boy.

"Must have been some *really* weird fumes. The aftereffects almost look like soul magic exposure," Zorian speculated loudly.

Zorian had expected *some* kind of reaction from Zach, but what he got was quite a bit stronger than he had imagined. Zach immediately sat straighter in his seat, eyes wide in realization. "Of course! That's why I'm still suffering the effects, even after the revert! The son of a bitch targeted the very thing that gets sent back—my soul!"

There was an eerie silence in the cafeteria as everyone stared at the crazy boy shouting nonsense in a crowded dining hall. Zach slowly lowered his hands, which had been gesticulating wildly, and mumbled an apology that was too quiet for anyone but Zorian to hear. Scattered laughter rippled through the gathered students for a few moments before everything finally returned to normal.

"Err...," Zach began, looking unsure. "Maybe we should continue this at the fountain, yeah?"

"I don't know," remarked Zorian carefully. "If you intend to be this loud, I don't think it will do much good."

"Oh ha ha," grumbled Zach. "So I got a little excited... not everyone is an ice cube like you, Zorian."

"Ice cube?" asked Zorian, an undercurrent of warning in his voice.

But Zach was already collecting his things, and Zorian could do nothing but huff in annoyance and follow after him. Still, Zach's little outburst answered a few of his questions. It wasn't his memories, or even his mind, that was being sent back—it was his *soul*. That would certainly explain why his spellwork and shaping skills didn't disappear every time he started over. It was common knowledge that magic was heavily connected to the soul, even if no one really understood the exact mechanism of their interaction.

When they finally reached the fountain, Zach seemed to be in a contemplative mood so Zorian took a moment to study the schools of colorful fish swimming in the basin of the fountain. He actually pitied the poor things, since they were unlikely to last long. The fountain had been in disrepair for years, and it was only due to the grander-than-usual summer festival that it had been renovated. How likely was it that the academy would continue to maintain it after the occasion passed? Not very. And it was even less likely it would be kept in a good enough condition for the fish to survive. Their days were numbered.

"Zorian…," Zach prodded.

"Hm?"

"Tell me… what do you know about time travel?"

Zorian blinked. Well. That was direct.

"Time travel?" Zorian asked with as much confusion as he could fake. "Not much, I guess. What's that got to do with anything?"

"Ugh, well…" Zach fumbled with words, scratching his chin nervously. "You'll probably think I'm insane, but I'm a time traveler of sorts."

Wow, Zach really didn't have a subtle bone in his body, did he?

"You don't look very old," Zorian remarked, trying to react as casually as possible. "If you come from the future, it must not be a very distant one."

"No, no, it's more like… the whole world resets itself on the night of the summer festival, and I'm the only one who remembers what happened."

That was an interesting way of explaining it, though the idea of a spell affecting the whole world was even more ridiculous than the idea of working time travel magic.

"I've lived through this month… gods, at least two hundred times by now," continued Zach. "Honestly, I'm starting to lose count."

"Wait, you're talking about it like you can't stop it," said Zorian, unable to keep a tiny bit of alarm out of his voice. Luckily, Zach appeared to be too agitated to notice.

"That's just it, I don't know if I can stop it!" Zach shouted, before he realized what he was doing and quieted down so as to not attract unneeded attention. "I was hit by this spell in the previous revert, and its effects didn't completely go away when I reverted into the past."

Zorian frowned. Previous revert? What about the other seven? Did Zach somehow skip those or did he simply not remember them? It occurred to Zorian that the aftereffects of the lich's spell could have been even more serious than what he thought he understood—what if Zach had spent the past seven restarts in a coma? Though that begged the question of why his guardian had reported him as missing instead of bringing a healer.

"I guess it really was a soul magic spell like you said," continued Zach. "I need to watch out for those from now on. Anyway, at first I thought it's just some nasty sickness that'll pass, and to a degree I was right. I already feel a lot better than I did this morning. It's just that it wasn't only my body that was affected. My mind has been a little spotty ever since I woke up."

Oh no…

"I don't remember how I started this time loop," Zach admitted, confirming Zorian's fears. "Or whether it was me who started it in the first place. My memory is full of blanks like that at the moment. I'm hoping it will all come back to me but…"

Zorian stared at the other boy, stony faced. Basically, they were both in deep shit.

Zach seemed to interpret Zorian's serious look a little differently, though.

"You don't believe me," he concluded.

"It's pretty far-fetched," Zorian said. If he hadn't lived through it, he wouldn't have believed Zach, no. "But I'm a pretty open-minded guy. Let's pretend you're right for the moment. What's that got to do with me?"

Zach arched an eyebrow at him, apparently incredulous about something.

"Huh," he said. "You're really different from your other self."

"My other self?" Zorian asked.

"Yeah," Zach said, nodding. "My memory may be spotty about some things, but I definitely remember you. Mostly because you kept dying at the start of the attack…"

Zach mumbled the last sentence in a quiet voice that probably wasn't meant to carry but did. Zorian pretended he didn't hear it.

"You're different than you used to be," Zach said. "You were more irritable, and always busy with something or other. You never believed me when I tried to tell you about the whole time travel thing—you thought I was trying to make fun of you."

Well… that kind of story sounded *exactly* like something his brothers would try to fool him with. And Zach did have a great many things in common with those two already.

"You've changed," Zach concluded. "You're a lot calmer. More laid-back, I guess."

Zorian frowned. He didn't think he had changed that much in personality, but he supposed it would be hard to *not* change when going through something like this. To say nothing of the fact that more than eight months had passed since the restarts had started for Zorian.

"So, wait... why did I change then?" Zorian asked. "Didn't you say the whole world resets itself?"

"Don't know," Zach shrugged, then gave him a speculative look. "Come to think of it, you were there too, weren't you?"

Zorian gave him a confused look. He wasn't going to get baited that easily.

"No, of course you don't remember," Zach sighed. "Do you at least feel a little different lately or something?"

"Come to think of it... yes. I chose different electives than I intended to, for no good reason really, and I did a bunch of other strange things ever since I came to Cyoria."

Zorian's motivation for saying that was two-fold. First of all, he wanted to see how Zach would react to the idea of another person going through the time loop with him. Secondly, he wanted to lay the groundwork for an explanation for why he'd be acting differently in every restart, in case he decided not to tell Zach about himself.

But Zach, to Zorian's surprise, seemed willing to buy in and believe him. Apparently even after all that time—seventeen years if the other boy had his count right—Zach still hadn't developed an ability to effectively read people. That, or Zorian was a better actor than he thought.

"Strange," was all Zach said.

"Yeah," Zorian agreed. "So... any advice a time traveler can tell a mortal like me? A secret spell of awesomeness, maybe?"

"To be honest, most of the spells I know are combat ones," Zach said. "I'm really good at combat magic, which is good because I need to be good at it. There is... something I'm trying to stop."

"Something involving the mysterious adversary that messed you up?" tried Zorian. He really wanted to work the invasion into the conversation but didn't know how to justify knowing anything about it. "Do you remember how *that* happened, at least?"

"Ugh," grunted Zach. "Mostly. I distinctly remember you being there, but you probably died right at the start of the battle—no offense, Zorian, but you aren't much of a fighter—and then I stupidly charged in, thinking myself invulnerable."

"Why would you ever think that?" Zorian asked, honestly confused. "That you're invulnerable, I mean. Doesn't it strike you as dangerously arrogant to perceive yourself as invincible?"

"Do you know how many times I've died in these reverts?" Zach said, throwing his arms out in frustration. "My memory is failing me again, but it was a lot. You tend not to take it too seriously after a while. And it's not like I was too far off. I just have to watch out for necromancy next time, right?"

"Not just necromancy," Zorian replied with a heavy sigh. "There is also mind magic to worry about. Aside from the obvious possibility of ending up as a mind thrall, you could also end up with more than a few gaps in your memory—you could have your whole mind blanked out. Then there's the possibility of having a geas forced upon you if you're too careless, which also binds to the soul as far as I know. Some creatures *eat* souls—like wraiths. That's another thing to worry about. And there are a couple of methods of sealing away a mage's ability to do magic, which might very well stay with you when you... 'revert'."

Zach was silent, but Zorian could have sworn he had grown even paler as he listened to Zorian speak.

"And that's just a couple of points off the top of my head," finished Zorian. "I'm only an academy student, and I don't know anything. It's obvious w—err, *you* are not invulnerable. Okay?"

Zorian swallowed heavily. That was close. It was fortunate that

Zach was so oblivious, because had the situation been reversed, he would have called Zach out on it ages ago.

"Wow, you almost sound like you care," Zach finally said with a nervous chuckle. "You really *do* believe I'm a time traveler now, huh?"

Zorian shrugged. "I'm not completely convinced, but it's not something that's worth fighting over in my opinion. If you say you're a time traveler, then we'll pretend you're a time traveler."

Yes. Until he got a better feel for Zach's character and understood more about the time loop, he would pretend.

When Zorian finally returned to school, having missed both the remainder of Essential Invocations and the following Magical Law lecture, he was beset by curious classmates and Ako. Ako was easy to deal with, since she only wanted to scold him for taking too long and warn him that she had made note of his absence in the attendance record. Zorian was pretty sure the only person, teachers included, who cared about what was written on that list was Akoja. As for the students asking about Zach, that was easy. It was an alchemical accident.

What? It's the excuse Zach used!

Unfortunately, many people also wanted to know why he had suddenly volunteered to escort Zach home, or what had taken him so long. Nosy, nosy people. And they were persistent too, refusing to leave him alone for the rest of the day. When Zorian finally reached his room, he immediately locked his door and breathed a sigh of relief. He finally had enough time to think about what he had discovered that day.

Zach had been confident he would be fine by the morning, and that his memory would come back to him. Zorian was not nearly as confident. A seven-month gap in his memory—and possibly existence—suggested something very serious had been done to him. Why hadn't Zorian suffered anything of the sort? Well… maybe he had. He had felt uncharacteristically tired in his first restart, but had written it off as mental stress. Maybe he had only been caught at the very edge of the spell and thus only suffered minor damage, or maybe his 'first restart' was only the first one he could remember.

It was a disturbing possibility, but there was not much point in dwelling on it.

And Zorian reasoned it wasn't that unlikely. The strange time travel effect he and Zach were under had essentially turned them into soul entities. A lich was, at its core, *also* a soul entity. They were mages that ritually killed themselves and tethered their souls to an object—their phylactery—before it could move on into the afterlife. If the form they currently inhabited ever got destroyed, they'd snap back to their phylactery and then simply possess someone. It would make sense for a lich to know how to fight another lich. And a method that worked against a lich would work just as well against him and Zach.

And Zach had stupidly said as much to the lich at the end of their battle! 'It's not like I'll be dead for good,' indeed! The lich may not have known what Zach was exactly, but a statement like that strongly suggested he was either a lich himself or some type of possessor entity, and from a practical standpoint the two weren't that different.

But that was all neither here nor there. The real question was: what was he going to do now? Even if Zach regained his memories, which seemed doubtful, he would certainly want to keep the time loop going until he found a way to defeat the lich. If the boy's previous altercation with the undead mage was any indication, that could take a while. And that was assuming Zach was the originator of the spell in the first place. If it happened once, it could have happened twice. He had a sneaking suspicion that Zach might be as much of a stowaway as Zorian was. Was there a *third* looping person running around?

As the bigger picture started to come into focus around Zorian, he realized that perhaps his desperation to end the time loop might be misplaced. Getting out might not necessarily mean going back to normal. The invasion was clearly more than a random terrorist attack, and Zorian somehow doubted that merely stopping it would be the end of it. Something very big was happening, and Zorian was a very small fish. A roach, as Taiven would charmingly say. Inside the time loop, he had a chance to secure his future. Outside of it, he was just another victim.

Besides, if Zach was to be believed, 'normal' for Zorian meant getting killed at the start of the invasion. He didn't care much for that kind of normal. In fact, the more he thought about it, the more it seemed to him this whole thing was a giant opportunity rather than an annoyance. Once upon a time, when Zorian was younger, he had dreamt of being a great mage. The sort that legends were made of, the kind that revolutionized whole fields of magic all by themselves. Over time, this dream had died as it became clear he didn't have the talent, the work ethic, or the right connections to make that happen. He was just a slightly above average civilian-born student with no special advantages to his name. But now? He had all the time he needed to rise above his peers and become truly great. Greater than Daimen, even.

He shook his head, abandoning that train of thought. He was getting ahead of himself. He needed something more concrete than a fuzzy notion of greatness to guide him—a clear set of goals to achieve and courses of action to pursue. But in that moment, the only things he could think of were harassing Zach for some tips, raiding the library for more spells, and leveraging his curious monetary situation to improve his alchemical skills.

He was leery about relying on Zach for help. Even if the boy would be cooperative, there was only so much he could learn from the other time traveler without revealing that he, too, retained his memories each time they reverted to the past.

The library was full of spells, of course, but anything that could be used for combat, crime, or spying was restricted, and he knew from talking to older students that teachers were really stingy with permission slips. Not even Fortov had succeeded in getting one, and he could charm a troll into not eating him.

Honing his alchemy skills was definitely an option. The only reason he had focused more heavily on invocation thus far was because he had to buy any ingredients he wished to work with, and he was trying to save money. A serious study of alchemy required a lot of funds, and alchemical ingredients were expensive. With his bank account spontaneously refilling after each restart, however, monetary concerns didn't limit him as much as they had before.

It wasn't much, to be honest. He needed a better plan. With another sigh, Zorian pulled out his trusty notebook and began to plot and write.

"Something I can do for you, sonny?" asked Kyron. "The class has been dismissed, in case you didn't notice."

"Err, I noticed. I just wanted to talk to you about something," Zorian said. Kyron gestured for him to keep talking as the last of the students filed out of the practice hall. "I hope you don't find this insulting, but your stated program seems a bit... easy. Practicing magic missile for a whole month seems rather pointless to me, since I already have a pretty good grasp on it."

Kyron stared at him for a few seconds. Zorian suppressed the instinct to shuffle nervously in place and returned the man's eye contact. Kyron seemed like the sort of person who would be impressed by that.

"I hope *you* don't find this insulting, sonny, but you just don't have enough power to be a proper battlemage," Kyron finally said. "Your shaping skills are rather impressive for your age, but you tire after only ten shots from the rod. And that just won't do in any serious combat."

"Well, I kind of know that," admitted Zorian. His reserves had increased slightly from what they had been when he first tackled the combat magic class, so ten was actually an improvement. "Incidentally, is there anything I can do about that?"

"Nothing I would recommend," Kyron said, shaking his head. "Your mana reserves will grow as your proficiency in magic grows, of course, but so will everyone else's. You will always be at a disadvantage against naturally powerful opponents, which would be most of the professional battlemages. Of course, I cannot forbid you from pursuing a career as a battlemage, but I would definitely advise against it in your case. There are plenty of magical disciplines where superior shaping skills are an asset, but combat magic is mostly about power."

"I see," said Zorian. He didn't intend to become a battlemage, but he had a feeling he was going to need to improve his combat skills, whether he liked it or not. At the very least he wanted to be able to deal with any stray winter wolves or trolls he might encounter during the invasion. "Though my point still stands. Since I can already do the spell well enough, and that's the only thing you intend to instruct us in for the foreseeable future, I can see little point in attending the class for the foreseeable future."

"Hmph," Kyron snorted. "Trying blackmail on me?"

"Er…"

"It's fine, I don't mind. And I *do* understand your point of view here…" Kyron rubbed his chin for a second, mulling something over in his head. "Wait here."

Fifteen minutes later Kyron returned with another spell rod, a small booklet, and four ceramic plates. He threw the plates towards Zorian, who hastily caught them before they shattered upon the ground.

"Good reflexes," Kyron complimented. "They're actually reinforced, so you don't have to worry too much about dropping them."

He took one of the spell rods they used in class and grasped it firmly in his hand. "Let me demonstrate something to you. Throw one of the plates to my left."

Zorian immediately complied, and Kyron wordlessly pointed the rod in the plate's general direction and released a spell. He shot wide off the mark, but the bolt of force actually homed in on the plate anyway, curving through the air to intercept it. The plate shattered into dust and sharp fragments.

"Again," Kyron said, his voice brisk.

Zorian threw another plate, and another bolt of force sped towards it. This one was different, however. It was longer and thinner, like an oversized needle. It hit the plate, but instead of smashing it to pieces, it went right through it, punching a hole through the center of the plate before dissipating.

"Throw the last two together," Kyron instructed.

Zorian tossed the remaining plates, and Kyron once again pointed the rod in their general direction. Zorian waited for the bolt of force, but nothing appeared. Instead, both plates were suddenly cut in half, as though by some unseen blades.

Kyron lowered his hand and began to speak.

"The reason I'll be spending so much time on magic missile is because it's a very versatile spell," Kyron spoke. "At its simplest, it takes the form of a shining bolt of force that travels in a straight line, delivering a concussive blast of force to whatever it impacts. This variant is often called the smasher, and it is a very simple and effective spell. A skilled mage can do so much more with it, however. You can use animation magic to make it home in on a target. You can sharpen it into a point that will pierce things instead of batter them, or create a blade that cuts—the piercer and cutter, respectively. You can fire multiple missiles instead of one—a swarm, even, if you have the reserves and skill to pull it off. And, of course, you can make the projectile invisible."

"Invisible?" asked Zorian.

"Yes," Kyron agreed. "A perfectly cast force spell is completely transparent. The lightshow you usually see is magical leakage resulting from an imperfect spell boundary. The speed with which combat magic is cast virtually guarantees that some mistakes in constructing the spell boundary will be made, and even if no mistakes are made, the large amounts of mana pumped into the constructs can easily distort or unravel some of the pieces."

"So I'm messing the spell up?" summarized Zorian, thinking of the brightly shining projectiles he always got when he used the rod. "Wait, your missiles normally shine too. Is that—"

Kyron chuckled. "Like I said at the start—there are plenty of magical disciplines where great shaping skills are an asset, but combat magic is mostly about power. Most battlemages can't even make a simple magic missile transparent, much less one of the higher level force spells. It doesn't hold them back any. Even I usually don't bother, since the benefits are so marginal. You, on the other hand, need every advantage you can get."

Kyron pushed the spell rod and the accompanying booklet into Zorian's hands.

"You are right that you won't learn much in class in the next month or so. The smasher may be simple, but more than half of your classmates are having trouble with it. You're the only one that truly has a good grasp on it. So read the booklet, find some targets to practice on, and make sure there is a friend nearby while you practice to get help if you screw up big. Oh, and don't hurt anyone with the rod I'm loaning you or I'll be mad. Come back to me in two weeks so I can see how you're progressing."

"Right," Zorian said enthusiastically. This went a lot better than he thought it would.

"Now get lost." Kyron gestured towards the door. "You've wasted my entire coffee break already."

Zorian dropped the stack of books on a nearby table and surveyed the shelves. He had decided to try his luck as a library employee again, hoping he would find a way to get around spell restrictions as an employee. Zach had been absent from class for a couple of days at this point, probably still suffering from the aftereffects of the soul spell, so Zorian couldn't simply trick the answer out of his fellow time traveler. And besides, he wanted to learn those book divinations he was promised before being brutally murdered and all.

But he wasn't in a hurry to get Kirithishli to teach him those divination spells. The magic missile variations Kyron had given him to practice were giving him enough problems as it was. Like Kyron had said, the problem was that shaping had to be done in an instant and involved shoving a great deal of his mana reserves into a hastily constructed spell boundary. That was easy enough when you just wanted a bolt that traveled in a straight line and smashed things, but trying to weave, say, a homing function into the spell was a chore to do in a fraction of a second. To say nothing of trying to eliminate all the little imperfections and make the bolt transparent.

But he had made progress. He could make the bolt curve towards a target even if his aim was a little off, and he had managed to make a flawless piercer yesterday. Progress!

"You're pretty good at this stuff," Ibery remarked beside him, putting a book on the shelf. "I'm surprised. Usually it takes a while for people to really understand the system we use here. I guess you worked in a library before, huh?"

"Uh, yeah," agreed Zorian. It *was* technically true. "It was... quite similar to this one in organization."

"It's not really surprising," Kirithishli said behind him, causing him to flinch in surprise. "All state libraries use the same system of organization. It's a standard enforced by the Society of Librarians. Hell, even the systems of other Splinter Nations are pretty similar."

"Because they all used to be part the same country?" guessed Zorian.

"It is debatable whether or not the Old Alliance could be considered a unified state," Kirithishli said. "The name says it all, really—it was an alliance more than anything. Arguably it was the attempt to turn it into a state that led to the Splinter Wars. But yes, being once part of the Old Alliance, the Splinter Nations inherited much of its administrative legacy, including library organization."

Zorian was starting to understand why Kirithishli had such strained relations with the current headmaster. He knew very little about the man, but what he did suggested he was very politically involved and… well, *patriotic*. And the country they were living in made its official position clear—there was no Old Alliance because the Alliance of Eldemar had never ended. It simply shrank. That this was a completely ridiculous claim was self-evident to citizens and foreigners alike, but most found it easier to humor the politicians. Kirithishli apparently went a step beyond typical arguments and denied there had been a predecessor state to be an inheritor of in the first place. Zorian could imagine the fiery, opinionated woman saying such things in the headmaster's hearing—perhaps not entirely accidentally.

"Hey!" called a familiar voice. "Is Zorian here? I heard—"

"Don't shout in the library, Zach," Zorian sighed. "Since you're back to your usual exuberance, I'm guessing you're all right now?"

"Yup!" Zach thumped his chest a few times. "Healthy like an oak. Got an hour to grab something to eat?"

"In case you haven't noticed, I'm working at the moment," Zorian protested.

"It's not an issue, Zorian, we're mostly done for the day," Kirithishli pointed out. Then she leaned towards him and whispered into his ear. "Unless you wanted to get rid of him and I'm interfering?"

Zorian waved her concerns away and followed Zach outside. As amusing as it would be to see what Kirithishli would say to Zach to get rid of him, he actually wanted to talk to the boy.

"So how come you sought me out?" Zorian asked. He thought he'd have to hound the boy to get more information, but it seemed Zach had taken a liking to him. He didn't know whether to be pleased or annoyed by that. It was convenient, but it increased the chances that Zach would eventually realize something was off with Zorian.

"You're the most interesting person I know of at the moment, and the only other person who believes me about time travel other than Neolu," Zach said.

"Neolu?" asked Zorian incredulously.

"She's an avid reader of speculative fiction and mysteries and is very imaginative and open-minded," said Zach. "A naïve dreamer, her father would say. It was surprisingly easy to convince her I'm really a time traveler. I guess she wants to believe it's true."

"Ah," said Zorian. He supposed that he knew now why Zach had involved Neolu so much during Zorian's first experience of the loop. "How many people did you try to convince, anyway?"

"All of our classmates and teachers, the headmaster, and the heads of every police department in the city. And a few nobles and other influential people."

How… persistent.

"Not very successful, I imagine," Zorian guessed.

Zach sighed. "That's putting it mildly."

Zorian frowned, suddenly realizing something. Why would Zach try to convince all those people he was a time traveler? That didn't sound like something a time traveler that came specifically to stop the invasion would do. It sounded more like something Zorian had briefly considered when he had realized how utterly out of his depth he was, but ultimately decided to scrap the idea because he expected the results to be more or less identical to what Zach got.

"Zach," began Zorian carefully, "what about those gaps in your memory? Are they…"

"They're still there," Zach said, a scowl marring his features. "I'm pretty sure they're not increasing anymore though, thank the gods."

"Hmm," agreed Zorian. "So you don't know how you achieved this time travel magic, then? I looked it up, and it's supposed to be impossible, you know? As impossible as drawing a square triangle, in fact."

"Well, it's clearly not that impossible, is it?" Zach countered. "But no, I have no idea how I did that. *If* I did that."

"If you did that," agreed Zorian. "From your comments, I'm getting a feeling you started these reverts as a common academy student. And I mean no offense, but the Zach I remember wasn't really the kind of person capable of inventing any spell, much less something as concept-breaking as time travel."

Zach chuckled nervously. "You're probably right. I used to be really bad at this whole mage business, didn't I? But enough of such depressing topics, because I've got good news for you!"

"Oh?"

"I heard you've been trying to learn combat magic."

"Where did you hear that?" Zorian tried to keep the alarm from his voice.

"Kyron told the rest of the teachers, the teachers told the administrative staff, the administrative staff told the janitors and other low paying workers, they told the students, and the students told me." Zach shrugged. "What does it matter? What matters is that I'm very good at combat magic thanks to the reverts, and I've decided to teach you. Think of it as a reward for believing me."

Zorian looked at Zach, speechless. He was going to help him

out on his own free will? Just like that? No need for any plotting or subtle maneuvering?

Almost disappointing.

"What?" Zach protested. "It's true, I really am good at combat magic! In fact, that's the field I excel at the most!"

Zorian couldn't ask for a more ideal opening than that.

"Not that I don't believe you," he began, "but how exactly did you get so good at combat magic? I mean, mages are really stingy about sharing combat magic. Even with these… reverts… why would a battlemage share their secrets with an academy student like you? Especially since you're… uh…"

"Known to be irresponsible," Zach finished for him. "To be honest, I didn't get the spells I know legally. I wouldn't recommend my methods of acquiring combat magic to anyone who isn't a time traveler. You tend to die a lot."

"Oh."

"Yeah. But you have me, so there's that. Come on, I know a quiet place to practice." Zach set off without waiting for a response.

Quietly wondering what he was getting himself into and if Zach's bright smile of confidence was luring him to his death, Zorian followed.

CHAPTER 008

Perspective

"Here we are!" said Zach happily, twirling around with his hands outstretched. "What do you think?"

Zorian studied the meadow in front of him, his eyes darting back and forth with suspicion. At first glance the area was just a large patch of grass surrounded by a ring of trees, but Zorian couldn't help but notice signs of obvious neglect. The grass was too wild and tall, and the space between trees was full of young saplings fighting for their own place under the sun. It was a good place to practice combat magic, but also a good place to hide a body. In an even remotely normal situation, Zorian wouldn't be caught dead following a complete stranger into a creepy, isolated place like this one. Oh, how far his perspective had shifted…

"I wonder what's keeping the saplings confined to that ring of trees," wondered Zorian aloud. "This meadow should be a copse of trees by now."

Zach blinked. "I never thought about that," he admitted. "You notice the strangest things, Zorian."

"I also wonder how a place like this can exist at all," Zorian continued. "I mean, we're in Cyoria. Land is very expensive here. Why is someone letting this place deteriorate like this instead of selling it?"

"Oh, that's easy," Zach said. "It's my land. Or rather, it's part of the Noveda family estates. It's supposed to be a private garden for the Head of House, or something like that, so no one could do anything with it unless they had my explicit permission. But since I hadn't even known this place existed before the reverts… yeah."

"Hm. I guess I should have expected something like that. Your home is pretty close to here, isn't it?"

"You know where I live?" Zach asked, surprise evident in his voice.

Crap. What to say, what to say…

"Of course I know where you live," Zorian said, looking at Zach like the boy was an idiot for asking. "Who *doesn't* know where the Noveda estate is located?"

A lot of people, probably. Zorian himself certainly hadn't known, not until he had tried to track Zach down in one of the restarts.

"Heh. I'm pretty famous, aren't I?" Zach said, grinning widely.

Note to self: Zach is easy to distract by appealing to his pride.

Zorian sighed. "So, is the great Noveda going to help me learn combat magic like he promised or not? Daylight's burning."

Zach snapped his fingers, apparently remembering just why they had come there in the first place. His hands blurred into a sequence of gestures, and several humanoids made of earth rose from the ground on the other side of the clearing.

Zorian gaped. Now *that* was impressive. Zach didn't even have to chant anything to cast that spell, and he went through the gestures with such speed Zorian had trouble remembering what they even were. Plus, those earthen constructs weren't just immobile statues—they *moved*. It was moments like this that Zorian remembered he was dealing with a vastly superior mage who had him beat in virtually every conceivable way. It was humbling, to say the least.

"Wow," he said out loud.

"It's not as impressive as it looks," Zach said. "They're nearly useless in actual battle. They make good targets though, since they're pretty resilient and reform each time you mess them up."

Zach fired a quick magic missile at one of the statues to demonstrate, hitting it square in the chest. The force of the bolt pushed the earthen construct back a step, and a web of cracks erupted from the impact point, but these quickly sealed themselves shut and the construct otherwise completely ignored the attack.

Zorian stared. "I don't believe this."

"What do you mean?" Zach asked. "They're just animated earth so it's—"

"Not them," Zorian protested. "The magic missile! No chant, no gestures, no spell formula, no nothing! You just pointed your finger at the target and produced a magic missile!"

Which, admittedly, was a gesture. Not one that should be sufficient to produce a magic missile, though.

"Oh, that," Zach said, waving his hand dismissively. "That's not terribly special either. That's just reflexive magic. When you cast a spell enough times—"

"Mana shaping becomes instinctive and you can start leaving out spell components," Zorian finished for him. Any serious mage had at least a couple of spells they knew so intimately they could leave out a couple of words and gestures and still get it working. "But getting a spell to work with something as simple as pointing a finger would take *years*!"

Zach simply grinned from ear to ear.

"Which, uh, I guess you had," Zorian concluded, feeling rather stupid. "This time travel thing is really convenient, isn't it? How many reflexive spells do you have, anyway?"

"You mean, how many are as reflexive as the magic missile I just showed you? Shield, hurl, recall, flamethrower, and a couple of other easy combat spells. There are a lot of spells I'm familiar with, but I can't exactly throw fireballs by pointing my fingers."

"Right," said Zorian sourly. He was getting way past humbling and straight into 'feeling mightily inadequate' territory. Better steer the conversation back to the lesson before Zach completely demoralized him. "So where do we start?"

"Kyron gave you a spell rod and told you to practice magic missile, didn't he?" asked Zach.

"Yeah."

"Well, let's see how that's working out for you first," said Zach, waving his hand in the direction of the earthen constructs. "Fire a couple of missiles at the mud people."

"Mud people?" asked Zorian incredulously. "Is that—"

"Probably not," Zach admitted. "I kind of forgot the official name of the spell, so I just refer to it as create mud people. It doesn't matter all that much since the spell is obscure and obsolete, and virtually no one except me uses it."

"I guess," agreed Zorian. He was tempted to ask more, but figured he would never get to actual spell practice if he kept distracting Zach with his questions. He pointed the spell rod Kyron gave him at the closest... mud person... and fired. He was a bit surprised when the construct tried to side-step his magic missile instead of soaking in the spell like it had when Zach targeted it, but that didn't save it—he had enough control of the spell to alter the missile's flight path, even if he couldn't get the bolt to home in on the target on its own. Of course, the bolt did very little actual damage to the construct, and even that repaired itself quickly. Undeterred, Zorian kept firing. His next shot was a piercer aimed at the head of the construct, which succeeded in hitting it squarely in the forehead but failed to actually punch through the animated earth. He tried to shape the next bolt into a cutter, but all he got was a diffuse blob of multicolored light that popped like a soap bubble halfway to the target. The next two were regular smashers, one of which missed when its target leaned to the side at the last moment.

Zorian stopped at this point, not wanting to completely deplete his mana reserves. He had demonstrated pretty much everything he had achieved so far, anyway.

Zach clapped overdramatically, completely ignoring the mild glare Zorian sent his way.

"You've only been practicing, what, for a couple of days?" asked Zach. Zorian nodded. "And you can direct your bolts already? You're a lot better than I thought you'd be."

"Oh?" asked Zorian, putting an edge in his voice—though Zach seemed unaware. "And why is that?"

"Let me ask you this instead: how many magic missiles can you cast before you run out of mana?" asked Zach.

"Ten," answered Zorian. He didn't see what that... oh. "Ah. Normally learning time corresponds to mana capacity, doesn't it?"

"Yup! The bigger your mana reserves, the longer you can train each day," confirmed Zach. "It means mages with larger reserves tend to learn faster than their less gifted compatriots."

"Assuming everyone is equally dedicated and equally good at shaping mana," noted Zorian.

"Assuming that," agreed Zach. "Though the difference in mana reserves tends to overshadow almost everything else. Do you know how many magic missiles I can cast before I run out of mana?"

Zorian hadn't forgotten Zach's seemingly inexhaustible mana reserves that he had demonstrated during the invasion, and was aware that the number had to be pretty high. Still, there was a limit to how big mana reserves could get. The booklet Kyron had given him said average mages can fire somewhere between eight to twelve magic missiles before running out of mana, while very gifted ones could manage as much as twenty or thirty. Furthermore, while mana reserves increased with age and practice, they were not unlimited in potential—for most people, the maximum was roughly four times the amount of their initial mana reserves, and sometimes less. Assuming Zach was in the above average range and that he had reached his maximum due to the time loop…

"Fifty?" he tried.

"Two hundred and thirty-two," said Zach, a smug smile on his face.

Zorian almost dropped the spell rod in shock, but in the end settled for staring at Zach like he had just swallowed a live chicken. Two hundred and thirty-two? What the hell!?

"Admittedly I'm at the extreme high end when it comes to mana reserves," Zach said. Understatement of the century! "And unlike you, I've spent years building them up, so they're as high as they're ever going to be. Still, even if you had a lifetime of practice, you'd probably never go over forty. That would make my reserves almost six times larger than yours. Quite a disadvantage to make up for."

"No kidding," agreed Zorian. "I'm guessing that's where you come in. Unless you've brought me here just to tell me how much I suck compared to you?"

"Hah! I admit, the look on your face when you realized how awesome I am was absolutely priceless, but that's just a bonus," said Zach.

He beckoned for Zorian to come closer and Zorian complied, allowing Zach to cast a completely unfamiliar spell on him.

Zorian felt the spell seep into his eyes, foreign mana straining against the innate magical resistance possessed by every living creature, and briefly considered snuffing the spell out before it took root. Not because he thought the spell was harmful, mind you, but out of principle. Zach just cast a spell on him without asking for permission or explaining what the spell did, which was a major breach of magical etiquette no matter how you looked at it. In the end he decided not to be that spiteful and simply reeled in his magical resistance, allowing the spell to do its work unopposed.

"You already have control over your magical resistance?" asked Zach. "Sweet! I usually have to teach people how to do that. Hell, *I* didn't know how to do that before the reverts."

Zorian frowned, ignoring Zach's comments in favor of trying to figure out what the spell actually did. It was concentrated in his eyes, so he should... see...

Oh.

A glowing, mind-bogglingly huge pillar rose into the sky, warping and undulating like a living being, occasionally spawning short-lived whorls of glowing matter along its length. It only took Zorian a moment to realize what he was looking at.

"That's how the Hole looks like under mage sight?" he asked, eyes glued to the spectacle even as he directed the question at Zach.

He knew the massive mana well around which Cyoria was built spewed vast quantities of ambient mana into the surrounding lands, but it was one thing to know it and another to see it in this manner. The massive column was thicker than any building and rose to dizzying heights as it left the underworld.

"Magnificent, isn't it?" Zach said. "Watching that huge geyser of mana rising into the sky always puts things into perspective for me."

"Mage sight shouldn't work in Cyoria, though," remarked Zorian. "Too much ambient mana saturating everything. Why aren't I blinded by a painful glow emanating from everything in sight?"

"It's an experimental variation that tries to filter out such noise, showing only the important stuff," said Zach. "It's not terribly reliable, but it will do for our purposes."

"Those being?" asked Zorian.

"I'll cast magic missile repeatedly and you'll watch what I'm doing for a while before trying to copy me," Zach said. "I'll be using the proper invocation this time, and I'll go at it as slowly as I can. Try to memorize the words and gestures, because you'll be using them instead of the rod Kyron gave you. A spell rod is more useful in combat, but for training purposes it's better to work with actual invocations."

Zorian was completely on board with the idea—he had been trying to find invocations for combat spells for a while. Zach was underestimating him, though. 'Try' to memorize? Zorian might not have Zach's absurd mana reserves, but his memory was very good. It took only one proper casting from Zach and Zorian had already burned the casting procedure into his memory.

Unfortunately, the rest of the session was a lot less impressive. Zach kept performing the spell a few more times before instructing Zorian to give it a try, upon which he found out that performing combat magic with classical invocations wasn't only slower than using a spell rod, it was a lot harder, too. Thankfully, the fact that he actually *saw* how the mana was supposed to be shaped during Zach's demonstrations drastically improved his learning speed, so he managed to fire off a passable magic missile in the end. He was completely out of mana by then, however, and Zach decided that was a good time to stop for the day.

Walking back to his apartment, Zorian was lost in thought. Zach's comment about the giant pillar of mana putting things into perspective for him seemed oddly applicable to his situation as well. Time loop or not, he would never beat Zach and people like him at their own game. Clearly Zorian couldn't bulldoze his way through with combat magic, like Zach intended to do. No, if he was going to get out of this in a favorable manner, he had to forge his own path.

If only he knew what that path was, though. At the moment, getting to the bottom of what caused the time loop and how the damn thing worked seemed to be just about the only thing he could do to help himself. Which was unfortunate, because he just didn't have the skills to unravel the mystery. He would need to spend some time improving his magical abilities, and time, at least, he had in spades. Probably. He could never be sure the time loop would continue happening, but Zach certainly didn't behave like it would end any time soon, and Zorian decided to follow Zach's lead in that regard.

He really wished he had someone other than Zach to ask for advice on how to proceed in his quest to improve himself. Typically, this was what a student's mentor was for, but he already knew what Xvim would tell him: more shaping exercises. And then he'd throw marbles at him.

Although… Ilsa had offered to take over his mentorship in more than one restart. Hmm.

Despite his desire for some additional help, Zorian delayed approaching Ilsa until he had completed a few sessions with Xvim. That would require a lengthy wait, but it would make it easier to complain about Xvim's mentoring methods, since he wouldn't have to explain how he knew so much about the man already. It wasn't like he didn't have anything to amuse himself with in the meantime—Zach was, if anything, even more enthusiastic about their combat magic practice sessions than Zorian was, insisting they meet up every day after classes. After two weeks of such practice, Zorian not only was able to weave a proper homing function into the magic missile spell, but had learned how to cast shield and flamethrower spells as well. He was keenly aware that his ability to cast such spells would amount to exactly zero against a human battlemage, but he also knew they weren't the only threats he faced. Those spells might buy him a second or two against a winter wolf or a troll, which could be the difference between life and death.

Zach returned to classes the day after their first practice session, apparently completely recovered. For a guy that had lost a good chunk of his memory, he was surprisingly exuberant. Zorian admired his fellow time traveler for his ability to maintain good cheer in poor circumstances, but Zach's attention-grabbing behavior only made his inexplicable improvement in skill that much more noticeable. It was almost a repeat of the very first time he lived through the month, only instead of hanging out with Neolu and that other mystery girl, Zach was hanging out with *him*. Which, of course, made Zorian a target for every curious classmate that wanted to know how Zach had suddenly become so skilled.

"What am I supposed to tell them?" he asked Zach. They were in the cafeteria, and he had noticed a couple students glancing at him a bit too often, doubtlessly waiting for the chance to talk to him when Zach left. "I can't exactly tell them you're a time traveler."

"Why not?" Zach asked. "Time travel. It's what I say every time they ask me how I got this good."

"You actually tell them you're a time traveler?" asked Zorian incredulously. He didn't know whether to laugh or bang his head against the table.

"Yeah," confirmed Zach. "What's the worst that could happen?"

Zorian felt a pang of phantom pain in his chest where, in another timeline, a masked assassin had stabbed him through and killed him. Did Zach honestly never experience consequences like that when trying to convince people of his story? Then again, he had said he tried to convince them he was a time traveler, not that he told them about the invasion. In fact, he didn't actually tell Zorian about that, either—he danced around the topic whenever Zorian tried to lead the conversation there.

"This could have all been avoided if you just held back a little in classes," Zorian said, sighing.

"I kind of like the attention," Zach admitted.

"Really?" asked Zorian. "I'm only going through this once and I'm already sick of it. You're saying the novelty of all that attention still hasn't worn off after, what, more than a decade?"

"Oh, come on, do you really think I spend these reverts attending classes, of all things?" scoffed Zach. "That got seriously old after the third revert or so. I spend most of the time doing my own thing. Hell, usually I'm not even near Cyoria! I only attend the classes when I want to relax or when I am feeling nostalgic. The only reason why I'm here right now is because I got kind of roughed up in my last revert and I'm still trying to sort out the holes in my memory. Oh, and because you've kind of caught my interest."

"Why did I catch your interest, though?" asked Zorian. "Not that I'm complaining or anything, but how come you're willing to invest so much time in me? Isn't it all going to be useless in the next revert?"

"That's a pretty cold way of thinking about things," Zach said. "I don't really think like that. I've tried to get to know all of our classmates in these reverts, even though some of them were pretty uncooperative, and I've never thought of it as a waste of time. This is the first time you've been this friendly, and I have no idea what exactly I did to cause that. It's best to make use of it while I can."

Zorian felt a knot of guilt build in his stomach. Not only had he never tried to get to know any of his classmates during the reverts, the idea had never even occurred to him. And this wasn't the first time Zach had insinuated that Zorian had been kind of a jerk to him in the past. Just what had happened between Zach and past-Zorian to leave that much of an impression?

"I see," said Zorian uncertainly, not knowing how to respond to that.

"I really do wonder about you, though," Zach continued. "You're so different from the Zorian I knew, I'm starting to wonder if you're really the same person."

"Who else would I be?" asked Zorian, honestly at a loss as to where Zach was going with this. He didn't appear to have figured out that Zorian was reverting, as he would say, so what was he getting at?

"I think I may have shifted timelines, or something," Zach said.

Zorian gave him an incredulous look. Shifted timelines? That's his explanation? Really? *Really really*? He almost revealed himself right then and there, just so he could tell Zach how silly that was. Almost.

"Or something," deadpanned Zorian.

"Whaaat?" protested Zach. "It could happen. Do *you* know how temporal mechanics work? No? Didn't think so."

"I did look up a couple of books about time travel after our first meeting," said Zorian. It was a lie, of course, but only a small one—he had sifted through time travel related texts, just not in this particular restart.

"And learned nothing," concluded Zach. "It's a total wasteland. All they write about is various ethical dilemmas and time paradoxes and whatnot. That was the first and last time I set foot in the academy library, let me tell you."

Zorian gave him a strange look. "That was a joke, right?"

"Which part?" Zach asked.

"The part where you only visited the academy library once."

"Err, well…," tried Zach, chuckling nervously. "What can I say? I don't really like to read…"

Zorian stared at Zach, wondering if the boy was pulling his leg.

He would totally understand if the old Zach, the one he knew before the time loop, told him he never set foot in the library. He wouldn't be terribly unique in that regard—many students never visited the library before their third year since they couldn't access the spell repository before their certification, anyway. But *this* Zach had lived through this month over two hundred times, and had access to the spells buried within its depths. And he had never tried to search through it. Because he didn't like to read.

The mind boggled. Well, Zorian's mind boggled.

"You've clearly read our textbooks," Zorian noted. "There's no way you'd excel as well as you do otherwise."

"Yeah, well, I didn't say I don't read at all," Zach countered. "Just that I'd rather avoid it if I can. I learn much better by practice anyway."

Funny, it was just the opposite with Zorian. He tended to learn much better when he had the chance to study the topic on his own before trying. He still thought it was a pretty serious flaw for a mage to avoid books, but Zorian had to remind himself that Zach was clearly achieving results somehow. Come to think of it, there was a serious shortage of anything dangerous in the academy spell collection, so a mage that was chiefly interested in the more restricted areas of magic would find the library of very limited usefulness.

"So, you learn primarily by mentorship?" guessed Zorian. "I'm surprised you can convince mages to teach you in less than a month. Don't they all require apprenticeships lasting several years before they'll agree to teach you anything useful?"

"Well, usually," said Zach. "But I'm the last Noveda, don't you know? I've had highly respectable mages tripping over themselves to teach me my whole life. Usually I just have to show up and tell them who I am and they're all too happy to help me out."

Zorian suppressed a wave of jealousy that washed over him. Zach was just making the most of his unique situation, just like Zorian would have in his place. It still bothered him, though, reminding him of how Daimen and Fortov could ask for and receive all sorts of help and concessions from their teachers, only for Zorian to fail in securing the same for himself. His parents had lectured him endlessly that the difference was in their attitudes—that if only Zorian was more sociable, more polite, more *everything*… he, too, could enjoy the same benefits. To Zorian, it always seemed like his brothers had some sort of invisible tattoo on their foreheads that only mages could see, and which marked them as somehow more special than him.

Zach wasn't his brothers, though, and didn't deserve to be the target for Zorian's personal frustrations.

"Convenient," Zorian said, giving his fellow time traveler a forced smile. Zach didn't appear to notice.

His jealousy aside, he was really starting to wonder if his assumption about Zach being an accidental stowaway like him had any merit at all. Zach had ridiculously huge mana reserves, probably the largest of any student currently attending the academy. He was the last member of a famous Noble House, enjoying all the prestige that came from that without having to deal with nosy parents who might be freaked out by Zach's sudden transformation. In addition to the power inherent in his name, the boy was also fairly charming and outgoing, further improving his chances of getting help from otherwise unapproachable high-circle mages. He was not your average spoiled prince, by any means—there was a lot of potential in the boy, if only he had enough time to bring it out. Which he now did. It was… convenient. A bit too convenient, in Zorian's opinion.

That was why, despite Zach's seeming friendliness, Zorian just didn't feel at ease with the boy. Not enough to reveal himself as a stowaway, in any case. Right now, his main advantage was that he was an outside element in this game Zach was playing. An unaccounted variable. He intended to use and abuse that advantage for all it was worth.

Whatever force was behind Zach, Zorian had no intention of revealing himself to it any time soon.

"Take a seat, Mister Kazinski," Ilsa said. "I suspected I'd be seeing you soon."

"You did?" asked Zorian.

"Oh yes," Ilsa said. "Usually students come knocking at my door immediately after a single session with Xvim. You actually waited until the second one, so points for patience."

"Right," said Zorian sourly.

"I can't transfer you to another mentor at this time, though, so I'm afraid you'll just have to bear with him for now," she said.

"I expected that," Zorian said. Why should her answer be any different than it was the last time he had asked her? "It's not what I'm here for."

"No?" asked Ilsa, raising an eyebrow.

"No. Since everything I've heard and experienced about Xvim suggests we'll never progress beyond the basic three, I've decided to be proactive about self-study. I've been hoping for some pointers from you— where I should start, what I should watch out for, that sort of thing."

Ilsa sighed heavily. "It's hard to give that sort of advice, Zorian. That's why the academy gives students mentors—because there is no one-size-fits-all solution. I suppose I could give you advice about my own subject, though. How good are you at the basic three?"

"Depends who you ask," said Zorian. "Most of the teachers from my second year told me I had them mastered. Xvim says I'm a shame to mages everywhere."

She snorted and handed him a pen. Actually handed it to him, instead of throwing it at him like Xvim would have. Ah, the joy of interacting with sane teachers...

"Levitate that," Ilsa said.

She wasn't even finished talking and the pen was already spinning above his outstretched palm.

"Oh, so you can already spin the levitated object?" Ilsa said, sounding pleased. "I bet Xvim was very happy with that." No, not really. "Do you know any other variation?"

"No," said Zorian. "Don't tell me learning those is standard procedure?"

"Not like Xvim is teaching them," Ilsa said. "But yes, most mentors will give students variations of the basic three to improve their shaping skills."

"And how many of those variations are there?" asked Zorian.

"Oh, *thousands*," said Ilsa, confirming Zorian's suspicions. "But most students only learn six or so by the end of their third year. Here."

She pushed a rather heavy book into his hands, patiently waiting for him to leaf through it. It described fifteen 'particularly interesting' variations of the basic three, five for each exercise.

"Let me guess: you want me to learn everything inside this book," Zorian said, sighing.

Ilsa laughed. "That would be a pretty neat trick. Didn't you hear what I said? Most people learn six or fewer... *in a year*. You'll probably be finished with the academy by the time you've learned everything inside that book. Assuming you want to, of course—I'm not making you do anything."

"Six in a year, huh?" asked Zorian carefully, an idea forming in his mind.

"That's right," Ilsa confirmed.

"What if I could master all fifteen before the end of the month?" asked Zorian.

Ilsa stared at him for a second before bursting into laughter. It took her a few seconds to calm down.

"My, aren't you the confident one? If you were really that good, I'd fill out the transfer forms right now, regulations be damned, and take you as my apprentice. I'd never pass up an opportunity to teach such a legend in the making. Not that I think you could do it, mind you."

Zorian just gave her a wicked smile.

Of course, there was absolutely no chance for Zorian to master all fifteen exercises in this particular restart, but that was beside the point. Thanks to the wonder of the time loop, he had far more than a few measly weeks to learn the contents of the book. It was even available in the academy library, so he didn't have to go to Ilsa in the next restart to acquire it. And who knew, maybe if he learned those he could get Xvim to cut him some slack, too. A man could dream.

Besides, the book was actually fairly interesting. Not only did it explain how to perform each variation in great detail, it also explained the reasons for including each particular exercise, as well as providing a background for understanding why the basic three were being taught to students in the first place. Zorian briefly familiarized himself with each of the variations before starting to read earnestly from the start.

Making an object glow, levitating it, or setting it aflame… these were very simple effects, requiring only rudimentary shaping skills. The levitation exercise, for instance, was just repelling force emanating from the mage's palm. It doesn't get much simpler than that. There were actually a lot of these simple effects, certainly more than the three they were taught, but these three were deemed a priority. Production of light, heat, or kinetic force were common components of many spells, giving the basic three the sort of general usefulness that most other simple exercises lacked.

The variations listed in the book, however, were not in the same category as these starter exercises. Although Xvim, Ilsa, and the book itself referred to them as variations, Zorian realized they might be better characterized as upgrades, or perhaps advanced versions. He hadn't realized it at the time, but the pen spinning exercise—which was the very first variation outlined in the book, albeit under a fancier name—occupied a category of difficulty far above simply levitating the pen above his palm. Not only did he have to maintain the levitation effect on the pen, he also had to shape an additional effect to make the pen spin. The variation was supposed to teach mages how to multitask by making them maintain two effects at once.

Though Xvim would have disagreed, Zorian considered his pen spinning exercise mastered, and the guidelines in the book seemed to agree with him. As such, he started poring over the other four variations of the levitation exercise, trying to figure out which one was the easiest. He quickly realized they were not only arranged in an ascending order of difficulty, but that mastering the later variations probably *required* mastering the preceding ones first.

Vertical levitation required him to make an object stick to his palm with attractive force, position his palm perpendicular to the ground and then make the object separate from his palm without falling down. The sticking part was easy, and something Zorian could already do. But making the object float off the palm without falling required that he balance the attractive force binding the object to his palm and the repelling force that made it separate from it. Without acquiring the ability to multitask from the pen spinning exercise, it probably would have taken forever to master this one.

After that came fixed position levitation, which required an ability to maintain the levitated object's position in space despite disruptions and changes in initial conditions. In other words, he had to be able to move his hand up and down, left and right, while keeping the levitated object static in space. It required the ability to balance attractive and repelling force he presumably acquired from the vertical levitation exercise, but this time he had to continually adjust the balance in response to changes.

And so on. Seeing how there was only one correct order in which these exercises could be learned, Zorian started practicing vertical levitation. Unfortunately, he wouldn't accomplish much in this particular restart.

The summer festival was approaching.

CHAPTER 009

Cheaters

"Majara," intoned Zorian, finishing the invocation with the word he wanted the spell to search for. He felt the spell reach out around him, scanning the books on the surrounding shelves for any mention of the word in question, and then poured some more mana into the spell to expand its radius. His efforts to overcharge the spell almost unraveled it, forcing him to spend several seconds stabilizing the spell boundary, but in the end the mana flow snapped into its proper place and the spell finished its task as planned. Seven golden threads flickered into existence, seemingly growing out of his chest and connecting him to various books in this particular section of the library.

Zorian smiled. The spell was one of the book divinations Ibery had taught him, one that sought out books containing a specified word or string of words. It was a somewhat fragile spell, failing if the number of positive matches exceeded a certain number—which was dependent on the caster's skill. It was mostly used to search for quotes or unusual terms.

Unusual like, say, the dead language of Majara. Zenomir hadn't been kidding when he had told Zorian that he wouldn't be able to find any books about it—there were no books specifically about the Majara language, and very few books even mentioned it. Until this moment, he had only found thirteen other books that contained the word, and most of them did so only in the form of a throwaway comment or two. It was possible that the knowledge he sought existed somewhere in the library, only in a format that was invisible to the divinations he was using. Ibery had only taught him the very basics of library magic, as she called it, so his searches were painfully crude in the grand scheme of things—but if that was the case, there was little he could do about it.

He glanced down at the threads growing out of his chest and waved his hand across them, watching it pass through without effect. He never got tired of doing that. Well, he probably would, in time, but the novelty hadn't worn off yet. The threads were an illusion, existing only in the privacy of his own mind. Every divination spell needed a medium through which it could present information to the caster, since it was impossible for human minds to process the raw output of a divination spell. A self-imposed illusion like the threads he was currently looking at was actually fairly advanced as divination mediums go, or so Ibery had claimed when he had tried to tell her he got the spell working within thirty minutes of being shown how to do it. He had a distinct impression she thought he was lying. He didn't really understand what was supposed to be so difficult about it—the threads were a purely mental construct that didn't even require much in the way of shaping skills… just visualization. It seemed pretty simple to him. Natural even.

He shook his head and followed after one of the golden threads until he reached a book it was attached to. It was a huge, intimidating, four-hundred-page book about the history of Miasina, and Zorian had absolutely no intention of poring over it until he reached the tiny part that actually interested him, so he cast another divination Ibery had taught him. This one highlighted every mention of the chosen word (in this case 'Majara') in shining green, so he simply flipped through the book till he caught a flash of green.

"Zorian? What are you doing here?"

Zorian immediately snapped the book shut and stuffed it back on the shelf. While he wasn't doing anything forbidden, he really didn't want to explain to Ibery what Majara was or why he was searching the library for any mention of it.

The retort he planned to use died on his lips when he finally turned to get a good look on his visitor. Ibery was a mess. Her eyes and nose were red, as if she had been crying recently, and there was an ugly purple splotch covering her right cheek and neck. It didn't look like a bruise, not exactly, more like…

Oh, hell no.

"Ibery…," he started hesitantly, "you wouldn't happen to be in the same class as my brother, would you?"

She flinched back and looked away. He sighed heavily. Just great.

"How did you know?" she asked after a second of silence.

"Brother dearest came to me earlier today," said Zorian. "Said he pushed a girl into a purple creeper patch and wanted me to make an anti-rash potion. I wasn't in the mood so I kind of blew him off."

That was a lie, actually. He had discovered, during the last three reverts, that Fortov was either unable or unwilling to track him down if he failed to return to his room after class. That was actually the main reason why he had spent the entire day in the library. Still, due to his rather unique situation, he knew what would have happened had he been present.

"Oh," she said quietly. "That… That's all right."

"No," disagreed Zorian. "No, it's not. If I had known he was talking about you, I would have helped him out. Well… helped *you* out. *He* can go die in a fire as far as I'm concerned." He paused for a moment, considering things. "You know, there is no reason why I can't do it now. I'll just have to stop by my room to pick up the ingredients and—"

"You don't have to do that," Ibery hurriedly interrupted. "It's… not that important."

Zorian took in her appearance one more time. Yup, she had *definitely* been crying before coming here. Besides, her choice of words was conspicuous—she said that he didn't *have* to do it, not that he shouldn't, and that it wasn't *that* important, not that it wasn't.

"It's not really a problem," he assured her. "The main reason I refused in the first place is because it was Fortov who asked, not because it was so difficult to do. Just tell me where to find you when I'm done."

"Um, I'd like to come with you, if it's not a problem," she said hesitantly. "I'd like to see how the cure is made. Just in case."

Zorian paused. That was… potentially problematic. After all, the alchemical workshop would be closed down this late in the evening, and he would have to employ some, uh, *unorthodox* methods of gaining access. But what the hell, it wasn't like she would remember this in the next restart.

They set off towards Zorian's apartment. Of course, having Ibery looking over his shoulder wasn't enough, so when he finally reached his room, he found another familiar person waiting for him. Specifically, Zach.

He wasn't terribly surprised to see Zach waiting for him, to be honest. The boy had been getting steadily more restless during their practice sessions as the summer festival approached, no doubt on edge due to the impending invasion. Not that he ever told Zorian about the invasion—Zach was stubbornly tight-lipped about that, regardless of how much Zorian tried to goad him into blurting out something. Recently, his fellow time traveler had questioned him about his plans for the summer festival several times, not so subtly implying that staying inside his room would be a bad idea. As Zorian still remembered quite vividly how one of the 'flares' had flattened his entire apartment building when the invasion started, he was inclined to agree with Zach on that one. Unfortunately, Zach seemed to have trouble believing this. No doubt he had come to Zorian's room again specifically to make sure that Zorian was going to attend the dance. Zorian wondered, as he had more than once, what had happened between Zach and his previous incarnations to produce this kind of impression. Had he really been that stubborn before the time loop?

Zorian walked up to Zach, who was sitting on the floor next to the door, completely oblivious to his surroundings while he concentrated on something on his palm. No, *above* his palm. A pencil, lazily spinning in the air. Apparently Zach knew the pen spinning exercise, too, and was currently practicing it while he waited. Zorian had a strong urge to throw a marble at Zach's forehead and demand that he start over, but decided against it.

Mostly because he didn't have any marbles on his person at the moment.

"Hello, Zach," Zorian said, startling Zach out of his reverie. "Are you waiting for me?"

"Yeah." He opened his mouth to say something else, but then he noticed Ibery trailing behind Zorian and snapped his mouth shut. "Err, am I interrupting something?"

"No, not really," Zorian said. "I just came to grab some alchemical supplies and then I'll go make something for Miss Ambercomb here. What did you want with me?"

"Eh, it can wait a while," Zach said dismissively. "What are you making? Maybe I can help. I'm pretty good at alchemy."

"Is there anything you're *not* good at?" asked Zorian with a snort.

"You'd be surprised," mumbled Zach.

Ibery watched their interaction in silence, but Zach was a fairly sociable person, so by the time Zorian returned from his room with a box of supplies the two of them were engaged in lively conversation. Mostly about Ibery's current condition.

"Man, I didn't know your brother was such a jerk, Zorian," Zach remarked. "No wonder you turned out to be such a... uh..."

He trailed off when Zorian raised his eyebrow at him, daring him to finish that sentence. Ibery's reaction was more vocal.

"He's not a jerk!" she protested. "He didn't mean for this to happen."

"He should have fixed it, though," Zach insisted. "Intentionally or not, it was his fault. He shouldn't have dumped his responsibility on his little brother like this."

"Nobody forced Zorian to do anything," Ibery said. "He's doing this out of his own free will. Right, Zorian?"

"Right," agreed Zorian. "I'm doing this because I want to."

He actually agreed with Zach, but chose not to say so. If he had learned anything about Ibery from spending an entire revert around her, it was that she had a massive crush on Fortov. No good could come from bad mouthing him in front of her. Besides, if he was to be honest with himself, Zorian had to admit he was incapable of being objective about Fortov. There was too much bad blood between the two of them.

Thankfully, the two of them quickly agreed to disagree on the topic and a comfortable silence descended on the group. Well, it was comfortable for Zorian—apparently Zach thought otherwise.

"Hey, Zorian," Zach said. "Why are we going towards the academy proper?"

"So I can access the alchemical workshop, of course," said Zorian. He knew what Zach was getting at, of course, but he was still hoping to get away without revealing one of his most closely guarded tricks.

No such luck.

"But all the workshops are closed this late in the evening," Zach said.

"Ah!" Ibery exclaimed. "He's right! They closed down two hours ago!"

"It won't be a problem," Zorian assured them. "So long as we clean up after ourselves, no one will know we were there."

"But the door is locked," pointed out Zach.

Zorian sighed. "Not to magic, it isn't."

"You know unlocking spells?" asked Zach in a surprised tone.

Zorian understood his surprise—unlocking spells were restricted magic due to their obvious abuse potential. Unless you possessed a special license, even knowing how to cast them was a crime. Not a particularly serious crime, but a crime nonetheless.

Perhaps it was good, then, that Zorian didn't know a single unlocking spell.

"No, I don't," said Zorian. "But it's just a simple mechanical lock. I can manipulate the tumblers telekinetically. Piece of cake."

They gave him a blank look. Like most people, they had no idea how locks actually worked and how easy it was to bypass most of them. Zorian, due to his somewhat colorful childhood, did. In fact, he could pick your average lock without using magic at all—it was just a lot slower than his telekinetic trick and required him to carry around a set of lockpicks.

He stopped in front of the door leading into the alchemical workshop and tried the handle. Like Zach said, it was locked. Shrugging, Zorian placed his palm over the keyhole and closed his eyes. He could feel Zach and Ibery cluster around him to get a better look and did his best to block them out. He needed total concentration for this.

He had developed this particular trick back in his second year after he got bored of refining the standard shaping exercises they had been given. It involved flooding the locking mechanism with his mana, using the resulting mana field as a sort of touch sight to get a feel for the lock, and then carefully moving the tumblers into proper position so he could neutralize the lock. It took him months of stubborn practice, but by now he was good enough at it to unlock most doors in thirty seconds or less.

Even warded ones. He didn't say this to Zach and Ibery, but the door he was trying to open was actually warded. Anything even remotely important in the academy was, including most of the doors. However, as Zorian had quickly discovered when he experimented with his newly-developed skill, low-level wards were very specific— they countered a handful of common unlocking spells and nothing else. Zorian's little trick was not a structured spell, and thus didn't trip these rudimentary wards at all.

The door clicked and Zorian tried the door handle again. It opened without resistance.

"Wow," said Zach as they all filed into the workshop. "You can open a lock just by pressing your hand against it for a few seconds!"

Zorian gave him a sour look. "It's a lot more complicated than that. That's just the visible part."

"Oh, I don't doubt that for a second," Zach said.

Still, while Zach seemed very impressed with Zorian's achievement, Ibery remained strangely quiet and kept giving him funny looks. This was why he hated telling people about his lock-picking prowess—most immediately assumed he was some kind of a thief. Well, that and he didn't want the academy authorities to find out about his achievement. They would no doubt change their warding scheme and then he wouldn't be able to do what he just did.

Fortunately, Ibery wasn't as quick to condemn as some people and got over her suspicions quickly once he started to prepare the salve. Strangely enough, Zach didn't know how to make one, even though it was fairly simple and Zach had demonstrated some mightily impressive alchemical work in class. He didn't appear all that interested in learning, either—apparently the anti-rash salve was too mundane for his tastes, and he was only interested in things like strength potions and wound closing elixirs. To Zorian, that sounded like trying to build a house without bothering to set up proper foundations, but it wasn't Zorian who was a decade-old time traveler. Yet.

"Aren't those purple creeper leaves?" Ibery asked, pointing at the small pile Zorian had placed on a wet piece of cloth.

"Yes," confirmed Zorian, wrapping the leaves into the cloth. "They're the main ingredient, though they have to be crushed first. Alchemical manuals usually claim you have to reduce the leaves into powder but it's not really necessary to go that far. You just have to use more leaves otherwise, but it's not like purple creepers are in short supply…"

An hour later, the salve was done and Zach was kind enough to conjure some kind of illusory mirror so Ibery could apply the salve on herself right then and there. Kind, but with an ulterior motive. While Ibery was busy applying the salve, Zach dragged Zorian away to the corner so they could talk in private.

"So?" Zorian prompted as Zach looked over his shoulder to ascertain Ibery was suitably occupied. "What is it?"

Facing Zorian once more, Zach reached into his pocket and pulled out a ring, which he promptly handed to Zorian. It was a featureless band of gold that reacted strangely when Zorian channeled some mana into it.

"It's a spell formula," Zach said.

"Magic missile?" guessed Zorian.

"Plus shield and flamethrower," Zach said. "Now you can use all three in actual combat."

Zorian looked at the ring with newfound respect. There was only so much one could cram into a spell formula, and it was mostly dependent on the size of the item used as a base. Turning something as small as a ring into a spell formula for three different spells, even if they were relatively low level, was a pretty impressive feat.

"Must have been pretty expensive," Zorian remarked.

"Made it myself, actually," Zach said with a grin.

"Still, that's a pretty valuable thing to give away to someone you barely know," said Zorian. "Why do I get the feeling I'll be needing this in the near future?"

Zach's smile disappeared and he became more subdued. "Maybe. I'm just making sure, you know. You never know when an angry troll might get a jump on you or something."

"How... oddly specific," Zorian said. "You know, you've been getting steadily more nervous as the summer festival approaches. And you seem oddly interested in making sure I attend the dance."

"You will, right?" Zach prompted.

"Yes, yes, I told you I will half a dozen times already," huffed Zorian. "What's so important about the dance, anyway? What's going to happen there, oh great traveler from the future?"

"You have to see it to believe it," Zach said. "It's possibly even more implausible than time travel being real."

"That bad?" asked Zorian, privately agreeing that an invasion of that scale was something he would have had trouble believing in if he had not lived through it.

"Just… try to survive, okay?" Zach sighed. Before Zorian could say anything else, Zach suddenly donned a mask of fake cheerfulness and spoke in a voice loud enough for Ibery to hear. "Wow, Zorian, I'm sure glad we've had this talk but I should really get going now! Have to be well rested for tomorrow! Bye, Zorian! Bye, Ibery! I'll see you both at the dance!"

And then he left. Zorian shook his head at the other boy's exit and walked up to Ibery, whose skin was now free of purple rash.

"Well, I guess we should go, too," Zorian said. "The academy normally doesn't have anyone patrolling after dark, but that idiot's shouting may have alerted someone to our presence."

"Oh. Um, right."

Zorian watched Ibery as they filed out of the workshop and he used his magic trick to re-lock the door. She seemed strangely subdued for someone who got what they wanted.

"What's wrong?" he finally asked after a while.

"Err, nothing's wrong," she said. "Why do you ask?"

"You don't seem very happy to be cured."

"I am!" she protested. "It's just…"

"Yes?"

"I don't have anyone to go to the dance with," she said. "I think the boy I was hoping to go with already has a date by now."

If her unnamed boy was Fortov, then yes, he most certainly did. In fact, he probably had found one weeks in advance, so there had never been much chance of her going with him in the first place, but he didn't feel the need to crush her dreams like that.

"Then you'll just have to do the same thing I will and go to the dance all by yourself, won't you," Zorian said.

She suddenly stopped and gave him an appraising glance.

"You don't have anyone to go with, either?" she asked.

Zorian closed his eyes and swore in his head. He'd really walked into that one, hadn't he?

Zorian was nervous. Ever since his very first restart, he had been assiduously avoiding the city on the day of the festival, not willing to get caught up in the invasion again. Being present within city limits could easily result in his grisly death, after all, and back then he hadn't been sure whether he would have another restart. That wasn't an option anymore, unless he wanted to clue in Zach that there was something wrong with him.

Bottom line was, he was stuck attending the dance, with the unexpected addition of Ibery as his date for the evening. He wasn't exactly happy with that. He didn't really have much of a plan for the evening, except to wait and see what would happen, but Ibery's presence at his side would no doubt limit him. Not to mention that he still remembered his disastrous evening with Akoja, and he had very little desire to live through a repeat performance, consequence-erasing time loop or not.

Speaking of his evening with Akoja, Zorian had to admit one thing about Ibery: she was a lot more reasonable and considerate than Akoja was. She didn't drag him out of his room two hours before the event, make him wait smack in the middle of the huge throng of people gathered at the entrance, or force him to chat with a bunch of people who only cared about his last name. She was also more interested in scanning the crowd for any trace of Fortov than paying attention to him, but that was okay—he was under no illusion that she had asked him out because she was actually interested in him. After a while, he decided to have mercy on her and informed her that Fortov was already inside, preparing for the performance along with the other members of the academy music club.

Naturally, Zach made his entrance in his usual flamboyant style. He caught everyone's attention when he arrived with not one, but *two* dates for the evening (Zorian didn't recognize either girl), and then further wooed people by demonstrating some impressive—and attention-grabbing—dancing. Apparently Zach had learned more than magic during these restarts. Zorian clapped with the others when Zach finally finished showing off and considered the merits of sinking some time into a non-magical skill. Not dancing, though. Or any other high society skill for that matter—honing those beyond the elementary level he had already grasped would require him to construct a mask so thorough he wasn't sure he'd be able to take it off afterwards. The benefits weren't worth selling his soul over, even metaphorically.

"This is a lot fancier than I thought it would be," Ibery noted, fingering the lacy tablecloth in front of her.

"It's obviously more than just a school dance," agreed Zorian. "I'm guessing the academy was organizing some kind of event for foreign dignitaries this year and then decided to simply merge it with the school dance."

"I guess," Ibery said. "They *did* invest a lot into making everything look good this year, and I doubt they did it for our sake." Ibery looked at the far end of the table, where Zach was entertaining a small crowd around him, his two escorts nowhere to be seen. After a few seconds of observation, she turned to Zorian and stared at him without speaking.

"What?" Zorian said, a little unnerved by her focus.

"I've been meaning to ask you…," she began hesitantly. "What is it between you and Zach? I mean, I know you're friends with him, but how did that come about? You seem very different from one another."

"It's a recent thing," said Zorian. "And it was mostly Zach's doing, to be honest. All I did was escort him home after he got sick in class one day, and he decided we were best friends after that. I sort of went along with the flow."

"So, you don't know about... um..."

"His sudden growth in skill?" guessed Zorian. He was actually surprised she hadn't questioned him about that sooner. Almost everyone else did. Of course, she would get the same shameless lie that he fed to everyone who questioned him about it. "I have no idea how that happened, but I can tell you it's real and not some kind of trick like many people have been suggesting. He has been tutoring me in combat magic for a while now, and he really knows his stuff."

"Yeah, I heard you were doing that," Ibery said, causing Zorian to frown. Being associated with Zach had made people disturbingly interested in his activities, no matter how mundane or irrelevant they might be. Having people scrutinize his every action was a novel experience. Novel and unwelcome. "Kyron has been kind of impressed with your growth, you know?"

Yeah... at least until he found out that Zach was involved, at which point it simply became one more thing that made Zach such a mystery, rather than a product of Zorian's own talent. Obviously Zach had some kind of secret teaching technique on top of everything else. Obviously.

But it's not like he was still bitter or anything!

"Impressed, right," said Zorian, a grimace twisting his features. "So, what do *you* think is behind Zach's amazingness?"

"Err, well... it's kind of silly," Ibery said.

Zorian gestured for her to go on. He always loved to hear the explanations people thought up to explain Zach. Much of the speculation wasn't serious so much as attempts to think up the most imaginative or humorous explanation, so he doubted Ibery's would be any sillier than some of the stuff he had been hearing all month long. His personal favorite was that Zach had performed an ancient ritual where you eat another person's brain in order to get their knowledge.

"Time dilation," Ibery said after a brief moment of hesitation.

Zorian blinked. Oh Ibery… So close, and yet so far away…

"I don't think any hasting spell is *that* effective, to be honest," said Zorian. "Zach isn't just a little better than he was. I'd personally put him around third circle, *at least*. I actually don't think he has any reason to attend the classes anymore, except that he finds it amusing to do so and flaunt his knowledge to everybody."

"I kind of noticed that," Ibery said, glancing momentarily to the small group of people surrounding Zach. "But I wasn't thinking of hasting magic. Do you know what the Black Rooms are?" Zorian shook his head. "There are rumors that powerful nations like ours have special training facilities that use extreme levels of time dilation. You go inside the facility, spend a couple of months or even *years* inside, and when you get out, only a day or two has passed outside."

Zorian's eyebrows rose at the description. If one of the major powers had something like that, why weren't the effects more keenly felt? None of the Successor States were shy about using their power. Surely such a tool would have been used to churn out trained mages on a mass scale by now.

"It's just a rumor," Ibery added. "Something between a conspiracy theory and an urban legend. I only know about it because one of my friends loves those kinds of things and she keeps insisting there is one such facility in the tunnels beneath the city. Supposedly they consume massive amounts of mana, so they must be located at mana wells."

"And the Hole is the biggest mana well there is," Zorian noted. "What's the explanation for such secrecy surrounding them? You'd think they'd be using it pretty intensively."

"They can't," Ibery said. "Or at least that's how the story goes. They have some kind of severe limitations on their use. Exactly how countries choose who gets to use the Black Rooms is where the conspiracy theory part comes in. The more conventional theories suggest they're simply top level facilities for training black ops super agents. The wilder ones are… well, wild."

Zorian thought for a moment. "It's a neat theory," he said. Far closer to reality than anything else he'd heard, though he'd never say that aloud, even as a joke. If she could take such a farfetched rumor seriously, there was a good chance she might actually believe him upon hearing the truth, and that would be very awkward at the moment. Maybe he should try to convince her in one of the next restarts? Something to think about, at least. "But if Zach spent years in one of those Black Rooms, why hasn't he visibly aged? And why exactly would they let Zach use one of them?"

"Well, it wouldn't have to be years," Ibery said. "It's not like anything he's done is *that* advanced. A couple months of intense tutoring could probably produce the effects we're looking at. And even if he spent years, there are potions that can halt your aging for a year or two. They actually work better on young people."

Zorian resisted the urge to frown as he realized something. As much as Zach liked to show off, he never really went wild with his abilities for all to see. If Zach were to demonstrate the sort of magic Zorian had seen during the invasion, neither Ibery nor anyone else would be dismissing Zach's prowess so easily. Then again, perhaps that was the whole point. Extremely skilled Zach was surprising, maybe even shocking to those who knew him before the change. Instant archmage Zach would probably be alarming in the extreme and inspire a matching attitude in people around him.

Perhaps Zach's behavior was a lot more calculated than Zorian had thought.

"As for why him?" Ibery continued. "Well, he's a Noveda. They were quite influential before their fall, and I don't just mean in the sense of being rich. They had their fingers everywhere. I could easily see some of that old influence surviving to this very day. Zach is the last of his line, and the fate of his House rests upon his shoulders. Perhaps this was simply a desperate maneuver by Zach's guardians to try to turn Zach into a worthy successor capable of returning the Noveda to their former glory."

With that thought lingering between them, the ground suddenly shook beneath them. Zorian had only a moment to catch sight of the alarm rising in Ibery's face when a deafening explosion shook the hall. Windows rattled, but didn't break. An uneasy silence descended upon the dance hall, broken only by the periodic rumble of more distant explosions.

"What... what was that?" Ibery asked, a tremble of fear in her voice.

She wasn't the only one asking that question. Agitated murmurs started traveling through the gathered crowd, steadily growing in volume and alarm. The ever-present pressure Zorian always felt while within a crowd intensified and... changed. What was usually just an annoyance pushing on the edges of his consciousness, suddenly became a suffocating blanket of fear. He struggled to remain conscious, his vision tunneling, as foreign feelings invaded his mind. What the hell was happening to him? He didn't remember anything about an attack like this from his previous experience of the invasion.

A minute ticked away. Then two. Zorian could practically feel the anxiety and agitation of the crowd steadily rising. The last (and first) time he had lived through the invasion he had been standing on the roof when that first barrage descended to earth and had been momentarily incapacitated as a result. At least, that's what he had thought. Perhaps he had been knocked out for quite a bit longer than he realized, because by his reckoning Ilsa and Kyron should have already rushed to the roof. He could see them arguing about something in a nearby corner, and neither made the slightest move towards the roof.

"Zorian?" Ibery's voice cut through his thoughts and Zorian had the impression she had been trying to get his attention for some time. "Are you sure you're all right? Maybe I should go find someone—"

"I'm fine," Zorian said, somehow managing to shove the oppressive feelings aside for the moment. The explosions had finally stopped, but that hadn't led to people calming down. If anything, now that immediate danger seemed past, they wanted answers, and they wanted them now. They were getting restless. Thankfully, the academy staff seemed to realize this as well. "Look, Ilsa is trying to say something."

"Please remain calm!" Ilsa said from the music stage, using the same magic that carried music evenly across the dance hall to make herself heard by everyone present. "My colleagues and I will go to the roof and open communications with the city authorities to find out what is going on. Please don't go anywhere until we return."

Well… that didn't do much to calm the crowd. If anything, they became even more unruly than they had been before Ilsa's speech, and some outright ignored her plea and rushed from the dance hall the moment she went up the stairs and out of sight. He couldn't judge them too harshly, since in another timeline he had done the exact same thing. On the positive side, the oppressive feeling lifted and reverted back to the familiar headache-inducing pressure. He breathed a giant sigh of relief.

"Hello, Zorian," greeted Zach, approaching the table. Of course he'd come to talk to him *now*… "Quite a commotion, huh? And I see you talked Miss Ambercomb into being your date for the evening! Congratulations! I never knew you liked older girls."

"I'm only a year older than him," Ibery protested. She glanced briefly at Zorian to see if he would point out that she had been the one to ask him and relaxed when she realized he wouldn't. Zorian had to restrain himself from rolling his eyes. "And how come you're over here all by yourself? Why don't you introduce us to your dates?"

If Ibery thought to fluster Zach by pointing out the plural nature of his partners for the evening, she was going to be sorely disappointed. And indeed, Zach only smiled at her, completely unaffected by the jab.

"They decided to leave early," Zach said, shrugging. "Probably for the best, considering what happened."

"What *did* happen, though?" asked Zorian. He didn't expect to get a straight answer out of Zach, of course, but it was worth a try.

"I guess we'll find out soon," said Zach, pointing to the bottom of the stairs leading to the roof. Ilsa was there talking to a group of students. After a couple seconds, Zorian realized that Akoja was among them and recognized several other faces as well.

"Who is she talking to?" asked Ibery.

"Class representatives, I think," Zorian said. "At least, the ones I recognize are all class representatives for their groups."

It was all so frustratingly slow. Maybe Zorian was expecting a little too much from a mere educational institution, but their response to the invasion was pretty underwhelming. At the very least, he had expected them to start evacuating people to the shelters by now, or organize some kind of defense force or... well, anything, really. He was getting the impression that Ilsa and Kyron didn't yet understand the severity of the situation.

Finally, Ilsa seemed to finish with her instructions and the crowd of class representatives dispersed, each beginning to gather their classmates into a group. Zorian bid Ibery goodbye and he and Zach moved to join their classmates.

Once everyone was present, Akoja told them the academy was going to use their limited teleportation capabilities to get foreign dignitaries and other important people out of the city, and that the students were to descend into the tunnels beneath the city to reach the shelters on foot. No teachers would be present to guide and defend them, being needed elsewhere, but the class representatives knew the way. Students had to know the evacuation routes in order to even get the position of class representative.

Zorian looked at Zach to gauge his reaction and saw that the boy's expression was grim and focused.

"All right," Zach mumbled. "Show time."

Zorian had a bad feeling about this.

Surprisingly, it wasn't Zach who raised the alarm. It was Raynie, of all people. How exactly she detected the winter wolves a few moments before they arrived, Zorian had no idea, but notice them she did, and she immediately raised the alarm. A lot of students didn't believe her, but most weren't willing to risk it. The entire procession of students started to move faster towards the small cylindrical building that marked the staircase leading down into the shelters.

They didn't make it before the wolves came.

Zorian wasn't a soldier and would never call himself an expert on tactics, but what the throng of students did upon sighting the horde of winter wolves charging toward them still struck him as monumentally stupid. They scattered. Those closest to the Dungeon entrance rushed towards it, but others immediately sought the closest shelter. He could hear Zach's frantic shouting, telling people not to separate from the main group, but his efforts were in vain.

Cursing, Zorian snatched Akoja by the wrist before she could bolt towards the nearby apartment building and wordlessly pointed towards the Dungeon entrance. For a moment he thought about explaining his reasoning in more detail, but he knew he didn't have enough time for that. He let go of her and started running, hoping she would have the presence of mind to follow him.

Thankfully, she seemed to, and as he let go of her hand and turned to run, several other students rushed to join them, seeking safety in numbers.

Around him, chaos reigned. The winter wolves were pouring in by the hundreds, and unlike the fleeing students, they were frighteningly well coordinated. Small groups of three to four wolves detached themselves periodically from the main body to intercept lone targets before rejoining the horde, using their superior numbers to flank and outmaneuver their opponents. Their white fur and the uncanny silence with which they moved made them seem like an army of ghosts risen from the underworld to punish the living. Screams. Shouting. Flashes of light and canine howls of pain, too—not every student was helpless. Up ahead, Zach was defending the entrance to the tunnels viciously, sending swarm after swarm of force projectiles that hit far harder than the average magic missile, felling scores of winter wolves with each volley. A number of people reached the safety of a nearby building and promptly barricaded themselves inside, ignoring the pleas of those outside to let them in.

Just as Zorian thought they would make it to the entrance without incident, his luck ran out. A large group of thirty or so winter wolves noticed them and moved to cut them off. Zorian and the other students halted, drawn together in a nervous cluster, unsure what to do as the pack continued to get closer, their path to the shelters cut off. Fighting the wolves was suicide. Zach was busy incinerating a group of war trolls that had finally made their appearance and wouldn't be able to help for a while.

"I told you I should have brought my sword," one of the boys groused. "But noooo, it's not suitable for a school dance, you said. You're too paranoid for your own good, you said."

"Oh, shut up," a female voice snapped back.

Zorian resisted the urge to fire off a couple of missiles at the approaching winter wolves. Even shaped as piercers, they weren't guaranteed to kill in one shot something as resilient as a winter wolf, and he still tended to fail quite often when he tried to weave a homing function in them. With no guarantee he would even hit anything, he had to use his mana intelligently.

Not everyone thought so, however. A number of people, it seemed, had a spell formula hidden on them in the form of a ring or a necklace, much like he did, and they launched missile after magic missile into the advancing wolves. Only one girl was capable of casting a proper homing bolt, so most of them missed. When they did hit, the simple smashers couldn't do lethal damage. They did, however, slow the pack down and force it to cluster together, since the girl that could fire homing bolts targeted any wolf that tried to detach from the pack to flank them. And that gave Zorian an idea.

The moment the pack got close enough, Zorian fired an overpowered flamethrower straight into their front line. Grouped together as they were, most of them were caught in the blast. The winter wolves, notoriously weak to fire, howled in fear and agony. This first blast was quickly followed by another, this one much larger and hotter than Zorian's, and the winter wolves promptly turned and fled. The ones that still lived, that is.

Zorian turned to see who had cast the second flamethrower and was surprised to see Briam there, staring smugly at the charred corpses in front of him. He was holding his fire drake in his arms like a living weapon, and the little lizard was licking its chops like it wanted to eat its kills.

So much for Zorian's theory that the drake was too young to breathe fire.

After a moment of shock at the sudden reversal, the students all scrambled into the building housing the Dungeon entrance and descended into the tunnels below. Zorian was immediately intercepted by a worried Ibery, who seemed extremely relieved to find him alive. Even though he knew her death wouldn't be permanent, he had to admit he was glad she survived as well.

Though, now that he could sit down and think about it a little, it wasn't that unexpected that she had survived. She was a fourth-year, and they had been at the front of the procession, which was very unfortunate, because fourth year students were, presumably, much more capable of defending themselves than third-years… and they were the ones who reached the safety of the shelters first, leaving their younger compatriots to fend for themselves.

"I didn't know you had any fire spells," Briam said from over Zorian's shoulder. Zorian turned to see the other boy stroking his familiar affectionately. "I guess that's one of the things Zach has been teaching you this past month, huh?"

"Yeah," Zorian admitted. He gave the fire lizard a dubious look, and the reptile stared back at him challengingly. "Did you really bring your familiar to the school dance?"

"Oh, no way," Briam said, laughing. "I'm not *that* attached to him. No, I used a recall spell to summon him to my side when the winter wolves started pouring in."

"Isn't summoning pretty mana intensive, though?" Zorian asked.

"Not if you're summoning your familiar," Briam said. "We're bound together, he and I. Connected through the soul. It's a lot easier and a lot less taxing to cast certain spells where they concern him."

An hour went by, with little to show for it. Hunkered down in the dim tunnel, Zorian listened to stories of people around him, trying to put some sense into what had transpired and thinking what he could change in the next restart to make this evacuation thing less of a fiasco. His thoughts were interrupted when a group of teachers finally stumbled into the shelters.

There were six of them and they looked tired and frightened, much like the students who gathered around them in search of explanations and assurances. The only one among them that inspired confidence in Zorian was Kyron, who remained as stoic as always. He was no longer bare-chested, opting to wear full body armor that resembled the chitinous shell of a saint bug, and a plethora of spell rods hung off his belt in addition to the combat staff he was firmly gripping in one hand.

Kyron had bad news—the attack on the academy was just one piece in an all-out invasion targeting the entire city. Zorian already knew this, of course, but everyone else was suitably shocked. The invasion was well prepared, and most of the defenders had been overpowered right at the start. The city was about to fall. Once that happened, the shelters would become a giant death trap. They would have to go outside and fight their way out of the city before the invaders could secure everything of critical importance and turn their attention to them.

This news did not go over well.

"Why don't you just teleport us out!?" someone called out as frantic voices began to fill the tunnel. "You're supposed to be able to do that!"

"Academy ward control has been subverted," Kyron said, his voice a bastion of calm. "The invaders have turned our own teleportation wards against us. We can't teleport in or out."

Zorian groaned. The enemy had control of the wards? How on earth had they managed *that*? The academy wasn't just some random house with a generic warding scheme—it should have been too secure and sophisticated for that!

The questions continued for a moment, but Kyron soon put an end to the disarray and started to bark out orders. They needed to get moving.

Zorian, however, was paying attention to something else. The student next to him, a stranger to Zorian, had been acting strangely ever since Kyron and his cohort entered the shelters, casting furtive glances here and there, his gaze darting around the tunnel. Zorian could practically feel the boy's eagerness and anticipation. For what, he couldn't say, but he had a feeling it was nothing good.

Zorian saw the boy reach into a pocket and withdraw a vial, concealing it in his palm. Then, his mouth curving in a wicked grin, he threw the vial to the floor and stomped on it with his foot, releasing a sickly green liquid. On instinct, Zorian sucked in a deep breath and fired a smasher missile into the boy, knocking him backward—but it was too late. Foul green smoke erupted from the broken vial, and the shelters erupted into chaos.

Thick smoke circled around Zorian, obscuring his vision, but the sounds of combat were unmistakable. He stumbled away from the source of the smoke, brushing past students wracked with terrible coughing. Though his lungs burned already, Zorian fought to hold his breath, glad at least that the smoke wasn't irritating his eyes. Through the green haze, he glimpsed a magic missile streaking toward his head—and threw up a shield just in time, the circular plane of force flickering into existence and soaking in the hit. As Zorian tried to orient himself, the shield wavered for a moment but held.

And then Zorian heard Kyron's voice boomed out a chant, and all the smoke around him rushed towards the teacher, as if caught in an invisible snare. As the air cleared around him, Zorian had just enough time to see Kyron holding his left hand in the air, a smoky green ball compacting itself above it, before another missile forced Zorian to return his attention to his shield.

He gasped in clean, cool air as the shield shivered in front of him, his chest aching with relief.

Before the attackers—who had likely teleported in under the cover of the smoke, because Zorian would remember a bunch of middle-aged men in brown robes if they had been present when he got into the shelters—could regain the initiative, Kyron snapped one of his hands and a shining whip flashed through the air. The invaders promptly fell apart, the upper halves of their bodies sliding off the lower halves like they had never been attached to one another at all.

Zorian stared at Kyron in shock. He knew the retired battlemage was capable, but seeing it was something else. The man had assessed the situation within moments and solved it with a total of two spells. He wondered what would have happened during the initial evacuation if Kyron had been leading the students. He couldn't help but think that Kyron would have found a way to repel the initial winter wolf rush without losing anyone. Certainly the students would be more inclined to listen to Kyron than their class representatives—the man had a certain aura of command about him.

"How… the hell… are you… still standing?" wheezed Zach from his knees nearby. Apparently he had breathed in some of the smoke and was affected just like everyone else. Even experienced time travelers could be brought down by some tricks, it seemed.

Zorian was about to answer when the ground exploded next to him, showering him with stone fragments and knocking him on his back. He heard screams, heard Kyron chanting something, but it was too late for him—the giant brown worm that emerged from the ground was far faster than it should have been and Zorian was in too much pain to move. He saw a huge toothy maw closing around him—and then he knew only blackness.

His last thoughts were that it wasn't fair. Just how many contingencies did these people have? These invaders were freaking cheaters!

CHAPTER 010

Overlooked
Details

Zorian's eyes abruptly shot open as sharp
pain erupted from his stomach. His whole
body convulsed, buckling against the object that fell on him, and suddenly he was wide
awake, not a trace of drowsiness in his mind.

"Good m—"

"No, it's not," Zorian interrupted. "How could
it possibly be a good morning? I got killed again!
Eaten by a giant worm this time. And waking
up like this is really starting to get on my nerves!
Couldn't the time loop have started a day later or
something?"

He stared at his little sister expectantly. She

stared back at him, confused out of her mind and probably a little frightened.

"Um, what?" she asked hesitantly.

Zorian wordlessly flipped her over the edge of the bed. She fell to the floor with a thud and an indignant yelp, and Zorian quickly jumped to his feet to better respond to any retaliation. Having learned his lesson during previous restarts, he then set out towards the bathroom before she could get her bearings.

She realized what he was doing, but by then he had already locked the door behind him. Her screams of outrage were music to his ears, especially since they eventually caused Mother to come after her and give her a scolding.

Maybe it *was* a good morning, after all.

Trains… Zorian hadn't really liked them to start with, but he was starting to develop an intense dislike for this particular mode of transport ever since he had been caught in this time loop thing. Travelling via train on a regular basis was almost as annoying as Kirielle jumping on him at the start of every restart. He had toyed with the idea of killing time by striking up a conversation with Ibery, so she'd be familiar with him when he got a job at the library, but scrapped the notion after a while. Mostly because he had decided not to apply for the job in this restart. Working at the library was fairly time consuming, and he had a much more promising project to work on—mastering all the shaping exercises in Ilsa's book so he could woo her into taking him as her apprentice. Library magic was useful, but getting rid of Xvim would be absolutely priceless.

He wouldn't be present in Cyoria when the invasion came either. Not in this restart, nor in any near future one. Even if he had to reveal his secret to Zach because of it, he'd take the first train out of town on the eve of the summer festival. He knew that the smart, responsible thing to do would be to stay in the city and note what was happening—how the invasion was progressing and what could be done to stop it. He knew this, but... it was too much for him. And not just because getting himself involved seemed to invariably lead to his death, either. The emotional rollercoaster of the 'evacuation' was hard on his nerves, but that was just a symptom of the real problem. He struggled with his thoughts for a moment as the landscape streaked by out his window, trying to identify the root of the problem. Every reason he could think of felt... not right.

And then it clicked. It was the helplessness. Every time his thoughts strayed towards the invasion, he couldn't shake the notion that the forces arrayed against him were vastly beyond his ability to handle, and that the only reason he survived as long as he did was through sheer dumb luck. It occurred to him that the manner of his most recent death could easily be an allegory for the entire event. So you repelled a murderous pack of winter wolves and reached safety, helped foil a traitorous ambush, and now you think the worst is over? No, stupid, a giant worm suddenly jumps out of the ground and bites your head off! How were you supposed to fight something like that? How was *he* supposed to fight something like that?

Maybe he shouldn't. A lot of things about the invasion seemed... implausible. About as implausible as Zach becoming a super-prodigy over the span of a single summer, Zorian learning all fifteen shaping exercises in Ilsa's book within the span of a month, or time travel being real. What if his theory of there being a third time traveler was correct and this person was the mastermind behind the invasion? It would explain a lot. Then again, it would also pose a lot of questions on its own... like why hadn't this hostile time traveler dealt with Zach already? The lich had already proved it was very much possible to hurt people like Zach and Zorian.

Regardless, he intended to involve himself again with the invasion only after he acquired some *serious* magic, or after he calmed down and felt emotionally capable of facing the situation. Whichever came first. It's not like he could study the invasion in any great detail if he kept dying at the very start of it, anyway.

Eventually the train arrived in Cyoria, and Zorian began his long trek towards the academy. He wasn't in a hurry this time, because he had finally found a spell to protect himself from rain in the last restart and was eager to try it. Well, he had actually found *several* protective spells meant to deal with rain and other adverse weather, but only one was within his ability to actually cast. That was okay, though, since the rain barrier spell was the one best suited for his purposes anyway—it offered the most complete protection, at the cost of being horribly draining to maintain. He could see why the mana drain would be a serious problem for people who wanted to use the spell extensively, but Zorian only needed it to last for an hour or two in an exceptionally mana-rich area of Cyoria.

Also, being encased in an invisible sphere that repelled water was just plain more impressive than the more subtle, sophisticated wards. The barrier actually worked on water in general, not just rain drops, so he didn't even have to worry about stepping into puddles and soaking his footwear. Seeing water on the road part before him as though he were some kind of celestial emissary was mightily amusing. And a bit of an ego boost, which was something he sorely needed after being so thoroughly outmatched by a toothy worm.

He'd probably never use the spell after getting out of the time loop, since an umbrella was good enough for most occasions and didn't consume any mana, but finding a store that sold them along his usual route from the train station had proved surprisingly difficult. Which, now that he thought about it, suggested that he probably *would* use the spell from time to time, since he doubted this would be the only time in his life he'd find himself without an easily acquired umbrella.

He shook his head. He really shouldn't be fantasizing about what he'd do after getting out of the time loop, since it didn't appear that would happen any time soon. He had to concentrate on the present... and boy did that sound weird, considering his situation. What was he going to do with Zach? He was sorely tempted to just admit everything to the boy so they could work together to figure out this mess. Impulsive though he was, Zach couldn't have gotten as far as he did without having a good head on his shoulders. Zorian didn't feel entirely comfortable with that idea, though. He strongly suspected there was more to Zach than it appeared, and he hated to charge in without knowing what he was getting himself into.

He decided to see how Zach interacted with him in this restart before making his choice.

"Zorian! Over here!"

Zorian glanced towards the happy-looking Benisek waving at him like a lunatic and wondered what he should do. He didn't really want to talk to him. Benisek might be his closest friend among the student body, but he was also rather irritating at times, and the restarts had begun to exacerbate that. In the end, he sighed in defeat and trudged over to the grinning boy. Time loop or no, it felt wrong to blatantly snub someone so visibly happy to see him, especially since he shared so much history with Benisek.

He did find it interesting that Benisek was present in the cafeteria at that moment, since that wasn't his usual behavior in the restarts. Unexplained divergences like this happened all the time, which was to be expected—there were at least two time travelers wandering around the time loop, changing things both inconsequential and crucial—but it was surprising to see a change this early in the time loop. Zorian had only arrived in Cyoria the day before. Usually it took at least a week until everything went off the rails, and even then a lot of things repeated themselves. Most teachers followed some kind of a fixed teaching plan, for example, and rarely deviated from it. As far as he knew, Fortov always came looking for him for help with the purple creeper salve, even though his incident with Ibery only happened near the very end of the time loop. Which, now that he thought about it, suggested the accident wasn't so accidental after all. It seemed suspicious for an accident to be so insensitive to changes...

"You just got to Cyoria, didn't you?" Benisek prompted excitedly the moment Zorian sat down beside him.

Zorian hesitated, then nodded. Benisek was only ever this excited when talking about a particularly hot girl or when he got a hold of juicy gossip material. Hopefully it was the latter, because there was no way Zorian would be staying otherwise.

"You're so not going to believe this!" Benisek said excitedly. "You know Zach? You know, Zach Noveda, last scion of the Noble House Noveda? He went to class with us these last two years."

Of course it was about Zach. He really should have known.

"Of course I know him," Zorian said. "He is... very memorable."

"He is?" blinked Benisek. He shook his head. "I mean, of course he is. I didn't expect you to know, though, since he's kind of a failure as a mage and you never interacted with him much."

Zorian shrugged. Truth be told, it was very rare for him to forget someone's name, regardless of the level of interaction or time lapsed. Even before the time loop, Zorian would have instantly known who Benisek was referring to.

"Anyway," Benisek continued, "Zach escaped from his family mansion yesterday."

"Err, what?" Zorian asked, incredulous. "What do you mean escaped? Why would he need to escape from his own mansion?"

"Well, that's the question, isn't it?" Benisek said. "Apparently he had an argument with his guardian that eventually descended into a full-blown magical duel. A duel which, get this, Zach *won*! Half of the mansion was trashed, and Zach fled into the city and has yet to be found. They're searching for him everywhere!"

"Um, wow," Zorian said, honestly at a loss for words. What the hell was *that* about?

"You said it," Benisek agreed. "I'm not sure I believe the official story, though. I mean, there's no way Zach could have taken on his guardian in a magical duel! Tesen Zveri is a seventh circle mage or something, and Zach barely passed his own certification! Then again, *something* sure demolished the Noveda mansion…"

"How do you know this?" asked Zorian.

"It's all over the newspapers," said Benisek. "Besides, everyone is talking about it. I can't believe one of our classmates would be involved in something like that. What do you think, Zorian?"

"Ben… I honestly don't know what to think about that," said Zorian.

And he really meant it. He didn't doubt for a second that Zach could beat the stuffing out of his guardian, seventh circle or not—the man was a politician, as far as Zorian knew, not a battlemage—but why would he want to do that?

"I suppose he won't be coming to class this time, then," mused Zorian out loud. Then again, he would not have put it past Zach to just walk into class as if nothing out of the ordinary had happened.

"I doubt it," Benisek said, laughing.

"Did he kill anyone?" asked Zorian. Benisek shook his head. "So basically he didn't do anything *that* serious. What's the worst that can happen to him if he simply turns himself in?"

"Well, Tesen must not be too happy with him now, and he's too influential to brush off, even for someone like Zach," said Benisek.

"Attacking one of the Elders of Eldemar is actually a fairly serious crime, and Tesen could really ruin Zach's day if he was inclined to pursue satisfaction. Not that I think he would, since that would just draw even more attention to what happened. This whole thing is a giant political scandal for him. I'm guessing Zach will come back after a month or so, after he cools off a bit, and Tesen will 'magnanimously' forgive him everything."

Zorian was silent. Zach had told him that it was rare for him to spend a restart in Cyoria, and even rarer for him to attend classes. In light of that, it had been foolish of him to expect Zach to be around in this restart. Zach may have found Zorian interesting in the previous restart, but probably not *that* interesting. Still, this was more than a little strange. If he had wanted to leave and do his own thing, couldn't he have just walked out of his mansion one day and kept going? Who would have stopped him? His guardian? Why would Tesen do that? The man was clearly very hands-off in his dealings with his charge, as evidenced by Zach's frequent absences from school during the last two years, as well as his abysmal performance prior to the time loop.

There was no obvious answer, and Zorian didn't feel like trying to track down Zach. He probably couldn't find him even if he tried, and he had more attainable goals to pursue.

Like getting out of Xvim's merciless clutches. What could be more important than that?

The rest of the restart was pleasantly uneventful. There was no Zach to deal with, since the boy never showed up in school and couldn't be found by anyone. After a week or so, the newspapers stopped covering the story because there were no new developments to justify the articles, and the rumors making rounds across the student body died down soon after. For his part, Zorian threw himself completely into mastering the exercises in Ilsa's book. He neglected virtually everything else, often skipping classes when he thought he could get away with it. Akoja was furious, since he was apparently ruining the attendance record of the class, and got Ilsa to corner him one day about it. Fortunately, Zorian's ability to get top grades on every exam, despite his spotty attendance, blunted the impact of Akoja's criticism, and Zorian managed to convince Ilsa he was working on a personal project that was taking most of his time… *not* skipping classes for the heck of it as Akoja claimed. He assured her the project would be finished within a month, and that he would resume attending classes regularly after the summer festival. She made him promise that he would show her what he was working on when he was done, and he enthusiastically agreed with her.

His single-minded focus produced results quickly—he mastered both vertical and fixed position levitation by the end of the restart. He didn't bother showing these advanced skills to Xvim, who was still having him work on the pen-spinning exercise, since he doubted he'd get a worthwhile reaction. Nothing seemed to please that guy.

He didn't stay in the city when the invasion came, of course. Without Zach's ring, he was even more useless in combat than he had been in the last restart, so it was doubtful he could have survived for long in the midst of it all. He did make sure to practice the combat invocations he learned from Zach each day, hoping to hone them into the same reflexive state that Zach displayed. That would take years of practice, of course, but that just meant he'd better start as soon as possible. He also didn't just leave via train like he usually did—he traveled by foot to one of the hills overlooking Cyoria and observed the city from there.

Watching the invasion unfold from such a high vantage point was not only a lot easier on Zorian's nerves than being in the thick of it, it also proved to be rather informative. It was interesting to see how the invasion played out in broad terms. It seemed to have several stages, the first of which was, of course, the disguised artillery magic barrage. The explosive flares mostly targeted three crucial areas—the city hall, the local military base, and one cluster of buildings that Zorian didn't recognize. The academy didn't appear to be a primary target, possibly because the invaders wanted it reasonably intact. Aside from the initial blast, the impact zones seemed to spawn scores of fire elementals that had to be dealt with. Fortunately, a lot of buildings in Cyoria were at least moderately warded against fire, because Zorian didn't doubt for a second that the entire city would've been aflame within minutes otherwise. Once the fire elementals had a few minutes to make a nuisance of themselves, monsters poured out of the sewers. The spellcasters only arrived after the initial rampage.

The battle was still raging when Zorian's watch finally hit two past midnight and everything went black.

All things considered, the army of monsters was the least destructive part of the invasion—if he could somehow prevent the initial barrage from crippling the city defense right from the start, or take out a lot of the attacking mages that followed in the monsters' wake… well, it was worth a shot when he finally had some skills under his belt.

The next three restarts were essentially the same, right down to Zach dueling his guardian and escaping into the night. Apparently that *wasn't* just a one-time thing, but a rather routine occurrence. The exact details varied, but every time he roughed Tesen up before setting off gods knew where. Unfortunately, Zorian couldn't find out anything substantial about Tesen—the man was a high-ranking politician, and thus not exactly approachable, and nothing in publicly available sources offered an explanation for Zach's apparent hostility towards the man.

His work with Ilsa's book progressed steadily, but he was, frankly, getting a bit sick of it. There was only so much incessant shaping practice he could stand before he lost all enthusiasm. Besides, Ilsa said most students progressed at a rate of six per year, and he was already more effective than that—something that he attributed to his unusual focus in the matter. How many people could afford to focus all their energies on shaping exercises? There were so many things vying for the typical student's attention that shaping exercises no doubt ended up near the bottom of their priorities.

His progress—and his boredom—drove him to visit Ilsa again in the hopes that he could get something out of her even if he hadn't quite mastered the entire book.

"What can I do for you, Mister Kazinski?" Ilsa asked.

"Well, I'm a bit concerned about the program you outlined in your first class," said Zorian. "I'm not sure I'll get anything out of it. I already have a solid grasp on all the topics you mentioned."

Ilsa raised an eyebrow at him. Hey, it worked on Kyron, why wouldn't it work on Ilsa too?

"I see," she said at last. "Would you mind if I gave you a couple of quick tests to confirm that?"

Confident he could deal with anything she tested him on, he agreed. Ilsa proceeded to rummage through her drawers and took out two different tests. One was an exact copy of the same test she would give to the whole class just before the summer festival, and Zorian proceeded to fill it out in ten minutes flat by sheer memory. The other was unfairly difficult, covering advanced topics that didn't come up in class at all. Zorian only managed to fill out a quarter of the questions before time was up, and he was fairly sure not all of his answers were correct.

Ilsa skimmed through them quickly and then nodded to herself.

"Your theoretical knowledge is pretty spotty," Ilsa said with a theatrical sigh, and Zorian had to stop himself from scowling. That was such bullshit! She gave him that second test just to make sure he failed! "Here… I'll give you a list of additional reading to study in your free time."

Two minutes later Zorian found himself practically pushed out the door, a piece of paper with hastily scribbled writing in his hand. He glared at the list of book titles, very much tempted to incinerate it on the spot. He was supposed to start on the variations of the flame producing exercise, anyway. But he didn't. He would not be defeated that easily! If he could survive Xvim's mentoring methods this long, he could definitely read a couple of theoretical manuals. He would be back. She could be sure of that.

"Good morning, brother! Morning, morning, *MORNING*!!!"

"Good morning, Kiri," said Zorian pleasantly. "Thank you for waking me up."

Kirielle stared at him for a couple of seconds and then huffed in disappointment at his lack of reaction and got off of him all on her own. Well damn—he should have tried that ages ago.

"You're no fun," she accused.

Zorian simply nodded in agreement.

"Mom wants to talk to you," Kirielle said. "Could you show me some magic before you go, though? Pleeeeease?"

Well… why not? He quickly cast the floating lantern spell, causing an orb of light to spring into existence above his palm. He had the orb fly around the room while he repeated the spell two more times, producing a different colored orb each time.

The new books Ilsa had told him to read were mostly yawn-inducing, but they did tell him something rather interesting. All those variations he had been practicing had more uses than just improving his shaping skills—they also allowed him to adjust certain spells more to his liking. The same variation of the light emitting exercise that allowed him to produce colored light also enabled him to change the color of the glowing orb produced by the floating lantern spell. Mastering a large number of light-related exercises would apparently also make light-based invocations more powerful and less mana intensive, and the same principle applied to other groups of spells as well... such as fire-related exercises improving invocations based around fire and heat, and levitation-based ones improving spells relying on telekinetic forces. He was a lot less annoyed at having to go through all the shaping exercises when he discovered *that*. Hell, if they were that useful, he'd probably see if he could find more of them when he ran out of the ones in Ilsa's book.

"More! More!" Kiri demanded.

Distracting Kiri with a few more orbs, Zorian quietly slipped out of the room and went to the bathroom before Kiri could realize what was happening. Why was she always so intent on getting there first anyway? That was horribly petty, even for Kirielle. He'd have to ask her in one of the restarts.

Unfortunately, he had forgotten about the multi-colored orbs of light by the time Ilsa came around to visit, so he thought nothing about inviting her into his room. He hastily swept his hand in front of him, causing them all to wink out of existence, but it was too late—Ilsa had already seen them and was looking at him curiously.

"That's not really a second year spell," Ilsa remarked, her eyes boring into his own.

"Daimen can be a pretty good teacher when he wants to be," said Zorian with a cheeky smile, shamelessly relying on Daimen's fame to deflect any concerns. Teaching first circle spells like that one to uncertified mages was illegal, but if Zorian had ever learned something in his life, it was that Daimen could get away with anything.

"And you know how to produce something other than white light," Ilsa noted. "Impressive. I guess this should be easy for you, then."

She handed him a very familiar scroll, and Zorian was just about to flood it with mana to break the seal when he realized something was wrong. Ilsa was studying him like a hawk, expectant and alert. She had never shown this much interest in his scroll-opening before, so what made this one special? He stared at the scroll for a couple of seconds, unable to see any difference between it and the one he had seen so many times before. Even the symbols on the seal were the same. Wait...

A moment later, he remembered where he had seen the symbols inscribed on the seal and promptly felt like banging his head against the wall. How... why... those sneaky little...

He had been doing it wrong! All this time he had been simply pouring mana into the seal to break it, when instead he had to channel mana into it in very specific ways so he could peel it off intact! It said so, right there on the seal! It required more mana control than simply flooding the seal with mana, but it was nothing he hadn't already been capable of, even before the time loop. All this time he had thought the symbols on the seal were purely ornamental in nature, but no, they were *instructions*. Instructions written in a somewhat obscure form, but still. How could he have missed that?

He directed his mana to flow along the sides of the seal, causing it to pop off without resistance.

"Well done," Ilsa said with a smile. "Not many students have such a firm grasp on their magic at this stage. I see someone is continuing in Daimen's footsteps."

Zorian smiled back politely. He mustn't scowl, he mustn't scowl...

"Unfortunately, I'm in a bit of a hurry so we'll have to continue this conversation later," Ilsa said. "Visit me in my office when you get to Cyoria. Now about your electives..."

Ilsa stared at him. He stared back. She glanced at the two completed exams on her desk and then returned her gaze to him, this time with a speculative look. Zorian remained silent.

It actually felt good to baffle someone like this, Zorian decided. Apparently Ilsa wasn't as cold-blooded about improbable skills as Xvim was.

"I must admit, I didn't quite expect this level of knowledge and shaping skill when I told you to come and see me," Ilsa said, her forehead creased in contemplation. "That second exam I gave you is the one I give to students at the end of their third year, and you only got two questions wrong. On top of that, you know ten different variations of the basic three, which is astronomical for a third year student."

She tapped her pen against the table, lost in thought.

"You may be a bit too advanced for what I intend to teach your group this year," Ilsa finally admitted. "My class is mostly there to make sure the students don't have any obvious holes in their shaping skills and theoretical knowledge, and to teach them a few miscellaneous spells that are of general utility to most mages. You're way beyond that. What am I going to do with you?"

"Transfer me away from Xvim so you can teach such a promising student?" Zorian tried.

She laughed at him.

"Sorry," she said. "You're good, but not *that* good. Besides… you should have it easier than most of Xvim's vi—err, *charges*. What with your amazing shaping skills and all."

"You'd be surprised how little difference that makes to him," Zorian said, sighing.

"Oh, come on, Mister Kazinski, you haven't even had a single session with him," Ilsa chided. "I'm sure that whatever rumors you heard were greatly exaggerated."

"Right," said Zorian, unable to keep himself from rolling his eyes. "Can you at least give me a written permit to skip your lectures? You said yourself I have nothing to learn there, anyway."

That wasn't quite what Zorian was after, but he supposed it was better than nothing. It would give him several free periods throughout the week, which wasn't terribly useful while he was inside the time loop (where he could just skip classes, consequence-free, if he needed more free time) but would come in handy when and if he got out of it. And besides, a written permit would cut down on Akoja's whining, if nothing else.

"No," Ilsa said. "I need you in class, if only to motivate the rest of your classmates to try harder. Don't worry, I'll make sure you're not bored during class."

Crap. Maybe he shouldn't have asked her that…

"In the meantime, I'm going to do you a favor," Ilsa continued. "While I am personally too busy to teach you, I will see if I can find another teacher willing to give you some private instruction. Do you have an area of magic you're particularly interested in? Personally, I would recommend you look into either divination or alteration, but it's your choice."

"Spell formulas," Zorian said firmly.

"Oh? Ambitious," Ilsa said. "It's a complex subject. Not something your shaping skills can help you with, either."

"I'm certain," Zorian confirmed. Spell formulas had fascinated him ever since he had first begun to learn magic, so there was no way he was wasting this kind of opportunity.

"Very well," Ilsa shrugged. "I don't foresee any problems, in that case. I'm sure Miss Boole will be ecstatic to have such a talented and determined student."

Miss Boole? As in, Nora Boole, the orange-haired maniac who expected them to read twelve books within a week and gave them sixty-question progress tests every other lecture? Zorian resisted the urge to sigh. Why couldn't he have a normal mentor for once?

CHAPTER 011

Limiters

"Why is your test longer than mine?" Benisek whispered to him hurriedly. "Did I lose a page or something?"

"You didn't," Zorian whispered back. "Nora is just testing me because… well, it doesn't matter. I'll tell you later."

Suppressing a sigh, Zorian continued pondering the advanced spell formula questions in front of him. As if the original sixty-question test hadn't been enough! Worse, Nora had taken a page out of Ilsa's book and decided to test him on knowledge that he technically shouldn't even have, because the additional questions had nothing to do with second year curriculum. Thankfully, he had actually read all twelve of her recommended books over the course of several previous restarts, so he wasn't *completely* stumped while looking at the piece of paper in front of him.

Still, the additional questions were encouraging since they suggested Nora was taking him a lot more seriously than she usually did when he asked for advanced instruction. In the handful of restarts he had attempted this, the results had been underwhelming—while enthusiastic about her subject, Nora Boole never seemed to believe he was as advanced as he claimed. All of his teachers were like that, as far as he could tell, with Kyron being the notable exception. Though now that he thought about it, that probably had more to do with the ease with which his proficiency with the magic missile spell could be demonstrated, rather than Kyron's inclination to believe his claims. In any case, the sheer speed with which things were finally happening gave him hope. He and Ilsa had talked only the day before and already Nora was testing him. That was absurdly fast since teachers liked to take their time about things like this. Zorian had expected the entire process to take a week, *at least*. Perhaps he had left an even bigger impression on Ilsa than he thought he had.

Good. It was nice to have a confirmation that he was actually making progress, rather than just wasting his time.

A few minutes later his peace was once again broken by Benisek. He gritted his teeth as the other boy started to pester him for answers. Zorian had begun to find himself steadily losing his patience with the boy as restart after restart went by. It wasn't really fair to Benisek—the chubby boy's behavior was no worse than usual—but the time loop made Benisek's antics annoyingly repetitive. He quickly scribbled answers to a handful of questions on a piece of paper and thrust it at Benisek. Benisek looked like he would say something to him in his not-whisper (Benisek whispered far too loudly for it to be called a real whisper), but Zorian silenced him with a quick glare.

As annoying as Benisek might be, Zorian wasn't ready to give up on him just yet. Whether that resolve would hold throughout the entire time loop remained to be seen, however.

"All right, time's up. Pencils down, everyone," Nora said, earning her a wave of protests from the student body. "Except for Mister Kazinski, that is. He can keep working on his second exam."

Zorian cursed internally as all eyes momentarily shifted towards him. She just had to announce that in front of the whole class, didn't she? He made a note to himself to watch what he said in front of Nora, since discretion obviously wasn't her strong suit.

Akoja hurriedly collected all the tests, lingering slightly longer near his desk so she could see what his special test was all about. After that, the class continued as normal. It was the exact same thing he had already listened to countless times before in the previous restarts, so he did his best to block it out and continue working on the test. Even with his unfair advantage, the test was quite hard. Spell formula in general involved a lot of mathematics and geometry, as the very name of the discipline suggested, and that automatically made it difficult for a lot of people... him included.

When the class ended, Nora asked him to stay behind while everyone else filed out of the classroom. She immediately started to look over his tests when the last of his classmates were gone, and Zorian watched her intently for a reaction.

Unlike Xvim, or even Ilsa, Nora Boole was a very expressive woman. By the time she had reached the end of the first test, he could see she was pleasantly surprised. She damn well should be, considering it was one hundred percent correct. When she started inspecting the second test, though, her face quickly morphed first into shock, then barely restrained glee. Evidently she liked what she saw. Finally, she set the test aside and met his eyes, giving him a penetrating gaze that actually caused Zorian to flinch a little. She reminded him of Zach and Kirithishli because she seemed to radiate a similar sort of... vibrancy, for lack of a better word. It was always a bit uncomfortable being around people like that, especially when they were focused solely on him as Nora was.

"Well...," she began, "I didn't expect that. Do you know why I gave you the second test?"

"Uh, no," said Zorian. "To scare me off?"

"Exactly!" Nora exclaimed. "Exactly!"

Zorian blinked, unable to believe she would actually admit that to his face.

"Spell formulas require bravery! They require passion!" continued Nora animatedly. Funny. Everyone else said they required patience and meticulousness. "They require determination! Anyone who is frightened by this little thing here," she waved the second test in front of his face, "will surely give up when attempting to delve into the truly difficult parts of the discipline. I had to make sure you wouldn't bail out on me."

Zorian was starting to feel a little unnerved by Nora's outburst. Was he signing up for spell formula tutoring or cult membership?

"Of course, I didn't actually expect you to solve any of the questions correctly," Nora said. "I just wanted to see if you'd leave it completely blank. Not that I'm complaining, far from it! Let's see..."

She went back to her desk and pulled a stack of papers out of a drawer. She frowned as she leafed through them, apparently unhappy about their contents, before finally setting them aside with a sigh. After an entire minute of silence, she glanced towards him and shook her head, as if suddenly remembering he was still there.

"Tell me, what are spell formulas?" she asked him. "And I don't want to hear a textbook definition. I want to hear it in your words."

Zorian opened his mouth for a moment and then quickly snapped it shut as he considered what to say.

"Come on," Nora encouraged. "Bravery, remember? Besides, I just want to know your opinion. There is no right answer."

Hah. There might be no right answer, but Zorian knew from experience that there was always a *wrong* answer. Always. But he supposed that, in this particular instance, silence was the wrongest answer of them all.

"It's the practice of using geometric shapes and various sigils to modify spells, usually in order to strengthen wards or amplify spellcasting," said Zorian.

"Really? How do they do that?" Nora asked, feigning curiosity with a smile.

"Err… they limit mana flow along pre-determined pathways?" tried Zorian.

"Yes!" agreed Nora. "They limit, that's exactly what they do! I can't tell you how many mages think they're some kind of inherent amplifier. Drives me crazy, I tell you. Of course, most modern crafters use special materials that *are* inherent amplifiers, but that's something else entirely. Anyway, you know the point behind structured spellcasting, right?"

"The narrower the effect of the spell, the more mana efficient it becomes. Structured magic creates a spell boundary to forcibly narrow down effect space into something manageable for a human spellcaster."

"And spell formulas are the exact same thing, only with more pronounced benefits and drawbacks," said Nora. "Since mages can take their time when crafting the spell formula, they limit the mana flow much more tightly than your typical invocation. This results in much greater potential benefits, but also makes the spell even more inflexible. And, of course, a tighter spell boundary leaves a smaller margin for error, so designing a working spell formula is a lot harder than designing a working invocation."

Zorian waited patiently until she was finished, not really sure why she was telling him these things—this was all basic theory that he had heard and read a thousand times—but unwilling to interrupt. Unfortunately, it appeared he would have to wait to hear what her point might be. She suddenly looked at the clock hanging by the door and blanched when she realized how much time had passed.

"Sorry, Mister Kazinski, I guess I got carried away. You better go to the next class before I get you in trouble," Nora said apologetically. Zorian shrugged—he had intended to skip the next class one way or another, but it probably wouldn't impress her much if he told her that. "I'll need a few days to set up a schedule for us, so I'll pass on the details to you via Ilsa. We'll have a blast working together, I can already tell."

He was just about to leave when she suddenly started talking again.

"Oh! I almost forgot. Make sure you see Ilsa sometime today. She has something she wants to talk to you about. Something about you returning a favor you owe her for setting this up…"

Now why did that sound so ominous?

Cyoria's main train station was always busy. There was a hurried feeling suffusing the entire area that Zorian found either annoying or invigorating, depending on his mood. When he was disembarking from the train, it served as a metaphorical bucket of cold water to wake him up from the long sleepy journey, and he welcomed it. When he was simply standing on platform number six, waiting for the train to arrive, it was oppressive and unwelcome, and he desperately wished he knew how to suppress it. Especially since the damned train was two hours late!

In order to amuse himself and pass the time, he had taken to harassing the numerous pigeons and sparrows milling around the place. Not physically, of course—that would not only be childish, but also cause people to stare at him—he was instead pushing his mana at them, trying to control them mentally. Of course, simply pushing mana at something and wishing for it to happen wasn't enough to do real magic, but it did seem to agitate them a lot. Typically, whatever bird he was concentrating on became increasingly erratic as seconds went by before fleeing away from the area after a minute or so.

Finally, *finally*, the shrill whistle of the incoming train broke him out of his concentration, and the local wildlife was spared further indignation. Zorian scanned the crowd of people disembarking from the train, searching for his target. He was technically supposed to hold a sign and wait, but he was confident he could spot the guy without a problem. There weren't going to be many white-haired teenagers on the train platform, after all.

It actually wasn't as bad as he'd thought it would be, this favor Ilsa had asked of him. Admittedly, helping a transfer student carry his luggage and showing him around the city would waste an entire day... but on the bright side, he was excused from attending classes. Besides, it would give him a legitimate excuse to approach Kael, the transfer student in question. The morlock boy was a bit unapproachable even at the best of times, and Zorian had been thinking of trying to befriend him. He really ought to find some friends beside Benisek, and Kael seemed like someone he could get along well with. If he turned out to be wrong... well, it's not like the morlock would remember any awkwardness between them once the time loop reset itself again, would he?

Finally, he spotted Kael disembarking and moved towards him to help with his luggage. It wasn't just an empty gesture of good will on Zorian's part. Kael was clearly struggling with his burden, probably because he only had one hand free to manipulate the heavy bags. The other hand was currently supporting a little girl that clung to Kael's side like a barnacle, observing everything around her with childlike intensity.

Kael was momentarily surprised when Zorian wordlessly started helping, but quickly went along with it. The little girl clutching his side was now staring at Zorian with undisguised curiosity, and Zorian wondered who she was. Was this his little sister? Her vivid blue eyes certainly reminded him of Kael, since the morlock had eyes of the exact same shade, but her hair was jet black, and she didn't look very much like a morlock to Zorian. And in any case, surely the boy wouldn't bring a child this young with him to the academy? Zorian kept expecting her mother to step out of the train and take the little girl out of Kael's hands, but no one else ever materialized.

Finally, the last of the bags was arranged on the platform and Kael turned towards him.

"Thank you," the boy said politely. For all the aloofness he had demonstrated, Kael was never actually rude. "I'm Kael Tverinov. I'm not normally this inept, but it's hard to handle the luggage with one hand. Kana has been rather clingy today, and I didn't have the heart to pry her off. The move was too stressful for her, I'm afraid."

"It's no problem," Zorian said. "I'm here to help, after all. I'm Zorian Kazinski, one of your classmates. Ilsa Zileti sent me here to help you with your luggage and show you around the city."

Kael gave him a startled look, clutching the little girl attached to his hip like Zorian was about to snatch her away.

"What?" Zorian asked, surprised at the alarm in the boy's posture. "Was it something I said? I didn't mean to offend."

Kael gave him a long, suspicious look, before finally reaching a decision of some sort.

"You didn't do anything, Mister Kazinski, and it is I who should apologize," Kael said finally. "Allow me to introduce myself again: I am Kael Tverinov, and this is my daughter, Kana."

Zorian stared at the morlock for a moment, before glancing at his... daughter. Kana gave him a shy wave but otherwise remained silent. She was very young, probably around three years of age, but Kael wasn't much older than Zorian. That would mean Kael would have been thirteen or so at the time of her birth. Huh. Talk about being a young parent.

"I see," he said finally. And he really did, too. Kael probably got enough grief from people around him over being a morlock without adding this sort of fuel to the fire. If Zorian were in his place, he would have done everything he could to keep this sort of thing from his classmates as well. "If you're afraid I'll go around telling all our classmates that you have a daughter, you don't have to worry—I understand the need for discretion in matters like this."

Kael breathed a sigh of relief. "Thank you."

"Don't mention it," Zorian said, waving him off. Considering the child's mother wasn't here with them, there was probably a very stressful story in there somewhere. Only a total jackass would set the academy rumor mill on the poor guy. He was a little curious as to how Kael intended to watch over his daughter while attending the academy, but supposed he had already arranged for a nanny of some sort for the child. "I'll just cast a quick spell to carry your luggage and then we'll be off."

Zorian quickly cast the floating disc spell, and a ghostly horizontal circle flickered into existence in front of them. It was a very useful spell that they were supposed to learn in Ilsa's class somewhere in the middle of the third year, but Zorian had been proactive enough to track it down during one of the restarts. It was similar to the shield spell in mechanics, but this particular force construct was mobile and optimized for supporting weight as opposed to absorbing blows. It dutifully floated after them as they started walking out of the train station.

"Interesting," Kael said. "I must admit that when Ilsa told me my education is severely lacking in many areas, I thought she was exaggerating. Is this what an average third-year student is like?"

"Well, no," said Zorian. "I'm actually way beyond what a third-year student should be. Though I'm hardly unique in my skill…"

Kael hummed thoughtfully.

"Why would your education be lacking, anyway?" asked Zorian.

Kael remained silent for a few seconds, and Zorian was just about to conclude the morlock wasn't interested in talking when the boy finally decided to answer.

"My education was… unconventional," said Kael. "I was a sort of unofficial apprentice to a village mage. One that wasn't a member of the guild. Her skills were somewhat specialized, so much of my proficiency with magic is a product of my own personal efforts. In other words, I'm largely self-taught."

Zorian's respect for the other boy rose a few notches after hearing this. Magic was hard enough to learn with proper instruction. For a young boy to go at it all by himself and get far enough to join a third-year class… though if he was such a genius…

"I hope I'm not being too nosy, but—"

"But why am I here now?" guessed Kael. "I got a pretty good offer from the academy, and it wasn't like I had anyone stopping me from leaving. My parents died when I was young, and my teacher… she got sick during the Weeping. As did my wife. Kana is the only family I have left."

Zorian flinched. "Oh gods, I didn't mean—"

Kael shook his head. "Don't worry about it, Mister Kazinski. If I was to fall apart every time someone broached that topic, I would have to become a hermit and avoid people completely. It is natural to be curious about these things."

Zorian still felt pretty terrible. He had pretty much assumed Kael had gotten some girl pregnant and later had to take responsibility for the child. But no, the guy had been married and everything. A bit shocking to marry and have children so young in this day and age, but hardly unheard of. He studied Kael out of the corner of his eye in the resulting silence. The boy looked very delicate, with a pale, willowy physique and gentle facial lines. Coupled with his shoulder-length white hair, it gave him a rather feminine appearance. Nonetheless, the boy clearly had no shortage of inner strength if he could move on after losing so many people to the horrible sickness. In Cirin, Zorian's family had known a woman who had lost her husband and both sons to the bloody tears fever and had never managed to move past her grief. She had actually blamed the entire Kazinski family for her tragedy, claiming they had used magic to curse her loved ones over some petty disagreement. Zorian would be the first person to admit he and his family were no angels, but that was just absurd. And kind of sad.

"There is no need to pity me, Mister Kazinski," said Kael, breaking Zorian out of his thoughts.

"Oh, I don't pity you," Zorian said. "I think you're very inspiring, actually. You're a single parent who somehow managed to find the time to teach himself magic to such a degree that a world-renowned institution acknowledged your potential. They gave you a scholarship, didn't they?"

Kael nodded. "I wouldn't be able to attend otherwise."

"They rarely give out scholarships," Zorian said. "Maybe five or six of them each year. You must be pretty amazing to have caught their attention like that."

"It's mostly my medical expertise," Kael said. "I made a vow to myself after… well, you know. I swore to myself I would become the best healer of our time and make sure a tragedy such as the Weeping can never happen again."

Uh… wow. Zorian didn't know what to say to something like that.

"I have made quite a lot of progress on that front, if you will permit me to be a little immodest," Kael said. "But… well, it's complicated. We can talk later, if you're still interested. Kana and I are rather tired from the journey and I'd like to retire for the day. Kana especially."

Zorian suddenly noticed Kana was starting to doze off on Kael's shoulder. She had been so quiet throughout his entire interaction with Kael that he had almost forgotten she was there. If only Kirielle could be that calm.

"Yes, sorry about that," Zorian apologized. "I got carried away. I'll have to give you a tour of the city some other time, then."

They spent the rest of the walk to Kael's apartment in comfortable silence.

"You were absent yesterday."

Zorian gave Akoja an annoyed look. She wasn't going to give him grief over that, was she?

"I was excused," he noted.

"I know," Akoja said. "I was just wondering where you were."

Zorian was about to tell her it wasn't her damn business where he went in his free time, but then he reconsidered. He was getting strange vibes off Akoja, almost as if she was… *concerned* about him. Very strange. Normally he would write it off as just another weird thing Akoja did from time to time—the girl seemed to possess a sense of logic all her own sometimes, one that not even her obsession with rules could explain—but his recent conversation with Kael stopped him. Was he too dismissive of other people? Up until yesterday, Kael had simply been 'that morlock transfer student' to Zorian… It brought back memories of his conversations with Zach and the other boy's remarks about Zorian's behavior in previous restarts, before he had become aware of the time loop.

"I was doing a favor for Ilsa," Zorian said, deciding the truth couldn't hurt. "Showing our newest transfer student around the city and such."

"Oh," Akoja said, glancing at Kael for a moment. The white-haired boy was sitting several rows behind Zorian, silent and aloof as always. He gave virtually no indication that he knew Zorian was in the classroom, but Zorian could feel the morlock's eyes on him from time to time. "Who is he anyway?"

"Kael Tverinov," Zorian answered.

"I didn't mean his name," Akoja huffed, realizing after a few seconds of silence from Zorian that he wasn't going to say anything else.

"Not sure what else to tell you," Zorian said, shrugging. "He seems like a good person to me."

"He looks kind of arrogant," Akoja remarked. "And girly."

"Well how judgmental of you," Zorian said with a frown. "You come off as a bit arrogant yourself, you know?"

So much for being nice to Akoja. She stomped off soon after that, but not before shooting him a nasty glare.

Resolving to be more understanding towards people was hard.

It took Nora Boole only two days to organize their first private lesson, and the moment Zorian stepped into the classroom Nora had reserved for them he realized she was taking this very seriously. It was a professional-looking workshop, the sort that students normally couldn't access without special permission from the teachers. Nora beckoned him forward, positively radiating excitement and enthusiasm. Suddenly he remembered why he had been pensive about receiving instruction from her. Considering the amount of homework and additional reading Nora assigned as a matter of course during her classes, Zorian dreaded finding out what she considered an appropriate workload for a promising student.

"Ah, you're too quiet!" she complained as he came to stand in front of her. "Courage, Zorian, courage!"

"Right," agreed Zorian half-heartedly.

"We'll make a proper crafter out of you yet, just you see! But first, let me just wrap up our discussion from last time. I was a little long-winded, but what I had been trying to build up to was that spell formula function as support magic. Magic affecting other magic. By itself, even the most elegant spell formula is merely a theoretical exercise. You need to actually cast the spells and anchor them to the spell formula before it's of any use. I note this because Ilsa seemed to think your skill in invocations would do you no good in my subject, which revealed a fundamental misunderstanding about the nature of the discipline. Which is very disappointing coming from her since she is… well, you know…"

"A teacher," finished Zorian.

"Yeah," Nora agreed, a little awkwardly. Teachers rarely spoke ill of one another, in Zorian's experience, so it was no wonder why she was uncomfortable criticizing Ilsa in front of a student. They did have to work with one another on a regular basis, after all, and undermining another teacher's authority like that could get ugly very quickly. Fortunately, only Zorian was present in this case, and he didn't intend to make trouble for either teacher. She seemed to realize this after a moment because she smiled and continued as if nothing had happened. "Anyway, I guess we should get you started on the beginner's cube."

As it turned out, the beginner's cube was a perfectly cubical block of grey stone, each side roughly ten centimeters long. The one Zorian was given was completely blank and smooth, but Nora showed him a couple finished ones as a demonstration. They were capable of heating up, shedding light, and floating in the air when activated, or when certain conditions were met. Basically, each finished cube was a crude magic item that used a couple simple spells and a whole lot of spell formula to produce a neat little toy. They were a standard training tool, according to Nora.

Zorian wanted one the moment he laid his eyes on them. Giving such a blatantly magical toy to Kirielle would probably keep her out of his hair for *hours*. It would be his secret weapon against her! Besides, a small floating cube would make a much more challenging target for his magic missile practice than the boulders and tree trunks he usually practiced on. Especially if he could somehow get it to dodge…

He wouldn't have to wait long to acquire one, as it turned out—crafting one was the first lesson. And not just any beginner's cube, either. Zorian had expected Nora to give him something easy for a start, but apparently she had something a little more ambitious in mind.

"These are too easy for you," Nora said. "No, I have something much more fun for you to work on. Here."

She handed him another cube, though this one was positively covered with spell formula. Zorian noted with rising dread that he couldn't make heads or tails of it. Hell, many of the sections looked like mere placeholders instead of working spell formula, being little more than stylized pictograms. Wait…

"As you may have noticed, I compressed the spell formula somewhat," Nora said. "Partially it's because there wasn't enough space on the cube to represent it fully in its raw form and partially to stop you from simply copying the entire thing line by line on the blank one I gave you earlier."

"Isn't that the whole point?" Zorian asked. "For me to study a working example to see how it's done, that is?"

"Absolutely. But I'm afraid blindly copying the spell formula from one cube to another won't teach you what I want you to learn. If I thought you needed to practice memorization and precision, I'd have you copy a dozen or so easy ones to start with, but I'm sure you're already beyond that. No one spends as much time on spell formula theory as you have without trying out some practical examples."

"Err, I never encountered anything like those cubes in the texts I read," said Zorian. "But yes, I have been using spell formulas from time to time. Mostly to establish an alarm perimeter around my bed during my second year—I had a really nosy roommate—and also to make some free lamps and heating plates."

Invocations didn't last long. Even if a mage poured more mana into them than absolutely necessary—and a spell could only be over-powered so much before it shattered from the strain—they inevitably degraded after a couple hours at most. The spell boundary degraded with time and eventually fell apart, regardless of whether the spell had enough mana left or not. As a consequence, if Zorian wanted his alarm spell to last throughout the entire night, or his makeshift lamp not to wink out every hour or so, he had to stabilize the spell bound-ary somehow. Spell formulas were the easiest and most reliable way to do that, so long as someone already crafted a stabilization formula for that particular spell and made it available to the public.

"It's not very surprising you never encountered beginner's cubes in your reading," Nora said. "They're mostly used for theoretical exer-cises. Not very useful. Most mages don't really care how spell formulas work—only that they do. They memorize the well-documented for-mulas and some quick-and-dirty methods of modifying existing ones, and then they only have to know when to apply which one. Then they say spell formulas are dry and boring. Hah! If only they knew the true mysteries of the art, the hidden beauty of numbers and geometry…"

Zorian listened stoically as Nora mumbled to herself about 'un-imaginative rabble' and 'sleeping in the bed they made for themselves' for a while. Eventually, she took a deep breath and plastered a pleasant smile on her face before turning her attention to him again.

There was no sane teacher in this school, it seemed. Zorian won-dered whether it was the stress of teaching itself, or if applicants simply had to be crazy to accept a teaching position here.

"But I digress," Nora said cheerfully. "I guess I should stop wast-ing our time and tell you what I want you to do. Here, let me dem-onstrate…"

The cube Nora wanted Zorian to recreate was quite complicated. At its core, it was a glorified lamp using a simple torch spell as its base. It could be activated and deactivated verbally by saying one of the several command words, and it needed to be able to discern the difference between the command word being directed at it and being used in another context. It had three different brightness settings. It conserved mana by not shedding light from any side that was covered by something—the side resting on the floor didn't shine, for example, and wrapping it in a blanket would cause it to turn itself off. Each individual side could be turned on and off by tapping it twice in quick succession. It could also be keyed to a specific person, taking orders from him or her alone.

Nora had told him not to worry if he couldn't duplicate it exactly—she only wanted to see how far he'd get on his own by the next time they met. That was good, because this assignment was far more complex than any spell formula work he had done up to that point. Their next session was Monday, so he had an entire weekend to work with, but he doubted he could fully rise to the challenge.

He had mixed feelings about Nora's teaching methods. On one hand, she was taking him seriously, and that was good. On the other hand, she seemed to think that throwing a person overboard was a perfectly valid way of teaching people how to swim, metaphorically speaking.

"Come in."

Zorian sighed before stepping into Xvim's office. What a wonderful way to end a week. For all her faults, he infinitely preferred Nora's way of teaching compared to that of Xvim.

"Zorian Kazinski? Sit down, please," Xvim ordered, not even bothering to wait for an answer. Zorian caught the pen the man had thrown at him with practiced ease, and then promptly caused it to float off the palm of his hand, gently spinning in the air. Woops. He hadn't meant to do that. Oh well, let's see what the man will say about that.

"Make it glow," Xvim barked out without skipping a beat, completely unfazed by Zorian's skill.

Zorian wasn't even surprised anymore. The pen promptly snapped back to his hand and erupted in a soft ghostly glow. He cycled through various colors without prompting from Xvim, occasionally changing the intensity of the light just to prove he could.

Xvim arched his eyebrow at him. "I didn't say you could stop levitating the pen."

Zorian's lips twitched in an aborted smile. If Xvim thought he would stump him with that, he was very much mistaken—combining two different shaping exercises was an obvious thing to do, and Zorian had already tried it. Moments later, the pen was spinning in the air in front of him, glowing.

Xvim tapped his finger on the desk thoughtfully. Was it possible? Had he really managed to give the man pause? The world was coming to an end! Zorian watched in anticipation, wondering what the crazy man would think up next.

"I suppose there is no point in testing your ability to burn things. That was always the easiest exercise of the three," Xvim mused. As a point of fact, Zorian was a bit deficient in the burning exercise… at least compared to the other two. Not that he was going to tell that to Xvim, of course. "Your essentials are… adequate. Almost decent, though not quite. Your attitude could use some work, but I suppose you at least have more tact than most of the unfortunates that haunt these halls. Plus, Miss Zileti has appealed to me on your behalf, asking me to be 'not such a hardass' towards you. As such, as much as I'd like to shake up your woefully shaky foundations, I'm going to reluctantly move on to something *slightly* more advanced."

To Zorian's great confusion, Xvim handed him a strip of cloth. What was he supposed to do what *that*?

"Err…"

"It's a blindfold," Xvim explained. "You put it over your eyes so you can't see."

"And… why do I need a blindfold again?" Zorian asked.

"We're going to train your ability to sense mana," said Xvim. "You're going to put the blindfold on, and then I'm going to throw these mana-charged marbles at you."

Zorian stared at the man incredulously. Had he really heard right?

"I'm either going to throw them over your left shoulder, over your right shoulder, or straight at your head. If you get hit by a marble, you lose a point. If you move when you don't have to, you lose a point. Otherwise you receive a point. We'll stop when you accrue ten points or our time runs out."

Yes, he really *had* heard him right. Thank you so much for your help Ilsa, thank you *so* much!

The next two weeks were busy, but routine. He directed most of his efforts towards mastering spell formulas, largely because Nora was very willing to indulge him—the harder he tried in their lessons, the more enthusiastic she became about teaching him. She even suggested they meet on Sundays for additional instruction, apparently not having any private obligations to distract her. He had learned much, but Nora set a grueling pace, and he was glad the restart was fast approaching. He doubted he could last much more than a month of Nora's teaching.

Interestingly, he seemed to be attracting attention from the teachers and students alike in this particular restart. Maybe it was due to him impressing Ilsa as much as he had, maybe it was the way he quietly went with the insane workload Nora gave him, or maybe Xvim had said something nice about him to the other teachers. Well, probably not that last part, since he had made little progress in mastering Xvim's marble game. In any case, he was getting a lot of attention for his efforts, which was rather curious. Most of the time, no matter how hard he tried in class, everyone was pretty flat about it. He thought about trying to leverage all that attention into something useful, but he was too exhausted by his studies to plot properly. Some other restart perhaps.

The attention had the unfortunate side-effect of wrecking any chance he had of befriending Kael. Associating with Zorian would surely bring great scrutiny on the morlock, something the boy was understandably concerned about, so Zorian wasn't surprised the other boy never sought him out. Frankly, he wasn't sure he could befriend the boy even in normal circumstances—the morlock had a daughter waiting for him at home and thus probably wouldn't want to spend his time after class socializing with friends.

Akoja was extremely pleased with him, though. Zorian couldn't really understand why, but she was.

And then it happened. Suddenly, without any warning as he brushed his teeth one morning before meeting Nora, there was a wrenching sensation and everything went black. He woke up, as usual, with Kirielle lying on top of him, looking smug.

There were two possibilities that Zorian could think of to explain this occurrence. The first one was that something or someone had killed him so fast he was dead before he realized it. He was skeptical of this, as he had done nothing to warrant an assassination, and he couldn't think of any natural force that could kill so suddenly and thoroughly. He hadn't even felt any pain before he died.

The second possibility was much more likely and also much more worrying. While he was minding his business, learning spell formulas in Cyoria, Zach was off somewhere in the world, doing insanely dangerous things—and dying. When he died, his soul was dragged into the past to start over… and it dragged *Zorian's* soul back with it.

Which would make Zorian soul-bonded to Zach.

Damn it.

CHAPTER 012

Soul Web

Zorian stomped into his room, closing the door behind him with far more force than necessary. He should have known he wouldn't find out anything about soul bonds that he hadn't already known, but it was still frustrating to come back empty-handed after spending an entire day in the library.

The books all repeated the same warnings he had received back in his first year: soul bonds were a dangerous and poorly understood branch of magic capable of causing horrifying side-effects if used recklessly. Every once in a while, some ill-informed couple decided that soul-bonding themselves together would be the most romantic thing ever, only for everything to end up in tears and lawsuits a few months later when complications surface. The main issue was that one of the participants usually started to mentally and spiritually dominate the other, making their partner more like themselves in mind and soul, not to mention disturbingly obedient and deferential. This was a good thing when binding animals as familiars, since it was almost always the animal that got dominated by the human, and animals tended to benefit from such domination by developing higher intelligence and better control over any magical abilities they possessed. Sapient beings usually had issues with someone magically subverting their entire personality and worldview, however. At least until the soul bond finished turning them into a servile clone.

Zorian ran a trembling hand through his hair and started to clean his glasses with the hem of his shirt to calm himself down. He really, *really* hoped he was wrong and that there was no soul bond between him and Zach. Zach's mana reserves were six times larger than Zorian's theoretical maximum, he was naturally more outgoing and confident, and—thanks to being in the time loop far longer than Zorian—was probably decades older than him, too. No points for guessing who'd be the dominant one between the two of them!

The worst thing about it was that he couldn't even go to someone for help. He was pretty sure the soul bond, or whatever it was, was responsible for him looping around along with Zach. If he asked someone for help, they'd insist on severing the bond. While he would normally be eager to agree to this, severing the bond would cause him to lose everything he had gained inside the time loop, memories included, once Zach started over at the end of the month.

Yeah, he was totally screwed.

He took a couple of deep breaths and put his glasses back on. Maybe he was being too fatalistic. Considering the sheer size of the disparity between him and Zach, he should have, if soul bonded, experienced some significant personality shifts, and he hadn't noticed anything of the sort. He certainly wasn't feeling submissive towards anyone, least of all Zach. He could very well be overreacting and overlooking some other, perfectly reasonable explanation for the unscheduled restart…

Someone was knocking. Who could possibly—

Oh. Right. Taiven.

He sighed heavily. Just what he needed right now. The knocking turned into banging, prompting him to finally open the door.

"Hi, Roach!"

"Hi, Taiven," Zorian said, not bothering to hide the suffering from his tone. "How nice of you to visit me. Do you want to come in?"

Taiven promptly did what she always did once he let her inside— she jumped on his bed and made herself comfortable. Zorian shrugged and followed. Best to get it over with quickly.

"Didn't you graduate?" he asked. "You said you were going to go into exploration. What happened to that?"

She gave him a sour look. "It's not that simple. No expedition is going to take a complete beginner like me with them. I need an established explorer to take me as an apprentice. I'm working on it."

"Funny, I heard you're working as a class assistant to Nirthak," Zorian remarked. "Isn't that going to interfere with searching for another master?"

"Well, sort of," she admitted. "But I'm not literally searching for another job at this point. I'm actually trying to build up my reputation and get people to notice me by doing missions and such. In fact, that's what I came to talk to you about—I'd like you to join me and a couple others on a job tomorrow."

"Sounds suspicious," Zorian said. "What could a measly third-year help you with?"

"Um, fill out our numbers?" Taiven answered. "We can't take the job until there are four or more of us, and we're one short of that."

"Well, why *does* the job require four people?" asked Zorian, knowing from previous restarts that this was the fastest avenue to shut down Taiven's excuses. "Surely the employer didn't include that stipulation without a reason."

"It's supposedly dangerous," Taiven huffed, folding her arms across her chest. "The old man is overreacting. The spiders aren't even that big from what he told us."

"Spiders?" prodded Zorian.

"Yeah," Taiven said hesitantly, apparently realizing she shouldn't have mentioned that. "Spiders. You know, hairy eight-legged—"

"Taiven," Zorian warned.

"Oh, come on, Roach, I'm begging you!" Taiven whined. "I swear it's not as dangerous as it sounds! We've been in the tunnels hundreds of times and it wasn't that dangerous at all! We can protect you easily!"

"Hundreds of times?" asked Zorian dubiously.

"Well, a dozen times at least," she relented.

Zorian was just about to tell her no, like he usually did at this point, but then he stopped himself. If the morning was any indication, he was likely to spend far too much time early in this restart considering the implications of being soul-bonded to Zach. A nice distracting stroll through the sewers might be just what the doctor ordered, so to speak.

"Sure," he said.

"Really!?" she squealed.

"Yes, really," confirmed Zorian. "Just tell me where to meet you tomorrow before I change my mind."

A few minutes later Taiven left, thanking him profusely and kissing him on the cheek—'for being a friend'—before running off to… wherever she had been going, he supposed. He hadn't asked, being too shocked by her kiss, innocuous as it may have been. He scowled, angry with himself for letting her affect him, but then let out a long exhale, resolving not to be harsh toward his subconscious. She was his former crush, after all.

He decided he had had enough of everything for the day and drank one of the sleeping potions he kept in his stash. Hopefully things would seem clearer after a good night's rest.

He felt more level-headed—and less hopeless—in the morning. He had been jumping to conclusions about his connection to Zach, he reasoned, and simply needed more information. He was tempted to skip classes for the day to have another go at the library, but he suspected that he lacked both the research skills and the access level to properly tackle a restricted topic like soul bonds. And besides, there was someone in his class he absolutely needed to talk to—Briam, the student with the fire drake familiar. Surely someone already soul-bonded to another being, even if it was to a magical animal instead of a human, could tell him more about those blasted things.

"I see your family has given you a fire drake of your own," he said conversationally, sitting down beside Briam and ignoring the threatening hissing of the fire drake. For some reason, the ill-tempered beast had never seen fit to attack him in previous restarts, so he didn't think it would start now. "Is he your familiar already?"

"Yes," Briam confirmed, clearly pleased with that. "I bonded with him just this summer. A bit strange, at first, but I think I'm getting the hang of it."

"Strange?" asked Zorian. "How so?"

"Well, it's mostly the bond being there, you know?" Briam said.

"So, the bond can be felt?" Zorian said speculatively, trying not to let his excitement show. He didn't feel anything. "Is that normal? Can everyone who is soul-bonded feel their bond?"

"No, not everyone," Briam said. "Only a tiny minority can, and nobody is sure why. I can, though. I guess I'm lucky that way."

Zorian suppressed a scowl. He had been hoping that the lack of any unfamiliar sensation meant there was no bond. Damn.

"You know," Zorian tried, "I've always had an… *academic interest* in familiars and soul bonds…"

Thankfully, Briam didn't find Zorian's interest in any way suspicious and was happy to indulge Zorian's curiosity. What Briam told him was interesting, to say the least. According to Briam, the soul bond spell was actually a ritual that took at least ten minutes to properly cast—usually more. Not something to be cast as a regular invocation.

There were a lot of things Zorian had experienced in the time loop that could qualify as signs of a developing soul bond, but it was hard to say how much of that was simply a consequence of the crazy situation he had found himself in. The effects were just too weak compared to what Briam told him should happen. His mana reserves were slightly larger than they had been at the start of the time loop, for instance, but the increase was nothing extraordinary. It could just as easily be a consequence of his regular combat magic practice instead of being caused by the soul bond trying to twist his soul to be more in line with Zach's. The spell that the lich had cast on them definitely hadn't been a ritual either… but then again, it *was* a lich. Who knew what kind of magic a creature like that had at its disposal?

All in all, it would appear he was lucky—the link between him and Zach was either very weak or of a different type. Or perhaps only half-formed? According to Briam, the bond required physical proximity and a lot of personal interaction between participants to fully mature. It was why he carried his fire drake everywhere he went at this point in time. Considering Zorian had only interacted with Zach to any great degree in one of the restarts, and that the boy spent virtually all of the restarts away from Cyoria, the bond may have never gotten the chance to solidify. If so, Zorian had to prevent it from fully forming—he would avoid contact with the other time traveler from now on until he knew more about what was happening.

Which, admittedly, could take a while, but Zorian could only hope that avoiding Zach as much as possible would prevent the bond from overwhelming him. He really ought to make a more detailed plan of study for himself. So far, he had been learning things rather haphazardly. There was no hurry, as far as he knew, and he didn't know where to begin anyway. Also, he had wanted to grow a little as a mage before breaking out of the time loop, since he would never get an opportunity like this again. That kind of disorganized approach was no longer appropriate, however—he wanted the soul bond broken as soon as possible, and that meant finding a way out of the time loop as quickly as possible.

But creating his plan would have to wait for another time because he had a meeting with Taiven and her friends scheduled for the evening. Why did he agree to this again? Oh yes, Taiven picked a really inconvenient moment and he had a momentary bout of insanity. He should have at least gotten some favor out of her for doing this. Oh well, live and learn.

Taiven had chosen an annoyingly distant meeting place—a park where one of her friends was a regular chess player—so Zorian had a long trek in front of him. He had never visited that particular park across the city, but the path towards it was somewhat familiar and he couldn't figure out why.

It was only when he stumbled on a small bridge just inside the park that he realized why. The bridge was where he had met that crying little girl whose bicycle had fallen into the stream, back before he was aware of the time loop. Come to think of it, he never visited this place after that, did he? There just wasn't any reason to, since he knew in advance there were obstacles blocking his path if he went this way. He peered curiously at the section of the creek beneath the bridge, trying to see if the bike was still there. Unsurprisingly, it wasn't. Yesterday's heavy rain had swelled the creek into a raging torrent, and the bicycle had, no doubt, been picked up by the currents and swept along.

The little girl wasn't there either, of course, but that didn't mean he was alone on the bridge. A small cat, probably quite young, sat between the bars of the railing, looking forlornly at the raging waters below. Zorian didn't generally stress himself about the plight of animals, but when the cat turned to look at him and their eyes met, he was assaulted by an intense feeling of sadness and loss. Unnerved by the experience, he picked up his pace, hurriedly leaving the strange cat behind him.

Finally, after nearly thirty minutes of wandering the park, he found the meeting place. Taiven really needed to learn how to give proper directions. It was a peaceful spot populated almost entirely by old people. As in, *really* old people. Taiven's group of teenagers stuck out like a sore thumb, but none of the elderly chess players surrounding them seemed to mind so Zorian decided not to let it bother him and cautiously approached.

Taiven's other friends were a pair of gruff, muscular boys that would look more at home in a boxing ring than at a mage school. One of them was currently frowning at the chess board in front of him, contemplating his next move, while Taiven and the other boy sat on each side of him. Taiven was clearly impatient and bored out of her skull, at one point actually trying to snatch a figurine from the board, only to be foiled by the players. The other boy was more relaxed, lazily observing everything around him like a guard dog. He pointed Zorian out to the other two.

"Roach!" Taiven waved. "Thank the gods, I was starting to fear you'd never show up!"

"I wasn't late," Zorian protested.

"Well, you sure developed a habit of cutting it close since the last time we saw each other," she accused. "But anyway. Roach, I'd like you to meet my two minions, Grunt and Mumble. Grunt, Mumble, this is my good friend Roach."

Zorian rolled his eyes. At least he wasn't the only one with a stupid nickname.

"Damn it, I told you not to introduce us like that!" one of the boys protested, though he looked as though he did not expect Taiven to change her habits. He sighed and turned towards Zorian. "Hi, kid. I'm Urik, and the guy playing chess is Oran. Thanks for helping us out like this. We'll make sure nothing happens to you, so don't worry about anything."

The chess player grunted, possibly in agreement. That must be Grunt, then.

"I'm Zorian," he said, leaving out his last name just as Urik had.

"Right!" said Taiven enthusiastically. "Introductions are over, so let's get going, shall we?"

"Not until I finish this round," the chess player said flatly.

Taiven's shoulders slumped in defeat. "I hate this game," Taiven whined. "Find yourself a seat, Roach. This could take a while."

Zorian clacked his tongue in annoyance. For once Zorian empathized with Taiven's impatience. He wasn't a big fan of chess either.

The Dungeon was an extremely dangerous place. Also known as the underworld, the Labyrinth, and countless other names, it was a staggeringly extensive network of caves and tunnels that ran beneath the surface of the world. At first glance, the place seemed like every mage's dream come true—ambient mana levels increased the deeper one descended into the endless depths, and the lower levels were practically swimming with useful minerals with fantastic magical properties. Unfortunately, mages were just one of the many creatures that thrived in such an environment. Monsters of all sorts lived in the tunnels, and the deeper one went, the stronger and more alien they became. Even the greatest of archmages had to take care not to go too deep when exploring the Dungeon, lest they come face to face with something they had no hope of defeating.

Cyoria, like many other cities, took advantage of the Dungeon beneath it when the city was being built. The topmost portion of the Dungeon was cleared of anything aggressive or particularly dangerous and then systematically walled off from the deeper levels. These tunnels were then modified into shelters, storage spaces, flood-control systems... and the city sewer system. Human settlements had used the Dungeon as a sewer for so long that several species of oozes and other monsters had adapted specifically to take advantage of this unique ecological niche, and humans often transplanted them from one city to the next when they built new settlements. Of course, the separation of this topmost layer from the deeper parts of the Dungeon could never be absolute—especially since many Dungeon denizens were very capable diggers. Regular maintenance was required to keep the whole thing functioning properly.

Cyoria's Dungeon boundary was widely known to have more holes than a sponge. It was a fairly young city, and the local Dungeon was particularly extensive. It grew too big, too fast, and a proper separation between layers was never completed. That was probably how the invaders managed to smuggle an entire army of monsters into the city—though how exactly the invaders mapped out the deeper layers well enough to find a route large enough for an army to pass through was beyond Zorian's comprehension. Just one more example of how ridiculously well prepared the enemy was.

Despite the obvious danger, Zorian wasn't too worried about following Taiven into the tunnels. Cyoria's underground wasn't the safest place in the world, but it was by no means a certain death sentence either. And he doubted the invaders were currently in there, since a giant army of monsters living just beneath the city would be impossible to hide for any length of time, regardless of organized the invaders were. No, Zorian was certain they would have to navigate their route on the day of the invasion to avoid detection. He would feel better if he had a focusing item for his combat magic, of course, but that was beyond his reach at this point. Nora's tutoring aside, he still wasn't good enough with spell formulas to make one from scratch, and he couldn't buy one without a permit.

Unfortunately, their employer didn't seem to share Zorian's confidence.

"This is the fourth member you found?" the old man demanded incredulously when he met them near a Dungeon entrance in one of the city parks. "Did he even graduate yet?"

Zorian looked at the scowling man waving towards him in a dismissive manner and promptly decided he could understand Taiven's irritation. If he was so worried about their ability to deliver results, he ought to cough up the cash to hire professionals. Frankly, Taiven and her group were probably the best he could hope to get, considering where he had looked for help.

The job itself was simple enough—the old man had lost a pocket watch in the tunnels while fleeing from a duo of giant spiders. He had tried to retrieve it, but when he returned two days later to the spot where he had dropped it, it was nowhere to be found. Personally, Zorian was sure it had been eaten by an ooze or some other metal-eating scavenger living in the tunnels, but the old man insisted it was still intact and in the spiders' possession. How he knew that was anyone's guess. What would a bunch of spiders, giant or otherwise, do with a watch? Perhaps they collected shiny things, like magpies.

"Nope," Zorian said, completely unrepentant. "I'm a third-year."

"A third year!" the man squawked. "And you think you can survive down there? Do you even know any combat magic?"

"Sure do," confirmed Zorian. "Magic missile, shield, and flame-thrower."

"That's all?"

"You get what you pay for."

"Look, what's your problem?" Taiven interrupted. "It's four of us versus two spiders. I could do this alone!"

"Just because I only encountered two doesn't mean there aren't more of them," the man grunted. "I don't want you to stumble on a whole hive of those things and get slaughtered. Those things are *fast*. And stealthy—I didn't even notice them until they were right on top of me. I'm lucky to be alive."

"Well, there's four pair of eyes among us," Taiven reasoned. "And we'll watch each other's backs, so good luck to them if they try to sneak up on us. I don't suppose you'll finally tell us what's so important about this watch?"

"It's none of your business," the man shot back. "Its only value is sentimental." He nodded towards Zorian. "I suppose the kid is right. I got what I could, considering the reward I'm offering. Just... don't get careless. I don't want the lives of a bunch of children weighing on my soul when I finally die."

A few minutes and a whole lot of pointless bickering later, Taiven finally led them all towards the nearby Dungeon entrance. There were guards stationed there but Taiven had a permit to go in and could bring people with her, so they were free to pass. That was reassuring at least—it meant someone in the permit office considered Taiven capable enough to keep less experienced non-combatants like him safe down there. Apparently she hadn't been talking completely out of her ass when she had said she could protect him.

The tunnels themselves were a lot less sinister than Zorian imagined, or at least this particular section was—smooth stone walls and nothing more threatening than rats wandering around. The stone covering the corridors reflected light pretty well, so the four floating lanterns they had hovering above them (Taiven insisted they all cast one and space them away from each other, so they wouldn't be immediately plunged into darkness on the off chance they encountered something that could dispel them) illuminated the tunnels quite nicely. Unfortunately, there was no immediate sign of either the missing watch or the giant spiders. Taiven seemed to think it would be easy to track down the spiders with a simple locate creature spell and was stumped when the spell—and all other divinations she tried, for that matter—came out empty.

As it turned out, Taiven and her two friends were more than a little specialized in combat magic and didn't have the faintest idea how to go about tracking down either the watch or the spiders once their rudimentary divination attempts failed. Eventually they settled on just wandering around, hoping they'd stumble on the spiders' lair and occasionally repeating the divinations with no change in effect. After about two hours of that, Zorian was ready to call it quits. He was just about to suggest they give up and come back the next day, when he suddenly felt very, *very* sleepy.

Being a mage required a great deal of mental discipline—shaping mana correctly required focus and the ability to visualize the desired result with crystal clarity. As such, all mages were, to an extent, resistant to mind magic and other effects targeting the mind. This practiced resistance was the only thing that kept Zorian on his feet, desperately fighting the sleep spell, instead of collapsing to the ground in deep slumber. In front of him, he saw Taiven and Urik sway on the spot as they tried to resist the spell as well. The other boy was already laid sprawled on the floor.

He struggled against the spell for a moment, and then the sleep effect just… withdrew. But before he could do anything, he was forced to his knees by a stream of memories and images that bored themselves directly into his mind.

Confusion. A memory of him staring at a particularly baffling spell formula problem, tapping his pen against the table in frustration. An image of two floating balls of water connected by a collection of ever-shifting streams of water flowing from one orb to another. An alien memory of a war troll tearing through delicate white walls that seemed to be made solely of cobwebs. A question.

[*Are you*—] the voice boomed in his mind, before collapsing into another psychedelic collection of images and alien memories. The deluge lessened for a moment, as if waiting for a response. Then it started again. Frustration. [*I thought*—] Brotherhood. Webs stretching across lightless chasms, orbs of light trapped within them. [—*don't understand me, do you?*] Sadness. Pity. More frustration. Resignation.

The flow of images abruptly stopped assaulting his mind and Zorian clutched at his head as though this could subdue the raging headache pulsing between his temples. As the waves of pain subsided slightly, he was able to look around. Taiven and her two friends were unconscious but appeared to be unharmed. There was no trace of an attacker. Crawling to the three other on his hands and knees, he tried to wake them up, but they wouldn't budge.

Deciding the best idea would be to get back to the surface before something decided to finish them off, Zorian promptly cast the floating disc spell and piled his three unconscious teammates on top of it before making a beeline towards the Dungeon entrance.

Forget the watch. He just hoped his head would stop killing him by tomorrow.

Zorian woke up disoriented and confused, waiting for Kirielle's weight to pummel his abdomen. He became vaguely aware of white walls and white bedsheets. He lay in a hospital bed, his limbs neatly tucked beneath a blanket. As his mind began to clear, he remembered the tunnels and the search for the watch—and then the strange attack on his mind. Had there been a voice?

He hadn't died, he realized, just had his mind scrambled—though this was actually far more worrying than merely dying. Any damage to his mind would carry over to the next restart, and every restart after that. He lay quietly for a moment, taking in his senses, letting his heart rate calm, until he was fairly sure he hadn't suffered any permanent damage.

A vague memory of a doctor concluding something similar surged back to him then, after a brief examination. Sleep, it seemed, had been the recommended treatment, prescribed gruffly and with considerable disinterest as Zorian was unceremoniously deposited in this small room. Some doctor. He didn't need a hospital for that. He wondered how Taiven and her two friends were faring—they had still been completely comatose when he had stumbled out of the Dungeon entrance and the guards had rushed them all to the nearest hospital.

"Finally awake, I see." Ilsa's voice came from the doorway and Zorian shifted in his bed to see her. "Do you feel up to talking or should I come back later?"

"Miss Zileti? What are you doing here?"

"As our student, the academy is obliged to represent you in legal matters," Ilsa said, approaching his bed. "This qualifies. How are you feeling?"

"I'm fine," Zorian said, shrugging a little against his pillow. He didn't even have a headache anymore. "I might as well go home once you finish questioning me."

"Questioning you?" Ilsa asked. "You make it sound sinister. Why would I be questioning you?"

"Err, well…" Zorian fumbled for words. "In my experience, the police tend to be hardasses towards witnesses. Just in case they're hiding something and all that."

For a moment Zorian thought she would ask him why he might have had that sort of experience, but she instead just shook her head and chuckled.

"Well, I'm not the police," Ilsa said. "Though I did come to ask you what happened. Your friends don't remember anything substantial, having been hit hard with that sleep spell."

"Are they all right?" Zorian asked.

"Yes," Ilsa confirmed. "They woke up yesterday with no ill effects. Your injuries were far more serious, medically speaking." She gave him a wry smile. "I think it was their pride that was hurt the most. A third-year resisted a spell they could not and saved their lives. Cyoria's Dungeon boundary is infamously… porous. If it weren't for you, they probably would have been dead by morning."

Zorian looked away uncomfortably. Is that why Taiven had never contacted him after that initial invitation to go with her at the start of each restart? He had thought she was being callous.

This was not, however, the only question on his mind. He could not fathom why he had been able to resist the sleep spell when they could not. As for what had happened next…it had hurt and had been severely unpleasant, but he didn't think it had been particularly malicious in intent. After all, he had been helpless and could have easily been finished off. The words, the images… it was as if something had been trying to talk to him but didn't know how to communicate with humans properly.

His mind flashed back to the alien memories. Webs. A lot of webs. Could it be the spiders? He had never heard of any sentient spiders with access to mind magic, though.

"I'm not really sure what happened," Zorian finally said. "After the sleep spell failed, I was immediately bombarded by a barrage of images that almost made me black out. It was very painful and disorienting. After it stopped, I tried to get my bearings in case further attacks were coming, but after a minute I decided to hightail out of there. I have no idea why the attackers stopped."

"Hmm," Ilsa hummed. "There are a lot of possibilities. Maybe, instead of walking into a deliberate ambush, you simply stumbled upon someone who didn't want to be seen and they moved to incapacitate you so they could slip away unnoticed. Maybe someone left a spell trap in that section of the tunnels for whatever reason and you set off the trigger. Maybe you resisting two spells in a row intimidated them into leaving. We may never know."

Yes, all valid possibilities. It certainly wasn't giant sapient telepathic spiders, no sir!

"Oh, and Zorian?" Ilsa continued, rising from her chair to leave. "You're forbidden from going down in the tunnels until further notice. I understand you wanted to help a friend, but it was still a foolish thing to do."

"Err, yes professor," Zorian agreed. "Understood."

"This is boring!" Taiven complained.

Zorian cracked one of his eyes open so he could glare at her.

"You said you wanted to make it up to me," he reminded.

"But I meant teaching you some kickass spells, not..." She scowled at the bowl full of marbles in front of her. "Not throwing marbles over your shoulders. Shouldn't I at least aim a couple at your forehead? I bet you'd be a lot more motivated to get it right that way."

"If you do that, I'm going to track you down to your room and suffocate you in your sleep," Zorian threatened heatedly. The whole reason he was having her do this was to practice this stupid trick without suffering through Xvim's methods.

He closed his eyes and took a deep breath. After a few seconds, he felt the mana-charged marble pass in the vicinity of his face but couldn't pinpoint over which shoulder it had flown.

"Left," he tried.

"No, right," Taiven. "Now you're just guessing, aren't you? Just give it a rest for today. You're not going to get anywhere once you get frustrated."

"No, I just need a couple of minutes to calm down," Zorian sighed. Taiven groaned in response and he opened both eyes so he could properly glare at her. "Why are you being so difficult about this, anyway? You know I can't ask anyone else to do this for me, right? I don't know anyone else who can aim their throws precisely enough, and none of them could keep charging marbles for more than half an hour without depleting their reserves."

"I know, I know." Taiven sighed. "And I'm glad you asked me for help. It's the least I could do after... well, you know. But you're not taking advantage of me properly!"

Zorian raised an eyebrow.

"Err, that came out wrong," Taiven said, chuckling nervously. "I meant I can do much more than this. My accurate marble throwing skills aren't my only gift. I know I must seem pretty pathetic for getting knocked out by a single spell but come on!"

"I never thought of you as pathetic because of that, Taiven," Zorian said. "But all right. What can the great Taiven do for me?"

"Teach you how to fight, of course!" she grinned.

"The magical way, I hope."

"You should never underestimate the usefulness of a fist to the face, even in a magical duel," Taiven said. "But yes, I meant the magical way. Were you telling the truth when you told the old guy who hired us you can cast magic missile, shield, and flamethrower?"

"Of course."

"Well, let's see them," Taiven said, waving towards a duo of dummies on the other side of the room. She had brought him to her home, which sat in a wealthy part of the city a short walk from the academy grounds.

"Err, won't your parents mind if I wreck their training dummies?" Zorian asked.

She rolled her eyes. "The whole reason I told you to come to my place was so we could train here. The whole room is warded and those dummies especially. You won't even scratch them, trust me."

Shrugging, Zorian quickly cast a magic missile, shaping it into a piercer and weaving a homing function into it so it would hit the head of the dummy. The bolt of force sped across the room and struck the dummy square in the forehead. The faceless wooden head of the dummy bent backwards with the force of the blow in a manner that would snap a real human's neck in several places. It then promptly snapped back to its default position as if nothing had happened.

"A decent magic missile," Taiven praised. "I like that you can cast one without a spell focus. I thought that would be the first thing I would have to teach you."

Then her hands blurred in a dizzying display of skill, the chant spoken so softly he barely heard it. A veritable swarm of magic missiles erupted from her, speeding towards the dummy with a lot more speed than Zorian's piercer and impacting it with enough force to lift it off its feet and smash it into the wall behind it. Though they were simply smashers, Zorian knew each individual bolt was a lot more dangerous than the piercer he had produced.

And she didn't appear the slightest bit strained by the effort.

"So, was there any purpose for doing that, other than rubbing in how far beyond me you are?" Zorian asked. "Firing that many magic missiles, even sequentially, would drain my reserves dry on the spot. I don't think I'll be repeating your feat any time soon."

"Err, really?" Taiven said. "I guess I kind of assumed your mana reserves are huge, like your brothers'. How many magic missiles can you cast in one sitting?"

"Eleven," Zorian said, pointedly ignoring her first remark. "It started out as eight, but I have increased it somewhat."

"Eight!?" Taiven gaped. "But that's… practically below average!"

Zorian knew nothing good would come out of blowing up at her. It was Taiven. She didn't really think before speaking, and if you were bothered by that you had no business interacting with her.

"Does that mean you admit defeat and we should get back to the marbles?" he asked with deceptive cheer.

"No!" she shrieked. "No, I was… I was just surprised, that's all. I wanted to teach you how to cast multiple magic missiles with one casting, but I suppose it wouldn't do you much good with such tiny mana reserves. You should make your every spell count instead of going for quantity. Show me your shield and flamethrower while I think of something."

After trying to burn a dummy to a crisp and failing, Zorian cast a quick shield, thinking just its existence would be enough proof for Taiven. Apparently not, as she immediately whipped a spell rod out of her belt and fired a small purple projectile at the shield. Zorian's eyes widened at the unexpected attack, but it splashed harmlessly against the semi-transparent plane of force and dissipated into a puff of purple smoke that soon wafted out of existence.

"What the hell was that!?" Zorian demanded.

"I was just checking if the shield can hold," Taiven told him. "The spell is harmless, just a simple coloring bolt that carries some force to it."

Zorian wanted to tell her his shield had held against a hostile mage that had been trying to kill him, but he couldn't really do that. He settled on giving her an annoyed look.

Eventually Taiven admitted she couldn't think of anything to help him with magic missiles and reluctantly started throwing marbles over his shoulders again. She made it clear to him, however, that she would enlist help from her parents in the coming days, and that this way of training was a onetime thing. Zorian was pleased when he managed to negotiate in at least an hour of marble throwing each session, in addition to whatever crazy scheme she would come up with eventually.

Truthfully, combat magic was only a side interest at the moment. He was starting to realize he couldn't keep blundering blindly through this. As much as he had wanted to advance his magical studies before finding the exit from the loop, he couldn't simply ignore the danger posed by the possibility of a soul bond—the longer he stayed inside, the bigger the chance of the bond activating in full force and devouring his will and personality. The mental assault he had experienced in the Dungeon simply highlighted that the time loop had its own dangers and that it was irresponsible to take them lightly.

A rough plan was forming in his mind. He needed to find out everything he could about the time loop—how it came to be, how it functioned, how he could get out of it, and what the nature of his connection to Zach was. As for the invasion, it seemed too conveniently timed to be a coincidence, so clearly it, too, was connected to the loop. Finding answers would require skills in divination, information gathering, and infiltration, so he resolved to focus his efforts there.

He would have to return to his apprenticeship in the library and learn all the tricks of that trade he possibly could within the constraints of the time loop. The academy library was an incredible resource, and he was sure he would have to use it extensively if he was to find answers to the questions that were plaguing him. His prior efforts there had not yielded much, but that was probably a consequence of insufficient authorization and lack of research skill on his part rather than an actual void of information on the topics in question. He needed to know how to bypass the protections on the secure sections of the library and how to search them efficiently once he got through. Kirithishli and Ibery were his best chance at succeeding. He would apply for the job in the library first thing in the morning.

And, though it was a bit late for it in this particular restart, he would once again impress Ilsa, then choose divination as his interest as she had recommended. If Ilsa was even halfway as motivated as Nora Boole was, he would have a particularly easy avenue on learning that otherwise tricky subject.

Satisfied with these plans, he was climbing the stairs inside his apartment building when everything went black and he woke up via Kiri jumping on him and wishing him good morning. It seemed Zach had died again. And only a few days into the restart, too. Zorian hoped Zach would get the hang of whatever he was attempting very soon, because being wrenched without warning into another restart could get old really fast.

He would soon learn he should really stop tempting fate with such thoughts.

CHAPTER 013

Any
Second Now

Zorian's eyes abruptly shot open as a sharp pain erupted from his stomach. His whole body convulsed, buckling against the object that fell on him, and suddenly he was wide awake, not a trace of drowsiness in his mind.

"Good morning, brother!" an annoyingly cheerful voice sounded right on top of him. "Morning, morning, *MORNING*!!!"

Zorian growled as he roughly pushed Kirielle away from him. The fifth time! Five times in a row the restart had terminated after only a handful of days! How many times would Zach need to die before realizing he should back off whatever he was doing for a while and try again later? Honestly, if it were him, Zorian would have reconsidered his approach after the second attempt…

He snatched his glasses from his bed post and stomped off towards the bathroom before Kirielle could gather her wits. The short, irregular restarts were ruining every plan he cared to make, not to mention disrupting his concentration. He really couldn't do anything substantial while this was going on, other than browse the library for helpful texts and hope Zach would quit killing himself on a regular basis. What the hell was the boy trying to do anyway?

Surely this couldn't go on for too much longer. Surely not ten or fifteen restarts, right?

Yeah. Yeah, that sounded about right…

"Hi, Roach!"

Zorian wordlessly gestured for Taiven to come inside before slowly closing the door and shuffling after her. He could feel her impatience at his sluggish pace, but he paid it no heed. He was deliberately stalling, trying to decide what to do.

He fully intended to have a chat with the weird telepathic spiders that inhabited the sewers, but it would be lunacy to go there at this point. There was no guarantee they would be as friendly as they had been the last time, and their mind magic made them dangerous even within a time loop. He needed a way to protect his mind before venturing into Cyoria's underworld, and so far, he had only found one ward in the academy archives that protected a caster's mind. Unfortunately, that particular ward blocked *everything* related to the mind, mind-based communication spells included. He needed something more selective than that.

But just because he was unwilling to descend into the Dungeon didn't mean he was content to let Taiven get herself killed by going there. He wasn't sure why he cared, exactly—pragmatically speaking, he shouldn't be bothered, since everything would be reset in a couple days and she'd be fine again. Still, he *was* bothered, and since he was forced to have this conversation repeatedly every few days, he might as well try to find a way to talk her out of going.

He didn't think for a moment it was going to be easy. Taiven was possibly even more stubborn than Zach.

"So, Taiven, how is life treating you?" he began.

"Eh, so so." She sighed. "I am trying to secure an apprenticeship, but it's not going all that well. You know how it goes. I got Nirthak to take me as his class assistant this year, so there is that. You wouldn't happen to have taken non-magical combat as one of your electives?"

"Nope," Zorian answered cheerfully.

"Figures," Taiven said, rolling her eyes. "You really should have, you know? Girls—"

"Love boys who exercise, yes, yes." Zorian nodded sagely. "Why are you here, Taiven? You tracked me down here even though I only moved in yesterday and never told anyone which room is mine. I suppose you used a divination to find me?"

"Uh, yeah," Taiven confirmed. "Pretty easy thing to do, really."

"Aren't these rooms supposed to have some sort of basic warding scheme placed on them?" Zorian asked.

"I'm pretty sure it's just rudimentary stuff like fire prevention and basic detection fields to warn the staff about fighting in the halls and attempted demon summonings and what not," Taiven said, shrugging. "Anyway, I'm here to ask you to join me and a couple of others on a job tomorrow."

Zorian said nothing, patiently listening as she gave her sales pitch. It was actually Monday she meant, not the next day—Taiven's definition of 'tomorrow' differed greatly from the standard definition—but other than that, she was actually fairly honest in her explanation of the situation. She even mentioned that there was a small chance they might encounter something very nasty in there, but emphasized that she and her friends were totally capable of confronting anything they might find. Right.

"Anything?" asked Zorian suspiciously. "You know, I happen to have read up on magical spider breeds, and they can be pretty powerful. A single grey hunter has been known to wipe out entire hunting parties of mages, and they're no larger than a human at their biggest. Phase spiders can literally jump on you out of nowhere and drag you off into their own private pocket dimension. Some of the breeds are even sentient and have mind magic at their disposal."

The last one was a joke in more ways than one. Dungeon ecology was a giant mystery, even to mages that specialized in it, and information about monsters that made their home there was very scarce. As such, it was probably not surprising that he hadn't found anything on sapient telepathic spiders in the academy library, even after conscripting Ibery and Kirithishli for the effort.

Was it just him or was the academy library a lot less useful than he had imagined it to be? Every time he tried to find something there he was disappointed. Then again, the things he was trying to find information on tended to be obscure, borderline illegal, or both.

"Oh, please." Taiven snorted dismissively. "Don't be so paranoid. As if something like that could be right below Cyoria. We won't be delving into the Dungeon's depths, for gods' sakes."

"I don't think you should go at all," Zorian insisted. "I'm getting a really bad feeling about this."

Taiven rolled her eyes, an undercurrent of annoyance in her voice. "Funny. I never took you for a superstitious guy."

"Time changes people," Zorian said solemnly, smiling internally at his private joke. "But seriously: I'm getting a *really* bad feeling about this. Is this really worth getting yourself killed over?"

Apparently this was the wrong approach to take as Taiven's temper flared immediately. He supposed she perceived his comment as an insult towards her skills as a mage. Before he could apologize and rephrase his argument, she was already shouting at him.

"I'm not going to die!" Taiven shouted irritably. "Gods, you sound just like my father! I'm not a little girl and I don't need to be protected! If you didn't want to come you should have just said so instead of lecturing me!" She stomped off angrily, muttering to herself about conceited brats and wasted time.

Zorian winced as Taiven slammed the door behind her. He wasn't sure why she had reacted so strongly to his words, but apparently pointing out the potential danger of the job was ineffective and only pissed her off.

Oh well, he hadn't expected to succeed in dissuading her on the first try anyway.

"Hi Roach!"

"It is a good thing you came, Taiven," Zorian said with a grave expression. "Come in, we have much to talk about."

Taiven raised an eyebrow at his behavior before shrugging and sauntering inside. Zorian tried to project a serious, ominous presence about himself, but it seemed to amuse her more than anything.

"So… I gather you wanted to see me then?" she asked. "I guess you're lucky I decided to drop by, then."

"Not quite," Zorian said. "I knew you would come today, just as I know you're here to conscript me into joining you for a sewer run."

"It's not a—" Taiven began, only to get interrupted by Zorian before she could gather steam.

"A sewer run," Zorian repeated. "Retrieving a pocket watch guarded by some very dangerous spiders from the top layer of the Dungeon under the city."

"Who told you that?" asked Taiven after several seconds of bewildered pause. "How could they possibly know? I told nobody where I'm going or why I'm visiting you."

"Nobody told me," Zorian said. "I had a vision about this meeting… and about what will happen should you descend into the tunnels."

Well, it *was* true in a way…

"A vision?" Taiven said, her expression one of disbelief.

Zorian nodded gravely. "I have never told you this before, but I have prophetic powers. I receive visions of the future from time to time, seeing glimpses of important events that will affect me personally in the days ahead."

It wasn't completely implausible—people like that did exist in the world, though their powers were quite a bit more limited than what he had at his disposal thanks to the time loop. From what he understood, their visions were less of a detailed recording of the future and more of a general outline of some upcoming event. The future was always changing, always uncertain, and trying to get a clear image of it was like trying to grasp a fistful of sand—the more you squeezed, the more it slipped through your fingers.

Unfortunately, while being prophetic was not impossible, Taiven clearly wasn't buying his claim.

"Oh really?" Taiven said challengingly, crossing her arms in front of her chest. "And what did this 'vision' of yours tell you about the job?"

"That it will be the death of you," said Zorian bluntly. "And me as well, should I choose to follow you down there. Please, Taiven, I know it sounds ridiculous, but I'm serious about this. The visions are rarely as clear as they were this time around. I won't go down into the sewers and you shouldn't either."

As seconds ticked past in silence, Zorian began to think she would actually listen to him. This impression was destroyed when she suddenly started laughing.

"Oh, Roach, you almost had me there!" she wheezed, breaking into uncontrollable chuckles after every couple of words. "Visions from the future… Roach, you have the funniest jokes. You know, I missed that quirky sense of humor of yours. Remember… remember that one time you pretended you were asking me out?"

How Zorian stopped himself from physically recoiling at that he would never know. She just had to mention that, didn't she? He forcefully pushed away the memories of that particular evening, determined not to dwell on it.

"Yeah," said Zorian emotionlessly. "What a funny guy I am."

Why was he trying to save her again?

"So…," she said, finally getting her giggles under control, "how *did* you know I was coming?"

"Hi R—" Taiven began, only to stop when she saw his vacant, hollow expression. "Whoa, Roach, what the hell happened to you?"

Zorian kept staring off into space for a few more moments before shaking his head, as if to clear his thoughts a little.

"Sorry," he said in a subdued voice, motioning her to get inside. "I just had an extremely vivid nightmare and I didn't get much sleep."

"Oh?" Taiven said, collapsing on his bed like usual. "What about?"

Zorian gave her a long look. "Actually, you were in it."

Taiven stopped fooling around and gave him a shocked look. "Me!? Why the hell would I be in your nightmare? You'd think a beautiful girl like me would automatically make for a pleasant dream! Now I *have to* know what it was about."

"I was walking through the sewers with you and two guys I have never met," began Zorian in a haunted tone, "when we were suddenly set upon by a swarm of giant spiders. There… there were so many of them… They just swarmed over us and started biting and…"

He took a couple of deep breaths, pretending to be on the verge of hyperventilating before finally calming down.

"I'm sorry, it's just… it was so real, you know?" he said, giving Taiven the most vacant stare he had. After a few moments he looked down on his trembling hands and balled them up into fists in a very exaggerated motion. "The feeling of their fangs sinking into my skin, the poison coursing through my veins like liquid fire… They didn't even kill us in the end, they just wrapped us in spider silk and dragged our paralyzed bodies off to their lairs to feed upon later. Such a horrid, vivid dream—I don't think I'll ever look at a spider in the same light again."

Taiven shifted nervously where she sat, looking extremely uncomfortable and vaguely ill.

"But it was just a nightmare," Zorian said in forced cheer. "To what do I owe this visit, anyway? Is there something you wanted to talk to me about?"

"N-No!" Taiven blurted out, a nervous laugh escaping her lips. "I just… I just stopped by to have a chat with one of my friends, that's all! How has life been treating you anyway? Aside from the whole… nightmare… thingy…"

She found an excuse to leave in a matter of minutes. He would later find out she went into the sewers anyway and never came back.

"Spiders?" asked Zorian, doing his best to appear alarmed. "Taiven, don't you listen to rumors from time to time?"

"Umm… I've been pretty busy lately," Taiven chuckled awkwardly. "Why, what do the rumors say?"

"That there are some mind magic using spiders prowling the city sewers," Zorian said. "Word is the city is trying to root them out, but the creatures are evading them thus far. They've been trying to suppress the information, since it would make them look incompetent and all that."

"Wow, good thing I talked to you then," Taiven said. "I never would have thought to put a mind ward on myself before going down there."

"You're still going down there!?" Zorian asked incredulously. "What makes you think this mind ward of yours is enough?"

"Mind magic is a subtle thing," Taiven said. "It uses tiny amounts of mana in very sophisticated ways, which makes it easy to counter with brute force. So long as you know in advance that you're going to face a mind mage, it's easy to make yourself effectively immune. Trust me, now that I know what to expect from those crawlies, I won't fall for their tricks."

Zorian opened his mouth to protest, but then reconsidered. Was Taiven right? Maybe he was looking at things from the wrong perspective. He was trying to get Taiven to *survive*, which didn't necessarily mean stopping her from going into the sewers.

"I guess," he finally conceded. "But I won't be going with you."

"Oh, come on! I can totally keep you safe!"

"Nope," Zorian insisted. "Not happening. Find someone else to go with you."

"How about—"

"No fighting," Zorian interrupted. "Look, there is no way to talk me into going along with this. Do tell me how the whole thing turns out afterwards, though. I don't want to have to check to see if you survived."

She actually did visit him a few days later and told him the sewer run was a failure as far as finding the watch went, but that nothing attacked them either.

Huh. Maybe Benisek was onto something when he spoke so highly about the power of rumors and gossip.

Zorian's eyes abruptly shot open as a sharp pain erupted from his stomach. His whole body convulsed, buckling against the object that fell on him, and suddenly he was wide awake, not a trace of drowsiness in his mind.

"Good morning, brother!" an annoyingly cheerful voice sounded right on top of him.

"Good morning, Kiri!" yelled Zorian back, engulfing the shocked Kirielle into a hug. "Oh, what a wonderful, wonderful day this is! Thank you for waking me up, Kiri, I really appreciate it! I don't know what I would do without my wonderful little sister."

Kiri wriggled uncomfortably in his grasp, not used to receiving such a gesture from him and unsure how to react.

"Who are you and what did you do to my brother!?" she finally demanded.

He just hugged her tighter.

"Something I can do for you, sonny?" asked Kyron. "The class has been dismissed, in case you haven't noticed."

"Yes, I noticed," Zorian said. "I just wanted your advice about something, if you can spare the time."

Kyron impatiently gestured for him to get to the point.

"I was wondering if you knew any means of countering mind magic," Zorian said.

"Well, there is your basic mind shield spell," Kyron said carefully. "Most mages agree that's all you need as far as mind magic protection goes."

"Yes, but that spell is a bit... crude," Zorian said. "I'm looking for something more flexible than that."

"Crude, yes," Kyron agreed, suddenly becoming more interested in the conversation. "Often useless, too. A simple dispel is enough to strip the protection off the target, and a proper mind mage will ensnare your mind before you even realize you're being targeted."

"Then why do most mages think it suffices?" asked Zorian.

"Do you know why most mind magic is restricted or forbidden?" Kyron asked. It was a rhetorical question, apparently, because he immediately launched into an explanation. "It's because it's most commonly used to target civilians and other mostly defenseless targets. Most mind mages are petty criminals that use their powers on the weak-willed and cannot be called a master of anything, let alone mind magic. It's rare for mages to encounter mind mages who know how to use their powers properly. Still, even a moderately talented mind mage can easily ruin your life, to say nothing of magical creatures with mind-affecting powers at their disposal. There are methods of dealing with mind magic without resorting to warding spells, but most find it easier to practice mind shield until it's completely reflexive and they can cast it on a moment's notice. Or just carry a spell formula for the spell on their person at all times."

"And these other methods are?" Zorian prodded after he realized Kyron wouldn't say anything more.

Kyron gave him a nasty smile. "I'm glad you asked. See, not too long ago, the combat magic class had a much more demanding curriculum, including what was called resistance training. Basically, the combat magic instructor would repeatedly cast various mind spells at students while they tried to fight off the effects. It was quite effective at making students innately resistant to common mind-affecting spells like sleep, paralyze, and dominate. Unfortunately, there were a lot of complaints from students who reacted particularly badly to it, and after a number of scandals where teachers and student assistants were discovered to have been using the training exercise as an excuse to punish students outside of proper channels, the practice was discontinued. An overreaction in my opinion, but I was overruled."

Zorian stood in silence for a moment, trying to digest this information. Was that really the best way to deal with mind magic? He understood the idea behind it—it worked on the same principle that shaping exercises and reflexive magic did, burning the defense procedures into his soul the same way repetitive movements burned certain reactions into muscle memory. It just sounded so… mindless. And probably very painful.

That's when he noticed Kyron was giving him a very predatorial look.

"How about it, sonny?" Kyron asked. "You think you have what it takes to go through it? I've been wanting to revive the practice for some time now, to be honest. I promise I'll go easy on you."

He lied. The very first spell he cast on Zorian was the nightmare vision spell. Whatever the spiders had to say, it better be worth it.

Zorian's eyes abruptly shot open as a sharp pain erupted from his stomach. His whole body convulsed, buckling against the object that fell on him, and suddenly he was wide awake, not a trace of drowsiness in his mind.

"Good morning, brother!" an annoyingly cheerful voice sounded right on top of him. "Morning, morning, *MORNING*!!!"

Zorian took a deep breath and focused on the image of what he wanted to achieve until it was so real he felt he could almost touch it. Billowing streams of mana erupted from his hands, invisible to the naked eye but easily felt by his senses—a mage could always feel his own mana especially while in the process of shaping it. In little more than a second, everything was ready and he set the effect loose on the little pest lying on top of him.

Nothing happened.

Zorian opened his eyes and let out a long, frustrated hiss. This was no structured spell he had been attempting, but pure unstructured magic—specifically, he had been trying to levitate Kirielle off of him by using the basic levitation exercise. He knew such an attempt would be much harder to accomplish than levitating a simple pen over his palm, but *nothing*?

"That tickled," Kirielle said. "Were you trying to do something?"

Zorian narrowed his eyes at her. Okay, that? That was a challenge.

"What can I do for you, Mister Kazinski?" Ilsa asked. "Normally I'd assume you were here to complain about Xvim, but you haven't even had a single session with him yet."

Zorian smiled brightly. That was the one bright spot in this series of short restarts—they always happened before Friday, so he didn't have to deal with Xvim while they lasted.

"Actually, I'm here to ask for advice on a personal project," Zorian said. "Do you know a training regimen that will allow me to lift a person telekinetically without casting a structured spell?"

Ilsa blinked in surprise. "As in, using pure shaping skill? Why would you ever have a need for that?"

"I sort of ran out of shaping exercises after mastering everything in Empatin's *Expanded Basics*," said Zorian. "It seemed like an interesting project."

"All fifteen of them?" Ilsa asked, a furrow in her brow.

Instead of answering, Zorian decided to demonstrate. He picked up a particularly large and heavy book from Ilsa's table and made it spin in the air above his palm. Spinning a book like that was actually much harder than spinning a pen, because a book was a lot heavier than a pen and had a tendency to snap open unless a mage used magic to force the covers shut while it was being levitated. That particular trick was something he had been taught by Ibery, of all people—she claimed that being able to keep a book shut while levitating it was a must-have for some of the spells she intended to teach him. Unfortunately, it took a couple weeks for Ibery to warm up to him and decide to teach him seriously, weeks he didn't have in these short restarts.

He made the book glow an ominous shade of red after a while. Using pure shaping skills to spin a book in the air while keeping it shut and making it glow with colored light was a pretty impressive showing from a third-year and should be ample evidence of his skills.

Ilsa took a deep breath and leaned back in her chair, obviously impressed.

"Well…," she said, "your shaping skills certainly aren't lacking. Still, hovering a person without a spell is… not really something there is a manual on. Nobody does it, as far as I know. If they have a need for on-the-spot levitation, they just carry an appropriate focus on their person at all times. Rings, usually, since they're small and unobtrusive. I really would recommend you focus on something else if you want to hone your shaping skills further. The number of shaping exercises in existence is virtually endless, and the academy library has quite a collection of them. Stone-crumbling and north-finding exercises are extremely useful, for instance, but they're typically not taught to most students due to time constraints."

"Stone-crumbling and north-finding?" asked Zorian.

"Stone-crumbling consists of placing a pebble on your palm and then causing it to disintegrate into dust. That's a flawless result, however, and most people are satisfied if they can get it to fall apart into sand-like grains. It's a useful exercise for those who plan to heavily focus on alteration spells, since the first step when restructuring matter is nearly always to break apart the existing state. North-finding is an exercise for diviners involving the use of a dummy compass to locate magnetic north. Those of sufficient skill don't even need the compass—they simply *feel* where north is at all times."

"Those do sound useful," agreed Zorian. "I'll definitely try to learn those. Still, are you sure you can't help me with my levitation problem?"

Ilsa gave him an annoyed look. "You're still not ready to give up on that? Why are so many talented students so intent on wasting their time on useless pranks?"

Zorian was about to object but then realized she was right. He was essentially trying to prank Kirielle. Ilsa reached out and snatched the book out of the air, causing Zorian to blink in surprise. He hadn't realized he had been levitating it through the entire exchange. He had stopped spinning it and it no longer glowed, but apparently levitating an object over his palm was so easy for him now that he barely even registered doing it. Huh.

His pondering was cut off when Ilsa threw the book on the table. It hit the wood with a deafening boom. She smirked as he flinched and gestured for him to pay attention.

"Like I said, there is no manual for this," she said. "And I've never tried something so foolish, either. So keep in mind that this is all pure speculation on my part, all right?"

Zorian nodded eagerly.

"The first thing I would do if I were in your place would be to stop relying on hands to levitate things," Ilsa said. "Focusing the magic through your hands makes the process easier, yes, but only for a certain category of tasks. In a very real way, levitating an object over your palm isn't true non-structured magic—the palm provides a reference point for the effect, which both guides it and limits it. If you mastered everything in Empatin's book, then you are familiar with fixed position levitation, yes?"

Zorian took a pen from a box full of them next to him and made it float above his palm. After a second, he moved his hand left and right, but the pen remained hovering in the exact same spot in the air, stubbornly refusing to follow the movements of his hand.

"A flawless demonstration," Ilsa praised. "But let me ask you this: does it not appear to you that fixed position levitation achieves its goal in a kind of convoluted, roundabout way? Why do you need an advanced shaping exercise to achieve something a simple levitate object spell can do as a matter of routine?"

Before he could answer, Ilsa reached out and twisted his palm sideways. The pen instantly fell to the table.

"Because using your hand as a reference point limits what you can do with the mana you're shaping," Ilsa said, leaning back. "Even though the pen appeared independent of your hand, it was only an illusion. A pretty baffling one, too. Why would you bother? Essentially, you placed a limiter on the mana flow—making it dependent on the position of your palm—and then tried to subvert that very same limiter to decouple it from your palm."

The book Ilsa had thrown on the table to catch his attention suddenly rose into the air. Ilsa didn't make a single movement, but he knew she was responsible.

Not the least because she was grinning at him.

"Look," she said. "No hands. Of course, this is just about the limit of what I can do without using any sort of gesture to help me out with the shaping. It is a hard skill to learn, but you probably won't need it in its pure form simply for the sake of this project of yours. You just need to reduce the degree to which your shaping depends on your hands and make it more flexible. Twisting your hand sideways shouldn't have caused the pen to plummet down like a rock."

"You just surprised me," Zorian said indignantly. "I don't usually lose control of my mana that easily."

"I stand by my words," Ilsa said with good-natured smile. "You are very impressive for a student, or even a regular mage, but you have a long way to go if you want to join the ranks of the truly great. But anyway, if and when you make some progress on that, you should try levitating some living being smaller than a human. *Much* smaller. Try insects for a start, then mice and so on. All in all, it should only take you…oh, about four years or so."

If she thought he would be discouraged by that, she was sorely mistaken. Not only did he have his doubts about the accuracy of her predicted timetable, he really didn't have anything better to do at the moment.

"I guess I better get started then," was all he said.

Zorian's eyes abruptly shot open as a sharp pain erupted from his stomach. His whole body convulsed, buckling against the object that fell on him, and suddenly he was wide awake, not a trace of drowsiness in his mind.

"Good morning, brother!" an annoyingly cheerful voice sounded right on top of him. "Morning, morning, *MORNING*!!!"

Zorian stared blankly at the ceiling above him, at a loss for words. He had lost track of how many restarts had passed since the short ones had begun, but the number was way more than the fifteen he had originally predicted. And nothing had changed since then—rare was a restart that lasted more than three days, and none of them went on for more than five. Whatever Zach was doing, it was lethally hard and Zach was too much of a stubborn ass to give up any time soon.

"Zorian? Are you all right? Come on, I didn't hit you that hard. Up, up."

Zorian ignored Kirielle who was currently pinching his side with ever increasing vigor. He stared at the ceiling without so much as twitching. The pain was negligible compared to a couple of particularly nasty pain spells Kyron had used on him during one of their resistance training sessions. Thankfully, Kyron never used any of them more than once per restart. Kirielle slapped him a few times and then pretended she was going to punch him in the face. When he didn't react to that, her fist stopped just before it would impact with his face.

"Umm… Zorian?" Kirielle said, actually sounding somewhat concerned. "Seriously, are you okay?"

Slowly, mechanically, Zorian turned his head to meet Kirielle's eyes, keeping his expression as blank as possible. After a few seconds of silent staring, he slowly opened his mouth… and screamed at her. She recoiled at the sudden outburst and let out a little scream of her own as her retreat caused her to tumble off the bed.

He watched for a few moments as Kirielle began to turn red from rage, and then he could no longer restrain himself. He started laughing.

He kept laughing even as Kirielle's little fists started to rain down blows on him.

Zorian's eyes abruptly shot open as a sharp pain erupted from his stomach. His whole body convulsed, buckling against the object that fell on him, and suddenly he was wide awake, not a trace of drowsiness in his mind.

"Good m—"

With an inarticulate yell, Zorian flipped Kirielle on her back and mercilessly started tickling her. Her shrieks reverberated through the entire house until Mother came up to his room and made him stop.

"Good morning, brother! Morning, morning, *MORNING*!!!"

A short silence ensued, broken only by the rustling of Zorian's blankets as Kirielle shifted impatiently on top of them.

"Kiri," he finally said. "I think I'm starting to hate you."

He was exaggerating, of course, but gods was this becoming annoying as hell. Amusingly, Kirielle actually appeared concerned by his proclamation.

"I'm sorry!" she said, hurriedly wriggling herself off the bed. "I was just—"

"Woah, woah, woah," interrupted Zorian, fixing Kirielle with a mock glare. "My little sister apologizing? That doesn't happen. Who are you and what did you do to Kirielle?"

Kirielle's appeared dumbfounded for a moment, but her expression quickly grew stormy as she realized what he was implying.

"Jerk!" she huffed, childishly stomping her foot for emphasis. "I do too apologize! When I'm wrong!"

"When you're backed into a corner," corrected Zorian. "You must want some pretty big favor out of me if you're this desperate to remain in my good graces. What's the story?"

He really did want to know, too. She had given no indication she wanted something from him all the times he had been through this, yet it must be pretty important to her if she was willing to apologize to get it. That didn't make much sense—Kirielle wasn't really a shy girl and had no problems with making her wishes known in the past. For a moment, he was tempted to conclude he had misinterpreted the situation but then Kirielle looked away and started mumbling something unintelligibly.

"What was that?" he prodded.

"Mother wants to talk to you," Kirielle said, still avoiding his eyes.

"Yeah, well, Mother can wait," said Zorian. "I'm not going anywhere until you tell me what you want from me."

She pouted at him for a moment before taking a big breath in preparation.

"Please take me with you to Cyoria!" she said, folding her hands in front of her in a pleading gesture. "I've always wanted to go there and I don't want to go to Koth with mother and…"

Zorian tuned her out, shocked at the revelation. How could he have been so *blind*? He *knew* there was something strange about the ease with which he could convince Mother not to make him take Kirielle with him, but he didn't want to question a favorable outcome and so ignored it. Of course it was easy… she didn't want him to take Kiri either! It was Kirielle who wanted to go. Mother was just making a token attempt so she could tell Kirielle she tried and failed. No wonder Kirielle always seemed so sullen on the way to the train station.

"Zorian? Please?"

He shook his head to clear his thoughts and smiled at Kirielle, who was looking at him with bated breath and hope in her eyes. Now how could he say no to that? That it would ruin Mother's schemes was simply a bonus.

"Of course I'll take you with me," he said.

"Really!?"

"So long as you behave y—"

"Yes! Yes! Yes!" Kirielle yelled happily, jumping around in excitement. He could never understand this boundless energy she had. He was never that exuberant, even as a child. "I knew you'd say yes! Mother said you'd refuse for sure."

Zorian looked away in embarrassment.

"Right," he said lamely. "Shows what she knows. Shall I assume, then, that you already have Mother's permission for this plan?"

"Yeah," Kirielle confirmed. "She said she was fine with it so long as you agreed."

Oh, that diabolical woman… saying no but making him take the blame for it. Looking back at it, the plan was almost magnificent in execution—she even gave him a lecture on proper attire and family honor to put him into a foul mood before springing the question.

With a sigh he put on his glasses and got out of bed. "I'm going to the bathroom."

A second later, his brain caught up with what he had said and he froze. Looking back at Kirielle, he was surprised to see she wasn't trying to race him to his destination and was instead looking at him in confusion.

"What?" she asked.

"Nothing," Zorian said, before walking out of the room. He supposed the only reason she did that in your average restart was to make him confront Mother as soon as possible. A poor move, since it only made him more annoyed at her, but she was only a kid and probably didn't think things through all that well.

It was going to be an interesting restart.

CHAPTER 014

The
Sister Effect

After telling Kirielle to pack her things for the trip, a task she took to with enthusiasm, Zorian filled his room with multicolored orbs of light and went down to the kitchen to face Mother. The lightshow was something he had begun to do in every restart, since he wasn't sure Ilsa would agree to arrange additional tutoring for him unless she stumbled on it. Not that it did him much good, since the short loops he was stuck in ceased too quickly, but he kept doing it regardless. Just in case. Who knew, maybe this particular restart would be the one where Zach stopped dying.

Mother studied him like a hawk as he descended the stairs, looking for any flaw in his appearance she could criticize. He knew from experience that she would find *something* to complain about, but he didn't really care. He was dressed well enough to avoid a protracted lecture about family honor, and that was all that mattered. For a while he had tried to use his time loop given foreknowledge to appear perfect in her eyes, but that hadn't worked on her. Talk about high standards. Maybe she really *was* deliberately trying to annoy him to make sure he'd refuse to take Kirielle with him?

Sitting at the table, he pushed the cold porridge to the side and started eating apples instead, ignoring Mother's annoyance at his spurning of her food. After she realized he wasn't going to say anything, she released a dramatic sigh and launched into one of her long-winded monologues, dancing around the real issue she wanted to talk to him about—the possibility of him taking Kirielle with him to Cyoria.

"Now that I think about it," Mother said, finally deciding to get to the point, "I never told you I'm going to Koth with your father to visit Daimen, did I?"

"You want me to take Kiri with me to Cyoria," Zorian pretended to guess.

"I… what?" She blinked, surprised for a second. Then she shook her head slightly and sighed. "She told you."

"Yup," Zorian confirmed.

"So much for picking the right moment like we agreed upon," Mother said. "I guess I should go and comfort her."

"Why would she need comforting?" Zorian asked. "I said yes. She was ecstatic. She's in her room right now, packing her things."

Mother looked at him as though he had suddenly started reciting classical poetry. Zorian didn't know whether to feel guilty or annoyed. Was it really *that* weird for him to agree to this? Before he had enrolled in the academy, he had spent more time with the little imp than anyone else in the family, Mother included. He was more of a parent to Kirielle than she and Father ever were! Really, if Kirielle had just told him she wanted to go herself instead of having Mother speak for her, he probably would have agreed to it—after some argument—even before the time loop had begun.

Annoyed. He was definitely feeling annoyed with her. He leveled a challenging glare at Mother, daring her to say something.

"What?" he snapped after a few seconds of mutual staring.

"Nothing," she said, schooling her expression into something unreadable. "I'm just surprised, that's all. I'm glad you're finally starting to think about someone other than yourself. Have you thought about housing?"

"I have," confirmed Zorian. "It depends on whether I'll have to pay for the arrangements from my own pocket or if you'll give me extra money for rent."

"Now you're just being insulting," his mother snapped. "Of course we'll give you rent money. When have we ever made you pay for essential living expenses by yourself? How much do you need?"

As if her own remark about him finally thinking about someone other than himself wasn't just as insulting. He was just responding in kind. But yes, Zorian grudgingly admitted she was right—his parents had many flaws, but they would never let him go hungry or homeless unless they were completely bankrupt themselves. He was the disfavored son, but a son nonetheless. They spent the next several minutes discussing living expenses in Cyoria, arguing back and forth about how much money he would need to rent a suitable place and feed Kirielle. He, of course, favored larger sums, and he knew enough about Cyoria's economy to give weight to his arguments. Mother made no secret about her surprise at his knowledge of rent prices in various districts of Cyoria—apparently she was under the impression such 'down to earth' knowledge didn't interest him. Zorian decided not to explain that he was keeping track of rent prices so he could move away from home at a moment's notice and instead tried to change the subject. He was not very effective in that regard—Mother was stubbornly fixated on that little factoid—but Ilsa's arrival saved him from her interrogation. Mother quickly excused herself, saying she was going to help Kirielle pack, but Zorian still led Ilsa back to his room when she asked him where they could have some privacy. He had to show her all those lights he 'accidentally' forgot to dispel, after all.

At first the talk proceeded in a fairly standard fashion, but the usual routine he was shattered when they reached the topic of living arrangements.

"According to this," began Ilsa, momentarily shaking a piece of paper she was holding, "you lived in academy housing for the past two years. I assume you intend to do the same this year, too?"

"Err, actually, no," answered Zorian. "I'm taking my younger sister with me this year, so I can't do that. Unless the academy makes allowances for such things?"

"It doesn't," Ilsa said.

"I figured," Zorian said, not really surprised by that. "We'll just stay in a hotel for a few days until I find a place to rent."

Ilsa gave him a strange look that Zorian had trouble deciphering.

"You don't have a place reserved already?" she asked.

"No," Zorian said. "The decision was a bit abrupt, so I didn't have any time to make proper preparations. Why?"

"I may have a solution for you in regards to that," Ilsa said, straightening her posture into a slightly more serious stance.

"You mean you know a place I could rent?" Zorian asked. Ilsa nodded. "That's… fortunate, I guess. What do you have in mind?"

"First of all, I want to emphasize that what I'm about to say has nothing to do with the Cyoria Royal Academy of Magical Arts," Ilsa cautioned. "This is something strictly between the two of us, understand?"

"Okay," said Zorian cautiously. He was getting slightly concerned now, but he sensed no deception or ill intent from Ilsa. He waited to hear what she was offering.

"A friend of mine is renting rooms at very reasonable rates…," Ilsa began.

After several minutes of questioning and reading between the lines, Zorian decided he would give Ilsa's friend a chance. Her 'reasonable rates' were a tad expensive, but it was manageable. Ilsa also said her friend loved children and would be all too happy to keep track of Kirielle while he was at class, which would be worth every piece he paid for the place—if actually true.

After that, the topic shifted to his choice of mentor (or rather, the fact that he wasn't allowed to choose one) and his choice of electives. Since he had pretty much tried out every elective he was even remotely interested in by now, his choices had become pretty constant at this point: botany, astronomy, and human anatomy. He chose them solely because he knew for a fact that the teachers of those particular subjects didn't care in the slightest if he chose not to come to class and because Akoja wouldn't choose any of them as *her* electives—and thus wasn't aware he was skipping them.

The moment Ilsa left, Kirielle came barreling down the stairs like a herd of elephants, ignoring Mother's admonishments about running inside the house. No doubt she had finished packing a while ago and had been simply waiting for Ilsa to leave so she could come out.

"I'm ready!" she grinned happily.

"You have everything packed?" asked Zorian.

"Yup!"

"What about my books?" asked Zorian.

"Why would I pack your books?" she scowled. "You can do that yourself, lazy ass!"

"Well, you did take them from my room and hide them under your bed," Zorian remarked.

"Oh!" Her eyes widened in understanding. "*Those* books! Umm… I guess I kind of forgot to give those back to you. I'll put them back in your room, okay?"

"What are you two talking about?" Mother asked as she approached from the kitchen.

"Nothing!" Kirielle said in a slightly panicky voice, whirring quickly to face Mother. "I just forgot something, that's all! I'll be right back!"

She quickly bolted up the stairs, ignoring Mother's repeated admonishment about not running in the house. Zorian looked at her retreating form with narrowed eyes. Why was Kirielle so frightened about Mother finding out she had been taking books out of his room? It was hardly the first time she had helped herself to his things, and Mother had never cared before. It was significant somehow, he just knew it.

He was starting to think he didn't know Kirielle half as well as he thought he did.

"I'm bored."

Zorian opened his eyes and glared across the train compartment at his little sister. He couldn't close his eyes for more than a minute without her saying something or kicking him in the knees with her pointy little shoes. And he had thought the station announcer was annoying.

"I can tell," he said, rolling his eyes. "What do you want *me* to do about it?"

"Play a game with me?" she said hopefully.

"Haven't we done enough of that already?" he sighed. "There are only so many times I can beat you at hangman before it gets boring."

"You were cheating!" she protested. "Asphyxiation isn't even a real word!"

"What!? Of course it is!" he shot back. "You're just—"

"Liar!" she interrupted.

"Whatever," Zorian scoffed. "It's not like that was the only game I won."

"So you admit you cheated in that one!" she concluded triumphantly.

Zorian opened his mouth to retort before he closed it again.

"Why am I arguing about this?" he asked out loud, though it was directed more towards himself than Kiri.

The sharp crackling sound that always heralded the voice of the station announcer stopped any further argument they may have had.

"Now stopping in Korsa," a disembodied voice echoed. A crackling sound again. "I repeat, now stopping in Korsa. Thank you."

"Oh, thank the gods," Zorian mumbled. Not only did arriving in Korsa mean three quarters of the journey was over, it also meant someone was going to join them in their compartment, thus giving Kirielle someone else to annoy.

Someone other than Ibery, though—he had decided to purposely avoid his usual compartment to ensure she and Kiri would never meet. He had a suspicion a conversation between them wouldn't end well. Kiri didn't like Fortov any more than Zorian did, and she was a lot less tactful about it.

"So many people," Kiri remarked, watching the throng at the train station through the window. "Are they all students like you?"

"Most of them, yeah," Zorian said. "Though not all of them go to the same school as I do. There is more than one academy in Cyoria."

"I thought mages were rarer than this," she said. "Mom says you need to be really smart to be one. Do you think I could be a mage too one day?"

"Sure," he said, shrugging

"Really?" she asked, a mixture of excitement and suspicion radiating from her voice and posture. Zorian supposed she half-expected him to use his agreement as a set up for a mean-spirited joke or something along those lines.

"Yes," he confirmed. "I don't see why you couldn't. You seem to be doing well enough in school from what I heard, so I don't see why your intelligence would be a problem. And it's not like our parents can't afford to send you somewhere, even if it isn't Cyoria."

Kirielle didn't answer, choosing instead to look through the window in silence and pointedly refusing to look him in the eye. He was just about to ask her what was wrong when the door to the compartment slid open, distracting him.

"Byrn Ivarin," the boy introduced himself. "Can I sit here?"

Zorian waved him in without a word. This was the boy who had inspired him to seek employment in the library in the first place. Byrn had been quite talkative then, so he would be a perfect traveling companion for Kiri. Even if he was disinclined to talk to someone so young, he doubted Kirielle would let him ignore her, and he seemed too polite to just plain snub her to her face. Hopefully he would keep Kirielle busy for the rest of the journey.

"I'm Kirielle Kazinski," his sister promptly introduced herself, "and that's my brother Zorian. Are you a student like Zorian? Can you do magic?"

"Err, well… yes," Byrn said, torn between desire to ask about the surname and a desire to be polite and answer Kirielle's question. Politeness won in the end. "I'm only a first-year, though, so it's not like I have anything to brag about."

Sadly for Byrn, he would have to wait for a while before he could ask about the surname—Kirielle was on a roll and promptly assaulted the poor kid with every question imaginable. Zorian soon found out that Byrn was an only child of two first generation mages from Korsa and that his family had pretty high expectations of him. Byrn was as excited to be away from his overbearing parents as he was about learning magic. That, at least, was something Zorian could empathize with.

"Three older brothers, huh?" Byrn laughed. "Poor you. Though… I kind of wish I had a few older brothers myself. My parents could have someone else to focus on every once in a while."

"I know what you mean," Kirielle said. "Ever since Zorian started going to the academy, Mother has no one but me to pay attention to. It sucks."

Zorian flinched in sympathy. He hadn't thought of that, but it shed a great deal of light on Kirielle's behavior over the past two years. Without Zorian there to act like a lightning rod for their mother's criticism, Kirielle's time at home probably took a sharp turn for the worse in his absence. A part of him was pleased that the little imp was forced to experience some of what he went through in his daily interactions with their family, but he mostly thought she didn't deserve something like that.

"So, I've been meaning to ask," said Byrn. "Your last name is pretty distinctive. Not that many Kazinskis walking around. Are you related to Daimen Kazinski by any chance?"

"He's our brother," Kirielle said.

"Really?" asked Byrn excitedly. "You know, I haven't heard anything about him in a while. What is he up to currently?"

"He's in Koth," Kirielle said. "I think he found something in the jungle but… I don't know. I don't really talk to him all that often. He's always traveling. You're more likely to find out about him in the newspapers than by talking to me. Zorian knows him better than I do."

Zorian shot Kirielle a quick glare for putting him on the spot like that—and on the topic of Daimen, no less! The little imp just stuck her tongue out at him. Hmph

"Daimen and I don't get along," Zorian said bluntly. "There is not much I can tell you about him that Kiri hasn't already."

"Oh," Byrn said, obviously disappointed. He let out a slightly strained laugh, trying to dispel the awkward atmosphere that had descended on the compartment. "And here I thought I would get some inside stories about one of my heroes. Though I suppose in a way I did, didn't I? It's a bit sad that he doesn't have time for his family."

"Hmm," hummed Zorian noncommittally.

The rest of the journey was uneventful except that Byrn decided to tag along with them for a while after they disembarked. Both Byrn and Kirielle were awed—and more than a little intimidated—by the sheer size and activity of Cyoria's train station, and Zorian decided to be nice and give them a brief tour around the place. The tour turned out to be not as brief as he had intended, however, because Kirielle insisted on browsing the stores. He tried to tell her that every shop in and around the train station sold massively overpriced merchandise (because they could, thanks to their favorable location) and that he wouldn't be buying her anything, but that didn't deter her in the slightest. She was 'just looking'. Byrn, for some unfathomable reason, sided with Kiri. He liked browsing stores, too, apparently. Madness.

Since they had wasted so much time, however, the rain had already started falling by the time they were ready to depart. Byrn had no umbrella, of course, and even if he had, the amount of luggage he carried would make a trek through the rain a problematic endeavor. Zorian reluctantly offered to help—the boy looked so miserable at this sudden turn of events that Zorian didn't have the heart to just walk away.

Besides, Kirielle wouldn't let him do that, and he didn't want to make a scene by dragging her away so they could be on their way.

"I really appreciate this, you know?" Byrn said, curiously brushing his fingers against the dome of the rain barrier spell surrounding them.

"I don't know what I would have done if it weren't for you. It doesn't seem like the rain is going to stop any time soon."

"For the last time, it's fine," Zorian said, trying not to sigh. "Really, I live to help."

Byrn covertly mouthed 'thank you' to Kirielle, who was unabashedly playing with the rain barrier by sticking her arms and legs outside the protective dome and then drawing them back in. She gave him a thumbs up in return. Apparently the boy knew whom to thank for his good fortune. Hmph. If he ran out of mana halfway to their new home after getting Byrn to the academy, it would be on her head. Rain barrier was quite draining, and he had to enlarge it so it would cover all three of them plus the floating disk that carried their combined luggage.

"This spell is awesome," Kirielle declared. "How hard is it? Do you think you could teach me how to cast this one? I won't tell anyone!"

"Oh, please," Zorian snorted. "You can't even *feel* your mana, much less shape it. It's not a question of legality, it's a question of skill. It would take months if you're some kind of genius, a year or two otherwise. Just wait until you enroll in a magic school yourself, okay?"

Kirielle immediately deflated.

In the end they managed to deposit Byrn inside the safety of the academy's own rain wards without issues before going their own way. In fact, they nearly made it to their destination before Zorian ran out of mana, causing the rain barrier to wink out of existence.

Emphasis on nearly. He hoped Ilsa's friend wasn't sensitive about people dripping on her floors.

"You should have waited! Honestly, what possessed you to walk around in this horrid weather? Kids these days think they're invincible…"

Zorian rolled his eyes at his host's scolding, not hiding his reaction in the slightest since she was busy rummaging through a set of drawers and wasn't really facing him. The rain would continue throughout the entire night—though he couldn't exactly tell her how he knew that—so waiting it out hadn't been an option. Besides, they would have made it just fine if Kirielle hadn't been so stubborn about getting Byrn to the academy grounds first. And a brief run through the rain wasn't exactly traumatic. So really, why was she getting so worked up about it?

His thoughts were interrupted by a towel hitting him in the face.

"There. You can use that to dry your hair," she said. "I'll go see if your sister needs any help. You just better hope she doesn't get sick from this, you hear?"

"She's not a sugar cube," Zorian mumbled. "She's not going to fall apart just because she got a little wet."

Either he had said it too softly for her to hear or she decided to ignore him, but either way she just walked past him and left the room. Unconcerned, Zorian sat down on a nearby chair to study the place they would call home.

Their landlord, one Imaya Kuroshka, was a lively middle-aged woman who quickly ushered them in when she found them, soaking wet, on her doorstep. She hadn't even asked for their identities before she had done that—it had required an introduction by Zorian before she realized they actually had a reason to knock on her door beyond getting out of the rain. Zorian was tempted to deliver his own scolding to the woman about naiveté and letting strangers into the house, but unlike *some* people, *he* chose not to be difficult. She seemed nice enough, all things considered. At the very least she didn't appear to be one of those landlords who tried to bleed their tenants of everything they could part with, though it was hard to be sure this soon.

He was irked, though, that Imaya seemed to consider them living at her place a done deal already. He had only agreed to check the place out, nothing more!

Once Imaya returned with Kirielle—who looked no worse for the rain—they started talking. Zorian had to steer the conversation back to the topic of their stay every once in a while, since both Imaya and Kirielle were content to let the conversation wander around if he let them. He also had to kick Kirielle a few times under the table to get her to shut up—Ilsa had told him never to broach the topic of marriage and husbands in front of Imaya for... some unspecified reason. Zorian liked it when people respected his privacy, so he was content to do the same for Imaya. He had warned Kirielle to abide by the rule as well, but her tendency to babble steered her into dangerous territory more than once.

Their arrangement was not exactly to his liking, in all honesty. Imaya's house clearly hadn't been designed for renting rooms—it was an average, if large, family home that had a bunch of empty bedrooms on the second floor. Zorian and Kirielle would be using one of them, and they would be sharing the rest of the house facilities with Imaya and two other tenants who were scheduled to arrive in the next few days. That was a lot less privacy than he was comfortable with. Not to mention that their room only had one bed, meaning he and Kirielle would have to share. He knew for a fact that Kirielle was a restless sleeper and a cover hog, so he was less than pleased. Thankfully, they were the only tenants at the moment, so Imaya allowed him to claim an additional room for himself at no extra charge, with the stipulation that he move back in with Kirielle when she found a proper tenant for it.

Zorian decided to quietly look into other places to rent tomorrow. Just in case.

Despite his novel living arrangements and Kirielle's presence, the next few days were fairly standard. He applied for the job at the library. He went to talk to Ilsa about advanced instruction and chose divination as a discipline he was interested in. He practiced various shaping exercises whenever he had some free time, concentrating mostly on the north-finding one since that exercise was supposed to help with divinations. Taiven tracked him down, despite his change of residence, and Zorian notified her about the 'rumors' about giant spiders capable of mind magic running around in the sewers to make sure she'd survive the encounter. Despite his misgivings, he decided not to leave Imaya's place since the woman did a masterful job of keeping Kirielle happy and off his back. For her part, Kirielle was remarkably well behaved. She spent a lot of her time drawing things. He didn't even know she liked to draw. She never did it at home as far as he knew. Maybe the trip had inspired her to take up a new hobby?

In any case, once those first couple days had passed, everything just… went off the rails. For one thing, the restart hadn't ended at that point and instead just kept going, which was noteworthy by itself. More importantly, however, he was once again asked by Ilsa to greet Kael and his daughter at Cyoria's main train station… only to find out that Kael had also rented a room at Imaya's place. For pretty much the same reason that he had, too—Ilsa had recommended the place.

So now he was living in the same house with his little sister, a teenage morlock and his daughter, and a landlord who didn't really act like a landlord. He was finally going to meet his divination instructor, Xvim would be throwing marbles at him again come next Friday, Ilsa apparently visited her friend's house on a regular basis, and Imaya invited Taiven to eat with them the following Sunday while she was trying to talk Zorian into following her into the sewers. Clearly things were going to be quite different this time around.

"I still feel like I'm taking advantage of you," Kael said, pouring a fistful of blue powder into a transparent glass container.

"And I still can't imagine why," Zorian said, not taking his eyes off the tiny blue mushrooms he was currently grinding into more powder.

"I stock your lab with ingredients, and you let me be your assistant while you do your work. You get to save a little money on reagents and I get some practical alchemical experience. What on earth is predatorial about that? Here."

He thrust the powdered mushrooms to the white-haired boy, who sighed in defeat and went back to work. Zorian took the time to look around the workshop without being too blatant about it.

Kael's workshop was pretty amazing considering it was really just a basement that Imaya had donated to the boy so he could convert it to his purposes. Kael had set it up immediately after his arrival, and Imaya had been surprisingly unconcerned about a mere academy student working with dangerous magical concoctions right under her home.

"Ilsa assured me Kael knows what he's doing," she had said when Zorian had tentatively broached the subject. Well, he probably did, but still.

As for equipment in the lab, it was on loan from the academy. According to Kael, it was rather outdated, but the morlock couldn't afford to be picky and was lucky to get anything at all.

"I just don't think the price of restocking my workshop is worth whatever experience you're going to get," Kael said while pouring boiling water into the powder-filled container and adding some weird little black balls that Zorian didn't recognize. "In fact, considering how good you are at this, I should probably be paying *you* for the help."

"Don't worry about it," Zorian repeated, hoping this time it would stick. He couldn't exactly tell the boy that his savings account would spontaneously refill when the loop restarted, so it was hard to explain why money wasn't too important for him.

Overall, his interaction with Kael was a lot friendlier this time around. Grudgingly, he had to admit Kirielle had a lot to do with it—she hit it off with Kana pretty quickly, despite the other girl being practically a baby, which seemed to put Kael at ease with both of them. After that, the two of them discovered they got along pretty well, and Zorian decided to help the morlock with his alchemy and learn something at the same time.

"This whole situation is terribly strange," Kael said after a minute of silence. "Not in a bad way, though. Kana is the happiest I have seen her in a while. I really am grateful to your sister for everything she has done for her, by the way."

"To be honest, I'm not sure how long it's going to last," Zorian admitted. "For now, she finds Kana cute and probably finds it pleasing to have someone pay such rapt attention to her. She tends to get bored really quickly, though. And in any case, she's only in Cyoria temporarily while my family is off visiting my brother in Koth."

"Well, that's too bad," Kael sighed. Then he grinned at Zorian. "Though I suppose you'll be relieved when she finally leaves."

"Well, who knows," Zorian said. "We'll see how things go. She's not so bad right now, so maybe she won't be a total pest like she usually is. I'm hoping some of your daughter's quieter personality will rub off on her in time."

"Oh, that would be such a pity," Kael said. "It would be a shame for such a lively girl to lose her spark of life. I wish Kana had some of that boundless enthusiasm."

"Shall we trade, then?" offered Zorian.

"No," Kael said, laughing. "Fetch me the water celery, please, and be quiet for a while. I need to concentrate on this part."

And so Zorian stood in silence, watched Kael work, and thought about what the rest of the month would bring.

CHAPTER 015

Busy Friday

Z orian felt the mana-charged marble approaching him, but didn't move. He couldn't tell whether it was aimed to the left or to the right, but he knew it wasn't aimed at his forehead. He could always tell when it was. Always. He wasn't sure how he could tell that with absolute certainty when he could not actually pinpoint where the marble was going, but he was grateful for it. He just wished he could replicate that success for the exercise in general.

The marble whizzed past him.

"Left," he tried.

"Wrong," Xvim said in a disinterested tone. "Again."

Another marble was thrown towards him. This one wasn't aimed at his forehead either. Not that surprising, really—Xvim had stopped doing that when he realized Zorian could identify those with perfect accuracy. It wouldn't do to give Zorian free points, after all.

"Right," he said.

"Wrong," Xvim immediately responded. "Again."

Zorian frowned behind the blindfold. Did it just seem that way or was he actually getting *worse* at this as time went by? Something was very wrong here. At the beginning of the session, he had been correct about half the time, but now he was constantly getting it wrong. He'd have thought he'd guess correctly every once in a while, through statistical inevitability if nothing else. There were only two possibilities!

That's why, when Xvim threw the next marble, Zorian quickly wrenched the blindfold off to see what the deal was.

The marble flew straight over his head.

That son of a bitch!

"I didn't say you could take the blindfold off," Xvim calmly said, as if Zorian hadn't just caught him red-handed.

"That's cheating!" Zorian protested, completely ignoring Xvim's remark. "Of course I couldn't guess correctly if you're not even going to abide by your own rules!"

"You're not supposed to guess, Mister Kazinski," Xvim said unapologetically. "You're supposed to *sense*."

"I *was* sensing," Zorian ground out.

"If you were, you would have realized what was happening far sooner, and you would not have needed to take off the blindfold to identify the problem," Xvim said. "Now stop wasting your time and put the blindfold back on so we can continue."

Zorian cursed Xvim mentally but did as he was told. As much as he hated to admit it, there was a lot of truth in Xvim's words. He had been mostly guessing over which shoulder the marbles were going, relying on gut instinct instead of a clear perception of its location and trajectory. But it was hardly his fault he couldn't reliably track a fast-moving object through its faint mana emissions—according to books, that was a highly advanced skill that took years to master! Honestly, asking a student to master this sort of thing in their third year was completely unreasonable. But completely in character for Xvim, he supposed. At least he no longer had to worry about being hit in the head anymore.

The rest of the session was typical, which is to say, repetitive and boring. Then again, what part of school wasn't boring at this point? He had been stuck in the time loop for little over a year now, and feigning attention during classes was starting to get hard. He was tempted to take a page out of Zach's book and go wander somewhere else for a few restarts, but he couldn't. For one thing, it would be irresponsible to waste time like that when he could be working on skills he would need to get to the bottom of this. For another, he didn't want to attract attention to himself. The memory of their interaction was probably still fresh in Zach's mind, and there was a possible third party to consider. Completely blowing off classes would be completely out of character for him and would raise a lot of eyebrows. He was already playing it close by taking Kirielle with him and skipping almost a quarter of his classes to do his own thing, but those changes were at least easily explainable. If his current course of action didn't produce results, he'd have to drop the masquerade to preserve his sanity, but that wasn't an immediate concern. He had more pressing problems to worry about, so he put off that issue for when and if it became relevant.

His session with Xvim done, he went to the library to report to Kirithishli. Normally he didn't go to work on Fridays, since dealing with Xvim tended to kill his mood very fast, but he seemed to have survived the session in better spirits than expected. He was getting used to the irritating man's antics, it seemed.

"Zorian!" Kirithishli greeted. "Good timing! We just got a new shipment today and Ibery had to go home early."

"Uh, okay," Zorian said slowly. He was about to ask what kind of shipment, but then he decided it was a stupid question. It was a shipment of books, of course. "What do you want me to do?"

"Just unpack the books out of their boxes and separate them into rough categories," answered Kirithishli, pointing in the direction of a small mountain of boxes. "I'll inspect them in more detail later to see what to do with them."

"You don't know what to do with them?" asked Zorian, baffled. "Why did you order them, then?"

"I didn't," Kirithishli said, shaking her head. "Someone donated their personal library to the academy. It happens from time to time. Sometimes people leave their books to us in their wills or people who inherit them don't have a use for them and can't sell them. A lot of old books are only useful as historical curiosities and sometimes not even that. Most of the books in these boxes will be disposed of, to be honest."

"Oh?" asked Zorian while opening one of the boxes and pulling out one of the books stacked inside of it. It was a manual on the cultivation of plums. The publisher information indicated it was twenty years old. "I'm surprised by that. I distinctly remember you saying that librarians should preserve everything they can rather than pick and choose what they think is 'good' or 'useful'."

"Oh, shut up," Kirithishli grouched, taking a half-hearted swipe at him that he dodged. "It's an ideal to be followed, not an unbreakable law. There is only so much space in the library, no matter how big it appears. And besides, most of these books are duplicates of ones we already have. Stop being a wiseass and get to work."

Zorian threw himself into the task, unpacking box after box. Kirithishli gave him a massive reference book of the most common volumes they received in these sorts of deliveries and told him to use it to separate the obvious duplicates from the rest. Using the reference manually to find the matches would be a total nightmare of course, especially since the letters were in a really tiny print in order to cram as many words as possible on every page, but Zorian knew it was designed with something else in mind. One of the spells he had learned from Ibery in the previous restarts involved making a list of terms you wanted to search for and then connecting the list via divination spell to a target book. It sounded a little pointless to him back then, but now he realized it was made with precisely this sort of thing in mind. And the huge, densely-packed reference book was probably made with the spell in mind, in turn.

Nearly two hours and twenty hastily scribbled lists later, he had separated the duplicates from the rest of the books and was in the process of leafing through one of the spellbooks he had found in the boxes when Kirithishli finally returned from wherever she had disappeared after giving him his assignment. His rapid progress surprised her, seeing how she had no idea he was so well-versed in library magic, and she apparently also found it a little disappointing.

"You're no fun," she sighed dramatically. "I wanted to show you that trick when I came back, after you spent two hours painstakingly searching for matches in that monster of a book. The expression on your face would have been priceless."

Zorian simply raised an eyebrow at her, but otherwise stayed silent. Kirithishli showed her maturity by sticking her tongue at him like a five-year-old, before eyeing the book he was leafing through.

"Found something interesting?" she asked.

"Not really," Zorian said, snapping the book shut. There was nothing particularly interesting in it anyway. "I sort of hoped I would find a book on powerful ancient magic and the like, but no such luck."

Kirithishli laughed. "Even if you did find something like that, it would do you little good. Contrary to what various adventure novels may have led you to believe, ancient magic is almost always inferior to what we have available now. Lost spells are usually lost for a good reason—generally for being too impractical, requiring ingredients or conditions that no longer exist, or because they would be considered massively unethical in the modern age. For example, you'd be hard pressed to find participants for orgy ritual magic these days, and Heruan volcanic spells relied on conditions present in one particular volcano that hasn't been active for more than two hundred years."

Zorian blinked. "Oh. Well, that's disappointing."

"Quite," Kirithishli agreed. "And even when those spells can be cast without issue, they tend to be infuriatingly inflexible and take a long time to cast. Mages of old didn't have the sort of shaping skills modern mages have, so they compensated by making their spells long and hyperspecialized. There were hundreds of color-changing spells, for instance, but most of them differed only in which color the spell changed the affected objects into. It has been a persistent trend in modern times to generalize spells, since better training methods allow modern mages to make up for the spells' lack of precision with the sheer control they have over their magic."

"Making a lot of old spells obsolete to a properly trained mage," finished Zorian. He had always known that most history books presented a heavily idealized image of their ancestors—their portrayal of the desertification of northern Miasina (he refused to call it Cataclysm, as if it was some natural occurrence beyond Ikosian control) and subsequent exodus to Altazia was proof enough that they were given a sugar-coated version of history—but he hadn't realized Ikosians were also crappy mages in addition to being shortsighted assholes. "And you have to be one if you plan to get certified," he went on. "You know, I've always wondered why so many really easy spells are classified as first circle ones. I thought it might be a deliberate policy by the guild to encourage certification, but I guess a lot of those were not nearly as trivial when they were first rated."

"That, but you also have to consider things from the perspective of the spell's maker," Kirithishli said. "It's a lot more prestigious and profitable to make a first circle spell than a zero circle one. So they almost never classify a spell as anything less than first circle, and the guild allows them to get away with it, probably for the very reason you stated. A determined person could probably get the guild to lower the classification on a lot of those spells, but you'd make a lot of enemies, especially among the spell crafter interest groups. It would be a thankless task, and you'd constantly have to watch out for people trying to roll back the changes."

Zorian digested this information in silence. He had no intention of involving himself in such high-level politics, of course, either in the time loop or outside of it. If there was one thing his parents had driven into his skull with their endless sermons, it was that his strengths did not lie in that area. Granted, that probably wasn't what those sermons had been designed to do, but that wasn't his problem. Still, things like this were useful to know. He'd have to prod Kirithishli for more stories in the future.

When Kirithishli told him to go home, Zorian was all too happy to oblige her. It had been a long (and boring) day, what with the regular classes, his session with Xvim, and working in the library, and all he really wanted was to go back to Imaya's place and relax. Sadly, it was not to be, because the moment he stepped out of the library, he was accosted by a shady looking man that had been waiting for him just outside the entrance.

Well, maybe accosted was a too strong a word—technically, the man in question was just leaning on a pillar next to the entrance, not blocking his path or even speaking to him. Nonetheless, the moment the man glanced up and their eyes met, Zorian knew the man had been waiting for him, and him alone. Middle-aged, dressed in a cheap, rumpled suit and unshaven, he almost looked like one of Cyoria's many homeless people, but there was a confidence in his posture that didn't fit that image.

Zorian halted in his tracks instantly, and an uneasy silence descended on the scene as they both analyzed one another. Zorian had no idea who the man was or what he wanted to do with him, but he wasn't inclined to be charitable. He had not forgotten the way he was assassinated in one of the initial restarts and had no wish to repeat the experience.

"Zorian Kazinski?" the man finally asked.

"That's me," confirmed Zorian. He didn't think lying would work, and it would be better to have a confrontation close to the library than to get ambushed in an empty street on the way home.

"Detective Haslush Ikzeteri, Cyoria's police department," the man said. "Ilsa sent me to be your divination instructor."

Zorian didn't know what to say. Ilsa picked a *detective* as his instructor? So much for the idea of talking his new divination instructor into teaching him the restricted divination skills he needed to actually investigate this time loop business. Why did it have to be law enforcement, of all things?

"That's great," Zorian said flatly. "I was wondering when Ilsa would find someone."

If his lack of enthusiasm bothered the man any, he didn't show it. The detective simply turned and walked away, gesturing for Zorian to follow after him.

"Come on, kid, let's go find a tavern to sit in," he said, shoving his hands into the pockets of his jacket.

Oh yes, a tavern—the perfect learning environment. Gods, not only was the man a detective, he was unprofessional as well. His unkempt appearance sort of suggested it right from the start, but Zorian always tried to not judge too harshly on appearances alone—too many people did it to him, and he always found it very annoying.

His thoughts must have been more visible in his demeanor than he thought they were, because the man quickly started to justify himself.

"Come now, don't look at me like that," the man said. "It's not like we'll be doing anything too serious today. It's been a long day for both of us, I think—you're tired, I'm tired, we don't know each other, and we'll accomplish nothing if we just jump straight into lessons right away. Hell, maybe we'll decide we don't like each other and call this whole thing off. So today, we're just going to share a drink and talk."

Okay, so maybe Haslush was smarter and more capable than Zorian gave him credit for. He had to stop judging people so quickly. Though…

"I don't drink alcohol," Zorian warned.

Haslush gave him a curious look. "Religious taboo?"

Zorian shook his head. He had never been very religious—the gods had been silent for centuries, and as far as Zorian was concerned that meant they either killed each other off or abandoned their creations to fend for themselves. Hell, listening to some of the stories from the age of gods, he couldn't help but think humanity was better off without them. They had a disturbing tendency to throw around plagues and curse entire cities on the flimsiest of pretexts. He didn't think it was a coincidence that humanity had only started to advance, both socially and technologically, *after* the gods had fallen silent.

"Bad experiences," he simply said, not wanting to discuss that topic any further.

"Ah," Haslush said, content with his answer. "That's okay, you can order some fruit juice or something. Hell, I can even show you a spell I use when I'm on duty but don't want to offend people by refusing an offered drink."

Now that sounded useful! Zorian looked at Haslush and the man correctly interpreted that as permission to go on.

"It's a neat little alteration spell that converts alcohol into sugar," Haslush said, raising his right hand to show a plain metal ring on his middle finger. "I have it imprinted into this ring so I don't have to visibly cast it—visibly casting a spell on your drink is often resented even more than outright refusing it, believe it or not. The moment I touch the glass the deed is done."

"Convenient," Zorian said appreciatively. That spell would have saved him so much trouble over the years. "But I thought organic matter cannot be restructured through alteration spells?"

"Usually not, but that's because most of them are impossibly complex and poorly understood, not because organic compounds are somehow impossible to replicate," Haslush said. He took note of each tavern sign they passed, apparently not merely looking for the closest one. "Both ethanol and glucose are fairly simple molecules and quite well understood, so there is no difficulty in converting one into the other." He suddenly stopped in front of a nearby sign, studying it for a moment before turning to face Zorian again. "I think this is a nice place. What do you think?"

Zorian's experiences with taverns were very limited and generally unpleasant, so he simply gestured for Haslush to go in before following.

It wasn't as bad as Zorian had feared: the interior of the tavern was dark and the air was a bit stale, but the tables were clean and the noise was manageable. Haslush picked a table in the corner and cast a long, complicated spell on it after they both ordered a drink. Probably a privacy ward of some kind.

Zorian expected the man to start interrogating him the moment the spell snapped into place, but it didn't play out like that. If Haslush was interrogating him, he was doing it too subtly for Zorian to notice. Hell, the man didn't even ask him about Daimen, which was always nice. Gradually, Zorian began to relax and started asking questions of his own. Questions like 'how come a detective has time and inclination to tutor a third year student in divination magic?'

"Hah." Haslush snorted into his drink. "A good question. Usually something like this would be the last thing on my mind, but yesterday my commander dumped a really silly case on my lap. Apparently there is a rumor circulating around the city about mentalist spiders lurking in the sewers, and I'm supposed to check it out." He rolled his eyes with a sigh. "Mentalist spiders, honestly...," he mumbled.

Zorian struggled not to let his surprise show and somehow succeeded—largely because Haslush was paying more attention to his drink than to him at the moment. He had started a rumor without even realizing it? He supposed he shouldn't be surprised. This restart, he had told Taiven about the spiders right in front of Imaya and his sister—between Taiven and those two, they probably blathered about it to a dozen people *at least*.

"Anyway, after work I went to meet with my good friend Ilsa so we could complain about our problems to each other over a drink or two. She told me she was having difficulty finding a divination tutor for a student. And at that point I realized I had the perfect solution for my problem. I could pawn off the case to some other poor schmuck, help a friend in need, and settle a long-standing argument between me and my commander in one fell swoop. See, a couple of years ago the bureaucrats in Eldemar decided to launch an initiative designed to entice more mages into careers in law enforcement. Only, instead of doing something concrete to attract new talent, they asked mages already working inside the police force to go introduce the profession to other mages on their own initiative."

"Ah," said Zorian. "So, you're supposed to do things like this anyway?"

"Yeah, but I've been kind of slacking off in that regard and my commander is constantly nagging me about missing my quota. Can you blame me though? We get paid extra for doing it, but it's a pittance considering the hassle."

"You know better than I do," Zorian said, shrugging. "How does, err, introducing me to the profession get you off the spider case, though?"

"I don't have time to do both," Haslush said. He frowned for a second and then shook his head, as if to clear it. "Yup. That's my story and I'm sticking to it."

The discussion petered out after that, and Haslush promised to meet him again after the weekend. Zorian was lost in thought as he went back to Imaya's house, wondering whether the spider investigation would produce any worthwhile results. Probably not, considering Haslush's dismissive reaction to it, but still. He'd have to prod the man for additional details after a week or so.

Zorian tapped his foot impatiently as he waited for Imaya to open the door. He had the key to the front door, but that was no help—Imaya had an annoying habit of leaving the key in the lock, and today was no exception. He couldn't enter without her help.

She probably liked it that way.

The sound of the lock turning brought his attention back to the door itself, which flung open to reveal a concerned-looking Imaya staring at him.

"Umm… did something happen?" he asked. Did Kirielle do something stupid while he was gone?

"I should be the one asking that," she said. "Where were you? You were supposed to be back hours ago."

"Uh…," Zorian floundered. "What's the problem? It's not like I'm coming in the middle of the night or anything…"

The annoyed look on her face told him he shouldn't have said that. Not that he understood why—it's not like there was a rule saying he had to rush back home after class, after all. Back in Cirin, his parents never cared what he did in his free time, so long as he didn't neglect his duties or embarrass them in the process. It was an alien feeling to have someone concerned for him just because he didn't come home on time.

"Look, I'm sorry but I had to meet with my divination instructor after class and the meeting sort of dragged on," he said. "Really, Miss Kuroshka, you're going to lose your nerves if you freak out every time I'm late from classes. It's not the first time I've been held up after class, and it's certainly not going to be the last."

She sighed and shooed him inside, apparently somewhat mollified by his speech.

"In the future, try to notify me when you're going to be late," Imaya said. "Surely there is some piece of magic that can transfer messages within city limits, yes?"

That was a good idea, Zorian had to admit. "I'll see what I can find," he promised.

"Good," Imaya said. "Your sister has been asking for you for a while now, you know?"

Zorian groaned. "She hasn't been a bother, has she?"

"No, she's a little angel," Imaya said, waving his concerns away. Zorian internally rolled his eyes at the idea of Kirielle being an angel. If Kirielle was so nice then why did Imaya want him to come home so badly? "She spent most of the day drawing, playing with the magic cube you gave her, and talking with Kana. Or should that be talking *at* Kana? I swear, that child is far too quiet. I must talk to Kael about it one of these days. It's not normal for a child to be so withdrawn…"

Zorian nodded, pleased that the cube he had made was such a success. It was nothing special, just a simple stone cube with a bunch of light-emitting sigils arranged into a childish puzzle. He had found a design in one of the books Nora had recommended to him back when she had been tutoring him in spell formulas and decided making one would be doubly useful: it would give him some practical experience using spell formula and give Kirielle something with which to pass the time.

"Sounds like she had fun today," Zorian remarked. "What did she need me for, then?"

Imaya gave him a strange look. "You're her big brother. She doesn't need a special reason to miss you."

"And the real reason?" Zorian pressed.

"Kana dozed off and your toy ran out of mana and went inert," Imaya finally admitted after a moment of silence.

"Ah," Zorian said, nodding. He had noticed the design had very little in the way of mana storage, but he wasn't feeling confident enough to redesign it while creating the cube. There was a reason why the cube had such rudimentary mana reserves, after all—large concentrations of mana tended to explode if handled inappropriately, and the cube was meant to be practice for beginners. Beginners who could totally botch things during the first couple of tries. Considering how many problems he had with simply recreating the design on the stone cube, he felt he had made the right choice when he had decided not to mess with the base design. He would simply make more of them if Kirielle still wanted to play with one—it was good practice, anyway. "She's in her room, I guess?"

"No, she's in your room, reading your books," Imaya said, her casual demeanor suggesting she didn't see a problem with this.

Zorian's eye twitched as he resisted the urge to march straight into his room and throw Kirielle out. In reality, he was lucky to have a room to call his own at all. Imaya still hadn't found anyone willing to rent the other room in the house, and Zorian was grateful for it, since it meant he could keep the room for himself. Unfortunately, his ability to keep Kirielle out of it was completely nonexistent. She had no inhibitions about coming and going whenever she pleased, and Imaya was even less inclined to stop her than their mother had been back in Cirin. She seemed to find Kirielle's behavior natural.

And the little imp knew it! She knew she could get away with just about everything, since Imaya liked her better than she did him, and she exploited it to the hilt. That's why, when Zorian loudly entered the room, she completely ignored him. She was lying on his bed with an open book in front of her, her feet comfortably resting on his pillow. As he watched her, she reached towards the plate of biscuits Imaya had brought her, intent on scattering even more crumbs over his bed sheets.

"Hey!" she protested. "Those are mine! Get your own biscuits!"

Zorian ignored her and studied the plate full of biscuits he had snatched away from his demonic little sister. "You know, originally I just wanted to get your attention and stop you from making an even bigger mess than you already have, but they do look kind of tasty..."

"Nooooo!" Kirielle wailed as he opened his mouth and threatened to swallow a handful of biscuits at once. She seemed reluctant to leave his bed to get them back, though. She probably knew he wouldn't allow her to claim her spot back easily should she ever relinquish it, clever little imp that she was.

"Tell you what," he said, closing his mouth and putting the biscuits back on the plate. "I'll give you your biscuits if you get rid of all the crumbs you put on my bed."

Kirielle immediately swept her hands over the sheets a couple times, pushing all the crumbs to the floor in front of the bed. Her task done, she flashed him a cheeky smile.

"Ha ha," said Zorian humorlessly. "Now go get a broom and do it properly. I'll eat a biscuit for every minute this mess remains in the room."

He punctuated his words by shoving one of the biscuits into his mouth. They were quite good, actually.

Kirielle let out a cry of protest and jumped off the bed in a huff. She unsuccessfully tried to retrieve her plate of biscuits, but when she realized she couldn't make him give it back—and when he ate a second one—she instead ran off to get a broom and a dustpan. Apparently she also complained to Imaya, because several minutes later the woman showed up with another plate of biscuits, cheerfully exclaiming that he didn't have to steal from his little sister if he wanted treats. Whatever.

Sadly, even after he recovered his bed from Kirielle's clutches, she still returned to his room. Currently she was sprawled over his chest, having collapsed atop of him when he closed his eyes for a second.

Zorian sighed. "Why are you still here, Kiri?"

Kirielle didn't answer at first, being too busy climbing over Zorian's body like he was an inanimate object that didn't feel pain and discomfort. Once she lay firmly on the bed with him, having wriggled sufficient free space for herself, she spoke.

"I'm bored," she said. "Your puzzle broke, by the way."

"It didn't break," Zorian said. "It just ran out of mana. I can make you a new one tomorrow if you want."

"Okay."

A short silence descended between them and Zorian closed his eyes to take a little nap.

"Zorian?" Kirielle suddenly prompted.

"Yes?"

"What's a morlock?"

Zorian opened his eyes and looked to the side, fixing Kirielle with a curious expression.

"You don't know what a morlock is?" he asked incredulously.

"I just know they're these white-haired, blue-eyed people," Kirielle said. "And that people don't like them very much. And that Kael is one. But Mother never wanted to tell me what the deal with them is."

"She didn't, huh?" mumbled Zorian.

"She said a young lady like me shouldn't talk about that kind of thing."

In the interest of avoiding an argument, Zorian refrained from making a snide comment about whether or not Kirielle qualified as a lady. Not even a derisive snort. Someone should give him a medal for self-control.

"Basically," Zorian said, "they're a race of underground humans. Though most of them don't live underground anymore. The disappearance of the gods hit their civilization hard, and the other denizens of the Dungeon have largely driven them out to the surface. Ikosian settlers sort of helped the process along by kicking them while they were down and burning down a couple of their more prominent settlements."

"Oh," Kirielle said. "But that doesn't explain why people don't like them. Sounds like they should be angry at us more than we should be at them. And Kael doesn't look like he hates us."

"Kael is probably totally ignorant of his ancestral culture. I understand a lot of morlocks are. And the reason people don't like them is that the old morlocks had some pretty barbaric customs. They liked sacrificing people to their gods and seemed to have been cannibals," said Zorian.

"Cannibals!?" Kirielle squealed. "They *ate* people!? Why!?"

"Hard to say," Zorian shrugged. "Ikosian settlers were more interested in condemning them for their practices than understanding why they did what they did."

"Well yeah, they ate people," Kirielle said. "That's evil and disgusting. Don't tell me they're still doing that?"

"Don't be ridiculous," Zorian scoffed. "The authorities would never let them get away with something like that."

"Oh. That's good. Is that why people don't like them? They're afraid the morlocks are going to eat them?"

"It contributes," Zorian said. "I've lost count of the number of rumors I've heard about morlocks supposedly kidnapping children off the street to eat them or what not. But there is more to it. The morlocks had their own brand of magic, which is currently banned just about everywhere, but a lot of morlocks still practice it. The guild calls it blood magic."

"Sounds sinister," Kirielle remarked.

"It does, doesn't it?" Zorian said. "There is no official information about what blood magic actually is, but most people think it has something to do with sacrifice. The story is that morlocks could use a ritual killing of a person or animal to power their spells. Modern morlocks can't exactly kill a bunch of people at whim, but supposedly they still engage in animal sacrifice, both for magical and religious reasons."

Kirielle snuggled in closer to him, shuddering.

"I'm glad Kael and Kana aren't like that," she said.

"Me too, Kiri," said Zorian, patting her on the head. "Me too."

CHAPTER 016

We Need
To Talk

Tearing out a piece of paper from one of his notebooks, Zorian wrote down a short message for Imaya, explaining that he had another of his divination lessons with Haslush and would thus be late today. He still didn't see what the big deal about being late was, but he really didn't want to argue about it.

Of course, writing the message was one thing and getting it to Imaya was another—he was at the academy currently, and it was a long way from there to Imaya's place. He was pretty sure he had a solution, though. He had found plenty of spells for long range communication, and although not many were within his ability to cast or suitable for his purposes, one of the spell combinations seemed promising. Basically, he was going to make a paper airplane and animate it to fly under its own power. A simple locator spell should guide it towards Imaya. The method worked when he had tested it with Kirielle, but that was over considerably smaller distances.

Undeterred by the somewhat experimental nature of his actions, he folded the note into a paper plane and cast his spells on it before flinging it out of the nearest window. It sailed away out of sight soon enough, tracking its target.

Well… classes were over, and the message sent. Time to find Haslush.

Somewhat unsurprisingly, Zorian discovered Haslush had arranged their second meeting in another tavern. Of course. Undeterred, Zorian walked into the place and tried to ignore the stares of the other patrons as he scanned for Haslush among them.

Haslush wasn't there. Zorian lingered on the threshold for a moment, wondering if he had the wrong place or if the detective had simply decided not to show. Haslush's directions had been vague, but Zorian was fairly certain he had followed them correctly. He was just about to leave the tavern to see if he had missed something when he realized it.

Something was wrong. He felt an almost unnatural desire to leave this place. If he hadn't spent a dozen or so restarts suffering through Kyron's resistance training, he probably wouldn't have noticed it, but there was a compulsion effect targeting him.

He pulled out his divination compass and murmured a quick locator spell, seeking out Haslush. The needle immediately pointed towards an unassuming brown-haired man in factory worker getup sitting in the left corner. Sighing, Zorian shuffled over to the man and sat on one of the chairs facing his table.

"Can I help you?" the man asked in a painfully scratchy voice, staring at Zorian with hollow, bloodshot eyes. Very creepy. Very uninviting.

Instead of answering, Zorian muttered a quick dispel. A wave of dispelling force rushed towards the man, disrupting the illusion. The creepy man melted away to show Haslush pouting at him like a little kid.

"I must say, I didn't expect that," Haslush said. "I figured you'd enter and leave the tavern at least three times before you figured it out. I dare say you just broke the betting pool—only two people bet on you getting it right away."

Out of the corner of his eye Zorian saw two of the bar patrons giving him a thumbs up.

"Can you drop the compulsion spell now?" Zorian sighed. "I don't think I'll be able to pay attention to you with it constantly hanging over my head."

"Oh. Right," said Haslush, snapping his fingers. Zorian's head cleared immediately and the desire to bolt out of the tavern evaporated.

"So what exactly was the point of that?" Zorian asked.

"I wanted to see where your observation skills stand," Haslush said, taking a sip from his glass. "Divination is one of the trickier magical disciplines because failure is not obvious. You could perform a divination flawlessly and still get nothing out of it. You could mess it up completely and not even realize you did something wrong. Ask the wrong question, interpret the results incorrectly, or fail to take an important variable into account and it's all just wasted effort. Experience can help you minimize those kinds of issues, but it helps to be naturally perceptive."

"I guess getting it right immediately means I scored really well?" Zorian tried.

"It means you're off to a good start," Haslush said. "We're not done yet."

And with that, Haslush reached out across the table and caught him by his wrist before he could pull his arm away. All sights and sounds around Zorian instantly disappeared, his surroundings replaced by an inky, silent void. The only things he could still see and hear were his own body and Haslush, who seemed to be sitting on thin air, his chair replaced by the same darkness that had consumed everything else.

"Don't," Haslush warned when Zorian tried to wrench his hand free of the detective's grasp. "It's a harmless spell, and it will disappear the moment we break skin contact. If it makes you feel any better, I'm suffering the same effects while it lasts."

"What's the point of this, then?" asked Zorian.

"How many people were present in the tavern when I used this spell on you?" Haslush said.

"What?" Zorian tried to look around him and immediately realized what the darkness was supposed to accomplish. "Oh. You want to see how much I noticed about my surroundings."

"How many people?" repeated Haslush.

Zorian wracked his brains for a moment. He'd had a pretty good look at the patrons when he had scanned them in search of Haslush, but he hadn't counted them. And it was possible someone had left the tavern while he was talking to Haslush.

"Twenty... three?" he tried.

"Close. How many trophies are lined up on the wall next to our table?"

Unfortunately, while Zorian had noticed the trophies, he hadn't given them more than a single glance. Haslush continued on with fifteen more questions in that vein, and Zorian soon no longer felt so confident about this. At last, Haslush let go of his hand and the rest of the tavern immediately appeared again.

"Oh, don't feel so down," Haslush said. "You're not half bad, really. And honestly, I wouldn't cancel our lessons just because you did poorly in something like this. How are you standing with divination, anyway? Standard second-year graduate or do you have something extra?"

"I know a bunch of library divinations and I have mastered the north-finding shaping exercise," Zorian said.

"What, north-finding exercise already?" asked Haslush, his surprise evident. Personally, Zorian felt that exercise was very easy. "Well, there goes the homework I intended to give you after today's session. Anyway, today I'll teach you how to analyze objects."

He reached into the pockets of his long coat and placed a number of objects on the table in front of them: a sealed envelope, an old pocket watch, a locked box, some kind of giant nut, a spell rod, and a fancy-looking glove.

"Analyzing objects is something I do a lot, so I figure it's a good thing to start with. Identifying what the object does, finding out who handled it last, what kind of magics and protections are placed on it… you could make an entire career out it, and some do," Haslush said. "I hear you're interested in a job at the spell forges so this is bound to be rather useful for you."

"Okay, what do you want me to do?" asked Zorian.

"I'll teach you the spells you'll need and then you can practice on these," Haslush said, pointing at the various objects on the table.

It was a very productive session after that, which got Zorian thinking. Based on the man's comments, Haslush was clearly somewhat high in Cyoria's police hierarchy. Maybe he could do something useful with the information about the invasion without tipping off the organizers? It might be worth dying once or twice to find out.

"I really must thank you, Mister Ikzeteri," Zorian said. "You are a lot better at this than I initially gave you credit for."

"It's fine," Haslush said. "I actively cultivate a somewhat unflattering façade. It helps people relax around me. So, what are you trying to butter me up for, anyway?"

Zorian sighed. How should he put this then?

"Could you put up some privacy wards first?" Zorian asked.

Haslush raised an eyebrow at the request but nodded in agreement. He quickly set up some sort of spells over their table and then waited expectantly. Zorian watched him work, hoping he'd have the chance to get the detective to teach him the protective spells.

"I have heard there is a plot to smuggle war trolls into the city during the summer festival after bombarding the city with artillery magic during the fireworks," Zorian said.

Haslush immediately sat up straighter, so at least it seemed Zorian wasn't going to get dismissed out of hand. Now he just had to make sure he didn't get carted off to the police station.

"And I don't suppose you'll tell me where you heard that?" asked Haslush suspiciously.

"Can't," Zorian confirmed. "It seemed reliable to me, though."

"I see." Haslush sighed. He poured some more alcohol into his glass and took a sip. "I hate the summer festival. Virtually all buildings have their warding schemes loosened while it lasts, the huge amount of visitors makes it hard to spot troublemakers in time, and the mayor and other bigheads want all sorts of stupid things done in preparation for it. It's a perfect time for criminals and terrorists of all stripes to go wild in the city."

Huh. Zorian hadn't thought about that.

"So, how are these people going to smuggle in goddamn war trolls of all things, and what are they trying to accomplish?"

"Through the Dungeon," said Zorian. "As for the purpose, I honestly don't know."

"Anything else you can tell me?" Haslush asked.

"Not really, no."

"Then I have just one more question," Haslush said. "Why are you telling this to *me*, of all people?"

"There are some very high placed people involved in this, and I'm not sure who I can trust," Zorian said. "You seem like a fairly influential person who is unlikely to be involved. And I'm hoping you won't drag me off to a cell for questioning."

He didn't actually know whether high placed people were involved or not, of course, but he felt it was a good bet they were. He failed to see how an invasion of this kind of magnitude could be organized without the cooperation of some very influential person inside city administration.

"I'm tempted," Haslush admitted. "But all you'd really have to do is claim it was all a prank and I'd pretty much have to let you go. The mage guild was founded because mages didn't trust civilian law enforcement to judge them fairly, and they guard their privileges jealously. The guild can get almost anyone released on the pretense of conducting their own investigation. You'd get a slap on the wrist for being stupid and I'd spend the next year being punished by my bosses for falling for a childish trick and antagonizing the guild."

"Um," Zorian fumbled. Haslush sounded more than a little bit bitter. He hadn't known Cyoria's police force harbored such resentment towards the mage guild.

"It's fine," Haslush said. "I'm not angry at you. I guess I'll do some investigating and we'll talk more about it after our next session. You try finding out more from these mysterious sources of yours."

Zorian left the tavern in a good mood, though it was somewhat dampened by his awareness that he might have just increased his risk of assassination. He could only hope Haslush would be discreet in his investigation.

When he got to Imaya's place, she told him that his message had arrived intact, but she was still fairly unhappy with him—apparently the paper plane had rammed straight into the back of her head, and that was dangerous. What if it had hit her face and poked out her eye?

Some people were never happy.

The house was calm, the only two occupants present being Zorian and Kirielle… and thankfully, Kirielle was amusing herself with doodling in her notebook instead of pestering him. That was good, because trying to levitate a snail, as Zorian was currently doing, was not at all easy. Not only was the snail alive, and thus inherently resistant to magic, but it was also actively fighting the levitation effect, twisting and bending in the air in an attempt to break free of the unseen force holding it aloft.

He was cheating a little—he was actually levitating the shell, which was largely immobile and much more solid than the actual snail. The real test of skill would be levitating a slug or something, but… well, he was having enough trouble with the damn snail at the moment.

"Poor snail," Kirielle remarked from the sidelines. "Why don't you let this one go and find another one to torture? It's going to end up traumatized if you keep this up."

"I'm not torturing it," Zorian protested, trying to split his attention between holding the snail in the air and talking with Kirielle. "It's completely unharmed. I'm not even sure if snail brains are complex enough to be traumatized. The damn thing is as enthusiastic about escaping as it was when I started this."

Kirielle looked as if she was about to argue but then just grunted and melted back into her chair.

"Where is he?" she said after a minute of silence.

"I don't know, Kiri," sighed Zorian. "Be patient. He isn't even late yet."

"Maybe we should start without him?" she tried.

"No, we should not!" snapped Zorian. The snail wobbled in the air, its eyestalks swinging wildly as it sensed its bonds weakening and redoubled its efforts. "Honestly, Kiri, you can be so callous sometimes.

The only reason I'm even doing this is because Kael asked me to. You should be thanking him for letting you participate."

"You're the one to talk about callousness," Kirielle grumbled. "You'd rather help a stranger you met a week ago than your own little sister. And I am grateful, I just—"

"Then be nice and wait," Zorian interrupted her, slowly lowering the snail into his hand. He clearly wasn't going to get any more work done. "He'll be here soon enough. If you want something to do, go release the snail back into the garden."

"What? No way!"

Zorian raised an eyebrow. "Weren't you just advocating for its freedom?"

"Well, yeah, but I'm not gonna touch it or anything. It's slimy and disgusting and eww."

Zorian rolled his eyes and put the snail into a small box by his side. He would release it outside later. A sound of the door opening signaled Kael's arrival.

"I'm here," Kael said. "I'm not late, I hope?"

"How did you know he was coming?" Kirielle asked suspiciously, turning to Zorian.

"Alarm spells," Zorian said dismissively. "And no, Kael, you're not late. Though Kirielle was impatient, as usual. Anyway, you said you need my help to catch up to third year curriculum, right? Which part do you need help with?"

"I really don't know," Kael said. "As I said, my education was somewhat spotty so even though I know a lot of things, there are things that formally trained mages take for granted that I'm not even aware of. Why don't you give me a brief overview of your first two years and we'll see where to go from there? Ilsa said she will test me three months from now, so I have plenty of time."

Zorian gave his sister a knowing look, but she was avoiding his eyes. He was sure that Kael knew exactly where he was deficient knowledge-wise, but Kiri had probably asked the morlock to play along for her, being largely ignorant about magic herself. He really didn't know why she was so adamant to learn magic Right Now, as opposed to later, in a proper school environment.

Honestly, as much as he cared for his sister and liked Kael, he probably wouldn't be taking Kirielle with him to Cyoria too often. He spent most of his time in the house dealing with Kirielle, Imaya, or Kael (and occasionally Kana), leaving little time for his personal self-study. Relatively speaking, of course—Kirielle already complained he spent too much time studying and not enough having fun or paying attention to her.

But all things considered, he could take it easy every once in a while. He could set aside a few hours for helping Kael study for Ilsa's test, even if the morlock would never actually live to take it during the time loop, and if Kirielle wanted to listen in, he'd be better off letting her than dealing with her pouting.

He gave them both a brief explanation of the first two years in the academy. Magic-wise, most of the first year was spent on teaching students how to consciously and consistently draw on their magical core by making them activate various magical objects. There was even a first-year class called Operation of Magic Items, which was exactly what it sounded like. They also worked on their memorization by doing increasingly complex strings of gestures and chants shown to them by teachers, a practice that would be useful for later study of invocations. The rest was theory: introductions to various magical traditions and disciplines and learning how to understand the basics of Ikosian language, biology, history, geography, law, and mathematics. Not all of it was strictly related to magic, but—

Zorian broke off his explanation, his alarm spell jangling at him.

"We'll have to pause for the moment," he said, looking at the door. "Someone is—"

Before he could finish, the door slammed open and Taiven barged into his room in her usual aggressive manner. She scanned the room quickly and then stalked towards him.

"...coming in," he finished with a long-suffering sigh.

"Roach!" she exclaimed excitedly. "You're just the man I... wait, am I interrupting something?"

"Yes?" Zorian tried.

"Never mind, it will only take a minute." She shoved a newspaper into his face. "Did you see this?"

He sighed and snatched the newspapers out of her hand so he could put them on the table and actually read the story she was gesturing at—and obscuring.

Academy Student Kills Oganj!

Yesterday morning Zach Noveda shocked the world when he announced in front of gathered reporters that he had slain Oganj, the feared dragon that had terrorized northern Altazia for more than a century. Naturally, such a bold claim requires suitable proof, which the young Noveda heir certainly delivered when he summoned the dragon's corpse for inspection. Alliance officials invited to the press conference have confirmed the body almost certainly belongs to the infamous Terror of the North, although further examination is necessary before they are willing to present Noveda with the promised bounty for killing the beast...

Zorian read the article in stony silence. He was dimly aware of Kirielle and Kael peering over his shoulder so they could see what had captivated his attention like that, but he didn't let that distract him.

Was this the reason for all those short restarts? Because Zach wanted to kill a dragon? Zorian wasn't sure what to think about that. On one hand, the mage dragon was a menace, and killing him was an impressive feat. On the other hand, it seemed like a waste of time and effort—what could Zach have gained from this other than combat experience? Dragon magics were of no use to humans, and Zach was already so rich that Oganj's hoard would have been relatively meaningless to him. Whatever game Zach was playing, Zorian couldn't figure it out. Did the other time traveler just do whatever popped into his head at any particular moment?

"Hey, Roach, you went to class with this guy, right?" Taiven prodded after a while.

"Yeah," he confirmed. "He was supposed to be in my class this year, too, but failed to show up when classes started."

"He ran away from home," Taiven said. "There was a recent scandal about that a week ago. They asked him about it in the article, but he kind of dodged the question."

Zorian nodded as he scanned the article further. Zach was quoted as saying he had 'a great number of disagreements with his former guardian' and refused to elaborate. There was an interesting story in there, Zorian was sure, but if the newspapers hadn't managed to dig something up, then Zorian definitely wasn't going to accomplish much by poking his nose where it didn't belong.

Zach also told the reporters, when prompted about his immediate plans, that he intended to go back to school 'for a few months'. Great. Zorian would have to lay low during the next few restarts until Zach got tired of the academy again.

"Isn't Oganj the dragon that annihilated an army sent to kill him?" Kirielle asked. "Or was that Mother just trying to scare me?"

"A small army, and Oganj lured it into a trap," Kael said. "The general seemed to think Oganj would wait in his lair while the army approached. Instead, he carved exploding runes into the walls of a canyon and lured the army inside. The only reason anyone survived is that some of the mages teleported out before the whole thing collapsed on top of them."

"And I heard he killed one of the Immortal Eleven, too," Taiven said. "So how the hell did this Zach guy kill the thing? Is he some kind of legend or what? Why didn't you tell me you had someone like that in your class?"

Zorian sighed. What the hell was he supposed to tell her?

"Let me put it like this," he said carefully. "During the first two years, Zach had trouble with just about everything. He was such a poor mage that people weren't sure if he would pass his certification, and you know how easy that thing is."

"That… doesn't make sense," Taiven said. "Even if this is a trick and Oganj isn't dead, he still summoned the corpse of a fully grown dragon. Even I can't summon something that big yet."

"I guess everything changed during the school break," Zorian said, shrugging. "Somehow he went from a borderline failure to amazing genius between years two and three."

"That's totally ridiculous," Taiven said, seizing the newspaper and crumpling it in her frustration. "How would that even work?"

"Time travel?" suggested Zorian shamelessly.

"Like I said, ridiculous," Taiven countered immediately. "Are you sure he wasn't faking incompetence?"

"I'm not sure of anything, Taiven," Zorian said. And he really wasn't—even after a whole year of being trapped inside the time loop he still felt the entire situation was all kinds of crazy. "And the few things I do know are so insane you wouldn't believe a word of it."

"Oh, now I just have to hear them," said Taiven, crossing her arms in front of her chest defiantly. "Go on, just try me."

"Tell, tell!" agreed Kirielle. Kael didn't say anything, but Zorian could tell he was curious as well.

Hm. He could tell them about the time loop, but even if they believed him, what would that accomplish? They were no more qualified to solve this mystery than he was, and if they went around telling that story to people, they could blow his cover to Zach or any interested third parties. Then again, he had already told Haslush about the invasion, so he was already playing with fire in this restart…

Oh, to hell with it, as if they'd ever believe him anyway.

"If I told you that Zach and I are time travelers perpetually reliving this first month of school, and that a giant army of monsters and hostile mages is going to invade the city during the summer festival, what would you say?"

Taiven raised her eyebrows at him.

"Well, go on," Zorian prompted.

"You're right," Taiven sighed. "I don't believe a word of it. So you're saying the things you know are *that* insane?"

"At the very least."

"Huh," Taiven said speculatively. "Sounds interesting, but you'll have to tell me those stories some other time. I kept you long enough, I think. See you around, Roach!"

Zorian watched as Taiven left before turning back to Kael and Kirielle. "So. Shall we continue where we left off?"

They both remained silent, staring at him.

"Um," he said. "Why are you staring at me like that?"

"Is it true?" Kirielle asked, her voice quiet. "Are you really a time traveler?"

Zorian opened his mouth and closed it again. What?

"Your friend may be too oblivious to recognize an answer couched as a hypothetical, but we're not," Kael elaborated. "You really do believe that, don't you? That you're a time traveler?"

"I… yes. If it's a delusion, it's a very convincing one," Zorian said carefully. "The magics I learn in each iteration of this month transfer over into the next one. Insanity doesn't give the victim spells and shaping skills."

"I don't understand," Kirielle complained.

"You and me both, Kiri," Zorian sighed. "You and me both."

"Perhaps you should explain from the start?" Kael suggested patiently. "Tell us what you do understand."

"I have lived through this month before," Zorian said after taking a moment to collect his thoughts. He hadn't expected to be explaining himself to anyone, nor was he sure exactly why he was choosing to be so honest. "The first time, before I knew about the time loop, I did not bring Kirielle with me to Cyoria."

"What!?" protested Kirielle. "Zorian, you jerk!"

"I lived in one of the academy-provided apartments and I went to classes like normal," said Zorian, ignoring her. He glanced at Kael. "You did, too, but I didn't know you then. However, we had an extra classmate."

"Zach?" Kael guessed.

"Yes," Zorian confirmed. "Unlike the previous two years I shared a class with him, this time he was amazing. He aced every test, he had mastered hundreds of spells, and he was good enough at alchemy to impress *you*, of all people."

Kael raised an eyebrow at him.

"Yes," Zorian assured. "It was like he had completely transformed during the summer break. At the time I didn't care very much—I was a little curious as to how he accomplished it, but it was not my business to pry. And then the summer festival came, and everything went to hell. Artillery spells descended from the sky on the city, and an army of monsters followed in their wake. As I was running through the burning city, I witnessed Zach fighting trolls and winter wolves. He was throwing high-level spells as if they were candy, fighting with a skill that no third-year student could possibly possess. He fared pretty well at first, but then a lich arrived at the scene and demolished him."

He paused for a moment to consider his next words. There was some relief, he realized, in saying everything out loud—and confiding in someone.

"And then what?" Kirielle asked. "What happened next?"

"What else?" Zorian scoffed, an edge in his voice as he remembered dying. "We died. The lich cast some kind of weird spell at us—a necromantic spell, I am told—and we were instantly killed."

"So how did you go back in time, then?" asked Kirielle suspiciously.

"I have no idea. All I know is that I was suddenly back in my bed in Cyoria, with you wishing me a good morning in that uniquely charming Kirielle way. At first I thought this was something the lich did, but then it happened again and again and again—and I only saw the lich that first time. Every time I die, or at the end of the summer festival if I don't, my soul is transported back to that morning in Cirin before I take the train to Cyoria."

They stared at him for a few seconds, and Zorian was already becoming certain they would suddenly start laughing and mocking him when Kirielle decided to speak again.

"So, you are a time traveler, but you can only go one month into the past and only until one specific day," she said. Zorian nodded. She understood that part a lot better than Zorian had expected. "And you don't control any of it, except by deliberately killing yourself."

"Yes," Zorian confirmed.

"You are the lamest time traveler ever," Kirielle opinionated.

And just like that the tension was broken.

Three days had passed since he had told Kirielle and Kael about the time loop and he was honestly a little bit disappointed by their reactions. They both seemed to believe him, but neither was terribly affected. Both of them were still asking him questions about it whenever they could catch him alone, and he knew Kael was researching time travel and soul bonds in his free time, but they continued to go about their business as if nothing was wrong. They weren't even giving him weird glances when they thought he wasn't looking or anything!

"I told you already, I've only been in the time loop for little over a year," Zorian told Kirielle. "I'm not even close to all-knowing and I can't answer these questions you keep asking me."

"I can't believe you've been going to school all this time," Kirielle grumbled. "I'd have quit after the second time."

"You'd have ended up mind wiped or enslaved to Zach in a heartbeat," Zorian retorted. "There is a reason I'm doing this slowly and carefully."

A gentle knock on his door stopped their argument short. Zorian was a bit paranoid about visitors ever since he had told Haslush about the invasion, and telling Kael and Kirielle about it had only increased that. Even though he had told Kael and Kirielle not to talk about the invasion in even an oblique way to other people, he could never be sure if they would listen to him. Especially not Kirielle. He kept expecting assassins to barge into the house at any moment, but his paranoia had thankfully been groundless so far. Since only Kael knocked so lightly, Zorian had a pretty good idea who it was.

"Come in," Zorian called out.

Instead of coming in, however, Kael opened the door and remained standing on the threshold.

"We need to talk," Kael said, a hint of nervousness in his voice. "Can you come into my room for a moment?"

"Is it about time travel?" Kirielle said, her face lighting up with excitement.

Kael smiled at her. "Kirielle, I know you won't like this, but can you wait in your room while I talk to your brother? It's related to time travel, but it's a bit... private."

For a moment it looked like Kirielle was going to complain, but then she shot him a speculative look and nodded in assent. As he watched her leave back to her room, grumbling all the way, Zorian had to admit he was a little jealous of Kael's ability to control Kirielle. She never listened to him when he tried that sort of thing.

Shrugging, Zorian followed Kael down the hall and into his room, where the morlock boy promptly dragged a chest from under his bed and retrieved a mysterious black book with no title on the cover or spine.

"I've been looking into your... problem... the last few days," Kael said. "I may have found something."

"You did?"

Kael opened the book and leafed through it for a few seconds before he found what he was looking for. He handed the open book to Zorian and pointed at the page.

"Based on the chant you memorized from the lich, and everything else you told me, I think this is the most likely spell he used," Kael said.

"Soul Meld," Zorian read aloud. "Requires at least two targets. Causes target souls to merge and blend into one. Typically used as a component in more complicated rituals, which in turn heavily modify the effects. If the spell is used in isolation, the resulting entity is virtually always rendered insane or otherwise defective from the stress of the merger. Commonly used in the creation of familiar bonds and soul bonds in general..."

That definitely sounded like a likely candidate for the spell, but Zorian couldn't understand how Kael had discovered this in only a few days while Zorian had been searching for a year. Frowning, Zorian leafed through the rest of the book. It was full of soul magic spells, and much of it was written in several unknown scripts that Zorian couldn't read. This... wasn't the sort of thing you could find in the academy library, least of all with just a student clearance.

Which meant this was probably Kael's personal book.

"Kael... are you a necromancer?" asked Zorian carefully.

"A difficult question," Kael answered after a short pause. "I do not enslave the dead or curse people. There is more to soul magic than that, though."

Well this was just great. He had revealed his secret to one of the few people who could actually do something to put him down permanently. And he had been scolding Kirielle about being reckless just a few minutes ago, too. He really was a giant idiot sometimes.

But hey, what's done is done, and at least Kael didn't seem hostile. If anything, the other boy seemed to be more afraid of Zorian than the other way around.

"I won't report you, if that's what you're worried about," Zorian said. Partially because he was deathly afraid of what the other boy would do to him if he tried. A necromancer, of all things... "You agreed to keep quiet about my secret, so it would be hypocritical of me to betray yours without reason. Still, necromancy? Err, I mean, soul magic?"

Kael gave him a weak smile. "It's an interesting discipline and unfairly judged. My teacher had an interest in it and I wanted to continue the tradition."

Tradition, right. Zorian thought about pressing the matter further but decided against it. Mistake or not, he could at least gain some benefit out of this—he'd just met a decent-seeming necromancer willing to answer his questions. How often does that happen?

"So, if the lich performed a soul meld on me, why am I still... well, me?" Zorian asked. "As I understand it, a spell like that would have fused my soul with Zach's completely. We would both cease to exist as individual people."

"Well, I must admit I am not an expert on soul magic by any means," said Kael. "My primary strengths are alchemy and medicine, with soul magic being merely a side interest. That said, I assume the spell was simply interrupted before it could complete the effect. I think it's entirely possible Zach committed suicide when he realized his soul was being targeted."

"It would have been a sensible course of action in his case," Zorian agreed. "Though he didn't exactly give me the impression that he was aware of the danger when I talked to him. I suppose it could have been the amnesia playing tricks on him."

"Or he may have a contingency spell placed on him, set to kill him if it detects unauthorized tampering with his soul. You already said he may not be the originator of the time loop. Whoever placed the magic on him was doubtlessly aware of the danger as the time loop you are trapped in is clearly the work of a skilled soul mage."

"Right. So, since the spell was only allowed to work its magic for a moment, we were spared from the worst effect," Zorian mused. "And I ended up with some kind of soul bond that drags me along for the ride. Possibly. There was obviously some soul melding involved, in any case. Can you find out what the spell actually did?"

"Maybe," Kael said slowly. "Although this would involve more spells. Soul magic spells, to be more precise. Are you sure you want to trust an evil, slimy necromancer with this?" Kael grinned a little.

"Yes," confirmed Zorian, rolling his eyes at Kael's dramatics. Maybe it wasn't the smartest thing to agree to, but he was honestly desperate for some answers and he was getting an honest feeling from Kael. He was usually a good judge of character. "It is true that I am leery of soul magic, but that doesn't mean I automatically hate you now. Go ahead and cast whatever spells you need."

After fifteen minutes of mysterious spellcasting with no visible results—or even any effects Zorian could feel—Kael was forced to admit that the only thing he knew with certainty was that Zorian definitely didn't have a classical soul bond with Zach. If he was connected to the other time traveler, it was through something more exotic and subtle than that.

"I'm sorry," Kael said. "I thought soul magic as high-level as this would be blatantly obvious, but I guess I was wrong. Maybe if I tried it on Zach…?"

"There is no way to examine him without telling him the truth," Zorian said. "I'm not sure I want to do that yet."

"Of course," Kael said. "Although I'm not sure what else I can do. I'd have to be a vastly superior soul mage to help you with this, and if you're right, I just don't have the time to become one. Even if you convinced me of all this right at the start of the time loop—and I'm not sure you could do that before I got to know you a little—one month is too little time to make significant progress in a field like soul magic."

"Uh," fumbled Zorian after a few seconds of silence. "Maybe you could teach me some soul magic?"

"You would be willing to do that?" Kael asked in mild amusement.

"You said there is more to soul magic than cursing people and enslaving the dead," Zorian said. "And I really do need answers that only soul magic can provide."

And if he learned soul magic, he would no longer have to trust strangers to mess around with his soul. If someone had to cast soul magic on him, he'd rather it was him.

"Though I'm flattered you are willing to set aside your prejudices, the truth is you would never be good enough for what you want to do with it," Kael said. "Although most soul magic can be performed by normal mages like you, the really sophisticated spells require a certain amount of soul perception—a skill that can only be gained by drinking a special potion made from a properly harvested dirge moth chrysalis."

"And is the potion rare?"

"Dirge moths spend most of their lives in the ground," Kael said. "They live as larvae for twenty-three years before emerging from the soil en masse as swarms of poisonous dirge moths. The moths live for exactly one day before laying their eggs and dying. In case you're curious, the last emergence of the moth swarms was less than a decade ago."

"So there will be no dirge moth chrysalises for at least another decade," realized Zorian.

Kael nodded. "And the potion requires a fresh chrysalis. They cannot be preserved."

"And there is no other way to gain soul perception?"

"Maybe there is, but I only know of this one," Kael said. "There are some rituals involving human sacrifice that claim to provide the same benefit to the mage, but I have never tried them and I suspect you would not want to, either."

"Definitely not," Zorian agreed.

After a few more minutes of discussion, Zorian left Kael's room, lost in thought.

He wasn't quite willing to give up on the idea of learning soul magic, but he had more than enough on his plate, so best to set it aside for now. There would be plenty of other restarts in which to try that later.

The moment he entered the room and closed the door behind him, he felt a very familiar touch on his mind, not unlike the moment in the sewers, yet more subtle and less alien, like cobwebs brushing against the edges of his thoughts.

He immediately panicked, his eyes darting from one corner of the room to another in search of his assailant while he tried to mentally block the presence from his mind. Despite his practice with Kyron, he found himself unable to do so.

[*So you are Open?*] a clear, confident voice resonated through his mind. Unlike the last time, there was no pain or confusing images involved… but that was somehow even more terrifying. In his last encounter, his opponent had seemed unaccustomed to dealing with humans. This one seemed to know exactly what it was doing. [*Interesting. You have met one of us before? This will be easier than I thought then.*]

There! Shadows moving in the corner. He readied a magic missile—but his whole body froze in an instant and refused to listen to him.

A dark shape suddenly leaped from the corner of his room and landed on his bed, directly in front of him. It was a spider, like he suspected, but it looked nothing like what he expected. Small for a giant spider breed, no larger than Zorian's torso, and a lot more compact than the spindly, long-legged varieties that people usually associated with spiders. Wracking his brain, Zorian identified it as a type of jumping spider.

As the creature turned to face him, Zorian suddenly found himself staring at a pair of giant, solid black eyes that gave the spider a surprisingly human-like face. Another smaller pair of eyes sat on its forehead, for lack of a better word, but the two big ones held Zorian's attention. The other thing he noticed, of course, was a pair of giant fangs that looked like they could pierce his skull with ease.

[*Greetings, Zorian Kazinski,*] the spider spoke telepathically. [*I have been wanting to meet you for a while now. You and I need to have a long, looong talk…*]

CHAPTER 017

Sympathy
for the Spider

For a moment, silence reigned (both literal and mental), as Zorian stared into the unblinking eyes of his adversary. Zorian didn't have a phobia of spiders, but it was hard not to be intimidated by a creature that could read your thoughts and have you completely at its mercy due to induced paralysis. He couldn't even try to physically overpower the effect, since the paralysis was purely of the mind—he was quite literally locked out of control of his own body.

The situation wasn't completely hopeless. As a mage, Zorian was resistant to mind reading almost by default. The ability to clear away stray thoughts and emotions and otherwise discipline their mind was a must for any aspiring mage. That said, controlling your thoughts for long periods of time was tiresome. It was only a matter of time until a stray thought escaped him and he slipped an important secret to the blasted spider. And resistance to mind reading would do him no good if the creature grew frustrated with his resistance and decided to take a metaphorical sledgehammer to his mind.

In the end, the spider decided to speak first. Or rather, communicate telepathically to him first, as that appeared to be its only method of talking to him. It made sense, really—the spider had no recognizable mouth from which to speak.

[You're untrained. It's a pity. I would have loved to trade techniques with a human psychic. I suppose it's to be expected, though, considering the unhealthy attitude towards mind magic your species has.]

…What?

[Why the confusion? You cannot possibly be ignorant of the Gift,] the spider said, torn between bafflement and amusement at the thought. [See, right there! You just sensed my emotions. What do you think that is, if not empathy?]

Zorian's brain froze for a moment. Him, an empath? That… that was ridiculous! He was neither social enough nor pleasant enough to be empathic!

[What a strange chain of thought,] the spider mused. [Aranea like me are all Open, yet there are plenty of loners and unpleasant individuals among us. I'm sad to say that some even use their empathy to purposely promote discord within the web.]

Zorian's mind was momentarily aflame with possibilities before he forcibly reined himself in and shoved those thoughts into the back of his mind. Focus! This was a horrible time to get distracted. He had a far more serious issue to contend with.

[You must be mistaken,] Zorian thought back, knowing that the spider would pick up on his thoughts. [It's far more likely you accidentally attached some of your emotions to the telepathic message you sent me.]

[There is no need to be insulting,] the spider immediately sent back. [I am an aranea matriarch. If I had attached something other than speech to our communication, it wouldn't have been by accident. But never mind—if you want to deny the obvious truth of your empathic abilities, I'll play along for now. What I want to know is what your quarrel is with my web. As far as I know, we've never done anything to you, so I'm baffled as to why you felt the need to send enforcers after us.]

What was she— Oh. The warning he gave Taiven to watch out for telepathic spiders and the subsequent search for the creatures. Right. Of all the things he had been worried about during this past week, having the spiders track him down for alerting the authorities to them had never even entered his mind. Funny how these things worked…

[I'm not sure if you'll believe me, but I never intended to send anyone after you,] Zorian sent. [All I did was warn a friend to watch out for you when she went to the sewers. It all seems to have spiraled away from there.]

[Why wouldn't I believe you? I am literally reading your mind as we speak,] the spider noted. [But that still doesn't explain how you even knew about us. We tend to be a tad secretive. Or, for that matter, why you felt the need to warn your friend to watch out for us, since we don't really attack humans without provocation.]

Well crap. How could he possibly explain that without revealing anything sensitive?

[I suppose this is something related to this time loop you're trapped in, then?] the spider asked innocently.

Zorian would have grit his teeth if he could. Damn it, how!? He had pointedly not thought about that!

[Your ability to control your train of thought is fairly impressive for an amateur, but it is a form of mental defense that only works if you know your mind is being read. I observed you and your group for quite a while before I executed this ambush. And while you are Open, and thus hard to read covertly, your friend and sister are virtually defenseless against my powers. They didn't even notice while I was trawling through their memories, much less when I skimmed their surface thoughts.]

Zorian felt like slapping himself for such an obvious oversight. Of course sharing his secrets with the likes of Kirielle would come back to haunt him—a secret is only as secure as its weakest link. He considered the situation for a moment before giving a mental sigh. It was hopeless. The spider had completely outmaneuvered him and currently had him over the barrel. The creature seemed reasonable enough, but he would have almost preferred that it was murderous—he could recover from death easily enough, but the things a skilled mind mage could do to him would linger with him on subsequent restarts.

[Your insistence on viewing me as an uncompromising threat despite no hostile moves on my part is honestly getting rather tedious,] the spider sent, and Zorian detected a distinct note of annoyance in her bearing. Zorian idly wondered how the esteemed matriarch would characterize her current ambush and her gross violation of his friends' privacy if not as hostile. [I came here to talk, not fight. The enforcers hadn't even managed to track us down, much less dispatch any of us, so there is no reason for hard feelings on my part. This isn't a revenge run—it's an attempt to defuse a situation before it spirals out of control. I know our kind looks frightening to your eyes, but please stop thinking of me as some slavering beast out to eat you or a sadist intending to torture you into insanity for absolutely no reason. We're no worse than humans, really.]

[I'm not sure that sets me at ease. Humans can be pretty horrible,] Zorian pointed out. [But I see your point. So, what now? The enforcers will get tired of their search quickly enough and leave you alone, and I have no intention of taking any further action against you and your… web. Problem solved, then?]

[Well, yes,] the spider agreed. [But in the process of confronting you I found something a hundred times more interesting than a human child with a grudge. You don't really think I'm going to just ignore the whole time loop business, do you?]

[I was kind of hoping you would, actually,] admitted Zorian. [It's not really your concern—]

[Oh, I beg to differ,] the spider interjected. [I just found out I'm effectively being memory wiped at regular intervals. I am *greatly* concerned.]

Zorian wracked his brain for a response that could dissuade her from getting involved but gave up after a couple seconds. He was getting an impression of resolve and stubbornness from the spider and had a feeling all of the arguments he could marshal were doomed to fall on deaf ears. He didn't know how he could read a giant spider's body language, but apparently he could. Maybe there was something to her claim of him being empathic.

[Look,] Zorian tried, [if we're going to have a serious conversation about this I would really appreciate if you released me from paralysis. This is very uncomfortable and I'd be a lot friendlier if I weren't frozen like this.]

[I don't trust you that much,] the spider told him bluntly. [All you have to do is scream and things could get uncomfortably messy.]

[I'm not going to do that,] Zorian assured. [That would just put my sister and friends in danger. I'm sure you could handle anything anyone in this house could throw at you.]

[Well, I'm not. I've lived too long to underestimate mages,] the spider said. [Tell you what, though. Why don't I simply let you go for now and leave? Later, when you calm down a little, you can descend into the city tunnels and track me down for a nice friendly chat in neutral territory where we both feel a lot safer.]

That… sounded like a great idea, actually. Well, except for the question of why—

[Why would you bother tracking me down when you can just pretend this never happened and ignore my existence entirely?] the spider surmised. [Well for one thing, I can tell you're interested in what I mean by you being Open, no matter how hard you try to hide it. You will never get a satisfactory answer unless you seek me out. Secondly, there is a reason why I accepted the idea that you're trapped in a time loop without so much as asking a question. I have important clues that could help you solve this puzzle and break out of the loop, but I'm not sharing them until I get something in return. I'm sure we can agree on a fair price. And finally, working with me isn't just going to be an unnecessary chore like you seem to think. I am a leader of a shadowy group of mind-reading spiders that have their feelers throughout the entire city—surely you can see we might be useful in making sense of this event?]

Zorian swallowed heavily as he finally realized the seriousness of the situation he was dealing with. Her group was that big and organized? He knew the spider before him was a representative of a larger group since she had introduced herself as an 'aranea matriarch', but he thought it was just a loose pack consisting of a dozen spiders or so at best. Suddenly the pitch-black eyes staring at him seemed a lot more threatening than they had been just a moment ago. Gods, what had he gotten himself into?

[I'm glad we are finally able to understand one another, Zorian Kazinski. Rest now, and we will talk when you're less tense.]

Zorian suddenly felt a smothering blanket of telepathic force press itself gently but firmly against his mind. He tried to resist, but the mental attack seemed to ignore his mental defenses entirely. Despite valiant efforts, Zorian soon blacked out. When he woke up a few minutes later, he was alone in the room and there was no trace of a giant spider anywhere in the house.

Afterwards, Zorian thought long and hard about the matriarch's 'offer' and ultimately decided he really didn't have much choice. He somehow doubted she would patiently wait for him if he ignored her for too long, and raising a fuss about her actions would attract unwanted attention to him and might cause the matriarch to retaliate out of spite. And since she knew about the time loop, she was bound to pick something that would haunt him beyond the confines of this particular restart. Of course, there was also the fact that some of the things she had said during their brief exchange interested him greatly. The potential benefits of hashing out a deal with her were simply too great to ignore.

That said, he had absolutely no intention of rushing to the damn spider at the earliest opportunity—that would just make him seem desperate. Let her wait for a while. It was a good idea to do some preparations before confronting the matriarch, anyway.

First of all, he needed to know more about these 'aranea' he would be meeting with. His previous searches for information about the spiders had left him empty-handed, but now he was armed with an actual name of the species and his search was much more successful. He found plenty of descriptions, though they were of much poorer quality than he had hoped. Apparently aranea were considered semi-mythical due to their rarity, and there were many conflicting reports circulating about them. Everyone agreed they were intelligent and magical in nature, but from there the details diverged wildly. Depending on the author, all manner of powers were attributed to them, from the ability to assume human form to the ability to manipulate shadows and other even more outrageous abilities. Zorian could see three possible explanations for this. One, the aranea had a dizzying number of subspecies, all with a wildly different appearance and abilities. Two, the authors were making stuff up. And three, the aranea were mages in the human sense, armed with a flexible spellcasting system capable of producing a wide variety of effects. Knowing his luck, it was definitely number three—the most worrying of possibilities. A group of one-trick ponies limited to mind magic was a dangerous foe, but one that could be countered with enough preparation. A group of mages utilizing a completely novel spellcasting system, whose limitations he was unfamiliar with? That was practically the definition of unpredictability.

Still, the aranea he had met had never given any indication of knowing any magic beyond the mind-based one, so maybe this group specialized in the field or something. Having a way to deal with their mind affecting abilities was certainly a must before confronting them. One of the books also suggested aranea were vulnerable to light-based attacks, being nocturnal in nature and lacking eyelids. It sounded plausible to Zorian, and he was pretty sure his spell formula skills were sufficient to cobble together some flash grenades. A few more general defensive measures and he should be set. Well, as set as a mage of his caliber and resources could possibly be—it wasn't much, but it would hopefully buy him enough time to flee if things turned sour.

The other thing he was trying to puzzle out was the matriarch's claim that he was an empath. The idea seemed so wrong to him. The stories he'd heard about empaths painted an image of a compassionate, sociable person possessing great wisdom, respect for tradition, and lots of friends. Zorian didn't really fit this mold. Did that prove anything, though? Empaths were so rare—among humans, at any rate—that any sort of fact about them was suspect. As strange as it may sound, he rated the opinion of a giant telepathic spider higher than those of human authors. If he really was an empath, however, why didn't he... well, know it? You'd think the ability to sense other people's emotions would be very obvious. He supposed it was possible that his abilities were too weak and erratic to manifest themselves in an unambiguous fashion. The obvious question, then, was how he could discern the truth.

Fortunately, empathy wasn't a particularly sensitive topic so nothing stopped him from asking Ilsa or other teachers for help and information. Before he did that, however, he decided to try looking for help closer to home. He had noticed their landlord had an interest in esoteric branches of magic even though she wasn't a mage herself. She had enough books in her house to stock a small library. It wouldn't hurt to ask, he supposed, and Imaya was a lot more approachable than anyone else he could reach.

He approached her while she was washing the dishes one evening.

"Miss Kuroshka, could you spare a minute?" he asked. "I'd like to talk to you about something."

"I told you to call me Imaya," she said, halting her task long enough to give him a mild glare. "And of course I can talk to you, but I have to finish this first. Pull up a chair and wait till I'm done."

Instead of doing that, however, Zorian moved to help her with her task. She'd be done faster if he helped, and it was a cheap way to score some points with her. She seemed momentarily surprised by his gesture but recovered her composure quickly and continued on as if his action was totally expected.

Once they were done, Imaya sat down at the kitchen table and motioned for Zorian to join her.

"So…," she began, "what exactly is weighing so heavily on the mind of my grumpiest tenant that he would come to me for counsel? The way you've been avoiding me this whole time, I might be excused for thinking you hated me."

"I don't hate you, Miss K… uh, Imaya," finished Zorian, correcting himself after seeing her cross look. "I've just been pretty busy, that's all. Kirielle kind of monopolizes all of my free time here."

"She is quite a handful, isn't she?" Imaya said. "Still, I can't see what a busy boy like you would want from me. You aren't trying to seduce me, are you?"

"What!? No!" sputtered Zorian. She was at least twice Zorian's age, for heaven's sake! "I am not—"

He stopped himself when he saw the barely restrained mirth emanating from Imaya.

"Very funny, *Miss Kuroshka*," he deadpanned, deliberately not calling her Imaya to spite her. "Very, very funny…"

"It was from my perspective," Imaya said, laughter dancing in her voice. "But I can see you don't take jokes at your expense too well, so let's just move onto the reason you sought me out."

"Well…," started Zorian, pointedly ignoring her remark about him being too sensitive about jokes, "it's actually magic related. I noticed you have a lot of books about esoteric magic in your home."

"It's a hobby of mine," Imaya said. "I always did have an interest in magic, especially the rare kind. I even went to a mage academy as a teenager, much like you. That's how I met Ilsa, actually—we were classmates back then. But… that was a long time ago."

Zorian nodded, accepting her last statement for what it was—a request not to pursue that topic further. He was fine with that.

"I assume you have read all of these books, then?" he asked.

"Each and every one of them," she confirmed.

"Did any of them perhaps relate to empathy?" Zorian asked. "Specifically, how can you tell if you're an empath yourself?"

"I did read something about that topic, though I don't have the book in question here with me." She gave him a curious look. "Why? Fancy yourself an empath?"

"Well… maybe," admitted Zorian. "I mean, it doesn't sound very likely to *me*, but I met an actual empath recently, and she seemed sure I was one, too. So I don't feel comfortable with just dismissing the possibility."

"Hmm," Imaya hummed. "And why do you think it's so unlikely if you've been told that you're one by another empath?"

"Shouldn't empathy be pretty obvious to the one who has it?" Zorian asked. "It's certainly not to me. Off the top of my head, I can't think of anything that would indicate I am one."

"Nothing?" Imaya asked curiously. "I find that hard to believe— the indicators of being an empath are so common and mundane that false positives tend to be a major problem. In fact, a lot of experts insist that there is nothing supernatural about empaths—that some people are simply a lot better at reading people's body language and environmental cues than most of humanity. It's far more likely that you're just ignoring the signs. For instance, can you honestly say that you've never had an instinctive 'feel' about a person you've just met?"

"Well, no, I can't say that," Zorian admitted. "I get feelings like that all the time. That isn't anything unusual, though."

"It might be," Imaya said. "Just how often do you get such hunches and how reliable are they overall?"

Zorian hesitated. "I get those feelings pretty much every time I talk to someone. They tend to be pretty accurate from what I can tell. Why? Is that so unusual?"

Imaya gave him a speculative look. "A bit, yes. Every time you talk to someone, you say? How about random strangers minding their own business? Do you get these… feelings about them, too?"

"Uh, sometimes?" Zorian admitted, shifting nervously in his seat. "Some people have really intense personalities, you know? You can pick them out of a crowd from the other side of the room without even trying."

"Interesting. How about groups of people? Can you make a spot judgment about the mood of a group without speaking to anyone?"

"Well, no," said Zorian. "Frankly, the pressure of being in a large enough group crowds out all other sensations. If I'm subjected to it long enough, I lose even the ability to make judgments about individuals, much less the group as a whole."

"The pressure?" Imaya asked, giving him a baffled look.

"It's a… ah, a personal problem," fumbled Zorian. "Every time I enter a big enough crowd, I feel this weird mental pressure that gives me a headache if I stay within it long enough."

Zorian shifted uncomfortably in his seat. He hated telling people about the pressure thing, since most people immediately assumed he was either delusional or making things up. His family, for instance, had never believed him when he tried to describe the phenomenon to them as a child, believing instead that he was making things up so he wouldn't have to attend social events. Eventually they grew tired of his claims and threatened to send him to a madhouse if he didn't admit he was lying, so he never brought the issue up again.

"That's… an interesting problem," Imaya said, her forehead creased in thought. "Tell me, is the pressure constant or does it vary according to some criteria?"

"It varies," said Zorian. "The more people there are in a crowd and the more densely they're packed, the stronger it is. It's also stronger if the crowd is…"

He trailed off as he suddenly realized something. Gods, he was so *stupid*!

"Yes?" Imaya prodded. "If the crowd is what?"

"…emotionally charged for some reason," finished Zorian lamely.

A short silence descended on the scene, and then Zorian rose from his seat and began angrily pacing around the room.

"Your empathic abilities are so strong that you literally feel the emotions of a crowd as tangible mental pressure bearing down on you," said Imaya after watching him pace around for a while. "And you think there is nothing to indicate that you're an empath?"

"It's not that easy! How was I supposed to know what the pressure was?" Zorian protested, nervously running his hand through his hair. "It's just… there. It has *always* been there, a constant annoyance that has been with me ever since childhood. Do you have any idea the sheer amount of trouble this has caused me? Isn't empathy supposed to be a boon? Most of the time I did my best to ignore it, vainly hoping it would go away in time."

"Well, yes," Imaya agreed. "Empathy is usually depicted as a great gift to the person who has it. But there are plenty of reports of empaths whose powers are so strong or volatile that they are crippled by them instead. Considering some of the horror stories I've read about, your case is relatively mild. It could have been worse."

'It could have been worse'—that could easily serve as a summary of his entire life so far. Oh well. There had to be a way to rein in his errant empathic abilities somehow, and he had plenty of time to find it. The aranea probably knew how, though he suspected he wouldn't like what they would ask in return.

"Zorian?" Imaya asked after a moment of silence. "I can see this is a somewhat sensitive topic for you, but can I ask you a question? Well, two questions, really."

"Sure." She had helped him, even if not how he had thought it would play out, so the least he could do was satisfy her curiosity.

"I get the feeling that you didn't like the idea of being an empath even before you knew what you do now," she said. "Why is that? Maybe I am projecting somewhat, but I can't imagine why you *wouldn't* want to possess an inborn magical ability. I hope you don't think you're a freak just because—"

"No, no, it's nothing like that," Zorian quickly assured. "I know a lot of civilian-born students react badly to anything that may make them… abnormal… but I'm not like that. No, the real reason I didn't like the idea of being an empath is… far more stupid than that. Actually, I'm kind of embarrassed to even admit it, so can we just move on?"

"No," Imaya said, a smirk on her face. "This I definitely got to hear."

Zorian rolled his eyes. Served him right for admitting it was embarrassing. At least she wouldn't remember this conversation once the loop reset.

"All right, but you can't tell this to anyone, okay?"

Imaya mimicked sealing her mouth shut.

"It's because empathy is usually portrayed as a *feminine* ability, one reserved for girls and girly men," admitted Zorian.

"Ahhh," nodded Imaya. "Of course a boy would be bothered by something like that."

"I'm not sexist or anything," Zorian hastily added. "But I already receive a lot of comments about my supposed lack of masculinity, and they're annoying enough as it is. I really don't want to see how bad they would get if they had this sort of 'proof'."

His family was the worst offender in that regard, especially his father, but he would keep that little tidbit to himself.

"I won't tell anyone," Imaya said. "And if it makes you feel any better, there is no evidence that empathy manifests itself more often in women than it does in men."

"I figured," Zorian said. "Very few magical abilities are gender specific, unless they're artificially designed to be that way."

"And I also think those people have no idea what they're talking about," Imaya said with a supposedly innocent smile that had a hint of mischief behind it. "I think you're a very handsome young man who will someday make some girl very happy indeed."

"T-thanks. What was the other question you wanted to ask, again?" said Zorian, trying to change the subject to something less embarrassing. She'd had her fun, no need to torture him further.

"I assume you will try to develop your ability further?" Imaya asked. Zorian nodded. "In that case, I'd like you to keep me informed about your progress. I find stuff like this incredibly interesting."

Zorian agreed, though it was essentially an empty promise. She would remember none of this after the next restart. Their conversation done, Imaya returned to her household chores and Zorian went back to his room to plan his visit to the aranea. He really didn't want to find out what the matriarch would do to him if he didn't show up soon.

"Well, this is it," Zorian said out loud, standing in front of the entrance to the sewers. The matriarch didn't tell him where exactly in the sewers she hoped to meet with him, but he knew where he had come across the spiders the last time, so he intended to start from there. "The point of no return. I once again offer you the chance to turn back. You don't have to risk your life with me, Kael."

He gave a pointed look to the morlock following after him, trying to use his newly found—perhaps newly recognized—empathic abilities to gauge the other boy's mood, but it seemed the morlock had his emotions too well controlled. That and Zorian had no ability to manipulate his empathy. Regardless of how Kael truly felt about this trip, he was clearly determined to see it through, though Zorian couldn't quite determine why. He had told Kael about the aranea matriarch's visit because he wanted to have someone to bounce ideas off of and Kael seemed like the best choice—not because he had wanted Kael to come with him. Kael, on the other hand, insisted that coming alone on such a meeting was the height of idiocy and that Zorian needed a partner to cover him. Zorian reluctantly agreed, not entirely comfortable with risking someone else's life, no matter how logical it was. Kael seemed amused that Zorian cared more about his safety than his own, considering that Kael would be restored to normal once the loop restarted and Zorian might not be, but Zorian's moral sense had yet to adapt to the implications of the time loop and he was horribly bothered by the idea of leading Kael to his death in the tunnels and leaving his daughter all alone in the world… even if it was only for a week or so.

"I told you to drop it," Kael sighed. "I'm definitely going with you. If nothing else so this aranea matriarch and I can have a conversation about ethical uses of mind magic."

Oh right—Kael was still kind of bitter that the spider searched through his memories in her quest to piece together what Zorian's motives were.

Zorian led the way when at last they descended into the tunnels. He chose his path carefully, occasionally leaving a magical trap behind them in the form of stone cubes covered in spell formula. If they had to flee, they could backtrack and draw any pursuers into the traps. Most of the cubes were designed to simply erect a forcefield to delay the attackers, but a couple had more… aggressive effects. At the very least, they ought to slow pursuers enough to give Zorian and Kael time to reach the surface.

Kael, meanwhile, was their anti-mentalist support. He had put a mind shield spell on himself and would remain under the spell's effects constantly. If the meeting at any point turned sour, Kael would immediately cast the spell on Zorian as well. Kael seemed sure that the spiders had a method of communicating with humans other than telepathy and suggested that they both use the spell right from the start, but Zorian knew he had to keep his mind 'open' if he wanted these talks to be in any way productive. His instincts, which Zorian now recognized as his uncontrolled empathic abilities, were telling him that aranea placed great significance on mind-to-mind communication. Shutting them out completely would be seen as an insult, even if they did happen to have alternative methods of communicating.

As they approached the spot where Zorian had first met the aranea during his romp through the sewers with Taiven, he felt a telepathic contact brush against his mind. Just as it had been the first time he had met the sapient spiders, this one was cruder, more forceful than the feather-light touch the matriarch had displayed.

A stream of psychedelic images and alien emotions hit his mind like a sledgehammer, causing him to stumble back in shock. Kael immediately shifted into defensive posture, but Zorian signaled him to stand down. He was pretty sure at this point that the aranea he was in contact with had no hostile intentions. It seemed more likely to him that this particular spider hadn't sufficiently honed his skills in communicating with the minds of humans, which were no doubt vastly different from those of its own kind.

As suddenly as it came, the communication stopped. The presence remained, however, and Zorian soon felt another aranea connect with him, using the first one as a sort of telepathic relay.

[Ah, so you've managed to find us in the end,] the distinctive mental voice of the matriarch spoke in his mind. [Good, I was beginning to fear I should have left instructions on how to find us. Stay where you are, please. I will be with you shortly.]

"She's coming," said Zorian to Kael, who nodded gravely.

They didn't have to wait long. The matriarch soon skittered into view, flanked by two other aranea guards. The fact that he was able to pick out the matriarch among the three aranea, despite the fact that all three of them were fairly identical to his eyes, was probably just another proof that he really was empathic. Things like these made him wonder just why he had needed a talking spider to point it out to him before figuring it out.

[I originally intended this to be a private talk between just the two of us,] the matriarch spoke to his mind. [But since you saw fit to bring a guard, I decided to do likewise. Oh well, at least you didn't shut me out of your mind like your friend did, so you're still better than most humans I converse with.]

"Kael isn't here just as a guard," Zorian said, speaking out loud for Kael's benefit. "He is involved in this thing as surely as you are, and I'd like him to participate fully in the discussion. Do you perhaps have a way to communicate vocally for his benefit?"

The matriarch seemed to consider this request for a moment before she suddenly started waving four of her front legs in front of her, tracing some complex gesture in the air. Zorian tried for a moment to decipher what she was trying to communicate before he realized she wasn't trying to talk to him.

She was casting a spell.

"There," a feminine voice declared from the direction of the matriarch, though her mandibles didn't move at all. "This is the aranea equivalent of the magic mouth spell with which you are no doubt familiar. It's just a sonic illusion, but it should be enough."

Huh. So they did have more than just mind magic in their arsenal.

"I thank you for your consideration," Kael said guardedly, obviously wary of the spiders but trying to stay polite.

"Far from me to refuse such a simple request," the matriarch said. Her voice indicated that she was obviously a little suspicious of Kael herself, probably because his mind was protected behind a mind shield spell. The spell made him immune to her abilities, but it also seemed to paint him as a threat to the aranea.

"Please, child," the matriarch scoffed. Zorian heard the words with his flesh and blood ears, but he also felt them broadcasted to his mind—she might be vocalizing her words for Kael's benefit, but she clearly wasn't going to give up communicating with Zorian 'the proper way'. "I could get past your silly human mind magic any time I wanted to. No, the reason I'm bothered by his mind ward is that it blocks me off from his mind completely. How am I supposed to trust him if he won't even let me read his emotions and surface thoughts? It's *rude*."

Zorian's mind boggled at the mindset that considered putting your surface thoughts up for scrutiny as being basic courtesy, but he supposed that's species differences for you. Kael didn't appear to be as understanding.

"Rude!?" he demanded, indignant at the accusation. "You think you have a right to just barge into people's minds as you please, no permission given or asked, and you call *me* rude!? You spied on my personal memories, damn it. I have every reason to protect myself!"

The matriarch sent Zorian a telepathic equivalent of a sigh, though no sound was vocalized for Kael's benefit. "So did I," she said calmly. "Your friend was a possible enemy that I needed to know more about, and you were one of the weak points I could target in order to get the needed information. Your mind was completely unprotected, after all."

"So why didn't you sift through Zorian's memories, then? Wouldn't that be quicker and more relevant to your quest?" Kael asked.

"Hey!" Zorian protested.

"I have limited myself to skimming his surface thoughts as a courtesy, because he is Open," the matriarch said. "Among aranea there is an unofficial custom to ask for permission before delving deeper into the minds of non-enemy psychics, regardless of species."

Kael narrowed his eyes. "And if a person isn't... *psychic?*"

"Flickerminds are fair game," the aranea matriarch said dismissively.

"All right, let's stop trying to piss each other off now and get back to business!" said Zorian with a clap of his hands, hoping to halt the argument before it got out of hand. "We were talking about the time loop and how you can help me with that. Before we get to that, though, I really have to ask—when you say I'm 'open', are you referring to my empathy?"

Kael gave him a surprised look at that, since Zorian never told him anything about being empathic.

"Being Open implies being empathic, but they are not the same thing. Empathy is just one of the powers available to you and a bit of a low-hanging fruit at that. But that's why you can use it, despite being completely untrained in the psychic arts. Openness often manifests itself as a low, uncontrolled empathy initially, coupled with a gift for divinations and the occasional prophetic dream."

"I… what?" fumbled Zorian, trying to wrap his head around this new information. Just when he had thought he had things a little figured out, something like this happened. What the hell was being 'open' or 'psychic', then? Was she saying he was a full-blown telepath or something?

"You could be that with enough training, yes," confirmed the matriarch, though he hadn't asked the question out loud. "I can teach you more about it… provided we come to some kind of mutually acceptable agreement about this time loop business."

"And what exactly do you want from Zorian in that regard?" asked Kael suspiciously.

"Why, my dear Kael, the same thing *you* want from him as well," the matriarch said with a hint of mockery. "I want in on this time loop."

For a moment Zorian wondered what she was talking about, but then his eyes widened as he understood what she meant.

"You want to keep your memories with each restart? To loop around with me and Zach?" asked Zorian incredulously.

Kael shifted uncomfortably in place, refusing to look at him in the eye. The aranea matriarch stared straight back at him without a hint of shame on her face.

"I… I guess I can see why you would want that," said Zorian hesitantly. "I mean, I'm not too happy about my situation, but even I can see that I'm benefiting massively from it. But you seem to have gotten the wrong idea—both of you." He glanced at Kael, but the morlock was still avoiding his gaze, no doubt concerned he had made Zorian angry. But it was confusion he would have seen in Zorian's face if he had looked. "The thing is, I don't know how to bring anyone into this loop. I don't even know how I got sucked into it, much less how to replicate it. I *can't* bring you into it."

"We didn't get the wrong idea, Zorian," Kael sighed. "We're not stupid. We know you can't do it now. We know you won't be able to do it by the time this time loop ends." He gave the matriarch a weak glare. "Or at least *I* know. Maybe the great aranea matriarch knows something this poor flickermind doesn't."

"I agree with the morlock," the matriarch said, refusing to rise to Kael's provocation. "It is highly implausible that you'd be able to bring us into the time loop as you are now."

"You've completely lost me at this point," Zorian complained. "What *do* you want, then?"

"My idea was to store memory packets in your mind, allowing your soul to ferry them when time resets itself," the matriarch said nonchalantly. "It's not quite as good as having your entire soul sent back, but it would be good enough for my purposes."

"And I would agree to that... why?" asked Zorian. That sounded like it would require some serious messing with his mind. Far more than he was comfortable with, in any case.

"I'm sure I can find something to tempt you with," the matriarch said, punctuating her message with a mental shrug. "You need information about the loop. I can give you that. You want to learn how to control your empathy. You need my help in countering the invaders. Need I go on?"

Zorian sighed and turned to Kael instead of answering her.

"I wanted to connect you with some people and have you figure out, with their help, how your connection with Zach works. Then you could apply that knowledge to bring me into the time loop," said Kael. "It would probably take quite a few restarts, and I don't have anything nearly as tempting as our esteemed matriarch over there, but on the other hand it is something that will definitely help you learn more about this time loop in the process."

Left unsaid was that those people Kael wanted to connect him with were probably all necromancers and that having them mess around with his soul was every bit as dangerous as letting the aranea tamper with his mind, and possibly more so.

"I see," Zorian sighed. "Well, I'll set aside your proposal for now, Kael, since that's not what we came here to discuss."

"That's fine with me," Kael said quickly. "I still have a lot to think about in that regard."

"Right," said Zorian. "Then let's move on to the details of the matriarch's proposal. Just out of curiosity, do you have a name? If we're going to do business, especially so sensitive, I'd like to know who exactly I'm talking to."

The matriarch didn't answer verbally. Instead, she sent a short burst of telepathy containing the same sort of psychedelic jumble of images and concepts that the less skilled aranea had bombarded him with in the initial greeting. Thankfully, this particular burst wasn't painful, just confusing—probably because it was so relatively short. After mentally dissecting the chaotic message in his head, he realized this was the name he had asked for. Translating the concepts into something appropriate for human communication proved a bit of a challenge, however.

"Spear of Resolve Striking Straight at the Heart of the Matter?" questioned Zorian curiously.

"As good an approximation of my real name as any," said the matriarch. "And yes, I know that's too unwieldy to use in human conversation. Your language is very crude, so it's hard to translate aranea names into it without ending up with such overdramatic-sounding drivel. You can just continue calling me matriarch and I won't hold it against you."

Kael snorted derisively at the matriarch's swipe against human speech, but didn't say anything. Zorian, for his part, was considering how to proceed.

"All right then," said Zorian. "You told me that there is a reason why you took the time loop seriously. Why don't you tell us what you meant by that."

Before the matriarch could answer, a loud roar pierced through the relative silence of the tunnel, quickly followed by several similar ones. The hair on the back of Zorian's neck prickled as he realized he knew what sort of creature made that sound.

A band of war trolls were coming their way.

CHAPTER 018

The Pact is Sealed

H e should have known, really. Every time he got even slightly closer to getting to the bottom of this mess, some complication sprang up to hamper his progress. It was uncanny. He was half tempted to conclude that the (as of yet unconfirmed) third time-traveler was deliberately sabotaging him, but in that case he would have expected something far more deadly than a pack of war trolls.

...and now that he thought about it, it was kind of scary how radically his perspective must have shifted during the last year if he started considering troll war bands a nuisance rather than an existential threat.

[Not this again,] the aranea matriarch complained telepathically. [How do those things keep finding us? I had the whole web warded against divinations and everything...]

Zorian filed in the back of his mind the fact that this wasn't the matriarch's first encounter with the war trolls, but at the moment he didn't really have enough time to consider that little tidbit in any appreciable detail. He exchanged a knowing look with Kael, and then they both turned around and started running in the direction they had come from. Zorian motioned for the aranea to follow after them, and received a thought of assent from the matriarch in turn.

[We can't outrun them,] the matriarch noted as they ran. [Especially us aranea. Aside from short bursts of speed, we're actually a lot slower than humans.]

[It's fine,] Zorian thought, certain that the aranea would pick up on it. [Kael and I prepared a couple of surprises for pursuers behind us. They should slow the trolls down enough for us to reach the surface.]

[Ah. An insurance against me in case the talks turned sour?] the matriarch surmised. [You hid it well from my surface scans. I would have been caught off guard if I had truly planned to double cross you. Then again, I don't think I could have caught up to you if you had decided to run anyway, so it was mostly a wasted effort. Or would have been, had there been no war trolls.]

[Information on aranea running speed is a tad hard to come by in human books,] Zorian thought irritably as he slowed down to let the aranea overtake him. They were just about to pass the first trap and he didn't want to seal the aranea on the other side of the forcefield along with the trolls. [Can't you use your mind magic to pacify those things?]

The war trolls rounded the corner behind them in a tightly-packed mass of green flesh, howling like lunatics and waving their huge swords and maces around like they were twigs. But Zorian was ready. He sent a pulse of mana into the pair of nearby sigil-covered cubes and a sheet of force sealed the corridor. It wouldn't last long if a bunch of trolls kept beating at it, but he had never counted on it being an insurmountable obstacle in the first place.

[Sadly, whoever is controlling them has learned to shield their minds against us after the first few conflicts,] the matriarch said. [It's not foolproof, but we won't be able to pick their defenses apart before they smash us into pulp.]

There was a terrible racket behind them, and Zorian chanced a glance back at the barrier to see what was happening. The sight that greeted him brought a pleased smile to his lips. The trolls had failed to arrest their momentum properly and ended up crashing head-first into the barrier. Probably because the relatively narrow corridor only allowed the trolls to advance in a single line and the ones in the back didn't let the ones in the front break up the mad charge. Or maybe they just didn't recognize the forcefield for what it was? No matter, the point was that they were currently all tangled on the floor in a great big confused mass. They would need some time to reorganize, which would give even the slow spiders enough of a lead to escape cleanly.

As an extra precaution, he activated the next two barrier traps as well, but the two cubes holding explosive traps he simply scooped up and took with him. They were weapons of desperation, truth be told, and he wasn't sure if he could activate them without blowing himself up along with the target. Besides, he was pretty sure they didn't have enough power to seriously damage a troll, being designed to handle much squishier targets.

Zorian was worried about how they were going to smuggle a trio of giant spiders past the entrance guards—but one look at the blank faces of the two men as the spiders scuttled into their view discarded this concern quickly. The guards continued to look around them, casually alert, and even nodded at Kael and Zorian. But their gazes seemed to slide right past the aranea as though over empty air. The aranea seemed to be able to edit people's senses in real time, effectively erasing their presence. Zorian had to admit he hadn't thought the aranea's mind magic was quite so... *subtle*. It would appear he was still taking them far too lightly.

But anyway, they were back on the surface and totally safe. Huh. He hadn't expected the whole thing to end so... favorably. When he realized a pack of trolls was coming after them, he fully expected he was heading for an early restart. It seemed good things *did* happen to good people occasionally. Still, as happy as he was at his current fortune, his talk with the aranea wasn't finished yet, so the four of them quickly relocated themselves in a deserted alley to continue their conversation.

"We should be safe enough to talk here," the matriarch said in her magically-assisted voice. "I can't sense the presence of any minds that don't belong here. Not even those blasted cephalic rats."

"The what?" asked Zorian.

"Another psychic creature with which we've recently come to share this city," the matriarch groused. "They look much like regular rats, except the top of their head looks like it has been sawn off, leaving their brains visible."

"Oh," Zorian said. "I actually saw something like that once, back in my original live-through of this month. I never went down that street in any of the subsequent restarts, though."

"Probably for the best," the matriarch said. "It is likely they are working for the invasion forces. They only appeared recently and the trolls started harassing us when we tried to exterminate them."

"Are the rats intelligent?" asked Kael. "You seem to be implying they're some kind of spies, yes?"

"They are psychic, like us," the matriarch said. "Their minds are telepathically linked to one another, forming a collective intelligence. Individually, they are little more than particularly cunning rats, but the more of them group together, the smarter they get. And the stronger their telepathic abilities become. They're small enough to get anywhere and the death of any particular rat is inconsequential. Each one acts as a relay for the full power and intelligence of the entire swarm. They're almost perfect spies, better than even us aranea. As I said, we tried to get rid of them before they could muscle in on our territory… but we failed to account for the fact they weren't working alone."

"Crap," Zorian said. "With those things running around the city, it's no wonder the invaders are so well informed. They could be pulling information straight out of people's minds without anybody realizing it. All they need to do is find one person that is privy to sensitive information and whose mind is unprotected, and they can blow a hole in the whole system."

"Yes," the matriarch confirmed. "Aranea can do something similar, but not nearly to the same extent. We're too big to move as freely through human settlements as cephalic rats do, and our individual members are not as expendable as individual cephalic rats. They can get into many places where we can't, especially warded ones—giant spiders trip defensive wards in ways that a couple of funny-looking rats do not."

Zorian frowned as he suddenly realized something. With these cephalic rats on the loose in the city and working with the invaders, there was no way the invasion organizers remained ignorant of the time loop in every single restart. Zorian himself had not advertised his situation much, but Zach did. Sometimes very visibly and explicitly, if Zach hadn't been speaking in hyperbole when Zorian talked to him. So whoever was controlling the cephalic rats knew about Zach being a time traveler in at least some of the restarts… and never did anything about it. Zorian found that difficult to explain. Did they just refuse to believe what their agents on the ground were telling them? That sounded uncharacteristically sloppy considering how well the invaders seemed to be organized otherwise.

"An interesting point," the matriarch said, breaking him out of his thoughts. "I'm beginning to understand why you're so reluctant to deal openly with this Zach. But we're getting distracted here, dancing around the real issue. You heard my offer, Zorian. I have been very generous about my information thus far, but I'm afraid I'm going to have to put my foot down now. I want a straight answer. Will you let me send a memory packet through you or not?"

Zorian sighed. What a difficult question. He wanted—no, *needed*—what the matriarch was offering… but he really didn't trust her with this. And really, how could he? Mind magic was only a hair's breadth better than soul magic in terms of abuse potential, and that was only because mind magic had well-established counters, whereas soul magic did not.

"You're asking a lot," Zorian complained.

"I offer a lot," the matriarch countered. "And besides, I'm taking as big of a risk here as you do. I have no guarantee that you will actually track me down in each restart and alert me to the memories I stored inside your mind. What stops you from playing along for a few restarts, until you've gotten everything you wanted from me, and then meticulously avoiding contact with me for the rest of the time loop? Nothing. I have taken a leap of faith and decided to trust you. Is it so wrong to expect a similar commitment from you in turn?"

A short silence descended on the scene as Zorian digested her words in his head. He supposed there was some merit in what she was saying, though he wasn't quite buying the idea that she was risking as much as he was. His risk was more final and immediate than hers.

Oh well. No pain, no gain.

"Fine," he said. "I agree to your terms."

"You are a braver man than I," Kael told him as they slowly walked back to Imaya's place.

Zorian absent-mindedly rubbed his forehead instead of giving him a proper answer. He didn't feel noticeably different in the aftermath of the procedure the matriarch had performed, but Kael was worried about possible dormant command spells that the matriarch may have implanted along with the memory packet.

"I actually had a reason to think it might not be as dangerous as it sounded," Zorian finally said.

"Oh?" Kael prompted.

"Yeah. I researched the limitations of mind magic before we went to talk to the matriarch, both the classical spellcasting type and the telepathic abilities of magical creatures known to use them. I even asked Ilsa and our combat magic instructor for advice. I probably made them really suspicious of what the hell I'm doing but whatever. Anyway, everyone seems to agree that even expert mind mages can't just rewrite someone's brain on a whim or in a stealthy manner. It takes a great deal of time and you basically have to knock the victim unconscious or they will be fully aware of what you're trying to do to them and will fight it with everything they have—physically and mentally. If the matriarch tried to do something truly terrible to me, we would have known quickly enough."

"I'm not really sure I could have done much for you, even if I had noticed the deal had gone bad," Kael said. "I do have some modest combat skills, but I doubt they'd be enough to fight off three giant spiders that are all within jumping distance of me."

"It doesn't matter," said Zorian, reaching into his pocket to retrieve one of his two unspent explosive cubes. He held the stone cube in his palm so Kael could see it. "All I had to do was send a pulse of mana into these and both the matriarch and I would have ended up in pieces. I very much doubt the matriarch could have incapacitated me faster than I can pulse my mana."

"Suicide?" Kael asked, sounding surprised. He shook his head. "I stand by what I said. You are a braver man than I."

"As Zach once told me, the time loop skews your perspective on dying," said Zorian, putting the cube back in his pocket. Now that he thought about it, his impromptu security system reminded him of the similar system that protected Zach from the lich's soul meld spell. He should probably start carrying something like this all the time, just in case. Something way lighter and less noticeable than two big stone cubes, though.

"It's still possible she used something less comprehensive than a full personality rewrite on you, though," Kael said after a few seconds.

"I know," Zorian said. "But you heard her. The memory packet should last for a year, at minimum. I plan to avoid the aranea in the next several restarts while I look for a way to examine my mind for such things. Even if the magical expertise is beyond me, I'm sure I can hire an expert to take a look at me."

"Ah. Good idea," Kael said, nodding. "Of course, that means it will be a while before you can question the matriarch again. She did say she wouldn't share any further information until you deliver the memories to her reborn self in the next restart."

Zorian shrugged. "An acceptable delay." It wasn't like he had nothing to do while he waited, and Zach had indicated he would be spending the next several restarts in Cyoria as well. Nor was this restart over. He wanted to see what Haslush would do about the invasion and how Zorian might be able to help—if he ended up staying in Cyoria during the summer festival at all, that is. He wasn't sure he wanted to do that, all things considered. "So... do you want to tell me your master plan for getting yourself into this time loop now or later?"

"Later," Kael grumbled. "I haven't even ironed out all the details in my head yet. Stupid spider and her big mandibles..."

"I'm pretty sure her speech didn't involve mandibles in any way, actually," Zorian said. "It was a pure sound illusion."

"Really? Wasn't my mind shield spell supposed to protect me from mind effects like illusions, even if they're beneficial?" asked Kael, frowning in confusion.

"The matriarch's spell wasn't targeting your mind. It created actual sound waves," said Zorian.

"But then it's a sound spell, not an illusion, no?" Kael stated more than asked.

"Officially, any spell that creates fake scenery is an illusion, regardless of the means it uses to do so. Many illusions are made primarily out of actual light and sound, but they're still illusions."

"That's... surprisingly imprecise," Kael said.

"I understand it's because a lot of actual structured spells from illusionary disciplines combine mental illusions with... well, let's call them physical ones. Theoretically, you could separate the two into different categories, and many tried, but in the end the Eldemar mage guild decided to just admit defeat and lump them together."

"How surprisingly practical of the guild, then," Kael said. "I guess even they get an attack of common sense from time to time."

Zorian said nothing. He didn't need empathy to deduce that his morlock companion had a bit of a grudge against the guild for some reason. Personally, Zorian thought the mage guild was doing a pretty good job overall, but he wasn't so impressed with them that he would defend them in front of others.

The rest of the walk passed in relative silence.

As the start of the summer festival approached, Zorian became more and more certain that Haslush wasn't going to do much about the invasion. He wasn't sure whether the man had decided Zorian's suspicions were merely a rumor or whether he was ordered to drop the issue, but he no longer seemed very interested in the whole matter. For Zorian, this was a sign that he should take Kirielle and get out of the city before the invasion began. He had no interest in getting murdered by the invaders again, and even less in having Kirielle die alongside of him.

He would have to see whether he could talk Kael and Imaya into leaving with them.

But although the date was fast approaching, such problems weren't a pressing concern yet. And in the aftermath of performing a series of mind-numbing tasks for Kirithishli that day, all he wanted was to eat and sleep, not plot. Conveniently, the moment he walked into the house he was assaulted by the smell of food wafting from the kitchen. Imaya's insistence on keeping her informed of his comings and goings was somewhat annoying, but Zorian had to admit it was convenient how she timed her meals to match his and Kael's schedules.

He entered the kitchen and was immediately tackled by Kirielle.

"Brother, I hurt my hand!" she wailed, waving her hand in front of his face. "Hurry, you have to heal it!"

Zorian snatched her wrist to stop her from flailing about and inspected the grievous injury. It was a shallow cut—a scratch really—that would probably heal on its own by the end of the day. Out of the corner of his eye, he could see Imaya trying not to laugh.

Zorian suppressed the urge to sigh. He knew his family would make fun of him if they knew he was an empath, but he honestly hadn't expected Kirielle to descend to this level. She *knew* he wasn't a healer, association between empathy and the healing arts notwithstanding. Though considering his excellent mana shaping skills, he would probably make a good healer with enough training… something to consider, at least.

Schooling his face into a serious expression, he slowly turned Kirielle's hand this way and that, pretending to study it in detail.

Finally, after a thoughtful hum, he looked Kirielle straight in the eye.

"I'm afraid there's nothing to be done, miss. We will have to cut it off," he concluded gravely. He then turned towards Kana, who was sitting at the table but studiously watching the entire exchange, and gave her a deep, meaningful look. "Fetch the saw."

Kana nodded seriously at him and made as though to leave the table, only to get stopped by a laughing Imaya, who assured her that he was just joking. Zorian was pretty sure the little girl understood that all too well and had just been playing along. Did they even *have* a saw in the house?

In any case, Kirielle wrenched her wrist out of his grasp at his declaration and pouted at him.

"Jerk," she declared, sticking her tongue out at him.

The meal was relatively quiet, except for occasional outbursts from Kirielle. But that was Kirielle—loud by nature, though Zorian was pleased to say she did have calm periods from time to time. Mostly when she was reading or drawing. It still surprised him a little every time he saw her do that, since it seemed rather out of character for Kirielle to be so absorbed in a book or a drawing. Doubly so because he knew from personal experience that their mother and father didn't think much of hobbies like that and tried to discourage them as much as possible.

After the meal, Zorian retreated back to his room, Kirielle following after him. Zorian didn't have the energy to chase her off and let her, but she seemed to be in a fairly agreeable mood today and left him largely at peace. He sat cross-legged on the floor and practiced his shaping skills, while Kirielle was lying on her stomach and drawing something on the floor, a small pile of papers scattered around her. Eventually, though, her pen stopped moving and she spent the next several minutes nervously chewing on the tip of it. Zorian was versed well enough in her tics by now to know his peace and quiet would end soon after.

"Zorian?" she suddenly asked.

"Yeah?" he sighed.

"Why do you study so hard?" she asked, giving him a curious look. "Even though nothing really matters in this time loop you're stuck in, you still keep working all the time. Don't you want to have fun from time to time?"

"You're wrong," Zorian said. "First of all, everything matters. You are what you do, and if I were to start doing stupid things just because there is seemingly no consequence for them, those actions would eventually come to define me. Secondly... I actually find studying fun. Well, maybe not all of it, but you get the idea." There was a short silence, but Kirielle seemed reluctant to continue the conversation, even though she clearly wanted to say something. Zorian decided to help her out. "Why do you ask? Is there something you would rather be doing?"

Kirielle's eyes darted between him and the pile of drawings on the floor several times before she finally reached a decision. She scooped up the papers into a neat stack and promptly plopped them into Zorian's lap.

"Can you look at my drawings and tell me what you think?" she asked excitedly.

Oh. Well, that wasn't too bad. He had never paid much attention to her drawings, especially since she tended to hide them whenever he tried to get a better look, but from what he had glimpsed they were pretty good. Hell, he was feeling in a good mood so he wouldn't even mock her... too... much...

Damn.

Zorian watched and listened in silence as Kirielle showed off the fruits of her labor, explaining what the drawings represented with a great deal of animated gestures. Not that she needed to do so, because the drawings were frighteningly realistic. She wasn't just good—she was freaking amazing. Zorian could swear he was looking at drawings by a professional artist rather than some childish drawings of his little sister. One of the drawings was a very detailed scene of Cyoria's cityscape that was so chock full of little details that Zorian was shocked Kirielle actually had the patience to put them down to paper, never mind draw them properly.

"Kirielle, those are absolutely amazing," he said honestly. He had intended to make a few jabs at her skill at first, but he honestly couldn't see anything remotely worth mocking in these. "Why on earth is Mother not bragging to everyone about having a budding little artist for a daughter?"

Kirielle shifted uncomfortably in his lap. "Mother doesn't approve of me drawing. She won't buy me any supplies and she yells at me whenever she catches me doing that."

Zorian gave his sister a baffled look. What? Why on earth would she do that? Mother was close-minded and status-obsessed, but not actively malicious. He picked up Kirielle's stack of drawings and leafed through it again, stopping at a very nice portrait of Byrn, the boy he and Kirielle had interacted with on the train to Cyoria. Kirielle hadn't seen the boy since, yet she was able to create a very faithful rendition of him, presumably by working from memory alone.

"Wait," he said suddenly. "Is that why you keep stealing my notebooks and writing supplies?"

"Ah! I thought you didn't even notice," she admitted. "Since you never complained about it to Mother. Thanks for that, by the way."

Well, he had never said anything because he thought Mother wouldn't do anything about it, even if she knew. But hey, all was well that ended well, and he certainly wasn't going to tell Kirielle the truth and destroy whatever gratitude he had just earned...

"What about the books, then? I suppose she disapproved of those, too?" Zorian guessed.

"Yeah," Kirielle said, clutching her drawings close to her chest.

"She won't buy me any. She says a lady shouldn't waste time with such things."

That he actually expected, truth be told. Mother didn't like it when *he* spent his time reading, so he imagined she would be none too happy to see her darling daughter picking up such a hobby. Still didn't explain why she didn't want Kirielle to draw, though.

"Well, that's Mother for you," said Zorian. Kiri seemed to be getting rather upset, and Zorian could totally understand. It would appear her situation had more similarities to his own than he had ever dreamed about. "Don't worry about it. It was the same with me at first. She'll lay off once she sees she can't bully you into submission."

"It's not the same!" Kirielle suddenly snapped at him.

Now what?

"Kiri…"

"You don't get it! It's not the same because you're away from home most of the year and she can't do anything to you while you're away! You and Daimen and Fortov are here, learning magic and doing whatever you want, *and I'll never get to do that!*" She buried her head in Zorian's chest, her tiny little fingers digging painfully into his arms. "It's not the same because I'm a *girl*…"

Zorian wrapped his arms around Kirielle, rocking her gently to calm her down while he digested what she was telling him. Finally, a realization hit him. Traditionalists in Cirin often held the view that educating female children was a waste of time and money. Hell, some of them even went against the law and refused to send their daughters to elementary school to learn how to read and write! It didn't help that mage academies tended to be rather expensive, even lower quality ones…

"They don't plan to send you to a mage academy…," Zorian concluded out loud.

Kirielle shook her head, her face still buried in his chest.

"They say I don't need it," she said, sniffing sadly. "They already have a marriage arranged for me for when I turn fifteen."

"Well, isn't that nice for them," said Zorian coldly. "You know what, Kiri? You're right. It's not the same. I had to defy Mother and Father all by myself… you, on the other hand, have *me*."

Kirielle peeled her face from his chest and gave him a searching look.

"You never wanted to help me before," she said. "Every time I asked you to teach me magic, you blew me off."

"I didn't understand what you were dealing with," Zorian shrugged. "I thought you were just impatient and didn't want to waste my time on something you were going to learn in due time anyway. But rest assured, if Mother and Father don't change their minds over the years, you will always have a teacher in me."

She stared at him for a few seconds before she snatched one of his arms by the wrist and gripped it in an oath-making position.

"Promise?" she asked.

Zorian squeezed her hand tighter, eliciting a yelp from her.

"Promise," he said.

Two days before the summer festival, Kael finally laid out his plan to Zorian. It was a lot less concrete than the matriarch's one, and basically involved talking to a number of individuals that Kael thought might know something about soul magic or time travel. None of them were in Cyoria, though, and would require Zorian to blow off school in order to travel across the country—and in some cases even across borders. The morlock also hinted that he knew a couple of individuals living in the Great Northern Forest, but he admitted it might be a bad idea to visit those until Zorian could actually defend himself properly. Zorian memorized the names and locations, but it would be a while until he could visit any of them.

The end of the restart was entirely uneventful. He, Kirielle, Kael, and Kana boarded the train heading out of Cyoria on the night of the festival and spent the last remaining hours playing card games to pass the time. Imaya refused to go with them, which was fairly unsurprising, given the suddenness of their request and their inability to adequately explain why.

And then, like always, Zorian woke up in Cirin with Kirielle wishing him a good morning. He didn't take her with him this time, which turned out to be a good decision as Zach did indeed show up at the academy. The other time traveler tried to strike up a conversation with him, but Zorian was determined to avoid him and gave him a cold shoulder. After a few days, Zach seemed to admit defeat and gave up, but Zorian could see that the other boy was watching him way more closely than he did most people. Zorian's freedom to act as he saw fit was consequently somewhat limited, and he mostly amused himself with honing his shaping skills, combat magic, divinations, and spell formula. He chose, in order to keep his distance from the matriarch, not to tell Taiven about the 'rumors' of giant telepathic spiders in the sewers.

An entire restart passed in this fashion. And the next one. And the next. In total, six restarts passed before Zach stopped approaching him at the start of each restart and otherwise paying attention to him. Despite this, Zorian was pleased with what he had accomplished.

He spent three of the six restarts learning from the ever-enthusiastic Nora Boole, with the other three focused on Haslush, and had become skilled enough with spell formula to create a lighter, more inconspicuous version of his explosive suicide switch. It was still a cube, though a much smaller one made of a combination of wood and stone. He made a habit of creating two of them at the beginning of each subsequent restart and attached them to his key ring so they would appear as an ornament.

He had discovered a mage in Cyoria who specialized in mind magic and paid the man to inspect his mind for implanted compulsions and other nasty surprises. This proved less productive than Zorian had hoped. The mage admitted he was rather baffled by the memory packet and couldn't confirm it only contained memories. He did confirm, however, that it was currently dormant and that no other magical effect was currently active in his mind. If there was a trap hidden in the memory packet, it had yet to activate.

Zach was once again at class in the seventh restart, but when he didn't so much as glance Zorian's way when they crossed paths, Zorian knew it was time to get down to business.

CHAPTER 019

Tangled Webs

O ne thing Zorian found interesting
about the restarts was that small, seemingly inconsequential choices exerted
incredible influence on what happened in the
restart. Conversely, actions that he felt should
throw everything out of whack often tended to
have muted, or even non-existent effects. Case in
point, the last time he had gone into the sewers
to meet the matriarch, convincing Ilsa to grant
him an access permit to enter the sewers had been
trivial. Thus, when Zorian marched into Ilsa's office a few days after the beginning of classes, after he realized Zach had decided to give up on

befriending him in this particular restart, he expected the request to be easily granted.

He was wrong. No matter how much he reasoned and pleaded, Ilsa refused to allow a newly-minted mage like him to risk his life in the underworld. He tried to demonstrate his—at this point rather advanced—combat magic skills, but Ilsa wasn't interested and simply shooed him out of her office. It took nearly an hour of fuming and pacing in his old room at the academy for Zorian to calm down and realize what the difference was.

Last time he came with Kael. A self-taught genius mage who was also a single parent and had probably dealt with danger before in his life. If Kael thought Zorian was ready to go down into the tunnels beneath the city and was willing to accompany him to boot to make sure he was safe, then that was good enough for Ilsa. This time he came alone, though. No Kael, no permit.

Not that Zorian was going to be deterred by such a minor setback, of course. He knew at least one person who already had a permit to go down there and might be persuaded to help him.

"Roach, I hate you. You do know that, right?"

Zorian released a long-suffering sigh, opting to keep an eye on the tunnel in front of him instead of turning around to look at Taiven. He didn't need to turn around to know she was making faces at him. "No, Taiven, I don't. After all, you only told me so five times already. Maybe I'll remember it if you say it a few times more?"

"I just don't get it," Taiven complained, ignoring his sarcasm. "You refused to follow me down here when I asked you, saying it's too dangerous. And then you come back to me a few days later, asking me to take you into the tunnels."

Yes, and he was very much regretting it. Why couldn't she have waited back by the entrance like he had asked her to? He still didn't know how he was going to explain aranea to her when they found the damn spiders. Hopefully the aranea would be savvy enough to hide in the shadows while he talked to them telepathically—kind of a hassle, but it would give him an opportunity to arrange a proper meeting in the future somewhere more accessible.

"I mean, were you trying to piss me off?" Taiven continued, undeterred by his lack of response. "Because I'm feeling pretty angry right now, let me tell you…"

"Taiven, please," Zorian pleaded. "I said I was sorry! How many times do I have to apologize? You of all people should understand considering how many times you pulled stuff like this on *me*."

"Not quite like this," Taiven grumbled. "At least tell me where we're going."

"I actually don't know," admitted Zorian. He had no real notion of where their home territory lay in the tunnels and was relying on one of the aranea scouts inadvertently contacting him by trying to read his mind. "I'll know it when I see it, though."

"Zorian, I swear, if this is your idea of a prank—"

"I'm totally serious," Zorian assured her. "I'm pretty sure we're getting close. It shouldn't take too—"

An alien presence skittered across the surface of his mind, withdrawing immediately when it realized its intrusion was detected. Its telepathic touch wasn't as subtle as that of the matriarch, but Zorian definitely received an aranea feel from it.

"Wait!" he protested, hoping that the aranea hadn't physically fled already. "I want to talk to you, aranea! I have important information for your matriarch!"

"Zorian, what the hell are you talking about?" Taiven asked, thoroughly baffled at his actions. "And who are you talking to, anyway? There is no one here."

Zorian said nothing. Seconds passed in utter silence as Zorian patiently waited for a response from the spider. Taiven seemed to be torn between feeling irritation at his behavior and agitation at the potentially dangerous situation. Eventually, the aranea decided to re-initiate contact...

...by stepping into the open right in front of him and Taiven.

Taiven gasped in shock at the appearance of the huge, hairy spider and immediately moved to draw her spell rod, only for Zorian to snatch her by her wrist and motion her to stand down. She gave him a baffled look before glancing at the spider in front of them. The aranea stood motionless, observing them silently with its huge, pitch-black eyes but not making any threatening gestures. Taiven seemed to realize that the spider was no threat at the moment and relaxed, moving her hand away from the spell rod attached to her hip.

"Zorian...," she began, radiating a mixture of anger and worry at him.

"I'll explain later, I promise," Zorian said with a sigh before turning to deal with the aranea. "And you! Couldn't you have been a little more discreet? Why couldn't you have stayed in the shadows and contacted me telepathically?"

The aranea reconnected to his mind and sent a burst of amusement at him. [If you wanted to speak to me telepathically, why haven't you called out to me telepathically to begin with? Aren't you psychic yourself?]

Zorian grimaced. If only it was that easy. Finding information about mind magic from his fellow mages was like pulling teeth since the mage guild took a very dim view on mind magic of any sort, no matter how benign. Nobody could tell him what being psychic meant, much less teach him how to telepathically contact someone. He did track down a spell that allowed a mage to establish a telepathic connection with someone, but the spell was painfully crude—it worked only on other humans, the target had to be willing and able to lower their spell resistance, and the link only allowed word communication devoid of emotional and other connotations.

[I am untrained,] admitted Zorian. [I don't know how to contact someone telepathically. I only know how to piggyback answers on a connection someone else made.]

He wondered about that, actually. Nobody taught him how to do it, yet the concept seemed to come naturally to him. Is this what it meant to be psychic? Perhaps being psychic simply meant he was some sort of instinctive mind mage with inborn skills in the field.

[That's so sad,] the aranea said. [You are incomplete. But I suppose it could always be worse. You could be a flickermind like your friend there.]

Zorian glanced at Taiven, suppressing a snort of amusement. It was a good thing he was talking to the aranea telepathically, because he could just imagine how Taiven would react if someone called her a 'flickermind'.

"What?" Taiven asked, apparently having noticed his look.

"Nothing," Zorian mumbled, shaking his head. [Miss aranea, I—err, you are a miss, right?]

It was hard to tell, but he was pretty sure the aranea he was talking to had a female feel to her. Plus, the aranea were led by a matriarch, so it would make sense for outsiders like him to mostly meet the female members of the species.

[All aranea are female,] the spider said.

[What, really?] Zorian asked. [How on earth does that work? Do you just divide like microbes or spontaneously get pregnant or what?]

[Nothing that exotic. It's just that our species is extremely sexually dimorphic, and the males are both smaller in stature and pretty much subsentient. We don't consider them real aranea,] the spider explained. [If you talk to one of us and they're smart enough to talk back, they're female. The males would probably attack you in lieu of conversation, though you're unlikely to ever meet one unless you somehow gain access to one of our settlements.]

Zorian digested that information for a few moments and then decided not to ask any further questions on the topic. It was interesting, but not really relevant at the moment, and he didn't know how long he had before Taiven snapped from the pressure and started throwing around spells and demanding answers. She wasn't exactly a paragon of patience.

[I'm sorry to be inconsiderate, but I really need to speak to the >*matriarch*<,] Zorian said, doing his best to reproduce and send the weird aranea 'spear of resolve' concept that the matriarch had given as her name instead of calling her 'the matriarch'. Hopefully this would help convince the aranea to take him seriously when he told them about memory packets from another timeline.

[I have been listening to your conversation with >Watchful Eyes That Miss Nothing of Importance< for a while now, Zorian Kazinski,] the familiar presence of the matriarch announced.

Zorian couldn't help but marvel at the ability she had to throw her mind to any location inhabited by a subordinate. How convenient.

[It is,] confirmed the matriarch. [Now. How about you introduce yourself and tell me how you know my real name? Then we can move on to this important information you have for me…]

[I am Zorian Kazinski, mage in training,] Zorian said. [And the reason I know your real name is that you told it to me yourself… right before you shoved a memory packet into my mind and told me to give it to you later.]

[I… don't remember that,] the matriarch said hesitantly.

[I know,] Zorian said. [If you had been able to retain the memory of that encounter you would not have bothered with putting the memory packet inside my mind.]

[That's quite a claim,] the matriarch said after a short silence.

[How do I know that you're telling the truth? This could be a trap. You could be working with the people that have been sending trolls at us all this time.]

[Honestly, I have no idea how to prove the truth of my words to you,] Zorian said. [Your other self was sure you would have a way to prove the authenticity of the memory packet, even without additional proof. You didn't provide me with any means to convince you.]

[I see,] the matriarch said. She was silent again as she thought it over. [Give me access to your mind so I can see this memory packet for myself.]

[Of course,] Zorian said, offering no resistance when the matriarch delved deeper into his mind. He turned to his companion, who seemed to be at the end of her wits as she watched his silent stare down with the giant spider. "Taiven, I'm communicating with the spider telepathically. Everything should be fine, but if I fall to the floor and start screaming in the next few minutes, feel free to blast it to oblivion."

He still had his suicide cubes with him, but it never hurt to take additional precautions. Taiven immediately nodded at his words and Zorian saw the aranea in front of him twitch her legs uncomfortably at the implied death threat. The matriarch said nothing, too absorbed in her work.

Several minutes later, the matriarch's presence retreated from his mind.

[I... I need to think about this,] the matriarch said, her voice sounding dazed. [Come back in three days and we'll talk.]

[Wait!] protested Zorian. [I need a way to get down here without going through any of the official entrances. Otherwise I will need to bring Taiven here every time I want to come down here, and I'm not sure she'll want to talk to me after this.]

Zorian was immediately blasted with a mental image of the local section of the tunnel system, along with eight different ways to access it from the surface without going through any checkpoints. Likening the underworld to a sponge suddenly didn't seem so farfetched. In any case, that was apparently the end of his conversation with the aranea, because the spider in front of him promptly leaped into the darkness and disappeared, leaving him alone with Taiven.

He cast a weary glance at said girl, only to flinch at the frown she was giving him.

"Okay, now that the spider is gone, I guess you can explain to me what on earth I just took part in. Start talking," she commanded.

Stupid aranea and their indiscretion… what the hell was he going to tell Taiven now? Hmm…

"Before we get to that I would like to point out that if you had waited for me at the entrance like I asked you to—"

"Zorian!"

"Just saying," said Zorian lightly. "Okay, here's the thing. I'm an empath. Do you know what that means?"

"Not… really…," Taiven said slowly.

"It means I can sense other people's emotions," said Zorian. "And sadly, the ability is currently only instinctive. I have no conscious control over it, and it often causes problems for me, so I have been looking for help in mastering it. Unfortunately, I haven't found any humans willing to help me, so I… broadened my horizons. The spider you saw was an aranea—a sapient, telepathic species of spiders that I hoped to talk into teaching me how to control my powers."

Taiven stared at him for a few moments, opening her mouth at one point only to simply close it soon afterwards. "And what did they say?" she finally asked.

Zorian shrugged. "They'll think about it."

Taiven shook her head in disbelief and started walking toward the exit, motioning him to follow.

"Let's get out of here, monster charmer," she said. "We should discuss things somewhere else. Somewhere I can sit down and have a drink."

He followed.

True to her words, Taiven led him into an open-air tavern so they could sit down and relax while they talked. Well, so *she* could sit down and relax—Zorian didn't find the experience all that fun, especially since she made him pay for her drinks out of his own pocket. Strangely enough, Taiven accepted most of his explanation without complaint, finding his decision to seek help from a species of monstrous spiders 'ballsy' rather than reckless and stupid, but things degraded from there. She was displeased that he had originally planned to meet with the aranea without backup and wanted to know whether he had done things like that before, and who had watched his back if he had. That kick-started a heated argument about the wisdom and necessity of 'going solo' and his ability to fight his way out should things ever go sour. Zorian honestly didn't know whether she was upset because he was putting himself in danger or that he hadn't invited her along with him.

Probably the latter, since she quickly started insisting that he take her with him the next time he went into the sewers to meet the aranea matriarch. She'd only get in the way and try to get him to spill his secrets to her, so he refused. Taiven didn't like that at all, but seemed to realize nothing would be gained by pressing the issue directly. Instead, she switched tracks and suggested she should help him develop his combat magic. Zorian knew this was a trap—that she simply wanted to wipe the floor with him in a 'friendly spar' in order to show him how overmatched he was against a serious opponent (and thus make him more amenable to take her along like she asked)—but he agreed anyway. He was curious how long he would last against her, and he had nothing to lose except perhaps his pride.

Drinks discarded, they retreated to the training hall in Taiven's family home. Zorian stood opposite her, the length of the hall separating them, an array of targets and practice dummies standing silent witness. He fingered his rod of magic missiles, trying to decide how to approach this… practice spar. The training hall was, according to Taiven, heavily warded to protect people inside from spell damage, but usage of lethal spells was still not recommended. And while the ban on lethal spells was appropriate and sensible for a spar, it completely eliminated a lot of his arsenal. He had never really put much thought towards battles that weren't the 'kill or be killed' sort, so his spell choices tended towards the destructive end of the scale.

"I see you invested in a spell rod," Taiven said with a confident smile. "Must have cost you quite a few pieces."

Left unsaid—but heard loud and clear—was the implication that the money was wasted. Zorian had no chance in hell of overwhelming Taiven's defenses with magic missiles, and they both knew it. That's why he didn't even intend to try. Getting into a battle of attrition with someone who had bigger mana reserves than he did was a fool's game. So Zorian had a different tactic in mind. The prominently displayed spell rod was a deception, intended to give Taiven the wrong idea about his opening moves. His real ace in the hole was the shielding bracelet hidden under his right sleeve.

"I made it myself," Zorian said. "So it didn't cost me anything."

"Really?" Taiven said, surprised. "I had no idea you were that good at spell formulas. I mean, I knew you were interested in them, but…"

"You have your talent for combat and I have mine," Zorian said smugly. He was quite pleased with himself for getting so good at spell formulas—not only was this something he had been interested in since before the time loop, it was also something that could easily ensure his financial independence once he found a way out of the time loop. Spell formulas were widely known to be a difficult field to master, and experts in the field were well paid for their services. Zorian was already good enough that he could start taking commissions, if he was so inclined, and he would only get better as he went through the restarts.

"Whatever. In the end, you are overmatched even in the equipment department, despite your fancy self-made spell rod," said Taiven. She stretched her hand out to the side. A staff mounted on the nearby wall flew straight into her palm. He knew it was a spell staff even before Taiven channeled a burst of mana into it and caused a series of glowing yellow lines to light up across its surface.

"Show-off," he said. He was definitely learning how to do that himself one of these days.

"Ready?" Taiven asked, pointing the staff threateningly towards him.

"Ready," confirmed Zorian, twirling the spell rod in his hand.

Taiven reacted immediately, sending a small missile swarm consisting of five magic missiles at him. She was fast, far faster than he, and Zorian could see in her face that she considered herself already victorious.

Determined to prove her presumptuous, Zorian raised the hand that held the spell rod to erect a shield and used his other hand to throw a vial of white liquid at her.

The missile swarm crashed into Zorian's shield like a hammer. If Taiven had been facing old Zorian, the one that existed before the time loop, then this would have been the end—any shield he may have erected to defend himself would have been sloppily done and would have broken like glass under the onslaught. But she wasn't. She was facing Zorian the time traveler, and that Zorian had almost two years of knowledge and practice under his belt.

In the grand scheme of things, two years was not a huge amount of time. Nonetheless, that was still two years of continual combat magic practice, most of it focused on a handful of spells, including shield.

His shield spell was nearly flawless. The plane of force was practically invisible when not under strain, and Zorian could overcharge it a great deal to strengthen it further.

The shield held. The missile swarm crashed against it ineffectually, causing the nigh-invisible surface to turn opaque under the strain but doing little else of note.

Before Taiven could collect her wits and try another attack, Zorian sent a mana pulse at the vial arcing towards her. The vial shattered in midair, as if crushed by some unseen fist, and a thick white smoke billowed forth from the spot as the liquid turned to gas.

The vial wasn't anything special, just a simple alchemical mixture that caused coughing fits in whomever inhaled it, but it was enough to incapacitate Taiven, who stumbled out of the smoke dazed and off guard. Zorian mercilessly used her moment of weakness to send a smasher straight into her torso, hoping that was the end of the fight but half expecting Taiven to throw a shield at the last second to save herself.

Something, perhaps his empathy, warned him to dodge when Taiven suddenly thrust her staff towards the incoming missile—and by extension, him. It was a good thing he did, because she didn't cast a shield. She launched a massive battering ram of force that batted his attack aside like a snowflake and continued towards him unimpeded. Sadly, his dodge was only partial, and while he avoided the main thrust of the attack, he was still caught in the outer area of effect. The attack sent him spinning like a rag doll and he soon found himself crashing head-first into the cold, unforgiving floor of the training hall, spared a concussion or worse only thanks to the cushioning wards in the room.

Since Taiven seemed to be more interested in coughing her lungs out than trying to finish the fight, he remained on the floor for a while, waiting for his head to stop spinning. Apparently he had made the coughing gas a bit stronger than he intended. He laboriously climbed back to his feet and walked towards the recovering Taiven.

"You have a very strange definition of non-lethal," he told her.

"Serves you right, you—" A series of coughs broke through. "—cheater!" she growled.

"I got you good though, didn't I?" Zorian smiled.

She huffed and swung her staff at him lightly, obviously expecting him to dodge the slow-moving object. In the interest of showing off, Zorian erected a shield instead, causing the staff to bounce off and wrench itself out of her hand.

Taiven looked at the shield with no small amount of curiosity and gave it a couple of good hard knocks. The plane of force didn't even turn opaque, much less give way to her hits.

"What the hell is that shield of yours made of, anyway?" Taiven asked. "It took five missiles without breaking and it looks… different. It's almost entirely transparent; I can see it only because I'm standing so close to you. During the fight, I didn't even see it until my attack hit. I thought you were trying to shield yourself with your hand or something at first."

"It's just a shield spell, just greatly overcharged and superbly executed," said Zorian. "I spent a lot of time practicing that spell."

"Still wouldn't have helped you without that stupid trick you pulled," Taiven said, her glare returning. "This was supposed to be a spell battle, dammit!"

"You said you wanted to see how I fight," Zorian shrugged. "By the way, how did you know where to fire that attack of yours? You had your eyes shut pretty tight from what I could see."

"Oh. That's just a little trick one of my teachers taught me," Taiven said. "I doubt it would help you much, though—it's pretty wasteful in terms of mana usage."

"What do you mean?" Zorian asked.

"Well, it's a pretty simple move that involves expelling a large quantity of mana and saturating the area around you with it. You can then sort of sense your surroundings through the resulting mana cloud. The information you gain is very rudimentary, but you can easily spot concentrated mana constructs like that magic missile you threw at me. I actually didn't know where you were, even with the aid of the mana cloud, but I figured that if I aimed in the direction from which the attack came, I'd probably catch you as well."

That sounded… awfully familiar. Zorian was pretty sure he used the exact same technique for his secret unlocking trick, except that he focused more on using the mana cloud as an extension of his tactile sense rather than perceiving mana sources. Of course, there was quite the difference in scale from flooding a lock with his mana to saturating the entire greater area around him. He simply couldn't afford to be that wasteful with his mana.

However…

"Taiven," he began, "let's say for a moment that I saturate a fairly large bubble of air around my head with this method. Would I be able to sense mana-charged marbles within that volume with this method?"

Taiven blinked and gave him a curious look. "I… suppose. You'd probably have to spend some time mastering the skill to get a cloud sensitive enough to detect such low-powered sources, though."

"But it would be easier than trying to sense mana-charged marbles with my inborn mana sense alone, right?" Zorian pressed.

"Way easier," Taiven confirmed. "Actually, just about any method would have been easier than *that*. Gods, you'd have to be, I don't know, archmage-level good or something to sense a mana source that weak with no spells or other aids."

Zorian suddenly felt incredibly stupid. Of course Xvim's task seemed impossibly difficult—he was doing it wrong! Xvim probably expected him to use a method like this to sense the marbles. The asshole just didn't bother giving him proper instructions on how to go about doing it. Or any sort of instructions, for that matter.

Gods, he hated that man.

Following an argument about who won their little spar (Zorian claimed it was a draw, Taiven claimed she totally won in the end), Taiven insisted on more rounds to resolve the issue, and Zorian saw no reason to refuse. He lost all subsequent fights, of course—Taiven was strong enough to simply overpower him if she so chose and he no longer had the element of surprise on his side. Still, he felt he had done well since Taiven actually had to work to bring him down. Even she admitted that if he caught his opponent off guard and was ruthless enough in his opening moves, he could bring down even professional battlemages, though she warned that he could easily get in legal trouble that way. The mage guild looked very dimly on people who escalated fighting into the lethal realm, even in self-defense.

And anyway, finding out what exactly Xvim expected of him made losing to Taiven a few times worth it all on its own. Most of the skill he would attempt to employ was already familiar to him, so it only took a few hours until he was able to create a diffuse mana cloud around his head. Granted, he couldn't really feel mana sources as such, but a marble was a physical object as well. Thus, when Friday came around and Xvim unveiled his oh-so-clever training method to him, Zorian calmly identified where the marbles were going as they zipped around—and occasionally at—his head. Xvim wasn't impressed, of course. He simply started throwing a quick succession of marbles at Zorian and demanded that he sort them by magnitude of mana emissions. Which he couldn't do, of course, since he was sensing them by more rudimentary means. But this didn't concern Zorian. Now that he knew what to do, he fully expected to master the skill properly soon enough. Possibly by the end of the restart, unless Zach decided to tackle another dragon or something similarly insane.

Fortunately, Zach's primary interest at the moment was trying to organize some kind of 'mother of all parties' that involved inviting the entire class to his mansion during the summer festival. Being aware of the time loop, Zorian was one of the few people who understood what Zach was doing. He was trying to get as many students as possible out of harm's way without having to explain anything to them. But Zorian had no idea what Zach planned to do with all those people when the attack started, or how he intended to deal with Ilsa and her insistence that attendance at the school dance was mandatory.

After a few days spent honing his mana bubble, Zorian returned to the sewers. Finding aranea proved very easy, since they were expecting him this time. Any doubts about whether or not he was going to be taken seriously were wiped out when the forward scout he met took him to a familiar figure. The matriarch had decided to talk to him in person, rather than simply project her mind through one of her subordinates.

[Well, I have had time to digest the memories my... 'other self' sent me,] the matriarch began. [The story is... not as implausible as you might think, and the memories contained some pretty damning proof. I suppose we should swap stories now, no? Of your experiences, I only know the basics you told your friends, and you know precious little of why I'm not scoffing at the idea of time travel.]

[I suppose that would make sense...] Zorian said carefully.

[But you want me to go first,] the matriarch surmised. [Very well. First thing you should know is that my web has been in a conflict with your so called 'invaders' for several months now. They were an infuriating but manageable opponent... up until a week ago, when they suddenly developed a disturbing amount of precognition about our tactics and abilities. They had counters for secret skills that have been passed on from matriarch to matriarch for generations and have never been used within living memory up until that moment. They had counters for personal abilities that were unique to a single aranea. They even seemed to know how we were going to react in response to their increased threat and aggressive moves. In short, the amount of insight they possess about us is downright implausible. Believe it or not, time travel was seriously discussed as a possible method by which they could attain such information.]

[Not divinations?] Zorian asked.

[We know divinations, child,] the matriarch said. [If there is a field of magic beside the mind arts that we excel at, it is that. It is good that you mention divinations, though, because they hold a piece of the puzzle as well. You see, our web routinely tries to forecast the future with divination, with varying amount of success—highly disruptive events tend to make any future forecasts useless. What do you think happened when we tried to forecast the future during the past week?]

[It didn't work?] guessed Zorian.

[Oh, it worked. It gave wildly different results every time we repeated the forecast, no matter how little time passed between one forecast and the next, but it worked. So long as we didn't try to extend the forecast beyond the day of the summer festival. Beyond that date, the forecast returns a blank. Each and every time. It is as if everything beyond that date simply ceases to exist.]

Zorian swallowed heavily. He had often wondered what happened to everything when the time loop restarted itself, but had ultimately dismissed the question as unknowable. He didn't know whether to be relieved that he had no need to worry about leaving a soulless corpse in some alternate reality or disturbed that everything was literally being deleted when the time loop reset.

[I'm surprised I hadn't heard about that,] he remarked. [You'd think that some of the human oracles would have noticed something like that.]

[You underestimate the difficulty of future forecasting,] the matriarch said. [It takes quite a bit of skill to read the future, and the
process is time consuming and tedious. It doesn't help that the results
are often useless… or worse, misleading. And even if you do bother
to forecast the future, odds are that you're only doing it for a few
days at a time, since the predictions get more and more unreliable the
further you try to extend them. My fellow aranea frequently complain
that such forecasts are a waste of time, and this despite the fact that
our oracles can actually achieve a small measure of accuracy in their
predictions. Still, I imagine you're right—someone in the above-world
has run the forecasts and encountered the same thing and chosen to
keep quiet. Nobody likes a doomsayer… well, nobody of any authority,
in any case. It would be nice to have independent confirmation of our
findings, but I suspect few diviners would feel comfortable sharing
their secrets with a bunch of giant spiders. Perhaps if a certain young
mage with an interest in divinations were to talk to them?]

[I'll see what I can do,] said Zorian.

[I'll give you a list of names,] the matriarch said. [Now how about
you give us some details about the time loop and your experiences in it?]

Zorian gave them a basic rundown of the situation, leaving out
many of the details he considered irrelevant and a tad too personal.
The matriarch had only given him the bare bones version of their story
as well, so he didn't feel too bad about that.

[That bond between you and Zach is really inconvenient,] the
matriarch remarked when he finished. [I don't blame you for not taking a chance with it, but are you sure you can't talk to Zach without
triggering it? Who knows what useful things the boy knows about
this whole thing? Surely if you inform him of your fears, he will agree
to keep his distance.]

Zorian wasn't nearly so sure. He knew Zach meant well, but he
always did have problems with patience and self-control, and none

of his previous encounters with the boy convinced him he'd changed all that much in that regard. Zach would probably find another time traveler immensely fascinating and keep pushing at the boundaries until the soul bond either activated fully or was shown to be harmless.

[I'm surprised you haven't already ripped the knowledge from his mind,] Zorian remarked. [Isn't he a... err, 'flickermind'?]

[He isn't psychic, but he does have some skill in shielding his mind,] the matriarch said, not at all ashamed to admit she had already tried to steal his memories. [Not well, but enough that I can't do more than read his surface thoughts. Now stop dodging the question.]

Zorian sighed. [Everything I found out about soul bonds suggests that there probably isn't any bond between me and Zach. Soul bonds tend to be really obvious to even basic detection spells. My divination instructor in one of the previous restarts showed me a spell for detecting soul bonds and I used it in school a few times. Every student with a familiar is clearly connected to their partner, and the two soul-bonded twins are also clearly bonded to each other. There is absolutely no link between me and Zach that I can see. There is no way an accidental side-effect of an offensive soul mutilation spell has such sophisticated effects when even properly created soul bonds light up easily on detection spells.]

[Curious,] the matriarch said. [What is it, if not a soul bond, though?]

[Kael thinks that when the soul merge was terminated by our deaths, the link between us was *cut* rather than carefully untangled. As a consequence, a piece of Zach's soul ended up fused to mine, and the reverse is probably true for Zach. The control function of the time loop probably got confused at that point, and rather than decide which one of us is the real Zach decided to simply loop both of us.]

[That would explain why Zach was absent during the first few restarts and why he was so very sick when he finally did show up,] the matriarch said. [You probably both spent a number of restarts in a coma while your souls healed and integrated all the foreign bits, but he probably drew the short end of the straw when the spell was cut and ended up with far more soul damage than you.]

[It would,] agreed Zorian. [And honestly, it's the most plausible explanation I've got.]

[So why don't you want to talk to Zach, then?] the matriarch asked. [Oh, I see… the third time traveler.]

[Yes. It's pretty obvious at this point that there is at least one more person inside the time loop besides me and Zach. That someone is aiding the invaders and has gods know how big of a lead on me in terms of time spent in the time loop, so I definitely don't want to catch their attention. And they know of Zach. I mean, they have to—he really isn't all that secretive about his status as a time traveler and his activities. But they aren't doing anything about it. Zach is clearly trying to fight the invaders, so why leave him unmolested?]

[Because his actions don't matter in the long run,] the matriarch guessed. [From what you told me, he's trying to become strong enough to personally contest the entire invasion force. There is not much chance of that happening, even if he has all the time in the world to prepare.]

[That, and he's possibly already been neutralized,] Zorian said. [I'm pretty sure that Zach is the key figure in this time travel business—the original time traveler. He has too much potential in terms of money, family legacy, mana reserves and so on. He could benefit from the whole time loop setup better than virtually anyone else, and I don't think it's accidental. Furthermore, if I am indeed in this time loop because I have a piece of Zach's soul fused to mine, that means it's him the time loop recognizes as the legitimate focus of the spell. The thing is, his past actions indicate ignorance of any sort of purpose or master plan, as if he had simply been dumped into the loop with no warning or information.]

414

[You think his memories have been edited,] surmised the aranea.

[I think Zach entrusted his secret to the wrong person,] Zorian said. [They couldn't just get rid of Zach—as I said, he is the key to this spell—but they could eliminate him as a threat. Shift his attention in a harmless direction and so on. But I'm not Zach. I am not integral to this time loop in any way and can be disposed of at whim. If I talk to Zach, and he's being watched, or if Zach is unable to keep his mouth shut in front of the wrong people, I could end up being... deleted.]

[Well...] the matriarch said. [You're certainly one paranoid human. Then again, that might be the only reason why you're still in possession of your entire memory, so maybe I shouldn't talk. You do realize you're going to have to talk to Zach at some point, right?]

[Hopefully not before I identify the third time traveler,] Zorian said.

[Then we should make it a priority to track this person down,] the matriarch said.

[How?] Zorian asked. [I don't even know where to start. It could be anyone.]

[Considering you said Zach managed to kill old Oganj single-handedly, it is clearly not just 'anyone'.]

[He wasn't always that strong, though,] Zorian pointed out. [In the first few restarts, any decent mage could have overpowered him, even some of our classmates. For that matter, it could be a matter of backstabbing rather than losing in combat—someone could have drugged him or lured him into a heavily warded trap area.]

[Even a classmate, you say?] the matriarch asked speculatively. [That's interesting. Didn't you say Zach is fairly obsessed with learning more about the rest of your class? He would probably think nothing of sharing a secret with one of them, especially since they're 'just' students... How well do you know them as a whole? Are any of them acting strange?]

[I'm… not really very close to any of them,] Zorian admitted. [I don't think I would know if they started behaving strangely, so long as they didn't go completely out of character. I can think of a few that I'm sure aren't time travelers but…]

[Try to investigate,] the matriarch said. [It would be terribly embarrassing if it turns out the third one was hiding in plain sight all along, no? Try to see if you can connect any of them with the invaders as well.]

Before they parted ways, the matriarch gave Zorian a list of human diviners that might know more about the irregularities related to future forecasting, and they agreed to meet in another three days. Zorian was a bit annoyed that the topic of his empathy and getting it under control never came up but he supposed the matriarch wanted to see how useful to them he was before investing their time to teach him their (possibly secret) mind arts.

But, he realized as he left the sewers behind and stepped back into the light of day, it was nice having someone on his side in this whole tangled mess.

He just hoped he wasn't making the same mistake with the aranea that Zach did with the person behind the invasion.

CHAPTER 020

A Matter of Faith

Z orian didn't like temples. Partially it was due to his bad experiences with them as a child, but mostly due to his inability to understand the reverence with which the priesthood spoke of the vanished gods they were supposed to be venerating. Virtually every story he had read or heard about the age of gods made the divinities sound like gigantic jerks, so why would anyone want them *back*? Nobody could ever give him a satisfactory answer to that question, least of all his parents, who were religious only so long as the neighbors were watching.

The temple in front of him did nothing to

dispel that unease. The large, dome-shaped building on the outskirts of Cyoria was larger and far more imposing than any other temple Zorian had previously visited, despite being described as one of the smaller ones in Cyoria. Still, the aranea matriarch had claimed this temple housed the best (human) future forecaster in the city, so his unease would have to be set aside for the sake of accomplishing the mission.

He hesitantly stepped towards the heavy wooden doors that served as the main entrance to the temple, warily glancing at the huge stone angels that flanked the doorway. Lifelike and grim-faced, the angels appeared to gaze down on him as he approached, almost certainly judging him and finding him lacking. Try as he might, Zorian couldn't completely dismiss his unease with the statues, since there was a very real possibility they were guardian golems or some other sort of security. Eager to move out of their sight, he was just about to open the door and walk inside when he noticed a series of images carved into the door and paused to study them.

Although the carvings were fairly stylized and disjointed, he recognized instantly what they were about. They formed a crude sort of comic, depicting a familiar story of how the world was created according to Ikosians—and by extension, most religions drawing their traditions from them. According to Ikosians, the world was originally a swirling, shapeless chaos, inhabited only by the seven primordial dragons. One day, the gods descended from the higher planes of existence and killed all of them save one. This last one they refashioned into the material world that humans now inhabit, turning her body into dirt and stone, her blood into water, her breath into air and her fire into magic. The vast networks of tunnels stretching beneath the surface of the world are dragon veins, now empty of blood but still flooded with magic emanating from the Heart of the World—the fiery, still-beating heart of the primordial dragon that rests somewhere deep underground. Far from being content with her fate, the World Dragon still rages against her bonds, giving birth to natural disasters like volcanoes and earthquakes. Unable to strike back against the gods themselves, the dragon takes her anger out on their favored creations—humans—by utilizing her heart, the one thing the gods have not seen fit to take from her. Pieces of it continually flake off from the main mass, giving birth to horrifying monsters, at which point said monsters begin their ascent to the surface to terrorize mankind...

And so on. Zorian didn't believe there was much truth in the old story, but the whole thing was pretty horrifying if one took it at face value. With gods like that, it was no wonder the Old Faiths were steadily losing converts to new religions that popped up after the gods disappeared.

"Can I help you with something, young man?"

Zorian wrenched himself from his musings to look at the man who spoke to him. He found himself facing a young, green-haired man in priestly robes, peering at him from within the dark interior of the temple. The man's relaxed posture and friendly smile set Zorian at ease, but he couldn't help but wonder about that green hair. As far as Zorian knew, the only people who naturally had green hair were members of House Reid, and it seemed rather out of character for one of them to go into clergy. That particular house was infamous for their links to crime syndicates.

"Maybe," allowed Zorian. "I am Zorian Kazinski, mage in training. I was wondering whether Priestess Kylae was around and willing to speak with me? Oh, and sorry about worrying you. I suppose I had been staring at the entrance a little too long."

"Junior Priest Batak," the man introduced himself. "And don't worry, a lot of people are intimidated by the gates. It's why I like to greet newcomers personally like this. As for Kylae... well, she is currently in the middle of a ritual, but if you're willing to wait an hour or so I'm sure she'll be happy to hear you out."

"Sure," Zorian agreed. This was a better reception than he had hoped for, to be honest—he had half expected the man to put him through some kind of religious test before allowing him to see the head priestess. Waiting an hour or two was a minor price to pay, really. "Err, so should I come back later or…?"

"Nonsense," the man scoffed. "Come inside and I'll make us something to drink while we wait. It'll be nice to have someone new to chat with for a change. We get so few visitors these days…"

Uh oh, it seemed that he might still end up being subjected to a test, only this one in the form of 'casual' conversation instead of something overt.

"Slow week?" Zorian asked as they entered the temple. The interior was pleasantly cool and fairly dark, with rays of multicolored light streaming down from several high-placed stained-glass windows. It was also completely empty. He was grateful for the lack of crowds, but it was unusual to see a temple deserted like this.

"I wish," Batak sighed. He led Zorian through rows and rows of wooden benches that filled the temple's main hall, his steps echoing hauntingly behind him. "More like a slow decade. The aftermath of the Weeping has not been kind to this place."

"What do you mean?" Zorian asked. "What does the Weeping have to do with this place?"

Batak gave him a judging glance before sighing heavily. "Though the gods have gone silent, the priesthood has never been completely powerless. Most priests have some skill with magic, and higher ranks can usually call upon the aid of angels and other lesser spiritual entities, but our real claim to authority came from various hidden mysteries that were entrusted to us before the gods departed to the unknown. Over time, a lot of those were stolen or otherwise lost, but the one thing where we were always unmatched was the healing arts. As such, when the Weeping Plague started spreading across the lands like wildfire, we were expected to do something about it. Sadly, not only were we as powerless against it as anyone else, our close contact with the infected quickly resulted in massive casualties within our ranks. With the subsequent shortage of qualified priests, peripheral temples like this one were all but abandoned, both by believers and by the Holy Triumvirate."

Zorian looked around him, but failed to see any evidence of decay in the interior of the temple. The temple was clean and intact, and the white marble altar draped in silk looked practically brand new. Plenty of stone statues were scattered throughout the building, seamlessly melding into the walls or support beams, and most of the remaining unadorned space was taken up by wooden panels that had various religious images carved into their surface, much like the main doors. In short, it was an absurdly luxurious building by the standards of rural temples such as the one in Cirin and better maintained to boot. Zorian was almost afraid to ask what Cyoria's main temple looked like if this one was not considered important enough to keep running.

Batak led him to a small, unassuming door next to the altar and ushered him to what was apparently a more informal setting. Rather than being a classical office, it was instead a combination of a kitchen and a living room, far messier than and not nearly as lifeless as the main temple had been. Batak immediately started preparing some tea while peppering him with questions—who he was, what he did, where he was from, who his family was, that sort of stuff. Innocuous enough so Zorian didn't mind answering honestly. Strangely, Batak didn't ask him a single question about his religiosity, something for which Zorian was glad. Zorian, in turn, asked a couple of questions about Batak and Kylae, trying to understand what they were even doing here if the temple was abandoned.

Batak was all too happy to enlighten him. Apparently the church leadership didn't feel comfortable with simply demolishing the temple… or worse, leaving it to the mercy of the elements and looters. A perfectly understandable sentiment, in Zorian's opinion. Not only would it be a shame to consign such a majestic building to oblivion, it would also be a blatant admission of weakness from the church. In the end, Batak and Kylae were assigned to the temple, ostensibly to keep the temple running but in reality more to keep it presentable and ward off thieves and squatters.

Finally, after he finished his cup of tea, Batak seemed to have decided he had danced around the issue long enough.

"So," said Batak. "You never did tell me why you're here, Mister Kazinski. Do you think you could perhaps tell me what you need to speak with Kylae about or is this too sensitive for the ears of a mere junior priest?"

Zorian thought about it for a moment before deciding it probably wouldn't hurt to tell the man why he was there. Future forecasting wasn't illegal or anything, after all.

"Well…," began Zorian, "for a start, I heard that Priestess Kylae is skilled at forecasting the future through divinations."

Batak stiffened slightly, but quickly forced himself to relax. His smile did slip off his face, however.

"She is," he said. "It is a difficult field to practice and I doubt anyone could claim mastery of it in any real sense, but she is as close to an expert as you're likely ever going to find."

"But there are other people who dabble in it regardless, one of whom has sent me to speak with Kylae about her findings," said Zorian, privately enjoying the mental image of the aranea matriarch hissing at him for calling her a dabbler in the field. "Some of the results she had gotten out of her predictions have been very… irregular."

All pretenses of good cheer had left Batak's face by the time Zorian finished talking. Silence stretched into uncomfortable seconds. Zorian was starting to wonder if the topic was somehow taboo or if he had otherwise insulted the man somehow when the junior priest spoke again.

"And these... irregularities... when exactly do they appear? How far into the future were the projections before they went haywire?"

It was at this point that Zorian realized: Batak already knew. He was no more a mere junior priest than Zorian was just an innocent messenger.

"There is only one real irregularity, and it appears on the day of the summer festival. Specifically, the prediction returns a blank beyond that date... almost as if the whole world disappears after that point. But you already knew that, didn't you?"

Instead of answering him, Batak spat out a very unpriestly curse and started pacing around the cramped room in agitation.

"I'll take that as a yes," Zorian said.

Batak stopped pacing to give him a wary look. After a few moments, the priest visibly forced himself to relax.

"I'm sorry," said Batak, "I didn't mean to be rude, it's just... well, it's probably best if I go and fetch Kylae now so we can discuss this together."

"Isn't she doing a ritual at the moment?" Zorian pointed out. He knew it was a very bad idea to stop magical rituals halfway through, but maybe the ritual Kylae was performing was purely religious in nature?

"Well, sort of," Batak said sheepishly. "I don't think she'll be terribly bothered if I interrupt her. Not for this, in any case. Please wait here while I go get her."

As Zorian watched the priest's hurried steps, he couldn't help but wonder why Batak was so spooked out by the termination date they uncovered. Zorian was certainly spooked, but that was because he knew exactly what was causing it, but to Batak and Kylae it shouldn't look terribly unusual. Much like soul-related magics, the field of future prediction was very poorly understood, and strange never-encountered events probably weren't unheard of. Zorian sincerely hoped that Batak's agitation meant they knew something important about the anomaly that he and the aranea matriarch had missed.

It wasn't long before Batak came back with a middle-aged woman in tow. Zorian's first thought was that she was surprisingly young for a high priestess, but he supposed with the manpower shortage among the priesthood they couldn't afford to be too picky about such things. For her part, the priestess gave him a long, searching look upon entering the room before offering a strained smile and sitting down next to Batak so that both of them were facing him.

"Hello, Mister Kazinski," she said. "I am Kylae Kuosi, the high priestess of this temple. I hear you want to speak to me. Specifically, that you wished to speak to me about future prediction?"

"About the termination date on the day of the summer festival, yes," Zorian confirmed.

A short exchange followed where they both confirmed they were indeed talking about the same thing and then the priestess leaned back in her chair and gave Batak a mild glare.

"I told you it was not a mistake," she said.

"And I told you it wasn't you who was the problem," Batak shot back. "I guess we were both right."

Kylae sighed before refocusing on Zorian. "I don't suppose you could introduce me to your master so I can discuss this directly with her? Not that I have anything against you, but you just don't have the necessary expertise and all your information is second-hand…"

"Sorry," Zorian said. "I'm afraid my 'master' definitely wishes to stay hidden. I agree she could help you better in person, but this is how things are at the moment."

And it was vanishingly unlikely that would change any time soon. According to current church dogma, aranea were classified as monsters—servants of the World Dragon, to be precise—and therefore not to be dealt with. Kylae and Batak seemed fairly liberal, as priests go, but probably not that liberal. Admitting he was speaking on behalf of a giant sentient spider would likely have led to him being forcibly expelled from the temple at best.

"If I may ask, though, why does this trouble you so much?" Zorian asked curiously. "I mean, I know why me and my, ah, master are concerned, but why do you have a problem with it?"

The priestess looked at him, one eyebrow raised. "And why *are* you concerned, if I may ask?"

"Trade?" offered Zorian, suppressing a smile in favor of the most innocent expression he could manage. Hook, line, and sinker.

The priestess shared a silent look with Batak, somehow communicating without words with her fellow priest. Apparently they knew each other quite well if they could manage that. Maybe they were lovers? If Zorian remembered correctly, priests were forbidden to have relationships with each other, and thus had to look for romantic options outside the church hierarchy, but it wouldn't be the first time such rules had been ignored. In any case, after a few seconds they seemed to reach a decision and turned again towards him.

"We will share our concerns with you, but only if you go first," the priestess said. "And be warned—I can tell when people lie to me. It is a supernatural ability and has never failed me before, so please don't waste my time with lies and half-truths."

Well. That was kind of inconvenient. Zorian didn't detect any attempt at barging into his mind, so whatever ability she had probably wasn't mind-based in nature. Was she instinctively divining the truth of his statements? Peering into his soul? He supposed she *could* be bluffing, but he somehow doubted it.

In the end, he decided to take a risk. He fired off a couple of divinations to make sure they weren't scried and that there were no cephalic rats around and then started to speak when they returned negative.

"Let's see if this will be a sufficient price for your help, then," Zorian said. "The reason we're concerned is that there is a well-funded, well-organized group of terrorists planning to take advantage of the summer festival to cause trouble. Some parts of their plan—like their use of artillery spells and war trolls smuggled through the Dungeon— are fairly pedestrian. But there is a more exotic component to their plans—one that wreaks havoc with future prediction by its very nature."

There was a brief moment of silence as the two priests stared at him incredulously.

"That... is not what I expected to hear," the priestess said. "Gods and Goddesses, this is way above my pay grade. I... don't think I want to know more, to be honest. I don't want to get involved in such things."

"Probably for the best," Zorian agreed.

"If that is indeed the true cause of the irregularity, though, then my own reasons to panic about it are largely misplaced," the priestess mused.

"I'd still like to hear about it, if it's not a problem," Zorian said.

"It's about the angels," Batak interjected. "Ever since the gods have gone silent, angels have, to some degree, taken their place. They can't grant magical powers to the priesthood or work miracles the way gods could, but they can be summoned in order to provide advice or give aid with their considerable personal abilities."

"And what did they say about the anomaly that got you so worried?" Zorian asked.

"That's the thing," the priestess said. "We can't ask them because no one has been able to summon them since about a week ago. We've been in contact with churches as far as Koth, and they report the same thing—even the most approachable of celestials are ignoring us. Hell, I've even heard rumors that demon worshippers cannot contact their vile masters any more. It is as if something has cut the entire material plane off from the spiritual realms."

Zorian swallowed heavily. A week ago… the start of the time loop, obviously.

"Quite disturbing, isn't it?" said Kylae. "Coupled with the timeline simply cutting off a few weeks from now, well, I must admit it had me very concerned. Finding out the two are basically unrelated certainly makes me rest easier."

There was further conversation after this, but none of it was terribly productive. He promised Batak and Kylae to be discreet about their troubles with contacting the spirit world and left.

Unlike the priestess, Zorian didn't feel like the conversation had eased his worries.

Following his visit to the temple, Zorian decided to sit down in one of the many restaurants scattered throughout the city and consider this new information with a bit of food and drink. There was no doubt in his mind that the severing of the link between the spiritual planes and the material one was caused by the time loop, but what that meant was less clear. Was the material plane the only one experiencing the time loop, isolated from everything else within some kind of time bubble? The fact that his current timeline seemed to literally end when the time loop restarted strongly suggested this. It seemed the spell wasn't snatching up a bunch of souls and putting them into their past bodies like he had assumed—it was literally rewinding time itself in the targeted area while leaving a couple of souls intact in the process. No wonder the spell was so easily transmissible. Compared to reverting everything one month into the past, the cost of looping an additional soul or two was probably utterly inconsequential.

And that, if true, was very disturbing. That was not human magic. A hundred or so mages in possession of a mana well and a whole lot of time to prepare could affect a medium-sized country at most. The time loop had to envelop the whole continent, *at least*, for the boundary to go unnoticed for more than a day. News spread fast these days. And, frankly, Zorian had a hunch the time loop enveloped the entire planet. This was like something straight out of the age of gods... But if higher beings were involved, why was the time loop allowed to go off its intended course so severely?

His musings were interrupted by the scraping of a nearby chair. Someone had decided to join him.

"Oh," he said. "It's you."

"Is that the way to greet a friend, Roach?" Taiven complained.

Zorian rolled his eyes at her.

"Hi, Taiven," he said blandly. "Fancy seeing you here. I mean, this place is pretty far from your usual haunts. It's almost as if you decided to track me down..."

"That's because I did," Taiven said. "What are you doing on the edge of the city, anyway?"

"I was visiting a temple nearby," Zorian answered. "Lovely architecture."

"You, visiting temples?" Taiven said with a laugh. Zorian didn't reply. "Fine, be that way. I won't pry. In case you're wondering, I'm here because I asked around to see if I could find a human empath that could help you control your powers."

"You did?" asked Zorian, suddenly a lot more alert and enthusiastic about this conversation.

Taiven smiled sheepishly. "I did find someone willing to help you, but I'm not sure whether it's something you're willing to go for. The woman in question is a healer in one of Cyoria's big hospitals and she's only willing to teach you if you agree to an apprentice contract with her and become a full-blown healer."

Zorian clacked his tongue in disappointment. He did intend to learn the basics of magical healing at some point in the future, but that was a long way off. Learning medicine wasn't something you do in your spare time. He'd need to dedicate most of a restart to mastering that one field and he had too many things on his plate as it was.

"No, that doesn't work for me at all," Zorian said, sighing. "I have nothing against healers but that's not the career I'm aiming for."

"Yeah, I kind of figured," Taiven said. "It really would be a shame to let all that work you sank into spell formula go to waste. I guess the spiders are still your best bet, huh?"

"Yeah," agreed Zorian. "Although… to tell the truth, they have been dragging their many feet in regard to teaching me. Maybe if they thought I actually had valid alternatives to their help they'd hurry up a little? What was the healer's name, anyway?"

Taiven narrowed her eyes. "You've been down there alone again?"

Uh oh.

"Maaaaaybe…"

She reached out across the table and cuffed him in the shoulder. It hurt.

"Zorian, you moron," she complained. "I told you not to do these things alone! Even if you trust the freaky giant spiders that much—and I don't really think you should—there are other things down there! No matter how capable you are, it's always smart to have another set of hands and eyes with you. Unless you think I can't keep up with you?"

"I don't think that at all," Zorian said. "I just didn't want to be a bother and…"

Taiven cut him off. "I already said I don't mind helping. You can't use that as an excuse."

"…and the aranea are kind of prejudiced against non-psychic people," finished Zorian.

"Non-what?" asked Taiven incredulously.

"Psychic. People who are like me and them. I don't quite fully understand what being psychic entails, but it seems to be some kind of instinctive affinity for mind magic. That's where my empathy apparently comes from—the aranea claim it's a weak form of mind reading and that I could do more once they actually deign to teach me."

Taiven seemed at a loss for words for a moment.

"You're reading my mind?" she finally said. "I didn't give you permission to do that!"

"I'm only getting vague impressions of your emotions, and not even that consistently," said Zorian with a long-suffering sigh. "Besides, that's why I'm meeting with the aranea—to learn how to not do that unless I want to. How did you think empathy works, anyway?"

"I guess I didn't," admitted Taiven. "But we're getting off track— why does me not being psychic matter to your new spidery friends?"

"How should I know? Prejudices rarely make much sense."

"Well go ahead and ask them the next time you see them!" Taiven said. "Because if you can't give me a proper answer the next time I ask, I'm going down there to ask them myself, with or without your permission. It's total bullshit!"

Though he tried the remaining names on the matriarch's list after his visit to the temple, none of the other future forecasters were in any way helpful to Zorian. A fair number of them didn't even want to talk to him, and those that did hadn't made long-term predictions and hadn't noticed anything strange. Well, one of them did *claim* to have done so and found nothing of note, but he was an obvious fraud and spent most of the talk trying to get Zorian to part with his money in exchange for a 'more detailed reading of the future'.

So Zorian turned to the matter of his classmates, as the matriarch had suggested, and the possibility that one of them was the third time traveler. Zorian didn't think there was much chance of that, but better safe than sorry. Besides, it was a good way to look for other clues he might have missed, and he had been thinking of getting to know his classmates better anyway.

Including him, there were exactly twenty people in Zorian's class—twelve girls and eight boys. Of those, there were three people he was almost certain weren't the third time traveler: Akoja, Benisek and Kael. The first two because he actually knew their normal behavior and personality well enough before the time loop and had interacted extensively enough with the both of them in various restarts to judge them unchanged, and Kael because of the events of the previous restart. Trying to write down everything he knew about the rest, he quickly found two classmates that were very suspicious: Tinami Aope and Estin Grier.

Noble House Aope had a very shady reputation. The House began its existence during the Witch Wars, when one of the major witch clans agreed to defect to the Ikosians' side if they were given the status of a formal House in return. The Ikosians, ever pragmatic, agreed. No doubt they thought they could milk the renegades for their magical secrets and then quietly sideline them until they could be officially removed, but that never happened. Instead, the Aopes rose through the ranks of the Ikosian political system, leaving a trail of broken rivals in their wake, until they eventually stood on top as one of the more prestigious Noble Houses in all Altazia. This extreme success wasn't a result of *just* being very competent politicians, though—Aopes were rumored to practice all sorts of dark, forbidden magic stemming from their witchy roots. Necromancy. Demon summoning. *Mind magic.*

Of course, this was all just a rumor. Certainly no one who valued their life and career would ever suggest that Tinami Aope, the first-born daughter of the current head of Aope household, was practicing forbidden magics. Perish the thought. And in fact, the girl was painfully shy and withdrawn and in general looked like she wouldn't hurt a fly.

That didn't prove anything, though. Beware of the quiet ones and all that. If there was one person in the class who had easy access to magics that could screw Zach over and hijack the time loop for their own ends, it was probably Tinami. Even better, her withdrawn nature would ensure that very few people knew her enough to realize she was acting strangely unless she did something totally crazy.

Estin Grier, the second suspect, was primarily suspicious because of where he came from. He and his family had immigrated to Altazia from Ulquaan Ibasa—the infamous Island of the Exiles. Since the island was populated mostly by mages exiled there in the wake of the Necromancer's War, that made Estin the second person who could plausibly have access to forbidden magics without too much trouble.

Also, Zorian was fairly certain that the mages leading the invasion force came primarily from Ulquaan Ibasa. The island was one of the few places where one could find enough necromancers and war trolls to explain the quantity of them present at the invasion. It was also the last recorded home of Quatach-Ichl, the lich general who had led the fight against the Old Alliance in the Necromancer's War and whose physical description matched almost exactly with the lich that had so thoroughly trounced Zach in that fateful battle where Zorian was dragged into the time loop.

Of course, those two were only the obvious suspects, and the third time traveler, if indeed present among his classmates, was no doubt far more cunningly hidden. Realizing he didn't know enough about people in his class to really make a judgment, Zorian decided to seek the aid of the one person who could no doubt tell him something about everyone.

"Hello, Benisek," Zorian said, sitting next to the chubby, talkative boy. "Can I ask you to do me a favor?"

"Sure," Benisek said. "What do you need?"

"I need basic information about everyone in our class. What's the latest gossip about them and so forth."

[Well, that is certainly an interesting turn of events,] the matriarch remarked. [A confirmation of the cut-off point in the timeline and another clue as to the true nature of this time loop is far more than I had hoped for. I must admit I hadn't actually expected you to find anything useful among human diviners, but there you go. I don't suppose you have anything on your classmates yet?]

[Not really,] Zorian responded. He had returned to the sewers at the appointed time, narrowly avoiding a rainstorm that had descended on the city at twilight. [I'm only starting with the investigation. Truthfully, this is bound to be a task spanning numerous restarts, so you shouldn't expect quick results.]

[Yes, of course. Well, I have nothing else to add so unless you have any additional questions, we can meet next week to check on each other's progress.]

[Actually, I have two questions,] said Zorian.

[Ask away, then.]

[First question: Can you explain to me what exactly you mean by 'flickermind' and why you disdain them so much?] Zorian asked. [You keep saying that word and it sounds terribly insulting and bigoted.]

The matriarch twitched her legs, emitting some complex emotion that Zorian couldn't decode with his limited empathic abilities. That tended to happen a lot, actually, since the aranea were so thoroughly different from humans in both body and mind.

[I apologize if we offend,] she finally said. [It had been quite a while since we had significant, sustained contact with a human, and there are bound to be misunderstandings and points of contention.]

[I notice you didn't actually answer my question,] pointed out Zorian.

[It is as you suspect: a flickermind is a creature that isn't psychic like you and me. I'm sure they can be wonderful people, but I—as well as most of my fellow aranea—find it hard to truly take them seriously. It's like meeting a society of people who are born blind. They can obviously manage without sight, but you'd probably still consider them fundamentally crippled.]

[You never did tell me what being psychic entails, you know?] Zorian pointed out.

[Everything, from the smallest grain of sand to the very gods themselves is connected through the great invisible web that suffuses all creation,] the matriarch said. [Psychic people are open to these connections and contact the minds of others, or even the universe itself, to perform what you humans call magic.]

[That explanation sounds… almost religious,] said Zorian.

[The great invisible web does feature prominently in our spirituality,] the matriarch admitted. [What was the other question you wanted to ask me about?]

[Ah, yes. I had found a human empath that might be willing to teach me some of her skills. I wanted to ask for your opinion—]

[No!] the matriarch interrupted. [That's a terrible idea! Your human empaths are bad teachers! Their 'training' consists of nothing but showing people how to shut off their link to the Great Web and keep it closed most of the time! They brainwash their students into believing that sensing emotions is all there is to their powers and that the rest of the mind arts are immoral! They make a mockery of the great gift!]

Zorian blinked in shock. He had intended to produce a reaction by broaching the topic in question, but he had no idea the matriarch would be affected this strongly! Anger and outrage simply *poured* off the matriarch, making it clear that she cared about this issue very, very much. For the first time since his first encounter with her, he remembered that she was actually quite a terrifying creature.

[That's a lot stronger denunciation than I expected,] Zorian admitted, forcing himself to remain calm. [Care to suggest an alternative, then? I really want to get this ability under control.]

[Have I not promised to help you with that?] the matriarch asked.

[And then you ignored the issue completely,] Zorian answered.

[I thought you needed time to come to terms with it. You didn't exactly act thrilled when I first informed you of your gifts. Maybe if you hadn't waited six months before contacting me, we would have been on the same wavelength?]

Ouch.

[But no matter,] the matriarch said, [this whole argument is pointless. If you want to learn how to use your gift effectively, I'll be happy to help. Come back tomorrow at this time and we can begin your lessons.]

She turned to leave before pausing and sending him one final parting burst of communication.

[And then, once you experience the Great Web in its full glory, you can go to that human empath and see for yourself who is right.]

CHAPTER 021

Wheel of Fortune

In the tunnels beneath Cyoria, Zorian sat cross-legged with his eyes closed, trying to sense the minds of nearby aranea with his own. That was the task he had been given by the matriarch as his first lesson, and it reminded him uncomfortably of Xvim's mana sensing exercise.

It wasn't going too well. That was another thing it shared with Xvim's bullshit lessons.

[It has only been three days,] the disembodied voice of the matriarch admonished him. [You've barely even started. Don't be impatient.]

"There's got to be a better way of learning this," Zorian complained. This kind of trial and error method was something he could have done without her help. As far as he could see, the only way the matriarch was really helping at the moment was by being an experienced practitioner ready to step in if something went wrong. Which, now that he thought about it, was quite valuable when messing around with something like mind magic. Or any magic, for that matter.

[That, and there is also the little fact that it's easier to sense and contact Open minds than those of… non-psychics,] the matriarch remarked, fumbling a little towards the end. [I somehow doubt you would find many Open individuals to practice on back on the surface. Fewer still would be willing to let you connect to them. Anyway. I realize that these initial stages are tedious and boring, but they are necessary. And if I have not explained things satisfactorily, I apologize, but I do not know how to do it any better. This ability is not something I learned, it is something I *do*. Aranea learn how to do this at a very young age, much like human children learn how to walk and talk. Can you explain to someone who has been paralyzed all their life how to move their legs?]

Zorian frowned. So he wasn't even able to master telepathic baby skills? Wonderful. Just wonderful. Taking a deep breath to calm himself, he tried to consider the task in front of him and how to solve it. Yes, yes, the matriarch insisted he should just keep trying until he eventually succeeded by sheer weight of effort, but he was a mage damn it! Mages did things smarter, not harder.

Being psychic meant being a natural mind mage. For all that the matriarch kept bringing her weird aranea spirituality into it, that's what it all boiled down to. A psychic could read thoughts and emotions, trawl through people's memories, hijack their senses and motor control, communicate with them telepathically and gods know what else, but all of it was mind-related. Even the matriarch admitted that aranea used modified human magic for things like her speech spell and the rest of their non-mentalist magical arsenal.

Divinations were the key, he felt. If psychic powers were mind-based, why did they also enhance divinations?

[Not all divinations,] the matriarch remarked from the sidelines, apparently following his train of thought. [Only the ones that put information directly into your mind. The Gift helps you interpret the results of such spells more easily, and since most high-level divinations pour at least a part of the information straight into your mind… well, you can imagine how useful that can be.]

With those words, something clicked in Zorian's mind. According to the books he had read about the mind arts in the academy library, spells that were meant to read people's thoughts were not terribly difficult *in principle*. The problem was that the result was totally incomprehensible to most users unless they spent years training themselves how to interpret it. Spells that aimed to establish telepathic communication also suffered this problem, though to a lesser extent—so long as the people in question spoke the same language, they could at least exchange verbal communication in such a fashion. In other words, human mind spells were remarkably like a divination that tried to simply dump its output into the mind of the caster… which wasn't something most mages were equipped to handle.

Taking it all together, it seemed obvious to Zorian that one of the defining powers of a psychic was their ability to make sense of information entering the mind directly—whether it was other people's thoughts or something more exotic, like divination results. Most relevant to him in that moment was the fact that it was a *passive* skill. Using it wasn't something he had to specifically activate, it was a state of being, so if he wanted to sense the minds of nearby aranea, perhaps he should stop trying to push his power out towards his surroundings and concentrate inward. He took a deep breath, visualized the results as motes of light around him and then just… opened his mind.

Blazing suns erupted all around him, including a couple in places where he hadn't expected there would be any aranea to begin with. Apparently the matriarch had brought more guards with her than she had openly displayed to him.

[Your first success,] the matriarch remarked, her telepathic probe breaking his concentration and causing the entire vision to burst like a dream. [Well done. Things should go a lot faster from now on. I'd congratulate you on your fast progress, but I have to be honest and admit I have no idea how fast humans usually progress in this.]

"Perhaps things would have gone faster if you had actually told me I was doing things wrong," Zorian said with annoyance. "Why didn't you tell me I was supposed to concentrate inward instead of outward?"

[I did; it's not my fault if you dismissed it as pointless aranean superstition,] the matriarch said airily. [And I actually didn't know that the problem lay there in particular. I suppose my tendency to respond to your thoughts makes you think I can understand them in totality, yes? The truth is less impressive, I'm afraid. Telepaths labor under many of the same limitations that plague human mind magic, it's just that we advance much faster in the field and don't need a structured spell to use our abilities. Unless you structure your thoughts into actual speech, the most I get from you from my surface scans is a very fuzzy image of your current emotional state and your general intentions. This is doubly true because you're human and I'm an aranea, two radically different species that don't even share the same general body plan, much less mentality.]

"Huh, so language and species *do* matter to a psychic," Zorian remarked. "I was wondering about that."

[It's usually not a big problem, since most creatures tend to think in words when they engage in conscious thought,] the matriarch said. [So long as two creatures speak the same language, they can freely engage in telepathic conversation, no matter how different their underlying thoughts. If they *don't* share a language… well, admittedly, not all is lost. Psychics *can* potentially communicate with completely alien minds. It involves structuring your thoughts into general concepts that are hopefully broad enough to be understood by the recipient but not so broad as to be meaningless. Unfortunately, this method is very crude and tends to be both painful and disorienting to the target. I believe you experienced it already when you met one of the less human-savvy aranea in one of the previous restarts.]

"So it's not just because you're more powerful that you speak with me so easily?" asked Zorian.

[No. I took the time to learn human language, mentality, and culture. As did a number of other aranea that occasionally interact with humans. However, our web is extensive enough that most aranea can remain largely ignorant of human ways while they go on about their business, which is why most of my guards are silent around you. Trust me, they aren't usually this withdrawn, but if they tried to talk to you, they'd just give you a headache.]

"Does that mean that mental attacks are easier than communication?" Zorian asked curiously. "I mean, if botched telepathic communication is practically a mental assault to begin with, it shouldn't take much to simply fry a creature's brain and be done with it."

[It's called a 'mind blast', and it's the simplest telepathic attack there is,] the matriarch said. [It's also the simplest one to defend against. You should really stop worrying about me attacking you. Aren't the explosives you constantly carry in your pocket enough to reassure you?]

"They help," Zorian said. "But in this particular case I wasn't alluding to the possibility of hostilities between us. I was just curious."

[Well, good. Anyway, we should get back to developing your mind sense before we get too off track,] the matriarch said. [You made your first successful stab at it, but it is far too shaky to be useable at the moment. You need to be able to sense minds around you instantly without having to sit still with your eyes closed and preferably while doing something else entirely.]

Zorian sighed. He was definitely getting flashbacks to Xvim.

The rest of the month was fairly unremarkable and mostly spent on honing the mind sense and trying to sense the intensity of magic sources through a mana cloud. Though the matriarch refused to teach him anything until he got his mind sense (relatively) mastered, he already noticed her lessons gave him some rudimentary control over his empathy—enough that he could keep it shut with enough concentration, but not enough to focus it on specific people or otherwise refine it. That alone made the lessons useful, since it ought to make social events infinitely more bearable for him.

And speaking of social events, Zach had been increasingly pushy about bringing him to his summer festival party. After the boy kept bugging him a few times, Zorian relented. Yes, it would bring him uncomfortably close to the other time traveler for the evening, but he was curious about how his empathy suppression would fare in a live situation and also how Zach's mansion looked from the inside. Besides, he was trying to get to know his classmates better, and this was a good opportunity to chat with some of them without looking completely out of character.

"Is it really okay for me to come with you?" Taiven asked as she walked beside him.

"For the last time Taiven, *yes.* Zach made it clear that the more people we invite along with us the better," Zorian said. Not surprising if you knew what Zach was trying to achieve. "Look, if you don't want to come—"

"Oh, no, I totally do. It's not every day you get a chance to attend a party at the Noveda mansion. It's just that I find it a bit strange, that's all. I'm kind of surprised you agreed to come—isn't this sort of thing anathema to you?"

"It's either this or attending the official dance organized by the academy," Zorian said. "My only real choice is to pick my poison."

"Ah, I see," Taiven said, nodding. "I guess that in that case this does appear to be a better option."

Zorian glanced at Taiven from the corner of his eye, feeling slightly guilty. The truth was that his main reason for inviting her along was to personally see how she would fare against the invaders. He knew she was a lot better than him at combat magic, but probably not all that much better in the grander scheme of things, and he wanted a comparison point that wasn't as ridiculous as Zach or an experienced battlemage like Kyron.

Then again, this was Taiven—she probably ended up fighting the invaders in every restart anyway, just not where he could see her. At least this time she would have the advantage of fighting alongside a combatant of Zach's caliber.

They had barely knocked on the door before Zach opened it and ushered them inside to a massive entry hall leading to a wide staircase. He had probably known they were coming the moment they stepped through the outer gate, now that Zorian thought about it—it would make sense to have some kind of detection field woven into the ward scheme that protected this place.

"I'm glad you decided to come," Zach told him as he led them towards the dining hall, where the party was apparently supposed to take place. "Considering how you've behaved towards me lately, I half expected you to ignore your promise to come and stay in your room."

"I don't know what you're talking about," Zorian said curtly. For one thing, Zach hadn't even bothered him all that much in this particular restart. Was the other time traveler trying to bait him into unmasking himself or had he simply spent so much time in this time loop that he was having trouble sorting events according to which time loop they happened in?

"Uh, what's going on here?" Taiven asked, looking between them uncertainly. "Is there something I should know or…"

Zach glanced towards her before turning towards Zorian and giving him a thumbs up. "New girl, huh? Man, you have a new one every time I see you. I wouldn't have pegged you as that kind of guy."

"What?" asked Zorian and Taiven simultaneously.

Zorian was honestly baffled for a moment but then realized Zach was mixing up his restarts again. Akoja, Ibery and Taiven: Zach had seen him with all three of them in various restarts. But that… that was totally different! None of them were even interested in him!

"Zorian is a man-whore?" Taiven asked in a worryingly calm voice.

"I am not!" Zorian denied hotly before focusing his anger at an amused-looking Zach. "And you! Stop spreading stupid rumors about me! I know for a fact you've never seen me with a girl until this evening! And you wonder why I've been avoiding you this whole month…"

Zach winced. "Sorry, sorry, I was just messing with you. Don't worry, I'm sure your girlfriend won't leave you over a couple of stupid remarks by yours truly. Or if she does, she was never worth bothering with in the first place."

"Oh really?" Taiven said. "You don't think he'd be devastated to lose a girlfriend as powerful, smart, and sexy as—"

"Taiven, don't you start too," sighed Zorian. "Zach, she's not my girlfriend. She's just a friend."

"Who happens to be female," Zach said, wiggling his eyebrows.

"Yes," Zorian said, gnashing his teeth in irritation.

"Ah well, at least you already have a girl to dance with for the evening," said Zach, his voice light.

Zorian kind of doubted that. Taiven was a very attractive girl, with a nice, athletic figure and the face of an angel, and she liked men who were similarly gifted in the appearance department. Chances were high that Taiven would find someone else to dance with once they hit the crowd. Zach maybe, if the way she was checking out his backside was any indication.

"You know, this place is pretty empty," Taiven whispered to Zorian as they walked. "I know he's the last of his House and all, but I can't even see any servants milling around."

"Most of the servants were dismissed from service by my guardian while I was still a small child," Zach said. It did not surprise Zorian that he'd heard her—Taiven was very poor at whispering. "Since my parents died while I was still a baby, he had free rein to do what he felt was necessary to keep House Noveda standing until I was old enough to take over. As part of that, most of the maintenance staff and other contractors were found to be unnecessary and were fired."

"And you don't agree with his actions?" Zorian guessed. He could definitely detect an undercurrent of hostility when Zach talked about his guardian, which fit in with the fact that he regularly brutalized the man at the beginning of a lot of restarts.

Zach gave him a curious look before sighing.

"Let's just say he and I have our disagreements and leave it at that," Zach said.

"You know, I never did find out what happened to your family," Taiven said. "How come you ended up being the last of your House?"

Zorian punched Taiven in the shoulder for asking such a question of their host and punctuated it with a firm glare when she shot him a scandalized look. He wasn't sure what she was scandalized about, though—did she really not realize how inappropriate her question was, or was she just surprised it was him hitting *her* for once instead of the usual Taiven-on-Zorian violence?

"Oh, leave her alone, she's just being upfront about her curiosity," said Zach. Somehow he knew what had transpired, even though he had his back turned to them when it happened. "I kind of like her attitude, to be honest."

"Figures," Zorian grunted. Now that he thought about it, Taiven and Zach both had the same devil-may-care attitude about things, so *maybe* it hadn't been the best idea to have them meet each other...

And with that, Zach launched into a protracted explanation of the Noveda House's downfall... most of which Zorian completely ignored in favor of studying various paintings and portraits along the way. Truth be told, Zorian had already tracked down all information about Zach and House Noveda that he could get his hands on, so very little of what Zach was saying was new to him.

While tragic, Zach's story was by no means unique, and could be boiled down to two main causes: Splinter Wars and the Weeping.

The Old Alliance was a complicated construct, a patchwork empire made out of a multitude of bickering, semi-independent states that only sometimes listened to orders coming from Eldemar, but for all its faults it was quite successful at suppressing outright warfare between its member states. Armed conflict was rare and highly limited in scale, especially since the Alliance had no major external enemies to defend against. Thus, when the Old Alliance shattered and its component states started mobilizing their forces for war, it was the first time in nearly a century that actual war would be waged in the region. And it would be a bucket of cold water straight into the face of every battlemage in Altazia—for it would be the first time ever that firearms were used in warfare on a mass scale.

Firearms had been known in Altazia for centuries by that point, but they were not held in very high regard by the generals and decision makers of Eldemar and other powerful countries. Initial attempts to make use of them had shown them to be unwieldy and almost as dangerous to the user as they were to the target. Artillery mages were a lot more mobile and effective than any cannon, and the less said about hand-held firearms the better. Still, enough people remained interested in them that the technology never died and gradually improved over time. However, even after naval powers started arming their ships with cannons and even when a couple of mercenary groups began using rifles successfully, handheld firearms were still ultimately seen as a dead end. There was nothing that riflemen could do that a properly trained archer couldn't do better, and bows and arrows were a lot easier to enhance with magic than rifles and their ammunition. The one advantage rifles had over alternatives was that they required almost no training before they could be used effectively, and countries of the Old Alliance had no use for barely trained conscripts.

Until the Splinter Wars, that is. With the dissolution of the Old Alliance, every state suddenly scrambled to arm itself for the coming conflict, and having a passable army immediately was more important than having a proper one in a decade. Smaller countries, inherently unable to compete with the likes of Eldemar when it came to magical might, invested particularly heavily in firearms as an alternative to combat magic. Eldemar, being one of the few countries with a fully functional traditional army, felt no need to play around with these 'commoners' toys'.

No one really expected firearms to be as devastatingly effective as they ended up being. Even the countries that made heavy use of them expected them to do little except stall the advance of classical armies and perhaps motivate them to look elsewhere for easier prey. Instead, massed riflemen armies absolutely savaged traditional ones, catching established powers completely off guard. Instead of larger powers gobbling up every minor power and city-state around them and then duking it out among themselves (the outcome everyone had been expecting), the larger powers ended up weakening themselves, often splintering into their component parts as their internal enemies smelled weakness. Although nations eventually adapted their forces and battle doctrines to firearms technology, the damage had been done, and every subsequent Splinter War only made Altazia's political fragmentation worse.

This was especially true because the Splinter Wars caused immense casualties to the mage Houses that were the intellectual and political elite of Altazia's nations. The reason was simple—being a battlemage was a highly prestigious occupation and many Houses used their military involvement as a way to gather influence and reputation, which they then used as leverage in furthering their political and mercantile interests. With the advent of the Splinter Wars, the demand for battlemages only increased, causing many more mages to enlist in the various armies in search of glory and wealth. This backfired spectacularly as casualties began to mount. Unfamiliar with the strengths and limitations of firearms, and often outright dismissive of them, many mages fell prey to snipers, artillery strikes, and massed rifle fire. Many noble Houses were thoroughly crippled by the losses they sustained, House Noveda being one of them.

House Noveda had been fundamentally a military House, even if they were active in a lot of other fields as well. According to Zach, House leadership considered military service to build character, and every male member was expected to serve at least a few years in their youth. Quite a lot of female members enlisted as well. Very closely connected to the Eldemar royal family and very traditionalist in attitude, the Noveda supported Eldemar's military ambitions whole-heartedly, conscripting every available battle-ready member into the war effort. As a result, when Eldemar began the Splinter Wars by launching a massive, multi-pronged assault on its smaller neighbors, House Noveda was right at the forefront of the offensive.

And they paid dearly for it.

Still, while House Noveda was heavily diminished in the immediate aftermath of the Splinter War, they were not yet done for. Given a few more decades, the House could have recovered somewhat and reclaimed its former glory and political influence. If not for the Weeping.

Nobody knew where the Weeping came from. It simply started to spread among the soldiers one day, a deadly, incurable disease that struck down everyone who contracted it, heedless of age, health, or even magic. Once a person contracted it, their death was all but certain—they would first collapse into fever and delirium, then become blind, and then blood would begin to leak from their eyes before they finally expired. Regular healers were useless, no magic could cure it, and even the church and its lost mysteries of the gods failed to halt its spread. In the end, nobody could do anything except wait for the disease to burn itself out, which it eventually did. As mysteriously as it appeared, the Weeping vanished after blazing across the entire continent.

The exact number of deaths from the Weeping was still debated, but most writers agreed that somewhere between eight and ten percent of Altazia's population perished in the epidemic. Some groups suffered more, while others were completely unscathed, seemingly without rhyme or reason. Zorian's family was completely untouched, for instance, which made them all very, very lucky. Conversely, Zach lost absolutely everyone to the Weeping. The few Noveda that survived the Splinter Wars all contracted the sickness and died, leaving a hollowed-out shell of a House whose only surviving member was a small child, too young to even care for himself.

"...which is how the whole sad story ends," finished Zach. "If nothing else, the Weeping finally put an end to the Splinter Wars. But that's enough of such depressing topics. We're here!"

Indeed they were, and boy was Zorian happy for his rudimentary control over his empathy—Zach's chosen meeting hall was a lot smaller than the academy dance hall, and the mood was a lot more informal and unrestrained, making the crowd denser and rowdier. This would have been pure hell in his normal state.

Just as he was contemplating the best way to go mingle with the other students—hopefully giving him an opportunity to dig for personal information while they chatted—the choice was taken from him. Taiven also wanted to mingle, though her reasons were almost certainly more benign than his, and she decided that the best way to do that was to have Zorian introduce her. Convenient.

He began with Kael and Benisek, who he knew he could talk to, then moved onto people that seemed like they wouldn't mind getting interrupted. Of course, in a group of this size, it was silly to expect it would only be them approaching others.

"All right, who else do you know here?" Taiven asked.

"Well, that tall, green-haired girl having a heated argument with those two guys is Kopriva Reid."

"Wait, she's *that* Reid?" Taiven asked. "One of those gangsters goes to the same class as you do?"

"Why, Taiven, are you suggesting that House Reid has something to do with organized crime?" Zorian asked with a small smile. "That's quite a serious accusation, you know. Nothing was ever proven, after all."

"Whatever. The bottom line is that I'm not going anywhere near the gangster princess. Anyone else?"

Zorian scanned the crowd again. To be honest, he had always found Kopriva to be a pleasant enough person to talk to, at least in their limited interaction. She was a bit blunt and had a habit of swearing like a sailor when things didn't go her way, but she never did anything… well, gangster-y. A small group of girls glancing his way suddenly caught his eye.

"See that group of five girls over there?" he said to Taiven. "That would be Jade, Neolu, Maya, Kiana, and Elsie."

"They look… giggly," said Taiven with a sour expression. "Pass."

"Oh, it's too late for that," said Zorian. "See how they're glancing in our direction? They've already noticed us and are debating how best to approach and interrogate us."

"Zorian, don't tempt fate," Taiven warned him.

"It's not tempting fate. It's knowing your enemy. They just saw one of their classmates walking around with a girl they know nothing about—there is no way those five would let that go without investigating," said Zorian, even as the group of girls he spoke of shared a nod and marched over in their direction. "See, what did I tell you? They're already coming this way."

Taiven gave him a quiet groan but then quickly schooled her face into a pleasant façade as the girls approached. Zorian understood her perfectly—he wasn't particularly looking forward to the upcoming conversation, but he knew it was coming the moment he had entered the room so he was prepared for it. And, while he didn't really think any of those five was the third time traveler, he had promised to himself he wouldn't skip over any candidates without giving them at least a cursory scrutiny.

This was going to be a long evening.

True to his prediction, once the introductions were done and the actual dancing had started, Taiven found herself some tall, handsome older student and left him to find someone else on his own. Whatever, he didn't like dancing anyway. He promptly used his expert skills at avoiding attention to retreat to the periphery of the dancing throng, seeking some out of the way corner where no one would bother him. He quickly noticed he wasn't the only one who had that idea. Tinami Aope seemed to have already found one such corner and was… looking pretty awkward, actually. Ho-hum. Somehow he doubted she *really*

wanted to be left alone, with a face like that.

"Hello, Tinami," he greeted, causing her to jerk in shock at being addressed.

"Um…," she fumbled. "Zorian, right?"

"That's me," confirmed Zorian. "Care for a dance?"

"Oh. Oh! But didn't you already come with a girlfriend? Won't she mind?" Tinami asked.

Zorian pointed towards the spot where Taiven was dancing with her partner. "Also, Taiven is just a friend, not a girlfriend."

"Ah," she said, fidgeting uncomfortably. Zorian wordlessly offered his hand to her. "Um, okay then…," she said, grabbing Zorian's offered hand with surprising forcefulness and dutifully following him onto the dance floor.

For the next thirty minutes, Zorian tried to engage Tinami in conversation with only mild success, and he suspected it was only because of these highly specific circumstances she was willing to open up even a little to him. She really was a very shy girl, and he somehow doubted she was secretly the third time traveler pretending. Her awkwardness seemed quite real, and surely a time traveler as old as Zach would have grown out of that by now?

"So as a hobby, you raise… spiders?" asked Zorian curiously.

"Tarantulas," she corrected insistently. "But, um, I kind of like spiders of all sorts. I know it's weird, but…"

"Nonsense," countered Zorian good-naturedly. What could possibly be weird about a shy, delicate-looking girl breeding big, hairy arachnids the size of a human hand? "Spiders are really quite amazing creatures. Though I prefer jumping spiders myself—those two giant eyes at the front somehow make them more human-like and relatable for me."

Tinami gave him an incredulous look before frowning. "You're making fun of me," she accused.

"Nope," Zorian countered with an easy smile. "In fact, there is a particularly large colony of jumping spiders that I visit on a regular basis. It's amazing what you can learn by observing the natural world."

Tinami narrowed her eyes at him and launched into a series of increasingly esoteric questions about spiders. Since Zorian had spent a great deal of time investigating various spider species as part of his research into aranea, he actually knew how to answer most of her questions. He then tried to turn the tables on her by asking her about magical varieties of larger, more monstrous varieties of spiders, gambling that her interest mainly extended to the smaller, 'cuddlier' breeds. He gambled wrong. Not only did she know more about spider monsters than he did, she also knew a great deal about monster species that only looked like a spider, such as various kinds of spider demons, and about monsters with spider-derived traits.

He wondered what would happen if he introduced her to the aranea, and decided he would definitely do so in one of the restarts. It was bound to be amusing, if nothing else.

"I see it didn't take you long to find a new girl once your lovely date for the evening left you," Zach said behind him, causing him to flinch. He turned and glared at the boy in response, wondering why he hadn't sensed him coming—he usually always... oh, right, he'd shut off his mind for the evening so the combined feelings of the throng wouldn't overwhelm him. The fact that he managed to keep it closed with no conscious effort even while being absorbed in conversation with Tinami was an encouraging sign for his developing mental abilities.

"Why are you here, Zach?" Zorian said, trying not to show too much irritation.

"I'm the host," Zach said. "It's my job to check up on the guests and see if they're having any issues with the service and whatnot. Though in this case I just wondered if you wanted to see the fireworks or not."

Oh yes, Zorian definitely wanted to see the fireworks and immediately said so. Thus, he and Tinami joined a sizeable group of people in the garden where they would have an unobstructed view of the sky. Zorian paid more attention to Zach than to the sky, though. If the matriarch's plan came to fruition, Zach was bound to have an interesting reaction.

Zorian had shied away from acting against the invaders and not just because he was too weak to contribute much. Sabotage was bound to attract the attention of the third time traveler, and Zorian didn't want to advertise his existence. Instead, he had limited himself to gathering information about the invaders and waiting until he was strong enough to survive hostile attention. The aranea had no intention of doing the same, however—the invasion forces seemed to spend most of the month leading up to the invasion wiping out the aranea as a coherent force, and the matriarch had no intention of sitting on critical information for the sake of deception. Fortunately, there was no way for the invasion leaders to connect the aranea to Zorian, and the matriarch agreed with him that he shouldn't get involved. He was far too useful as a scout and memory carrier to risk revealing himself recklessly.

But she wanted to act, and so, at their meeting three days prior, he and the matriarch sat down to discuss a plan of action. Zorian had observed the progress of the invasion from various points in the city during the last few restarts, and he was convinced that the best and easiest way of derailing it was to prevent the initial artillery barrage that preceded the invasion proper. This was especially true because he knew exactly where they were firing from—triangulating the location of their firing positions was absolutely trivial when it involved tracking a brightly shining projectile moving relatively slowly across the sky. Unfortunately, he had never managed to get close to one of those firing points to see what kind of defenses they had, since he was killed both times he attempted the feat. The matriarch agreed that assaulting those positions before they could fire was likely to be the best way to strike a critical blow to the invaders, and the plan was put in motion.

The fireworks started… and not a single artillery spell accompanied them. The look of increasing bafflement on Zach's face was priceless.

"What's wrong, Zach?" Zorian asked innocently. "You act like you've never seen fireworks before."

"Err, no, I mean I have, it's just… never mind," Zach said.

Zorian shrugged and turned to Tinami, offering her a hand. "What do you think of going back inside for another dance?"

"Um, yes!" she agreed enthusiastically. "Let's!"

Slowly, the people got tired of exploding lights in the sky and streamed back inside, leaving a frowning Zach staring alone at the sky.

Zorian's good mood was short lived. While the invaders were indeed hard-hit by the lack of their initial bombardment, the invasion wasn't called off, and they appeared to have made Zach's mansion one of their primary targets, probably because that's where Zach was and they were specifically targeting him. Perhaps if the students had witnessed the artillery spells hitting the city, Zach could have used that to assume control and organize some kind of proper defense, but as it was the attack caught them all completely unprepared. Not even Zach, with all his mighty magic, could stop the flood of invaders gaining entry into the mansion, after which several groups of students were isolated from the main group containing Zach. Zorian was in one of those.

He, Tinami, Taiven, Briam and four other students he didn't know had ended up barricading themselves in one of few untouched rooms in the mansion, desperately trying to keep the invading forces at bay. The four unknown students were almost entirely useless, but the other three were worth their weight in gold. Briam had summoned his trusty fire drake to his side the moment he realized they were under attack,

Taiven knew how to cast some kind of incredibly destructive fire vortex that actually made the invaders reluctant to continue their attack for ten whole minutes, and Tinami… well, she was clearly no stranger to fighting and behaved completely differently in a combat situation than she did during normal interaction. She didn't know any fire spells, but she did know how to fire some kind of purple beams that caused even the biggest of war trolls to collapse to the ground screaming. The beams did no obvious damage, so he assumed they were simply pain spells, but that was useful enough on its own. And Tinami didn't spam those beams mindlessly, instead concentrating on causing pileups, breaking up charges and interrupting enemy spellcasters.

"Zorian, I really hope you'll be done soon, because this position is rapidly becoming untenable," Taiven shouted.

Zorian ignored her, carefully inscribing the last set of explosive runes on the walls of the corridor behind them. You didn't rush this sort of task, unless you fancied blowing yourself up before the enemies even got to you. A minute later, he finished the set and rose to his feet, his knees cracking painfully from the long period he spent crouching.

"Done!" he shouted. "Everyone retreat through the corridor!"

Just as Briam, Taiven and Tinami had covered him while he set up the explosive runes, he now focused on covering them while they fled deeper into the mansion. Some—mediocre—assistance came from one of the other boys, who began firing magic missiles at the war trolls. The trolls soaked in the hits with ease as Zorian shouted at the student to aim instead for the more vulnerable mages supporting the trolls. Zorian, aware that he didn't have the mana reserves to tank the entire enemy assault force, knew the value in taking the mages out of the equation first. Raising the spell rod he had smuggled into the mansion, he fired a weak disintegration beam towards the floor just in front of the mages' feet. The beam gouged a jagged line in the floor, sending billowing, irritating clouds of dust in the air. That should at least mess up their aiming.

Turning his attention to the rapidly approaching war trolls, he knew he had very few tricks capable of stopping the charge, and none that could be employed on a moment's notice. But he could try. Drawing on a significant portion of his mana reserves, Zorian hit them with an overpowered flamethrower.

It didn't kill them—Zorian's flamethrower wasn't strong enough, and these war trolls seemed to be particularly tough ones, brought to deal with them after Taiven cast that flaming vortex spell—but it broke their charge, and Zorian used that momentary reprieve to conjure another cloud of dust with his spell rod and fled down the corridor after the rest of the students. The other boy had broken his position and run ages ago, the useless coward, so Zorian could only hope the trolls' confusion would last long enough for him to gain some distance. He wasn't fast enough to outrun a war troll.

Mid-stride, a furious screech erupted around him, and he could suddenly hear one of the war trolls rapidly gaining on him. Damn it, he hated dying.

A sinister purple beam suddenly cut through the air next to his head, hitting the war troll behind him. The monster screeched again, this time in pain, and collapsed to the floor. Zorian gouged another line in the floor with his spell rod, cloaking the corridor in more dust, and then he was pulled inside their newest sanctuary.

"Thanks," he said, breathing heavily.

"Um, you're welcome," Tinami said, fiddling with the silver amulet she was wearing and watching the dust cloud covering the corridor for any sign of movement. The amulet seemed to be the spell formula she was using to cast the purple beams.

"Here they come," Briam said.

"Remember the plan," Taiven said. "Let them all advance into the corridor before triggering the explosive runes."

"What if they notice the trap?" one of the unknown girls asked.

"Then at least they'll be hesitant to push forward so insistently," Taiven said.

They didn't bother closing the door to the room in which they'd taken refuge—that would just result in them being pelted by wooden splinters and shrapnel when the mages forcibly broke down the door. They had lost two students before they learned that lesson.

Sure enough, there was a barrage of concussive beams and battering rams preceding the war troll charge. After Briam and Taiven repelled the initial approach with a fairly anemic defense, the mages moved into the corridor to provide support, sensing that victory was near. That's when Zorian released a mana pulse towards the nearest cluster of explosive runes and the entire corridor collapsed in a deafening explosion. A huge plume of dust and gravel rushed into the tiny room they currently occupied, but Taiven was ready and immediately created a large bubble of clear air to stop them from choking to death.

"Well." Taiven coughed, having been too slow to shield them from all of the dust that had permeated the room. "That should stop them for a while. Still, we have a bit of a problem. This room is a dead end. The only exit is this corridor and the window to the outside."

"The outside is swarming with enemies," Zorian said.

"We don't have much choice, though, do we?" Briam asked rhetorically. "We can't stay here."

"How are we going to get down?" one of the other girls asked. "We're on the second floor. We can't just jump out of the window."

"Hmm… all right, how many of you know how to cast the floating disc spell?" asked Taiven as she raised her own hand.

Zorian was the only one who raised his own hand to match.

"Ugh. Fine, that will have to do, I suppose. Okay Zorian, I'm going to go first and get these four dead-weights down and you follow after me with those two."

"Hey!" one of the dead-weights complained.

"Sorry, but I call it like I see it," Taiven said pitilessly. "Let's go, before even more of these assholes converge on our position to see what the explosion was all about."

Zorian waited, with spell rod at the ready, until Taiven and her four passengers had made it to the ground, then created a large floating disc of force of his own outside the window. He climbed out and jumped on it, closely followed by Briam and Tinami. He let himself breathe a sigh a relief as the disc began to descend. There were no enemies waiting for them at the bottom, Taiven had successfully touched down, and his disk was not giving any indication of failing under the combined weight of people standing on it. The moment he let himself think they were safe, though, a flock of iron beaks suddenly appeared from around the corner of the mansion. Zorian swore angrily.

There was really nothing he could do to deal with a flock of iron beaks, and Briam and Tinami weren't much better. There were about fifty of them, so even if he could snipe a couple out of the sky, it wouldn't mean a thing. Tinami probably couldn't make that pain beam of hers home in on a target, and iron beaks were very agile flyers. As for Briam, his attack options seemed to be strictly limited to his fire drake, and there was no reason for the flock to approach close enough to be caught in its fire breath when they could just rain their iron feathers on them from distance.

Zorian fired off a homing piercer anyway and noticed out of the corner of his eye that Taiven had launched a small swarm of seven homing magic missiles. Eight iron beaks fell, but it was a drop in the bucket—and then it was the iron beaks' turn. The air in front of him blurred and a cloud of glittering feathers were streaking at them.

Faced with the choice of trying to tank several hundred magical iron feathers or trying to survive a fairly dangerous fall, Zorian knew which one he wanted to chance. He immediately dismissed the floating disc and all three of them promptly plunged towards the ground.

This would probably be the end of this particular restart—knowing his luck, he was going to break his neck when he hit the ground—but on the bright side he managed to evade the deadly feathers! As he tumbled through the air, his eyes briefly met with those of Briam's fire drake, and he couldn't help but think it was glaring at him. It was hard to tell when that thing was angry, though, since it always looked pretty pissed off to Zorian.

Suddenly, just before they were about to hit the ground, their fall was halted and they touched down as gently as a feather. Before Zorian could ask what happened, a huge swarm of flaming missiles erupted from somewhere behind him, annihilating the entire iron beak flock.

"You know, Zorian," Zach said behind him, "sometimes I wonder if you have a death wish. How do you get yourself into these kinds of situations? You're almost as bad as me!"

"I don't know what you're talking about," mumbled Zorian, climbing to his feet and helping Briam and Tinami rise as well. Strangely enough, they didn't seem angry at him for what he'd done. Shaken by the experience, but not angry. Perhaps they didn't realize he'd dismissed the disc on purpose.

"Well, I'm glad to see another group of survivors, but we should really get going," Zach said. "It's not safe staying out in the open like this. Come, I know a place where we'll be reasonably safe."

Zorian looked around him. A surprising number of students had survived the attack and were dutifully following after Zach. Actually, they probably survived precisely because they were following after Zach. In any case, Zorian and his group decided there was no harm in joining the group—it's not like they had a better idea anyway.

They didn't get far before the attackers returned in force. Zorian heard Zach swearing something about bad luck and scoffed. This was no bad luck—the attackers were clearly tracking Zach's movements and targeting him directly. Did Zach even take any precautions to make sure it took something more than a couple of easy divinations to track him down? Knowing Zach, probably not.

But Zorian had other things to worry about, because while Zach was occupied with another flock of iron beaks, a giant brown worm erupted from the ground and started wreaking havoc right in the middle of the student throng. Zorian had only met those things four times so far in the various restarts, and he already hated them—they could move through earth almost as if it was water, and their hides were utterly impervious to physical force. They weren't particularly vulnerable to fire, either. Zorian watched impotently as the worm single-handedly shattered student formations, sending them scattering in panic so they could be picked off one by one by the winter wolves circling the throng.

Tinami apparently didn't want to just watch. She fired one of her purple beams at the worm and finally achieved some results. Namely, she got the worm to scream out in pain before immediately swinging its toothy maw in her direction, its murderous attention now firmly focused on her. Uh oh.

With a roar that promised revenge, the worm dived back into the ground. Zorian immediately closed his eyes and tried to block out the sounds of battle, focusing on his mind sense, trying to track its movements. It wasn't too hard—even if the worm wasn't psychic, it was the only mind that was below ground and thus easy to pick out from all the rest. He opened his mind, keeping track of the worm's mind as it swam underground. Tinami seemed rooted to the spot, aware that she couldn't separate too far from the group lest she be picked off like the rest of the students that made that mistake... and therefore couldn't really escape the worm.

Just before the worm was about to surface, Zorian wrenched Tinami to the side and dropped an explosive cube where she had been standing. The worm erupted from the spot only a moment afterwards, its toothy maw snapping shut around the clump of earth… as well as the explosive cube. Even as it swung its head in their direction, Zorian activated the cube, and the worm shuddered and started screeching and thrashing like mad before violently vomiting some of its pulped innards. The worm's convulsing tail thwacked into Tinami, sending her flying to the outer periphery of the battlefield, where she lay unmoving. Zorian quickly ran up to her and was relieved to see she was still breathing and had no obvious wounds. He shifted his attention back towards the worm, hoping that it had finally died while he had not been paying attention to it.

The worm swayed in the air as if drunk, and for one sweet moment Zorian thought he'd won—but then the worm swung its head straight towards him and roared out a challenge. This time it didn't bother to dive into the ground, instead stretching out to an impressive length far faster than a creature of such size should be able to.

He didn't die. The worm stopped a hair's breadth away from his face, straining against some invisible bonds before suddenly turning to the side and biting down on the winter wolf that had been trying to sneak up on Zorian while he was distracted.

[I was just in time, I see,] the voice of the matriarch spoke into his mind, and then she physically appeared, jumping out of the shadow of a nearby tree like it was the most normal thing in the world.

"Thanks," Zorian said. "But I'm not sure why you're here. I thought we agreed there should be as little contact between us as possible during the invasion."

[I decided that updating your memory packet with the information we found out today is more important.]

Zorian sighed and glanced around. Everyone was too busy fighting for their life to pay much attention to them, and it wasn't like the aranea was easy to spot in the gloom of the night.

"Make it quick," Zorian said, and the matriarch immediately set to work. Anything that tried to sneak up to them was dealt with by the giant worm, which was apparently still under the matriarch's control.

And then, after five minutes, she vanished back into the night, and Zorian picked up Tinami and tried to rejoin Zach, but he had barely gone five steps before a jagged red beam filled his vision, plunging his world into darkness.

CHAPTER 022

Complications

Zorian woke up in his bed in Cirin, Kirielle wishing him a good morning in that charming manner of hers. He was annoyed both at himself for not paying more attention to his surroundings and at the unknown attacker that did him in. Of course he would survive war troll charges and angry worms only to get killed by a simple sneak attack.

He passed the train ride sketching magic item blueprints in his notebook. Most of them were trivial things, like plates that kept the temperature of a meal constant or explosive traps that triggered on their own when certain conditions had been met, but he was toying with the idea of designing a practice dummy. He had found a combination of alteration spells that should allow him to construct a dummy out of wooden scraps and soil, but making the animation core was no simple task. And then, even if he managed that, he would have to design a warding scheme to etch into the dummy's surface, lest it disintegrate when he started hurling spells at it… possibly in an explosive manner, showering him with wooden splinters and shrapnel. He should probably also add at least a weak self-repair function, to prevent the dummy from falling to pieces from micro-fractures and such…

He didn't expect to finish this project in the current restart.

In any case, this time Zorian didn't wait much before contacting the aranea. Upon entering his room, he spent an hour crafting a rod of magic missiles for basic self-defense and then promptly marched off in the direction of the nearest Dungeon entrance.

Unlike his previous attempts to look for aranea, he wasn't simply walking around, waiting to stumble upon their scouts—he was trying to sense their minds with his brand new mind sense. Sadly, he sensed nothing except an occasional rat and—

He stopped, sensing a mind of unusual strength from one of the rats ahead. He mentally ordered his floating light to intensify for a moment and was rewarded with the disquieting sight of a rat missing the top of its skull.

For a full second, Zorian and the cephalic rat stood still and watched one another in indecision, trying to decide on a course of action. Then—gently, hesitantly—the rat extended a telepathic probe at him, trying to worm into his mind. For one small moment, Zorian considered trying to take it on telepathically, but then discarded the thought as stupid and risky. He was completely untrained in telepathic combat, and this single rat was merely a conduit for the entire cephalic rat collective. Instead, he drew his brand new spell rod and fired a magic missile at it.

The moment he reached for his spell rod, the rat immediately dropped its telepathic probe and tried to run. It was too slow. The bolt of concussive force slammed into the tiny creature with a loud crack, pulverizing its bones and crushing it into paste.

Well, so much for that. Zorian extended his mind sense as far as he could, trying to sense the rest of the collective, but found nothing. Either this one was an isolated scout or the rest had some method of hiding from his scans.

By the time he decided to move on, the pulped body of the cephalic rat was already being enveloped by a green, translucent mass of crawling gel. The oozes that patrolled these walled-off sections of the Dungeon were artificially engineered to be less dangerous and aggressive than their wild counterparts, but Zorian was never a fan of tempting fate and did his best to side-step the things as he moved past them. Acid burns were hard to heal, even with magic.

When he finally did find the aranea, the meeting was pretty disappointing. The aranea he met was one of those that didn't know how to talk to humans, so it took him ten minutes of telepathic pantomime that left him with a raging headache, and once the matriarch did show up, she basically told him to get lost for a few days until she came to terms with the contents of the memory packet.

Not an unexpected turn of events, but he had been hoping that the matriarch had refined her memory packet into something that could convince her past-self a bit faster than last time. The matriarch was a bit pushy and conceited, but it was nice to talk to someone about the time loop. Also, the truth was that there was little he could do to unravel the mystery of the time loop without assistance from the aranea other than steadily gathering magical skills and keeping his eyes open.

As he walked back to his room to sleep off his newly-acquired headache, he tried to think of a way to advance faster in his magical studies. He needed a teacher. One willing to teach him spells most instructors would consider too dangerous for the likes of a freshly certified student. Who did he know that would... oh.

That just might work.

The next day, when Taiven came to recruit him for her little sewer expedition, she found him practicing combat spells on one of the academy training grounds instead of sleeping in his room. He could have easily warded himself against her divination spells at this point, but having her track him down was part of the plan: he was hoping to recruit her as a sparring partner—and possibly teacher.

He had always thought he had gotten over Taiven's (oblivious) rejection of him, but apparently there was still some lingering resentment remaining because he had noticed something very important in the previous restart. Something he should have noticed way sooner, had he not been unconsciously ignoring her and pushing her away. Taiven was not at all opposed to helping him out, especially if the help was somehow related to combat. Why was he insisting on learning combat magic alone, without an instructor, when he was friends with someone who specialized in that very field of magic?

He tried not to look at her out of the corner of his eye to judge her reaction to his magic missiles, needing instead to focus on making each one as mana efficient as possible, but he could tell she was watching him thoughtfully. He was hoping Taiven would offer to help on her own when she saw him practicing, and he wasn't disappointed. She did, however, attach a condition to her offer.

"So, in conclusion, I get a month of instruction from you, free of charge, in exchange for joining you on this sewer run of yours?" Zorian asked.

"Yup!" Taiven said happily, looking very satisfied with herself. Zorian could guess why—she had found a way to pressure him into accompanying her, and all it took was promising to do something she was inclined to do anyway.

"I suppose that's okay," said Zorian, mentally considering how he should approach the search for the watch. He could, of course, simply trail after them and let them fumble around for a while—it's what Taiven expected him to do, and he was pretty sure the aranea wouldn't 'attack' while he was present. However, after some thought, he decided to take a different route. "I have a request, though. I am on speaking terms with a colony of sapient spiders living in the sewers, and I have a sneaking suspicion they're the ones that supposedly took the watch. I'd like to try actually talking to them before you go in and start burning things."

Taiven gave him a curious look. "You are friends with a bunch of giant, sewer-dwelling spiders?"

"Pretty much," Zorian said. He would describe the aranea as acquaintances and allies of convenience instead of friends, but she didn't have to know that. "I trust you and your friends can keep that a secret? I'm sure you can see why spreading this around might cause problems for me and the spiders both."

"Don't worry, I'm not a tattletale," Taiven said dismissively. "And I've yet to see Grunt and Mumble engage in any kind of gossip, so your secret is safe with us, oh great monster charmer. You think they'll just hand us the watch if we ask?"

"If the client's story is not made up, then yes. I don't see what use they would have for a pocket watch. But anyway, I have a request for you before you run off to do your thing."

"Oh? And what's that?"

"Teach me a fire spell more destructive than flamethrower," Zorian said.

"How big are your mana reserves?" Taiven immediately asked, not at all perturbed by the request.

"Magnitude twelve," Zorian said.

"Hmm, a little lower than I thought, but decent enough I guess," Taiven said. Zorian decided not to respond to her comment about the underwhelming nature of his natural reserves, lest he inadvertently reveal that he was actually an eight. "What kind of spells are you looking for, anyway?"

"Preferably something that can one-shot a troll," Zorian said.

Taiven looked at him like he was crazy. "What? Roach, you're far too green to go around picking fights with trolls. What the hell are you on?"

"Just humor me, Taiven," Zorian said, sighing. "Besides, this is pure self-defense—I won't be picking fights with anything."

Taiven snorted. "Says a guy who goes around meeting giant spiders in the sewers in his free time. But all right, I guess if you're going to do stuff like that, you'll need some stronger spells under your belt. I expect an explanation about that soon, though."

"After the summer festival," agreed Zorian smoothly.

"I'll hold you to that," Taiven said, poking him painfully in the chest. "Now, there are two spells that kind of fit your criteria, fire bolt and incinerating ray. Neither will kill a troll unless you can hit the troll in the face with them. The bolt can home in on the target and is cheaper in terms of mana use. The ray is far more damaging, but also far more of a mana hog and you'll need to worry about your aim."

"Teach me both," said Zorian. The bolt seemed like something that would be more generally useful for someone like him, but he needed the raw power as well.

"You sure you have the shaping skills for this, Roach?" Taiven asked. "'Cause this kind of spell isn't going to fizzle out if you fail—it will blow up in your face."

Zorian snorted derisively. "Trust me, shaping skills are not something I'm lacking in," he said. He raised his arm into the air, palm pointed towards the earth, and willed some of the dust and dirt to rise towards it. The dry, loose material that covered the training ground slowly rose towards his hand in a diffuse pillar, coalescing into a rough sphere just below his palm.

Once he was satisfied with the size of the sphere, he pointed his palm towards one of the targets and willed the mass of dirt rapidly forward, catapulting it towards the dummy. Sadly, the impromptu construct was too structurally unsound and disintegrated into dust halfway towards the target, ruining the effect somewhat.

It didn't make the feat any less impressive to Taiven, though.

"Damn, that was impressive as hell," Taiven said. "How can you do that? I don't think *I* could do that... Lift a rock off the ground, sure, but diffuse material like soil? That's a pretty advanced exercise. Hmm, if your shaping skills are that good, I guess there are a few more spells I could teach you…"

Zorian smiled. This had definitely been a good idea.

During the next several days, while he waited for Taiven to gather her team for the journey into the city's sewers, Zorian got a crash course in combat magic from his friend. Taiven took a surprisingly broad approach to the topic, opting to teach him as many different spells as she could manage instead of having him practice a few until he had a firm hold over them. She claimed that he already had a core of spells he was properly proficient in and that he needed a variety of options more than he needed a new ace in the hole, but she later admitted she was testing him, trying to discover the limits of his shaping skills. Something she didn't end up finding—Zorian's shaping skills were better than hers; every spell she could cast, he could as well.

Not all of the spells she taught him were of the typical offensive sort he expected from her. Some of them, like the spider climb spell that allowed him to cling to sheer walls and other stable surfaces, the featherfall that allowed him to survive high falls, or the various comfort spells that blunted temperature extremes and other environmental conditions, could be more properly classified as survival spells. Nonetheless, Taiven insisted that sometimes the environment itself was just as dangerous to a mage as his living opponents, and that he needed to know these spells if he was going to waltz around the Dungeon and similar places.

She was also fairly horrified by his lack of defensive spells. Not just a lack of any defensive barriers more substantive than the basic shield, though she wasn't happy about that either. No, she was talking about wards. Wards, since they were slow to cast, were fairly useless once a fight was underway, since they were slow to cast, and few opponents would give a mage the time needed to cast them during a battle, but Taiven claimed they were absolutely essential for a mage who expected to get into a fight. In any situation that wasn't an ambush, basic wards could improve spell resistance and counter common spells. And if you actually knew something about your opponent's spell repertoire and specialties? Then you could really ruin your opponent's day with a few choice wards. This was the reason why humanity had been steadily encroaching on monster-held territory with every passing year—most magical creatures only had a handful of inborn magical tricks and abilities to draw from and once you knew what they were you could devise a perfect counter for them in advance.

Unfortunately, you could only stack so many wards on top of each other before they started to interfere with each other and the whole edifice collapsed, and some of them inherently interfered with each other's operation, so knowing how to combine them effectively was a bit of a specialist skill. Taiven was not very proficient with wards herself, being more offensively focused, so he would need to find somebody else for anything beyond the basics.

However, most of the spells she taught him were various offensive and defensive energy projections, largely ones revolving around fire and force, but also some spells based on cold and electricity. Among other things, Zorian could now cast the ever-famous fireball spell… exactly twice before he ran out of mana. So not very useful, honestly, but Taiven claimed that any mage worth their name should be able to cast a fireball, and that the utility of such spells would naturally increase along with his mana reserves.

"Actually, I'm curious… is there some way to speed up the growth of mana reserves?" asked Zorian. "I know that artificially increasing them has bad side effects, but is there some kind of training method that would speed up natural growth?"

Taiven looked at him, her expression apprehensive. "Technically, yes," she admitted. "It's as simple as using mana-intensive spells to constantly exhaust your reserves. It would kick the growth of your reserves into overdrive. However, that kind of unnatural growth would completely wreck your current shaping skills—your normal growth of reserves is so slow because your soul is making sure your control over mana doesn't slip. Ruining your shaping skills just to speed up the growth of your reserves would be really short-sighted, Roach. Please don't do it. I never would, and you know I'm not exactly the most responsible girl. Surely you can wait for a few years for them to grow on their own?"

Well, he certainly wasn't pressed for time at the moment, Zorian had to admit. "I suppose that makes sense," he said. "I guess the reason why mana reserves plateau after a while is that there is only so much power a soul can safely handle. Increasing the cap artificially after that point messes up the mage's shaping skills with no hope of ever regaining them. No wonder everyone recommends against doing it—no matter how benign the enhancement process, the result is still more power and less control over it."

"There is always a trade-off between control and power," said Taiven. "It's just not apparent most of the time, since very few people try to develop their shaping skills to their limits. Many mages think that having more mana is always better. They reason that they can always work harder on their shaping skills, whereas increasing mana reserves without bad side effects is essentially impossible. It's not true, though. No matter how much time they spend honing their shaping skills, people with huge mana reserves are outright incapable of performing some particularly finesse-focused spells—things like advanced mind magic, detailed illusions, and complex alteration constructs."

"Wait, you're saying that I'll lose the ability to cast finesse-based spells as my mana reserves increase?" asked Zorian in alarm.

"No, no, I'm talking about your *natural* mana reserves—your inborn capacity before you start to increase it through regular spellcasting. About magnitude. Most spells, even highly sophisticated ones, are designed for average mages—magnitude eight to twelve, in other words. You're twelve, so still comfortably within the intended range. Hell, I've heard of one particular fifteen magnitude mage who became a damn good illusionist, so even if you tip over a little it will hardly matter."

Considering Zorian's real magnitude was eight, he apparently had nothing to worry about. Still, it did make him wonder about Zach, who, as far as Zorian could estimate, seemed to have magnitude in the low sixties. How did that kind of monstrous power factor in Taiven's scheme?

"How about people with really high magnitude?" asked Zorian. "How high can you go before finesse-based spells become impossible?"

"I've never seen hard numbers, but I'd guess around magnitude twenty or so," Taiven shrugged.

"How about the really high numbers?" Zorian asked. "Something like magnitude sixty?"

Taiven blinked, seemingly baffled by the question. "Well, that would be downright inhuman!" she said finally. "Is that even possible? Anyway, I'm not sure whether that would even be a good thing, even for a battlemage like me. Anyone with such mana reserves would have to spend years longer than their peers just to gain the basic level of proficiency expected of a certified mage. Maybe as much as a decade even, I don't know."

Zorian thought about what a relative failure Zach had been before the time loop and frowned. He had thought that Zach had simply been a lazy slacker, but maybe there was more to it than that? Then again, he had a feeling Zach was a special case. Those inhuman mana reserves were just that—completely outside the human range. He hadn't found any records of people like that in any books, and most of the experts he had asked flat out told him such people didn't exist outside of myths. Also, while Zach had been a crappy mage, he did succeed in getting certified, so his huge mana reserves clearly weren't as crippling as they should have been.

Maybe it was a Noveda House bloodline? One that gave their family huge reserves without the crippling loss of control, perhaps. Of course, the Novedas publically claimed they had no bloodline, but it wouldn't be the first time a House had lied.

"I hesitate to even bring this up," Taiven said, breaking him out of his thoughts, "but if you're really desperate for a short-term mana boost, you can always absorb ambient mana faster than you can assimilate it. I'm sure you're aware of the drawbacks, though…"

Zorian nodded. There were two main forms of mana available to the mage: his personal mana and the ambient one that emanated from the underworld. Personal mana was something that all things with a soul possessed in varying amounts, and it was attuned to the person producing it—it bent easily to its creator's will, and was innately more malleable and controllable than anything else they might use to power their magic since it never resisted the caster's efforts to shape it. Ambient mana, on the other hand, was both harder to control and toxic to living beings. Not enough to kill a mage just for using it once, but any substantial, prolonged use resulted in sickness and insanity. The mages of old believed that ambient mana was tainted by the World Dragon's hatred for humanity and shunned its use, but modern mages had discovered a few tricks to making use of it. One was by using it to power items, which had no minds to corrupt or bodies to sicken. The other was to assimilate the ambient mana into their personal reserves, negating its toxic properties. While the process of assimilation was too slow to power actual spells, being able to regenerate personal reserves faster was useful enough that the skill spread far and wide. These days, every student of magic was taught how to do it along with the other basics of spellcasting.

"I'll get sick," Zorian said. "And possibly go mad if I keep using it constantly."

"Right," Taiven said. "Using raw mana on a regular basis is pretty stupid, but if you're in a real bind… well, it's better to spend a few days bedridden with a fever than end up dead."

"You've used it before," guessed Zorian.

Taiven gave him a furtive look. "Uh, maybe once? Or twice?" She shifted her stance, looking uncomfortable. "But keep quiet about that, will you? Most combat mages have done it a couple of times in their life, but guild inspectors don't accept 'everybody's doing it' as an excuse."

Zorian made a gesture over his mouth, indicating that his lips were sealed. It's not like she didn't know plenty of things that could get him in trouble.

"Let's just get back to the lesson, oh great teacher," Zorian said. "Since you're so intent on teaching me mana-intensive fire spells, how about that fire vortex I heard you can cast…"

When the time came, Taiven and her two friends let Zorian take point as he led them towards aranea territory. They had already tried and failed to divine the location of the watch, which wasn't terribly unusual if it really had been taken by the aranea. The aranea had been engaged in a shadow war with the invaders for some time, Zorian knew, even before the time loop had begun, and their anti-divination wards were top-notch.

[We meet again, Zorian Kazinski,] the matriarch spoke telepathically to him. She was surrounded by six honor guards, though only two were actually visible while the other four hung from the ceiling, masked by some kind of invisibility spell. Zorian only knew they were there because he could sense their minds. [And once again you bring additional guests with you. Three of them this time. If this pattern continues, we'll have to find a more spacious area to house them all after a few more restarts.]

[Funny,] Zorian sent back. [But actually, this is the group I was with when I first met the aranea. We were looking for a watch supposedly in your possession then, same as we are now. Sound familiar?]

"What's going on?" asked Taiven. She and her two friends were lingering a few steps behind Zorian, looking apprehensively at the three spiders in front of them. "Why are you just staring at them?"

Before Zorian could say anything, the matriarch started waving her front four legs in the air for a while and then spoke for all to hear.

"What's this about a watch I hear?" she asked, turning her two biggest, forward-facing eyes at Taiven.

It took a few minutes of explaining and clarifications, but in the end the matriarch finally seemed to remember the event in question.

"Oh, now I remember," she said. "Though the man in question certainly wasn't any kind of innocent passerby, and the 'watch' is no simple time-keeping device. He and a few other thugs assaulted our web and he dropped his bauble when we chased them off."

[He's one of the invaders,] the matriarch told Zorian telepathically, so only he could hear. [Or at least he works for them. You say you saw him? Excellent, we finally have an entry point into the organization. A face, a name, and personal contact, even if brief, should be enough to divine where he lives. You do know his name, don't you? Excellent. Hopefully he gave his real one. Did you shake hands with him when you accepted the job? No? Try to shake hands with him when you give him the device. Maybe put a tracking spell on it if you know how...]

Somehow, the matriarch was able to participate in two separate conversations at once, speaking out loud to Taiven and her two friends as she spoke telepathically to Zorian. Zorian himself was not similarly blessed and mostly tuned out her explanation to Taiven in order to absorb what she was telling him mentally. Finally, she seemed to realize this and cut her telepathic communication with him short, allowing him to pay attention to what she had been saying out loud.

"...so I'm not sure what the device is for, but it's clearly a magical item of some sort," the matriarch said. "It's useless for us aranea, but we are well familiar with the concept of trade. We were hoping to trade it to some of our human contacts for something we can actually use, but since it's our dear friend Zorian that's asking for it, I guess we'll give it to you as a favor. I'm sure Zorian will make it up to us... eventually."

"Uhh...," fumbled Taiven, looking at him uncertainly. "Is... that okay, Roach? Are you...?"

"Yeah, I'm fine with that," Zorian said. Although as far as he was concerned, he didn't really owe any favors to the matriarch for this.

[I only said that for the sake of appearances,] the matriarch told him telepathically. [It would be suspicious if we just gave it up for no reason. Besides, as far as *I'm* concerned, you will repay my generosity by helping me track down your employer so we can wring him for information.]

"Fang of Victory will go and retrieve the bauble," the matriarch said out loud, causing one of the two visible honor guards to suddenly skitter off into the darkness. "I'd ask you to warn your employer against further aggression against us, but it's probably best if he doesn't know you spoke to us."

"Why did he attack you anyway?" asked Taiven. "You seem nice enough to me."

"Most places will kill sapient monsters as a matter of course, if they find them within their borders," Grunt said. He and Mumble had both been pretty quiet thus far, so it was a bit startling to hear him speak up all of the sudden. Taiven gave him a dirty look for his remark. "What? I'm just saying he didn't need a reason. Their presence would be offensive enough for some people."

"It's a little more complex than that," the matriarch said. "Humans clash with other sentient races, that is true, but that's because most of them are highly territorial, murderous, view humans as food, or all three. On occasions where that wasn't the case, humans have shown themselves willing to make exceptions and take a more… nuanced approach. There are several dragons that deal with humans in a peaceful manner, the lizardmen of Blantyrre have long been a trading partner for human nations, and many of the Splinter States bordering the wilderness have made secret or not so secret pacts with various spirits and monster clans living within their nominal borders."

"You've thought about this a lot," Zorian remarked.

"Though not well known, we have been peacefully interacting with humanity for quite a long time now," the matriarch said. "The aranea have been living in the deeper levels of the Dungeon for as long as this city has existed. When the foundations were being laid, several campaigns were launched into the local sections of the Dungeon to clear out the threats lurking inside it. However, this power vacuum also allowed weaker races like aranea to move in and find a foothold. The Dungeon around the Hole is prime real estate for magical creatures of all breeds, as you probably know, and the competition was fierce. Fortunately, while we aranea lacked the brute strength or destructive magical abilities of some of our competitors, we are far more willing to cooperate with humans to our mutual benefit. We contacted some of the humans that were willing to cooperate with us and gave them information about our mutual enemies—their strengths and weaknesses, where they lived, the timing of their attacks and movements… everything they needed to wipe them out, or at least weaken them to the point where we could finish the job. Information gathering has always been our specialty."

Zorian found himself fascinated by the story and more than a little surprised that the matriarch was willing to say all this in front of Taiven and her friends. Then again, Zorian had never told them that aranea were mind readers, so their minds were completely unshielded. The matriarch probably had a pretty good sense of how likely they were to cause trouble for her. And they weren't going to remember anything about this when this loop ended, either.

"Although giving information to humans helped us as well as them, we rarely did it for free. In return for our secrets, we demanded some of your own. Our human allies used the information we provided to make a name for themselves and further their careers, and in return they taught us some of your magic and helped us adapt it for our own use. Armed with our very own system of structured magic, the aranea grew in strength and versatility, solidifying their hold over this region and making the web that lived beneath Cyoria the most prestigious of aranean webs. The resulting prosperity caused their numbers to swell, and they sent a never-ending stream of colonists and breakaway webs to the surrounding region, where they proceeded to evict or subjugate every lesser aranean web they encountered. But although these aranea left Cyoria in search of their own destiny, no place had the prestige or opportunities that Cyoria offered, and thus many viewed their mother web with envy and resentment. In time, a number of these colonies banded together and, armed with the experience of fighting the lesser webs for territory, drove the original web out of their homeland. It would not be the last time Cyoria changed hands. The conquerors were soon evicted by another group of invaders, and this group was evicted by another, and then they were evicted by us. We are the fifth web to hold this place and while our position is secure at the moment, any sort of weakness could cause the neighboring webs to get... restless."

"Huh," Zorian said. "So if you were, hypothetically speaking, absolutely decimated by someone and had your numbers severely reduced?"

"Our neighbors would launch a few probing raids at the very least," the matriarch said. "But anyway, my point is that humans and aranea are not, nor have they ever been, enemies. Well, barring some... isolated incidents. On both sides. In fact, it has been my explicit policy to encourage closer links between this web and humans living in Cyoria. I hope the day will come when aranea will be able to walk the street above in open daylight, just like any other citizen."

"And I suppose you hope the humans will defend you from outside threats, like any other citizens," Grunt said. "Like, say, from those rival webs that want to take your territory?"

"I confess that possibility does factor rather heavily into my thinking," the matriarch admitted. "The city authorities would be a lot less inclined to stand by and watch if we had an established, formal relationship with them."

"So is this your recruiting pitch?" asked Taiven. "Are you trying to turn us into your agents?"

"More contacts are always helpful," the matriarch said. "But no, I'm not trying to recruit you. I just sensed you were worried about Zorian's association with us and wanted to assuage your fears somewhat. Anyway, Fang of Victory is coming back with the bauble, so we'll have to cut this short here. Talk to Zorian if you ever want to chat with us again."

Sure enough, the matriarch's honor guard soon returned with the watch. Zorian half expected the spider to return with the watch gripped in her fangs, but it actually came back wearing a leather harness full of pouches, one of which held the watch. For a moment Zorian wondered how they had crafted the harness, which seemed like it would be complicated without hands, but then realized he was being a bit foolish. The matriarch had already said they traded with humans for many things—this must be one of them.

Moments later, they said their goodbyes to the aranea and were on their way back to their employer, prize in hand.

"I don't know what to think," Taiven said when they had put some distance between themselves and the aranea. "They seem nice enough, but it's a bit disquieting to discover we have an entire colony of these things living beneath the city, pulling their strings over gods know how many people."

"Yeah," agreed Mumble quietly. Zorian could definitely see why Taiven called him what she did—he tended to talk really softly, making his speech very hard to understand sometimes. "Did you know Cyoria is kind of famous for its spider silk? The merchants who sell it are really cagey about where they get it in such quantities and have declared their source a trade secret. Most people think they have managed to create a spider species that can be farmed effectively and have a giant farm hidden somewhere, but I think it's pretty obvious now where they get it…"

Zorian mostly kept out of the conversation, alternating between listening and studying the device they had retrieved from the aranea. It was, as the matriarch had said, a magical item of sorts—shaped like a pocket watch, but not one. The hands didn't move, and the screw that should have allowed a person to wind it was fused with the casing and seemed to be simply an ornamental bump put there to make the illusion superficially convincing. He tried to channel mana into it, but that didn't result in anything substantial. Likely the device required the user to channel mana in a very specific manner, as many complex magical items did.

The lessons in divining the secrets of magical items that Haslush had given him really paid off here. The fake watch was a ward scanner, designed to guide and enhance divination spells meant to seek out weaknesses in complicated warding schemes so they could be broken or bypassed more easily. To put it bluntly, it was a thief's tool. Zorian thought it likely that the owner of the watch had probably been trying to identify a hole in the aranean defenses.

Still, while the purpose of the device was readily apparent to his divination spells, its method of operation stubbornly remained a mystery. After several unsuccessful attempts to pry the casing open without damaging the device, he finally decided to try something… experimental. He extruded a mana cloud from his hands, just as he did when picking locks, and directed it to trickle into the device's insides through the gaps and misaligned seams. The resulting information was fuzzy, but told him that the inside was filled with brass gears and crystals. Prying it open would damage the delicate components. How then…

Ah, so that was the trick! The hands of the clock weren't just static—they were nothing more than an image painted on the glass cover. Zorian pressed his finger against the glass cover and pushed it into the casing. There was a soft click from the inside, and when Zorian released the pressure, the cover immediately flew open, revealing a complicated interface full of dials and sigils. A *very* complicated interface. He wasn't going to figure this out in the hour or so they had until they reached the client.

He was so taking this thing apart to see how it worked in one of the future restarts.

They finished the job without complications. Zorian opted not to put a tracking spell on the device, since he didn't know how sensitive it was and didn't want to ruin it. That turned out to be a good choice, as the man immediately cast several diagnostic spells on the device once Zorian handed it over, one of which Zorian knew was designed to detect simple tracking spells. Once the transaction was complete, Zorian insisted they shake hands, claiming it was traditional in his village to do so after a successful business deal. The man rolled his eyes and mumbled something about yokels but humored him anyway. Mission accomplished.

After they all shared a drink in a nearby tavern—Taiven insisted and wouldn't take no for an answer from anyone—the group separated. Zorian immediately descended to the sewers again and went back to the aranea.

[A ward reader, you say?] the matriarch asked. [It makes sense. He and his friends had been hanging out at the edge of our territory for a while, trying to stay hidden. I'm surprised he hired a bunch of students to get it, though.]

"Yeah, I'm not sure what he was thinking," Zorian said. "Seems like a stupid idea to me."

[We'll find out in a few days, if all goes well,] the matriarch said. [That said, there are other things we must discuss. I believe I told you in the previous restart that I happened upon some important information.]

"You did," Zorian agreed. "I was wondering what that was about."

[The invasion, of course. First of all, your guess was correct—they are indeed from Ulquaan Ibasa.]

Zorian scowled. "I knew it. Why? Are they out for revenge or is this just sheer opportunism?"

[A bit of both,] the matriarch said. [They resent you for their exile and they think you're weak now that the Splinter Wars and the Weeping wiped out most of your battlemages. But that's not the important part. The important part concerns a question so simple I'm honestly not sure why neither of us thought of it. Namely, why exactly did the invasion think they could conquer Cyoria in the first place?]

Zorian opened his mouth to answer 'with the aid of the time loop, duh', but then quickly closed it again. According to the matriarch, this invasion had been in the works far before the start of the time loop. Clearly, someone associated with the invasion was brought into the time loop eventually and started feeding information to them to make the whole endeavor scarily effective, but what about before that? Without knowing exact locations of Cyoria's defenses, their initial bombardment would have been a lot less damaging than it was. And without knowledge of the academy's exact ward scheme and how to bypass it, their assault would have been rife with challenges, perhaps even doomed from the start. And on top of all that, the matriarch claimed the aranea had been successfully keeping the invaders out of Cyoria's underworld before the time loop. Given that, the invasion had never really stood a chance.

"Perhaps they didn't," Zorian said. "Intend to conquer it, I mean. Cyoria is pretty important to Eldemar, but it's not the capital nor the industrial heartland. It's the seat of Eldemar's mage guild and the home of the world's most prestigious mage academy, neither of which is likely to cooperate with the invaders. Most likely they just intended to do as much damage as possible. If they cripple Cyoria and keep Eldemar's magical might busy, it would give them the opportunity to strike elsewhere."

[You're very close,] the matriarch said. [They were indeed trying to cause as much damage to the city as possible, but it was to be much more than a simple distraction. Apparently the date of the summer festival is magically significant. It is the day of the year when the barriers between planes of existence are the weakest. In fact, the weakening begins exactly one month before the date, gradually increasing until it reaches its peak on the day of the festival. And this year's summer festival is even more special than usual. I'm afraid that we aranea don't know much about astronomy, seeing as we live largely underground, but it seems this year's summer festival coincides with a,] she paused, as though recalling the words, [planetary alignment?]

Zorian took a deep breath, a shiver running down his spine. Of course! How could he have missed it? The planar alignment only took place roughly every four hundred years. The last time it occurred, a city of mages took advantage of it to teleport their entire city all the way from Miasina to the southern coast of Altazia, performing the largest feat of trans-continental teleportation to ever be recorded. If someone wanted to mess around with space and time on a grand scale, this was *the* time to do it.

"Yeah, that *would* explain a lot," Zorian finally said. "Like why the time loop was initiated now, of all times. But wait, how does that help them to do more damage to the city? Did they intend to teleport Cyoria into the sea or something?"

[No. First of all, they intended to summon a large number of high-level demons to help with the invasion. This was why they were willing to go through with the attack, despite their lack of success against us and their inability to do much to the academy and its wards. Demons, especially high-level ones, are virtually immune to mental attacks and highly resistant to magic. The aranea would be massacred in no time at all, and the mages would be too busy fighting for their lives to help out the city's more mundane defenders. Those same defenders would be up against trolls and fire elementals, who are immune to firearms, with winter wolves and iron beaks acting as support.]

"That... that's horrible," Zorian said after digesting that for a second. "Why aren't they doing that now?"

[They can't, remember? No summoning anything while in the time loop. The whole material plane has been cut off from the spiritual ones,] the matriarch reminded him.

"Oh yeah," Zorian said. "I guess that would throw a serious wrench in the works. I wonder if they actually went through with the invasion before they had an agent inside the time loop. They would have surely known their plan was doomed without demonic support."

[They probably would,] the matriarch said. [The demons were ultimately a distraction, same as the rest of their forces. The invasion leadership didn't actually think they were enough to do more than cripple Cyoria and they wanted it completely wiped off the map. No, the real target lies with the area around the Hole. While the defenders were busy fighting for their lives, a group of mages would secure the place and enact a grand summoning ritual.]

"Ugh," Zorian grunted. "Let me guess: a really big demon."

[No. They wanted to summon a primordial.]

Zorian's stomach knotted as he felt the hair on his arm rise. "What!? But… that would leave the whole city a lifeless crater! What about their own forces!?"

[Expendable,] the matriarch told him bluntly. [Everyone high enough to matter was ready to teleport away at the first hint that the summoning was successful, the rest were disposable pawns that were never actually expected to survive. Besides, you'll notice that the actual invasion force is really light on human mages. Only a minimum of Ibasan mages was necessary to maintain some control over the various demons and monsters. And you're actually rather optimistic in your damage predictions. The Ibasan leadership hoped that summoning the primordial with the help of the biggest mana well on the continent would give it enough power to linger on this plane for weeks. If so, it would rampage across large swaths of Altazia before finally running out of power or until the Altazians managed to organize a group of mages strong enough to banish it back to its realm. Then Ulquaan Ibasa could just swoop in once it's gone and mop up the demoralized survivors.]

Zorian was honestly at a loss for words. On one hand, the plan was utterly crazy, and a large part of him wanted to say it would never work. Where did they even find a ritual to summon a goddamn primordial of all things? But still, he'd watched the invaders bulldoze through Cyoria's defenses far too many times to discount them like that. If they thought the plan could work, it probably could.

"Where did they find mages willing to do the summoning?" Zorian asked. "They must have known they'd be killed by the primordial's rampage before they can escape, being so close to it and all. And do you happen to know which primordial it was?"

[The summoning would be done by the Esoteric Order of the Celestial Dragon… probably known to you by the name Cult of the World Dragon. Apparently they are willing to sacrifice their lives in order to summon one of what they call the 'Great Mother's children'. Those of their members not involved with the summoning are helping the invasion forces as regular mage support or simple saboteurs, in the case of more mundane members. Actually, now that I think about it, they are probably acting as the invaders' inside agents in general; we'll have to infiltrate their group deeper for more information. Anyway, no, I don't know which primordial. Just that it was one of the land-bound ones—the Ibasans didn't want to risk it suddenly deciding it wanted to visit their little island and flying over.]

"I'll bet," Zorian said. "Of course, all this means we have a problem on our hands. No matter how formidable the invasion is while we're trapped inside the time loop, it will be even more fearsome outside of it. They will have additional demon support on top of everything we've already seen, and we'll have to spend some of our time thwarting the primordial summoning. I want to say those cultists are just totally crazy and couldn't summon a crippled imp, much less a thrice-damned primordial, but the possibility is just so catastrophic we can't afford to risk it."

[Yes, this indeed complicates the matter considerably,] the matriarch agreed. [My original plan was to keep thwarting the flow of the invasion until the third time traveler is forced to reveal themselves, either through sloppiness or frustration; lure them into an ambush and mindrape them into catatonia; find a perfect counter for the invasion over several restarts; and then finally find a way to break the time loop and deal with the invaders once and for all. The part about dealing with the third time traveler still seems workable, but finding a perfect counter will clearly be impossible with such a large variable missing while we're inside the time loop...]

Zorian was a tad queasy about how matter-of-factly the matriarch spoke of destroying a person's mind, but he had to admit he knew of no other way to deal with the third time traveler. The only other way involved destroying his soul, and that was arguably even more morally reprehensible. Plus, he didn't actually know how to destroy someone's soul. And hopefully never would.

"Right." Zorian sighed, suddenly tired. "What a day. Do you have any other bombshells to throw at me?"

[Well... not as such, no. However, these recent developments mean that I will not have much time to teach you this month. Fortunately, you are at the level where you don't really need a high-level user like me to guide you, so I have found you a suitable replacement. Zorian, say hello to Enthusiastic Seeker of Novelty.]

One of the aranea that had accompanied the matriarch, a rather small and twitchy individual that seemed to have trouble staying still, suddenly jumped down from the ceiling and landed in front of him.

[Hi! I am Enthusiastic Seeker of Novelty and I will totally be your teacher this month! I know you humans have trouble with our names so you can just call me Novelty. I don't mind!] She circled around him as she spoke to him telepathically, looking like some kind of weird puppy inviting him to play with her. [Anyway, when the matriarch asked for volunteers to teach you, I was like: 'this is your chance, Novelty'. I was totally game! They won't let me help with defense because I'm supposedly too young, but they told me you're a baby at this psychic stuff and I can totally take care of babies! And hey, you can teach me stuff, too! I was always curious about you humans, like how you can walk on your hind legs without tipping over all the time or...]

Zorian tuned out her chatter in favor of giving the matriarch a glare.

[Does she come with an off button?] he asked telepathically.

The matriarch simply projected a mixture of amusement and satisfaction in response.

CHAPTER 023

Lighting the Fuse

O n the surface, getting saddled with Novelty seemed like a recipe for endless frustration and annoyance—she was an impatient, impulsive chatterbox who seemed to have no concept of personal space, always hovering uncomfortably near him and poking him with her front legs. Zorian was not afraid of spiders, but that kind of close physical contact was just too much.

In short, she was a spider version of Kirielle. And he only tolerated Kirielle's antics as much as he did because she was his little sister.

Despite this, Zorian was actually glad to have met her. Her personality certainly left a lot to be desired, and he often had to keep her focused on their lessons instead of going off on weird tangents, but she was still a wealth of information on both psionics and aranea. And unlike the matriarch, whose every explanation sounded like a thinly-veiled manipulation attempt to Zorian, Novelty didn't have a single deceptive bone in her body. Most of the time she said what she meant, and it was painfully obvious when she tried to shift the subject or fudged the truth. It was a refreshing change of pace from his previous interactions with the aranea.

Novelty remained blissfully unaware of his thoughts, often too engrossed in other distractions, such as inspecting Zorian's alchemy equipment. That was another difference between Novelty and the matriarch—Novelty couldn't read his surface thoughts unless he structured them very slowly and clearly aimed them at her. It made him much more relaxed about her presence than he would have otherwise been.

[Humans build so many strange things,] Novelty declared after inspecting the glass vials by sight and touch. Zorian didn't know whether aranea were usually this fond of touching things and Novelty was simply unrestrained in her interactions with him or if the spider in front of him was simply a physical sort of girl, but Novelty certainly liked to touch the things she was studying. Annoyingly, this included him as well as random inanimate objects, but at least she seemed to have finally internalized the idea that he didn't like her climbing into his lap.

[How did you even make this? It's the same kind of transparent rock you use for those 'window' things, but I have no idea how you managed to carve it out in this kind of shape. And it's so smooth, too… I know those branching upper limbs of yours are better at manipulating things than our legs, but this is crazy. You know, the aranea once tried to keep human thralls to create things for us, but it was a huge hassle and it turned out it's much easier to just trade with humans for what we need. You humans don't seem to fare too well underground,

492

and kidnapping humans always seemed to anger the rest of the human communities a lot, even when they weren't of the same clan or anything. And... uh, that was a really long time ago and we totally don't do stuff like that anymore and you should forget everything I said about that, okay?]

"Uh-huh," said Zorian dubiously before deciding not to pursue the issue. "For what it's worth, the transparent rock is called glass, and it's not really carved. It's made from sand, which is heated until it turns molten and therefore malleable and then shaped by sticking long tubes into the resulting molten mass and blowing air into it."

Novelty turned around to focus all of her eyes on him. [How, in the name of grandmother's shriveled egg-sack, did it occur to one of you to do *that*? Do humans have some sort of magical stone sense or something?]

"Err, no," said Zorian patiently. Explaining stuff like this to Novelty was annoying, but it made her much more willing to share things with him in turn, so he would labor on. "Humans have always been mucking around with tools of various sorts. We're pretty fragile in our natural forms, so building things is a matter of survival. We use crude tools to fashion better tools, and then those better tools to fashion more precise tools, and so on. I don't really know how glassblowing came into existence, but it didn't just magically pop into someone's head all of a sudden."

[I don't really think you can be considered fragile,] Novelty said dubiously. [You wield incredible magic, and you pretty much conquered the surface world with it.]

"Not all humans wield magic," said Zorian. "Only a small number of people are mages, and the number was even smaller the more you go back in time."

[Most of your tools sound a lot like magic to me, to be honest,] Novelty said. [You take rocks and stuff and perform complicated rituals on them to turn them into these wondrous creations that no amount of web-weaving can duplicate. It's the part that fascinates me most about you humans—this weird building magic of yours. I was kind of hoping I could learn some of your secrets while I teach you, but it looks like that will be pretty difficult because, you know,] she waved her front legs in the air for emphasis, [I haven't got these 'hands' you humans use for everything. Not that I'm giving up or anything! I'm definitely going to figure something out!]

"Well, you already told me you are learning to be a mage, so you could always resort to actual magic," said Zorian. "Fabrication spells are a thing, after all. Granted, you'd have to understand the properties of materials you're working with and the engineering principles of the things you're trying to create, but if you're serious about being a crafter that's pretty much a must anyway."

[I'll be honest and admit I have no idea what you just said,] Novelty said after a brief silence. [But I'm guessing you were trying to be encouraging so thanks!]

"Right," Zorian said, sighing. "We've gone on another tangent. Let's focus on the lessons again."

[But those lessons are so boring!] Novelty complained. [You already know most of this stuff; it's just a matter of practicing, and you can't do that all alone in your room, anyway. You are practicing, right?]

"Sure am," Zorian agreed. "I spend most of my classes trying to sense my classmates and other students in the building. Not like I get anything else useful out of classes these days. It's going pretty well, but I still have to concentrate pretty heavily to achieve any kind of range. I've also tried sensing their emotions, but that is still pretty hit and miss. Are you sure no one is going to detect me doing that? Because I'm going to land in pretty hot water if somebody detects me messing with people's minds."

[I keep telling you, no one is going to detect anything without invading your mind first,] Novelty assured him. [I totally went and asked other aranea about that, since you keep asking about it, and they confirmed it. Basically, sensing minds and basic empathy doesn't involve any delving into other people's minds. I know you don't believe in the Great Web and all, but imagine a kind of mental plane that permeates everything. Minds create ripples on this mental plane, like stones thrown into a pool of stagnant water, and those who are Open can use these ripples to locate other minds around them and divine some basic facts about them. Stuff like species and their general mood.]

"Huh. That does make sense," Zorian said. "So, sensing minds and empathy are really two aspects of a single ability to perceive this mental plane of yours and interpret the 'ripples' propagating through it? Do you know if mental shielding spells have an effect on this?"

[Oh, definitely,] confirmed Novelty. [The basic shielding spells that mages like to use will pretty much ruin your ability to use empathy on them. Too much interference. Detecting them, on the other hand, becomes even easier. Any mind-affecting spells make a mind 'noisier' to a psychic, even defensive ones. *Especially* defensive ones, now that I think of it. Well, except for that one infamous spell called mind blank that actually causes a mind to disconnect from the Great Web, making a person completely undetectable to mind sensing and utterly immune to mind-affecting magic. Pretty terrifying stuff, that.]

Zorian knew of the spell she was talking about. Mind blank was well known as a kind of 'ultimate defense' against mind magic, but the spell was infamous for causing psychological problems if miscast or used too extensively. A number of mages paranoid about people invading their minds had gone insane after leaving it permanently on, giving it a somewhat poor reputation. There were other, less drastic protections that were sufficient in most cases.

"That's strange," Zorian said innocently. "The matriarch told me that no flimsy human magic could shield me against her if she was determined to get me, but here you're telling me there is a spell I could learn to make myself completely immune to psychic powers."

[Ah, well, you see…] Novelty fumbled. [She was actually right because, because those are totally different things, yes? A shield is one thing—we can totally batter it down or bypass it. If you take yourself off the Great Web, though, it's like you aren't there at all! You first need to sense a mind to connect to it, and if you can't connect to it—]

"I get it," Zorian interrupted. "No telepathic link, no aranean mind magic. And you can't connect to something you can't sense telepathically. Hmm, clearly the creator of mind blank knew a thing or two about psychic powers. It sounds like the spell is designed specifically to defeat them."

[The idea isn't that revolutionary,] Novelty grumbled. [A sufficiently skilled psychic can disconnect from the Great Web with some effort. It's called 'going dark'. It's a pretty shady skill, though, mostly used by assassins, thieves, and saboteurs. Anyway, the problem isn't just the mind blank—it's the fact that any mage powerful enough to cast it is also powerful enough to take on the entire aranean web all on their lonesome. We have ways of dealing with people like that, but I totally can't tell you because the others would have me dismembered if I said anything about it. Since, you know, secret defenses and stuff.]

"Right," Zorian said. He had no intention of creating problems at home for Novelty, so he wouldn't pursue that topic further. Their super-secret defense plans probably boiled down to 'collapse the entire tunnel on top of them', anyway. "So, mind blank is a psychic skill translated into a spell. Not that surprising, I guess. Mages love taking the abilities of magical creatures and turning them into spells for their own use."

[Really?] Novelty asked. [But I thought human magic is so good that there is nothing you can learn from others. The matriarch is always talking about how amazing your magic is and how no one can match it…]

"No, that's completely wrong," Zorian said. "Mages of Ikosian tradition—which is virtually every mage you're going to encounter—are pretty much all about taking other people's magic and making it their own. The entire system of structured magic is specifically designed to be expanded upon as needed. It's true that we rarely find something worth learning among other magical traditions these days, but that's mostly because we already stole and traded for everything that was worth taking."

[That's... not quite the story I was told,] Novelty admitted.

"Don't feel too bad—most humans also think our entire magical tradition sprang up fully-formed in the early days of the Ikosian Empire," Zorian said. "But back to our conversation about mental defenses. You said an aranea could batter down or bypass defensive magic other than mind blank. Does that include you personally?"

[Of course! Who do you take me for? If I couldn't fight telepathically, I'd have been devoured while still at the hatchery!]

Zorian blinked. "What, seriously? As in, actually get eaten or...?"

[Err, no, not *literally* eaten. We haven't let the hatchlings eat each other ever since... err, actually, let's not talk about that. It was just a figure of speech, that's the important bit. Anyway!] Novelty hastened to change the subject. [I don't know how it works among humans, but newborn aranea are confined to the hatchery during the first few months of their existence. There are usually a lot of us, and we're all cooped up in this tiny boring room with nothing to do but pester the caretakers for stories and pick fights amongst each other, and the caretakers don't like it when the hatchlings fight physically with each other. They are a lot more lenient about... *experimenting*... with our psychic powers, though. A bit of telepathic roughhousing is to be expected, so you pretty quickly learn the basics of defending your mind.]

Zorian tried to imagine the scenario Novelty just described and abandoned that train of thought with a shudder. He made a mental note to avoid being near aranean hatcheries at all costs, just in case the issue ever popped up in the future.

"That's... interesting... but not quite what I was asking. I meant countering defenses, not defending yourself," he said finally.

[You can't win a fight by only defending,] Novelty scoffed. [I don't really understand this weird divide between mental attacks and defenses you insist on. Striking back is a crucial part of any worthwhile defense. Even a weak counter-attack forces your opponent to spend some time and focus on their defenses and weakens their own attack.]

"I guess I keep forgetting that psychic powers aren't discrete spells, but more of a manifold manifestation of a single holistic ability," Zorian admitted. "Still, retaliation doesn't have to be mental. If I could stop your mental attacks long enough, I could just punch you or cast a spell on you to make you stop. Considering I know nothing about telepathic combat, that's probably the smartest option for me anyway. And that brings me to my proposition—I want to see how my magical defenses fare against your capabilities. I'm going to cast a few mind shields and you're going to do your best to take them apart. What do you say?"

[Honored matriarch gave me strict instructions about when I can progress with your lessons,] Novelty said hesitantly.

No doubt accompanied by strict instruction about what she wasn't allowed to teach him *at all*. Zorian was under no illusion that the aranea intended to teach him anything but a small fraction of their psychic skills. While the aranea seemed to worship their ability in some sense, and sought to encourage its spread among humanity, they clearly regarded most of it as a personal secret. Hell, some of the things the matriarch told him heavily implied they kept some things secret even from each other, never mind from outsiders. Not to mention it would be rather foolish of the matriarch to teach Zorian how to do some things, since he could, if he chose, promptly use those skills against her interests. For instance, he was quite sure that

Novelty had been given strongly worded instructions not to tell him anything about memory manipulation, since that would allow him to mess around with the matriarch's memory packet and potentially feed her forged information.

Still, Zorian was fine with that. He had already got more out of the aranea than he thought he would have, and in case he ever got greedy for more than the matriarch was willing to provide? Well, there were more aranea than the ones beneath Cyoria, and Novelty had made it clear they didn't really talk to each other much. If he traded for a single secret with ten different groups, he could easily amass far more knowledge than any one group would be comfortable with him having… for additional irony, he might even trade them a secret he got from one of the other groups he traded with. It was a classical trick that Ikosians used when dealing with tribal groups, and the time loop only made it easier.

But if he ever wanted to do such a thing, he needed to have some way of defending his mind. He got the impression that aranean tribes outside of Cyoria weren't nearly as friendly as the matriarch and her tribe, and mind effects transferred across restarts. The matriarch had promised to teach him 'the basics of telepathic combat', which he translated as 'inadequate to threaten us, but good enough to ward off cephalic rats and random mind mages.' But first Zorian wanted to know how human mind magic fared against the average aranea.

"We aren't 'progressing my lessons', because you're not going to teach me anything," Zorian insisted. "It's just an experiment. I want to see how my spells fare against you."

[All right, I'm totally game, then!] Novelty agreed, suddenly enthusiastic. [But, uh, you're not allowed to attack me physically in response, okay?]

"That would kind of defeat the purpose of the experiment," agreed Zorian.

[Right. So are we assuming I'm attacking from an ambush or that I'm pressed for time?] Novelty asked.

"The difference being?"

[Well, if I was attacking from an ambush, I would try to simply bypass your shield entirely through superior skill. It's very effective when it works, but slow to set up, so the target needs to be preoccupied with something or unaware of the attempt. On the other hand, if time is of the essence, I'd just batter down the shields with brute force. It's faster but more mana expensive. Oh, and it's kind of hard to judge the exact amount of force needed to break through a defense without also damaging the mind it was defending so, uh… let's just assume I'm attacking from ambush, okay?]

"Yes, let's," Zorian deadpanned.

The next hour was as frustrating as it was instructive. Novelty took the whole thing as a game, improving as time went on, despite Zorian's futile attempts to refine his defenses through repeated castings and spell combinations. It was rather embarrassing to see the over-excitable, scatterbrained aranea go through his spells like they didn't exist in thirty seconds flat. Granted, those thirty seconds would be enough for him to incinerate her in real life, but that presumed he was in a position to do so, and that might be an unwarranted assumption. What if she was hidden from him? What if she was behind some kind of wards? What if she wasn't the only attacker?

But a little embarrassment was worth it. He now knew that his best defense against aranea (and other psychics, he supposed) was actually the basic mind shield spell. Other, more sophisticated spells couldn't seem to cope against Novelty's telepathic attacks.

[Most of the spells you used were really easy to trick and bypass with a few feints and a bit of careful timing,] Novelty explained. [They were all based on simple defense patterns and always reacted the same to my attacks. That magic shell you used to surround your mind with, though… it's such a crude thing, but I have to admit it gave me trouble. No patterns or anything fancy, just a solid, unyielding mental barrier. I don't think I'd be able to bypass it at all if you hadn't kept messing up the spell every time you cast it.]

"I was messing it up?" asked Zorian in surprise.

[Yeah. The shell had these minute imperfections in it that I used to slip past it. I don't think those were supposed to be there,] Novelty said.

Hmm. What she called minute imperfections sounded like a normal result of a usual spell boundary. Very few mages could cast a spell flawlessly, and they rarely needed to—minute imperfections rarely mattered except under very special circumstances.

But apparently this was one of those special circumstances. Zorian suppressed a sigh—he could already hear the ghostly voice of Xvim in his head lecturing him about the failures of today's mages and the need to practice until you could do the spells *right* instead of good enough.

In retrospect, he was just asking for trouble with that line of thought.

When Zorian arrived at his weekly session with Xvim, he fully expected to get an hour of his usual crap from the mentor… which in this particular restart meant taking a bundle of thin sticks and trying to incinerate one of them without singeing the rest of them or burning his hand in the process. Admittedly, Zorian noticed that Xvim seemed to be eyeing him with more intensity than usual when he came in, but it was hardly out of the ordinary for the teacher to act strangely.

But Zorian hadn't even taken a seat before Xvim decided to speak to him.

"I have heard you have been casting fireballs," Xvim said. "Is that true?"

Zorian forcibly stopped himself from scowling at the man. Him making a comment like that was never a good sign. Xvim was never impressed with anything Zorian did, so no doubt he found something objectionable in his combat practice with Taiven. How the hell did the man even find out about that?

Xvim's face gave nothing away, and Zorian had already tried to use his rudimentary empathy on him to no avail, trying to see what made the annoying man tick. Xvim had incredible control over his emotions, and virtually nothing fazed him or truly set him off.

"I can cast the spell, yes," Zorian said carefully, as if talking slower would help him evade whatever minefield Xvim had set up for him with his question. "Admittedly only at minimum power, but—"

"So that's a no, then," Xvim deadpanned. He stared at Zorian, his expression stern, as if challenging Zorian to contradict him. Fortunately, Zorian was far too wise to get worked up over Xvim's proclamations by this point, so they simply stared at each other in silence for a few moments. Eventually, Xvim broke eye contact with an overdramatic sigh. "Mages these days, always rushing into things half-baked. I expected better from you. There is nothing wrong with being interested in combat magic, but immediately going for the flashiest, highest rated spell in your reach is unwise. A half-powered fireball is no fireball at all. You should have concentrated on building a solid base until you could do it *properly*."

"Well," Zorian said calmly, "why not show me how it's done, then?"

In response, Xvim wordlessly drew a stack of cards from his drawer and threw them at him. Zorian instinctively caught them before they could collide with his head, too used to his mentor's antics to be surprised at the move.

"Cards?" he asked, turning them over in his hands. They looked like regular playing cards, except their faces were replaced with squares, lines, circles, and other geometrical shapes.

"Cards," Xvim confirmed. "Specifically, cards made out of mana absorbing material. Those sigils on the corners expel any mana the cards gather, radiating it away into the surroundings. It takes a lot of mana to affect them in any way."

"And I'll be affecting them?" Zorian guessed.

"You'll try, I'm sure," Xvim said airily, pointedly rearranging the pens on his table instead of looking at Zorian. "They're very hard to affect for mages of such meager skills as yours. To make the story short, you'll be trying to burn the shapes painted on the cards—and only the shapes. You may begin when you feel ready."

Zorian stared at the cards for a moment. He suspected he knew what the point of this exercise was—he had to use a lot of mana, and he had to use it instantly or the corner glyphs would simply radiate his mana away. That was pretty much the basic challenge of all combat magic: shape a lot of mana quickly without messing up the spell boundary too much.

He took a deep breath, picked a card that looked easiest to him (it was just a circle in the middle, how hard could that be?) and poured a sizeable chunk of mana into his first attempt.

Other than the corner glyphs glowing slightly, nothing happened.

Damn it. This just might be a little harder than he thought it would be.

After failing to affect the cards a few times and then overdoing it and burning a few to cinders, singeing his fingers in the process, Zorian finally managed to burn some blurry shapes that were clearly inspired by what was drawn on the card—instead of an irregular hole through the center of the card. Predictably, Xvim had some very disparaging things to say about that.

Eventually, Zorian ran out of mana and had to stop. What kind of shaping exercise was so mana intensive you could actually run out as you practice? The Xvim kind, apparently. Instead of simply sending him away, though, Xvim then proceeded to lecture him about the proper way of gathering ambient mana. According to him, ambient mana could be assimilated faster if one sat completely still and focused on doing absolutely nothing else. So not very useful, all things considered, but probably crucial if he intended to complete Xvim's newest exercise in any sort of reasonable time-frame.

Then, as a parting remark, Xvim casually remarked that they were going to continue their lesson tomorrow. That it wasn't even a school day didn't bother Xvim in the slightest.

"Good," Xvim concluded. "We have a whole day, then. We will need the time from what I saw today."

It wasn't an isolated occurrence. From that day on, Xvim insisted on practice sessions every single day, monopolizing every bit of free time Zorian had. Why did Xvim suddenly decide to do that, when he usually never interacted with him outside their assigned meeting times? Hell if Zorian knew. It was certainly annoying, though.

The aranea, on the other hand, had their own frustrations. Trying to track down the ward-breaker that hired Taiven's group to recover the watch turned out to be fairly easy, but getting access to him was anything but. In addition to being good at breaking and analyzing wards, the man was also good at building them, and he was a very capable mage to boot. The aranea lost two of their members trying to corner him and eventually gave up on him for that particular restart, focusing on other leads for the moment.

They still did their best to counter the invaders during the summer festival, of course.

The next two restarts were much the same—the aranea gathered information about the invaders, sometimes asking Zorian to speak for them if they had to interact with someone openly, and started a limited

assassination campaign among the cultists and other invasion collabo-
rators they identified. Zorian learned combat magic, aranea mind arts,
and tried to survive Xvim's lessons without punching the man in the
face. Their efforts were steadily bearing fruit—the invasion went more
and more haywire with each subsequent restart—and the matriarch
hoped their mysterious third time traveler was going to show up soon.

The biggest surprise to Zorian, was that Novelty actually remembered their interactions in previous restarts. It seemed the matriarch had
decided not to monopolize the memory transfer like Zorian thought
she would, and was instead including the memories of six different
aranea in that memory packet of hers. Novelty, being something of
Zorian's personal trainer by now, was deemed important enough to
be included in that elite company, something the young spider was
very smug about.

But Zorian began to feel it was time for a change of pace. Two
restarts full of Xvim were enough for him, and Taiven had taught him
most of what she knew about combat magic anyway.

He knocked on the door to Ilsa's office and waited for her to
invite him in.

"Good morning, Mister Kazinski," Ilsa said with a hint of amusement.
"I wasn't expecting you until Friday. I suppose you've heard some stories
about your mentor, then?"

"No, I already know what kind of person Xvim is. That's not why
I'm here," Zorian said. "No, I'm here because I want to learn how to
teleport."

Ilsa blinked in surprise. "That's... quite ambitious. Leaving aside
the question as to why I should spend my time teaching you that, what
makes you think you're even capable of casting such a spell? Even the
simplest of teleport spells are very difficult."

"A fair question," Zorian admitted. "How about a demonstration?"

"By all means," Ilsa laughed, motioning him to go ahead. Zorian didn't need empathy to see she didn't think he was capable of impressing her.

Well then—challenge accepted.

Moving in smooth, rapid succession, Zorian demonstrated every difficult shaping exercise, every complicated spell he had learned over the past two years in the time loop. Every written test or theoretical question she fielded against him he countered with a perfect answer—sometimes because he honestly knew the topic, and sometimes because she tended to ask the same questions each time he tried to impress her. And then, when she was still reeling from the realization that he was skilled enough to graduate from the academy right at that moment if he wanted, he pulled out several magic objects from his backpack and started explaining his spell formula experiments to her. While she did not teach the subject, Zorian knew from previous restarts that she was very knowledgeable in the field and could appreciate the difficulty of what he was showing her.

"I'm surprised you haven't applied for a transfer to a tier one group with these kinds of skills," Ilsa remarked after a moment of contemplation when he was finally done.

Ah yes, the tier 1 groups—the academy's answer for students too advanced for the normal curriculum. Sadly, the prestige of belonging to one of those groups meant that many people did everything in their power to place their child into one of them, and that meant the actual lessons couldn't be *that* much more advanced from normal ones, else all the people who bought or otherwise arranged for their presence there couldn't keep up. Zorian had heard all sorts of things about those groups, good or bad, but the general picture seemed to be of a bunch of social climbers looking down on everyone else. Nothing that Zorian wanted to be a part of.

"I believe I can get more things done through independent study," Zorian said. "If I truly thought my classes had nothing to offer me, I would just test out."

"Don't be too hasty," Ilsa warned. "I'm sure you can find the academy resources useful for another year or so. You aren't *that* advanced."

The academy didn't like it when people tested out. They publicly prided themselves on being able to help even adult mages, never mind gifted children. Graduating early implied that the student had nothing left to learn from the academy and was considered a bit of a slap to the institution's face. You didn't get any money back for finishing early, either.

All in all, Zorian didn't really intend to test out—that wouldn't do anything except create bad blood between him and the academy. Still, he always found that sprinkling some light threats into negotiations helped the other side take him more seriously.

Ilsa continued to think in silence for a while, rhythmically tapping her pencil on top of a folder full of written tests that Zorian had speedily filled out earlier in the meeting. He didn't interrupt her, although he considered the long silence a bad sign. In all likelihood this attempt was a waste and he would have to try another approach in the next resta—

"All right, here is my offer," Ilsa said suddenly. "I will take on your mentorship in place of Xvim. I will give you instruction in advanced aspects of illusionism, alteration, animation, and conjuration. If you impress me with your dedication, I will then include lesser dimensionalism spells in that list. If you prove yourself adept at those... *then* I will teach you the basic teleport spell."

Zorian blinked. What? That was way more than he had asked for! Not that he was complaining, but...

"That sounds better than I hoped for," Zorian said. "What's the catch?"

"Well, first of all, I'm expecting you to be my personal assistant," Ilsa said. "I've been trying to get one for the past two years, but the headmaster refuses to pay the salary and finding a skilled person willing to work for free is understandably difficult. Anyway, you'll mostly be dealing with the large number of tests and homework I get every single day, and I may also ask you to take over some of my first-year teaching responsibilities. Or any other random task I think of that I consider below me, really."

Annoying, but a fair price for what she was offering. In fact, this whole thing sounded remarkably like—

"And you'll officially become my apprentice," Ilsa continued. "If I am going to teach you advanced magic and trust you with my work, I want to have some kind of legal hold over you."

—like that. Normally Zorian would be very leery of signing an apprentice contract with someone he barely knew considering the contracts were designed to make life miserable for an apprentice who violated the agreement. But the risk was nearly nonexistent for him, given the fact that the contract would vanish in a matter of weeks.

"Oh, and you'll be taking over the position of class representative for your group," Ilsa suddenly added.

Zorian winced. Not only was that a thankless, horrible job, it was also already taken.

"Akoja is going to be devastated," Zorian mumbled. He felt kind of bad at stealing her position, especially since he didn't actually want it in the first place, but there was no way he was missing this chance.

Ilsa laughed. "Zorian, the reason I'm giving you the position is that Akoja doesn't want it anymore. She says she hates the position—that everyone shuns her because of it and that I should give it to someone else. Unfortunately, I haven't received any offers to switch with her. Not from anyone I trust, anyway." She gave Zorian a knowing look. "You were one of the people she recommended for the position, but I didn't even bother asking you about it. Everything I heard about you suggested you wouldn't accept."

"And you were absolutely right," Zorian agreed, still a little shocked. Akoja didn't want to be the class representative? But the girl lived for that stuff! And anyway, if she didn't want to do it then why did she perform it with such dedication? If Zorian was stuck in a job he hated, he would do as little as possible or even mess up deliberately so Ilsa would feel pressured to replace him as soon as possible. Why couldn't Akoja do the same? "The only reason I'm accepting this now is because the rest of your offer is so good."

"So we have a deal, then?"

"Yes, but I have a question and a demand," said Zorian. "First, why do you want to teach me those particular subjects? And second, I want to learn the teleport spell before the summer festival."

"I somehow doubt you'll manage to master the prerequisites for the teleportation spell in little less than a month," Ilsa said. "But in the *highly theoretical* case you actually do so, I have no problem fulfilling your demand. Why are you so dead-set about that spell?"

"It's a bit of a dream of mine to be able to do that," Zorian said, offering a shrug. "In my mind, teleportation has always been one of the ur-examples of what a proper mage can do, should be capable of."

"Interesting. Out of curiosity, what are the other things a proper mage can do?" asked Ilsa.

"Make a force field, create a magic item, produce a fireball, repair broken objects, and turn invisible," Zorian said. "I can already do the first four, and the fifth one is illegal without special permits."

He was already working on acquiring an invisibility spell anyway, but she didn't have to know that.

Ilsa gave him a knowing look and Zorian might have worried she was reading his thoughts if he weren't certain he could detect any casual intrusion into his own mind.

"To answer your first question, I chose those disciplines because they're my own specialty," Ilsa said. "It's only proper for an apprentice to learn his master's specialty, is it not?"

"Sure," Zorian agreed. "I'm not sure what all of those things have in common though. Aren't specialties supposed to be more focused?"

"Well, when I was a young mage, I, too, had a bit of a dream," Ilsa said. "Specifically, I wanted to master true conjuration."

Zorian blinked. "As in, the creation of real matter out of thin air? Isn't that a myth?"

"That's the current academy stance, yes," Ilsa agreed. "Pre-Cataclysm sources claim that powerful mages could manage the feat, but all the spells to do so have been lost and no one has been able to recreate them in modern times. Many mages think they never existed and assume the old records are making things up or describing something other than actual matter creation. Anyway, as a young mage, it was my dream to recreate those spells, so I studied anything I thought could be a path towards that goal. Modern conjuration basically involves making solid illusions, so it was somewhat natural to start with illusionism and then progress to conjuration. And then, since true conjuration involves working with real matter, I moved onto alteration spells dealing with fabrication of items."

"And... did you have any success?" asked Zorian curiously.

"Depends on your definition of success," Ilsa said. "My ultimate goal was to design a spell that would summon material from somewhere else without the caster having to know exactly where the materials are coming from. That was how I imagined ancient Ikosians could 'fake' matter creation. I found a certain level of success, but the spell I made only works in a specially prepared room and the mana cost of the spell varies wildly from casting to casting depending on what I'm trying to conjure. And there was that embarrassing incident with the gold creation part of the experiment swiping these ancient coins from a nearby museum…"

She shook her head. "A story for another time. I have to get to class soon, anyway. I'll prepare an apprentice contract for you to sign tomorrow so be sure to drop by when you have the time."

The next five restarts were both hectic and boring. Hectic in that there was always something that needed to be done, and boring in the sense that little of it was truly novel. He steadily improved his various skills, the aranea were becoming highly adept at countering the invaders in various ways, and Zach seemed to have finally accepted that something highly unusual was going on in the background, and that he wasn't the cause.

There was little chance of Zach identifying Zorian as the source of these changes since the sheer magnitude of them tended to drown out everything Zorian personally did. The aranea always started each restart very aggressively, giving anonymous tips to Cyoria's police department, assassinating a few people, and even spreading a few rumors around. The result was that by the time Zorian entered his first class, the changes had already propagated throughout the whole city, academy teachers and students included. Zach didn't appear to suspect Zorian as the ultimate cause, or any other classmate for that matter.

Zorian was starting to agree with Zach in that regard—the third time traveler wasn't in their class. Zorian had, through various excuses, talked to all of them, using his new position as class representative in the previous five restarts to assist in this endeavor. He had also employed his slowly improving empathy to gauge their reactions to suggestive hints that would only make sense to a time-looping person. He found nothing to implicate any of them.

All in all, things were going pretty well in Zorian's opinion, especially the most recent restart. He had finally managed to learn the teleport spell from Ilsa, Zach was actually starting to get smart about countering the invaders instead of simply trying to take them all on through his combat skills, and the most recent invasion attempt had failed to conquer the main academy building or the student shelters because the aranea somehow managed to influence academy leadership into adjusting their warding scheme.

But the matriarch was getting impatient. Something was making her more and more nervous with each passing restart, and she refused to tell him what, giving flimsy excuses every time he asked. She seemed to be focusing most of her energies on some kind of personal project, which she described as 'information gathering' and 'following a hunch', and whatever results she was getting were clearly disturbing her. Zorian strongly suspected she had discovered some kind of vital information about the nature of the time loop, and she refused to share it with him for whatever reason. He was honestly kind of bitter about that. What could possibly be more disturbing than what they already knew about the phenomenon?

Regardless, the matriarch was insistent that the third time traveler had to be found, and the sooner the better. Once Zorian confirmed that they weren't in his class, she became convinced they, like Zach, weren't even present in the city most of the time. In all likelihood they simply gave critical information to the invaders at the outset of each restart and then went to do their own thing. If they wanted to get their attention, the invasion would probably have to be a *spectacular* flop.

Accordingly, the matriarch laid out her plan for the next restart, one that would definitely be impossible to ignore...

CHAPTER 024

Smoke and Mirrors

Zorian would be the first to admit he wasn't the easiest person to get along with. He was unsociable, irritable, and tended to assume the worst of people. He had always known that, even before he had died and gotten stuck in a mysterious time loop, but he had also always felt he was justified in his behavior. Indeed, if anyone had been foolish enough to criticize him about it before the time loop, he would have reacted with all the subtlety and grace of a disturbed rattlesnake.

Now… well, he still felt he had good reasons to behave the way he did, and he wasn't going to win any friendliness contests any time soon, but the time loop had changed him. Made him calmer and perhaps a tad more considerate to people around him. He hadn't had an argument with his family in years, his financial independence was all but ensured once the time loop was over, his growing magical prowess had done wonders for his confidence, and the sheer scale of his current problem made all his previous frustrations seem rather petty in comparison.

Thus, when Kirielle kicked him in the knee for the third time in as many minutes, he pointedly didn't snap at her. He didn't even sigh in exasperation. He just continued staring out of the window, watching the fields fly by as the train sped ever closer towards Korsa.

"I'm bored," Kirielle complained.

Zorian gave her a curious look. While the wards protecting the train disrupted mana shaping, they had only a rudimentary effect on his empathy, and what he was detecting from Kirielle wasn't boredom—it was a mix of excitement, anticipation and apprehension. As far as Zorian could tell, such complex mixtures of emotions appeared to be the most common 'emotion' that people experienced, and they were almost entirely indecipherable at Zorian's current level of skill.

"What's really bothering you?" he tried. Her mind immediately burst into a flurry of activity, and she opened her mouth to say something before losing her courage and lamely disguising her attempt to speak as a particularly deep breath. Huh, so she wasn't just being restless…

"Nothin'," she muttered, averting her gaze and despondently picking at the hem of her blouse.

Zorian rolled his eyes and kicked her lightly in the knee. Despite doing the exact same thing to him only few moments ago, she proceeded to send him a nasty glare. Unsurprisingly, her attempt at intimidation failed utterly—she was about as frightening as an angry kitten.

"Tell me," he insisted.

She gave him a long, suspicious look before relenting.

"Will you teach me some magic when we get to Cyoria?" she asked hopefully.

How troublesome. The smart, reasonable response would be 'no'. She wouldn't see much success in a single month and she would forget everything she had learned, but more importantly, this particular restart was going to be extremely busy as it was.

"…I'll see what I can do," Zorian said after a few seconds of tense silence. Well, tense for Kirielle—he was pretty sure she had literally stopped breathing while waiting for an answer.

"Yessss!" she crowed, pumping her fists in the air in triumph.

"But in exchange, I'll want your help with something," he added.

"Fine," she immediately agreed, not even asking what exactly he had in mind. "Hey, can you—"

"No," Zorian immediately said. "The train is warded to disrupt mana shaping. No one can cast spells in here."

"Oh," Kirielle deflated.

Truthfully, Zorian was bending the truth a little. The ward on the train that disrupted mana shaping was very weak and rudimentary, meant to deter overeager students and casual vandalism, and was little more than an annoyance to a proper mage like Zorian. He could overpower the ward with ease, but he had analyzed it in detail during the previous restart and knew it reported any significant spellcasting to some remote location. He'd rather not get chucked out of the train before reaching Cyoria just because Kirielle wanted a free show.

Kirielle opened her mouth to say something else but was promptly interrupted by a sharp crackling sound that heralded the voice of the station announcer.

"Now stopping in Korsa," the disembodied voice echoed. "I repeat, now stopping in Korsa. Thank you."

Well, at least their compartment would soon have another occupant for Kirielle to bother.

"So many people," Kiri remarked, watching the throng at the train station through the window. "I didn't know there were so many people going to that school of yours."

Zorian, who was amusing himself by trying to count the number of people on the train station using his mind sense, made an absent-minded sound of agreement. While he was no longer totally oblivious to the world while using his mind sense, it still took most of his attention to get anything useful out of it. After half a minute of trying to separate the tightly-packed mass of people into discrete individuals that could be counted, however, he decided the task was beyond him at his current level and refocused back on Kirielle.

"Why are mages so rare if there are so many people studying to become one?" she asked.

"They aren't terribly rare," Zorian said. "It's just that most mages coming from rural areas don't stay there once they finish their studies. I totally understand them too. I know *I* have no intention of coming back to Cirin when I graduate."

"What!? Why!?" Kirielle protested.

Zorian raised his eyebrow at her. "Do I really have to answer that question?"

Kirielle huffed and crossed her arms over her chest in obvious annoyance. "I guess not. But that means I'll be all alone with Mother and Father then. That sucks."

"Just pester Mother to let you visit me often," Zorian said. "She'll cave in eventually, especially since you'll be the only means through which they can maintain contact with me. Father doesn't care about either of us, so he'll follow Mother's lead on this."

Kirielle gave him a weird look. "I can come and visit you?"

"Any time you want," Zorian confirmed.

"You don't think I'm annoying?" she asked.

"Oh no, you're definitely annoying," Zorian said, smiling at her mutinous expression. "But you're still the only part of our family I actually like. And I bet you find me annoying too."

"Damn right," Kirielle huffed, kicking him in the knee again for good measure.

They watched in silence as people boarded the train and sought out empty compartments for themselves and their groups. But as the empty compartments dwindled in number, the expected additional passengers arrived: Ibery and Byrn. Unexpectedly, two other girls he had never met before also stepped inside. But no matter, maybe it was better this way. The larger the audience he had for this, the better. Now all he needed was an opening.

He didn't have to wait long.

"Well, your brother is far better than mine," one of the new girls said to Kirielle after his sister explained who she was and why she was going to Cyoria. "I'm pretty sure mine would have done just about anything in order to avoid taking his little sister along with him."

"I almost decided not to bring her, what with the whole Cult of the World Dragon incident," Zorian interjected. "But then I figured they're probably just a bunch of crazy idiots anyway. I mean, if it was so easy to summon an army of demons, all of Altazia would have been a burning wreck by now, wouldn't it?"

All conversation stopped as everyone turned to stare at him as though he had grown another head. Zorian feigned confusion and gave them all a blank look.

"What?" he asked finally.

"What... exactly are you talking about?" Byrn asked carefully.

"You didn't hear?" Zorian frowned, shifting uncomfortably in his seat. "The Cult of the World Dragon issued a threat... well, technically a proclamation of intent but whatever. They intend to summon an army of demons on the day of the summer festival. The planar convergence scheduled to occur on that day will be the most powerful one in centuries, so this is apparently a once in a lifetime opportunity for them."

"You're serious," Ibery half asked, half stated.

Zorian shrugged. "It's what they said. And Cyoria has a lot of those crazies running around, so I think I'm justified in being a little concerned."

"Cyoria has a lot of Dragon Cultists?" Byrn asked, obviously more than a little incredulous.

"It's the Hole," Ibery said with a sigh. "It's something of a holy location for them, being a huge gaping hole in the ground of uncertain depth that continually spews mana into the air. They think it's a direct conduit to the Heart of the World."

This unexpected contribution to the conversation had Zorian smiling internally. He hadn't known that about the Hole and Ibery had saved him from having to make things up. It also served as a reminder that he ought to read up on the Cult's actual beliefs one of these days instead of simply thinking of them as a bunch of crazies. Know your enemy and all that.

The conversation didn't linger on the cultists and their goals for long, and his fellow students soon shifted to other topics. Zorian allowed it, not interested in pushing the issue. He had no idea if this exchange was going to have any meaningful effect on the restart, but it cost him nothing to try and start the rumor mill a little early.

The first domino was set.

Much like the last time Zorian had taken Kirielle to Cyoria, Byrn and Kirielle decided to tour the train station for a while before they moved on to the city proper. By that time, of course, it was heavily raining. Unlike last time, Zorian was now in possession of a warding necklace he had made while waiting at the station in Cirin, so keeping the rain barrier up around the group didn't strain his mana reserves in the slightest. Consequently, he decided to be nice and didn't argue at all when Kirielle insisted they accompany Byrn to the academy.

Byrn's appreciation was obvious and the other boy asked to keep in touch when they reached his destination. Zorian gave him directions to Imaya's place and told him to drop by when he had the time. He was pretty sure Imaya wouldn't mind in the slightest and, while Zorian himself didn't care much for the boy, he could see that Kirielle got along pretty well with the first-year.

And speaking of Imaya, their initial meeting went a lot better than it did last time. The fact that they didn't introduce themselves by frantically banging on the door and dripping rain water all over her floors probably helped with first impressions. Hell, she didn't even protest much when Zorian insisted he had something important to take care of and went out into the rain again.

The important thing he had to do was speaking to the aranea, of course, to give them back their memories, but this time he bore additional gifts—five stone discs that acted as telepathic relays, drastically improving the ability of aranea to coordinate their actions across large distances. Naturally, the sixth disc remained in Zorian's possession so he didn't have to descend into the sewers every time he wanted to speak with the matriarch.

Unfortunately, that also meant the matriarch could contact him as often as she pleased, regardless of what she might be interrupting.

[You know, when I told you to contact me as soon as possible, I didn't really mean you should reach out to me in the middle of the freaking night.] Zorian had bolted upright in bed when the matriarch's voice had seeped into his sleeping consciousness a moment before. He poured as much of his annoyance and crankiness into the message as possible, though he still wasn't very good at attaching emotions and images to his communication. He knew she would get the right impression. He took a deep breath to orient himself. [I'm not sure about aranea, but we humans actually have to sleep during the night to function properly.]

[My apologies,] the matriarch sent back. She didn't sound sorry at all. [It's a fascinating device you've gifted me with. Most impressive.]

[Not really. It's pretty shoddy as far as magic items go. I took a lot of shortcuts in order to make so many and it shows. It's a fairly large, heavy disc made out of solid stone, so it's not very inconspicuous or portable, and it has a lifespan of only two and a half months.]

[That's still a month and a half longer than needed,] the matriarch remarked.

[True,] Zorian agreed.

[I assume you can make versions that will last longer?]

[Yes, of course,] Zorian said.

[Could other artificers duplicate your work?] she asked. [Or is this something you came up with yourself?]

Zorian frowned. Why would she need other artificers when she had him? Did she plan to ditch him after they left the time loop or something?

[It's something I came up with,] Zorian said. [Other artificers would have to design a blueprint first. That could take a while.]

True, but misleading. He had designed the relays on his own, basically from scratch, but it honestly hadn't been that difficult. He suspected any good maker of magic items could design one within a month or two… provided they were either psychic themselves or had a psychic on hand for testing purposes. She could figure out that little detail on her own as far as he was concerned.

[I see,] she said. [Well, I guess I shouldn't keep you awake any longer. I just wanted to tell you I've reviewed the memory packet and am convinced it is genuine.]

Zorian rolled his eyes. As if there was any doubt. Apparently having gotten what she contacted him for, the matriarch cut the connection and left him alone in his bed again. Well, alone in his head at least—Kirielle was very much in the room with him, a fact she immediately reminded him of by taking advantage of his momentary distraction to appropriate the last bit of bed covering he had managed to keep away from her thus far. He gave her a nasty look for that, but she just snuggled deeper into her cocoon of stolen blankets, blissfully unaware of his ire in her realm of dreams.

He sighed. There was no way he was going to be able to go back to sleep. He quickly cast a silencing ward on the room and then slowly extricated himself from the bed, taking care not to wake up Kirielle. She was annoying, yes, but it wasn't her fault his sleep was ruined.

But if he couldn't sleep, he could at least start working on an improved design for the relay discs—namely, one that included an off button.

After surprising Imaya by already being awake when she woke up, Zorian went out into the city to hit the stores. The plan he and the matriarch had hashed out involved the creation of a lot of magic items on his part, and that meant buying material components and specialist tools. Not to mention that there were a few things he had to buy if he wanted to seriously start teaching Kirielle how to be a mage.

He really hoped Kirielle would charm Kana in this restart like she had the last time around—while Zorian himself was decently skilled in alchemy and could manage on his own if he had to, Kael's help would be invaluable for some of the projects he had planned.

"Zorian! Over here!"

Zorian snapped out of his thoughts and quickly made his way towards the person calling him. Benisek was exactly the person he was looking for. He quickly sat down next to the chubby boy and exchanged a bunch of pleasantries before getting to the reason he had tracked the boy down.

"Ben, my friend, you won't believe what I found out during our school break," Zorian said. "I still don't understand what they were thinking when they came up with that stuff. It's like something out of a bad adventure novel."

"Do tell," Benisek said, leaning forward.

"Well…," Zorian began, suddenly feigning reluctance, "it's kind of confidential, you know. I'm telling you this in strict confidence because we're friends, so don't go spreading this around, okay?"

Noting that he was about to tell him something confidential and warning him to keep it to himself was crucial—it meant Benisek would spread the story around twice as fast as he normally would.

"Of course," Benisek said pleasantly. "You know me, Zorian. I would never betray your trust like that."

Zorian couldn't help but smile. "Thanks, Ben. I knew I could count on you."

Having told Benisek all about the nasty terrorist plot to bomb Cyoria during the summer festival, Zorian went back to Imaya's place to wait for Taiven and her offer of joining the sewer run. He amused himself by creating one of those practice cards that Xvim had him hone his shaping skills on. He had planned to simply buy a stack of them from one of the stores he had visited that morning, but they were a lot more expensive than he had expected, a fact that increased his respect for Xvim slightly, given how much the man was spending on Zorian's training. Zorian's list of complaints about the man was several pages long, but it seemed that being cheap wasn't among them.

He was still impressing Ilsa into taking him on as her apprentice, of course. Cheap or not cheap, the man was incredibly frustrating and only tolerable in small doses.

He finished painting the glyphs on the corners of the card he was making and started binding the necessary spell combination. Kirielle, who was in the process of drawing a nearby vase of flowers, briefly looked up from her sheet of paper when she noticed him casting spells, but quickly went back to her work when she saw the lack of lightshow or other impressive visual effects.

He hoped that Benisek would keep silent about the source of the 'rumor' Zorian had told him. He probably would—Ben never revealed his sources if he could help it, since he liked to pretend he had some super-secret sources to draw information from rather than just spreading rumors from his fellow students—but Zorian had a contingency plan to follow even if someone with official authority came to confront him about the story. The fact that the aranea were currently also spreading the same story in several different places should help mask where exactly the whole thing had originated in the first place.

He was just putting the finishing touches on the card when Taiven burst into the kitchen and locked onto his position.

"Hey, Roach, nice place you got here," she said, plopping down on a seat next to him and peering closer to look at his work. "Ooh, I know what that is. I've been meaning to get some, one of these days, but I always end up spending my money elsewhere. How many did you buy?"

"None," Zorian said. "They were too expensive for my taste so I decided to make my own. This is the only one I made so far."

Taiven raised her eyebrow at him, looking amused at his claim. Zorian frowned, not liking the expression—she didn't believe he could make a card like this? This was nothing! He thrust the finished card into her face with a scowl.

"Try it out," he told her.

Sighing dramatically, Taiven took a deep breath and… frowned. Zorian felt a mixture of surprise and frustration burst from her and realized she had tried to burn the circle he drew onto the card and failed.

"You couldn't do it, could you?" Zorian grinned.

"You made it wrong!"

"Did not!" Zorian protested. "You just suck!"

"Do not!" she shot back. "Why don't you do it if you're so special, huh?"

"Hmph," Zorian scoffed, snatching the card back. He positioned the card so that she could see the results of what he was about to do, noting that Kirielle was also paying close attention, and then flashed his mana into the card in a practiced manner.

The circle—and *only* the circle—momentarily shone red from the heat before collapsing into ash. Zorian blew a gust of air into the hole to scatter the remains across the table and then smugly handed the spent card to Taiven. He crossed his arms and waited for her reply.

"Ahem," a mature female voice interrupted the scene from behind him. "You will, of course, clean up this mess you've made on my table, won't you, Mister Kazinski? Oh, and I would like to warn you that I will bill you for any property damage you inflict on my material possessions with your… experiments."

Zorian turned and gave Imaya a big, friendly smile. She rolled her eyes at him and gestured towards the ashes on the table. Hanging his head in defeat, Zorian went to get a rag from the bathroom, ignoring Taiven's soft laughter behind him. Just for that he was tempted to blow her off when she asked him to accompany her to the sewers.

Briefly. The fact was, he definitely needed to go with her this time.

"So, what was it that you needed from me anyway?" Zorian asked as he sat down next to Taiven again.

"Ah, well, I was wondering if you'd join me on a little expedition…"

Zorian patiently listened to her explanation before revealing he had contacts with the aranea and requesting that they try talking to them first before barging in, spells blazing. Much like in previous restarts where he had brought the issue up, Taiven accepted him hanging out with giant sewer-dwelling spiders easily enough, but this time she also had an additional request.

"Since you apparently think you're good enough to walk around the Dungeon all by your lonesome, meeting sentient monsters and gods know what else, I would like to test your skills a little," Taiven told him. "Plus, it doesn't hurt to know what your actual combat skills are if you're going to accompany me and my team into a potentially dangerous situation. You do know some combat skills, don't you?"

"Plenty," Zorian assured her.

"Good. Come to my place tomorrow at noon so I can see for myself," Taiven said. "You're sure they're going to hand us the watch if we ask nicely?"

"If they have it," said Zorian. "That guy who gave you the job doesn't sound all that reliable to me. I don't believe for a second that he didn't know what the aranea are, yet he still sent you go get a pocket watch from them. Either he's trying to get you all killed or... hell, I don't know what his game is there."

"If the watch is something very valuable or very illegal he might not want to send someone who could recognize what they are hold-ing," Taiven frowned. "Just how dangerous are these spiders of yours? I mean, even if sentient, they're still bound to be vulnerable to burning and such. Maybe he thought we would just bulldoze through them without talking?"

"Aranea are all mages," Zorian said. It wasn't strictly true, as only a small minority of aranea was armed with a true spellcasting system, but psychic powers were versatile enough to count as a sort of specialized spellcasting system. "They are especially fond of mind magic, illusions, and stealth. And they have a telepathic link to one another so they will know and remember you if you massacre some of their outposts. And then you'd have a bunch of magical spiders with a grudge looking to ambush you or lure you into a trap the next time you descend into the Dungeon."

"Shit," Taiven said. He felt a spike of anger from her before she reined it in and forced herself to calm down. "That asshole better have been ignorant of the danger or I'm reporting him to the nearest police station I find. That's practically a murder attempt!"

"Let's talk to the aranea first and see what they have to say," Zorian quickly said. He didn't want Taiven to confront the man and then cancel the whole thing. "I guarantee they won't attack you so long as you have me with you."

Taiven gave him a long, unreadable look.

"What?" he asked.

"Nothing," Taiven said. "it's just that… I thought I knew you, but now it turns out you have this whole secret life I've never known about until now. It's a bit unreal."

"Yeah!" Kirielle suddenly piped in. She had been silent throughout their discussion, but apparently she had been listening to everything with rapt attention. "How come you never told your own sister any of this!?"

"Oh, that one is easy," Zorian replied smoothly. "I didn't want Mother and Father to find out, so telling you would have been foolish. Do you have any idea how many times you've gotten me in trouble by spilling my secrets in front of our parents?"

"Oh, come on!" Kirielle whined. "I was a little baby! I didn't know anything! You can't possibly still be angry about that?"

"No, of course not," Zorian mumbled uncomfortably. "I did just tell Taiven about the aranea right in front of you, didn't I?"

Taiven shook her head sadly, rising from her seat. "You keep too many secrets, Roach. I feel a little hurt that you felt you couldn't confide in me but I was never one to hold a grudge so I'll let it go. Just don't expect this to be the end of it. I'm going to pester you endlessly until I get the whole story. See you tomorrow."

"Wait," Zorian said. "Actually… yeah, there is something I need to tell you. All of you. Miss Kuroshka, I know you've been eavesdropping on us for a while now so you might as well sit down for this."

Imaya whirled around from where she was fiddling with the cutlery and placed her hands on her hips, giving him an angry look.

"I was not doing any such thing," she told him, "I was simply minding my own business, and in my own kitchen no less. If you didn't want me overhearing your conversation you should have taken it elsewhere."

"My mistake," Zorian agreed easily, seeing no value in pointing out that she had been polishing the same spoon for ages. "Kiri, do you remember how I promised to teach you spellcasting in exchange for a favor back in the train?"

"Yeah?" Kirielle confirmed hesitantly.

"Right, a little background first. I am what is commonly known as an empath—a person who can sense other people's emotions. Unfortunately, up until recently, my powers have been kind of running amok. There was nobody I could turn to for help… at least not on the human side of things."

"The spiders," Imaya surmised.

"Yes," Zorian agreed. "Aranea are all innately empathic. Thanks to them, I now have more or less gained control over my empathic abilities, though it will take years of practice to truly refine them into something reliable. Follow me so far?"

"What am I feeling right now?" Kirielle asked.

"I actually don't know," Zorian admitted. "People's feelings are rarely simple, and unless they are feeling one emotion very strongly,

I'm reduced to educated guesses based on my previous interactions with the person. The more time I spend around someone, the easier I can read them."

"But isn't she your sister?" Imaya asked. "You'd think that if anyone was familiar enough it would be family."

"Our family is…," Zorian hesitated, searching for a proper word, "slightly dysfunctional, I guess. I try to stay away from them most of the time, so I haven't interacted with Kirielle as much as you might think. And I'm not the only one keeping secrets around here—Kirielle is also keeping a lot of things close to her chest. I guess we don't really know each other all that well, sibling bonds notwithstanding."

There was a brief silence as everyone digested that admission, but the awkward atmosphere was quickly broken by Imaya clearing her throat.

"Well," she said, "I guess it's a good thing you're both here now to reconnect."

"Yeah!" Kirielle immediately agreed. "Hey, do you think I could be an empath too?"

"Sorry, Kiri, but I'm pretty sure you aren't," Zorian said. "I would have been able to sense it if you were."

"You can sense other empaths?" Taiven asked.

"I can sense all minds around me, empath or otherwise," Zorian said. "I also get some basic information about each mind—how complex their thoughts are, their species, their gender, stuff like that. Empaths light up like little suns on my mind sense, so… sorry, Kiri."

"It's fine," she said dejectedly.

"You can sense people all around you, regardless of obstacles?" Taiven asked. Zorian nodded. "And the range on that ability is…?"

"If I'm busy with something else and just running my mind sense in the background? About ten meters," said Zorian. "If I'm specifically concentrating on scanning the environment? Easily ten times that.

However, if there are a lot of minds around me, I have trouble processing the information and they all sort of start to blend together in a confusing, headache-inducing mass. I mostly just shut my empathy off when I'm around big crowds."

"Roach, I am so recruiting you for my team," Taiven said. "I've been trying to find a tracker for my team for a while now! Now all we need is to teach you some divination spells and—"

"Already done, thank you," Zorian said. "I am quite proficient in divination."

"Even better!" Taiven said. "You're hired."

"We'll see," Zorian said.

"Fascinating," Imaya said. "I've never heard of that aspect of empathy, though I guess it makes sense that someone who can sense emotions can locate other people through it. But that's not what you wanted to talk about, is it?"

"No, it's not. It's not common knowledge, but empathy is just an initial expression of a much more... dangerous ability. A sufficiently skilled empath can bridge the gap between minds and connect with any person in range in order to talk to them telepathically, read their thoughts, fool their senses, or mess with their memories. And aranea have been teaching me how to do that."

He paused to gauge their reactions. The lack of immediate panic or outrage was encouraging.

"I have no intention of doing that to any of you without permission," Zorian said. "But at the same time, I need someone to practice on. The aranea aren't very suitable for this—their minds are too alien for a beginner like me to understand. I need a human volunteer, and I'm hoping you'll help me out, oh sister of mine."

"You want to read my mind?" Kirielle asked.

"To put it bluntly, yes," Zorian said.

"And if I say no, will you still teach me magic?"

"Absolutely," Zorian said. "It's a request, not blackmail. I'll just have to find someone else to help me if you refuse."

"Well, okay," she said. "I guess I'll help you. But you can't talk to anyone… about the stuff in my head. And you have to tell me all about your secrets in exchange!"

"Sure," Zorian smiled. "Sounds like a fair deal to me."

Revealing his empathy and his need for a human to practice on went off surprisingly well, Zorian reflected. Sure, Imaya had been avoiding him ever since and Kirielle gave him these weird looks, but none of them were terrified of him—just mildly uncomfortable. They were taking the revelation much better than he had predicted they would.

And then there was Taiven, who was apparently not at all bothered by his admission that he was learning how to read people's thoughts. She didn't even mention it when they met up to practice combat magic the next day.

"You ready, Roach?" she asked, twirling her combat staff in her hand.

"I'm ready, yeah," Zorian said, gripping his spell rod tighter.

If he knew anything about how Taiven thought—and he did—she would immediately go on the offensive. Her battle philosophy basically boiled down to 'attack hard and you won't have to defend'… though she could defend too, if pressed. He had no way to win a protracted fight with her, even if he was technically a better mage than she was, so he would have to resort to trickery if he wanted to prevail here.

Eking out a win against her would be immensely satisfying. He couldn't wait to see the look on her face when she lost to little old Roach.

He'd have to work for it.

A single blink after they began and already five magic missiles were homing in on him. He let them crash uselessly against his shield and responded with a somewhat exotic electrical spell. A beam of electricity shot towards Taiven, who erected a basic shield of her own to tank it.

Halfway towards its target, the beam split into three smaller beams—one pivoted to the left of Taiven, the other to the right, and the third one arced straight up into the air. A moment before impact, they all changed their paths again and crashed against her from three different directions, completely bypassing the shield in front of her.

It wasn't enough. Somehow, Taiven had managed to smoothly transition from a single-direction shield to a full aegis before the beams managed to reach her. Zorian threw a couple smoke bombs around the training hall to blind her, relying on his mind sense to tell him where she was, and started casting a complicated spell that wasn't etched into his spell rod the moment his location got obscured by the smoke.

Taiven responded by casting several gusts of wind to disperse the smoke—and blow him off his feet if she happened to catch him in the area of effect. She had just about stripped him of his smokescreen when he finished the spell and felt his mana reserves drain almost completely dry.

A bright beam of concentrated force shot out from his hand and slammed into Taiven's shield. The shield flared at the point of impact, shattering almost instantly, and Taiven was lifted off her feet by the impact and thrown violently across the floor. She didn't get up, rendered unconscious by the impact.

Zorian grimaced, feeling a little guilty. It was clear he had overdone the spell. Without the interference of the training hall's wards, she might have been grievously injured—or worse—by his ray of force.

After casting a few divinations to make sure she was mostly okay and not bleeding internally, Zorian allowed himself to smile. He would have to work on his restraint, but it *was* a victory. And she hadn't been any gentler towards him in their previous fights, so she hardly had any right to complain about excessive force. He couldn't wait to see her face when she woke up.

"Come on, Roach," Taiven growled. "Find those spiders of yours so we can be done with this mission. I'm getting sick of this place already."

Zorian sighed and refocused on scanning his surroundings. It would go much faster if Taiven wasn't snapping at him every other moment. If this was Taiven's reaction to losing, he wasn't sure it would be worth it to repeat his success. Talk about being a sore loser.

"Hey," a male voice whispered into Zorian's ear, breaking him out of his thoughts. "What happened between you and Taiven to get her so bothered, anyway?"

Zorian glanced at Grunt and considered how to answer for a second. He decided to be blunt and truthful.

"I beat her in a spar," he said. "She thinks I cheated."

Grunt gave him a considering look. "You beat Taiven in a spar? Aren't you a third-year?"

"Sure am," Zorian agreed, before he noticed a familiar presence on his mental map. "Oh hey, there they are."

After the initial introductions were completed, Taiven immediately moved onto the reason they were down in the tunnels in the first place, only to get disappointed.

"So you don't have the watch?" Taiven asked.

"Alas, I'm afraid the next group of attackers managed to break into our treasury and escaped with a great many of our artifacts, including the watch we claimed from the thief," the matriarch said, her voice heavy with regret. "I do know where their base is, however."

This was all a bunch of bullshit, Zorian knew. The watch was indeed somewhere else—specifically in one of the forward outposts that the invaders used to launch attacks on the aranea—but it was there because the aranea had put it there. The idea was for Taiven and her group to stumble onto the outpost, realize they'd discovered something big—bigger than they could handle—and then report it to the authorities.

It was Zorian's job to make sure Taiven and her group survived the encounter with the invaders.

"How convenient," Zorian scoffed. "Now if we want to get the watch, we have to take out some of your enemies."

"A happy coincidence," the matriarch said easily. "We both get something out of it, after all—you get the location of the watch for free, and I get to deal with one of my problems without risking my web. Now... do you want the location of the base or not?"

"Just who are these enemies of yours, anyway?" Taiven asked.

"I don't know exactly," the matriarch said. "The attackers consisted of a mage controlling two war trolls, but the base is guaranteed to have more forces than that."

"War trolls!?" Taiven blanched. "Hell, that is way more than we signed up for!"

"The guy is definitely not paying us enough to confront war trolls with mage support," Mumble said quietly.

"Maybe we should check it out anyway?" Zorian tried. "Like, from a distance? I may be able to sense their numbers."

"Yeah," Taiven said after considering things for a few moments. "Yeah, we should check it out at least. No offense to the matriarch here, but a bunch of guys running around the sewers with tamed war trolls sounds a bit... implausible. Maybe she saw something else."

"I suppose it's possible," the matriarch allowed. "I haven't actually seen trolls before and wasn't personally present when the incident occurred, but they sounded very much like the trolls humans speak of."

"Right," Taiven said, nodding. "Where did you say this base was again?"

The base wasn't actually in the city sewers. That part of the Dungeon was somewhat patrolled and monitored, and it would have been impossible to hide a large mass of soldiers there for an appreciable length of time. For that matter, the aranea didn't actually live in the sewers either, although they considered them part of their territory. Instead, both the aranean home base and the various invader outposts were situated in what was known to Cyoria authorities as the 'intermediary layer'.

It was not particularly rare for mages to descend into the intermediary layer, but it was not a common occurrence either. The intermediary layer was too dangerous for a casual stroll by an unarmed civilian but mostly devoid of anything valuable that would attract Dungeon delvers and other adventurers. The city hired mercenaries to sweep through the place every few years and get rid of any obvious threats that had set up residence, and they usually also picked the place clean of anything valuable, leaving something of a barren wasteland behind. For those who wanted to challenge themselves against the denizens of the underworld and search for riches, the Hole and its direct access to deeper levels was the natural place to start. Most visitors from the city consisted of the occasional thrill-seeking student and scattered patrols to keep an eye on things.

The invaders had timed their invasion well. The city was so focused on the summer festival and everything that entailed that attention on the Dungeon had diminished beyond the norm. Given the short span of time the festival required, there would be no expectation that any serious issue could arise while the city's attention was elsewhere— especially with little to no indication that anything untoward was afoot. But now...

"Holy shit," Taiven whispered, peering from behind their cover to look at the camp again. "They've got a freaking army there!"

"Get down, you idiot," Grunt growled at her, pulling her down behind the boulder they were using as cover. "Do you *want* them to see you? If they notice us, we're dead. There must be at least a hundred trolls down there and twenty handlers."

"Sorry," Taiven said. "It's just… so unreal."

Zorian had to agree. He was expecting it and yet was still surprised at the scale of what they were seeing. Then again, this was why the matriarch had chosen this particular base out of the twelve of which she was aware. The others were smaller and much better hidden, but this particular base was situated in a large open cavern and had enough artificial illumination that a human observer could see the whole camp easily from a sufficiently high vantage point… like the one they were using, for example. In fact, their hiding spot was pretty much *perfect* for observing the camp.

Something tickled at the back of Zorian's mind.

He silently ran his fingers against the wall of the tunnel that had led them there. The stone surface was bumpy but smooth. *Far* too smooth to be natural. The rock they were hiding behind was the same.

He smiled a little to himself, admiring the matriarch's preparedness. Unless he was mistaken, they were crouched in a tunnel crafted by an aranean mage—conveniently placed where Zorian and the others would find it with ease. Not only that, but it seemed the mages below were unaware of its existence. Guards were stationed near the other two tunnel entrances he could see, but there was a distinct absence of patrolling near theirs.

Well, whatever. Time to do his part in this charade. He pulled out a mirror from his backpack and silently cast a scrying spell on it. The base had a divination ward, of course, but it was grounded in the notion of stopping people from realizing that the base was there to begin with. Since Zorian knew that the camp existed and where it was, and was in fact right next to it, the entire ward was pretty much useless against him.

After five minutes of watching the camp through the mirror, Taiven decided she had seen enough and motioned for him to cancel the spell.

"Let's go," she said. "I want to get out of here before our luck runs out."

They almost made it out without complications. Almost.

As the four of them approached one of the seals between the sewers and the deeper layers of the Dungeon, they suddenly came face to face with a duo of hooded mages flanked by four trolls. For a moment, both parties halted and tried to make sense of what they were seeing, neither group really expecting to stumble upon each other. Zorian noted with annoyance that their mental presence was somehow muted—no doubt a countermeasure against the aranea—and cursed himself for thinking that his opponents wouldn't have some way of dealing with mind sense.

The impasse was broken when one of the mages ordered the trolls to charge.

To their credit, Taiven and her teammates didn't hesitate when faced with four charging war trolls. They raised their staffs to blast the attackers, but Zorian decided to concentrate on the mages instead and fired a small missile swarm of four piercers, two for each mage.

Several things happened simultaneously. One of the mages dropped whatever spell he was casting and raised a shield to successfully thwart the missiles coming towards him. The other was less skilled and fumbled his shield—both piercers hit him straight in the chest and he went down in a heap, blood streaming from his wounds. Grunt and Mumble used quick flamethrowers to halt the charge of the trolls, but while three of the trolls did flinch away from the flames, the largest, best-armored troll lurched forward, a little dazed but unharmed.

Taiven hit them all with a battering ram of force, intending to knock the whole group down and give them some space, and for the most part succeeded—the three recovering trolls and the surviving mage were hurled deeper into the tunnel and away from them, but that one troll at the front held its ground.

Raising its massive mace overhead to strike, the troll screamed out a challenge, its shout staggering them like a physical blow, not unlike Taiven's battering ram, though far less powerful. For the briefest of moments, Zorian considered the strange implications of a troll demonstrating magic other than the regenerative capabilities that made them infamous, but the moment fled when the troll surged forward.

Frantically, Zorian erected a large shield in front of the group, trying to buy time. This troll, however, proved smarter than those he had faced before, smart enough to recognize the shield for what it was. Halting its charge, the troll smashed its mace into the shield with great force—once, twice, three times. The shield shivered, then broke, and the troll kicked Zorian in the chest, catapulting him backwards where he collided with Grunt and Mumble and interrupted whatever they were about to cast.

Unimpeded by Zorian, Taiven was able to complete her spell and a vortex of fire surged forward. The flames finished off the surviving mage and the more vulnerable three trolls, but left the lead troll merely singed.

And very, very angry.

"Shit," Taiven said quietly, as the troll raised its mace for a killing strike.

Even though he knew her death wouldn't be permanent, even though he had known there was a chance for this to happen when he had agreed to participate in this plan, Zorian found himself completely horrified at the idea of watching Taiven get crushed to death. Killed because of him and his plots and schemes...

He reached out to the troll's mind and noticed it was no longer being muted. While Taiven's spell failed to incinerate the troll, it seemed to have burned out whatever protected it from mind magic. Rather than try any sort of sophisticated attack, Zorian simply flooded it with meaningless drivel, blasting its mind with random telepathy.

The troll flinched in shock and spasmed, halting its attack and dropping the mace it was holding. Zorian immediately threw two explosive cubes at its feet.

"Taiven, get back!"

She didn't have to be told twice, immediately snapping out of her daze and scrambling backwards out of the troll's reach. Zorian activated the bombs as soon as he judged her in the clear, and the troll was enveloped in a deafening explosion.

Somehow, it still survived. Blood coursed from its wounds, and the blast had dropped it to its knees. One leg was bent at a terrible angle. But Zorian could already see its flesh knitting together.

Damn it, what was it with this one troll!? Was it a super-troll or something?

And then two ice blue beams impacted directly into the troll's chest, courtesy of Grunt and Mumble, and the creature immediately froze over and went still.

"Is it finally dead?" Zorian asked in the sudden silence.

"I don't know and don't care," Taiven said. "Let's get lost before we meet another one."

Zorian took a deep, shuddering breath and nodded in assent. A single step sent pain lancing through his leg, but there was no indication the limb couldn't take the weight. He was just in for a painful week.

"This better be worth it, you damn manipulative spider," he mumbled quietly.

[So, it's done?] the matriarch asked.

Zorian gripped the stone disk in his hand tighter. [Yes. I just said so, didn't I? Thankfully, there were no actual casualties, though it was close. In many ways our close brush with death works in favor of your plan, since Taiven is really pissed about these people now and determined to bring them to justice. She is going to report the whole thing tomorrow to the city authorities. I sincerely hope it wasn't you who arranged for us to stumble onto that group, miss Spear of Resolve, or I'll be very angry with you.]

[Don't worry, I had nothing to do with it,] the matriarch assured him.

Zorian sighed. [Right.] Maybe he was being paranoid, but the matriarch's behavior had grown ever more secretive over the past few restarts and he wouldn't put it past her to change her plans without telling him. [How about you? Is your task done?]

[Yes,] the matriarch confirmed. [I have contacted Zach and told him that the aranea are aware of the time loop.]

CHAPTER 025

The Unexpected

Zorian stared at the stone disc in his hand in silent contemplation. It was done. Zach finally knew he wasn't alone in the time loop. True, the other boy didn't know about Zorian being one of the time travelers—the matriarch had presented herself as the time traveler and made no mention of Zorian—but he couldn't help but feel it was only a matter of time. There was no way that Zorian could fool the other boy for more than a couple of restarts now that the idea of there being other time travelers was no longer totally ridiculous in Zach's mind. Assuming he even wanted to. After all, if this plan of theirs worked and the third time traveler was neutralized, there would be no reason not to introduce himself to Zach immediately afterwards.

[So,] Zorian said, [how did Zach react to your... introduction?]

[Confusion, surprise, and outrage,] the matriarch responded. [He had become aware that there was someone else looping with him. It was the only way to explain all the wide-scale changes that began to take place in the last handful of restarts. He was very confused about how they came to be and why they didn't come to talk to him, though, and was considering doing something eye catching to get our attention. The idea that the other time traveler is a giant talking spider caught him off guard but I don't think it will be a problem in the long term. He doesn't appear to be arachnophobic or a human supremacist. But he was angry to learn of the existence of a *third* time traveler who had wiped his mind. He was so irate, I was forced to cut our meeting short.]

[Understandable,] Zorian said. [I know that aranea consider memory editing to be business as usual, but humans tend to flip out over such things. Do you think he bought your story about you being the other time traveler?]

[Actually, I said there are *several* aranea time travelers. That I had a way to bring other people into the time loop. Technically true, and makes us look like a bigger threat.]

[Not sure if that was really necessary,] Zorian mused. [Or even wise. What we have planned already should be sufficient to annoy the third time traveler into confronting you. Making yourself look more dangerous than you already are is just going to make this person more cautious and dangerous.]

[You're overthinking things,] the matriarch said. [We're trying to set a trap, not engage the enemy in battle. Given that our enemy hasn't responded to our provocations so far, I think that getting him to take the bait is a bigger priority than worrying what happens once he does. As you have yourself stated, and as Zach has learned so painfully over the course of this time loop, there is only so much a single mage can tackle on his own. However capable our opponent is, he's not walking off from a well-prepared ambush.]

[Right,] Zorian said, though he remained unconvinced. He was far less certain than she was about that plan, but he didn't have a better idea to offer. And it had occurred to him that if one of the matriarch's plans went disastrously wrong, she might be more forthcoming with information in the next restart. [So do we have Zach's support on this?]

[He will help, yes,] the matriarch confirmed. [I didn't have to offer anything to make him cooperate. He even asked for a list of targets so he can help us soften up the invading forces in advance. Very earnest and straightforward, that boy. Quite unlike you and your rampant paranoia, I might add.]

Zorian narrowed his eyes, gripping the stone disc in his hand a little tighter. Was that it? Was the matriarch trying to replace him with Zach? Someone more trusting and easier to manipulate?

Was Zorian going to be next on the chopping block once the threat of the third time traveler was gone?

That settled it—he would have to reveal himself to Zach sometime soon, regardless of how this ambush turned out. There was an advantage to anonymity, yes, but it was massively outweighed by the danger of allowing the aranean matriarch exclusive access to Zach. That could end up *very* badly for Zorian.

[You've been silent for a while,] the matriarch noted. [You do know I was just teasing you, right?]

[I was just thinking,] Zorian said, glad that the relay disc gave him an opportunity to hide his true thoughts. The disc made it impossible for the matriarch to read his thoughts unless he specifically sent them to her. It wasn't really a safeguard he had consciously installed, more like a consequence of their shoddy construction, but Zorian was pleased with the end result all the same. [What about the money? I'll be running out of savings soon, you know.]

[I'll be able to get you about 20,000 pieces by the end of the week. Will that be enough?]

[For the ingredients? Sure,] confirmed Zorian. [If we have to hire experts, though? I'm not so sure. Good experts are expensive, especially if you're hiring them on a tight schedule or expect them to be discreet. Hopefully Kael will agree to help us, or else I'll probably have to hire an alchemist.]

[I'll leave that to you,] the matriarch said. [You understand the problem far better than I do.]

There was a brief silence as both Zorian and the matriarch considered what to say next, if anything.

[Listen,] the matriarch suddenly said. [Did you know that the aranea sometimes scatter small memory packets into the minds of their males?]

Zorian blinked. What? What did *that* have to do with anything?

[No,] said Zorian hesitantly. [I can't say that I did.]

[Well, we do,] the matriarch said. [It's a useful way to leave secret messages if you know what you're doing. If you break the message into sufficiently small chunks and embed it carefully enough into the targets, it's virtually impossible for anyone without a key to find them, let alone piece them together into a coherent whole.]

[Why are you telling me this?] Zorian asked.

[Just in case,] the matriarch responded. [Aranea males are far smaller than females and very, very cowardly. They're frightened by fire and loud noises just like any other animal, and most divination spells designed to track aranea do not register them as the same type of creature. Most of the time when an aranean settlement is destroyed, a lot of males will survive the destruction. Leaving messages encoded in their minds is a good way to leave messages from beyond the grave.]

Zorian frowned. So the matriarch *did* acknowledge that the ambush could go wrong… but why would she leave a message for him in such a roundabout, complicated way?

[If you have something to say, why not just tell me?] he asked.

[It's probably nothing,] the matriarch said. [And you worry too much as it is. This is really just a precaution in case of the worst outcome. Novelty will give you the key when you see each other next time.]

Before Zorian could continue the discussion, the matriarch cut the connection.

"Very mature," Zorian mumbled, throwing the disc on the bed beside him. Still, as annoying as the matriarch had become, she had been nothing but helpful so far. He would give her the benefit of the doubt. Maybe she really did have good reasons for her secrecy.

Still, it wouldn't hurt, after this restart, to begin fashioning some precautions of his own. Just in case.

At Cyoria's train station, Zorian settled onto a bench to wait. He was early and Kael's train wasn't due for some time, allowing Zorian a moment to amuse himself by messing with the pigeons milling about on the platforms.

Animal minds were paradoxically both harder and easier to affect with psychic powers than human minds. More difficult because simpler minds were harder to sense and pin-point, less so because their thoughts were easier to discern and subvert once a psychic finally achieved a connection.

The pigeons weren't that hard to sense—not if he had a direct line of sight on one and could devote all his attention to the task—so there was little the birds could do to defend themselves against Zorian's experimentation. He simply sat on his bench and systematically targeted pigeon after pigeon, practicing his skills. Sometimes he simply tried to make sense of their rudimentary minds without alerting them to his intrusion, other times he tried to flat out hijack their senses or puppeteer their body. Neither task was going terribly well, but it was something to pass the time with and he did have *some* success. After the fiftieth pigeon or so, he could distinguish a pigeon that was hungry, sick, or in pain from those that weren't. He could make a pigeon stumble or freeze up for a second, or frighten them until they fled as far away from him as possible.

Actually, that last one was extremely easy. Considering the effect was almost identical to the spook animal cantrip he had learned back in his second year, he shouldn't have been surprised. But it did give him an idea… mind spells that affected animals weren't restricted as heavily as spells that targeted humans. Hell, some of them were freely available in the academy library! It might be a good idea to try some in one of the future restarts and compare the results with what he could achieve with his psychic powers.

For now, though, he concentrated on another idea—one that would draw the pigeons to him rather than making them flee. He could choose to produce this result by seizing complete control, but instead he began to attempt to simply dampen a pigeon's fear and influence it into approaching him on its own. This was, he learned, far more difficult than achieving fear. The pigeons were already inclined to bolt at the slightest provocation, so it didn't take much to send them running. Enticing them to approach a strange man with no food that kept staring at them went against their instincts.

It took over twenty tries, but he gradually learned how to steer the pigeons towards him. With one last attempt, he chose a speckled brown bird and was pleased when it didn't immediately startle as he probed its mind. Perhaps more fearless than its comrades, this bird seemed more interested in playing along. It slowly meandered close and then briefly took flight in order to land on the same bench Zorian was occupying.

It cooed and stared at him, and when Zorian stretched out a hand and scooped it up, it did not resist in the slightest.

Success! Zorian reached into his pocket and offered the docile pigeon some bread. It was only proper to reward such a cooperative experiment subject.

And his achievement was just in time too, since Kael's train was arriving at the station. He put the pigeon down on the bench and left to help Kael disembark.

"Kael Tverinov? I'm Zorian Kazinski, one of your classmates. Miss Zileti sent me to help you settle in and show you around the city. Don't worry about your daughter; I know the value of being discreet."

Kael gave him a searching look before nodding. "I appreciate the help, Mister Kazinski. As well as your silence. Lead the way, if you will."

"It's no problem at all," Zorian said, creating a floating disc of force and loading the other boy's luggage on the platform. "We live at the same place, after all."

"We do?" Kael asked curiously.

"Well, yes. Or at least we will if you have rented a room at the place Miss Zileti recommended to you. She recommended the same place to me when I told her I'm bringing my little sister with me this year and sought alternatives to academy housing."

"Your little sister?" asked Kael, shifting Kana in his hands. The little girl studied everything around them with her bright blue eyes but remained resolutely quiet. "Why did you choose to bring her with you, if you don't mind me asking?"

"Our parents went on a trip to Koth and someone has to take care of her. And, well, that someone has always been me in cases like this. I don't mind all that much, really, and the owner of the place seems to be good with kids."

"Well, that's a relief," Kael said. "To be honest I had great reservations about coming here, and I worried Miss Zileti overstated her friend's fondness for children in order to convince me to enroll."

"I don't think you have a lot to worry about. Imaya, the owner of the place, seems honest and friendly enough. And I'm an empath, so I can usually tell."

Kael gave him a sharp, questioning look.

"Too sudden?" Zorian asked. "Sorry, but I wanted to get it out of the way first. I know some people can't stand the idea of someone knowing their private emotions, but I don't think I can keep it a secret from someone that I'm going to share a roof with on a permanent basis."

"If you aren't worried about living with a morlock, I don't think I have the right to complain about you being an empath," Kael said, shaking his head. He gave his daughter a sad look. "Truthfully, I am a little envious. Kana is so quiet most days, I sometimes wish I could peer into her head and see what she's thinking about."

Kana immediately wrapped her little hands around Kael's head and gave him a quick kiss on the cheek. Kael snorted derisively and ruffled her hair, a smile dancing on his lips.

Kana 1, Kael 0. Quiet she might be, but Kana clearly knew how to deal with her father effectively.

Imaya's kitchen was crowded. Crowded and loud. Between Zorian and Kirielle, Kael and his daughter, Ilsa, Taiven, and finally Imaya herself, the room was as full as it could comfortably be and there were constantly at least two simultaneous conversations going on at any particular moment. Strangely enough, Zorian felt comfortable being there. In the past, a gathering such as this would have annoyed him terribly, and he would find some reason to excuse himself as soon as possible. The difference, he realized, was that he was no longer in a gathering of strangers. This was the first time he actually felt he belonged in one of these things, instead of being a barely-tolerated intruder constantly scrutinized for weakness and misbehavior.

He still remained mostly quiet, of course. But it was a comfortable silence.

"…and then Grunt and Mumble hit it with polar beams and froze it solid," spoke Taiven animatedly. "I don't know whether that really killed it, but it put it out of the fight long enough for us to run for it. Most harrowing experience of my life, let me tell you. I'm really glad Zorian was there—if I had chosen any other third-year student as filler, I don't think I'd have survived that encounter."

Zorian fidgeted in his seat, a little uncomfortable at the praise. If it weren't for him, Taiven wouldn't have encountered that troll in the first place, so he didn't feel like he had done her any favors.

"While it's indeed impressive that Zorian can contribute in such a fight, I'm going to have to insist you refrain from bringing him along to your Dungeon delving in the future," Ilsa said with an amused smile. "He's my apprentice now, and it would look absolutely terrible on my record if I let my apprentice be killed by a rampaging troll or some other monsters immediately after signing the contract."

"Err, yeah…," Taiven fumbled. "Well, I have no intention of going down there for a while. I reported the incident to the police, but the cleanup will probably take months, and the place is too dangerous for me and my group at the moment."

"A wise decision," Ilsa nodded. She then shifted her attention to Zorian. "And the same principle holds for you. I don't want you taking such risks in the future. I will ignore the issue this once, since you were helping a friend and the situation escalated beyond anything that could reasonably be expected, but from now on consider all excursions into the Dungeon forbidden until further notice."

"Of course," Zorian immediately agreed, having no intention of actually honoring the restriction.

"And I want you to consult me before doing anything similarly dangerous in the future," Ilsa warned. "Is there anything else I should know about?"

"Not really," Zorian said. Ilsa gave him a hard stare. Hmm, maybe he should throw her a bone to distract her with before she starts actually monitoring him. "Well, I'll be meeting my aranea tutor on a regular basis, but she's totally harmless. Wouldn't hurt a fly, despite being a giant spider."

"Ah yes, the spiders," Ilsa said with obvious distaste. "Don't worry, Imaya has already told me about your… condition. I wanted to speak to you about that, but I'll wait until we can meet in a more private setting."

Zorian nodded, appreciating Ilsa's discretion. Kael still didn't know about the full extent of his mental abilities and Zorian didn't believe this was the time to reveal them. He was a bit disappointed that Imaya had told Ilsa about his 'condition' without asking for his permission. It was by no means unexpected, but still disappointing.

"I'm curious," Kael said. "If your teacher wouldn't hurt a fly, what does she eat? I'm pretty sure all spiders are strict carnivores."

"Mostly rats and stray dogs," Zorian said.

"Rats?" Kirielle asked in disgust.

"I'm told rats can get pretty big in Cyoria," Zorian said.

"Ho boy, can they ever," Taiven confirmed. "I swear I once saw one of them stalking a cat instead of the other way around…"

"She's just telling fisherman's tales," Imaya quickly assured the disturbed-looking Kirielle. "I've lived here my whole life and have never seen anything like that."

"How do you know that stray humans aren't also on their diet?" asked Ilsa.

"According to Novelty, the idea is about as likely as a group of humans hunting an occasional dragon in order to put some meat on the table—that is to say, not very. There is almost always easier prey around," answered Zorian. "Not that aranea are harmless, far from it, but if they kill me it's not going to be because they want to eat me."

"Novelty?" Kael asked.

"That's the name of the aranea tutoring me," Zorian said. "Well, technically her name is Enthusiastic Seeker of Novelty, but that's unwieldy and she doesn't mind if I shorten it."

"That name sounds stupid," Kirielle said.

Zorian opened his mouth to tell her that 'Kirielle' was also a stupid name when he thought better of it. For one thing, it was best to reserve immature bickering for when they were alone. For another, he had just thought up a much more amusing and diabolical idea.

"Want to meet her?" Zorian asked.

"What?" Kirielle asked.

"Novelty. Want to meet her?"

Kirielle stayed silent, mulling it over. "I don't know. I don't like spiders. They're disgusting."

"Well okay," Zorian said, shrugging. "I just figured you'd jump at the chance to meet with a member of a reclusive race of magical creatures that very few humans can boast having spoken to. Once in a lifetime opportunity and all that. But I guess I understand—"

"Umm, well…," Kirielle fumbled. "Actually, I changed my mind. She's not going to try to touch me, is she?"

Of course she was going to try and touch her. Novelty wanted to touch *everything*. By her own admission she once stuck one of her legs into an open flame in order to see what would happen.

"I'm sure she'll keep her distance if you ask politely," Zorian told her.

How he kept a straight face after telling her that, he'd never know. Sometimes he surprised even himself.

The conversation continued for a while after that, but eventually began to peter out. Ilsa and Taiven excused themselves and left, while Kirielle amused herself with trying to teach Kana how to draw. Of course, unlike Kirielle, Kana was a typical child with age-appropriate (that is to say, appalling) drawing aptitude, but neither Kirielle nor Kana seemed discouraged by that. Zorian excused himself and went to his room to see if he could get some work done before Kirielle decided she was bored.

It was not to be, though. Barely a minute after he had sat on his bed, Kael showed up and knocked on the doorframe to get his attention.

"Am I interrupting something?" he asked.

"No, I was just considering what to do with myself. Did you need something?" asked Zorian.

"Sort of," said Kael. "I just came to tell you that you don't have to dance around the issue of your mind magic any more. I already figured out you're not *just* an empath."

"Kirielle told you, didn't she?" Zorian sighed.

"Not so much told me as gave me enough clues to figure it out. She's a chatty kid. But there is no need to be angry at her. It's not like I'm going to turn on you just because you're learning how to read people's thoughts."

"Thanks," Zorian said. "Although quite frankly, it would be kind of hypocritical of you to shun me for dabbling in forbidden magics, mister junior necromancer."

Kael immediately flinched back in shock and gave him a wide-eyed look. "W-What!? There is no way..."

Zorian gestured for him to quiet down and Kael immediately shut up and peered down the corridor to make sure no one had been listening. Zorian knew they hadn't been—he could feel that all of the other residents were still back in the kitchen. His scrutiny done, Kael quickly stepped into the room and closed the door, then leaned heavily against it.

"How?" he asked. He sounded more panicked than menacing at the moment, but Zorian knew that could change at any moment if he didn't get a satisfactory answer.

"Do you know the arcane lock spell?" Zorian asked.

"I... yes," Kael said, still sounding rather dazed.

"Lock the door, then, and I'll make sure we're safe from any stray divinations," Zorian said, and immediately started casting a temporary divination ward on the room. It wasn't anything fancy, but it would ward off simple scrying attempts and hopefully notify him if anything more complex targeted them. Not that he really thought they would need it, but it was good practice and you could never be careful enough.

Five minutes later, the room was as secure as Zorian could make it on such short notice and Kael looked increasingly impatient. Zorian decided to get on with it. He opened his mouth and began to speak.

"Let me tell you a story of lost time and a month that refuses to end..."

Unpaid teenage labor was an age-old tradition among mages. While the ancient apprentice system had largely been replaced with specialized magical academies, and the quality of young mages had improved drastically as a consequence, there were some things that simply couldn't be learned in the classroom. In those cases, a mage needed a mentor—someone to show them the tricks of the trade, teach them unique skills and spells they had developed and did not share lightly with others, or just plain connect them with the right people. Said mentors usually had plenty of work they considered beneath them, ideally of a sort that took advantage of their student's magical ability and prepared them for their future vocation.

Ideally.

As Zorian trudged towards his classroom, half an hour before any of his fellow classmates, he reflected on the fact that life was rarely ideal. In practice, a lot of work given to apprentices consisted of tedious, dull, repetitious chores to which the mentor would never stoop. The duties of the class representative, for instance, were largely one giant waste of time. In the previous restarts, this fact hadn't bothered him all that much—the job was fairly easy, so long as you didn't take it as seriously as Akoja did—but this time he had so many things vying for his attention that he resented this additional duty being piled up on top of it all. Maybe he shouldn't have talked Ilsa into taking him as her apprentice this restart but, well, what's done is done.

He yawned. He supposed he was just cranky today since he had gotten very little sleep last night. His conversation with Kael had gone on for hours as the other pressed him for details and answers to a host of questions. While Zorian didn't begrudge the other boy for wanting answers and considered the time well spent, he kind of planned to use that time to read through the research assignments he had collected from his classmates on Ilsa's behalf—assignments he had to give back to Ilsa today, complete with corrections and grade recommendations. He had thought his knowledge from previous restarts would make the task a child's game, but apparently something about their massive changes to this restart caused Ilsa to give out completely different topics for research and he had to actually read everything from scratch. He ended up spending most of the night dealing with those stupid things and then had to get up half an hour earlier in order to be at his post at the required time.

Peering into the classroom, he saw that Akoja was already inside. He rolled his eyes at her excessive punctuality and marked her down as present on his little attendance sheet. The blackboard was full of horrible drawings, love confessions, and other garbage, but he knew better than to wipe it clean right now—a clean blackboard was utterly irresistible to some of the idiots in his class, and they would no doubt make a mess again by the time the teacher finally showed up. Who knew, maybe if he left it alone long enough, Akoja would take care of it on her own initiative, as she was sometimes wont to do.

The next to arrive were—surprisingly, since they weren't normally early birds—Aneka and Armie, the (in)famous Ashirai twins. The Ashirai family consistently produced soul-bonded twins, and the two sisters he shared his class with were no exception. Zorian had considered asking them for help back when he thought he was soul-bonded to Zach, or at least questioning them about the mechanics of soul bonds, but eventually decided it would be a bad idea. For one thing, mage families tended to jealously guard their family magics, and it was obvious that the Ashirai family was trying to become an official House with their own magical specialty centered around their soul bonds. Asking too closely about their family trait could have ended up blowing up in his face spectacularly, and Zorian hadn't been willing to risk it, time loop or not. A second concern was that the twins were unreliable. Benisek-level unreliable. They were giggly little twits who took nothing seriously and wouldn't keep quiet even if he paid them.

No, it had definitely been smart to stay away from them.

Next to arrive was Kael, who looked as though he also hadn't slept much. They exchanged only a few words before the morlock boy decided to retire to his seat, but Zorian could already see there would be more questions in the near future. Lovely. He had forgotten how inquisitive and interested in the time loop Kael had been the last time he had been aware of it.

Briam, Naim, and Edwin were marked down as present next. Briam gave him a wave as he passed, his other hand holding his fire drake familiar, while Naim and Edwin were too absorbed in their conversation to take notice of Zorian. Zorian didn't really mind. It wasn't like he knew either of them all that well. Naim was a first-generation mage, much like Zorian and Akoja—a child of a soldier who rose to the rank of general in the wake of the disruptions caused by the Splinter Wars. Edwin's parents were golem makers, and they had clearly passed on their enthusiasm for the craft to Edwin. He was always tinkering with various mechanisms and making blueprints, even during lectures or other times he should have been concentrating on something else.

The next to come was Raynie, the red-headed mystery that transferred into their class in the previous year. She was reserved, polite, extremely attractive, a good student and absolutely refused to tell anyone about her family or origins. The only one who knew anything concrete about Raynie was Kiana, another of his female classmates, and she was resolute in her silence.

And so it went, student after student, until the list was complete and he could finally slip inside and try to rest for a bit before class started. He absent-mindedly erased the blackboard with a single alteration spell, causing the chalk to simply peel off the surface and fall to the floor, and sat down to wait.

"No, Ben, you cannot turn in your assignment a week from now," Zorian growled. "The deadline was yesterday. I have to hand them over to Ilsa today. Don't you see the problem here?"

"Come on, Zorian, this is what friends are for," Benisek complained. "What good is having your best bud as the class rep if you can't ask him to cut you some slack?"

"You're not asking for a favor, you're asking for the moon," Zorian told him, giving him a flat stare. "I *cannot* help you in this regard."

"But I really, *really* can't get another demerit." Benisek gave him a hopeful smile.

"Tough," Zorian said. "I guess you should have thought about that before you decided to completely blow off another assignment from Ilsa. You already know she can't stand students boycotting her homework."

"She's completely ridiculous!" Benisek said. "What kind of teacher gives out three assignments during the first week of the year?"

"Umm," a new voice cut in. Zorian silently offered a prayer to whosoever was still listening on the spirit planes for the interruption. He had been contemplating how thoroughly he'd have to strangle Benisek to get him to shut up. This wasn't the first time he was suffering through this conversation, but he usually wasn't so tired when dealing with his… sort-of friend. He was honestly rethinking his connection with the boy at this point.

As it turned out, the interruption was by Neolu, though Kiana and Jade were hovering close behind her. All three were holding a sheet of paper.

"I know the deadline for the assignment was yesterday, but I was sort of wondering—"

"If you could turn it in now?" Zorian finished.

She nodded furiously and extended the paper towards him.

"No," Zorian deadpanned.

"Seriously?" Jade piped in. "You're going to make a big deal out of this?"

"Yes?" Zorian asked rhetorically.

"Why don't we just leave this here," Kiana said, placing her assignment on his desk, "and you can decide whether you want to bother with them when Benisek is done annoying you and you cool down a little."

"Hey!" Benisek protested.

"Sure," Zorian said. "You do that."

Zorian patiently watched as the three of them left their assignments on his table and filed out of the classroom, waited until Benisek finally gave up on convincing him to… write Benisek's assignment for him, he supposed? And then he calmly fished out a pen from his backpack and wrote 'LATE' at the top of each sheet of paper before unceremoniously shoving them into his backpack along with the other assignments. There, let Ilsa decide what to do with them.

"Why are you still here, Ako?" Zorian sighed, turning to the last person remaining in the room. "Your assignment was flawless, if that's what's worrying you."

"I'm glad you decided to take the position from me," she said. "I don't think I could have gone through another year of it. When I accepted the position back in our first year, the teachers said it was a privilege. That there were benefits for the class representative. That it commands respect. But it was all a sham and by the time I realized that nobody was stupid enough to take the position from me."

"Hey…," protested Zorian lightly.

"I'm not saying you're stupid for taking it," she immediately clarified. "You accepted it because it was bundled into your apprenticeship. You were far smarter about this than I had been."

"More like less naïve," Zorian said. She flinched at his remark; apparently he hit too close for comfort. "Why did you sink so much effort into it if you hated it? Why not just boycott the whole thing?"

"Because it would be wrong," she said vehemently. "You shouldn't shirk your responsibilities. And I had accepted the class representative duties as my responsibility."

Zorian gave her an incredulous look.

"What?" she challenged. Defiant. Daring him to tell her she was wrong.

"Nothing," Zorian said. He didn't want to argue with her. Ever since he had started to develop his empathy, he had become increasingly certain she had a crush on him. A small one, but it was there. And while he didn't return her feelings at all, he also didn't want to hurt her. And he would have hurt her if he started talking to her honestly—they were two very different people with different worldviews and ideals, for all that Akoja seemed to think they were alike.

"Listen, Ako," he said, rising from his seat. "I spent most of last night reading through the assignments and I'm not the best person to hold a philosophical discussion with right now. Can we table this for another day?"

"You shouldn't have procrastinated until the very last day," Akoja said. "That's almost as bad as what those three did."

"No, it isn't." He hefted his backpack in one arm and rose from his seat. "And it's impolite to preach like that. See you around, Ako."

"Wait!" she said. Zorian could suddenly feel a wave of nervousness emanating from her, and the fact she was wringing her hands under her desk and looking anywhere but in his direction completed the impression. "I… can we talk? Not now, but… I'd like your opinion on something."

Crap. This had never happened before in any of the restarts. What set her off? He really hoped this wasn't a love confession; he couldn't afford that kind of drama right now.

"Can it wait until next week?" he asked. "I will be really busy the next few days."

"Yes," she immediately agreed. "That's perfect. I need to gather my thoughts on the subject anyway. I'll… I'll tell you when I'm ready."

"You wanted to see me?" Zorian asked as he peered into Ilsa's office.

Ilsa gestured him to come inside, too busy sipping on her tea to give a verbal response. Zorian sank into the visitor's chair and promptly handed her all of the assignments he had collected from the students. She glanced at them before setting them aside and taking another sip from her cup.

For a minute or so, she just kept silently scrutinizing him. Finally, she put down her cup and sighed.

"I wanted to talk to you about your experimentation with mind magic," she said, drumming her fingers on the table. "I'm sure you're aware of the rather illegal nature of most mind-affecting magic, but since it's the product of an inborn ability rather than access to restricted spells and literature, some allowances can be made. The Empath Association goes to great pains to make a distinction between empathy and mind reading, and to claim one is just a logical extension of the other is… novel. And more than a little controversial. Nonetheless, my discreet inquiries into the subject have discovered there is indeed a known link between the two abilities, so your story holds water."

"Technically, empathy and mind reading are indeed different. Empathy is a passive skill with no mental intrusion involved, while mind reading requires one to actively invade the mind of another," explained Zorian. "It's just that every empath is capable of mind reading with the right training."

"Oh? Interesting," said Ilsa. "I'm surprised more mages haven't stumbled upon that fact, then."

"I thought about that, actually," Zorian said. "The aranea are born with the ability. They speak to each other telepathically as their normal mode of communication, they have telepathic scuffles as kids, they use it to hunt their prey, for just about anything. It's natural that they would refine and build upon the ability, exploiting it to its logical extreme. Human empaths, on the other hand, are rare and isolated, so most of them have to rediscover the wheel alone, so to speak. It doesn't help that few people are willing to let someone read their mind, so any 'training' is almost certainly illegal, or at least highly disreputable. So most people who discover their latent telepathic abilities are either going to keep mum about it or become outright criminals. There probably are a fair number of empaths who have discovered they can delve into mind reading, but they certainly aren't going to admit it to anyone."

"Excellent reasoning," Ilsa praised. "And actually, it is the issue of training partners in particular that I wanted to talk to you about. I understand your sister has already agreed to help you with your training, but I am given to understand that having a wide variety of targets to practice on would be preferable, yes?"

"Yes."

"Believe it or not, one of the students has issued a request for someone to help them train their mind magic. Understandably, none of the teachers are eager to have a student mess around with their heads. But simply refusing it is… politically unfeasible."

"You want me to step in and take a teacher's place," Zorian surmised.

"It would benefit both of you," Ilsa said. "You both want a target to practice on, and you're both more qualified to help one another when it comes to mind magic than any of the teachers the academy has at its disposal."

"And if the other student protests this?" asked Zorian. "I mean, they may have wanted someone to practice on, but that doesn't mean they're willing to let someone else practice on them in turn."

"Then it wasn't a simple case of the academy refusing a request out of hand, now was it?" Ilsa said, giving him a conspiratorial grin. "But I very much doubt the student in question would make a fuss about that. What do you say?"

Zorian hummed thoughtfully. While there was a risk that the other side might find out about the time loop from his thoughts, he did possess some rudimentary mental defenses and was familiar with the limitations of mind reading. So long as he didn't let the other student trawl through his long-term memories, he should be fine. And he had to admit he was curious about this other student dabbling in mind magic.

"All right, I'll give it a try. Who am I going to be working with?"

"One of your classmates. Tinami Aope," Ilsa said.

Zorian blinked. Tinami was… wait, of course it would be her. Aopes were rumored to dabble in mind magic, among other things.

Not all rumors were malicious nonsense. And it would explain why Ilsa knew about the request in the first place, come to think of it.

Besides, hadn't he promised to himself to introduce her to the aranea at some point to see what would happen? Yeah, he was totally fine with this.

"Hello, Tinami," Zorian said, walking into the empty classroom Ilsa had reserved for their lessons. "Am I interrupting anything?"

"Umm," she fidgeted. "I'm actually waiting to meet someone…"

"For mind magic practice, right?" he asked. Her eyes widened in response. "That would be me. I will be your partner today, if you will have me."

"Umm, ah, I was… I don't want to be rude, but I was kind of hoping for an expert…"

Huh, so Ilsa hadn't told her who was going to teach her? Strange.

"I'm a natural mind mage," Zorian said. "I'm the closest thing the academy has to an expert on the topic. Why don't we try this and you can leave in a huff if I can't satisfy you, okay?"

She immediately flushed scarlet and looked away, her feelings cycling between embarrassment and outrage. Uh, maybe he should have worded that better…

"Bad choice of words, let's pretend I said something else," Zorian said quickly. "Anyway, I'm surprised you didn't know who would be teaching you. How much did Ilsa tell you about me?"

"Just that you need someone to practice on, too," Tinami said quietly. "I don't really mind. I have enough mental discipline to keep sensitive things from my surface thoughts most of the time."

"Likewise," Zorian said. "And I won't allow you to look into my memories."

"R-Right," she agreed. "I mostly just wanted to practice telepathy and mind reading. The spells are not hard to cast, but actually using them takes a lot of practice."

"Well, feel free to go first," offered Zorian.

Just for the occasion, Zorian had memorized portions of a biology book describing various forms of wild plants native to Cyoria and the surrounding region, and simply recited them in his head while Tinami tried to read his thoughts. Not only did this ensure he wouldn't reveal any sensitive details, it actually made her job easier. It was a lot simpler to read someone's thoughts when they thought in concrete words and sentences, as opposed to a confusing stream of consciousness that composed the vast majority of people's thoughts. In fact, the matriarch had explained to Zorian that it was simply not possible to read people like a book—unless they were literally reciting text in their heads like he was doing at the moment. Otherwise, a large amount of guessing and extrapolation were involved, and no mind reader could completely understand another sentient being.

But they could get pretty damn close.

"Why are your thoughts full of information on plants?" Tinami asked with a frown.

Apparently, Tinami didn't know that. The Aope style of mind magic training was very crude, and boiled down to throwing a kid into the swimming pool and hoping they didn't drown. A bit disappointing, really. He eventually shifted to reciting sequences of numbers and imagining simple geometric shapes.

"I guess I owe you an apology for doubting you," Tinami said. "You really do know your stuff. Do you want to try now?"

Zorian nodded and then focused on her, homing in on the glittering star he saw in front of him through his mind sense and connecting with her mind.

[Are you sure you're ready?]

She yelped and jumped in her seat. "W-What?"

563

[Telepathic communication,] he explained.

"But… you didn't cast a spell," she frowned.

[I don't have to. As I said, I'm a natural mind mage. I can sense all minds in my vicinity and I can connect to them if I want to. Right now I am talking to you telepathically, but if you're ready I will expand my awareness to your surface thoughts.]

She closed her eyes for a second but then frowned and opened them again.

"Wait," she said. "I don't understand. If you made a telepathic link between us, why can't I use it to talk to you telepathically?"

[I suppose that's how it works if you use a structured spell for it?]

"Well, yes. I mean, there are various sending spells that simply send a mental message to someone, but you need to cast them again and again every time you want to send something to the target. If you want a proper mental conversation with someone, you create a telepathic link between them and yourself. The main issue being that people often don't know how to filter their thoughts well and end up sending inappropriate things over the link."

[Hmm, I guess you could say I continually 'send' messages over the link I established between us. I don't know how to establish a two-way link yet, I'm afraid,] Zorian said contemplatively. The aranea had never mentioned anything about two-way telepathic links, and in retrospect it was obvious why—a psychic could use an established link to reply telepathically regardless of who the maker of the link was. Every aranea was psychic, so why would they bother with two-way links? It was something he would have to figure out on his own, probably. [Anyway. Are you ready?]

"Yes," she said, nodding. "Feel free to start."

Unlike him, Tinami didn't resort to text or numbers, and instead did her best to imagine a random scene out of her life in as much detail as she could render. The scenes were wholly unexceptional—

one of Ilsa's lectures, an inconsequential conversation between Jade and Neolu as they talked next to Tinami, a walk down the street... It was all very visual, but still very challenging. His little sister was still much harder to read, ironically because she wasn't trying to hide anything from him. Her disjointed, stream-of-consciousness succession of thoughts was next to impossible to figure out unless he engaged her in conversation and made her focus on one particular issue. But Tinami was smoother and less random.

"Okay, I'm officially jealous," Tinami said. "I've been practicing this for three years with my mother and her friends, and I'm nowhere near this good."

"Don't feel too bad," Zorian said. "I have... an unfair advantage."

"So do I," Tinami said. "My family has been dabbling in mind magic for generations, and I have their advice to guide me. It's frustrating to realize just how much raw talent can mean in a field like this."

"Ah, it's not just raw talent," Zorian said. "I, too, have a teacher with generations of mind magic practice."

She raised her eyebrows at him. "There aren't very many of those," she remarked. "I'm pretty sure my mother would know if any of our rivals had adopted a new student."

"Not many human ones you mean," Zorian said, smiling. "Your mother definitely wouldn't know, not unless she keeps tabs on the many colonies of telepathic spiders scattered throughout Altazia."

Tinami stared at him in silence for a moment before leaning towards him, her eyes bright with excitement.

"Telepathic spiders? You mean... you have actually met one of the legendary aranea?"

Legendary? Zorian almost scoffed, but he supposed that the spiders were very good at hiding themselves. While there were humans who knew about them, very few seemed to be willing to advertise their connections to the aranea colonies. Zorian didn't think it was because of intimidation from the aranea—or at least not *just* because of that. In all likelihood the mages that were 'in the know' simply wanted to preserve their monopoly on the business with the aranea and didn't want rival mages butting in and demanding their piece of the pie.

"Her name is Enthusiastic Seeker of Novelty," Zorian said. "Would you like to meet her?"

CHAPTER 026

Soulkill

The temple was just as imposing as it had been the last time Zorian had visited it— the same guardian angels glaring down at him, the same deserted feel to the building, and the same creation story carved into the heavy wooden doors. This time he studied the carvings on the door more closely than he had the last time, since some of the images were rather interesting in light of things he had discovered after his first visit. Specifically those carvings depicting monsters that had sprung up from the World Dragon's flaking heart. These were clearly primordials. They had the whole 'impossible patchwork creature' look that seemed to be a primordial's one defining characteristic, and they matched the descriptions of well-known primordials he had read about.

The unholy cross between scorpion, dragonfly, and a centipede was clearly Hynth, the Locust Lord, whose bronze carapace was impervious to just about everything but divinely-forged weaponry and whose four pincers could tear steel like paper. The ability to release clouds of biting, devouring insects from pores on his body completed the image of a living natural disaster. The cluster of wings hanging above Hynth was probably Ghatess, who was allegedly a ball made out of multicolored bird wings—and *only* bird wings—and created storms and tornadoes wherever it went, funneling matter into the center of its sphere where it seemed to just disappear without a trace. The boar-crocodile-porcupine thing was Ushkechko, a beast made out of indestructible black glass that poisoned anyone who so much as scratched themselves on one of its numerous bladed protrusions and could fire said protrusions like arrows at opponents. The slug-like entity covered in eyes and mouths was—

"Can I help you with something, young man?"

Zorian wrenched himself from his scrutiny of the door to look at Batak. The last time he had been here he had asked to speak with Kylae, but this time the man in front of him would suffice. He might even be preferable, considering Kylae was supposed to be a master diviner. He gave the man a nervous smile and spoke.

"I... wanted to have a talk with you, if it's not too much of a problem."

"Of course!" the man said happily, quickly ushering Zorian inside. Zorian recalled from last time that the temple didn't receive many visitors. It must be a pretty lonely existence to serve as custodian of this place. Before long they were both seated at a small table in the kitchen-like room that Batak used to receive visitors, a pot of tea steaming in between them.

"Please, tell me, what did you want to discuss?" Batak said after some small talk, raising his cup to his mouth and taking a long sip.

"I wanted to ask about primordials," Zorian said.

Batak promptly choked on his tea and spent the next few seconds coughing.

"Why *cough* would you want to know about *them*?" the priest asked incredulously.

"I'm… not sure I should tell you. I don't want any trouble."

Batak gave him a curious look, but Zorian sensed a note of worry in his mind.

"Well, I'm not sure whether you know or not, but there is a rumor spreading around that some people are going to try to disrupt the summer festival," Zorian began.

"I've heard about that, yes," Batak sighed.

"Well, a few days ago I went with some friends into the upper levels of the Dungeon to do a job for a client. A simple find and retrieve job, but we ended up running into an underground base full of war trolls and nearly died in the process. The police are keeping it very hush at the moment, but I understand their investigation revealed it wasn't the only base down there. Somebody has spent months preparing a beachhead for this attack and they have a lot of assets to burn…"

After more than an hour of explanations and clarifications, Batak seemed to accept that the attack was something a lot more serious than he had thought and, more importantly, that it was just a distraction for an attempt at primordial summoning. Thankfully, everything Zorian was telling him was true, so whatever method of truth detection the man was using had no reason to flag Zorian as anything other than genuine. The fact that Kylae had experienced a prediction blackout probably did a lot to legitimize his claim in the priest's eyes, since the successful summoning of a primordial could explain the failure of her divinations. Which was exactly why Zorian had come to this temple in particular, rather than, say, the main temple in the city.

"I'll notify the church hierarchy. They should be able to spare a squad or two of investigators to check it out," Batak said. "Especially if they have solid proof rather than just an anonymous tip. Do you have anything in writing, perhaps?"

"Here," Zorian said, retrieving a stack of documents and notebooks from his bag and handing them over to Batak. "This is everything I have about the invasion. I tried to be as thorough and methodical as possible. I'd really prefer if my name was not mentioned anywhere, though."

Batak eyed the stack speculatively. "I cannot guarantee that. If your name comes up during the investigation—"

"It won't," Zorian interrupted.

"Well, then I don't foresee any problems," Batak shrugged. "A bit odd of you to have so much information on this group if you're not a defector from their ranks."

Zorian said nothing.

"All right," Batak said, perking up and shaking his head slightly as if to clear it. "Are you still interested in hearing about the primordials or was that just a ploy to get my attention?"

"I'm still interested, yeah," Zorian said. "I'm really curious why they felt the need to organize all this just to summon one."

"To be fair, I don't think knowing more about the primordials will satiate your curiosity in that regard," Batak said. "Anyone who wants to summon one of these things is clearly insane. But no matter—tell me, what do you know about the primordials in the first place?"

"They're some kind of powerful spirit hailing from ancient times," Zorian tried. "Like fey or elementals, only older, weirder, and far more dangerous."

Batak sighed. "I knew you were going to say that. In the future, when you're interested in some aspect of the spiritual world, please consult religious texts first before delving into mage-written works. I know the church can be a little biased about a lot of things, but we really do know our stuff when it comes to the spirits and everything related to them. Ever since the gods fell silent, spirits are the only thing we have left, so we have done some extensive work on them. And we don't hide what we know."

Zorian nodded sheepishly. It had never even occurred to him to look at religious texts on the topic. He blamed his town priest back in Cirin, a bigoted old hypocrite who kept making problems for Zorian whenever they crossed paths and consequently had soured the church as a whole for him.

Batak drummed his fingers on the table for a few seconds, gathering his thoughts.

"All right. First, let me tell you something about actual spirits. I'm sorry if this is already familiar to you, but it's important to understand spirits before you can understand why a primordial absolutely cannot be one."

Zorian motioned for him to continue.

"Spirits are, from a practical standpoint, divided into two main groups: outsider spirits and native ones. Outsiders spend most of their time in their own spiritual worlds and can only ever enter ours if summoned by someone from this side. Demons and angels are the most famous of outsider spirits, though lumping all demons into a single group is mostly done for human convenience—there is no demonic equivalent to the angelic hierarchy and two demons are as likely to fight each other as they are to cooperate on a common goal. Native spirits exist on the material plane by default. You already mentioned elementals and fey, which are the two most common types of native spirits. It is likely that native spirits were once outsider spirits that gradually adapted to life in the material world, as they share the key feature that all spirits have. Namely, that they don't really have bodies in the way humans and animals do. They are disembodied souls that need a vessel in order to interact with the world around them."

"So, spirits are soul entities," Zorian mused. "Like liches or body snatchers."

"Yes, very much like that," Batak agreed. "In fact, some spirits are very much body snatchers and prefer inhabiting bodies of humans and animals. And it's likely that the process of transformation into a lich has been developed by studying spirits and the way they interact with their vessels. Anyway, on to primordials. Primordials have bodies. Actual flesh and blood bodies. Most people, even mages, assume they're spirits because of their strange forms and remarkable resistance to damage, but they really have more in common with dragons and other magical creatures than with spiritual entities. Spirits tend to be weird because their bodies are usually just ectoplasmic shells, which they can twist into whatever unnatural form they feel like taking. Primordials are creatures of the material world, just like you and me."

"But wait," Zorian said. "If primordials are not spirits, but more akin to a magical creature, how are the attackers planning to summon one?" asked Zorian.

"They aren't," Batak said. "I didn't want to interrupt you while you were talking, but you almost certainly misunderstood something there. Primordials can't be summoned since they're down here with us already. Bound, forced into sleep, and locked away, but still with us. What they can be is *set loose*."

Zorian felt a shiver run down his spine. The primordial wouldn't disappear, he realized. The Ibasan invaders thought they were summoning a fancy demon to go romp over their enemies, but that thing was never going back to its home plane on its own. It didn't have one.

"Why were they sealed away?" Zorian asked. "Why not just kill them?"

"Primordials don't die the way most things do," Batak said. "They are a remnant, a relic of the age when the world was still fresh and the World Dragon had only just been bound at the center of our world. They are her original children, the purest expression of her rage and hate, and they have found ways to strike out at humanity and the gods even in their death. They spawn smaller, weaker primordials in their death throes, and often inflict corrupting effects on the area in which they died. Even the gods found the aftermath of one of them dying to be difficult to deal with, so they eventually just contained the lot of them and trapped them in remote corners of the earth."

"And the attackers believe one of them is in Cyoria."

"Apparently," Batak said. "I wouldn't know personally—no one has ever seen one of these prisons within living memory and written records are deliberately vague about their locations. Still, historically speaking, Cyoria had effectively *been* a remote corner of the world up until relatively recently. So I suppose it's possible. Strange that no one has ever found any indication of it in all this time, especially considering how many mages delve into the depths of the Hole on a regular basis…"

"I see," Zorian said. He excused himself soon afterwards. While interesting, this truthfully didn't change much and his task had already been done.

Zorian was feeling pretty pleased with himself for organizing this little event. While setting up Kirielle for a meeting with Novelty was done purely for amusement and sheer curiosity at how Kirielle would react to Novelty's antics, introducing Tinami to Novelty was… well okay, it was also mostly done for the sake of his curiosity and amusement. But that didn't mean he wouldn't take advantage of it to gain something from little miss 'forbidden magics' Aope. Like, say, getting her to teach him the invisibility spell. He knew, just *knew* that Tinami had been taught that spell, restricted magic or not, and he was totally right! So now he had finally completed his 'list of spells every proper mage should be able to cast', and all it took was promising to do something he had intended to do for free, anyway

And the cherry on top? Novelty loved him for promising to bring her two new humans to meet. He hadn't needed to persuade her because she thought he was doing her a favor!

Yes, Zorian was feeling very pleased with himself. Now all he had to do was wait with Kirielle until their two guests showed up and then stand back and watch the fireworks. Novelty would come first and meet with Kirielle to start with, since that meeting was bound to be shorter and more casual, and would then remain to greet Tinami when his classmate eventually showed up at Imaya's place. He wasn't expecting any problems, but just in case something happened beyond his ability to handle, Zorian had arranged for a bit of insurance…

"So aranea are about the size of a dog?" Kirielle asked.

"A big dog," Zorian said. "But Novelty's not scary at all, and I'm sure you'll get along splendidly. She reminds me of you, actually."

"A giant spider reminds you of me?" Kirielle asked him, sounding surprisingly threatening for a nine-year-old.

"You'll find out why soon enough," Zorian said, more amused than anything. "She's coming over as we speak."

He had been devoting only half of his attention to his conversation with Kirielle, trying to train himself to pay attention to his mind sense and talk at the same time, and had thus immediately noticed Novelty when she came in range, despite the fact that she had tried to dim her mental presence to surprise him. He immediately launched a telepathic attack on her and she promptly dropped her attempt at stealth in favor of a short mental wrangle that resulted in Zorian being quickly booted out of her mind. Despite his poor showing, Zorian was pleased. He had been doing such 'greetings' for a few days, ever since he realized that Novelty didn't consider such telepathic 'play-fights' hostile. Compared to his initial results, this was absolutely amazing.

It was kind of amusing that Novelty refused to teach him actual telepathic combat due to the matriarch's orders but had no qualms helping him practice in such a fashion. In fact, after his first few attempts, she began to initiate the mental tussles herself, or tried to stalk and surprise him like she did today. He supposed she didn't think of it as teaching—it was just a game as far as she was concerned. She would be rather cross with him if she ever caught him thinking it, but she really was still a child in many respects.

[That was barely any better than yesterday,] Novelty complained, apparently not sharing his optimistic self-assessment. [This is why I think we should have gone with my idea for teaching you. It would have been a million times faster than our lessons so far.]

[You are not locking me in one of your hatcheries,] Zorian told her.

[But you'd have left a master of telepathic combat within a week!] Novelty protested. [Well, master by human standards, anyway.]

[No,] Zorian responded. He suddenly became aware that Kirielle was tugging on his shirt. "What is it, Kiri?"

"You drifted off," she said.

"I was just talking to Novelty," he said. She gave him an odd look. "Telepathically, I mean."

"Oh," Kirielle said, her eyes widening in realization. "I'm so jealous you can do that. I wish I could talk to people without being overheard. It would have been *so* helpful around Mom."

"Don't I know it," Zorian sighed. "So many things would have been easier if I could have done that earlier. Though maybe it was a blessing in disguise—a lot of people back in Cirin would have freaked out if they started hearing voices in their head and mind magic abuse is punished very harshly by the mage guild. Anyway, let's go introduce you to Novelty."

575

To her credit, Novelty hadn't immediately rushed in towards Kirielle and started to crawl all over her. To *Kirielle's* credit, she didn't immediately scream in fear and try to hide behind him upon seeing a huge black spider hop into the room. Instead, the two of them faced each other square on, standing a good deal of distance from each other, and carefully scrutinized one another.

[A mini human!] yelled Novelty telepathically to them both, breaking the stand-off. [Great Web, she's so much smaller than you! Can she even talk yet?]

"W-What!?" Kirielle protested. "Of course I can talk! I even learned how to read and count last year! What do you think I am, a baby!?"

[Oh, you *can* talk, that's excellent! Excellent! I actually *was* afraid you were a baby,] Novelty admitted, skittering left and right to take in Kirielle from different angles. [Not that there is anything wrong with being a baby, but I got assigned as a babysitter for *soooo* long and it gets *soooo* boring after a while, you know? They're all so needy and grabby and they never know anything interesting…]

"Um, yeah," Kirielle said. She shot Zorian a suspicious look, but he was maintaining his impassive façade through superhuman will. His lips only twitched into a smirk once she returned her attention to Novelty. "I guess I can understand that. But I'm definitely not a baby anymore! I'm nine years old, and that's a lot!"

[Wow, that *is* a lot!] agreed Novelty. [You're only a year younger than me! How come your brother is so much bigger than you, then?]

"He's… older than me?" Kirielle tried. "Wait, if you're ten, aren't you just a kid like me?"

[No way!] Novelty protested. [I went through the maturation ceremony last year, so I'm totally an adult of the tribe and no one can say otherwise!]

Zorian watched as Novelty and Kirielle went through a clash of cultures in miniature, gradually coming to an understanding of sorts.

They both complained about not being taken seriously by people around them (it was a mystery as to why; no, really) and exchanged some information about their respective species. Zorian actually learned a few new things about the aranea that he had never really thought to ask about. Apparently aranea had a lot shorter lifespan than humans did, with fifty-five years being considered positively ancient. He had known they could spin webs, but apparently the webs weren't at all involved with hunting prey and were instead used exclusively as construction material to make walls, bridges, and so on. He had also thought they were fully subterranean in nature, with only Cyoria's colony interacting with the surface so heavily, but it turned out they all preferred to hunt on the surface and only used the Dungeon to build their settlements.

Eventually, Novelty decided to try her luck and approached Kirielle, which resulted in his brave little sister immediately backpedaling and cutting the meeting short. Zorian wasn't at all surprised by this turn of events, but he was impressed by the restraint shown by both parties. Hell, Kirielle even indicated she might not be averse to the idea of another meeting in the future.

[Aww,] Novelty wilted, drooping pitifully over the couch she was currently occupying. [I scared her away.]

"She did say you could meet her again in a few days," Zorian pointed out.

[But I wanted to talk some more,] Novelty telepathically pouted.

"Just give her some time to digest the whole thing. And don't try to hug her next time."

[But humans love hugs! I totally read so in one of your books!] Novelty protested.

Zorian thought about explaining to her that that wasn't universally true among humans. His parents had never really been big on physical contact with any of their children, really, and Zorian couldn't remember the last time he was hugged by anyone other than Kirielle.

Not that he was particularly crazy for hugs himself, mind you. He decided against it.

"I'm afraid that aranea just don't have what it takes to give a proper hug," Zorian nodded sagely. "Sad but true."

[Do we really look so ugly to you humans?]

"Scary," Zorian corrected. "The word you're looking for is 'scary'. You probably shouldn't have spent so much time lovingly describing how your fangs can easily punch through bone and hardened leather or how you kill your prey by driving said fangs into your victim's neck and severing the spine."

[But cats do the same thing, and cats are cute! You explained so yourself!]

"And then you butted in to note that cats are 'yummy', thus completely invalidating my attempt to make you seem less threatening," Zorian noted.

Novelty sent him an unintelligible telepathic message accompanied by a note of annoyance. Zorian just shrugged and went back to his book while they waited for Tinami to show up.

"Oh. My. Goddess," Tinami said, staring at Novelty like she was the best thing ever. "She's *beautiful!*"

[Well yes, I don't want to sound arrogant, but I have been told I'm quite a looker,] Novelty preened, standing a little straighter and trying to appear more dignified.

"And she really does talk telepathically, just like the stories say!" Tinami exclaimed. She turned towards Zorian. "Wherever did you meet one of them? How did you befriend her? Can I touch her? Do you think she'd teach me her ways if I ask? Do you—"

"I don't think I'm capable of pulling off the 'yes, yes, no, yes' routine so one question at a time, please," Zorian said. "Also, most of those questions you should be asking Novelty here instead of me."

"Oh! I'm sorry, I didn't mean to be disrespectful and ignore you," Tinami said, turning back to Novelty. "I was just excited and it felt natural to talk to the guy who brought me here. To be honest, I was half-convinced this was his idea of a prank and already had a little curse prepared—"

"Hey!" Zorian protested. "That's totally illegal!"

"—but I guess it won't be necessary now, and that's probably for the best," Tinami continued blithely as though he hadn't interrupted. She took a deep breath. "I'm Tinami Aope, by the way."

Thirty minutes later, Zorian found himself unceremoniously booted out of the room so they could have some privacy. Ungrateful scum, the both of them. He debated spying on them with a scrying spell, but considering their conversation mostly consisted of Tinami fawning over Novelty and the young aranea feeling very smug about the attention, he really wasn't missing much. He remained close by for another half an hour, but after a while it became obvious he wasn't needed (nor much wanted) and he entered the room to tell them he was going for a walk.

The moment he was far enough from Tinami that he could no longer feel her on the very edge of his mind sense, he found a quiet corner and shrouded it in some basic anti-divination wards.

"You can come out now," he said to no one in particular. The matriarch promptly stepped out of the nearby shadowed corner, fading into visibility. The trick was somehow less impressive now that he could duplicate the feat and become invisible himself. "So?"

[She is neither a time traveler nor is she connected to the invasion in any way,] the matriarch said. [And as far as she knows, neither is her family.]

Zorian nodded. He had expected that—the Aopes were part of Eldemar's ruling elite and tied far too tightly into its power-structure to participate in a wild stunt like this invasion, and Tinami was too genuine to his senses to be constantly pretending—but it was nice to have a confirmation. "You had no problems with her mental defenses?"

[She had them, but they were of the wrong sort, much like the 'advanced' ones you demonstrated to Novelty,] the matriarch said. [I'm certain she didn't notice my intrusion, and I did nothing except look so there should be no traces left for anyone to find.]

"And she couldn't have fooled you?" Zorian asked. "I've read plenty of stories where people are pretending to be dominated by a spell cast by the villain, only to surprise them when they let their guard down."

[Must be a human mind magic thing. I can't see that sort of thing happening to a psychic. Well, unless the target has constructed a fake mind on top of their real one and fooled the attacker into thinking it was the target's actual mind. But that almost never happens. Constructing a fake mind that is actually convincing is enormously challenging.]

Zorian blinked. He hadn't even known that constructing fake minds was possible.

"Well, sorry I bothered you with this, I guess," Zorian said.

[Nonsense, it was a reasonable suspicion and I actually found a number of useful details by trawling through her mind. Not only is her family not at all friendly towards the invaders, they are likely to be quite annoyed about their plans. Cyoria is their powerbase and they don't want it ruined. And since Novelty is back there, charming the young Aope heir, we will have an easy way to get in contact with the Head of House. Getting such a prominent Noble House on our side will guarantee that the evidence of an invasion plot is taken seriously. Have you spoken to the priest?]

"Yes," Zorian confirmed. "He said the church would send someone to look into it."

[Yet another proof of our legitimacy,] the matriarch stated with satisfaction.

"Hopefully I won't get pulled in for questioning," Zorian said. "I don't think my half-truths and understatements could stand up to professional investigators."

[My web is trying to divert any ongoing investigations away from you, so it shouldn't be much of a problem,] the matriarch said. [We've already ambushed and killed three different investigation groups by the Cult of the World Dragon, and we've been subtly redirecting official Cyorian investigations towards us.]

"You?" asked Zorian in surprise.

[It has been decided that this restart will serve as something of a test run,] the matriarch explained. [As I've told you before, my web's goal is to eventually reveal ourselves to the city at large and join the population as rightful citizens. While full disclosure would be too disruptive for what we're currently trying to achieve in this restart, we've decided to reveal ourselves to a number of prominent people in Cyoria—both to coordinate the response to the invasion better and to sound out their reaction to us.]

"And?" asked Zorian, honestly curious.

[It's mixed, so far, and the fact we're bringing news of an impending invasion doesn't help. We've overheard several 'secret' meetings that discussed how to deal with us in a hostile manner, thankfully with the conclusion that they should wait until after the summer festival before acting. But there has also been talk about how Cyoria can profit from our presence.]

"Which you have no problems with."

[Nobody wants to kill the goose that laid golden eggs,] the matriarch said. [No offense to your kind, but I trust your greed more than I trust your compassion. I talked to Zach again, by the way. You were right. He doesn't remember any restarts being cut short for any reason whatsoever. You dying doesn't seem to reset the time loop.]

"I knew it," Zorian said. "Even Zach would have realized something was wrong if he kept restarting every time I was killed before he was. This is more proof that Zach is the anchor of the loop."

Zorian had at one point toyed with the idea that there was an actual mind behind the time loop—a god who had decided to break the Silence, perhaps, or a very powerful spirit. However, there were a lot of little ways in which the situation matched better with the idea of the time loop being a spell of some sort and none was so clear as the way the spell was treating time traveler detection. Clearly, on some level, the spell knew it was Zach who was the anchor of the time loop and that everyone else was a tagalong. However, at the same time, it could get easily confused (via a little soul blending) into including multiple people into the awareness of the loop. That sounded more like a dumb spell function trying to reconcile incompatible directives with each other than a willful, intelligent mind making a judgment call.

The trouble was, a spell implied a human caster. And a human caster shouldn't be able to roll back time *once*, much less repeatedly.

[If we manage to provoke the third time traveler into revealing themselves, most of the questions about the time loop should be answered easily enough,] the matriarch noted. [I suspect they know what the time loop is and how it functions.]

"Yeah," agreed Zorian. "Let's hope so."

Days passed. When Zorian was not attending to one of his numerous obligations (he'd never try to do so many things at once in the future!) he alternated between creating the various traps and items needed for the ambush of the third time traveler and helping the aranea root out the cephalic rats from the city.

Choosing and preparing the ambush site had fallen mostly on Zorian's shoulders in the end. The aranea knew how to make traps and ambushes, of course, but most of them were based around lethal force or mind magic assaults. Considering that the third time traveler almost certainly knew how to counter aranean mind magic and that they wanted him or her alive, little of it was useful for their purposes. Thus it fell to Zorian to design something that would contain and disable their target, or at least distract them until the aranea could strip them of their mental defenses and do their thing. Kael contributed by helping Zorian make a mixture of powerful alchemical sedatives for disabling purposes, and the matriarch served as his assistant since she was the most capable aranea when it came to structured magic and knew a lot about the local mana flow of the settlement. She would also be the one to lead the execution of the actual ambush with her fellow aranea, so she had to be extremely familiar with how the trap was going to work.

In the end, Zorian decided upon a three-part trap set in the middle of the aranea settlement. The first part was a fairly exotic effect on the floor that temporarily turned stone to liquid. The effect would only activate for a moment, immediately shutting off and turning the stone back into a normal solid state once the target sunk to their knees into the rock floor. As far as Zorian could tell, there was no easy way for a mage to get themselves out of the rock once the effect ended. The spell couldn't be dispelled any more than the ashes of a book destroyed by fireball could be dispelled into a pristine state, and trying to blast the rock off was liable to blow the caster's legs along with it. The only convenient way of getting out was to phase or teleport out, which is why the second part of the trap was a dimensional lock that would shut down most dimensional shenanigans. Finally, the last part involved dousing the combat area with smoke infused with powerful sedatives Zorian made with Kael's help.

It was a bit simple, but Zorian had read that the best plans are always simple. Just in case, though, he had built backup traps in several other aranean caverns. These were a lot less sophisticated ones, though, generally relying on explosions. A whole lot of explosions.

Aside from that, Zorian had made a great deal of combat equipment for the aranea who would take part in the ambush: shielding discs that they could strap to their bodies to shrug off some of the weaker attack spells, stone cubes and alchemical vials that produced a variety of effects when set off, and some equipment for himself and a handful of mercenary mages that the matriarch had discreetly hired as additional muscle during the ambush. Of course, in an ideal scenario, Zorian wouldn't have to fight anyone at all and the equipment he made for himself would be a useless waste of time… but really, what were the chances of an ideal scenario? Things had been going a little too well for him as it was.

As for the hunt for the cephalic rats, that had actually been his own idea, and he had been pleased that he had thought of something the aranea, with all their connections and psychic might, hadn't. The basic idea was to capture one of the rats and then use that specimen as a connection for divining the location of the rest of the rats. Not quite a novel idea to the aranea, but they thought heavily in terms of mind magic and tried to follow the telepathic links connecting the captured rat to the rest of the hive mind—something that quickly failed, since the main collective promptly cut the connection with any captured rats. Zorian, on the other hand, used good old locator spells—divinations meant to find and keep track of all sorts of things, so long as the caster had something connected with what you're trying to find. A cephalic rat, even if disconnected from the collective, was sufficient for those divinations to work.

Though catching a rat to experiment on had been a less than pleasant task, Zorian was able to follow the connections until he located the main swarms, four in all, and then, with a handful of aranea acting as support, herded them into tight formations that could be wiped out with a single fireball spell. By the end of the month, the cephalic rats had been effectively removed from the equation.

Not only that, but when he finished torching the fourth rat swarm, one of the aranea assigned to guard him during the operation admitted she finally understood why humans had a reputation of being dangerous.

Zorian wasn't the only one who was busy. Kirielle persisted in trying to learn magic, with more stubbornness and diligence than Zorian had ever seen from her. She was doing very well for a complete beginner, but the sad fact was that she was closer to him in talent than, say, Daimen or some other child prodigy. Novelty had become something of an unofficial liaison between the aranea and House Aope, and as a consequence was subjected to a crash course in diplomacy and proper conduct by the matriarch—something she constantly complained about to Zorian whenever they met. Tinami, for her part, was much more interested in her lessons with Zorian once she learned more about what it meant to be psychic, and appeared to be working on some kind of personal project that consumed most of her free time. Zorian suspected, from the snippets of thoughts that briefly bubbled into her consciousness during their lessons, that she was trying to somehow artificially make herself psychic. Which struck him as extraordinarily dangerous, since it meant messing with your own mind and all, but that was House Aope for you. Kael was also pursuing some kind of personal project that he refused to disclose to Zorian, though it apparently had something to do with spell formula because he kept borrowing Zorian's books on the topic. Zorian didn't pry—out of gratitude for all the help Kael had provided throughout the month—but he didn't think Kael acted purely on generosity and hadn't forgotten just how fascinated with the time loop the other boy had been. He couldn't help but consider when the other boy would approach him about what he *really* wanted from Zorian.

Apparently when was 'just before the summer festival'.

"Hello, Zorian," Kael said, peering into Zorian's room from the hall. "Are you doing something?"

"Not really. I'm just waiting for Akoja to show up so that I can go to the dance," Zorian said. "She's bound to show up early, so she'll just interrupt me if I try to get anything done. What is it?"

Ah, Akoja. He still wasn't sure why he had asked her to be his date for the evening. Probably because she gave every indication that she wanted him to, and he didn't want to make her sad for no reason. Not that she had actually come out and said it, though. She'd even chickened out on the meeting she had arranged with him and made it look like she wanted some school advice instead of... well, whatever it was she had really wanted to talk about. Hopefully she would be a little less pushy this time around and the evening wouldn't be as catastrophic as it had the last time they went out.

"I have... a gift and a request," Kael said. Zorian mentally translated that as 'a bribe and a demand'. "First, I have been thinking about your stories of previous restarts and couldn't help but notice the presence of a powerful lich on the side of the invaders. Those are... very hard to deal with, especially with classical magics."

"But not with soul magic?" surmised Zorian.

"Well, sort of. It's not easy, even with soul magic, but there are some tricks you could pull on a lich if you knew how to mess with souls. The thing you need to remember is that a lich's soul is automatically pulled back into their phylactery when their physical form is destroyed. This is because destroying their body severs the link between their soul and their body... obviously. Still, if you could sever the link between the soul and the body—something that is a lot easier to do with creatures whose soul is artificially connected to the body through magic—then their soul would immediately be wrenched back to their phylactery, even if their body is technically intact."

"They'd be effectively banished," Zorian concluded. "It wouldn't kill them, but…"

"The process of possessing a new body is not that fast for a lich. They need a whole day, at the minimum, and that's assuming they already have a new body ready to go. Banishing the lich back to its phylactery is as good as killing it, at least for your needs."

"You're telling me you can teach me a spell to do that?" asked Zorian excitedly.

"Well, no," said Kael, promptly popping Zorian's bubble. "And it would be of dubious value even if I could. The spell requires you to touch the target."

Zorian winced. "Yeah, I don't see myself getting within touching range of the lich."

"So I got you this instead," Kael said, handing him a small silver disc reminiscent of a particularly large silver coin. Closer scrutiny, however, quickly made it clear it was some kind of a spell tool, being covered in spell formula instead of typical imagery common to currency.

"I don't have to touch the lich!" Zorian realized after studying the coin for a few moments. "I just have to make sure the coin touches him!"

"Yes," Kael said. "I noticed your fighting style seems to be based around items, so I've imbued the spell into that disc. It should work but I make no guarantees, so use it at your own risk. I tried to make it as small and non-threatening as possible, but…"

"But there is no way to be sure the lich will let it touch him," Zorian finished for him. "Trying to keep a strange item thrown by your enemy from touching you is common sense. I don't suppose that hitting the target's shields is sufficient, is it?"

"I'm afraid not."

"Yeah, that's what I was afraid of. Thanks anyway. What about your… request?"

"Well… the truth is I want a favor in exchange for helping you. I know you're almost certainly going to make further use of me in future restarts, and I have no problems with it… except I want to get something out of it, too."

"I'm not sure what I can do for you that won't be rendered hollow by the restart, but okay," Zorian said. "What is your wish, oh great Kael?"

"I want the same thing you're already doing—to use the time loop to improve my skills. In case of magics that require shaping skills and the like, this is clearly next to impossible without being brought into the time loop, but there is a magical discipline that is far less dependent on shaping skills. One that I happen to be quite good in."

"Alchemy," said Zorian.

"Exactly. Now, practicing alchemy on my level involves a lot of experimentation—testing the effects of your brews, improving them, and designing original concoctions. These things take a lot of funds and a lot of *time*, but once you have a recipe for a potion…"

"You want me to help you design finished potion recipes and then give you the result in subsequent restarts, thus allowing you to refine your recipes further and then take *those* results and—"

"Exactly!" Kael said. "And then, when the time loop ends, you're going to give me the fruits of this labor and I will have saved myself months, possibly years of work! You'll have to memorize the recipes, since we know any written work I produce will vanish, and it will require you to delve more deeply into the intricacies of alchemy than you currently do, but I think that works out in your favor, actually, since you rely on items so much."

As it turned out, Kael had spent most of the month running various experiments and promptly brought Zorian a notebook filled with the results. There was a lot of text there, but Kael explained that Zorian only really needed to memorize the last two pages, which listed which avenues of research were dead ends and outlined a partially finished recipe for some kind of anti-fever potion. Kael explained that giving him those results in the following restarts wouldn't just help Kael improve his craft, but would also allow Zorian to convince the other boy he was really a time traveler far faster than would otherwise be possible. Not seeing the harm, Zorian spent the rest his time until Akoja arrived memorizing the pages and then leafing through the rest of Kael's research. It wasn't every day that a mage got to scrutinize another mage's research methodology, after all, and Zorian could use some pointers for the future

"Zorian, your *girlfriend* is here!" Kirielle called, trying to sound teasing but just ending up mocking and annoying in the process.

He bit back a response, then called out, "Coming." Setting the notebook aside, he went to greet Akoja, who was trying not to look too awkward in front of Imaya and Kirielle. And failing miserably, as she seemed completely at a loss for how to deal with his sister's light-hearted teasing and Imaya's advice on what to do if Zorian got too grabby during the evening ('kick him in the crotch' seemed to be the gist of it). After a few minutes, he decided to have mercy on her and dragged her away from those two so they could be on their way.

It was time to get this show on the road.

The evening had been going splendidly. Akoja was still rather frustrating, but with the date not being a mission from Ilsa this time around, she wasn't nearly as insistent on dragging him along to pointless introductions. She instead settled for criticizing him every five minutes and in general being far too self-conscious and high-strung for what was ostensibly a casual dance. As for the invaders, they were far from the efficient fighting force they had previously been. Zorian kept monitoring the situation through the telepathic relays he had left with the aranea, and it was obvious that the whole invasion had unraveled at the seams. While the city hadn't believed that the invasion would be on the scale described by the aranea and had vastly understaffed their response forces—and even this had been considered an overreaction by a significant portion of the leadership—they had taken some precautions and the attackers were a mere shell of their usual strength due to the lack of forward bases and a whole lot of assassinated leadership. There was no initial bombardment because the artillery mages had been ambushed before they could strike, the academy had opted to change their warding scheme so the attackers couldn't just teleport wherever they wanted to go, and their invasion routes were being actively contested by defending forces that continually swelled as the city realized the scope of the invasion and drew on all the combat assets available to it.

From within the confines of the dance hall, Zorian was almost prepared to breathe a sigh of relief—at which point the door to the hall was suddenly and violently blown into bits, showering the unfortunate guests who stood too close to the entrance with a rain of splinters and concussive force. A few moments later, amid the dust and the screams, three people strode into the hall.

At the center was the lich, just as Zorian remembered it: an imposing skeletal figure, its bones black and vaguely metallic-looking, wearing a crown and a suit of metal armor. It held a scepter in its skeletal hand, completing the royal-like appearance. To the left of the lich stalked a woman clad in black clothing reminiscent of a military uniform—simple pants, heavy leather boots, and a plain jacket with a crest sewn on it—difficult to make out from Zorian's distance, but seemingly featuring a skull. Who the hell puts a damn skull on their crest? She gripped the hilt of a sword strapped to her belt, her expression stony and severe, and Zorian couldn't help but notice that her pale skin and coal-black hair swept back in a tight pony tail gave her a...vampiric air.

...she *was* a vampire, wasn't she? Gods, every time he thought the Ibasan force couldn't possibly be any more sinister, they pulled a new card out of their deck.

The final part of the triumvirate wore a blood-red robe which covered them from head to toe. The face was invisible behind a patch of darkness that seemed to fill every open portion of the robe, obscuring the wearer's features. Unlike the lich and the vampire girl, who looked aloof and imposing, Red Robe, as Zorian immediately thought of the figure, walked carefully and scanned the shocked crowd with interest, his cowled head swinging left and right in search of something. Or someone, as it turned out: the moment the dark emptiness within the hood locked onto Zach, the figure stopped and spoke.

"Him," Red Robe intoned, the masculine voice magically distorted and resonant, pointing his staff at Zach.

As if to punctuate the statement, a small stream of war trolls and robed mages suddenly poured into the dance hall through the broken door, and everyone snapped out of their daze and realized they were under attack.

All chaos broke loose.

The plan Zorian and the aranea matriarch had made assumed that the third time traveler would attack Zach, overpower him, and then pull the information about the aranea out of his mind. Zorian was not sure about a lot of these steps, but a big one was the idea that Zach could lose against the third time traveler so easily. For all his flaws, the other time traveler seemed to be a capable combatant.

It did not take long for Zorian to understand that Red Robe was the third time traveler, and his chosen method for beating Zach was immediately obvious—by not coming alone. Zach seemed to have problems tackling the lich on its own, and with Red Robe and the vampire girl joining the undead mage, the outcome was never in question.

Admittedly, Zach was in a room full of mages who also fought against the three attackers, but the other forces they had brought with them served their purpose as distractions and tied down most of them. Kyron tried to help, as did a couple of others, but they just weren't on the level of their opponents.

But they certainly tried. Kyron summoned a glowing whip of force that severed the arm of the vampire girl at the shoulder, and then used the same whip to seize and fling her sword, which burned with a purple fire and ate through forcefields. It was this that finally confirmed his suspicions that she was some kind of undead, as her severed stump didn't bleed at all and the sudden loss of an arm only seemed to inconvenience her. She promptly pulled out a knife with her other hand and resumed her onslaught.

Red Robe was actually bloodied by one of the students when they managed to overpower his aegis with a coordinated barrage of magic missiles, but when the salvo petered out, Red Robe conjured his own missiles and calmly sent them to take the students down.

As for the lich, he was utterly unfair—nothing seemed to scratch those bones of his in the slightest. Zach actually managed to blow his shiny armor to bits with some kind of black bolts and even knocked the thing's crown off its skull, but nothing ever made a mark on the bones. What the hell was that thing made of?

With reluctance, Zorian didn't involve himself. The plan didn't call for it, and quite frankly he was likely to end up dead if he tried. He did help put down a couple of war trolls and disposable mages that ventured too close to his position, but other than that he just watched uneasily as Zach was slowly taken apart by his three opponents—

—until Kyron blasted the vampire with enough force to send her flying across the hall. She landed next to Akoja.

Zorian had been separated from Akoja at the outset of the attack and decided not to rejoin her, since she was clearly terrified and would want him to stay away from any danger while he personally didn't intend to completely stand on the sidelines while people died. But as he watched the vampire rise to her feet once more, as he saw those dead eyes fixate on Akoja, he knew he had only a moment to act. Lobbing a low-yield explosive cube at the vampire's feet, to halt her in her tracks, he then poured most of his mana into an incineration beam aimed straight at her chest.

Beam spells weren't Zorian's ideal form of combat magic: they dealt a lot of damage, but they were also very mana intensive and it was easy to waste most of the beam's power on the surroundings if you couldn't keep the beam constantly on target. And in a room packed this tightly with panicky civilians, 'surroundings' and 'innocent bystanders' were often one and the same. But Zorian knew he needed to kill the vampire girl quickly, before she could regain her balance. She was extremely fast and her blades could cut through force fields with ease, meaning he'd get his throat slit the moment she got close to him, so he had to use the most damaging spell in his repertoire. Thankfully, she was sufficiently dazed by the explosion that Zorian didn't have any problems keeping the beam on target and he knew from watching her fight against Zach and Kyron that she was vulnerable enough to fire.

He kept the beam on her for a full five seconds, reducing her to little more than a heavily charred skeleton and a pile of ash.

Akoja seemed to be in shock, both at the sudden lunge towards her by a crazed undead woman and at the brutal method of her destruction. The other students around him were watching him with a mixture of fear and awe. Red Robe had eyes only for Zach. The lich, though…

Oh crap, the lich was staring at him.

Indeed, the lich took one look at the smoking corpse of the vampire girl and then locked its hollow eye sockets with Zorian, its gaze seeming to look right through him. Kyron used the moment of distraction to launch another one of those glowing whip-things that severed the arm of the vampire girl like it was paper, but instead of moving out of the way, the lich simply snatched the whip out of the air with one of its skeletal hands, its finger bones closing around the thread of severing light with no ill effects that Zorian could see, and pulled. Kyron let the whip dissipate almost immediately, but not enough to maintain his balance. The lich promptly fired an angry red beam of jagged light and drew a line between Kyron and Zach. They both went down in a spray of blood.

"Watch it!" Red Robe yelled. "That could have killed him! I told you, I need him alive!"

"I grow tired of this," the lich responded. "He is alive enough for your purposes, and this way he'll struggle less. And you should watch your tone, little whelp—you're not in charge here and I could kill you whenever I want without anyone batting an eye. Enough of your 'information' has turned out to be incorrect that your value is being questioned."

"I told you, we have a leak," Red Robe said. "That's why I need Zach intact."

"You don't need him intact to rip the information from his mind," the lich said. "Do your thing and be quick. There are already reinforcements from the city on the way here."

Red Robe seemed to want to say something, but the lich had already returned to scrutinizing Zorian. Red Robe bent down to Zach's motionless form and began casting a complicated spell before placing a hand on Zach's head.

Zach's motionless form suddenly blurred into action, as Zach revealed himself to have just been pretending to be unconscious and tried to punch Red Robe in the face. Sadly, while Zach wasn't totally unconscious he wasn't in top form either, and Red Robe deflected the attack before slamming Zach's head into the floor several times until he went limp. The Red Robe then began casting the spell again.

The lich chuckled hollowly. "*Now* who's being too rough? You could've cracked his skull with that stunt. Living beings are such fragile things…"

Red Robe ignored this, his hand now pressed to Zach's forehead. Though Zorian could not see the face within the darkness, he sensed the figure was concentrating. "The aranea?" Red Robe said after a while. "I can't believe it, I'd never have thought those thrice-damned bugs would be… no matter, I have to go. Time to go tie up some loose ends."

"The aranea were never part of the—" began the lich, but Red Robe already teleported away. "Hmph. I am killing that fool when I meet him later. He's more trouble than he's worth."

He turned back to Zorian after a few moments, and people around him edged away from him.

"I hated her, you know?" the lich said conversationally, pointing at the smoking remains of the vampire girl. "She thought she was so much better than little old Quatach-Ichl. I was a relic, she said, while she was the next generation of undead or some bilge like that. Now look at her, killed by a precocious student with a simple fire spell. Still, while I find the situation amusing, I can't exactly let you get away with it, you know? She was kind of important, much as it rankles me to admit, and I can't just go back home and say: 'Remember that Zoltan House heir you told me to take care of? I kind of lost her!' The Head of House will at the very least want your head for this, if not your soul."

Crap, crap, crap. He'd killed an heir to a Noble House? The confirmation that the lich was Quatach-Ichl barely registered as he tried to figure out how to survive the encounter with his soul intact.

"I don't suppose you would accept a bribe to pretend you couldn't catch me?" asked Zorian with as much calm as he could muster. He took the silver disc Kael had given him from his pocket, rubbed his thumb across the spell formula, then flung it at the lich—

—who reached out a skeletal hand and snatched it out of the air.

The moment his fingers closed around the silver disc, he froze in place for a moment before collapsing to the floor like a puppet with its strings cut.

Zorian exhaled heavily, thankful that Quatach-Ichl considered himself all but invulnerable—not an unwarranted assumption considering those weird bones of his—and thus didn't bother knocking the disc aside with a shield or some other spell.

"What?" one of the students behind Zorian asked. "What happened? What the hell did you do to him?"

Zorian ignored him. Instead he rushed towards Kyron and Zach. He began to examine their injuries, but a moment later an older student knelt by his side and told him she had medical training. His heart pounding still, Zorian took a breath and moved out of her way. Pulling a telepathic relay out of his pocket, he closed his eyes in order to contact the aranea and see what was happening on their front.

It had started so well. The red robed intruder, presumably the third time traveler, had walked blithely into the trap, his confidence buoyed by the familiar layout of aranean defenses near the entrance, as well as several victories against the sentries that the matriarch had purposely sacrificed in order to lull the enemy into a false sense of security. The moment he was near the center of the room, the floor turned to liquid and he sank into it before it froze solid again.

The aranea and the human mercenaries the matriarch had hired for the evening attacked immediately, dousing the area in sedatives and disabling spells.

But something was wrong: the sedatives didn't seem to have any effect on the robed man, and many spells also failed to have any effect. Even stricken immobile, the man somehow managed to defend himself effectively, exploiting any openings to fire off strange purple beams that slew anyone they hit instantly. They were slow to cast and only targeted single opponents, so their losses were light, but it was still frustrating. Finally, one of the purple beams hit one of the human mercenaries and his companions lost their nerve, responding with a barrage of glowing lances that tore straight through the robed man's shield and impacted his chest.

For a moment, the matriarch was afraid that they had killed the man, rendering her preparations and plotting meaningless… but the reality turned out to be far worse than that. Instead of erupting into a shower of blood and gore, the robed man simply… turned into smoke.

And Zorian understood, in the same moment the matriarch did, that their opponent hadn't been the third time traveler. Not really. It had been merely an ectoplasmic shell infused with some of his skill and magic. A simulacrum, meant to test the waters and distract them.

A cone of purple light washed over the area, instantly slaying all of the human mercenaries and scores of her loyal aranea. She turned to sound a retreat to—

Zorian jolted awake from his trance as his connection to the matriarch was violently severed. Watching the events unfold from her perspective had been strange and mildly unpleasant, but this was trivial considering the sudden end of the transmission. The matriarch was probably dead. And the rest of the aranea would likely soon be as well.

They had failed. All that preparation and they had still failed. Damn it.

"Zorian?" A raspy voice from the floor near him broke him out of his thoughts. It was Zach, conscious again, a heavy bandage wrapped around his head. "You with us again? You kind of drifted off."

"Yeah," Zorian breathed out. "I'm… fine."

"They say you killed the lich," Zach said, pointing weakly towards a pile of black bones some distance away from them. A couple of braver students were clustered around the fallen body of the lich, whispering and pointing. "How the hell did you manage to do that?"

"I severed the connection between his soul and his physical vessel, thereby causing it to snap back into his phylactery. He's not really dead, just banished."

"Oh," Zach said. "Still, that's… I never managed to do anything even close to that. How… how is it that you knew how to do that? You… are you…"

"I need to go," said Zorian, rising to his feet.

"Hey, wait!" Zach said, trying to get to his own feet before wincing in pain and giving up on that idea. "You can't just ignore me, Zorian! Zorian!"

He could. And he did. Akoja, too. He moved through the crowd, without seeing it, mentally plotting the path to the nearest sewer entrance. Nobody moved to stop him.

"Zorian, you ass! I swear I'm going to punch you in the face the next time I see you!" Zach shouted behind him.

"Sorry, Zach," Zorian whispered to himself. "But this takes precedence."

By the time Zorian reached the aranean settlement, the whole place was dead, and Red Robe had moved on somewhere. Probably to hunt down any fleeing aranea that had scattered into the city—Zorian knew that a number of aranea were above ground at the time the ambush had been taking place. Whatever the reason, Zorian thanked his good fortune and started examining the place for additional clues about what had happened and for any surviving male aranea.

The fight had been fierce, but Zorian could see that most of the damage to the settlement had been inflicted by the aranea themselves through the use of the spell cubes he had gifted them and their own traps in a futile attempt to halt Red Robe's advance. Red Robe killed incredibly cleanly, leaving no mark of damage on the bodies of the fallen—it was those strange purple spells obviously, but why was he taking such pains to kill all the aranea so bloodlessly when he could have hurled a fireball and simply fried the lot of them?

He had been thorough, though, whatever his reasoning. Zorian didn't know whether the man was unaware that the aranea males were not intelligent or simply didn't care, but there were as many male corpses among the dead as female. And despite the precision of the killings, the scene was one of fury and rage, strangely at odds with the relative composure Red Robe had shown in the dance hall. He had even wiped out the children's crèche, for gods' sake! Yes, obviously killing them all would ensure that he got any time travelers amongst them, but still. They would all be back in the next restart anyway.

Disturbing. Even though the emotional impact of seeing an entire settlement butchered down to the last child was blunted somewhat by their obvious non-human anatomy, Zorian was still sickened and disturbed by the cold-hearted brutality of the third time traveler.

Well. Maybe the matriarch's message from beyond the grave would provide some answers. With the help of his divination compass and his mind sense, he slowly tracked down the surviving males one by one and extracted the pieces of the message they held.

There were two parts to the message, Zorian soon realized. The first was a simple narration—a voice message left to him by the matriarch explaining her actions. The second was a detailed map of Cyoria's underworld, with several locations marked as important. Both messages were incomplete, due to the thoroughness with which Red Robe had hunted down the aranea, and the matriarch had seemingly prioritized the map as the more important of the two, since several males had redundant copies of some of the sections of the map.

As the time loop inexorably inched towards its end, Zorian took stock of what he had managed to piece together.

[Missing] …mean things went awry. I know you think I had it coming by rushing into this but… [Missing] …simple: the time loop is degrading. I can't tell how long it will be before… [Missing] …can leave at any time. Thus, stopping him was… [Missing] …can only ever be one winner in this game. I am truly… [Missing] …hope it won't be necessary, but just in case I put in a map to… [Missing] … whole other continent. I didn't think it was possible, even with the help of… [Missing]

That was it. The map was also full of holes, although Zorian noted he still currently had what was an incredibly accurate map of Cyoria's underworld by commercially-available standards.

Before he could really consider the message at length, the loop ended and everything went dark.

Zorian's eyes abruptly shot open as a sharp pain erupted from his stomach. His whole body convulsed, buckling against the object that fell on him, and suddenly he was wide awake, not a trace of drowsiness in his mind.

"Good m-!" Kirielle began, only to get cut off as Zorian immediately lurched upright into a sitting position, sweeping Kirielle into a crushing hug. The suddenness of the motion shocked Kirielle into a few seconds of silence as Zorian took several deep breaths to calm himself down.

"What's wrong?" Kirielle asked, wriggling inside his grip but not really trying to break free of his hold. Zorian promptly let her go and tried—and failed—to think of a good answer.

"N-Nothing," he exhaled. "It's just a nightmare. I'm sorry for worrying you."

And it really was a nightmare. All their manipulation and preparations, all his combat practice, all the tricks he had thought of, and they *still* lost. They lost miserably. The aranea… they had been hunted down like stray dogs and massacred. Why? What could the third time traveler hope to accomplish with such pointless brutality? And the message the matriarch had left him didn't explain much of anything, either.

"Like I was really worried," she huffed, giving him a sharp poke and jumping away from him. "Mother wants to talk to you so you better hurry down."

"Right," Zorian said, getting up and making a motion towards the door. Predictably, Kirielle sped away to occupy the bathroom, and Zorian immediately locked the door to his room once she was gone and started pacing around like a caged tiger.

He needed to warn the aranea, and he needed to warn them as soon as possible. He wasn't going to bring Kirielle with him this time and the moment the train disembarked in Cyoria he was… no, no, no. That was too slow. Far too slow. Considering Red Robe's actions in the previous restart, and the fact that he 'knew' they were time travelers now, Zorian wouldn't put it past him to butcher them all at the start of the restart this time.

The aranea needed to be warned right *now*, not by the end of the day. He would have to teleport directly to Cyoria. He mentally apologized to his mother and Kirielle, since they were going to have a fit when they realized he had gone missing from his locked room, and started casting.

He couldn't teleport straight to the aranean settlement. The aranea had actually warded most of their settlement against teleportation, and in any case the aranea lived deep underground. Teleporting underground was a bad idea—between the sheer amount of rock in the way and the magical interference created by heightened levels of ambient mana, which only got worse around a mana well like Cyoria's, there was a good chance he'd end up killing himself. As much as he needed to hurry, killing himself in a teleportation accident was even worse than being late, and he had no mana to waste either. Teleporting to Cyoria's teleport beacon was going to be hard enough on its own for a mage of his meager capabilities in the field.

Teleportation had a reputation of being dangerous among most mages. This was because, at its core, the classical teleportation spell wasn't a pure dimensionalism spell—it had a substantial divination component that divined the exact coordinates of the location the caster was trying to reach, and if the caster set up the divination wrong... well, all sorts of weird and unpleasant things could happen. Then there was the fact that some people really didn't like people teleporting into their home and territory and set up wards that didn't cause teleportation just to fail, but to fail *catastrophically*. Such wards were illegal but used by a certain type of people anyway.

Other than that, though, teleportation was a fairly safe and convenient method of transportation. So long as your destination wasn't behind wards. Or underground. Or somewhere you've never set foot in. Yeah.

Ah, whatever, the point was that it could get him to Cyoria in mere moments. Cyoria thankfully had a teleport beacon in the city that funneled travelers into a central location and simultaneously made teleportation easier and less mana intensive for a mage. That meant that Zorian wasn't going to spend most of his mana on the teleport, which was a very good thing.

His world shifted unpleasantly—he still wasn't skilled enough with the spell to produce a smooth transition like Ilsa could manage—and suddenly he was at Cyoria's teleport redirection point. As tempting as it was to immediately descend into the Dungeon and seek out the aranea, he had to think of his own safety first. The aranea could be saved in some other restart, but if he got captured by the third time traveler, all would be lost. He had to wait half an hour or so until his mana reserves regenerated enough that he would feel safe descending into the Dungeon, so he set off in search of a store where he could buy some equipment as there wasn't enough time to make his own.

Well, except for the trusty pair of explosive cubes that he made at the beginning of every single restart. He had to be able to kill himself in an instant if something went wrong. This had been true in the past, and it was even more important now. Thankfully, their creation process was almost instinctive to Zorian by now, and it took very little time to make them.

He slipped into the dimly lit interior of the closest magical store, the sole customer at such an early hour, and began to browse. He was soon disappointed to discover that their selection of spell rods—those he could legally purchase—was very underwhelming. He settled on a shielding bracelet and a rod of magic missiles, but everything else useful required permits he didn't have.

Zorian decided to approach the shop keeper, just in case he could convince the man to… bend a few rules. "I hate to sound like a crazed killer or something, but don't you have anything more interesting in your selection?" He tried to keep the impatience from his voice but didn't think he succeeded.

"Of course, but I can't really sell them to you without getting into trouble, can I?" the merchant said with a radiant smile, not at all disturbed by his question. "The mage guild keeps a close eye on the sale of spell rods and such, and it's not worth it for a few coins. Sorry." Zorian was about to turn away when the man's gaze narrowed into a shrewd expression. "But might I suggest a somewhat… unorthodox choice?"

He reached beneath the counter and withdrew a plain wooden box. He placed it carefully on the counter, then, with great fanfare, showed Zorian the contents.

Zorian stared at the contents for a few seconds, thinking it over. It was unorthodox yes, but…

"I'll take it," he said.

The man gave him a knowing smile and started to write up a bill.

He knew something was wrong the moment he approached the aranean settlement without being intercepted by the sentries. He should have been intercepted by now, especially since he had been deliberately inflating his telepathic presence to be as noticeable as possible. But no one came to confront him, and no one answered his vocal greetings. It was unnerving, and as Zorian drew nearer to the settlement, an undercurrent of dread began to seep into his mind.

Was he too late? But he came here as fast as reasonably possible!

He finally encountered one of the aranea in the tunnels, then another not far away. Dead, both of them. There was no sign of physical damage Zorian could see, either on the corpses or the environment, and he could detect no magical residue to indicate heavy spellwork. It looked eerily like the aftermath of Red Robe's attack in the previous restart. He promptly stopped to cast three different protective spells on himself: non-detection to stop simple divination, invisibility to hide from sight, and a spell to increase his natural spell resistance. He didn't know what those purple beams were, but they looked like direct effect spells rather than simple projection attacks, so spell resistance should work against them. Finally, he took out a cheap scarf he had bought back on the surface for this very purpose and wrapped it around his head to hide his identity. His invisibility would vanish the moment he cast a spell, and he wanted to be prepared.

Then he proceeded more carefully into the settlement proper.

It was a graveyard. Everywhere he looked there were dead aranea, silent and motionless, legs curved inward and glassy black eyes staring at nothing. The terrifying thing was that there was absolutely no sign of struggle anywhere he looked—no spell damage, lingering mana concentrations or groups of corpses piled together as they attempted to delay the attacker at some chokepoint. In fact, most of the aranea seemed to have simply dropped dead in the middle of some mundane activity, such as feeding on a rat corpse or making a sculpture out of webbing.

After trying to piece together what happened, Zorian was tempted to conclude that the third time traveler enacted some kind of wide-scale area of effect ritual that duplicated the effect of those purple beams of his and killed every aranea in the settlement in a single moment, before they even realized what was happening. The problem was not *every* aranea had died. Some of the males, skittering away from Zorian now, had survived. It didn't seem likely that they had merely been far enough away from the settlement given that the distant sentries had succumbed.

After capturing several males and delving into their minds, he began to notice something. All of the males he captured felt... familiar to him. He had delved into their minds before, in the previous restart when he was retrieving the matriarch's message from them.

No. It couldn't be! The aranea weren't time travelers so why would—

The air sizzled behind Zorian, and a flash of light brightened the darkness around him—a portal opening. Zorian whirled, hoping to see Zach.

A foolish hope, perhaps.

For a moment, Red Robe and Zorian stood in silence, staring at each other, each surprised by the other's presence. Zorian's invisibility didn't seem to be effective. The third time traveler was in the exact same getup he had used before—a blood-red cloak that covered every inch of his body and wreathed in some kind of protective spell that made his face a featureless patch of darkness beneath the hood.

The moment was broken when the Red Robe whipped out a spell rod in a swift, practiced motion and fired a swarm of five magic missiles at Zorian. Caught off guard, Zorian could do little except soak in the hit with his shielding bracelet. The shield held, but Zorian knew he wasn't going to win any fights with someone who had bested Zach. He managed to fire a disintegration spell at the ground between them, throwing clouds of dust into the air and allowing him to disengage from battle.

He ran.

He didn't go far.

Although he tried to lose Red Robe by using his familiarity with the tunnel network around the aranean settlement, Zorian soon realized he simply wasn't fast enough. He had never been physically fit, and was just a teenager, whereas Red Robe seemed to be an adult and a capable runner. The small amount of time Zorian bought himself with his diversion soon melted away as he tried and failed to lose Red Robe in the maze of tunnels.

Desperate and unsure what else to do, Zorian eventually slipped into a crevice in the cavern wall, reinforced the divination shield on himself, and hoped the Red Robe would think he had fled down the closest tunnel.

"You are shielding yourself from divinations," Red Robe said in his distorted voice as Zorian tried to sink further into the crack. "Good. At least you're smarter than that fool Zach. Can you believe that even after all these decades in the time loop, he still hasn't learned how to hide himself from the most childish of locator spells? You, on the other hand, have been in the time loop for, what? Three, four years? And you already know how to shield yourself from my soul perception."

Zorian said nothing, desperately wracking his brains for a way to lose the man. It was fortunate that Kael had taught him how to shield himself from soul sight, because Red Robe was apparently a motherfucking *necromancer*!

If he hadn't understood why his invisibility had been useless, he'd be dead already.

"They're permanently dead, if you're wondering," Red Robe continued. He didn't seem to be able to pinpoint Zorian's exact location, but he could clearly tell he was around. And he was slowly getting closer to Zorian. "When I killed them in the last restart, I didn't just kill their bodies. No matter how many times the time loop repeats itself, the aranea will always start the time loop dead, their bodies present but their souls forever gone. Soul magic is so fascinating, isn't it?"

Even though he had been suspecting it, Zorian still felt his heart drop at the admission. The aranea... were dead permanently? That's... He felt a storm of outrage and guilt building up within him, but then he ruthlessly crushed it. Now was not the time. There would be time for breakdowns and self-recriminations later, but now he had to make sure that there would *be* a later.

"But I'm not as violent and unreasonable as I might first appear," Red Robe said conversationally. "If you tell me the names of other people the aranea have brought into the time loop, I promise I will leave you alone. I might even teach you a thing or two."

Zorian blinked. Is that why Red Robe hadn't flooded the whole room in fire to flush him out? Because he thought there might be more time travelers beside him? Huh. In retrospect, that seemed like a reasonable conclusion: the matriarch did claim such to Zach, after all.

Suddenly Red Robe surged forward, snaked an arm into Zorian's hiding place, and snatched him by the shirt. Before Zorian could react, the other mage slammed him into the rough wall of the cavern several times, sending bolts of pain coursing through Zorian's neck and back. He blinked, trying to force away the darkness burrowing into his vision, trying to stay conscious. His hands scrabbling at Red Robe's grip, Zorian fought to free himself, but he had never been particularly fortunate when it came to physical gifts, and Red Robe's strength was utterly superhuman, completely out of proportion with his size and build.

"How many others have the aranea brought into the time loop?" Red Robe asked menacingly, his dark face looming close to Zorian's, all pretense of politeness dropped.

Someone else might have been tempted to lie, but Zorian knew it was best to stay quiet. A statement could be divined for hidden meanings and veracity. You could not divine the meaning of silence.

"Oh fine, have it your way," Red Robe said with a dramatic sigh. "I guess I'll just have to rip it out of your mind like I did with Zach. Regardless of what those arrogant bugs told you, the aranea aren't the only ones capable of mind magic."

Zorian felt the other mage trying to connect with his mind, but he immediately realized the attempt was incredibly crude and simplistic. Zorian was better and he knew it. Not willing to let this mistake on the part of his opponent go to waste, he promptly clamped down on the connection and blew Red Robe's telepathic attack to bits before counter-invading his mind. Knowing he had no experience with subtle attacks, he simply proceeded to blast the Red Robe's mind with an undirected telepathic scream. Red Robe flinched back and tried to terminate the connection. When that failed, he reached for his spell rod, but Zorian caused his hand to spasm and it promptly slipped between his fingers and clattered to the floor of the cave.

After several seconds Zorian realized that, while the other mage was no match for Zorian when it came to telepathic combat, he wasn't defenseless either. Zorian couldn't overpower Red Robe mentally, and the moment his concentration dropped the other mage was going to sever the connection and beat him to a pulp in the physical world. He tried to commandeer the Red Robe's limb to release its grip on him so he could flee but the hand remained resolutely wrapped around his neck.

Well, fine then. Zorian reached to his belt and retrieved the revolver he had bought from the merchant, emptying the entire cylinder into Red Robe at point blank range.

The ear-shattering shots broke Zorian's concentration on the mage's mind, but as the first two bullets impacted Red Robe's chest, he immediately released Zorian in favor of erecting a hasty shield around himself. The last four bullets pinged uselessly against the plane of force the other mage had managed to raise in front of him, but the damage was already done. Blood seeped through the robe, staining it a new shade of crimson.

Zorian fled, hoping that Red Robe's fresh wounds would inhibit his pursuit. No footsteps pounded after him, but a disintegration beam narrowly missing his head told him his opponent wasn't out of the fight yet.

"You shot me!" the Red Robe's voice yelled hysterically behind him. "What kind of mage uses a gun!?"

Zorian didn't grace this with a response and instead opted to keep running. The idea of simply activating his bombs and killing himself was tempting, but he realized that would be a horrible idea. His opponent was a necromancer—suicide wasn't going to protect him from Red Robe, not in any way that mattered. It wasn't like the time loop was going to reset itself when he died—it only did that for Zach.

No, he had to find a way to kill himself such that Red Robe could not recover his body afterwards. After wracking his brains for a second, he accessed the map the matriarch had left for him and searched for something... there! A tunnel leading to a long vertical shaft that ended in a giant underground lake. It was marked as dangerous. That probably meant there was something living there, ready to eat anyone who ventured into the waters. His body would likely be eaten long before Red Robe could recover it. He sped off towards his destination, Red Robe constantly on his toes, not nearly as crippled by his wounds as he should have been. He shot him in the chest, for gods' sake! Twice! What the hell did he do to himself to get that kind of resilience? Some kind of forbidden ritual, maybe?

Red Robe's patience, however, seemed to be gone. A vortex of crackling blue lightning flooded the corridor. Zorian's muscles locked up in painful knots—but the mage was too late.

Zorian had already lurched over the edge of the vertical shaft. Inertia did the rest.

Zorian tumbled through the air, a strange amusement bubbling through him despite the agony under his skin as he considered the irony of Red Robe trying to keep him alive. The dark water below loomed. Everything had gone silent. And then Zorian activated the explosives in his pocket just before he hit the surface of the water. His world ended in light and pain.

End of ARC I

Thank You All! Please Read!

Thank you all so much for picking up *Mother of Learning: ARC 1*! The journey from serial to wide publication has been a long and arduous one, but we got there in the end, in no small part due to the enthusiasm of all of you reading this now!

On that subject, a quick note:

Please, please, consider rating and reviewing *Mother of Learning* on Amazon, as well as any of your other favorite book sites. Many people don't know that there are thousands of books published every day, most of those in the USA alone. Over the course of a year, a quarter of a million authors will vie for a small place in the massive world of print and publishing. We fight to get even the tiniest traction, fight to climb upward one inch at a time towards the bright light of bestsellers, publishing contracts, and busy book signings.

Thing is, we need all the help we can get, and that's where wonderful readers like you come in!

That's it! Regardless of whether or not you choose to review, thank you again for taking the time to read *Mother of Learning*, and we will see you in *ARC 2* very soon!

All the best,
Domagoj Kurmaić
aka
nobody103

Nobody103
aka Domagoj Kurmaić

is just your average accountant from Croatia who
thinks way too much about fantasy and sci-fi, and
occasionally puts his thoughts into writing.